PORTO LÚA

PORTO LÚA

DAVID GREEN

atmosphere press 2023

Also by DAVID GREEN

Atchley

The Garden of Love

Centaury with your staunch bloom
you there alder beech you fern,
midsummer closeness my far home,
fresh traces of lost origin.

Paul Celan rendered by Geoffrey Hill

I was born in the Casa das Flores. Jasmine and wisteria were the elemental breath of my bed, and the sweetness of night I took for the scent of my mother. Sometimes I would waken to that scent thinking she was near only to discover I was alone and had to wait until morning before I could see her again. As I listened to closing doors and quiet conversations, I revisited the evening ritual of my exile where I kissed my father and grandparents goodnight, took my mother's hand, and climbed the stairs to my room. She helped me undress and tucked me in and, when the night was mild, opened the windows before she left. The sea lay just beyond the roofs of the town, and I could hear the sound of waves washing over the pebble shore and feel the salt air enter my room, stirring my hair and cooling the linen sheet where I pressed my face. On clear summer nights, a glassy light of pale mauve lingered on the horizon, and, when stars emerged from the depths of the sky, deities of night rose from the darkened corners of the room. Following the shadow of the earth, they brought their forgeries of fear and desire to haunt my sinking consciousness and rule my restless sleep.

On those nights when I woke and lay unaware of the hour, I moved in and out of dreams like one making his way across tenebrous gulfs on vanishing islands of light. Sometimes, if the sky was clear, I would sit beneath the eastern window and gaze at the bright array of stars rising over the silhouette of the mountain behind our house like a city shining on the shore of a dark sea. Drawn by a desire to know what lay beyond the neighboring fields and wooded lanes, I imagined climbing the stone paths of the mountain to reach the stars and drift far from this world into the blue and white fires that burned like the dying love of ancestral souls—for even then I had some notion of the mysteries of the night. When clouds obscured the sky, I passed the time by naming the objects in my room, carefully recalling as many as I could to ensure their presence when the light returned, or by considering each unfamiliar sound in order to identify its source: the footsteps of a neighbor returning home or the branches of a tree brushing against the barn. And some nights, as I listened to drops of rain falling from the roof, I felt the bed and floor and ground give way beneath me as if I were falling down a well, rushing past layers of earth and stone, disappearing into the darkness, into the night of another world, through banks of clouds and mists of mountain forests, though shadows of valley depths, opening onto yet other worlds, blue tunnels beneath a sea of ice, white petals in a dark rain, elusive dreams in the fall of sleep.

The scented night, the whispers of the sea, give way to summer mornings: a basket of red geraniums, a whitewashed wall, a yellow strip of sunlight on a gray wooden floor. The air is cool from the chill of the sea, and through a window framed by jasmine, the sky is clear and blue. Beyond the garden wall, white smoke rises from a smoldering fire. Like incense on the moist air, it drifts through the garden where carmine bougainvillea and blue clematis contend for light. In the shadow of the barn, the mossy crust of a midden heap—ashes piled with dry ordure—is breached by blue thistles and bristling nettles. Blackberries and ivy grow along the walls, and yellow-tipped fennel surrounds the pillars of a stone granary crowned with a finial on one end and a cross on the other—hedging our bets with the harvest gods. Lined with burdock and alder trees, the lane behind the house borders dry-stone walls centuries old that climb the slopes of Mount Aracelo, enclosing a legacy of ruin and misery. Thin lines rising for hundreds of yards, they reach as far as the granite boulders that mark the edge of a forest called Caos.

As the sun clears the mountain, it first strikes the clouds above the sea, then the orange roofs of Porto Lúa and the tallest trees in the alameda, and finally the narrow lanes leading down to the quay. Paving stones shimmer with soapy water tossed from stoops, and on cool mornings, steam rises above the reflections of sunlight. As the air warms, it yields its odors of moss and stony must, urine and bleach. In the port where father anchors his boat, gulls skid sideways on the wind, as if glancing off a solid sky. Others roost on the masts of red and green and blue boats that rock back and forth with the swells. On the quay women wearing straw hats are repairing nets and stacking lobster traps to dry in the sun. The motor of a fishing boat, the barking of a dog, and the bells of Nosa Señora do Mar fade into the blue sky overhead. While father speaks to his friends on the launch, I sit between two iron rings on the edge of the quay hanging my feet over the water, framing the reflections of clouds between them. Below me bright green beards of algae cling to the granite blocks of the wall. Halfhearted waves roll in lazily from the open water and gently slap the stones. A few dead hake are lying broadside, flashing silver in the sun, while cockles, sand, and shingle stones shift in the currents, and the tentacles of anemones rise swirling like the arms of dancing maenads.

On afternoons in midsummer, clouds gather and move up the coast on the southern breeze. Boiling slowly in the distant heat, they darken the silver water of the bay with blue shadows. Strengthening winds chafe the surface of the sea as fishermen take in their sails. Honeysuckle and wild roses hanging over the walls in back lanes and alleyways sway abruptly, fitfully. Shutters bang in the street. Suddenly rain hits the windows like a spray of pebbles. And stops. And starts again. Glass panes tremble in the wind. Doors rattle at their latches. In the street, damp gusts stir the dust and sand as raindrops patter flatly on the stone. Soon the roofs of houses are wet in the rush of rain passing with the freshened scent of earth and stone. People stand in doorways as the eaves shed beaded curtains of runoff that pours into the streets and descends the slopes in liquid fans. Within minutes the storm passes, and the clouds break up in wraith-like dissolution, exposing the blue sky beyond. The arms of women swing open a series of shutters, and granite outcrops on the mountain gleam in the sunlight.

There were three houses beyond ours in Rúa dos Loureiros, and for many years the street ended in a muddy lane that wound through a thicket of broom toward a fragrant pasture called Campo da Graza. Like the other houses, ours was separated from the street by a dry-stone wall of brown schist. A small wooden gate opened into the front yard where the walk was bordered on both sides by violet buddleia and pink and white roses. My great-grandfather had planted four camellias in the yard, two on each side of the walk, and privet hedges marked the end of our property to the north and south. The only other trees were a large palm that towered over the street and an old fig that grew beside the kitchen window. Next to it was a rain barrel where grandmother would draw a bucket of water in the morning to wash her face. She believed there was no time in heaven, and if she washed with rainwater, the aging of her skin would slow. The house was built of fitted granite stones embossed with gray and yellow lichens. Beside the door, white tiles with blue letters spelled "Casa das Flores." To the right was a large kitchen. Against the facing wall was a black iron stove with brass hinges and handles, a sink cut from granite, and a sideboard where we kept the Pickman china salvaged from the *John Tennant*. At the back of the kitchen, separated by a half wall, was a storage area where there was a tall wooden cabinet and a zinc tub for baths and washing clothes. The room to the left of the front door had once been the stable, but for as long as I could remember had housed old barrels, a broken windlass, a wooden plow, the wheels and tongue of an oxcart, tin lanterns, and some old netting and rope. Everything was covered by a layer of dust older than I was.

The stairs to the second floor were worn by generations of boots and pocked by woodworms. As they rose, they narrowed, and each was a little higher than the last. The walls were cold, chalky plaster bowed with age. On the second floor, a long hallway traversed the length of the house. There were four modest rooms. Those of my parents and grandparents were in the front, and my room and a guest room were in the back. At both ends of the hall was a small window and a flowering plant on a pedestal table. On the wall between my room and the guest room was a silver mirror that had been draped with black linen since the death of my great-grandmother. On the opposite wall was a photograph of my great-grandparents. Sepia-toned and cracked, they stood aging in their youth before long curtains printed with an oriental motif. In the bottom right-hand corner were the words "Valmonde, Astorga." I never discovered what they were doing there. Perhaps it was their honeymoon. Next to the photograph was a framed telegram dated September 26, 1917, reading, "Got drunk. Not Drowned." As a young man, grandfather had boarded a steamship in Coruña to look for work in America. The day after he arrived in Havana, he was booked to take another ship to Buenos Aires, but that night he got drunk and missed his departure. The ship went down in a hurricane off the coast of Cuba. From the southern side of my room, I could look down the coast and see part of the harbor and Illa da Luz, but I preferred the rooms on the western side of the house where full-length doors opened onto the balcony, and evening light entered soft and warm like the touch of grandmother's hands. The window frames were painted blue to guard against witches, and there were small holes in the mortar that opened to spaces in the walls where bees could build their hives. Trap doors in the bedrooms allowed us to harvest the honey, and being stung was a small price to pay for the sweet brown liquid.

In the sullen, persistent rains of late winter, father shoveled loads of straw and dung over the thin soil of the fields to sooth the wounds of the plow and produce our meager harvests of corn, kale, potatoes, and wheat, which we ground in a watermill on the river and sewed in meal bags that hung from the storeroom ceiling. On the southern edge of the property were two small orchards, one of orange and lemon trees, and one of apples. Running between them were several rows of grapevines supported by heavy wires resting on granite posts.

We had chickens for eggs, an ox to pull the hay cart, and two donkeys in a small field behind the barn. And every spring we bought a young pig and raised it as a member of the family. Our neighbors to the south named theirs after the great philosophers and those across the street after the Bourbon kings, but we adhered to no particular theme. At the end of the year, it was customary for the men in the neighborhood to gather at each house to slaughter that family's animal. For two weeks during the waxing moon of November, one could hear the squeals of death on the street as first one house and then another dispatched its family pet. And for those two weeks, one might hear a neighbor calling out "Democritus" or "Alfonso" and see a fugitive pig trotting down the street after a daring escape involving injury and profanity. But it was a short reprieve.

We hung the carcasses from a granite post in the garden to drain the blood and preserve the meat. Then mother and grandmother separated the cuts to make chitterlings, bacon, serrano, fried rind, and lard, which was used for both cooking and soap. Over the winter months and into spring, we consumed the flesh and several organs, but saved the bladder, which was dried and used to store olive oil. Because of its central role in the economy of our family, the health of the pig was of critical importance and a topic of conversation second only to the weather. One year a creature named Romeo grew ill and died from an undetermined cause. Whether the result of enchantment or disease, its demise had been puzzling and gruesome, and the animal was therefore unfit for consumption. We buried it quickly and relied on a diet of fish and vegetables through the winter and spring.

Though we produced most of our own food, the money we needed to buy tools, household goods, and clothes came from the sardines and mackerel that father caught. At first light, summer or winter, he sailed out beyond the cape and returned later in the day with his catch packed in wooden crates of ice. Before coming home, he carted them across the quay to the market where mother sold them in a stall we rented from the town. Dating from the end of the nineteenth century, the building resembled a church with a peaked tile roof, clerestory windows, and large, trefoil openings at both ends where sparrows flew in and out. There was one long corridor with stalls on both sides. On one end, the women sold produce, cheese, and meat. The rest sold fish and shellfish. They were dour creatures for the most part who wore white aprons, rubber gloves, and nets to cover their hair. They watched the shoppers with discerning eyes and shouted their specials of the day in cadences approaching song. A stall consisted of a space roughly eight feet wide and ten feet deep fronted by a slightly tilted granite slab with a ridge at the lower end and a small hole where the ice melt and blood ran out onto the cobbled paving. As lobsters stretched their legs in a slow dance of death, mackerel, hake, sea bass, congers, sardines, white tuna, and shrimp lay in a glittering landscape of crushed ice staring vacantly with their black button eyes upward at the hell of air that poisoned them with emptiness. When a customer decided on a particular fish, mother cut off its head, slit its belly, and dug out its guts with the precision of a surgeon. Scales that had once reflected the dim light of ocean depths covered everything, and the odor of the sea, born in those depths, clung to shoes and clothes, satchels and hands.

While my parents were working, grandmother kept the house and garden: she washed the clothes and cooked and made jam, and several times a week met with the ladies of the lacemakers' guild in an old chocolate factory. Built by a Colombian immigrant in the 1890s, the building was a large room with pebbled windows, a pressed tin ceiling, and green wooden doors. I spent many afternoons there sitting on a wooden bench beneath a glowing light bulb listening to gossip and inhaling the odor of waxed tiles as the bobbins clacked. My grandfather's principal occupation was sitting in the shade of a chestnut tree smoking cigarettes. Sometimes, when it wasn't too hot or too cold or too wet, he tucked his pant legs into a pair of boots and took a hoe to the vegetable garden behind the house. After scraping the earth a few times, he would complain about his back and seek the shelter of the chestnut. If I was around, he would direct me to pick up the loose stones in the yard and reward me with a spoonful of honey on a wedge of bread. When he was feeling particularly good, the two of us would gather firewood on the mountain or harness the ox and haul seaweed up from the beach. And when I was a little older, he showed me how to make salmon putchers from willow branches and where to place them on the river.

At this time in my life, the mountain, like the clouds that stretched across the western horizon, was a place of enchantment. In the afternoon sun, the sea-mist turned its peaks into a fabled land far from the cold fields and damp stones of our few acres. Bathed in that light and creased with shadows, its colors changing as quickly as emotions, the granite massif was like a living presence in our lives. It was our ancestral home and our history, and for generations it had protected us from the rest of the world, but at the same time, it had blocked our horizons to the east and pressed us to survive on the shores of an unpredictable sea. We called the two peaks on the summit the portals of heaven. Between them lie the ruins of Onde se Adora and the headwaters of the Deva, a mountain river that rushes to the sea through a deep canyon cut in the pink granite. Listening to these waters cascading down the valley, Roman slaves shifted boulders to build a road through forests of oak and pine in order to extend an empire to the edge of the world. Before the Romans, the Phoenicians came up from the south on African breezes, and the Celts came down from the north beneath rays of stormy light. And before them were the twilight people, mystics and saints of forgotten faiths, who sought the western shores in order to know the infinite in this life. They followed the stars over mountains and plains and wasteland moors in order to worship the setting sun. Some returned to their homes dreaming of paradise. Some died along the way and were buried in granite cairns with their halberds and daggers. And some stayed to farm the slopes of the mountain and fish the sea.

My mother's side of the family came from Casa Sagrada, a village on the northern face of the mountain below the summit where there is a cave associated with the birth of Santa Lupa. Most of the houses in the village have been abandoned, but once a year people return to celebrate the saint and leave offerings of flowers and candles. My father's family came from

Lonxe do Sol. Although people there share our name, we have lived in Porto Lúa for four generations. The village rests on a rocky outcrop in the gorge of the Deva where the air is filled with a perpetual mist, and because the light is indirect for much of the year, there is a sense of being in a place outside time. Like my family, most of the people in Porto Lúa came from the mountain, and even the name of the town is thought to have originated there.

Before I was old enough to have any idea of the world at large, father decided he and I would climb the mountain so I could learn the ways of the past.

"At his age he won't remember anything," mother said.

"He will," father replied.

"He won't. He's too young."

But believing I was more impressionable at an early age, father was not to be deterred. So on a spring morning when the shadow of the mountain was still on the sea, we set out along the cart path behind our house provisioned with warm blankets and enough food for three days. As we approached the Deva, we turned left onto the Roman road and began to climb its crooked bed of stones rutted by the ironshod wheels of oxcarts. In places our progress was partially impeded by rocks that had tumbled down from the earthen embankments where the roots of pine saplings and clumps of gorse clung to thin soil. During heavy rains, parts of the road had become a channel for the water that coursed down the slope piling up dead leaves and pine needles and depositing a powdery mica sand in the natural craters and cups of stone before merging with one of the several streams that crossed the road and dropped into the gorge of the Deva. As we passed through tunnels of overhanging trees, the air was cool and seasoned with the odors of pine and moss. Every now and then we turned to look down at the sea and fields below us but didn't stop until we came to a clearing where a stream ran alongside a group of boulders. We drank from a shallow pool, and I filled the bottle I carried in a bag over my shoulder. In the shade beside the stream, we ate a lunch of broiled sardines and apples and then climbed the boulders for a view of the coast. The wind was blowing hard, and far out at sea passing clouds left indigo shadows on the sparkling surface. In a glance we could see all the world I had ever known. Among the tesserae of walled fields, father pointed out landmarks and geographical features. After identifying a large expanse of brilliant green as Campo da Graza, we found our street and house, and then Nosa Señora do Mar, the alameda, and the market. On the headland, we located the lighthouse and beyond that, faintly through the sea-mist, the gray silhouette of Illa da Luz.

After eating, we continued through the oak and pine forest above the Deva, but hadn't gone far when we came upon two old women dressed in black walking down the mountain toward us. They told us they had come from a village near Santiago and had been traveling for five days. They were taking the souls of their late husbands to Porto Lúa, they said. Father gave them some bread and a few pesetas and wrote down the name of the street where they might find accommodations. They called upon God to bless us and proceeded on their way.

We left the Roman road late in the afternoon as sunlight poured through the forest in bright yellow rays and made our way along a path cut from a granite cliff toward Lonxe do Sol. Two hundred feet below us, the rushing waters of the Deva echoed off the walls of the gorge to drown out the sound of the wind in the trees. In places, the trail was overgrown with gorse and ferns, brambles and broom, and winter rains had washed out stones along the edge of the precipice and brought down others from above, making the passage more dangerous than father had remembered. At that time, Lonxe do Sol was a village of two dozen houses clinging to a pier of granite that jutted into the mists of the canyon. Its location must have been chosen for defensive purposes in the past as there were few natural amenities, and the air was cold and damp as the winds rising from the sea condensed into a rolling fog just below the houses. Perhaps the most impressive aspect of the place was the pink granite of the valley that created a pale aura of light in the swirling mists and the white smoke that rose from several chimneys. We walked down a muddy street littered with straw and manure as dogs, like the companions of Cerberus, barked from the darkness of sheds and stone barns. Father knocked on the door of the last house and called for my grandfather's cousin. An old woman across the street leaned out her door to inform us the man was dead, but his son was working in the fields near the church. She spoke in a way that was difficult for me to understand, and I was surprised when father answered her in the same way.

We returned to the entrance of the village, but rather than go back the way we had come, we took a path that led north across a fertile plain where the residents of Lonxe farmed dozens of small plots of potatoes, corn, and kale enclosed by stone walls. Outside the walls, grazing in an open pasture, were herds of goats and sheep. We found Xosé, the son of grandfather's cousin, plowing one of the fields behind a large black ox. He stopped working and greeted father by his name. They spoke about his father's death and the old family house, and then we crossed the Roman road to a small church surrounded by a grove of oak trees. Xosé pointed out several stones in the yard inscribed with the name of our family. One rested at the head of the man we had come to see. The mound of earth was still fresh, and flowers lay scattered here and there around the grave. As they conversed about our relatives, we walked down to the edge of the cemetery where a stream had washed away a grave whose headstone lay half submerged in the roots of a white willow. Another, from the distant past, had been used in the foundation of the church. Over time, fieldstones had become headstones, and headstones had become hearthstones or found their way into the walls and floors of houses as the monuments of the dead provided shelter for the living. The unadorned church had a low-pitched gable roof and an obelisk finial at its peak rather than a cross. Inside, the air was close and musty. There were no benches and the walls and floor were cold stone. I imagined my ancestors kneeling on that floor praying for their simple needs.

We said goodbye to Xosé as it began to grow dark and continued up through the oaks in a gathering fog. Not far from the church, standing in a yard uncluttered by human activity, was an isolated stone house. Father opened the wooden door with a brass key and lit a candle as we entered. The windows and roof were intact, but dampness and worms were working through the rafters that held the roof in place. I had a distinct feeling of having been there before. There was no furniture, so we rested our bags on the floor beside a granite hearth in the kitchen and started a fire. As the stone walls began to warm, we walked through the rest of the house. There were six rooms altogether, and though moisture had taken its toll on much of the wood and plaster, the floor was mostly solid, and there was still a hand-carved banister going up the stairs. On the second floor, we found an antique cradle and hand-painted porcelain bowls from a shipwreck.

"My grandfather's grandfather built this house by hand."

"That was a long time ago."

"Your family lived in this village for many years before that. Your great-grandfather was born here in the room above the kitchen. When I was your age, my father brought me here. At that time his aunt was living in the house. When she died, it was abandoned, and the trees grew up in the yard. Before that, you could see much of the coast from here and Illa da Luz."

I tried to picture the man who had built these walls, who

15

had gathered the stones and fitted them. Who had cut and milled the wood to build the floors and stairs and ceilings. People had been born in this house, and they had died in this house. And now there was no one left to maintain it. Slowly it would return to the earth. The stones would disperse as they fell, and the wood would rot, and one day a patch of ivy would be all that was left to mark the site. We went outside and sat on the threshing floor under rusting arbor wires and grapevines that had run wild. The fog had cleared, and the stars shone like glassy grains of sand in a black stream. They seemed brighter than they appeared at home, and I wondered how close they were. We ate the rolls we had brought with us thickly spread with lard and drank the water I had collected from the stream. In the starlight, the remnants of a wall that had once enclosed the yard resembled a jawbone of broken teeth. Father reached over and picked up a handful of dirt and let it run through his fingers.

"This was once the garden that fed your family. Remember this. Remember everything you see because one day you'll be the only one who does."

"I will."

That night we slept on the floor of the room where great-grandfather had been born. Winds from far off over the sea shook the casements on their hinges, and the floor creaked as the kitchen below it cooled. The house seemed to breathe the night air with lungs of damp stone. As I lay between sleep and wakefulness, I saw my ancestors walking through the rooms and hallways as they did when they were still alive. Their faces were white like the moon, and their clothes were tattered like a bed of leaves. I wondered if they too had grieved over a dead pig. Then I heard a woman ask, "Will he recognize us? Will he know who we are?" I called out, "yes," but she continued speaking as if I wasn't there.

In the morning, heavy rain beat against the windows and

filled the yard with standing water. As we waited for it to stop, father took me into the living room where the wooden floor was stained with rot, and cobwebs laden with dust canopied the corners of the ceiling. He slipped the blade of his pocket-knife into a crack in the wall beside the fireplace and, with a back-and-forth motion of the blade, removed a chip of stone. From the hollow where the stone had been, he retrieved a small dark object, which he polished on his shirt and handed to me. I studied the smudge of metal carefully. It was a silver medallion. Years later I would learn its origin was Roman.

"Your great-grandfather found this when he was digging in the garden. Put it in your pocket and fasten the button. Don't lose it. There is no point in leaving it here."

When the rain stopped, silver shafts of light pierced the probing mists that rose among the trees. Scattered randomly across the yard, wild irises and daffodils bloomed purple and yellow against a gray and green background of stone and forest. As we returned to the road and continued our climb toward the summit, the clouds moved away to the north. The light seemed purer, the sky a deeper blue.

The morning air, stirred by the spring wind, carried the scent of vernal grass, of eucalyptus, of moss and wild onions. These distant, cloudy peaks were not as I had imagined them from our gardens and fields, but were rather a hard and rugged place where the gorse was thick and the mud was deep. When we stopped to rest, I watched the random play of sun and shadow in the pines and felt the fresh wind on my skin. Overhead, a green light shone through the new leaves of a horse chestnut where the delicate branches were like the leaden cames of a stained glass window, and for a moment I was in a sanctuary of light, a place sacred to the presiding spirits of the mountain.

At midday we reached Porto Ventoso where the road passes through a natural palisade of granite columns. At the entrance of the opening was a rusty iron gate that had been mortared into the rock decades, if not centuries, earlier to prevent people from reaching the summit. But one of its hinges was broken and someone had pulled it to one side. We passed through a narrow canyon of immense boulders and then through the rubble of three stone walls to enter the forest of Agro Vello. A cool wind rushed through the birches and acacias that were still dripping from the morning rain. Below them, the ground was covered by a gravel of pink granite, brown acacia leaves, mountain lilies, ferns, and wind flowers.

We emerged from the forest, still ascending, through a landscape of stone where only a few trees and bushes were able to withstand the Atlantic winds. The road finally leveled off in a saddle pass between the portals of heaven, two granite peaks hung with vines and small trees like the gardens of ancient temples. Where the road from the east first came within sight of the sea was a statue of St. Peter holding the keys of heaven, and at the foot of the northern portal were the ruins of Onde se Adora: broken outlines of foundations and piles of stone engulfed by ivy. On the edge of this ground, overlooking the Atlantic, was a tall monolith of smooth, pale granite known as A Noiva do Ceo. At the base of the stone, pilgrims had carved crosses to advance their passage to the next world, and on the flat stones around it were cupmarks where oils once burned to illuminate the path at night. Father explained that people used to come here every summer on the morning of the solstice because they believed the shadow of the stone pointed the way to paradise. We walked through a field of boulders to a granite ledge that looked over the top of a coniferous forest toward the sea. The sun had already passed into the western sky, and the wind was blowing hard enough to drive the hawks back that were hanging in the air overhead. From this height, Porto Lúa was a small cluster of orange roofs between the bay and the green fields surrounding the town. South, beyond the headland, the coast was visible past a series of capes interspersed with thin white beaches until it disappeared in the sea haze over the *ría* at Louro. The surface of the sea was as smooth as hammered tin, and reflected the sun with a dull shine. Like spilled cream thinning out across blue marble, high clouds extended toward the distant horizon at the edge of the world where to my imagination there was the promise of a place yet unknown.

We returned to the road and crossed a single-arch keystone bridge over a brackish slough where the headwaters of the Deva trickled through the bog grass and formed a narrow ravine that passed the southern portal and dropped into the gorge to the south. At the base of this peak, carved out of a natural cave, was a chapel so old that the cruciform figures etched on its walls in the distant past had largely been worn away by penitents touching them as relics. We entered a round door cut from the rock as a group of pilgrims dressed in black were coming out. Two women sat on a stone bench along a wall. One was holding a heather besom, and the other was resting with her eyes closed. They appeared to be waiting for us to leave. The altar was a narrow ledge of stone at the back of the cave where green algae covered the walls. In an alcove to the right were sarcophagi carved into the stone floor as if molded from soft mud. Candles were burning in small pots in niches along the wall. Father lit one at the request of grandmother, and we went back into the sunlight.

We left the road and followed a path along the stream as it cut a deep gash through the brown turf exposing the granite bedrock below. Spongy clumps of peat clung to the side of the gash staining the rocks with acidic runoff. As the stream descended, it gathered volume from small tributaries that seeped down through the rocks, and one could hear the low roar of a waterfall echoing off the cliffs of the deepening gorge. As we approached the level of the clouds, the wind subsided, and the blue smoke of burning wood rose to greet us. Cutting back and forth along the path, we reached a series of watermills and a small settlement of round stone buildings. In a field nearby were several horses and a dry-stone pen full of sheep. Several dogs lying in the grass outside the building where the fire was burning lifted their muzzles to sniff the air and barked a series of alerts. A short man with the shadow of a beard came out and quieted the dogs. He greeted father and shook his hand, studying it for a moment.

"A fisherman."

"Our people are from Lonxe."

"Many people have left the mountain."

"I brought the boy up to show him the old ways."

As the man looked at father's hand, I looked at his. It was reddish-brown from the stain of blood, and his nails were purple. He invited us inside where we found several hunters smoking the carcasses of wild boars. Without rising from their rough stools, they nodded a greeting and offered father a cup of wine.

"It's strong enough to reveal the secrets of the earth," one of them said.

The walls of the building were blackened by generations of smoke, and the men seemed inured to its presence. The legs of the stools where they sat were fashioned from saplings, and the seats were woven from strips of bark. They were all older and worn by life. None had a complete set of teeth. They lived in a village on the eastern slope of the mountain, and because their ancestors had lived in Onde se Adora, they considered the summit of the mountain to be their home. Several times a year they brought their animals to graze in the high pastures and camped for a week or two to hunt while the women cleaned the chapel at Onde se Adora and tended the graves of their ancestors.

Father asked the man who had greeted us if he could tell

us more about the history of the mountain and the local names of its landmarks. As the dogs ran before us, we walked back up to the path until we were once again above the clouds and crossed the ravine of the Deva to reach the edge of a cliff where we climbed a large boulder to survey the landscape without obstructions.

"What is the name of the hollow below us?" father asked.

"That is called the pit of forgetfulness where people throw away the things that cause them sorrow. Like the possessions of the dead."

Pointing to little stone walls in the crevices of the southern portal where eons of heat and frost had split niches in the seams of rock, he asked, "What are those walls for?"

"That's where the bones of our ancestors are buried. They were put there so they wouldn't pollute the fields."

"Do you remember those times?"

"No, no. That was in the time of the Celts," he said, meaning "pagans."

"And the peak itself? What is it called?"

"It has many names."

"What do people commonly call it?"

"Each calls it according to his own view of it. In truth, it changes with each name it is given. So I suggest you give it your own, and you will never fail to recognize it."

"If we give places different names, how will we ever know we are talking about the same place?"

"How can we ever talk about the same place if it is always changing?"

"What do you call it?"

"I call it the southern port, but my wife calls it the port of the sun. Other people call it the gate of false dreams."

"What about its counterpart across the way?"

"That's the northern port, which my wife calls the port of the moon, or of true dreams. I knew a man once who called it the gate of Capricorn."

"Why Capricorn?"

"Because the souls go up through Capricorn."

It was already early afternoon, and if we wanted to avoid spending the night on the summit, we needed to begin our journey down the mountain. When father asked the man if we could get to Lonxe do Sol without returning to Agro Vello, he told us to follow him back to the encampment where he showed us a trail through the trees that ran along the cliffs above the Deva. At this height, sheltered from the north wind and warmed by the sun, the southern face of the mountain was covered with heavy vegetation. The cool air that rose from the shadows of the canyon entered the forest in ghostly rags of fog, and for hundreds of yards, the path was like an underground passage through dense foliage, twisted black boughs, glistening ferns, and grasping tangles of briar. Fallen trees and boulders became banks of moss among bowers of ilex and ivy, and the living bark of oaks was encrusted with delicate fans of blue lichens. The roar of water falling below was more noticeable as we left the cover of the trees and looked out over the sheer walls of granite where pines and gorse were clinging precariously to narrow fissures in the stone. As we continued our descent and dropped into the shadow of the ridge on the other side of the valley, the air grew cooler. We reached Lonxe in daylight, and, after spending another night in the family house, arrived home late in the afternoon of the third day of our trip.

I returned tired and hungry, and my feet were battered and bleeding. Because mother viewed me as a willing accomplice to father's adventure, and therefore deserving no sympathy, I was left in the care of grandmother who prepared a warm bath for me and a bowl of hot *caldo*. In the days immediately following our return, it rained incessantly, and in the semidarkness of those spring showers, when the morning light and the afternoon light were indistinguishable, I tried with little success to recall the faces of the men I had seen and the canyon walls and the stones of the forest path. At best these impressions were weak and fleeting like the reflections in windows we pass in the street. But when the sun returned, and the moisture in the air evaporated, and the gray stones of the walls and houses brightened, I began to dream in concert with the emergent light—waking dreams—memories conveyed on the warm spring air. I could see the kitchen in the house at Lonxe, the boars hanging in the dark hut, and the headstone half submerged among the roots. One morning as grandfather was smoking beneath the chestnut tree, I sat on the grass beside him and, looking up into the green canopy overhead, I lost any sense of where I was and returned to the sun shining through the leaves of the chestnut on the mountain. However insignificant such moments may seem, they have stayed with me and lent themselves to the character of my life. Not so much to the person I appear to be, but to the life that lies within.

Sometimes at night when I was unable to sleep, my thoughts turned to the lives of the people buried in the niches on the mountain and to my forbearers who had lived in the house in Lonxe. They were now somewhere in a place apart, somewhere I vaguely associated with the stars. One night I dreamt I was lying in the house at Lonxe when I heard the dull roar of fire. Following the sound, I opened the door to another room where blue flames swirled in the darkness and ghostly bodies flew back and forth seeking an opening into the night. I woke crying and was comforted by grandmother who sat with me until I could fall asleep again.

"I have spent many nights in that house," she said.

"Were you frightened?"

"No. It's a good place. I was glad to be there. When I was first married to your grandfather, I used to load the oxcart with wooden crates of cockles and sardines wrapped in leaves of kale and drive it over the mountain. He had cousins living in the house then, and I would stop and spend the night with them. The next morning I set off for the villages to the east. The people of the interior were not fond of shellfish, but they ground up the cockles and spread the powder over their yards to strengthen the shells of their chickens. I did this because we needed the money. Sometimes when people couldn't pay, I brought back tools or bags of wheat, which we sold in the market or to passing ships."

"You weren't afraid to be alone?"

"I was afraid of wild animals. But I was mostly afraid of the spirits who dwell in the forests and caves."

"What would they do?"

"Well, they might wrap you up in a fog and cause you to lose your way."

"Did that ever happen to you?"

"Oh, yes. Sometimes the clouds would close in, and you couldn't see your own boots. And sometimes I encountered a wild pig or a vicious dog. But I had a conch shell I used to announce my presence in the villages, and if I ever had any trouble, I would blow on it. There were more people living on the mountain in those days and people traveling on foot, so sooner or later someone would hear me and come to help."

She was a small woman with gray and white hair pulled back in a bun, black eyebrows, and gentle, blue eyes. I told her about Xosé and the wild boars and the pilgrims we met, and asked her why there was a gate across the path at Porto Ventoso.

"Many years ago the church tried to keep people from going to the summit by putting in that gate. There's one on the eastern side too."

"Why did they want to keep people from going to the summit?"

"Because of the old beliefs."

"What kind of beliefs?"

"Things from the past."

"Is that why we lit a candle?"

"Yes."

"And that's why there are pilgrims? And people buried on the mountain?"

"Many years ago when people lived on the summit of the mountain, the moon was much closer than it is today. Before crossing the western sky and descending beyond the horizon, it passed just above the portals of heaven. Its white mountain peaks stood out against the black sky like shards of broken porcelain, and it lit the earth with a soft milky light. It was so bright people could work in their fields at night, and sometimes they would see the dust of its cold plains falling over their houses and fields. Even today people believe that when a person dies, the next full moon receives his soul and carries it through the stars to the heaven of light. For thousands of years people have come to Porto Lúa so that when they die their souls will know the way to heaven."

As a result of the strenuous climb of the previous week or the subsequent cold rains, or both, I contracted an aggressive fever and chills. Doctor Romalde was called. He examined me carefully, poking at my gut and inspecting my tongue, and declared that I had a case of Chinese flu and should rest and drink plenty of water. Thinking the doctor might reconsider his diagnosis, mother asked how I could catch an illness from China when I had never left Porto Lúa.

"It's from pigs."

"But our pig is from Curra."

Alarmed at the possibility of losing another pig, she lavished an inordinate amount of attention on the beast, which by all appearances was perfectly healthy, and the task of looking after me fell once again to grandmother who fed me cloves of raw garlic and applied a poultice of herbs to my forehead.

When the fever and chills worsened, and I was passing in and out of consciousness, she appeared to doubt my recovery, and rather than reassure me that the illness would pass, tried to comfort me with descriptions of the world to come.

"The souls of some children go to the eastern sky," she said, "and the souls of others go to the western sky; the former dwell among fresh gardens and flowers and greet the rising sun, and the latter dwell at the edge of the stars where the setting sun fills them with nostalgia for all things past. To the north are empty plains of blue and to the south lies a green sea covered by soft white mists."

"Where will I go?"

"You, child, have a western soul. You will dwell in the fading colors of the western sky."

"How far is that from Porto Lúa?"

"Very, very far. Long ago, when people still worshipped on the mountain, a great king asked his advisors the same question, but none could answer him. So, seeking the burial place of the gods, he went to the sea and built a boat and set out to find evidence of their presence, the light they had left in their passing. He sailed farther than anyone had sailed before. To the south he saw the Hesperides hanging over their island paradise, and to the east, the moon rising over the dark land, carrying the souls of the dead. As he sailed on beneath the coursing dead, the sea filled with glowing forms of life and small white mountains of ice. Far from all that he had known, he continued westward through days of blue emptiness and nights of dark origins, seeking the land of the dead. A gentle wind from the east carried the boat over rolling swells and falling troughs until he reached the edge of time where he found the haunt of the old gods who lingered in the green and yellow dusk of their extinction. And then, passing through the final curtains of light, the king came to the realm of death. The sky was a pale gray, like an ancient wall of stone, and the ivory moon descended into the sea. The souls of children and kings, of mothers and saints, gathered over the dark water like white blossoms on a spring night. In the faint glow of the afterlight, he heard their sighs and whispers, and wept at the sight of so many faces. 'Take us back to the sweet land of our birth,' they said, 'back beyond the river of forgetfulness where we left our lives in the dust.' But there was nothing he could do. Their place had been appointed since birth. With the answer to his question, the king returned to his people, and since that time they have passed down his story and wondered at the beauty of the evening light and at all those souls languishing beyond the horizon yearning for their lives."

After the worst of the fever had passed and I was well enough to walk, grandmother took me to the tree of evil. One morning she waited at the top of the stairs until my mother and father had left the house, and then wrapped me in one of father's old jackets and placed a leather cord bearing a small jet amulet around my neck. She took two clean white rags from a drawer in the kitchen, folded them neatly, and tucked them into the pocket of her overcoat. We went out in a soft rain and crossed the orchard to the gate in the far wall. Huddled beneath a black umbrella, we followed the same path I had taken with father down to the Deva and then turned left and climbed the slippery stones of the Roman road. The clouds brightened as the glancing rain slit the fog that bloomed cold and white among the pines and freshened the rugs of moss that covered stones and logs. As we went higher, the rain diminished, but the fog persisted, approaching and retreating, like a curious animal following our progress through the dripping woods. After climbing for more than an hour, we left the road and took a narrow path along a stream lined with ferns and brambles through an old growth of pine and eucalyptus trees.

I must have been quite feverish still because as we proceeded, I could sense the vital presence in everything I saw, and felt that it supported and sustained me, even welcomed me, not as in a dream, but in a more vivid reality. The light, the air, the sight and sound of every object provided a sense of comfort, assuring and complete. The drops of mist falling on twisted scraps of bark were articulate and clear, intent like a voice. Even the blue glimpsed briefly in the eastern sky seemed aware of my presence.

We passed through the woods to an open field where the bracken and calamint beside the stream had been pressed close to the ground. "Spirit swept," grandmother said. "They come at night to bathe in the water and leave before the dawn." Just beyond the point where two trees cross above the stream, a spring pours out of the rocks into a blue granite pool like the pure blood of the earth welling up from deep veins. Vapors rose over the surface of the pool the way steam rises over water about to boil, and through the heavy air, I saw a woman standing above us on a cliff.

"There's someone watching us," I said.

Grandmother glanced up at the woman. "Mother Ambages. We'll have good luck."

There were offerings of candles and carnations on the bank of the stream, and on the slope behind us was a laurel tree with dozens of white rags tied to its branches. As the wind stirred, the rags swayed with the rhythms of the air like a flock of white birds waiting for the fog to lift. Grandmother took the rags from her pocket and, leaning over the edge of the pool, soaked them in the water that came from the depths of the earth. She told me to take off my jacket and shirt and then she pressed one of the rags to my chest and one to my head. As I stood shivering in the cold, wet air, she rubbed the rags over me and uttered a strange prayer. I felt sacrificial, a small gift to an unknown god. Then she tied the rags to the tree. Over time they would disintegrate in the wind and rain, and, as they did, the darkness removed from my body would be dispersed up the slopes and into the sky or down through the valleys of the mountain—wherever the wind might carry it.

I was sick for another two weeks. To the point where mother was afraid I had pneumonia. But at least the evil was gone. When I finally recovered, I emerged from the dark agitation of my fever into the sunlight of warming days. But wherever I went, the thought of those rags still hanging on that tree worried me. Perhaps the malevolence might follow the streams of air that poured down over the rocks of the mountain and find me again. To take my mind off this fear, or perhaps because she shared it, grandmother asked me to accompany her to the headland to gather yellow blossoms of gorse to make her summer spirits. We crossed the Deva on the Roman bridge south of the quay and walked out a stone path through isolated fields of kale until we came to a wild terrain of the tough, spiny plants that grew where past fires had burnt a forest of pines and left a dusty, insipid soil. We pushed our way through the scrub that rose several feet above me picking the flowers from as high as we could reach and placing them in the cloth satchel grandmother carried over her shoulder. We did this every morning for a week, breathing the fresh sea air as we followed the paths of wild horses over worn ridges that crested like storm waves bearing a flotsam of yellow flowers. The vertical light of the noon sun seemed to darken the landscape with its intensity as we worked our way down to coves of riven granite where the foaming sea-wash boiled and the gorse grew with perverse tenacity.

After a night of heavy rain, grandmother declared the malevolence absterged from my body had been washed away, and I no longer needed to fear its presence. But I must still be wary of the mountain, she said, because of its power to alter our perceptions and make us the fools of its mysteries. She cautioned me not to stray too far up the slopes behind our house, but as children will, I wandered. Knowing nothing of boundaries, I explored back stables and kitchen gardens, fresh streams and forests, and the caves inhabited by shepherds and the mountain dwellers who sold wild berries and firewood in the market. Sometimes when the sun was low over the Atlantic and the crowns of trees were red above the haze like embers glowing in an ash pit, or when the grasses were silver in the moonlight and the song of the thrush poured out of the orchard, I felt I was no longer in this world, but had stumbled unexpectedly through an opening into those mysteries.

On the morning of Palm Sunday, grandmother removed a belt containing a sachet of elderflowers and a ribbon of cloth embroidered with the phrase *qui in tribulatione salvus erit* whose purpose was to guard against the maledictions of her enemies.

"I won't be needing this anymore."

"Why not?" I asked.

"A light has entered my heart and replaced the world of things."

"What kind of light?"

"Last night I dreamt there were blackbirds in the fig tree discussing the nature of God's kingdom. When I called to them, one of the birds flew down and perched on the window sill.

"'How do you know these things?' I asked.

"'Because we fly into the light,' it said. 'People believe they are different because they build houses of stone, but they can't fly, and they die like every other living thing.'

"'Why are you here?'

"'We come from your mother.'

"'God rest her soul.'

"'She is waiting for you.'"

Grandmother sat quietly during Mass wearing an expression of contentedness, thinking, no doubt, more about her conversation with the blackbird than the service of the palms, or "reeds," as she called them. As Father Ithacio took the

opportunity of the Lord's triumphal approach to death to de-
nounce the barbarities of our rural practices, she was far away
at the threshold of another life beyond the meekness of his orthodoxy. Like a child dancing to her own song.

The revelation of the blackbird was confirmed the next
night when a procession of the dead descended over the sea to
enter her dreams. As they approached her window, she recognized them as the recently deceased of Porto Lúa and accompanied them to the summit of the mountain where her ancestors had gathered to welcome her. She took off her boots to
call down the moon, and together they waited until it drew
close enough for them to leave this world. She woke before
dawn, made herself a cup of coffee, and read the grounds.
Where the brown particles clung to the white ceramic, she saw
an image of paradise.

I found her sitting peacefully on the stone bench in front
of the house seeming to share the joy of the birds, but thinking
of other things. I sat down beside her. She told me about her
latest dream, and when she finished, I asked her what she was
going to do.

"First, I have to collect the threads of my shroud," she said.

"Do you want me to bring your sewing basket?"

"No, child. I'm stitching a patchwork of memories to dress
my soul."

She laced up her boots and reached for a sweater on the
rack just inside the door.

"Where are you going?"

"I have goodbyes to say and ghosts to visit."

"May I go with you?"

"Of course," she said. "When I am gone, you will be my
eyes and ears, my witness, my memory."

Although the town was still in shadow, the morning sun
was already shining on the headland and the waters of the bay.
We went down Rúa do Olvido to the plaza and turned north

into the old part of town, a warren of densely packed houses and slatted *hórreos* on the edge of the water. Constructed from crudely cut stones, many of the houses were in ruins, and all were stained by the sea air. The streets, which were originally paths and pedestrian alleyways, were too narrow for anything larger than a cart to pass. Here was the house where Alonso Pinzón had slept on his return from America and the ancient Capela de Santa Lupa, situated a few feet above the highest tides.

According to legend, there had been a Roman temple on this site that had disappeared along with other traces of an ancient port. Built by the Visigoths in the seventh century, the chapel had served the families of fishermen for hundreds of years and hosted many funerals without a body. Its ceiling was low and vaulted with heavy granite blocks. The nave was dimly lit by a stand of votive candles, and above the altar hung a miniature wooden ship. Condensation from the sea air dripped continuously in its alcoves, and not far below the broad, flat stones of the floor was a cave where waves washed in at high tide, and the souls of the drowned would return to hear their requiems.

Grandmother showed me the font where she had been baptized, a half-shell of granite hollowed to a shallow depth and resting on a pedestal of rock carved with symbols of male and female fertility. Then we walked down a side aisle past statues of San Lorenzo, San Sebastián, and San Bartolomé. Each held a palm of martyrdom in one hand and in the other the instrument of his agony—a griddle, an arrow, and a flaying knife. I imagined them fighting against the enemies of their faith and the grisly ordeals of their torture. As we knelt in the front row, grandmother bowed her head before the statue of Santa Lupa. Though lacquered, its painted white face had been flaked by centuries of sea air. Its cheeks were pink, and its eyes were blue, and, testifying to its sacred status, a wire halo of stars circled its head. In one hand it held a sword and, in the other, a rope secured to the neck of a wolf. I studied the child-like semblance of the saint hoping to feel something of her sanctity, but my mind wandered to the resonance of the dripping water and the rush of the sea beneath our knees.

Back outside, we continued down passageways of shadow and stone where purple flowers grew from mossy walls and stale bedding hung from porch rails to absorb the scent of spring air. Knowing nothing of their origins, grandmother pointed out the medieval archivolts and broken pieces of fluted columns in the foundations of the houses we passed. In a narrow lane lit only by indirect light, we stopped before the house where she was born. It had crumbled in from the top, and a rotting beam lay across the width of the ivy-covered pit where the cellar had been. The doorway was low, as if crushed by the weight of the lintel, to suit the statures of a previous age. A scallop had been carved out of a flat stone in the wall, and over the years grooves had been cut in the granite sills of the small windows by iron latches. At the corner of the street, fresh mountain water poured through the mouth of a sea horse that jutted from the stonework of a small fountain. Grandmother held me up to stroke the head of the beast for good luck the way one might pet an indulgent mastiff.

Like someone leaving a home of many years, who goes through each room one last time, she led me through the streets, crisscrossed overhead by lines of drying clothes, taking her leave of the blue shutters, the whitewashed houses, and the fragrance of ferns sprouting from schist walls. In Rúa das Sombras, low arcades, whose granite columns were stained with algae and leaching mortar, enclosed both sides of the street. Here salvagers and merchants of all sorts, iron-mongers and tinkers, a wayward Berber and a Basque, sold their treasures on collapsible tables: the wooden head of a mermaid, the personal effects of drowned sailors, English razors,

Phoenician maps, tin lanterns, New World coins, watches, pinchbeck jewelry, African talismans, counterfeit relics, flotsam fathomable and unfathomable, a pitchfork with broken tines, and rows of pastel shirts wrapped in plastic. At the end of the street, we crossed a small plaza where a single olive tree grew, and a magpie dug at a heap of garden refuse. Two men sat in the shade of the tree playing dominos on a board placed over a wicker basket while a woman leaned out a window to watch the clouds pass. The day was growing warmer.

We entered the main plaza through the Rúa dos Olores, a passage no more than a yard wide that shared a wall with the house of the reclusive Madame Zafirah. As we walked single file down the corridor of stone, I felt the intoxicating power of each odor hanging in the air evoking sensations like memories of dreams. The warm aromas of garlic and coffee contained the heat of sunbaked streets, the casual echoes of busy kitchens, the laziness of the midday meal; the tang of eucalyptus and moss steeped the air with a piquancy that in time would be confused with musty stones and the mists of gray afternoons; the exhalations of the blue sea, a burning cigar, the pungent blossoms of red geraniums colored my affections with a distant hunger; and the sweet perfume of furtive lovers hidden in the crevices of those walls would one day remind me of a love I never knew.

Across the plaza, a breeze blew in from the sea dispelling the diesel exhaust of a delivery van and the scent of cats that lived in the shadow of the market. Standing under the plane trees trimmed in pollard fashion that lined the quay beside the market were seasonal shepherds, stone cutters, a knife sharpener, a letter writer, and a pig gelder who sang their trades to the men and women who passed through the iron gate. Because she had worked in this building for more than forty years, grandmother knew them all. How they had become what they had become, who had maligned them and who had blessed them. And she knew the building so well she could tell you the hour by the position of sunlight on the flagstones and which stones were loose and spattered careless feet with bloody water. She knew which shoppers would buy hake and which mackerel and how to read the feigned indifference on their haggling faces. When we reached our family's stall, she rested briefly on the stool behind the counter as mother spread generous handfuls of ice across the granite slab in anticipation of father's arrival. I sat on an empty crate beside a green tank of lobsters and watched the creatures clamber over each other searching for a deeper cold, while on a dolly in front of me lay a wooden tray of fish an hour or two beyond their capture in the margins of the sea, an hour or two beyond their death throes, beyond gasping for their heavy element.

After stopping at several stalls where grandmother greeted old friends and exchanged pieces of gossip, we left the market through the south gate and walked toward the center of the plaza. To the right, near the Roman bridge over the Deva, was a row of one-story houses built, according to the plaque on the first house, by "The Society of the Immaculate Conception for the Benefit of the Widows and Orphans of Seafarers 1760." On the same side of the plaza were several large houses with white galleries and a store owned by the mayor's wife, María Dolores. To the left was the palace of El Conde de Curra, the town hall, O Galo, the most popular bar in Porto Lúa, a *pensión*, and an old guild hall used as an office by a fishermen's cooperative. In the middle of the plaza was a round tower dating back centuries. Every time a child was born, a stone engraved with his or her name and birth date was added to the top row. Since stone was considered to be more permanent than paper, there was no other record, and so, during periods of war, conscription officers had to requisition ladders to find their men.

On the eastern side of the plaza was a thirty-foot wall of

liver-colored schist where pink and purple wild flowers grew. Above it was the alameda, which could be reached from the plaza by one of two stairways that converged halfway up the wall under a trellis covered with wisteria. A stone balustrade stretched along the top of the wall, and next to the stairs was a lookout with a view of the port. During the heat of the day, people slept on benches beneath the magnolias, camellias, oaks, and palms that cast cool shadows. Two great eucalyptus trees scattered their seeds over the promenade marked off by mossy stones and low iron fences painted red and white. Mica dust sparkled in the sunlight, and at night, electric bulbs on wires stretching from tree to tree gave off an orange glow. Just inside the eastern entrance, level with Rúa das Angustias, was a fountain surrounded by a scruffy boxwood hedge, while on the western side, above the plaza, was a statue of a mounted general no one could name from a war no one remembered. Roughly between the two was a gazebo where the band Fanfarrias played on Sundays after marching through the town. Every day, rain or shine, Xosé de Arcos stood under a magnolia near the fountain selling fresh fruit from a wooden cart, and from noon until six o'clock, including feast days and national holidays, a man from Asturias named Señor Morcín stood at the entrance with a box camera mounted on wheels waiting to photograph strollers and lovers for a few pesetas.

Grandmother and I settled on a bench beside the balustrade as she caught her breath after climbing the stairs. From that height we looked out over the buildings on the plaza and the plane trees on the quay. The noon sea was bright blue. She was silent for several minutes, her sight fixed on the far horizon, and then said simply, "Before we were married, your grandfather and I sat in this same place every evening. I was shy then, and he was very handsome. We would hold hands and talk as peacocks screamed like cats in the darkness."

When the bells of Nosa Señora do Mar rang the Angelus,

we got up to continue our walk, but stopped for a moment before leaving the alameda to have a photograph taken by Señor Morcín. In black and white, now yellowed along the edges, it captures an image at odds with my memory: an old woman wearing a black sweater, a simple black dress, and black stockings looking directly into the camera with great dignity, and a boy with tousled hair squinting uncomfortably in a patch of sunlight. She was fixing the things of this world in her mind to last well into the next, and I was creating a future out of a past I had never known. We took Rúa do Olvido up the hillside to Rúa dos Loureiros. The way is so narrow that sunlight only reaches corners in the street for a few hours in the summer, and some of the houses are so white one could imagine walking through a crevasse at the bottom of a glacier. Except for the heat. We passed our house without stopping and the blossoming privet at the edge of the yard and then the cinder block wall at the end of the street. Someone had placed a long plank over the rutted pool at the entrance to Campo da Graza. The sun had dried the wood, momentarily arresting its inevitable transformation into a brown stain of decay, and we stepped across avoiding the worst of the mud. Clouds, formed by the midday heat, churned slowly upward, shutting out the sun over the sea, but leaving gaps over the field where its rays shone through like the light of religious paintings.

Pursued by horseflies, we abandoned the field, cutting down the hillside on a rocky path through the gorse to Nosa Señora do Mar where we sat on a stone bench to rest. Projecting from the wall above us, carved from granite, was a skull mounted on a plaque containing words barely legible that grandmother read out loud: *Como tu me ves, te verás. Como tu te ves, me vi.* She considered them for a moment and then walked into the uncut grass and weeds of the churchyard, surveying the premises for the site of her grave. I imagined the dead lying beneath me and wondered whether they had sat where I was sitting and had considered those who had gone before them. One day, I thought, the last person to die will have to lie unburied unless covered by grass and falling leaves. Grandmother stopped in an area near the wall where there were no headstones but an abundance of wildflowers.

"This is the place. Here. This patch of clover."

She came over and sat on the bench beside me.

"I don't want you to go."

"I can't stay here forever. No one can."

"But you don't have to go now."

"Don't worry, child. It won't be me. Even this isn't me. This wrinkled skin and these old bones. I'm still the girl I always was, just like you'll always be the boy you are today. I'm not this old thing. This is just an appearance and appearances change. I'll be happy to leave it in the world of appearances."

"Have you finished making your shroud?"

"Not yet. Tomorrow I'll visit the mountain one more time and then I'll be ready."

I was not old enough to comprehend the fact of death. I understood that people had come into the world and departed from it, that there were people buried in the ground beneath me, that there were bones on the mountain and souls that travel through the sky, but I couldn't connect the bones on the mountain to those hidden in our bodies nor the souls in the sky to the love and care of anyone close to me. The dead had always been dead because their lives had never been a part of mine, and the living had never not been and therefore would always be.

From the churchyard we went down Via Sagrada to the plaza and the store run by María Dolores where grandmother purchased a black dress and a black scarf, and then declared she would never buy another article of clothing. When we arrived home, she laid the dress and scarf across her bed.

Mother and father arrived a little later. The morning's

catch had been slight, so we ate potato omelets and turnip soup instead of fish. When father learned that grandmother and I had made a pilgrimage through the streets of Porto Lúa so she could say goodbye to the places of her life, he told the story of a man who had purchased his childhood home and restored it in every detail to resemble the way it had been during his youth with the same furniture and fixtures arranged just as he had remembered them. He sat in his favorite chair day after day reading old newspapers again and again until he lost contact with the outside world and died of loneliness.

"You can live in a world of memories, or you can go about your business and live your life, enjoying your family and friends," he concluded.

"This will be my last meal with the family," she said.

"If that's the case, you should be in church lighting candles and saying your prayers."

Her last wish was to visit the village of her ancestors, so early the next morning she fastened a harness and saddle to the tractable, even-tempered donkey we called Baltasar. The creature shuffled back and forth in a cloud of biting flies as it endured the leather straps that cut his skin and shook his head as if to express his opposition to the plan. There were mangy, scabrous patches on his flanks where he had rubbed himself against trees and stone walls, and his ears and muzzle had been scarred by gorse in the fields where he grazed. As the rest of the family watched from the back garden, grandmother and Baltasar ambled up the cart path toward the Roman road.

Just before noon, she appeared in the doorway scratched and bruised. With no addition or nuance, she looked at father and said, "That beast wasn't shy of heaven and neither am I." She took off her boots and left them inside the door. Then she went upstairs, put on her new dress and scarf, and climbed into bed.

We eventually learned the donkey had collapsed and died

in the road, and two men passing by had pushed it over the edge of the cliff to become a feast for crows and any creature that could descend the rocks. That grandmother hadn't shared the same fate was a matter of chance as she had fallen off the animal to the left rather than the right. But having the good fortune to avoid the depths of the canyon did not deter her from her desire to leave this world. When she woke the next morning, still sore from her ordeal, she summoned the family to her room and announced she had lain down for the last time.

"I shall not rise again," she said. "My wants will be simple, and the child can keep me company."

Father played along, appearing to accept the decision with equanimity, but mother was perplexed.

"Who is going to look after the house and take care of the child when you're gone?"

"Fioxilda."

"Fioxilda is not well enough to come home."

"Then find someone else."

True to her word, grandmother never left her bed. My views on death were formed by what I witnessed over the following weeks, and I concluded that departing from this world is a matter of choice, a release to be desired. Her room became the place where she fulfilled this desire, and, because of this, the objects it contained were endowed with enduring mystery. In later years, they came to possess an enchantment inseparable from the love I felt for her. I longed for her through them and perhaps also longed for the days of my own life lost as surely as hers. If the kerosene lamp, the nightstand, the pier glass, the bedspread, the brass door knobs had appeared in the arcade of merchants, they would have had little worth, but in the sunlight dispersed through the yellowing curtains, through the lens of time, of loss, they became a means to return to those moments, to those days I had spent beside her waiting for her to die.

Because mother was working in the market, father was fishing in the waters beyond the cape, and grandfather was contemplating the virtues of tobacco in the yard behind our house, it fell on me to keep grandmother company. In the mornings, I took her a plate of bread and jam and watered the flowers on the balcony. I learned to make coffee with the right amount of milk and sugar, and when her feet tingled or grew numb, I rubbed them to improve their circulation. She slept in the afternoons as clouds crossed the ocean sky and the sun appeared on the western side of the house. Gentle air, conveying the scent of tidal wrack and salt, blew the curtains inward, like the dress of a dancing woman, while, half-awake, I listened to the bees in the wall and the distant drone of motors on the sea. As the curtains lifted on the light wind, flashes of sunlight fell across the room. Over the years, it had been enough to fade the crimson cushion on the chair where I sat. As if color was life and the sun was time, drawing the life out of the objects it touches, leaving them pale images of themselves.

Grandmother taught me songs she had learned as a child and told me stories of the people and places of Porto Lúa. But mostly we talked about the old ways on the mountain. How isolation and austerity had preserved the wisdom of the past.

"In those days people believed we come from the stars, and the character we acquire depends on the path we take as we enter this world. We become who we are by our willingness to accept or reject the illusions it offers. And when we die and return to the stars, we leave these illusions, like our bodies, behind."

"Is that what you believe?"

"When you were born, I took you out to the night sky and held you up to the moon. I did that because the world has lost its enchantment. I wanted to ensure you would live your life blessed by the old beliefs. People spend their lives looking for answers, but the answers are right there. They've always been there. Every night when the moon is in the sky. If you know how to see, you will see. If you know how to hear, you will hear. The moon speaks with the authority of eternity. When you are older, you will go to the mountain and learn its secrets for yourself."

"What's an illusion?"

"Something that's not real."

"Why is the world an illusion?"

"Because it is full of things that come and go in time, and time itself is an illusion."

"Are we an illusion?"

"Life is like a light passing through the darkness. One day your body will return to the darkness, and your life will return to the light. It is the good of all things, the source of all living things. It touches everything and gathers all things into itself. We were created by it and belong to it, but are separated from it for a time by the shadows of our bodies. Compared to the light, the day is like the silence that gives meaning to words. When a soul first leaves this world, it is bewildered by the brightness like a child looking at the sun. It recognizes nothing, does not know where to go, nor what to do. Only gradually does it grow strong enough to seek the light. But if it is weak, it will remain behind, forever lost, troubling its family and friends."

At night as I lay in bed, I thought about what she had said. I wanted to believe what she believed, but could not reconcile myself to the loss of all that was familiar. Some nights I lay awake until dawn. And one morning I watched a pink half-moon set in the gray-blue sea and wondered what it would be like to ride that ship of light over the distant waves beyond the horizon.

During the second week of her self-imposed confinement, grandmother began to lose track of time. The hours flowed together, sometimes uphill and sometimes down; sometimes they spread out as if across a broad flatland thinning under the sun, and sometimes they narrowed as if rushing through a deep canyon. At dinnertime she asked why I brought her fish for breakfast and in the evening wondered why the dawn was so slow to arrive. Thinking he was doing her a favor, father bought her a clock. It was the first we had ever owned because in the past no one had needed one. We knew the hour of the day by the sun or, when it was cloudy, by the songs of birds. We woke to the rooster, began work with the lark, and slept to the nightingale. The seasons we measured by the stars and the habits of animals. When Arcturus appears at dusk, winter is over. When the cuckoos call, it's time to plant. When Sirius rises with the sun, and the oxcarts squeak with the heat, it's time to cut wood and harvest potatoes. And when the Pleiades reappear and the cranes migrate, it's time to slaughter the pig.

Though it lacked a hospital, a bank, and a pharmacy, Porto Lúa did have a clockmaker, Don Horacio, an expert handler of time, who maintained a shop on the plaza between Rúa do Olvido and Rúa das Angustias. Every afternoon at a slightly different time, depending on the angle of the sun, he picked up his awning crank from the corner where it rested and unfurled the red and green canvas that protected his storefront from incursions of light. The sun, he claimed, disturbed his clocks, hastening the movements of gears and springs as it invaded the shadows where time slumbered in the lethargy of summer afternoons. Curiously, for a man who measured time, he kept no regular hours. When he was open for what little business he had, he could often be found next door playing dominoes with the barber Fulgencio, or, when Fulgencio was busy, pacing up and down the street wearing an expression of great expectation, as though something important were about to happen. His hair was cut so short his scalp looked like sandpaper. He wore thick glasses with a loupe mounted on the right lens and tied a short apron under his jacket. On the counter where he worked were tin and brass and mother-of-pearl dials. As if exhausted by their efforts to time the timeless, measure the measureless, these taciturn faces of age and oblivion sat on yellowing sheets of newsprint in a dusty chaos of warped wooden shells and oiled gears. Working alone in the dust and shadow, Don Horacio was no mere craftsman, but a sage centuries beyond his proper metaphysic, an alchemist of emptiness, searching for the ghost of time, peering through his loupe at the wheeling gears and escapements and tiny screws the way a mariner might look to the stars when lost at sea.

Father and I arrived late one afternoon and found him sitting on the bench outside the barbershop. He opened his door, took up his station at the counter, and pushed aside a box of ratchet wheels, plates, pinions, pendulums, and a miscellany of gears, screws, and springs. Noticing my interest in the contents of the box, he raised it before my eyes, swept his hand over it, and referred to the bits and pieces of metal as parts of the net he used to capture time. Then he put the box on a small shelf beside the counter and turned to father.

"What can I do for you?" he asked.

"We'd like to buy a clock."

"What kind of clock?"

"A clock for an old woman who can't keep track of time anymore."

"One with stars and a moon," I said.

"That's not too expensive," father added.

"I believe I have what you're looking for."

He went to his backroom and brought out a wall clock made of dark wood with a bright ivory-colored face and neat, hand-painted Roman numerals. In the upper left-hand corner were several stars and in the upper right, a quarter moon. He opened the back of the case and took out a key that was taped to the inside panel. He wound and set it for us and we were on our way.

When we entered grandmother's room, she was sleeping, but woke up as father prepared a mount on the wall.

"What's that?"

"We bought you a clock."

"Why?"

"So you'll know when it's time for dinner."

"It's time for dinner when I'm hungry."

As soon as father left the room, she instructed me to take a scarf from a drawer in the armoire and drape it over the face of the clock. When father came in the next morning to wind it, the key was gone. He looked at grandmother, and then he looked at me.

"Where is it? I didn't spend money on a clock just to have it sit on the wall."

"I don't want a clock."

"What do you want?"

"A funeral."

"You'll have to die first."

"I want a funeral before I die."

"Why would you want a funeral before you die?"

"To see who comes."

After some discussion, father and mother agreed to humor her, but only on the condition that if she didn't die in the next two weeks, she would get out of bed and resume her normal life. They still didn't believe anything was seriously wrong with her. Because the request was impractical and might even be sacrilegious if it culminated in a funeral Mass, they decided to fulfill their promise by inviting a single mourner, Simple María, to a visitation at the house. That way they could not be accused of ignoring her wishes, but at the same time, they would avoid any repercussions they might suffer for deceiving their friends and neighbors with a false decease.

And so the preparations began. When father asked her

what kind of coffin she wanted, she said she preferred a plain pine box. After lunch he and I went down to the lumber mill near the quay and ordered wood cut to the specifications he had calculated.

"Isn't that extravagant?" mother asked. "First the clock. Now this."

"She's seventy-four," he said. "We'll need it eventually."

When the wood arrived, father and I carried it into the barn where he set about making the box. In the meantime, mother took an old death notice from a drawer and carefully copied its design onto a white card, drawing a black cross and writing the letters *D. E. P.* and grandmother's name in old-fashioned script. Early the next morning, I delivered the card to Simple María and then helped father carry the coffin to my grandparents' room.

Since a corpse is always barefoot, grandmother removed her stockings and lay beneath her blanket. As mother applied her death make-up, I took my position by the front door, playing the role of usher in this theater. A little after ten o'clock, María, a tall woman with bright rosacea cheeks wearing a blue smock over a black dress, rubber boots, and a broad-brimmed straw hat, appeared at the gate. I led her upstairs to grandmother's room where mother and father were waiting for her. She took her place behind mother and whispered her prayers as she went through a decade or two of the Rosary. When she finished, she clasped mother's hands and expressed her condolences. Then mother led her down the stairs and received one further set of condolences before closing the door behind her with an obvious sense of relief.

The plan might have worked if it hadn't been for the crucial oversight of assuming Simple María wouldn't think to mention what she had witnessed to everyone she met. A few minutes after her departure, an old woman leading a cow encrusted to its shanks in mud and manure stopped before our house and made the sign of the cross, and just when grand-mother had given up hope of receiving any more guests, an-other appeared in our doorway with thick, black eyebrows, no teeth, and a face cracked like dry earth. More curious than pi-ous, she entered, climbed the stairs, and stood in a corner praying, much to the consternation of my parents. She was soon followed by the ladies from the lacemakers' guild who arrived wondering why they hadn't received a formal notice. Father was required to say a few words, and mother quickly went to work baking an *empanada* for the company.

As grandmother lay closely scrutinized by those seeking some assurance of an afterlife in her cryptic smile, I watched the flies light on her eyes and forehead and wondered how she could bear their presence. But she maintained her impersona-tion of death with perfect composure as the women whispered their prayers and clicked their Rosaries. Until, looking for a friend whose voice she hadn't heard, she opened her eyes just enough to squint through the lashes. For a moment everyone stopped. Then, as if released from a spell, the women of the guild, first one and then another, cried out in fear and aston-ishment. One of them knocked over a chair in her startled re-treat. Another fell to her knees, made the sign of the cross, and rose again as quickly as a spirit ascending the ether. Another lost her boot as she stumbled hastily toward the door. But there father stopped them. Having previously considered the possibility of such a discovery, he had the presence of mind to shout, "It's a miracle. Thank God. Your prayers have been an-swered." To doubt or question this proclamation would have been to doubt or question the will of God and the efficacy of their own piety, so the women, still discomposed from the shock, collected themselves as mother crossed the room to check on grandmother who had closed her eyes again as if nothing had happened. "She's alive," she said, and then turned to the women and declared how blessed they were to witness the restoration of their companion. Father thanked the women for coming, praised them for their devotion, and quickly steered them down the stairs and out the door with a piece of *empanada* to compensate them for their trouble. As soon as he had closed the door behind the last woman, he went back upstairs, folded his arms and stood beside the bed waiting for grandmother to offer an explanation. With no sense of the fear she had inspired or the pandemonium that had ensued, she calmly asked, "Where is Marcella?"

I was assigned the task of inviting the widow Marcella to what could be described as the epilogue of grandmother's mock funeral. Having already been apprised of the miracle by one of the ladies of the guild, she reluctantly agreed to follow me up the hill to our house. She wore a heavy brown overcoat, men's trousers, and tennis shoes, and when she walked, she took long strides with a wide gait and swung her arms vigorously up and down, like a foot soldier striding forth to battle. Known in Porto Lúa for being able to smell odors in the dreams of others, she once beat her late husband when she smelled the perfume of another woman as he slept.

Despite their years of friendship, the conversation was brief.

"Did anyone tell you?"

"Loli."

"But you didn't come."

"I'm here now."

"I meant for my funeral."

"It's not a funeral until you're dead."

"But I *am* dying."

"I'll be back when you finish."

"I won't be here."

"Then I'll see you in heaven."

As Marcella was going out the front gate, father entered with the only man in Porto Lúa who could verify the miracle and save the family from disgrace, no less an authority than Father Ithacio. As they were going up the stairs, he asked father why he hadn't been summoned earlier to perform the sacrament of Extreme Unction. Father explained that her death had not been expected. When the priest saw grandmother's emaciated body, he must have doubted this explanation. And from the expression on his face, it was also clear he was skeptical of the miracle, but he kept his suspicions to himself and embraced the awakening as divinely inspired because the net result—strengthening the faith of people—justified his approbation. He heard her confession, which included nothing about her recent attempt to deceive her neighbors, and administered the Sacrament. When he was leaving, he told father and mother he agreed that a miracle had occurred, and he would write a letter to the archbishop's office testifying to the fact. It was evidence, he said, of the success of his ministry and the infinite mercy of God.

Grandmother pretended to be asleep when father returned to her room. He picked up the chair that was lying on its side and placed it beside her bed.

"You can get up now. Your funeral is over."

She opened her eyes.

"We had an agreement," he reminded her.

"You only invited Simple María. That wasn't the agreement."

"The ladies from the guild were here."

"Only because she told them. If you had invited Marcella in the first place, everything would have been all right."

"How could it have been all right? You're not dead. Were you going to stay in your room until you were?"

She crossed her arms over her chest and closed her eyes again.

"What are you doing now?"

"Preparing."

"For what?"

"My eternal rest."

"You're not going to hang around the house and frighten people, are you? Or be upset when we don't talk about you all the time?"

"No. I've had enough of chickens and pigs."

That night was the Feast of St. John, and before it was dark, grandmother instructed me to take a wine glass out to the spring behind the orchard and fill it half full. When I put it on the table beside her, she asked me to bring her an egg as well. She cracked the egg, separated the yolk from the white with the skill of a card sharp, and poured the white into the glass. Then she told me to leave it on the balcony under the waxing moon. The next morning I retrieved the glass, and she studied the pattern that had emerged overnight.

"That's what I thought."

"What does it say, grandmother?"

"It says I need to get my affairs in order."

"How will you do that?"

"I'm going to make my will and tell my story."

"I'll bring some paper and a pen."

"No. I can't write anymore. You'll have to remember what I say."

"I can draw pictures of the stories to help me remember."

"Good."

I returned a moment later with a pen and a paper bag that I tore into several sheets.

"Are you ready?"

"Yes."

"Let's start with the oxcart. It came from my father. Grand-father won't need it anymore, so we'll leave it to your father. The plates and clothes and linens, everything in my dowry chest and lacework, goes to your mother unless Aunt Fioxilda wants something. My bobbins, pins, hooks, and pillow go to the ladies of the guild."

To me she left what she called her most precious possession, the curiously diverse and seemingly random stories of
her life. She began by retelling the tale of crossing the mountain with her cartload of cockles and sardines. But this reminded her of the years when she and grandfather and some
of their neighbors used to harvest ice. When they were first
married, the winters were so cold the Deva would freeze above
Lonxe do Sol and, at a high falls, form an ice cliff ribbed with
glistening columns. From a steep path along the bank, they
could reach the area below the falls where the river was frozen
in a thick sheet over a level bed of granite. There they camped
and cut the ice with chisels and hammers, and when they had
filled their cart with clear slabs and covered them with straw,
they brought their cargo down the mountain and stored it in a
cave near the river. And there it kept, cooling their supplies of
butter, milk, meat, and cheese. When they took a break from
their work, they would rest in the chamber behind the frozen
curtain of the falls where mist had coated everything in layers
of frost, creating sculpted thrones and footstools in what she
described as their palace of ice. Late in the afternoon, when the
solstice sun dropped into the southwest corner of the sky, they
would stand among the glazed walls and statuary and sing or
silently watch the vapor of their breath in a blue light that
seemed to emanate from deep within the ice itself.

The light in the cavern reminded her of the stained glass
windows of Nosa Señora do Mar, and she continued with a
story about the church that occurred many years later, well
after the Civil War, when General Molinero visited Porto Lúa
for a fishing holiday. He commandeered the house of El Conde
de Curra for his entourage of officers, government officials,
and photographers, and early on the morning after his arrival,
he sailed around the headland on a yacht accompanied by a
diver who ensured a successful catch with fish from the

market. After the excursion, he returned to town for an outdoor lunch and an afternoon Mass. During the war, the people of Porto Lúa had suffered greatly at the hands of the general's army. To avoid being drafted, the local men of age had fled to the mountain, and out of spite, the soldiers stationed in town had persecuted their families and even attempted to bury many of the remaining men alive. So when word spread that the general was going to attend Mass at Nosa Señora do Mar, grandmother collected wild lilies from the Campo da Graza and hurried across the hillside to the church where she managed to persuade the Guardia Civil to let her enter to arrange the flowers. Once inside, she barred the door.

The general's procession of black sedans stopped beside the churchyard gate just as a heavy shower began to fall. Curious onlookers gathered along Via Sagrada, but were pushed back by security officers as the great man emerged from a phalanx of soldiers carrying machine guns and black umbrellas. Indifferent to the crowd, he walked across the yard followed by a young soldier who struggled to keep an umbrella over his head. The general was no more than five feet tall and teetered from side to side as he walked. His large head was concave on one side, and because of its resemblance to a pork kidney, people called him *El Riñón*. His mistress followed a few steps behind. She was a tall, blond woman dressed in an elegant black gown spattered with gray mud. As the general and his companion stood in the rain, the Archbishop, a monsignor, and several members of the security detail tried to pry the door off its hinges but gave up after His Excellency broke his toe. A butcher's table was brought from a nearby house and Mass was celebrated in fewer than five minutes while the rain beat down on the humbled assembly and grandmother watched from a gap in the door of the church. As soon as Mass was over, General Molinero retreated through the rain-glutted mud and disappeared into one of the cars behind a wall of umbrellas. It was his last visit to Porto Lúa.

Returning to the stained glass, grandmother explained that when the window depicting the final Station of the Cross was destroyed by lightning, a replacement was designed by a man named Andrade who wore a handlebar moustache and a coat his great-grandfather had taken from a French officer after the battle of Ponte Olveira. When the parish had raised enough money for the window, he sent a sketch to a manufacturer in Germany who produced the glass and sent it to Porto Lúa by ship. By the time she knew him, he had long white hair, but even at his age, he still enjoyed staring at the window for hours as the sun brought out different colors at different times of the day, and occasionally he lifted his hand to touch the glass as delicately as a man reading braille. In the lower right-hand corner of the window was a white skull. One morning after Mass, he turned to grandmother and asked, "Do you know the story of this skull?"

"Is it from Golgotha?"

"No, not Golgotha. It represents the trials of a man named Fidelio who lived by himself in a little house near the river. Because he was getting old, he became forgetful and began to fear the loss of his mind. Sometimes at night, he would waken from his sleep and cry out in fear that he would no longer be himself. One night he woke to find the devil standing beside his bed. 'I am here to make you a deal,' the devil said. 'I will give you a sound mind for another ten years in return for your soul.' The devil gave him a week to think about it and when he came back, Fidelio agreed because he wanted to remain him-self for as long as he could. He went about his business and over the next few years was pleased with the agreement he had made. His thoughts were clear, and he could remember details of his youth with an accuracy uncanny for his age. But over time, he began to feel his heart weaken and a shortness of breath. Then his muscles began to give out, and he felt a palsy invade his arms. He went to an old woman who gave him some herbs which he burned to call down the devil. 'I am dying,' Fidelio told him. 'No,' said the devil, 'your body is dying. Your mind is perfectly sound.' 'What's the point of having a mind if you don't have a body?' 'I don't know,' said the devil. 'That wasn't what you asked for.' And so, as you might expect, Fidelio fell into a state of despair and within a few weeks died alone in his bed.

"When he found his body decomposing around him, he cried out for help, but no one heard him. After several days, his neighbors noticed his absence and called on the priest to investigate. When they discovered a voice emanating from the decaying flesh, they suspected the work of the devil. After the priest blessed the body with a spray of holy water, they wrapped it in blankets, and in the middle of the night carried it up the mountain to Agro Vello where they buried it in a grave marked by a circle of oaks. But boars or wolves or foxes scattered the bones, and the skull came to rest, if such a skull could ever be said to rest, a few yards from the Roman road where pilgrims and shepherds could hear it speaking. Hour after hour, day after day, deprived of any other way to pass the time, Fidelio went on talking to himself and anyone else who would listen. He spoke of his desire for hell and how people should be on their guard against the tricks of the devil. When the devil got wind of this, he appeared one night wrapped in a dense mountain fog and asked Fidelio why he would say he had been tricked. The voice of the old man begged to be released from their contract, but the devil refused because he was greedy for every soul he could get. 'There is no place worse than this,' Fidelio said. 'Being with you in hell will be a blessing—not a punishment, but a reward.'

"Concerned that hell would be a pleasure compared to the torment of the soul's current state, the devil reconsidered the deal, but freeing Fidelio would mean losing the agreement, so he was at a loss. He decided to take the old man's soul to Illa da Luz and down into Boca do Inferno where he would be able to witness the various tortures of hell for himself. But when they returned to the mountain, Fidelio remained adamant that he would prefer those tortures to the torture of being kept inside a muddy skull for another five years. Since he had nothing else to do, Fidelio had plenty of time to think about how he could secure his release. Knowing the devil would not agree to anything he might suggest, he proposed that he receive a new body, even that of an animal, until the years of their agreement had passed. 'If that is what you want,' said the devil, 'I can't give it to you, but because hell is only hell if it is worse than where you are, I have decided to free you from your skull without giving you a new body. You will still be lost in the emptiness of your existence, but not sitting in mud with ants and worms to keep you company. In five years I will return to claim what is mine.' However, as soon as Fidelio was released from his skull, he rose up over the forest and disappeared into the mists above the portals of heaven. Five years came and went, but as long as he remained silent, the devil could not find him and take him to hell. That is how the soul of Fidelio outsmarted the devil, and to this day people are aware of his presence on the mountain, and sometimes when the devil is not around, they can hear his laughter on the wind."

Out of breath from the exertion of speaking for so long, grandmother concluded with the incongruous pronouncement that she did everything she could for her family and remembered the day she was stung by a wasp gathering apples for their favorite preserves. As she was telling these stories, I scrawled lines of hieroglyphics across the sheets of paper. There was a cart loaded with rectangles of ice and a general with stars on his chest and a skull with black eye sockets and an open mouth, and finally a wasp and an apple. When I finished the last drawing, she asked me to "read" the stories back to her. With some corrections, I was able to make sense of most of what was there. And in this way, several of the most memorable events of her life were retained in the picture gallery of a child.

"Keep these pages, and when I am gone, remember what I have told you. Someday this will all be different. The houses and streets will change, and the world will belong to people who will know nothing of what it was like to be here now."

To honor her request, I repeated the stories she told me as I was falling asleep at night or walking through the fields, and when I learned to write, I set them down with as many other stories as I could remember in a little exercise book, and, as I gained greater facility with the language, I went back and filled in the gaps of the narratives with descriptions meant to complete her accounts in ways consistent with my memory of the events.

By the end of the third week of her self-imposed confinement, grandmother had stopped eating. She drank a little broth, but grew thinner, seemingly by the day, until her legs resembled a pair of pine saplings. Given the extent of her decline, it was no surprise she succumbed to a fever. Sensing for the first time that she might in fact be in danger, mother insisted on giving her a concoction of apple vinegar, honey, and chopped garlic and wrapped her feet in rags soaked in egg whites. But she refused to take any medicine because she had no desire to forestall the inevitable. One morning as the fever intensified, she thought she had been taken outside, immersed in a stream, and baptized again, but it was only the cool air pouring through the window.

Hoping to lift her spirits, mother asked if she would like to go for a walk around the yard.

"I can't walk. I'm dying."

"You can't try?"

"I don't want to try."

"But if you were to exercise a little, you might feel better."

"There comes a point where nothing gets better and everything gets worse."

"What is it? What's wrong?"

"I told you. I'm dying."

"It's as if you want to die."

"I do."

"Why would you say that?"

"Well, for one thing, I won't have to worry about dying anymore. For another, I'll never have to gut another pig or plant another crop. There'll be no more boots to break in. No more hair to cut. No more teeth to fall out. No more burning in my joints. No more aching in my back. No more trembling in my hands. No more freezing in my feet. The lines in my face will never get any deeper, and the skin on my hands will never get any thinner. My eyes will never get weaker, and my breath will never get shorter. I bequeath all of that to you."

"There are still many things to enjoy in the world. Look at the sky this morning. And the broom blossoming on the mountain."

"How many more skies do I need to see? How many more flowers do I need to smell? There has to come a last sky, a final flower. A memory remembered no more. The time and place gone forever. I'm finished. I've done what I was here to do. I'm tired of this. Tired of the same old walls. Tired of trying to keep everything together. Trying to keep it going. Trying to keep myself going. Make myself last one more year. Then another. I feel like a dead tree ravaged by termites. I want to be free of this life. I'm tired of what grows and grows old. Of what is learned and forgotten. What appears and disappears. Tired of the foolishness of life. Tired of eating only to be hungry. Sleeping only to be tired. And all the while losing everything I am. For what? I'm ready for the light that burns without end in the ever-brightness of the afterlife. Listen. Can you hear that? It's the music of heaven."

"That's Fanfarrias," father said. "It's Sunday."

Despite grandmother's protests, I was dispatched to the home of Dr. Romalde. Because he was the only practicing physician within miles, he was known simply as *o medico*. That's not to say he was certified, licensed, or registered in any official way. He often told the story that he had settled in Porto Lúa after a career as a knife-thrower in the circus. "I learned to stitch with a needle and thread," he would say, "because sometimes I missed my target." People doubted the story because his glasses were so thick no one would have trusted him to see a target, let alone throw a knife at it. He wore a brown felt hat and a long tan coat with a white scarf. His eyes were close together, and his large nose made a right angle downward from the bridge—like Cicero's, he said. When he looked at people, he tilted his head back to see them through the bottom lens of his glasses and seemed to sniff the air like a connoisseur sniffing a glass of wine. Every now and then, he struck a well-placed blow to the right side of his belly to purge the bile from his liver. He knew a great deal about the history of Porto Lúa and had written a short treatise on the Suevian influence in the area, but his mission in life, as he conceived it, was to fight the superstition of its people. By any measure, he was unsuccessful. When his housekeeper developed a painful condition in her leg, his own daughter took her to Madame Zafirah who uttered several incomprehensible lines and pushed the pain through her leg and out through her toes.

The examination was brief. Although grandmother refused to speak, she accepted the indignities of Dr. Romalde's intrusions with indifference. He pushed and probed her abdomen. He tapped her chest and listened. He lifted her eyelids and looked. He pressed her tongue and felt her neck. Finally, gazing at his watch, he took her pulse. When the examination was complete, he asked father about her diet and state of mind.

Then he deliberated. We watched the process in his eyes and the subtle movements of his face as he considered all the possibilities, rejecting one and then another. Several times he shook his head and muttered, "This is an unusual case."

"Is there anything we can do?" father asked.

"There's nothing. Nothing you can do. Nothing I can do."

"Nothing?"

"There is no cure."

"What is it?"

"She's dying."

"From what?"

"Her imagination."

That evening grandmother asked for her bed to be moved closer to the balcony so she could see the moon. It was nearly full as it passed over the house and spread its light across the sea. Mother and father kept a vigil beside her bed throughout the night, and grandfather sat in the hallway just outside the door. I sat quietly in a corner of the room listening to the tide going out on the shingle. It is the sound I will always associate with her death. In its slow departure, the sea seemed to draw her from us, toward the distant edge of the world.

"I am in that place again. The moon is very bright."

"It will be full in a few days."

"The words are far away like a circle of sky at the bottom of a well."

"That's all right. You don't have to say anything."

"After so many years, I am running out of things to say."

"Try to rest."

"It comes like a bouquet of shadows."

Her last day began beneath an ashen dawn. Fog rose from the earth to become clouds. Clouds fell from the sky to become fog. A dog howled among the boulders on the edge of Caos, and on streets devoid of color, the odors of seaweed and manure mixed with chthonic vapors that seeped from cracks in the earth like the decay of buried gods. Through the shifting atmosphere, the sun appeared pearl-like, a lucent planet that had strayed too close. When the warming day had cleared the condensation from the air, smoke from breakfast fires rose in white columns above the houses, and the coolness of dawn retreated to shadows and coverts of damp stone. Death was also there. Waiting patiently, discreetly. In the thin walls of her heart. In the whiteness of her hair. In the tired bones that sought their rest in the earth.

Grandmother lay with her head tilted forward as if she were looking over the edge of creation. Her mouth opened like a gaping cavern as she took her breaths in short, deep gasps and then let her head drop back to the pillow, willing herself away, or, rather, not willing anything anymore.

"Bring the child here."

"He's here."

She reached her hand out, and I took it in mine. White marble speckled with liver-spots, the skin on the back of her hand was bunched in tiny waves like the wind-blown sea viewed from a height. The veins were blue rivers lying in shallow channels between thin levees of bone. A trapezoid of sunlight fell across the bed, and her dress smelled like old canvas in the hot sun.

"I'm going to go soon. I want you to remember what I tell you."

"I will."

"Life will give you many good moments and many moments of pain. Enjoy the pleasures. Endure the pain. Don't fear what is unknown. Remember what I have taught you. Go to the mountain to learn its secrets. Will you remember?"

"Yes."

She slept briefly and then woke to ask for her glasses because she wanted to see God more clearly. She spoke confusedly as if to her mother, believing she was in a stranger's house resting in a pale, northern light. She described fir trees at the edge of a forest and children playing in a vanishing dusk. The diversions of daily life that had shielded her from death were breaking down, fracturing into a host of broken dreams. Flies circled in the middle of the room. A rooster crowed. The trapezoid of light had moved to brighten the wooden floor.

"I know it's coming and still it surprises me," she said. "The way cold grass surprises a child on a warm summer night."

And then she let go, falling beyond the reach of this world into the capacious light of her memory, a light one could only imagine from her life: sea-salted air and the scent of pine, a girl's tokens of love, of grief, iron rims sounding on granite paths, the faintest crescent moon, pink and white camellias, and the smell of straw in sunlight.

Grandfather walked into the room and told grandmother that his coffee was cold. He looked at her the way a child might look at its injured mother, then took her wedding ring from her finger, slipped it on his own, and left. He slept in the barn for the next few weeks and only returned to his room when his arthritis became so bad he could barely move.

As soon as grandmother had taken her last breath, I was told to open all the windows and doors in the house as well as boxes, jars, and cupboards for fear her soul might be trapped. Then I checked all the glasses, pots, and bowls for standing water and poured it out because a soul will cleanse itself before leaving a house, and no one wants to drink its sins. When this was done, I was sent around the neighborhood to deliver the news to Father Ithacio, the ladies of the guild, Marcella, and anyone else who looked familiar. Within an hour, the house was full of guests who had overcome their skepticism to stop by and pay their respects. Father Ithacio, who was standing at the foot of the bed, surreptitiously took a pin from his cassock and pricked grandmother's toe just to be sure. When there was no response, he began to pray. Women washed the body with sponges dipped in rainwater from the barrel beside the fig tree. Then mother sprinkled some of the water over a tightly cinched bundle of rosemary and lit the leaves to create a dense smoke to purify the air. Before the sun set, one of the women took the bed sheets outside to expose them to the sky, while another placed candles along the Roman road to help grandmother's soul find its way to the stars. In keeping with custom, for the next month, no sharp tool was used in the house, no furniture was moved that might confuse a soul, no fire was lit in the stove or hearth, no meat was cooked, and nothing was swept because one might inadvertently anger a soul by interrupting its peace or forcing it to leave before it was ready.

The funeral took place two days later. A sickly air, hot and humid, settled in over the small plots and gardens along Via Sagrada where overhanging trees sun-teased the paving stones with sultry light. I sat with my parents and grandfather in the front row of Nosa Señora do Mar listening to Father Ithacio retell the miracle of grandmother's revival and extol the virtues of her life even though she had had little interest in his strict interpretation of the articles of faith. As he spoke, my imagination made a theater of the church and a play of the proceedings where actors performed their roles to the amusement of grandmother's soul. Light from the cancel windows filled the sanctuary with an amber grace while the nave was ribbed with bright beams of color that fell from the stained glass to warm the ancient atmosphere of wood and incense and earthy stone. In this light, particles of dust rose like rainbow-colored gulls circling above the bay, and when the sun struck the luminous green on the damp walls and columns of stone, the reflected light reminded me of the glow beneath the leaves of the chestnut tree.

There had been some discussion over whether grandmother had ended her life deliberately or succumbed naturally according to the will of God. Fortunately, the miracle confirmed by Father Ithacio allowed her to be buried in the place she had chosen within the bounds of consecrated ground.

When Mass was over, we followed the pallbearers in a procession of several dozen mourners to the gravesite accompanied by the keening of a self-designated chorus of wailers. As we stood beside the hole dug by Facundo, the parish sexton, father called her name one last time in a ritual summons to ensure she was no longer with us, and then she was lowered into the ground by four men, two on each side, slowly releasing a pair of muddy ropes. Father placed his hands on my shoulders as I stared into the well of darkness. In the black earth of its walls, glazed by the glancing blows of Facundo's shovel, I saw several small pieces of bone that had migrated in the slow terrestrial tides from the broken coffins of forgotten graves. As she went deeper into the ground, I imagined her in a small boat dropping from a davit through the charlock and chamomile, the burdock and thistle, like one leaving her home on a familiar shore forced by circumstances to travel through unknown regions of night to a timeless place where daylight never comes.

One of the men paying out the ropes was too old or weak to maintain his grip, and as his end slipped through his hands, the little wooden box father had built plunged to the floor of the grave, and one could hear the tiny body of grandmother slip to the side of the coffin as it came to rest in its eternal mooring. As the sunken earth received her sunken flesh, and clotted dirt pitched by the handful rained down on the pine boards followed shortly by shoveled earth sealing the vault of her fate, I remembered what she had told me about the light she expected to encounter, but I could not reconcile its promise with the darkness that fell over her narrow sky forever.

When the breach in the wall between the living and the dead had been filled, Father Ithacio finished his formal obsequies and gestured to the group of mourners that the services were over, but grandfather, who had said nothing for two days, stepped to the mound of fresh earth and addressed his wife in a low voice: "We ran out of time, Tilde, but it was a good life. The living world is waiting to follow you into the ground. Take possession. Lead the way. The earth is now your home. Make your memories there of other days and other nights, of other fields and other skies, and when we come to join you, you will tell us stories of how it goes."

Because of the fear that a soul will follow its family home after a funeral, we departed from the route we normally took on our return from church. After Sunday Mass, grandmother used to stop in Via Sagrada to chat with her friends as they left the company of worshippers to enter their gates. So rather than continue along that street, we cut down a narrow flight of stairs between two houses and came out on Rúa dos Castiñeiros, which led down to the old part of town where we turned back and went up Rúa do Olvido and then on to Rúa Loureiros. For the next month, we took a similarly circuitous route home on Sundays and changed the times when we ate and slept in an effort to confuse or frustrate grandmother's soul. We also took the precaution of never uttering her name. If she heard it, she might think she was still needed and there-fore be tempted to linger in this world rather than proceed to the next. Similar to the way adults will use a code when speak-ing in the presence of children, we adopted a word we recog-nized as referring to her, but not obviously so. Because she was small and sometimes querulous, we chose "sparrow." For ex-ample, mother asked if anyone knew where sparrow had put the clothes pins or whether sparrow had used butter when making a certain kind of bread. And on several occasions grandfather said that he and not sparrow should have gone first. But sometimes he forgot himself and the purpose of the subterfuge by suggesting a place be set for sparrow at the ta-ble. Rather than chiding him for these remarks, mother let them go because she believed that he, as she put it, would soon be "singing with the sparrow."

I left the house shortly after returning from the funeral and walked through Campo da Graza. The person I had been when I had last walked through the field with grandmother was gone as surely as she was. Just as I had never known what it was like not to be, I had never known what it was like not to be with her. My life to this point had been a dream that would never return, and memories of the things we had experienced together were now inescapably a source of sorrow. As I crossed through the deep grass, a bank of clouds approached from the sea, concave like a cupped hand, nacreous like mother of pearl. Settling in over the town and fields, the clouds slowly broke apart, and the sun shone through in long, clearly defined rays. I half expected a revelation of some sort, as if nature should concern itself with my loss, but there was nothing. And I was left wondering how a world where everything seemed to be interconnected and whole could sustain such a loss with complete indifference.

From the high ground of Campo da Graza, I looked down on Nosa Señora do Mar and below it the rocky coastline and the expanse of sea mirroring the sun as far as the horizon. To the left a row of whitewashed houses stained green and gray from the sea air descended the slope along Via Sagrada. Weathered shutters opened above a grape arbor, and a woman in a flowered apron leaned out to check the sky. To the north, farther up the coast, Cathedral Rocks rose from the white surf like the ruined towers of an ancient city. Everything I could see and hear was like an outdated belief. The things of this world had deceived me for too long, and I abandoned the assurance of their presence as one might abandon the hope and trust one has placed in a false prophet. Nothing fresh, nothing fair found its way into the emptiness that possessed me. My thoughts were confused, and I couldn't sustain an interest in anything. The first time we experience such loss, like the first time we experience love, we are forever removed from the life we have known.

A few days later, I entered grandmother's room. On the far wall, silenced at her insistence, was the clock we had bought from Don Horacio. It was still covered by the scarf I had hung from its finial corners. I walked around the room carefully inspecting the cover on the bed where she had lain, the curtains that blew in like a woman's dress, and the lamp that had kept her from the darkness. Her touch was still fresh on the brass knob of her closet, the items on her dresser. Gray hairs nested in her brush and lay scattered over the scarf she wore to church on Sundays. I don't know if I was helping myself adjust to her absence or tormenting myself with the loss. Perhaps they're the same thing. Perhaps the pain is the process of adjustment. This was the first time I had seen these objects in her absence, and though I would come to cherish them, they now seemed disloyal in their independence. They were so closely associated with her in my mind that their continued presence suggested an ungrateful disregard for the life that had endowed them with significance; I was both attracted by the memories they contained and offended by their willingness to survive her. I felt the same sense of injustice in the kitchen where the bowl of sugar she had filled before her confinement was still half full. It didn't seem right that she would not be there to see it finished. Or to use the tablecloth she had mended without her sitting beside me.

The objects that spoke most eloquently of her life were her boots, which were still standing by the front door where she had left them. To a perceptive eye, the angle of wear on the heels revealed her distinctive gait, and the vamps, creased by the way she had raised her legs on her toes when seated, were etched by gorse and abraded by the granite stones on the many paths she had walked during her final years. Even dry, the mud that clung to the leather was like a map of her movements. On the ankles was the swampy muck measuring how deeply she had sunk on the path to Campo da Graza. Caked between the heels and soles was reddish dirt from veins of iron-laden earth on the mountain. Sparkling along the seams of the sole was the mica powder that had settled in the natural basins of granite boulders, while the toes were encrusted with the green ferment of ox manure plastered with the yellow impasto of undigested grass. And from the beach where she had collected seaweed for the garden, sand stuck to the mud like a dust of blue and pink and citreous diamonds.

Night was the time when I felt her absence most acutely. Sleep was intermittent, and without the distractions of daylight, my imagination was free to follow every inducement of fear that rose from the darkness. Still unsettled by how little difference her death had made, I knew the world would treat me with no more regard—that I was an unnecessary part of a whole that had as little need for me as I had for a single stone on the shore of the ocean. To alleviate the isolation, I continued to slip out of bed and sit beneath the window on the eastern side of my room. I watched the stream of stars that passed overhead and measured its motion against the darkened peaks of the mountain. I felt the roll of the earth and the unity of the trees and stones and sea, and of all the living and the dead. And I took comfort from the thought that we were carried along together by an unknown impulse, rolling ever under that stream of light.

Sometimes I imagined climbing the northern portal of the mountain and sitting on a large boulder at the highest point as the moon passed overhead. It moved with the patience of age, peering through the windows of sleeping men and women, shedding its light on uninhabited mountains and snow-covered fields where wolves prowl wary of its presence. Its white deserts and gray craters, its fields of ancient debris, glided past, crossing the sky above me and finally drifting away through the stars toward the faint glow of light above the sea on the western horizon. But invariably my thoughts returned to grandmother. Like any child, I suppose, I wondered what it was like to be in a box deep in the ground and on one occasion crawled under my bed and lay in the dusty, narrow confines beneath the pine slats to feel what she had felt, to fall through the darkness of the grave and forever into the sunless earth.

Two weeks after her death, we commemorated her birthday with a meal of fresh vegetables and fruit and afterward recalled some of the stories she used to tell. To my parents' surprise, I was able to repeat her account of General Molinero's visit as well as the history of the stained glass window in great detail. Later that night, as I was lying awake thinking about her, I heard the vines around the casements rustle and noticed a faint blue light moving across my room. And then I saw her sitting at the foot of my bed.

"Don't be surprised, child."

"Why are you here, grandmother? We opened the window to let you out and came home from church a different way so you wouldn't be tempted to follow us."

"I have to wait for the increase of the moon, and I want to make sure you are all right before I leave."

"I'm all right."

"But you worry that I am alone in the churchyard."

"Yes."

"There is no need to worry. I'm not in the churchyard. I'm speaking with you."

"But you have to go back."

"No. I told you before—I'm not those rags and bones."

"What was it like?"

"Leaving this world?"

"Yes."

"The first thing you notice is you are no longer breathing. And the people around you seem very far away. You are more alone than you have ever been."

"And then what?"

"There is light. Just light. Nothing else. Only emptiness. Not a place or a thing that is empty, but emptiness itself. Like floating inside a sunlit fog. You are like a bird flying over the sea searching for an island where you can rest, but the only islands are your thoughts, and as soon as you reach them, they disappear into the emptiness. Each time you come to yourself, each time you reach the purchase of yourself, you disappear again. Then through the fog you begin to see what look like clouds, darker than the emptiness, coming toward you, and then more appear, and as they grow darker, they begin to take shape, and at length you realize they are the images of your mind, the place of memory, where everything you have ever seen and imagined is present. Not just Porto Lúa, but other towns, and forests, and the sea, and the places of dreams, and the stories you heard as a child. And there are also the people you knew."

"Am I there?"

"Yes. Of course you are there. You are there now."

"But I have been here the whole time. We have been here where you left us."

"You are here for you, but there for me."

"Where is that?"

"In the light. The light that existed before there was life. The light that fills the sky, the sea, the flowers of the garden, and the marrow in your bones, but is none of those things. Being in the light is so much more than being in the world, which is only a single thought at any moment. Think of something else and it is gone, but the light always was and always will be."

"Then it doesn't matter if you're forgotten."

"No more so than what happens to the people in your dreams when you awaken in the morning. In the world you will come to be as though you had never been. If you live your life this way, you will be blessed. If you die this way, your soul

71

will be free. But it is not easy. The soul is attached to the world by habits and desires that hinder its return to the light. To be free, you must say goodbye to all of that forever. I must leave now."

"Can I go with you?"

"Not yet."

"Why?"

"Just as you must know sadness to know happiness and darkness to know the light, you must learn to know this world before you can know what lies beyond."

"Will you be back?"

"No. But if you doubt that I was here and what I said is true, go tomorrow and look for a rose on my grave."

The next morning when I told my parents I had spoken to grandmother, father said I had dreamt or imagined her, but after breakfast, mother took me aside and questioned me carefully.

"Why did she come back?"

"She said I shouldn't worry, and then she told me what it was like."

"What it was like?"

"Yes."

"Are you sure you didn't imagine this?"

"She said if I doubted she was here, there is a rose on her grave to prove it."

Mother knew I hadn't been out of the house that morning and couldn't have had the opportunity to visit the churchyard. She decided there was only one way to verify my story, so we walked down the hill and up Via Sagrada. In the cemetery, on grandmother's grave, was a red rose that had been cut within the last day.

Convinced that I had actually spoken to grandmother, she gave me the rose to keep, and that night and for several nights thereafter, she sat with me into the early hours of morning, but grandmother didn't appear. A few days later, when she was working at the stall in the market, a buyer from Muros said that during the previous week he had seen grandmother walking along the coastal road at dawn. Mother asked the man if he was sure it was her.

"Of course I'm sure. I've known her for forty years."

Worried that she had overlooked the needs of grandmother's soul, mother waited until the bells at Nosa Señora do Mar struck midnight and then took me to Rúa dos Mortos where the boundary between the living and the dead dissolves on the threshold of the hour, and souls return in defiance of nature to rectify the injustices of their lives or seek prayers to aid them on their journeys through death. It is a place where old women supplicate the darkness to hear disincarnate children whisper of neglect, or spouses speak of torment in the damaged inflections of the dead. Dogs avoid the street, and believers wear garlic or silver amulets when they come in the night.

The paving stones in the old part of town were wet from intermittent rain and fugitive encounters with a tentative fog. Dripping condensation from the roofs of medieval houses, the lazy trickle of water from a fountain, and our own footsteps were the only sounds in the small square at the head of the street. An oil lamp in the window of an ancient house on the western side of the square was the single source of light. Cast through the branches of a laurel tree, the glow of the lamp shone on the pavement like the entrance to a subterranean realm of fire. Carved in the lintel above the door of the house, a palm and sword revealed a past association with the Inquisition. The building to its right was constructed of large granite blocks with no windows where legend claims apostates and unbelievers had been tortured and killed. Because they had suffered violent deaths, their souls were thought to walk the street and gave it its name.

We crossed the square with a respect for the dead bordering on trepidation, but were nevertheless confident in our mission—for we were there, or so we assumed, at the bidding of one who had gone before us, one who would protect us. If there were other spirits abroad in the night, it was to be expected. The line between the living and the dead in Porto Lúa was as indistinct as the line between belief and imagination, and the possibility of an incursion from the other side would not move us from our course. We waited patiently just inside the doorway of an abandoned house keeping what mother called a "vigil of snails." Occasionally a living creature ran past in the dripping shadows, and at one point I noticed a woman across the street beside a cistern who neither moved nor spoke the entire time we were there. After what may have been half an hour, we heard a weak, but high-pitched sigh issue from the darkness. Neither of us could locate its source or verify that it belonged to grandmother and not the devil or some other spirit, so we stepped out of the doorway and into the square as mother answered cautiously, repeatedly asking,

"Do you recognize the boy? Tell me, are you here for us?"

After a brief silence, an attenuated voice whispered, "Yes."

"Where are you?"

"Don't come too close. You'll frighten the boy."

"What can we do for you?"

"I'm cold."

"Would you like some clothes and a blanket?"

"Yes."

"Stay here. We'll go and get something warm for you. We'll be back."

On the way to the house to fetch the clothes and blanket, I told mother I didn't recall grandmother saying anything about the cold in our conversation or even expressing any material needs, but she ignored me and took a heavy woolen blanket from the closet in my room as well as a pair of grandfather's woolen trousers and a shirt from his room. By the time we returned to Rúa dos Mortos, it must have been close to two o'clock. We left the blanket and clothes on dry ground inside the doorway where we had been standing and returned home without any additional communication.

The next night we went back to the house where we had left the blanket and clothes and discovered they were gone. Mother announced our presence by reciting the first words of the Introit of the Missa defunctorum: *Requiem aeternam dona eis Domine, et lux perpetua luceat eis.* There was no response and so we waited as we had done on the first night until we heard another sigh in the darkness.

"Is there anything else we can do for you?" mother asked. "Is there any message you want us to pass along?"

"There is no message but the plea of a hungry soul."

"Tell us what you want."

"There is nothing to eat in the next world, and a soul still needs its sustenance."

"Will bread be enough?"

"Yes. Bring me bread."

We went home, just as we had done on the previous night, and returned with the provision the voice had requested. Mother wrapped the bread in a tea towel and left it in the doorway of the house but hanging from a hinge where the rats would not be able to reach it. The following night, the bread and towel were gone, and the voice expressed one final need:

"There are many tolls and fees in the next world, and I have nothing with which to pay my way."

"How much do you need?"

"Twenty pesetas."

Mother left the money in a hole in the doorframe. The next night it was gone, and though we waited until the first rooster crowed, the voice failed to return. We went back one more night, but again heard nothing and maintained no more vigils.

Mother felt blessed that she had been able to alleviate the needs of grandmother in the next world and was praised for her efforts by Father Ithacio.

But her satisfaction was short-lived. A few days later, as she was crossing the plaza on her way home from work, she saw a stranger wearing grandfather's shirt and trousers sitting outside O Galo drinking a glass of cognac.

"Where did you get that shirt?" she demanded.

"I found it in the street."

"You found it in the street?"

"Yes."

"Not in a house?"

"What difference does it make?"

"What if I were to tell you that's the shirt I gave my dead mother?"

"What if I were to tell you the dead have no need for shirts?"

"You would profane the dead?"

"I would tend to the living."

"Let the curses of every mother fall upon you and drag you to hell. And when they do, there will be no one to mourn and no one to care."

Before walking away, she spit in the glass of cognac the man had bought with our money. He laughed, poured it out, and ordered another. But his fate was sealed. God in His mercy granted the stranger no foreknowledge of his death, allowing him to leave this world in a state of oblivious intoxication. For the next few weeks, he was seen drinking in the alameda and on the benches along the seawall. Then one morning, his body was found floating in the water near the benches. Unknown and unmourned, he was buried without ceremony beneath an unmarked stone in a corner of the churchyard where the weeds had grown rank over forgotten graves. Upon hearing the news, mother expressed no remorse over the harshness of her curse, saying simply, "At least he had a decent shirt and trousers for his burial. That's more than he had before."

On the hottest days of summer, stray dogs slept beneath the plane trees along the quay where the seines were piled, and the town was scented with the sweat of women. When the sun finally relinquished its hold on the day and drifted toward the horizon, its low rays gilded the paving stones of the streets and plaza before giving way to a soft reddish glow that lit the roofs and façades of gray and white houses for a moment or two and was gone. The running lights of small boats returning for the night shone on the pink and silver surface of the bay. Gulls ceased their quarrels, content to mutter in quiet coves, and men gathered in the gloom of O Galo where the light that fell from lamps was too weak to escape the darkness of their faces.

One evening after the sun went down, and the trees and boulders on the mountain were barely visible, I was in the yard behind our house collecting dead branches and brush to use for kindling. Father had gone to the center of town, and mother was in the kitchen preparing supper. Over the mountain a storm had gathered, and momentarily the clouds, sculpted by soft nocturnal light, opened like a baroque altarpiece of blue marble to reveal a full moon surrounded by a silver sky. Lightning flashed within the clouds followed at some length by a low rumble of thunder, and then, as the clouds closed in around the moon, a sheet of luminous rain began to fall across its narrowing path of light. Rising from the forest, wide swaths of mist that people call the ventilations of heaven gathered in banks below the storm and spread slowly downward in a white blur like dimly seen cascades. Emerging from these falling clouds, seeming to float over the stones of the road, a pale figure stood out against the growing darkness. At first I thought it was a lonely revenant visiting from the graves of Lonxe do Sol, but as it grew nearer, it seemed to be a celestial creature with two white wings drifting down the mountain like a white blossom on a black stream disappearing and reappearing behind the trees along the road.

I called to mother to tell her an angel was approaching from the clouds, but she didn't respond. It cut toward the house through the orange and lemon orchard and entered the gate at the end of the garden. Hoping I hadn't been seen, I hid behind a wall and heard it cross the threshing floor and descend the steps where I had been standing. A man spoke, and mother began to cry. I crept to the door and saw a tall man in a damp gray suit drop a bedroll from one shoulder and a duffel bag from the other. He sat at the table as mother filled a cup with hot coffee and whipped a bowl of eggs for an omelet. When I slipped inside the door, the man reached out his great hand and placed it on my head.

Mother nodded to me and said, "Greet your uncle, child."

His fingers were dark like the roots of an old tree, and his face was so brown I couldn't tell where the sun damage stopped and the dust started. I stood back and stared at his black boots.

"That's the soil of Castile," he said.

"Castile," I said.

"When you're older, you'll come with me. We'll set out walking until we reach the moon."

"Such nonsense," mother said. "He doesn't understand that sort of talk."

But I did. In my own way. I hadn't seen my uncle since I was too young to remember, but as I stood back and studied this man at our table, I recognized him through his resemblance to my father, and in the weak light of the naked bulb hanging overhead, in the blue smoke of burning egg, I formed a memory of singular clarity that I would forever associate with his promise to take me to the moon.

"How did you know?" mother asked.

"I felt the beats of her heart dying in my own."

"You missed the funeral."

"I was too far."

The whiteness of his eyes appeared brighter in contrast to his earthen face, and he had not shaved for weeks. He had a kindly expression, but there was a deep weariness in the stillness of his gaze at odds with the unruly whimsy of his beard. He had come from an army of reapers and binders who used to cross Castile cutting the summer wheat and rye with sickles in the old way, gathering the sheaves by hand as they bent over in the fields with the morning sun on their backs and straw in their hair. They slept during the heat of the day, and at night, carrying their clothes and beds, their sickles and sledges, set out for the next job. Singing their descants to the summer moon, they walked down blue roads beneath a sky they knew as well as the land.

In her rush, mother prepared a place for Uncle Teo on the far side of the table where I usually sat, which left me with my back to the kitchen on the side reserved for guests. Noticing I was disconcerted by something, he leaned back and reached into his pocket.

"I brought you a coin," he said. "It has a horseman on it."

I smiled and said, "I thought you were an angel."

"Maybe I am."

He showed me a magic trick where he picked up two stones, placed one in each hand, and pressed them together to make a single stone. Then we ate a supper of eggs and bread. The dark green leaves of the fig tree pressed against the southern window, and a crease of salmon sky was still visible beneath the clouds in the west. Moths fluttered around the kitchen light in the dim interior of oily smoke and steam. Grandfather came home first followed shortly by father. They greeted Teo warmly and, after eating the rest of the eggs, opened a bottle of grandmother's *aguardiente* to celebrate his return. As Teo told them about the summer harvest and the long journey from Castile, mother cleaned the dishes, as people used to do, with fine white sand, and scrubbed the brass handles of the stove with ashes from the hearth. Then she gave me a pair of scissors, paste, and colored paper to keep me occupied and sat down next to father resting her chin on the palm of her hand as the conversation turned to grandmother's mock funeral and miraculous recovery.

On the wall to my right hung a calendar with a photograph of brightly colored fishing boats anchored in the port at Muros. It was cheaply printed, and the colors were garish—the sky unnaturally blue and the boats too red and green—but to me there was an enchantment in the intensity of those colors, as if I were seeing them for the first time. In reality, it was nothing more than an inexpensive way of advertising maritime supplies and a modest decoration in the home of working people—that had been out-of-date since the year I was born. Yet, as ordinary as it was, it presided over the meals and conversations I shared with my family throughout my childhood, and on that night it provided a model of composition as I attempted to re-create the boats and water with my bits of colored paper while my family spoke of the past and the lives and fates of their friends and neighbors in Porto Lúa. When I thought mother might notice I had stayed up past my bedtime, I pretended to listen to the conversation more intently hoping my interest would earn me a temporary dispensation from my exile to bed until I was too tired to hold my head up and slipped through the veil of a fading consciousness and someone lifted me and carried me upstairs as the muted conversation drifted off into the night.

Since grandmother's death, Mother had been waking me before she left for work, but because Uncle Teo was in the house, she let me sleep in. When I went downstairs, he was taking a bath in the zinc tub behind the kitchen. As soon as he heard me, he looked around the partition and asked,

"What are we going to eat for breakfast?"

"I'll make something for you, Uncle Teo."

As I cut several wedges from a round loaf of bread, he dried off and then went to the backyard where he retrieved a shirt and pair of trousers that had been drying in the morning sun. I spread the irregular wedges with a pasty lard the color of sand, and we ate breakfast on the stone bench beside the front door.

"What do you want for your birthday?" he asked.

"My birthday was last winter."

"Yes, but I wasn't here, so we'll need to get you something special to make up for the delay."

On our way down Rúa dos Loureiros, we came across an itinerant African with several rugs slung over his shoulder. He was tall and slender and wore a suit that was too short and a green, yellow, and red knit cap.

"Rugs for sale."

"Not today," said Teo.

"Not tomorrow," said the man. "Not the next day. I know."

"You know what?"

"I know your mind. For one *duro* I will tell you where you got your shoes, and for another I will tell you how many children your father had."

"All right, but then you have to allow me to win those *duros* back and two more by answering my riddle for you."

The African smiled and agreed.

"You got your shoes on your feet, and your father didn't have any children—your mother did."

Uncle Teo gave him the two *duros*.

"Now answer my riddle."

"All right."

"What is greater than God, more evil than Satan, and will keep you from dying?"

The African thought for a minute and said, "I don't know."

"Nothing."

The man laughed and paid Teo the two *duros* he had given him and two more.

As he walked away, he turned and shouted, "It was worth the money. I'm going to use that to make more."

"These winnings should pay for a couple of haircuts," Teo said.

There was one barber shop in Porto Lúa. It was a small room with a large plate glass window next to Don Horacio's shop. On days when the weather was fine, Fulgencio the barber and Don Horacio sat at a small iron table with a marble top outside the barber shop drinking coffee and playing dominoes. They were often joined by Benito, also known as O Gordo, who rolled down Rúa do Olvido in a wheelchair made from a salvaged captain's chair, plywood, and bicycle wheels. He had mutton chop sideburns, a few oily locks on the top of his head, and a gruff voice that sounded like a cinder block being dragged across pavement. As soon as he saw us, he called out,

"*Carallo*! Look who's here."

"I'd say he hasn't had a haircut since his last visit," said Fulgencio.

"Not since Medina del Campo," Teo answered, "and I want one for the boy too."

They left their dominoes and half-empty cups of coffee on the table and led us inside where there was a chair unlike any I had seen before with a padded headrest, a brass footrest, crimson leather upholstery, and a foot-operated lift. It also served for dentistry since Fulgencio, in addition to being Porto Lúa's only barber, was its principal puller of teeth. Behind the chair was a mirror set in a large wooden frame and a mahogany counter scavenged from a shipwreck where razors, scissors, combs, and pliers sat in a jumble of mugs and jars beside a stack of white towels and folded white sheets. Fulgencio had been one of the handsomest young men in Porto Lúa and had maintained his vanity well beyond middle age. While working on a customer, he turned the great chair toward the mirror and addressed both his client and audience across the room in their reflection, but too often he was looking at himself, studying his own expression and movement as he gesticulated with the razor, comb, or brush that was in his hand at that moment.

"Always a challenge to shave a Celt," he said, as he watched himself lather a brush, "with copper wires for a beard. I may have to buy a new razor after this."

"Where's Armando?" Teo asked.

"You haven't heard?"

"No."

"Succumbed to drink."

"Perished."

"Out of fear."

"Of what?"

"Of dying, of course."

"Drinking as much as he did, he was afraid he would die prematurely like his dissolute father had done."

"So he drank himself to death."

"So he did."

"Time weighs more heavily on the shoulders of those who can bear it less," said Don Horacio.

"How old was his father when he died?"

"Armando had always believed he was thirty-eight," said the barber. "And so when our friend turned thirty-nine, he thought he had escaped the curse of his paternity, and to celebrate he went to his father's grave to drink with his ghost. But when he woke up in the churchyard the next morning, he discovered his father had lived to forty-two. So for three years he was beset by severe anxiety and died of acute alcohol poisoning two weeks before his forty-second birthday."

"He was a good man but for the bottle," said Don Horacio.

"*Carallo!*" cried O Gordo. "A cursèd life."

After his haircut, Teo asked Fulgencio to show me the famous painting he kept hidden among the mirrors and bottles and broken chairs of his storage room. With the choreographed flourish of a bullfighter in the ring, the barber removed the sheet over Teo and tossed it into a wicker hamper. Then he excused himself with a bow, passed through the door at the back of the shop, and returned momentarily with a plaid blanket whiskered with bits of straw and folded into a rumpled square. As he opened it, dust and mold rose like black smoke, and the white husk of a wood louse fell like a bead to the floor. He dropped the blanket on an empty chair and proudly held the painting up to the light entering the front of the shop. The yellow of an incandescent dusk shone brightly in contrast to the silhouette of a woman riding a donkey down a road. To the right, balancing the composition, was a maritime pine whose dark branches were pierced by the light the way a resurrection glory might shine through stained glass.

"This was painted by Picasso when he was living in Coruña. He was only a few years older than you are."

"It will give you something to aspire to."

"Where did you get it?"

"I won it playing *birisca*."

I had no idea who Picasso was and didn't think to inquire how such a famous painting could be won in a card game or be sitting in a windowless room behind a barber shop in Porto Lúa.

Fulgencio propped the painting up against the mirror for all to admire and then lifted me up and placed me in the upholstered chair. He took his soap dish and brush, lathered my face, and pretended to shave me with the dull side of the razor. The lights flickered several times and went out, so the group returned to the street where Fulgencio wrapped me in a white sheet and gave me my first professional haircut. As I leaned back in the chair, I noticed one, and then another, ivory butterfly fluttering down Rúa do Olvido like the first snow-flakes of a winter storm. Then several more appeared behind them. Some settled on the purple flowers growing in the crevices of buildings while others gathered in clusters on the damp walls. By the time Fulgencio had finished cutting my hair, the sky was full of them. As Teo and I walked across the plaza, we seemed to follow them, but any direction one chose would have given the same impression: they were floating across the blue sky in every direction like drifting clouds of apple blossoms. I imagined the beating of so many wings could reverse the direction of the wind and send light sallies of air over distant hills and towns announcing their arrival in the stirring trees. A donkey had broken free of its tether and was standing in the middle of the plaza as children and their parents stopped to watch the sky. One mother told her daughter the butterflies had come from distant lands and were carrying the souls of infants across the sea to paradise.

Over the door of the shop owned by María Dolores was a sign in the form of an escutcheon that hung from an iron pike perpendicular to the building. It read simply, *Ultramarinos*. The premises had once housed the stagecoach office, and there was still a mounting block carved from stone in front of the building. It was one of the first stores in Porto Lúa that did not carry rope, netting, buckets, tobacco, saws, lanterns, or corking machines. María Dolores began by stocking exotic foods from overseas, but gradually specialized in what she knew best: men's and women's apparel, hosiery and shoes, towels, yarn, First Communion clothes, pictures of the Sacred Heart of Jesus wrapped in thorns, devotional candles, and women's lingerie displayed on pinkish manikins, whose anatomical details caused an uproar until the offending parts were filed down and painted over with a color that was much too dark, leaving an impression worse than before. Added later, at the back of the store, were shelves of insecticides, detergent, cologne, scented soaps, toys, and a variety of other unrelated items.

The owner herself greeted us as we entered. She was meticulously dressed and liberally embellished with lipstick and rouge; her manner was courteous, and she called the rare man who entered her store, regardless of his class, *cabaleiro*. In a cruel twist, her detractors called her *cabalo* because of her prominent teeth and long head. Her hair was straight and fell down her back as if deadened by the tedium of her conversation, and her large brown eyes studied her customers from beneath coffee-colored lids. With stout legs, she walked with short, quick steps, hammering the wooden floor with her heels as if to punctuate her presence.

"*Bos días, cabaleiros*. How may I help you?"

"I have something in mind for the boy."

Teo nodded toward the back of the store and then, without waiting to be directed, walked down an aisle to a shelf stocked with devotional candles decorated with images of the Holy Family, the Virgin and Child, and the resurrected Christ, as well as two Paschal candles bearing the Greek letters alpha and omega. Above the candles, gathering dust in a net of blue yarn, was a plastic soccer ball marked with black pentagons and white hexagons. Teo took it down from the shelf and handed it to María Dolores.

"This is what we want."

She led us back to the front of the store where Teo took a handful of coins from his pocket and paid for the prize as I stood beside him with an expression of wonder and gratitude. I had never received a gift this valuable and my birthday was still months away.

The butterflies had almost disappeared by the time we went back outside, but the donkey was still there eating a carrot from the hand of a Romani trader. Haze rose over the bay to brighten the afternoon light but dull the clarity of the day.

When a butterfly landed on my head, Teo was delighted.

"Behold," he said, "the sacrament of truth has touched you through this messenger. You will know more than the physical world can hold."

"That's a lot," I said.

We went down the cobbled lane in front of the houses built by The Society of the Immaculate Conception for the Benefit of the Widows and Orphans of Seafarers and descended the steps at the southern end of the port where the Deva enters the sea. The retreating tide had exposed a hard, flat beach littered with oxblood pebbles and broken shells. The force of the river's current kept the inlet clear and deep, but dark green clumps of seaweed had washed up on the beach, blown from the harbor by the north wind. Teo and I tossed the piles of kelp and bladder wrack back in the water, marked off a pitch in the sand, and set up goal posts of driftwood we gathered from the base of the seawall. Under his instruction, beneath the late summer sun, along the bubbling edge of the shifting tide, I learned to play the game.

Timing our trips when the sea was out, we returned to the beach every day. One morning the children next door saw us leave the house and joined us as we walked down the hillside to the shore. Ramón was six years older than I was, María was my age, and Miguel was a year younger. Ramón and María formed one team, and Miguel and I formed another. We raced back and forth across the sand passing the ball, crowding each other out of the way, falling, getting up, falling again, scoring, and shouting in celebration. When the ball veered off course and landed in the water, Ramón swam out to retrieve it, and when we grew tired, we lay on the beach and listened to the waves encroaching on our pitch as the clouds moved slowly overhead. Teo watched us from the shadow of the seawall for a little while and then went home to help grandfather repair the roof on the barn. He knew what he was doing, not just as far as roofing goes, but as far as what we needed after the loss of grandmother. Even though he did little of the actual work, grandfather felt he was once again contributing to the needs of the family, and I was out of the house, exercising in the freshness of the morning air.

I had been living too much under the influence of night—my thoughts produced by its emptiness—but in the sunlight, these thoughts disappeared, drawn up like vapor into the ether. Feeling my heels press the hot sand, my bare feet licked by the foam of waves, I laughed with my friends in the light of our freedom, the joy of our bodies. We were so young, and life was so new that we were still able to take pleasure from the simple fact of being. And so I learned to live two lives, or, rather, I learned to live between two lives. One on the outside, engaging with others in the brightness of day, and one within attempting to reconcile myself to the indifference of night.

Where the seawall stopped, littoral grasses grew in the gaps between boulders that had been brought in to protect the embankment against the surging tides of storms. Nervously protecting their nests, small birds flitted among the granite slabs and sea spurrey as kittiwakes passed overhead. Retreating from the sun one afternoon, we climbed over the tumble of rocks and followed the northern bank of the Deva beneath the Roman bridge as far as the first step of falls where an abandoned fishing boat rested in the silt exposed at low tide. We waded in and with cupped hands bailed stranded minnows back into the river. In the verdurous tunnel of the wooded gorge, willows leaned over the water caressing the current with their slender branches like women washing their hair. Softly downed by a terry sheen of moss, the muscular trunks of oaks were bound by nets of living ivy and the thick dead vines of its antecedents that clung to the bark like snakes frozen in a predatory advance. There were lilies and irises growing along the bank, patches of watercress in the shallows, and long, green banners of aquatic weeds rippling in the current. Shouting above the roar of the water, we climbed to a cool hollow where mist from the falls gathered in crystal globes on the leaves of ferns. Soaking our pant legs with the moisture, we walked through the green forest light to a layered bluff that provided a lintel to the cave grandmother had called the ice house. Inside were brick cabinets with rusty fittings and moldy wooden doors, and on the ground were piles of decomposing straw and the abandoned nests of small mammals. Kings of the castle we had claimed, we imagined furnishing it with homemade chairs and holding our solemn conclaves in its musty air. We spent the rest of the afternoon fashioning spears and swords from the alders in the grove and vowed to protect our cave against any Roman, Celt, or Moor who might seek its shelter.

By the time we returned to Rúa dos Loureiros, it was late. We said goodbye to each other in the dusk light and entered our homes for supper. I had seen less of Uncle Teo since he had started working on the roof. He and grandfather had hauled several cartloads of pantiles and battens up from the quay and had already constructed a frame from rough timbers and crossed it with the slats. At night he met his friends at O Galo to pass the time drinking Ribeiro and playing cards. So unless I pitched in and helped around the barn during the day, the only time I saw him was at the table for the evening meal when most of our conversations centered around people and events of the past, but after my day of exploration, he must have noticed the scratches on my skin or burrs in my hair and asked me what I'd been doing.

"We went up the river from the beach," I said.

"And what did you find?"

"Near the bridge there was an old boat lying in the water, and farther up the river was the ice house grandmother told me about. It's really just a cave."

"Did you find any ice?"

"No. No one uses it anymore."

"Do you know why?"

"No."

"A long time ago, ice came to Porto Lúa in mule carts built of heavy wood and tightly sealed. The blocks of ice were buried in straw, and water dripped from wagons on hot summer days. People bought the blocks and stored them in the cave with their cheese and butter."

"Grandmother said they hauled the ice down from the mountain."

"That was before my time."

"Why don't they bring it in carts anymore?"

"Because electricity arrived."

"Arrived from where?"

"From dams in the interior."

"Bankers in cahoots with the government build the dams and flood the towns and then sell the electricity as if anyone could own it," grandfather added.

"You've seen the granite posts and cables coming down the mountain through a clear swath in the forest."

"Yes."

"A small army of men camped on Aracelo and cut that swath and strung the cable in order to bring electricity over the mountain, and every year or two some of them return to reattach the cable when the storms blow it down. The town bought a subscription to use the electricity and lit a ring of light bulbs around the plaza and along the quay. They were first switched on one evening to great fanfare by the mayor. People stood silently in awe as the filaments in the large, clear globes began to redden, like worms glowing in a fire. As they turned orange, people started to clap, and, as they turned white, a cheer went up from the crowd. Then the filaments dimmed, accompanied by a sigh and brightened again, a cycle they repeat even to this day. Most of the people had no interest in receiving electricity and said they could not see any advantage in it and that it was simply another trick by the government to take money out of the pockets of working people, but some people decided it wasn't so bad when the first ice machine and radio arrived in Porto Lúa."

"Uncle Teo?"

"Yes?"

"Where do you live?"

"Here and there."

"Why don't you live in Porto Lúa with us?"

"I guess I just got used to going from place to place."

"Because of the war," grandfather said.

Teo leaned back in his chair and lit a cigarette. The conversation was suspended for a moment as he blew the first draw of smoke out and watched it rise toward the light bulb that hung from the ceiling.

"Did you ever shoot anybody?"

"That's enough for tonight," said mother.

"What happened?" I asked.

"Many things. Many bad things."

"But you won."

"No. No one wins."

"Why not?"

"Because when the disagreements have been forgotten, and the ideals of a former age have passed into history, the dead are still dead and gone forever."

"That's enough," mother said. "You're going to give him nightmares. You can continue this conversation tomorrow."

She took me upstairs and sang a song to help me fall asleep, but I stayed awake long enough to imagine myself in battles of my own played out in the woods above the Deva where I defended the ice house with my alder sword.

The following morning a warm wind blew off the sea, and the clothes hanging on the line behind our house rippled and snapped like a string of nautical flags. In the high branches of pine trees beyond the orchard, fledgling crows cried out weirdly like infants schooled in the voices of the damned. Farther to the south, testifying to the patience of an ageless land, an oxcart creaked slowly up the hillside between the ruins of granite houses toward narrow fields of corn and kale. I found Teo on a ladder nailing the battens to the trusses on the roof of the barn. Grandfather was sitting on a mound of old tiles smoking. I had not forgotten the conversation of the previous night and was single-minded in my search for answers. After sitting beside grandfather for several minutes listening to their conversation, I could no longer contain my curiosity.

"I want to know why Uncle Teo left."

"Still thinking about that?"

"You said it was because of the war."

"It's because the army came to Porto Lúa looking for conscripts."

"And to arrest the communists and socialists, the leaders of the fishermen's syndicate, Bachiario, and anyone else they could find who might not agree with their views."

"What's a conscript?"

"Someone they force to join the army."

"What about you, grandfather?"

"I was too old to be of much use. And your father was too young."

Teo came down from the roof and sat on the sawhorse he was using to cut the battens. There were bits of chaff and sawdust in his hair picked up from the wooden strips he had carried on his head.

"It began one morning in a dense fog just above Praia Branca," he said. "Ánxel Varela was plowing a strip of land when he looked up and saw several soldiers approaching with their rifles leveled. He raised his arms and shouted, 'I am a loyal son of His Majesty, the King. Shoot me if you will.' The soldiers ignored him and continued to march forward, disappearing into the fog. A few moments later, there were bright flashes in the white mist followed by the thunder of explosions and gunfire. Someone called out, 'For God's sake, it's me.' Then everything went quiet. When the sun finally broke through the fog, the soldiers were able to orient themselves and found the road to Porto Lúa. By the time the sky had cleared, several personnel carriers and numerous infantrymen were crossing the Roman bridge into the plaza, filling the air with black diesel exhaust.

"It was a busy time of the day, but as soon as people caught sight of the soldiers, they disappeared into the narrow streets and alleys of the old town and hid behind shuttered windows. The soldiers tracked down Xosé Pombal, Porto Lúa's constable, in the toilet at O Galo. He found a ladder for them, and they placed it against the Tower of Names. When they had compiled a list of all the men between the ages of sixteen and forty, they fanned out across the town knocking on doors. The penalty for those evading conscription was death, once in a summary execution. I was sitting in the kitchen when I heard a gunshot not far from our house. An unassuming fisherman who worked for the syndicate was staying with his sisters when a group of soldiers knocked on the front door looking for him. He leapt to the roof of an adjacent shed in his night clothes and ran down the street where he was shot in the back. The guard blocked off the street and removed the body, leaving thin streams of blood and red pools between the paving stones."

"There were informers who helped them find people."

"Father Ithacio was one of them."

"What did you do, Uncle Teo?"

"I went outside to see what was going on and heard another shot. Then one of our neighbors came running up the street to warn people that soldiers were assembling at the bottom of the slope. I looked at a pool of rainwater in the street and thought how if I am shot and suffer the pains of death, that pool will remain there to reflect the sky. The world will go on without me. In that moment I understood more clearly than I ever had that a man must rely not on a deceptive sense of justice or some hope in the rightness of things, but on his own wits and effort to determine his fate, and so in less than a minute I said goodbye to everyone in the house and took a blanket, a knife, and a loaf of bread and ran up the lane past the orchard to the Roman road."

"Did they follow you?"

"They did not. The effort was too great for them, and they were afraid of ambushes in the forest. I went to Lonxe do Sol for a few days and then lived in a cave called Casa Xoana with several other men. The people of Lonxe gave us food and blankets and an M93 Mauser they used to shoot wolves."

Grandfather dropped his cigarette on the ground. Although he could barely remember what he had done the previous day, his recollections of the war were clear and precise.

"Your father and I witnessed what happened next. With the help of the priest and other collaborators in town, the soldiers marched all the men who were reputed to be Communists or Republicans down to the main plaza. They were joined by anyone the soldiers could find who appeared to be between the ages of sixteen and forty. The commanding officer, Colonel Florentino, ordered them to line up against the wall beneath the alameda.

"'You have a choice,' he said. 'You may honor your homeland, your families, and your God by stepping forward to join us, or you may die a dog's death and be forgotten.'

"Then he called on each man to state his name and decision. To those men who refused to speak, he assigned names based on a distinguishing feature of their capture or appearance. For example, when he came to a man found hiding on the edge of the forest, he called out, 'Félix Caos, one arm longer than the other.' And a man with an unusual birthmark on his forehead he called, 'Marco Zapato, birthmark in the shape of a shoe.' When none of the men chose to step forward, the colonel gave an order for them to be blindfolded. Women, children, and old people gathered on the edge of the plaza. Several of the women had to be restrained. Others fell to the ground weeping. Father Ithacio declared that those to be executed were blessed for they knew the moment of their death and therefore had the opportunity to confess. Only three did. The soldiers lined up in a row facing the men, raised their rifles, and, on command, fired. To the colonel's surprise, one of the prisoners dropped to his knees and toppled forward hitting the pavement with his face. A young soldier no older than a boy dropped his rifle and began to cry. '*Imbécil!*' shouted the colonel. 'How do you confuse live bullets and blanks? Look at their markings!' He took the young man's pistol from its holster, threatened to shoot him, and struck him across the face with the butt of the weapon, breaking his nose.

"Then Colonel Florentino walked past the prisoners and said, 'I have allowed you to live, but I have the power to have you shot.'

"One of the men responded, saying, 'And we have the

power to let you shoot us.'

"The colonel walked back to the man who spoke and said, 'You're not afraid.'

"'No.'

"'Either shoot us or let us go,' another man said.

"'I have something better in mind. For this you can thank your friend who talks too much.'"

"What did he do?" I asked.

"He called for a carpenter."

"A carpenter?"

"He counted the number of prisoners and ordered him to build thirty-three coffins with a thick pane of glass on the lid where a corpse might look out. Then, when the prisoners had been locked in the market under an armed guard, he called for Xosé Pombal.

"'This is only a fraction of the men we're looking for,' he said. 'Where is the mayor of this town?'

"'On the mountain hunting.'

"'On the mountain?'

"'Yes. He hunts boar this time of the year.'

"'You tell him to be in his office tomorrow morning at eight o'clock, or we will burn every building on this plaza.'"

Grandfather took another cigarette from his pocket and lit it.

"Did he find the mayor?" I asked.

"Don Andrés was a young man then, and because he was a member of the Partido Galeguista, he had made himself scarce at the first sign of trouble. After stopping by his house, Xosé found the mayor hiding in Capela de Santa Lupa, and when he told him what Colonel Florentino had said, Andrés was beside himself with fear.

"'What are we going to do?' he asked. 'I can't turn myself over to them. They'll shoot me.'

"'We can't let them destroy the town either,' said Xosé.

"As Don Andrés and Xosé were discussing the problem, the mayor noticed they weren't alone. Sitting in the front row of the church was Cotolay, an *inocente*, who spent entire days there staring at the cross over the altar without saying a word to anyone."

"I know who Cotolay is."

"In those days he used to wash himself with mud, dry himself with gypsum, sleep on ash pits and dung heaps, wear a tunic of horsehair, and proclaim himself the mayor of the City of God. He walked through the streets at some distance from others because he feared their shadows. If touched by one, he would bathe in the sea for the length of nine waves. At night he had terrifying visions that the souls of the damned had returned to rule the world disguised as the living. When his illness was especially troublesome, he would stand in the middle of the plaza and cry that God's greatest mistake was creating human beings.

"'The answer to our problem may be sitting right over there,' Don Andrés said.

"'Cotolay?'

"'Go to my house and tell María Dolores to give you one of my shirts, a tie, and a black suit. And my sash. Oh, and a pair of shoes too. They should fit. If not, we'll cut up some rags and stuff them into the toes. And bring a couple of bottles of my *aguardiente*.'

"In addition to his reputation as an eremite, Cotolay was known for his high consumption of, and low tolerance for, alcohol, a fact Don Andrés used to his advantage. After Xosé returned, the three of them had a drink together, but only Cotolay continued to imbibe throughout the evening. At two o'clock in the morning, Xosé and Don Andrés dressed him in the suit and sash and helped him down the darkened streets until they reached the back entrance of the town hall. They left him sitting in the mayor's chair strapped in with a belt so he wouldn't fall over. Then Don Andrés went back through the narrow streets of the old part of town to a boat that he took across the bay to Illa da Luz. The next morning, just before eight o'clock, Xosé took the belt off Cotolay. Then, on the hour, opened the door to the town hall and escorted Colonel Florentino upstairs where the acting mayor, wearing the suit and sash, was still asleep. When Xosé woke him, he jerked his head up and stared at the light coming in on the balcony.

"'Where am I? Everything looks like glass.'

"'At work, your honor. You must have dozed off. Colonel Florentino is here to see you.'

"Cotolay looked at the clothes he was wearing and then looked around the room. He had enough understanding to know where he was even if he had no idea why he was there.

"'I've come to your town to arrest its traitors,' the colonel said. 'Where can I find the rest of the Communists, Socialists, and atheists, and a heretic called Bachiario?'

"'They're with God,' answered Cotolay.

"'With God?'

"'God is everywhere.'

"'I'm going to ask you one more time, and I want a straight answer. Do you understand? Where can I find these people?'

"'Pray with me, colonel.'

"Florentino turned to Xosé, who was standing by the door. 'What's wrong with this man?'

"'He's very religious, sir.'

"'Does he ever make sense?'

"'All life in praise of God.'

"'I'm as religious as the next man,' the colonel said, 'but right now I want some answers. Both of you come with me.'

"They went downstairs and out the front door of the town hall into the plaza. When people saw Cotolay wearing the mayor's sash, they started laughing. Thinking they were laughing at him, the colonel fired a shot in the air.

"'Did you hear his confession, Cotolay?' someone called out.

"Prompted by the irreverence, he lunged toward the crowd, sweeping his hand before him as if gathering their wits with his clawed fingers. They drew back from him, forming a semicircle. When another heckler called out behind him, he repeated the gesture, and the crowd drew back again so that he found himself encircled by his neighbors with the colonel by his side.

"'*Coño!*' he shouted. 'How can a man confess his sins to another man? How is that? Did a man create men? Who among you has the power to forgive? Who among you can take away the sins of the world? That's why the priests hate me. But God knows. God knows the iniquity, the hubris, the license. The philosophers are no better. They steal our happiness with their tricks of reason. *Coño!* They waited too long to kill Socrates. Empedocles knew what to do. They fill your head with ideas of the eternal and tell you to bear up under the torments of life. Give me a man who howls in his pain like a wolf at the moon. The hypocrites hate me because I show them for what they are.'

"'You,' the colonel said to Cotolay, 'that's enough.' Then he pointed to two people at random in the crowd and asked them if they knew Cotolay.

"'Yes, sir,' they replied.

"'And who is he?'

"'He's our mayor, sir.'

"'Let's see what the priest has to say.'

"With Cotolay and Xosé walking beside him followed by his soldiers, the colonel ascended Via Sagrada to Nosa Señora do Mar. Inside they found a young farmer named Caamaño standing at the altar wearing a cassock.

"'Where is the old priest who spoke to my men earlier?'

"'Father Ithacio has gone up the mountain to serve the

99

people of the villages. He should be back in a week or two.'

"It was true that Father Ithacio was on the mountain, but he wasn't there serving the people. After the priest had given the colonel a list of names, a group of men took him to Lonxe do Sol in the middle of the night and locked him in a storage cellar beneath an abandoned barn.

"'Who are you?' asked the colonel.

"'Father Antonio.'

"'How long have you been here?'

"'I'm just visiting, colonel. To help out while Father Ithacio is on his mission.'

"'Do you know who this man is?'

"When the colonel turned to Cotolay, he found the *inocente* struggling with two of the soldiers as he attempted to kneel before the altar.

"'Never mind, Father. I see what's going on here.'

"Colonel Florentino led the group back to the plaza where he formally invested Cotolay with civil authority in the town and, in a public announcement made from the balcony of town hall, informed the people of Porto Lúa that his men were there to ensure the edicts of the mayor were carried out in full. Then he invited the *inocente* to speak. Cotolay stepped forward to the front of the balcony, looked around the plaza and said, 'I must confess that until today I had wondered whether I was a madman dreaming of being the mayor or the mayor dreaming of being a madman. This morning when I woke up, I realized that I am in fact the mayor of the City of God, that this is my office, and you are my people. The Almighty had a choice when He created me and that was to create nothing or to create something. By creating something other than Himself, He created what was less than all-good. But this relative evil is still a higher good than nothing because it demonstrates God's love. And yet that was not enough. God also gave us the gift of free will, the ability to do good and to do evil. Because we are less than all-good, we must use our free will to deserve God's love. Therefore, I call upon you, the citizens of the City of God, to obey the following edicts. Shoes and socks must be removed during Mass. No one is allowed to approach me when the moon is full. Demons will be discouraged from interrupting religious services by the frequent interjection of imprecations. Fourteen will replace the numbers one and four. And all holes where entry may be gained to other worlds will be anointed with holy unguents and closed.'

"The next day Colonel Florentino decided to punish those who had fled to the mountain by rounding up their families and trying them as collaborators who had helped their sons and brothers and husbands escape in defiance of his orders. His soldiers went to every house where his informants had told him a young man had been living before the arrival of his troops. They broke down doors and dragged old men and women, young boys and daughters, down through the streets to the plaza where they were questioned."

"Did you and father have to go?" I asked.

"Yes. We went willingly and explained that Teo had by chance left to find work two days before the soldiers arrived. They kept us there for several hours, and when they could find no informant to dispute this story, they let us go with the warning that hiding or aiding a fugitive of the state could result in immediate death. The families who could offer no better story or who could not agree on a story were detained. In one case, a child contradicted the sworn statement of her father, and the poor man was taken to the market and held with the other prisoners. Tables were brought out from the town hall, and the soldiers tried to form juries, but people were afraid of what might happen to them when the soldiers left and refused to serve. Then Colonel Florentino ordered his men to press-gang every adult they could find into jury duty, but these involuntary jurors invariably found the defendants innocent and were in turn put on trial for subverting justice.

"The making of coffins was slowed by the increasing number of people the colonel sent to the market. By the time they were finished, three weeks later, the total number of prisoners had risen to forty-eight, including Xosé Pombal. The coffins were placed on oxcarts and carried up Via Sagrada followed by the prisoners and the soldiers with their bayonets fixed in place. When they reached the cemetery, the men, who were by this time unwashed and emaciated, were given shovels and told to dig their own graves. As the soldiers watched with guns drawn, the prisoners dug deep pits in the mud long enough and wide enough to accommodate the wooden boxes. Then their hands and feet were bound, and they were placed one by one in the coffins. Before the lids were sealed, Colonel Florentino asked each man to tell him who the principal agitators in the town were as well as the names of the men who were hiding on the mountain. None of the men answered, and so the lids of the coffins were nailed shut and lowered into the earth. 'If you change your mind,' the colonel shouted, 'you can wink through the window, and we will retrieve you. Otherwise, rest well. That will be your bed until your flesh becomes the earth.' As women were weeping on the grass behind him, he gave his troops the signal to begin shoveling dirt into the graves.

"If the colonel had taken his eyes from the grim labor of his men and the faces of the living corpses to glance at the mountain for a moment, he might have seen the reflection of the sun off the barrel of a rifle and a man poised among the boulders and then a small flash of light. Barely audible above the sound of the wind coming off the sea and the earth raining down on the wooden coffins, a shot rang out. It missed. The colonel turned to look. Before the report of the second shot reached us, we heard what sounded like the flick of a finger on taut wool and saw a red spray flash over the green grass, and then Colonel Florentino, all his power gone forever, leaned forward, stroking the air for support, and collapsed into the mud. In the seconds that followed, the soldiers paused, awestruck by the horror, and then another and another exploded in bright red bursts. As the remaining soldiers dropped their shovels and fled down Via Sagrada, the mothers and wives of the men in the coffins pried off the lids while the old men and boys picked up the rifles of the fallen soldiers and followed the others down the hill to the plaza where their trucks were parked. But the vehicles had been sabotaged, and the soldiers were isolated and exposed in the open space. Those who sought the cover of the trucks died in flames when the fuel tanks erupted in the crossfire and the rest were killed after a brief exchange with men hiding in the buildings and alleys around the plaza. You can still see cracks in the stone pavement caused by the heat of the fires. Within hours, the burnt-out shells of the trucks had been hauled to a deep cove off the headland and dumped in the sea, the scorched stones of the plaza had been washed and scrubbed, and the bodies of the dead had been buried in a remote field on the mountain. Two men stole dynamite from a quarry on the eastern side of Aracelo and towed an abandoned fishing boat around the headland to an estuary where the coastal road crosses a wide sandy inlet. They anchored the boat beneath the bridge and destroyed it with a powerful explosion that effectively sealed Porto Lúa off from any approach by land except over the mountain."

"Did more soldiers come?"

"They did not. People expected them to and were afraid, but none appeared. One morning an unidentified plane circled in the sky and dropped a single bomb in the harbor before flying off, but there were no other sanctions against the town, and no one ever came in search of the lost soldiers. It was as if nothing had happened."

"The war was fought in many places," said Uncle Teo, "and

Porto Lúa was not important enough for the army to spend their resources here."

"For many years the town was abandoned by the government and received no mail. There was no contact with the outside world except by sea and over the mountain. The roads fell into disrepair. The electricity stopped. And no one seemed to care. There was still trade as people went back and forth to Muros in their boats bringing olive oil and gasoline and nets and buckets. But we survived on our own and in some ways were better off than we had been before. When the coastal road was widened and resurfaced, a new bridge was built with steel and cement, and Porto Lúa was once again a part of the world."

"What did they do to Father Ithacio and the mayor?"

"Father Ithacio was left in the barn in Lonxe do Sol until the war ended. When he returned to Porto Lúa, he had aged significantly and been forgotten by the archdiocese. He was still accepted as the priest, but for several years he was only allowed to leave the rectory to say Mass and officiate at religious ceremonies. At the same time, three other informants lost their boats and homes and were forced to leave Porto Lúa. Even though Don Andrés returned from Illa da Luz when the soldiers were killed, Cotolay remained in office for another year because people decided they would rather close the holes to other worlds than listen to long-winded speeches."

"What did you do, Uncle Teo?"

"I lived in Casa Xoana for a few months, but the cave is windy and cold in the winter, so I traveled east toward the Pyrenees. To avoid the military, I took up with smugglers who travelled at night and provided safe houses during the day."

The sun was now setting behind Illa da Luz rather than the open sea, and the yellow mornings of late summer had begun to give way to dense fogs that rolled across the bay to revive the ferns and patches of moss that grew on the stone walls around our house. Uncle Teo would be leaving soon. I could tell because he had taken up the tasks he had avoided since his arrival: darning his trousers and visiting Fulgencio to have a tooth pulled.

I thought of him alone among the lights of a strange city, among strange people, and, if he went far enough, among the inflections of a foreign language.

"Where are you going?"

"I don't know yet. I'll head east until I find work."

"Until you reach the moon."

"Yes."

"Maybe someday I'll go with you."

"Maybe you will. Maybe someday we'll cross the mountain together and pass through the towns and villages of Galicia and León and Castile and see the towers and domes of great cities."

On his last night in Porto Lúa, Uncle Teo bought a round of drinks for everyone at O Galo and walked home alone in the darkness. The next morning he gave father money to buy sheets of polished granite to mark the graves of grandmother and grandfather as well as his own, unless, as he put it, he never made it back. I helped him retrieve his clothes from the line where they were drying and, after he had packed his few possessions and taken an emotional leave of the family, walked with him up the lane behind the house. We stopped along the way to pick blackberries from the hedge, and I asked him if he wished he had a home somewhere and family of his own.

"Sometimes I think about that," he said. "I ask myself what a different life would have been like. But all lives are journeys of sorts. When you travel from place to place, you leave behind cities and towns and the friends you make, and when you stay in one place, you still travel through time and lose your loved ones and friends or they lose you. A journey is like a story, and even if we leave everything we acquire on the journey behind, we will always have the story."

We continued walking until we came to a shady spot under an oak tree a mile up the Roman road where he hoisted his bedroll and duffel bag more comfortably on his shoulders and told me it was time for us to say goodbye.

"As you grow older, you'll need to carry more of the burden in your family. Help your mother and father, and especially grandfather. Work hard and do what your parents ask you to do."

"I will," I said.

"I know you will."

He disappeared through the trees and then reappeared higher up where the road curves south above the gorge of the Deva. He waved one more time, and I waved back. Then with his two wings brightly lit by the morning sun, he ascended the mountain toward the sky.

The rest of that summer, time moved at the pace of my discoveries. María, Miguel, and I scavenged the rocks and beaches along the shore looking for shells and sea glass, and when the days were hot, we returned to the banks of the Deva to explore its colony of watermills. These were small stone huts with tile roofs that descended like steps along the falling contours of the mountain. Some were still in use and locked, while others had been abandoned to the elements. The roofs of the latter had typically collapsed, and their millstones had been removed, but water continued to flow through their races lined with moss and partially hidden beneath overgrowths of brambles and ferns and nettles and milkweed blown on sea winds from the New World. In one of the channels beside a dense thicket of alders and young figs, we built a dam with bricks from the ice house and reinforced it with large stones to create a pool which we stocked with small fish caught in a bucket and carried up from the river. The plan was to keep them there until they grew large enough to sell in the market and use the money to finance our futures in football, but after a heavy rain, we returned to find the bricks and stones scattered down the race and the fish gone, presumably carried through the channel to more tranquil waters in the deep pools of the river below.

My chores included feeding the pig and chickens first thing in the morning and cutting grass for the ox with a small sickle. I helped Marcella and some of the other elderly people in our neighborhood by running errands for them and delivering messages. In the afternoons I closed down the stall in the market with mother, and on several mornings when the breezes were light, I accompanied father to the waters off the headland to learn how to sail and drop the nets. With grandfather I set several putchers on the Deva and to my great surprise returned to find a salmon in one, which mother cleaned and served for dinner.

Though more conscious of the need to make myself useful around the house, I still had time to kick the football back and forth on the street, bouncing it off walls until Ramón and Miguel heard me, and we went down the hill to the beach rather than play in front of our houses where the pavement was marred by fills of broken tiles, patches of rough cement, and piles of manure. The summer sun had turned the grass pale brown, but the fields were still full of late flowers. Blue and purple morning glories covered the walls of gardens and lanes, and the fruit in the orchards was growing ripe. In the evenings when we returned from the beach, the streets shone as if encased in amber, and the hum of cicadas softened the lingering heat of cloudless days.

Every year on the first of September, the faithful of Porto Lúa celebrate the Feast of Nosa Señora do Mar. It's not the date established by the liturgical calendar and celebrated elsewhere because the townspeople have their own reason for giving thanks. On this day in 1755, a ship foundered on the rocks off the headland in a violent storm. All the crew members were destined to perish until the Blessed Virgin appeared at the height of the storm to calm the sea for long enough to allow rescue boats to reach the men and carry them to the safety of the harbor.

This year, like every other, the day began with fireworks hissing into the sky and exploding over the bay with a concussive boom. They were followed by a reenactment of the rescue in brightly festooned boats, a Mass to honor the Virgin, and finally a procession from Nosa Señora do Mar through the streets and plaza to the manor house of El Conde de Curra. A doll clothed in blue satin, crowned with a tin halo, and seated on a swaying *litera* led the way followed by Father Ithacio in a black soutane and lace-fringed surplice dispensing holy water with sprigs of hyssop. Don Prudencio, El Conde, came next, then Don Andrés and his family, then a series of oxcarts carrying children dressed in traditional costumes, then the Gallardo brothers playing their bagpipes, members of the search and rescue team, ladies of the lacemakers' guild, and finally Fanfarrias. The route of the procession crossed the Roman bridge and continued down the coastal road past a few stone houses before turning into a cobbled avenue lined with American maples. The retinue, announced by a cacophony of bagpipes and brass instruments, entered the grounds through the front gate and completed the journey at a small family chapel where, with traditional rites, the *litera* was left before the altar on the gravestones of El Conde's illustrious ancestors. When the ceremony was over, the children and their families dispersed throughout the estate along gravel walkways arranged in quincunx patterns and bordered by manicured boxwood hedges. The men and women, carrying baskets of food and wine, claimed cool spots beneath hundred-year-old oaks and chestnuts to nap or play cards while the children went off to explore the wonders of the property. Some gathered around a fountain where streams of water poured from the mouths of Neptune's steeds, while others dangled their feet in the lily pond between languid nymphs of stone.

The house was a long rectangular mansion built of dark granite blocks and flecked, like the walls surrounding it, with pale blue and saffron lichens. The original building was a twelfth-century crenellated tower. In the eighteenth century, the main body of the house was built, and in the nineteenth, the great-grandfather of the current resident added a terrace with a stone balustrade where Fanfarrias installed themselves to play throughout the afternoon. The family's heraldic shield was carved in stone above the main entrance that opened onto a series of stairs leading down to the lawn where one of the servants had saddled a donkey for children to ride. Late in the afternoon, after we had eaten a light meal with our parents, we were assembled by the same servant with a series of whistles to visit the barn where El Conde kept a collection of exotic animals that included a llama, an ostrich, a miniature horse, a tame ocelot, and a pair of mating peacocks. Throughout the afternoon and early evening, wherever we went, we could see a woman dressed in a white gown watching us from an upstairs window. Just after sunset, she descended the front stairs with her arm linked through her father's to greet the children. As Don Prudencio stood beside her, Doña Esperanza asked each child several questions and gave him or her a peseta from a velvet purse. She was rarely seen in town or even in the full light of day, and no one knew her well enough to speak to her directly.

An ethereal figure, this aging maiden took obvious pleasure in the presence of the children since she had none of her own. Her father had sent her to a convent in Coruña to be educated, and there she had fallen in love with an older man who either died at sea or disappeared to the New World. No one knew exactly what happened, but from the age of sixteen she had refused to change her clothes or cut her hair, as if preserving those aspects of herself that he had known would somehow preserve his presence in her life. Despite her rank in society, she had been married to the memory of the man in a ghost wedding, a ceremony typically conducted for young women who lose their fiancés at sea which allows them to enjoy the status marriage confers and to receive the benefits paid to the widows of misadventure. Most people believed Doña Esperanza had insisted on the marriage because of an intemperate passion. Heartbroken over her request and the lost hope of having an heir, her father had nevertheless granted it, and she was officially married in a small ceremony in the family's private chapel.

After placing a bright peseta in the hand of each child, Doña Esperanza led the group to an iron gate behind the house and opened it with a large brass key. Inside was a garden hidden from public view by high schist walls topped with stone globes at regular intervals. Comprising roughly four acres, the pleasure ground contained numerous isolated paths where one could easily lose oneself among the dense hedges and groves of azaleas and rhododendrons, jasmine and verbena, wild roses and orchids, blue hydrangeas and laurels. It was a world unto itself as different from the surrounding fields and vegetation as the imagination is from reality. Indirect light from the evening sky, from the glowing peaks of the mountain, and from a rising moon created shadowy specters in the woods along the main path where we were greeted by statues of Pan and Narcissus. Swallows sliced the air, hurtling across the sky, as wood pigeons called their fluted notes from a row of elms. At that time of the year, chill air rose from the sea and crept up the coast to infiltrate the garden with a vague scrim of thinly layered fog. Against a pale cerulean sky, the spoke petioles of a traveller's palm fanned out like the silhouette of a feathered headdress while the inverted brushes of araucaria branches seemed to sweep the atmosphere of its emptiness. Blooming magnolias tested the darkness with cool white torches, towering cypresses trembled like black flames, and late-flowering lindens intoxicated clouds of gnats with the sweetness of their scent.

Entranced by the perfume of verbena and the song of a nightingale, I left the other children and wandered along a path that tunneled through a boxwood arbor and, farther along, through a bower of privet and orange trees bent with ripening fruit. Here and there gaps among the branches of the trees allowed a faint luminosity, moonlight or its reflection off high clouds, to guide me deep within the shadows. I continued walking, hoping to discover the mythical creatures my parents had told me lived in the topiary garden among the boxwood camels and elephants, obelisks and corkscrew spirals. After an unsuccessful search through the paths and cul-de-sacs of the garden, I tried and failed to find my way back to the other children. Confused and tired, I sat down beside a glazed white urn beneath a long trellis of climbing roses and fell asleep. When the garden was cleared and locked for the night, my parents assumed I had gone home with María and Miguel, and hadn't realized I was absent until it was too late. By the time they returned to the estate, the lights were off, and the front gate was closed. It was the first night I had ever spent alone. I woke from my sleep and walked around with no conception of the time, bathed in the pale light of the moon that cast bluish shadows beside the ornamental hedges and illuminated the gravel paths and ghostly statues with a dim, unearthly whiteness. At some point, I lay down on a bench and fell asleep again. When a chorus of birds broke the dawn silence, I made my way back to the iron gate where mother and El Conde's gardener soon found me. She placed her hand under my jaw and lifted my head to study my eyes.

"Did the moon speak to you?" she asked.

"Yes," I said.

"What did it say?"

"It told me stories of a place where everything is white."

She looked at the gardener with an expression of dismay. "The child is moonstruck," she said and took my hand and led me home.

The lazy blue sky. The trilling of insects at midday. Hollyhocks blooming beside a fisherman's cottage. It was easy to think summer might last forever. But the idyll would soon be over. For many, the threshold of the year occurs in the calm depths of winter when the sun lies low on the southern horizon and the days neither shorten nor lengthen, but for me the transition between one year and the next, when we live in both and neither, occurs with the coming of fall and the cool air that brings death to the fields and forests. Unlike the showers of summer, September's storms are driven by contending seasons where the impatient north descends to claim the earth and sky from an intractable south. As if in sympathy with the world around me, I was torn by seasons of my own. The shimmering air above the sea, the brilliant sun, had taken me out of myself and filled my dreams with impressions of light and color: a lemon sky in a garden of white blossoms and green canopies, idle fields of poppies and purple flax, pink clouds at dawn. These dreams of summer flowed like a river without continent, its watershed the sky, but like the north winds that penetrate the stone canyons of the mountain and bring the first hint of winter's killing frost, gusts of fear passed through my thoughts with each day of fading summer. A sense of loss returned, and I wondered, young as I was, if there is no will but chance, no destiny but darkness.

One night when rain was pelting the windows, and the wind was lifting loose tiles from roofs and tossing them clattering down the street, I dreamt I was fishing with father. In the depths of the sea I saw ghostly images, fearful apparitions, graves dug into the water like caisson shafts, and liquid smoke floating up through schools of scavenging fish from charnel grounds and mud-caked bones. When I turned to father, he was gone. I began to suffocate from the sulfurous fumes that rose with the smoke and heard muffled cries of terror and grief and then what seemed like great volume without sound. My heart pounded in my chest in short, hard strokes like a hammer on steel, and the blood in my eyes clouded the edges of my sight. Out of a red and violet shadow, a small glass coffin floated toward me. Then it opened, and grandmother's soul emerged like a vapor of dawn rising over a darkened horizon.

Crying quietly, alone as only a child can be, I went to my parents' room and woke my mother. She sat in a chair holding me as grandmother had in the past. I told her of the terror I had felt and the overwhelming sense of loss.

"There is no reason to be afraid. You know she is gone," she said.

The mere fact of her death had not ended her presence in my life. We live in a world of our making where there are certainties more tenable than facts. Despite the bedside vigil, the burial in the black earth, the departure of her ghost, grandmother had remained a part of my life. I had continued to hear her voice and feel her love. Through her I had come into this world, and I had never known what it was like to be without her. My connection to her was as real as it had ever been, even though she was no longer there—like a mooring line wrapped around a bollard and tautly stretched over the harbor, but on the other end secured to nothing.

No assurance mother gave could alleviate my fears, and I continued to wake with a sense of dread, understanding, with a clarity known only in the darkest hours of night, what it means to be gone forever. As if the truth forces itself upon us in those moments when we are least able to protect ourselves, when the illusions of human artifice, habit, and the distractions of our daily lives belong to another world, when our practiced evasions have been caught off guard, and all our art and guile fail us. We sense, even as children, that when we come to an end, it is the end of something that never was, that our lives are no more real than our dreams of lives we have never lived.

It was a Sunday in early autumn. The ground was wet from a night rain. When the breeze stirred, the trees shed a second rain, and a few yellow leaves shook free from the alders in the lane behind the house. Every day the arc of the sun dropped a little lower over the southern horizon, and the flaxen light on the sides of the houses and the stone escarpments of the mountain was clear and bright against the fair blue sky. After church, Mother and I opened the windows and doors upstairs to let cool, fresh air circulate through the house and spent the afternoon cleaning the spare room in anticipation of my aunt's arrival. From what I could gather, there were reservations about bringing her home, but I wasn't sure what they were. The benefits, on the other hand, were clear. For one thing, she could help look after the house while mother and father were working. That included taking care of me as well as grandfather. And for another, according to the doctor at the convent, living with her family might help to steady her nerves. When I asked mother what this meant, she explained that some people need more rest than others.

There was one taxi in Porto Lúa. It was owned by Paco Carreira, a former postman from Noia who kept a small library in the trunk of the car. He and father went to Santiago early that morning and were due to return late in the afternoon with Aunt Fioxilda. After helping mother prepare the room, I busied myself in the orchard collecting windfall apples for the pig and waited for their arrival with a mixture of excitement and curiosity. When the car finally appeared early in the evening, mother went out to take Aunt Fioxilda's valise from father, and he and grandfather carried a crate containing her belongings up the walk. I stayed behind in the doorway. I had imagined her to be similar to grandmother, but as she neared the house, I could see she was as little like grandmother in her bearing and expression as she could be. She kept her metal gray hair under a black scarf, except for a lock that fell over her forehead. Cup handle ears stood out on the sides of her head, and her black eyebrows were raised as if fixed in a permanent state of suspicion while the shadows beneath her high cheekbones gave her face a skeletal appearance. Her teeth were clamped together at the incisors, and she heightened the effect of tightness by pressing her lips together. This caused the muscles at the corners of her mouth to rise slightly, giving her the appearance of a feigned smile. Her thinness was emphasized by the straight black dress and stockings she wore, so that her breasts were like beads of wax frozen on a candle.

"How was your journey?" mother asked.

"All these cars and commotion disturb the peace of resting souls."

"How do you know they're disturbed?" father asked.

"How could they not be?"

"How are things in Santiago?" mother tried again.

"There are too many people to tell." Then she looked down at me and asked, "Is this the boy?"

"Yes," mother said.

"Is he a good boy?"

I did my best to make a pleasant face.

"He's a very good boy."

"Well. Where is his room?"

"Next to yours."

"He should be all right there."

Sensing father's impatience and attempting to head off a confrontation, mother quickly added, "He'll be fine. Let's get you something to eat after that long trip."

"I'll put a sprig of laurel in his room and a *signo-Salomón* on the threshold," she said. "There'll be none come for you on my watch, boy."

My parents glanced at each other with obvious concern as if they understood something that still eluded me. At dinner she asked me if I understood the wages of sin. I didn't. I mean I didn't understand why someone would pay us to sin. That was one of many words or phrases she used that left me wondering what she meant. For example, when she was in mother's way at the kitchen table, she excused herself by saying, I'm sorry I'm holding up progress. On another occasion she exclaimed that she was thoroughly possessed by a headache. And when she gave up thinking about something she couldn't understand, she said, I am too tired to bewilder myself any further. Apart from her unusual way of speaking, there were no other signs of what was to come, and the rest of the evening went smoothly. After dinner, she cut a bunch of laurel branches from the hedge in the garden and, under mother's supervision, bound them in the form of a cross and hung them from a nail above the door of my room.

I was already in bed when mother took her to her room. Creaking stairs were followed by creaking door hinges and then heels crossing the wooden floor in the room next to mine. After a brief conversation, mother left her on her own. Every sound now anchored my imagination and kept me from drifting away into the darkness. I watched the flash of the lighthouse beacon on the wall and wondered how I had escaped calamity before the laurel cross was hung. Furniture scraped across the floor. Then there was the sound of some kind of commotion and several sharp knocks on the wall. Then the shouting began. There were accusations and incitements as if the house had been invaded by a host of warring spirits. Within the space of ten minutes I heard addresses to Saclas and Nebroel, rallying calls to Michael and the armies of heaven, and finally celebrations of victory in song. Father labored up the stairs followed by mother. He knocked on her door. The singing stopped.

"It's all right," he called. "There's no need for that."

"I have made a vow," she said.

"We're going to sleep soon. The house needs to be quiet."

I listened for a while longer, but that was the end of it for the night, and eventually I fell asleep.

The next morning at breakfast all were assembled but Aunt Fioxilda.

"They told us she was getting better," father said.

"It will take time," mother said. "Maybe when she gets accustomed to her new surroundings, she'll be better. Maybe it's the lack of familiarity."

"She's no stranger to this house."

When she came downstairs, she acted as if nothing had happened. I lingered at the table after eating my eggs in order to observe whether she said or did anything out of the ordinary, but she appeared normal and conversed with the rest of the family about the weather and our neighbors and distant cousins who lived in Coruña and other equally inconsequential subjects, thereby removing most, if not all, of the trepidation I felt in her presence. She ate her bread like everyone else and after breakfast offered to wash the dishes as mother got ready for work. The more I saw of her, the more familiar she seemed, and I noticed for the first time the resemblance between her eyes and those of grandmother.

She spent the rest of the day visiting the cemetery, looking up some of her friends, and gathering flowers on the lower slopes of the mountain. Dinner was as unremarkable as breakfast. Mother complained about a woman in the market who didn't clean her fish the right way and was eventually going to poison someone. Aunt Fioxilda talked about her visit with one of grandmother's friends in the lacemakers' guild. But that night as I was lying in bed, it all began again. First I heard her speaking to herself. Then came the sound of shifting furniture as she cleared the field of battle. Loudly denouncing their attempts to corrupt her, she refused the wealth the demons offered, and when they promised her absolute power over worldly kings, she called forth the legions of heaven and clattered into battle with the weapons of God. Once again, father knocked on her door and after a brief exchange, all went quiet. At the first opportunity the following day, he attempted to put an end to these holy wars by reasoning with her, but she explained that she had taken an oath before God to struggle against evil and defended her efforts as necessary:

"These demons are incarnations of the darkness that would deny me the uniqueness of my soul and the souls of everyone in this family. They enter our minds and whisper their lies. They tell us we are nothing against the darkness. You have had such thoughts. The boy has had them. That's why you sent for me, and with the help of God, I will defeat them."

If you understood her premises, her answers made perfect sense. She saw the health of the mind, the health of the body, and the health of human society in terms of the health of our souls. What she couldn't clearly explain was how the shouting and knocking about in the bedroom of an old house in the middle of the night actually protected those souls.

During the day we went about our lives as we had always done and at night waited for the battle to begin. Mother discovered that the banging came from the handle of a mop Aunt Fioxilda used to joust with her adversaries, and the scratching sound was made by a paring knife she used to record her victories in rows of crosses on the wall. At one time or another she had hosted the most prominent saints of the church, conversed with them, and sought their advice on the best way to defend us from evil. No less important to her mission were the archangels she petitioned as reinforcements in her battles when Leosibora, Armazel, Abrasax, Barbelos, and Balsamus came in through her window, which she believed to be the gaping mouth of hell. Conditioned to expect father's knock on the door, she hurried to complete her battles, and most lasted no more than five or ten minutes After a round of scuffling and muted cries, she declared victory for another night, satisfied that she had proven her loyalty to God. When the moon waxed, the intensity of her conflicts increased. The battle cries were louder and more urgent, the clattering more chaotic. I thought it odd how the presence of this source of light in the darkness could cause her so much torment. Looking back now, I think it provided just enough light to provoke her imagination, but not enough to correct it.

On the night when the moon was finally full, a paroxysm of fervor caused her to break the glass in the eastern window of her room. Despite her angry protests, mother deemed it prudent to remove the candles that burned during the battles, and when father replaced the glass, he decided to nail the shutters to their frames. But demons have a way of passing through walls of granite and continued to invade our house as I lay in bed awaiting their arrival. Some nights she sang so loudly that Miguel said his family could hear her next door even though the windows and shutters were closed. They were mostly religious songs, but some were folk ballads about spurned lovers or lost children.

Things came to a head a few nights after she broke the window when the consequences of her visions extended beyond the confines of our house. Among the demons who massed in ranks several deep along her wall, she caught sight of Father Ithacio. Skilled in the ways of deceit, he fought her with every trick in a devil's repertoire, changing shapes and using curses and incantations, but armed with only a crucifix and her prayers, she ultimately vanquished him along with his retinue. The next morning at church during the Introit of the Mass, she stood up and revealed that she had seen him among the soldiers of hell. There was a stir among the members of the congregation as the old priest tried to humor her by saying he was actually a double agent for God.

"I suppose you were a double agent when you betrayed the people of Porto Lúa and drove Bachiario into the mountains."

Father Ithacio burned bright red and replied, "And I would do it again to protect the Fatherland from the heresies of the past, from pagans and godless barbarians, from Communists and Jews, atheists and Masons, and anyone else who attempts to subvert the will of God."

"The army of God is on my side," she continued. "I have seen the truth standing before me. The righteous shall prevail."

Several people in the congregation applauded as Aunt Fioxilda held her ground. Then she walked out the door and did not return to church during the tenure of Father Ithacio, which would soon be over.

Exasperated, father arranged for Paco to drive the family to Muros where he had scheduled an appointment for her with a doctor under the pretext of having her hearing checked, but the questions the doctor asked to test her hearing were meant to test her mind. After the examination, he took father aside and asked, "What do you want me to do? How is she any different from anyone else around here?" In the days that followed, there was some talk about taking her back to the convent, but no decision was reached, at least not in my presence, and so she stayed. She lived in a world different from ours and saw things no one else could see. At night she left pieces of bread on the sill of the kitchen window in case a soul happened by unannounced. She took her shoes and stockings off to increase the efficacy of her prayers and never knotted her hair or shoelaces. She created chaos points around the house with fretted twigs to block the paths of malevolent spirits and refused to allow anyone to sweep after sunset for fear of upsetting a wayward soul.

Because Aunt Fioxilda hadn't spent much time around children, it took her a while to get used to me, but after a few weeks, my willingness to listen to her stories led her to believe I might have some promise as a protégé, and she began to take me with her in the evenings when she walked the narrow lanes of Porto Lúa seeking to assuage the loneliness of forgotten souls. She sensed the dead everywhere and shared their concerns as if they were alive. When the town dug up the flagstones in the middle of the streets to replace the unsanitary channels beneath them with sewage pipes, she asked, "Who will pacify the dead now that they have been disturbed?" Naturally we spent a great deal of time in the cemetery where she placed bowls of *caldo* on the graves of those she knew and pieces of bread on the graves of those she did not. On grandmother's grave, she left religious medals to pay the tolls on her journey to the next world. When the churchyard emptied after a funeral, she would remain for hours beside the grave. She held a crucifix in one hand and worked the gauds of her rosary in the other to ensure no evil spirit could steal the soul of the departed. I asked her how we could tell the good souls from the bad.

"The good have a scent and the bad have an odor."

"What's the scent?"

"Like heaven after a rain or like the colors of a rainbow."

"And the odor?"

"That of burning flesh."

I could guess what heaven smelled like because I knew the fragrant scent of air after a rain, but I had no idea what burning flesh smelled like apart from the odor of cooked meat.

It wasn't long after we started our evening walks that she began to allow me into her room, but only during the day when the light filtered through the cracks in the shutters. Everything was very neat. Even the crosses carved in the plaster wall. But there was an acrid staleness in the air of a room too long closed and damp in the corners. She herself smelled of sour cotton, and the odor seemed to infect the woodwork and curtains and sheets. The room was decorated like a shrine. There was a faded color print of Jesus tending his sheep, crucifixes on the dresser made from different stones, metals, woods, and glass, and above her bed, a framed print of St. Lucia holding a gold plate with two eyeballs lying on it, which she gave me on my next birthday. The crate she brought with her contained old letters, several small cotton bags with drawstrings, a pillow embroidered by an abbess in León, black blouses and skirts, which constituted her wardrobe, a book of novenas, a Bible, and the writings of Ambrose and Priscillian. The most precious item in her possession, however, was a bar of Italian soap given to her by a Vatican prelate. It was still wrapped in a white ribbon and textured paper bearing aquarelle images of wisteria and lilac. She kept it on the table beside her bed and smelled it every night before she went to sleep claiming that it enabled her to dream of a past life. The sweet floral scent, she said, revived indistinct memories and shadows from just beyond her reach.

The flowers she collected on the mountain were not displayed, but rather used to prepare an ointment that she rubbed on her skin. Next to a jar of petroleum jelly were yellow and blue petals, several white trumpet flowers, minced leaves, spiny fruits, and purple berries, all of which she crushed and pressed to extract their juice.

"What's it for?" I asked.

"To see in the dark."

"But you have a light."

"A different kind of darkness. A different way of seeing."

"Different in what way?"

"You see light and darkness, life and death, spirit and matter, good and evil. When I use my ointment, the boundaries between these things cease to be, and I see darkness in the light, death in life, the profane in the sacred, and evil in the good. I go where others cannot. Where the sun is smaller than the smallest star. Where the earth is a mote drifting through the night. I pass through the boundary between this world and another where boulders are the bones of a living creature, with flesh of earth and blood of air, that feeds on time. To you, skin is soft and stone is hard, but to stone, skin is like water, and to water skin is like stone. To the dead, our light is their darkness. Our life is their stone. So much exists beyond common sight. Why do we consider time to be the origin of things and lives only alive that resemble our own? Death lies not in the earth, child, but in ignorance of the truth."

Despite her long absence, many people in Porto Lúa still remembered Aunt Fioxilda and believed in her powers over the invisible world. When word of her return spread, she was frequently summoned to vitiate the evil of envious neighbors, provide an apotropaic shield against malefic spirits, or enhance the fertility of the earth by appeasing the local genii. Her willingness to help others was so great that she fixed a bell in her room and ran a cord down the side of the house so they might call her in the middle of the night without disturbing the rest of the family. To engage the spirits of the air, she wrote charms on pieces of paper and attached them to trees and bushes. When the rain had blurred the ink, and the sun had bleached the paper to the point where no words could be deciphered, she considered her petition complete. Spirits of the earth were a different matter. To coax a field to produce healthy crops, she buried smooth river stones etched with uterine forms at strategic points around its perimeter, and then, as if to marshal their power to control the influences of good and evil, she recited Latin verses from one of her books. One day when she was called to rid a garden of voles or shrews, a plague typically attributed to the spells of vengeful neighbors, she asked me if I would like to come along. When we reached the garden on the far side of the Deva, she cautioned me not to move erratically or swing my elbows broadly since I might anger one of the spirits she was trying to placate. As she walked barefoot down the cold furrows of the garden, she sprinkled a powder that smelled like dry blood over the damp soil and uttered unintelligible imprecations. After crossing the garden back and forth in all directions, she declared victory over the sorcery, and we returned home. When the issue was of a more personal nature, for example, impotence, hair loss, infertility, or matters of love, she prepared a recipe of various herbs wrapped in leaves and tied with tendrils of bryony that the person was to wear in the pockets of his or her clothes. "Comestibles of the soul," she called them.

She contributed to the family economy by charging those who could afford it a few céntimos for her services and by making dolls of the most popular martyrs whose fates were most torturous. She had spent much of her time at the convent learning this craft and for many years had supplied the archdiocese with replacements for previous generations of statues in out of the way country churches. The small cotton bags in her crate contained glass beads, scraps of silk, and woven locks of her own hair that she used to decorate and vivify carefully painted bits of wood that became the heads and hands of iconic saints. Working together at the kitchen table, we held small stones to the head of San Esteban as the glue dried and bent wire into the shape of San Lorenzo's griddle. I asked her to tell me the stories of their martyrdoms, and as she did, I drew gruesome depictions of their grisly deaths. Because Father

Ithacio had stopped going to Capela de Santa Lupa, it was left to the women of Porto Lúa to keep it maintained, and Aunt Fioxilda naturally took it upon herself to restore the various statues on its altars. Humming or singing as she worked, she scraped away flakes of old paint from the faces of the saints and gave them new life with pale white skin and rose cheeks. Painted eyes she replaced with blue or green beads and when the vestments of a figure were tattered or spotted with mildew, she dressed it in crisp, bright new robes. Her crowning achievement, however, was the restoration of the statue of the Virgin Mary, a large plaster object which took two weeks to paint and dress. Her stole was the blue of a warm autumn day, and her halo the color of the light that edges the horizon's clouds just before sunset.

My natural curiosity and ability to remember so much of what I saw and heard led Aunt Fioxilda to conclude I might have some promise as a scholar, but before she decided whether it was worth her time and effort to educate me, she thought it best to determine whether I had been chosen by God for a higher purpose.

"What do you want to be when you grow up?" she asked.

"A saint," I said. "I want to write a Gospel."

"You want to be a saint."

"Yes. And I want to write a Gospel."

"How do you expect to write a Gospel when Jesus is no longer living in this world?"

"I'll write what He says in my prayers."

This response must have impressed her because she declared to mother and father that she had found me apt and would begin to plan my lessons that night. I was very pleased by this unexpected development because I would soon be able to render the stories I had collected in hieroglyphs in the more precise medium of language.

To teach me the rudiments of reading and writing, she

began not with Castilian, but with the Galician spoken in the towns and fields where we lived. She wrote the letters of the alphabet carefully in copperplate script on a large sheet of butcher paper and repeated their sounds until I had memorized each. Then she put them together to make words. When it was my turn, I stared at each letter before sounding it, and when convinced I had it right, ran them together to create what resembled the words I heard spoken. As much as the sounds pleased me, the pictures I saw in the groups of letters pleased me even more. Perhaps because I was so accustomed to my hieroglyphs. In one word I saw a bowl. In another, an adze. And in another, the patterns of mortar between the stones of a wall. I was especially fond of the words *madressilva*, which I saw as a mountain with its peaks of *d* and *l* and the falling waters of its double *s*, and *volvoreta*, which contained the shapes and fluttering motion of the creatures it conveyed. I imagined not just a single butterfly, but all members of the species and all the colors that I had seen floating above the gardens and fields. In each word I possessed the imagination's ideal of the object I wished to convey. Though the forms of the words seemed arbitrary, they were no more so than the random patterns in nature which strike us with their beauty—the constellations of night, fallen leaves in a streambed, the profiles of sea-worn boulders. Making this connection between the letters on the page and the sounds I had heard my entire life gave me access to mysterious correspondences. I saw languages everywhere and believed that I could unlock the secrets of clouds and trees, of stones and earth, the stars in the sky, the finite shadows of the infinite. It was as if I was experiencing the world again for the first time, refreshed, renewed, reinvigorated. Not only could I capture what was around me, I could possess it permanently—make it my own— even create what had never existed before through unique combinations I could record on paper. As if I had found a new substance with which to fashion as many worlds as I could imagine.

We moved on from short, simple sentences conveying prosaic observations to the homilies of Origen, some of which Aunt Fioxilda had translated from Latin and kept in a yellowing folder on the cabinet beside her bed. Although I had no idea what he was saying, I could identify many of the words, and for this effort she rewarded me with a diary she bought at María Dolores's shop. I was moved by the physical beauty of the book and wondered if my words would ever equal its splendor. It was bound in three-quarter faux morocco leather and inside the boards were covered with marbled paper. She inscribed it with the date and a brief description of the reason for its presentation and across the top of the first page wrote the following passage from the *Vita Sancti Fructuosi: Post haec revertens ad locum illum solitudinis supra memoratum, et devotionem quam dudum parvulus elegerat, iam perfectus implevit.* I took it with me wherever I went. To me its pages were a vast white sky waiting to be filled with an apotheosis of words—an invitation to chart the world of my experience with magical evocations of form and sound.

One morning after the mist had risen, Aunt Fioxilda and I gathered rotten apples from the orchard to augment the kitchen scraps we fed the animals. The fishy odor of fermenting mud mingled with the acidic scent of decaying fruit, and in the rainwater that collected on stone surfaces and in the ruts and footprints of the path, dead leaves decomposed in brown pastes and slush, adding an odor like stale tea to the air. Later in the afternoon, as she hung sheets and clothes on the line to dry, I sat on the threshing floor writing down the words she dictated in order to test me. The stone was dark and cold with the dampness of the season. Above, the sky was clear and blue. The yard, embowered by a mosaic of red and yellow leaves, relieved the melancholy of the season with a few late flowers.

Shaken by the wind, some of the leaves broke free in fluttering trains, rising like small birds into the sky or scattering in flocks over the walls and hedges. In the slow departure of the sun, those that drifted up into the saffron light shone like sparks sent skyward from the flames of a forest conflagration. The dry inflorescence of autumn grasses blushed between the lengthening shadows of barns and houses, and milkweed floss escaped from seedpods like souls rising from common graves to ascend the heights of the mountain. As Aunt Fioxilda turned to face the western light, her face softened, as if revealing, for a brief moment, the youth she had once possessed.

She could be openly contemptuous toward those who were lazy-minded or who made a show of their ignorance. Our familial bond as well as my youth mitigated the harshness of her judgment toward me, but I was still unnerved by the fear of her censure. During our lessons, she checked my mistakes with a grimace or sigh and encouraged my progress with an occasional nod, but for the most part, her expression gave little away, and I had to divine her feelings from circumstances and imagine what lay in her heart. Uncertain of her past, I filled the unknown with my own fantasies. I concocted scenes in my imagination where she harangued Church scholars in rooms filled with the incense of old books and led an army of hooded cenobites into battle against the malevolent ghosts of a great cathedral. And when I lay quietly in my room at night, I tried to see what she saw in the darkness—the hideous faces of the demons that haunted her, and I sometimes wondered, given her authority on so many subjects and her claim to see a world no one else could see, whether she was right about those demons and the rest of us were wrong.

When she did reveal her feelings about something, the subject often appeared at random. For example, one afternoon when she was cleaning a fish, she related how she had once found an American half-dime in the belly of an eel and believed it had come from the pocket of a drowned sailor, a young man, she proposed, who had gone to sea disappointed by love. I noticed her eyes grow moist and thought it odd that a fillet of mackerel could have this effect. On another occasion, she mentioned a donkey that had lived in the garden behind the convent in Santiago. Speaking of the animal with a certain affection, she told me how she used to treat the sores around its muzzle with a special salve. No doubt these feelings inspired a similar affection for our remaining donkey, and on a warm day late in October, when the flies were biting with renewed vigor, she massaged its ears and testicles with petroleum jelly.

When the weather was fair, we walked the paths on the lower slope of the mountain collecting wild berries and the hulls of walnuts that she used to dye wool stockings and sweaters an earthy brown. One day in a clearing near Casa das Bestas, she directed my attention to a large slab of stone where people in the past had carved out dozens of cupmarks. She asked me if I could guess what they were for, and I said I could picture them holding oil and wicks to light the way of pilgrims at night. She considered my answer for a moment, but then explained they were in fact created to resemble the place where a woman's body receives the soul of a child. Making one of these holes was like a prayer to call a soul down from the stars. On the way home, we cut across the mountain to the spring where grandmother had washed the evil from my body. In the woods above the pool, Aunt Fioxilda showed me a monolith of blue granite she called "the bell" and related how the priests of Porto Lúa used to strike it with a silver rod to make it speak in times of drought. I told her I had seen Mother Ambages there last spring and asked if she knew her.

"Everyone knows Mother Ambages. Your great-grandparents and their parents knew her. They say she is a goddess, the goddess of paths, who was punished with the body of an old woman because she once loved a man. Some day when the gods relent, she will return to them, but until that time, she must walk in the mists and fog of the mountain."

"I'll pray for her in church."

"No, these are different gods."

"Do they have a church?"

"Their church is nature. They dwell in the mountains and rivers and fields. They have their roles in bringing good and evil, may bless and disrupt, but they are not God."

"How do you see things no one else can see?"

"Part of me was born into this world and part of me was not."

"What's the part that was not?"

"The part on the other side of everything you see. Think of this life as a dream where you are surrounded by empty images, and then you awaken to a world where there are more colors than you have ever seen, more sounds than you have ever heard, more life than the bodies of plants and animals can contain."

Looking back now, I realize Aunt Fioxilda was still living in a time before the disenchantment of the world, still engaging the mysteries of nature, of life and death, creatively without the explanations of modern science. At that time most of the people of Porto Lúa felt the presence of souls or spirits around them or held equally improbable beliefs in the supernatural. It wasn't really a matter of religion, of Christian versus pagan. It was more an attempt to interpret the world as one interprets a dream, to find the hidden significance of things, and to maintain an ancient compact with the earth that had enabled our ancestors to survive its fateful contingencies. However unsophisticated her explanations, they gave meaning to her life according to her needs—that is, they satisfied her need to understand it and fostered an appreciation for its beauty and purpose.

To this day I remain in her debt. Not just for cultivating my imagination and a faith in the value of my convictions, but for introducing me to the broader world of books and ideas. My father had little interest in such things, and my mother only had a few years of education. For her part, Aunt Fioxilda seemed gratified to have the opportunity to mold a young mind, but she was also susceptible to the fear that despite her efforts I might turn out like other men she had known, men like Uncle Teo, who, according to her, lacked tenacity, men whose "vagrant interests" led them to become "wandering Cains." This concern became more acute when Fulgencio gave me a travel book he kept in his shop. Though she was grateful to him for encouraging me to learn, she was also wary of a book that might plant wayward ideas in my head, and so she did her best to dispel any incipient wanderlust by countering the author's romantic tales of places with harsh descriptions of their flaws.

"Madrid," she informed me, after we had read a captivating account of the city, "is full of lonely people. It is a great stage of fools who drink too much and argue over nothing. They make laws for themselves and change them every time their interests change. We have had the same laws since before there was ever a Madrid to speak of. We have acted as a community in order to survive. We grow crops to feed animals. The animals feed us and our crops, which feed more animals. Our lives are that simple. We live in an ocean of time, and we are far from any shores.

"Barcelona is just as bad. And the same thing is true of Seville except they have orange blossoms in the spring, and magnificent stained glass, and carriage horses that wear knit caps. That is all true. But not cause enough to live there."

"What about Santiago?"

"Even Santiago is too crowded. Except at night when it's raining. That is the best time to walk its streets. When the lamplight reflects off its wet stones, and the balladeer is hidden in the shadows of an arcade."

Despite her efforts to check my curiosity, the more we read, the more I wanted to experience these places for myself. I wanted to see what Uncle Teo had seen, and at night when I stood beside the window in my room and looked out at the mountain peaks, I tried to imagine the towers and domes of the cities that lay beyond.

Up to this point in my life, my world had been circumscribed by Mount Aracelo to the east, the bay of Porto Lúa to the west, Muros to the south, and Cathedral Rocks to the north. To these four coordinates were added the metaphysical poles of celestial blue above and fearful caverns of dripping pitch below. But that world became a little larger on the second day of November, the Día de Todas as Almas. My family gathered in the kitchen for an early breakfast and then walked down to the port before the sun was up. Grandfather carried a small box containing some of grandmother's clothes and her rosary. Father carried a grill and bucket of sardines. Mother carried a blanket as well as bread and wine. Like many of our neighbors who had lost a family member within the past year, we climbed aboard our boat and joined a small fleet of *dornas*, their canvas sails full breasted in the wind, and set out across the bay to Illa da Luz. Father Ithacio and two acolytes were in the lead boat together with Don Andrés. I sat in the front of ours with Aunt Fioxilda. Overhead the sky was gunmetal blue, but in the east, it was flush with the first light of day. As the sun rose, a cold wind picked up, and the sea began to spit from cresting waves. One after another, they hit the bow like a granite curb and dropped it again with a rainbow spray that fell over us like a cloudless rain.

The island lay too far out to offer the town much protection from violent storms, but was close enough to be a familiar presence in our lives. It was a calendar by which we measured the seasonal path of the sun and a barometer by which we predicted the changing moods of the sea. In the summer, we rose to its reflection of morning light and retired as its shadow lengthened across the bronzed water of the bay. Few fisherman ventured beyond its outer banks, and, despite the ships we could see outlined on the horizon, the older generation still considered it to be the boundary of the known world and the entrance to another. The story of the king who sought the burial place of the gods was one of many told of those who dared to pass into the realm of light. Enhancing its reputation as a gateway to the next world, a gaping shaft in the rock on its southern slope was believed to be the mouth of hell.

As we approached Illa da Luz, a sun-brightened mist skirting the shoreline lifted and dispersed giving way to blue sky. Except for a sandy cove, the eastern side of the island was girdled by a sheer granite cliff shimmering in the morning sun as water leached out from the turf above. We entered the cove at low tide. On either side of us were brown boulders covered with foul-smelling wrack. Above were wind-blown fields of broom and heather. The blue and green and red skiffs hit the shingle one after another as startled seabirds rose overhead lighting on narrow ledges. We pulled the boats up the beach and unloaded baskets of food, bottles of wine, and rusty braziers. Accompanied by several women, the two acolytes carried Father Ithacio's trunk up a stairway cut into a deep crevice in the wall of rock and made their way to a small chapel isolated among the maritime grasses and gorse near Boca do Inferno. While they prepared Mass for the souls of the dead, the rest of us spread blankets over the sand and started fires to cook an early lunch.

I asked mother why we had brought a box of grandmother's personal objects.

"To commemorate her passing."

"But why leave them here?"

"So there is something familiar to guide her."

"What about the mountain?"

"What about it?"

"I thought souls went to the mountain to wait for the moon."

"The custom is to go to Illa da Luz, and since the moon passes over the island anyway, it's all the same."

Once the fires were lit, father joined his friends to play cards in a shelter of pines beside the cove. To keep me occupied, he gave me a small packet of salt and told me if I could sprinkle it over the tail of a bird, it wouldn't be able to fly. And so for half an hour I crept back and forth along the beach through patches of thrift and sea-spurrey, hiding here and there among the rocks, hoping to catch a seagull or sandpiper, but when I saw María and Miguel arrive with their father, I returned to the cove to greet them, and together we set off to explore the island. From the path to the chapel, we crossed over a high ridge of deep grass and bell heather to Laxe dos Defuntos, a splinter of rock on the western shore. On a grassy perch sheltered from the wind, we watched the steady surge of swells break over the rocks and ebb in lacework wreaths of foam. Then we climbed through the shattered detritus of fallen boulders to the highest peak on the island, a lichen-gray column of granite resembling a bell tower. Patrolling the air above the ledges of their raucous nursery, scythe-winged gulls railed and gibbered their displeasure at our presence. Overhead a cloud drifted past like a parasol floating on the wind. To the east, we could see Porto Lúa and the reddish violet peaks of Aracelo through a gray shroud of haze. To the west, far out at sea, white clouds created islands of shadow as ephemeral as dreams of paradise.

To escape the shifting wind, we moved inside a shallow cave formed by an overhang of rock. All around us were the strange shapes of boulders sculpted by the wind and rain. As we looked out over the landscape, we imagined ourselves the nobles of a great castle surrounded by an extensive fortification. When the wind picked up, we moved to the back of the cave where María discovered several small crosses carved on the wall. I told them how Aunt Fioxilda had marked her wall in a similar manner.

"Our father thinks she's crazy," said Miguel.

"Does she really fight with demons?" María asked.

"I'm not sure," I said.

"Are you frightened?"

"No. Maybe at first. But not now. She's teaching me how to read."

I drew the letters of the alphabet in the damp soil and taught María and Miguel how to write several words. Then I showed them how to write their names. María asked me what it was like when grandmother died, and I told them her soul had gone to the mountain and not the island.

"Who died in your family?" I asked.

"Our aunt," María said. "She lived in Carnota."

"We were late because mother wouldn't come."

"She didn't like her."

"No one liked her."

"I liked my grandmother," I said.

Before returning to join our families, we decided to descend the landward side of the peak to see the ruins of a settlement where the foundations of round houses were visible through a leafy mesh of ivy and brambles. As we made our way over a series of ledges sharply studded with feldspar and quartz, we could feel a light mist of salt spray on the cold wind. I crouched low in the wind and moved to the edge of a long, narrow boulder to look for a path, but the drop was sheer on all sides. As I backed away from the edge, a seagull appeared out of nowhere and struck me on the right shoulder. The blow was so hard and the wind was so strong that I was knocked forward and for a moment struggled to right myself before losing my balance with nothing between me and a serried row of boulders twenty feet below, but as I reached out instinctively, grasping at anything, I caught María's hand. She leaned back, bending her knees to counter my weight, and pulled me to safety with such force that we fell together on a level surface several feet from the edge. As I sat upright, it took me a moment to gather myself and realize that if the wind had gusted more strongly, or if María hadn't caught me, I would have been lying on the rocks below. We continued to climb down to level ground and talk and laugh as if nothing had happened, but, like a person who has survived an accident or a near fatal illness, I was now aware of a possibility that had never been real to me before, and for years, when I looked out on the island, I was reminded of the inscrutable balance among the experiences of life, its dangers and risks, that make us vulnerable at any moment to an unexpected fate.

As we reached the ruins, we heard my father whistling above the buffeting wind and saw him standing deep in the grass halfway to the chapel waving his arms to get our attention. We arrived late for Mass, which, as if to compensate for what we missed, lasted well over an hour. Because so many people had died in Porto Lúa that year, the six rows of kneelers on either side of the nave were full, and many people had to stand throughout the ceremony. Aunt Fioxilda, who still refused to attend a Mass said by Father Ithacio, maintained a daylight vigil for the soul of her sister at Boca do Inferno. At the end of Mass, we deposited the box containing the clothes and rosary of grandmother in a stone crypt in the foundation of the chapel known as the vestuary of souls and joined our neighbors in the cove for a dinner of pork and sardines. In the boat on the way back to Porto Lúa, Aunt Fioxilda told me how she had seen ghosts rising from the black opening of the cave and heard voices greeting them from across the sea. As the island receded in the distance, the afternoon sunlight glistened on her arms and hands still oily with the herbal salve she prepared from the flowers and berries of the forest.

During the two weeks that followed the Día de Todas as Almas, before the cold rains and fog of winter settled in, farmers burned the stubble in their fields and stored the last of their harvests. Everywhere the air was filled with the pungent smoke of burning weeds and straw. We fattened our pig on acorns for weeks until he was so heavy he couldn't move without dragging his belly through the mud. On a Saturday morning men from the neighborhood gathered in our yard to catch and slaughter the animal who seemed to know what was in store. In the childlike screams of the beast and the ratcheting sound of the blade sawing down through its spine, I found the subject of my first story. Although it was lost long ago, I remember that it was written in an unaffected style devoid of subtlety or moral overtones. I simply recounted what I saw: the seizure by the tail, the hammer to the head, the jowly throat slit deep, the flush of red gore, the hoisting of the carcass, the blood splatter on shoes and hands, the sawing to separate the portions, and then the bacon we would eat for a year. When Aunt Fioxilda saw me at the kitchen table with my diary, she sat down beside me.

"What are you writing?"

"A story."

"What is it about?"

"The death of Enrique the Pig."

"What are you describing that's blue?"

"His eyes. Like the sky."

"It's good to tell these stories at your age," she said, "when the words are still fresh in your mouth."

We moved downward through the cycle of the year in darkness like a traveler passing through a valley at night. Along the way he sees the lights of an isolated village, and finds in it brief refuge before setting out for the next. When the nights were long and the days were darkened by cloud and fog, the isolated points of light on our horizon were the feast days of mid-winter. From O Nadal we proceeded to O Dia dos Santos Inocentes, and from there to Noite de Ano Novo, and then on to Os Santos Reis, and in February, A Candelaria, and, finally, near the end of winter, we reached O Entroido. The most memorable of these was Noite de Ano Novo, for on that night, according to tradition, El Conde de Curra opened his palace to the public. Though opulent by comparison to other buildings in town, with only two stories, it was nothing like the palaces I had seen in Fulgencio's book. There were four windows across the top floor, and on the lower, two on either side of the portal. Those above opened to small balconies enclosed by railings of black ironwork. In the center of the building, dividing these windows into pairs, was the family coat of arms carved in granite. Directly below it was a thick wooden door studded with iron clavos and held in place by halberd strap hinges.

This year was the first I was allowed to attend the celebration, and I was pleased to be admitted into the company of adults. After giving our coats to a servant, my parents and I crossed a tile mosaic of mermaids and leaping dolphins and climbed a broad oak staircase that led to El Conde's office on the second floor where the festivities were held. On the stairs we caught up to an old woman from the mountain who grasped the banister and paused every step or two to take a deep breath. Father reached up to help her, but she was so intent on meeting her host that she barely noticed. She was heavily bundled in layers of skirts and sweaters beneath a ragged coat, perhaps all she possessed, like the pistil of a flower wrapped by its petals. When she reached the top of the stairs, she curtsied to Don Prudencio and, taking his hand, whispered, "If your majesty permits."

"I'm not the king, my dear, but your neighbor. Come in and enjoy yourself." Then gently shaking free of her hand, he turned to me, looked at mother and asked, "Is this the young man who spent the night in our garden?"

"It is. And moonstruck he is to this day," she said as if I were a strange creature she had encountered on the road.

"Wonderment is a joy in children," he said.

"The wonder is he's not worse," said mother, pleased with her reply.

Father nodded his agreement. "He'll have to do, your honor. He's all we've got."

We took a few steps down a hallway and entered a large room already crowded with guests. To the left, in the middle of the wall, was a granite hearth, wide as a park bench, and stacked with flaming logs. Above it, an old mirror with a maculate tain tilted precariously forward on a frayed wire. A gift to El Conde's great-grandfather from Amadeo I, it was set in a heavy rococo frame of gilt rocaille and acanthus garlands. Dark tongue-and-groove wainscoting lined the other sides of the room below hand-painted wallpaper of classical arcades and floral sprays. The antique furniture was worn, and the colors of the silk upholstery, once elegant greens and golds, had faded in decades of sunlight to reinforce a general air of decline. Overhead the ceiling was decorated with interlinking quatrefoils around a crystal chandelier, and in each of the four corners, opening outward, was a plaster wreath of victory. On the right was El Conde's desk. Behind it were portraits of his antecedents as well as of his daughter as a child. On this night the desk was flanked by four wing chairs, and in front of it, a podium had been installed for the grand event that had brought the town together.

Every year we celebrated Noite de Ano Novo with a contest to determine the best poet in Porto Lúa. Every year Don Prudencio entered one of his odes, and every year he won. There was always one other participant who read, a shepherd named Evandro, but no one expected him to win. In reality it was not a contest at all, but an unspoken compact between El Conde and the town. He demonstrated the ancient practice of *noblesse oblige* by providing the citizens of Porto Lúa with a night of food and drink, and to his mind, the elevating influence of poetry. And they, in return, offered him the laurel crown, a wreath of fresh sprigs cut and woven by María Dolores for the occasion. A year when he did not win would have been off to a very inauspicious start. The matter was simplified by the fact that Don Andrés was the sole judge of the contest and to some extent was indebted to El Conde for the office he enjoyed. This year, however, things were complicated by Father Ithacio's decision to submit a poem and his assumption that the sacred nature of his work would secure his victory. Had he been correct in this assumption, it's possible I would have gone through life with only a rudimentary education or none at all.

The administration of the local school, which had been closed for several years, was among the official duties Father Ithacio had neglected as the pastor of Porto Lúa in response to the way he had been treated since his arrival, especially during the war. Though Don Andrés was pursuing a plan to secularize the school, funding was a problem. In the meantime, the parents of children affected by the closure were not overly concerned because they assumed the school would eventually open again, and three or four years of education acquired at any age would provide all the knowledge necessary for lives spent working in the fields or at sea. Even when the school was open, it was not unusual for students to attend for no more than a few years, and in some cases, depending on the economic circumstances of their families, they didn't begin their studies until the age of nine or ten.

The antipathy between Father Ithacio and the people of Porto Lúa that led to the abandonment of education began with his first sermon when he railed against the old ways, what he called the devil's enchantments, and did his best to undo centuries of superstition. He preached against the vestiges of Manichaeism and decried the magical unguents people prepared from the precipitates of the moon. He denounced the incantations they uttered over fields newly sown and the verbal grotesques they recited to protect their crops against blight and the relentless heat of the midday sun. Angered by his misfortune in finding himself in such a place, he cursed his congregation from the pulpit as backward heretics. But to no effect. His reproofs fell on deaf ears. In time Father Ithacio came to accept that he would pass his life among barbarians. Like a Roman legionary sent to the fringe of civilization, he had been sent to this outpost at the edge of Christendom. He could only fight for so long in the fog of superstition and ignorance and made no secret of his desire to return to the capital. When someone dressed a pig in a cassock and set it loose in church, he pleaded with his bishop for a reassignment. But none came.

Years after the war had ended and Porto Lúa had reconnected with the outside world, Father Ithacio attempted to redeem himself in the eyes of his superiors by agreeing to smuggle Nazi refugees to South America. They came at night in military vehicles carrying suitcases and wearing leather and furs. Father Ithacio welcomed them to the rectory and fed them lamb and shellfish at a time when many of his parishioners were nearly starving. At midnight he watched the waters off the headland for a flashing point of light and then, in violation of the prohibition on his movement, led his charges through the back lanes to the quay and down the ramp where a skiff waited to take them and as much fresh produce as they could carry to a ship farther out in the bay.

Ignored by his bishop and scorned by his parishioners, Father retreated to his library and domestic life with his housekeeper, Rosa, who was the daughter of a servant in the house of Don Andrés's father. Awkwardly tall as a child with thin hair and severely crossed eyes, she was slighted by other children and later by young men, and spent much of her time alone. When she was eighteen, Father Ithacio hired her to cook and clean. Within in a year she gave birth to a son, an indiscretion he attempted to conceal for as long as possible. Not that it mattered. Few thought any less of a priest who fathered a child. In fact, most people in Porto Lúa preferred to have a man of God who was also a man. But his orthodoxy was so disliked by the parishioners of Porto Lúa that Don Andrés used this as an excuse to write to the bishop to request his removal. An ecclesiastical secretary responded by saying it is not up to mayors to make such decisions and so Father Ithacio remained.

At half past eleven, the table in the middle of the room lavished with fruit and wine was moved to the back wall, and the poets took their seats beside the podium as Don Andrés delivered his annual New Year's speech in which he deftly managed to note his own accomplishments without taking any credit away from El Conde and the hard-working citizens themselves. Then the contest began. According to custom, Evandro went first. Although he had little formal schooling and knew nothing of Latin, his poems were naturally steeped in the

Roman ideal of *rusticitas*, reflecting the traditional values of piety and industry. He composed them during the long hours he spent watching his animals and preserved them in a memory more prodigious than any other I have known. He eschewed old Silvanus and the Naiads and Dryads of educated poets, but on occasion included the names of local nymphs and forest gods. On this night he praised the virtues of those who live off the land and the hermit in his solitude, and compared shepherds and the forest dwellers to the stars in the sky for the beauty of their lonely souls. When he concluded, there was polite applause and some shouting from the country people. He smiled for the first time that night and bowed awkwardly as Don Andrés shook his hand.

Don Prudencio went next. He began with the arrival of Sanctu Iacobu in Spain and his burial in the Arca Marmónica and proceeded to extol the heroic exploits of Pelagius of Asturias and Rodrigo Díaz de Vivar on the field of battle. As he was commending the achievements of Diego Gelmírez, I stared at the red light reflecting from the tip of a crystal shaft in the chandelier overhead and watched it change from red to orange to yellow to green to blue to violet as I moved my head slowly to the side. I began to associate each color with a different figure from the past, so that Fernando II was yellow, Isabel I was green, and Philip II was blue. By the time I turned my attention back to El Conde, he was glorifying the city of Alcalá de Henares which gave birth to the greatest Galician of all, Saavedra de Vilarello. He went on to praise the generosity and gracious spirit of the old nobility, and then the lengthy peroration culminated with a lament over the errors of Alfonso XIII and a prayer for unity and a blessing for the future of the country.

When El Conde concluded, Don Andrés applauded enthusiastically and stepped to the podium where he declared that Don Prudencio would one day make Porto Lúa as famous as Virgil's Mantua, Dante's Florence, and Petrarch's Arezzo.

Beaming with pride, he took the wreath in both hands and held it up to the audience, but just as he did, Father Ithacio stood and placed his manuscript on the podium. Realizing he had forgotten to give the priest a chance to read, the mayor courteously pretended the contest had not yet concluded.

Father Ithacio's white hair clumped in thick locks at the back of his head and curled unwashed over his collar. As he glanced over his manuscript, his thin lips tightened in a straight, gar-like smile. He wore a black cape that had been blessed by the Archbishop for the purpose of spiritual prophylaxis and conveyed an unremitting interest in the world with small, black eyes. Because he watched people surreptitiously in sidelong glances, he was sometimes called "the pharaoh."

He raised his pig bristle eyebrows, drew a deep breath, and began.

"Poetry is like the surface of the sea, which belongs to neither the sea nor sky. I am the sea and you are the sky. Where we meet is neither you nor me—is both you and me together in God's love."

Don Andrés was perplexed. "Is that the poem?" he asked.

"Not at all. It is a prelude."

Someone in the front of the room whispered, "It sounded like a poem to me."

"With respect, Father, we all thought it was a poem and a good one."

"It was not a poem, but rather a way of explaining how poetry works. That is why you mistook it for a poem."

"Very well, then. Proceed."

> "Sing a song in your heart.
> Tremble there a while,
> Stirred by God's Love.
> Sing if you will,
> For on the morrow,

Sorrow shall not prevail."

"Was that the poem?"

"Yes, of course it was the poem."

Father Ithacio wiped his brow with a handkerchief.

"Well, it was a little short, but very good nevertheless. Very good. Maybe next year you'll beat out Don Prudencio."

"I'm not here to win, but to make the most of the gifts God has given me."

Shortly after the presentation of the laurel crown to Don Prudencio, the table was moved back to the middle of the room and at midnight those in attendance celebrated the New Year by drinking generous glasses of Codorníu and eating Portuguese grapes.

Father Ithacio attributed his defeat to the vengefulness and backwardness of the people of Porto Lúa. However, rather than resign himself to the judgment of Don Andrés or the ignorance of his audience, he used the occasion to strengthen his resolve to write. He would no longer pander to the public taste by limiting his talents to simple songs. Scrupulous in avoiding the sin of pride, he would devote his abilities to sacred themes and decided to unleash his genius in a Pindaric Ode on the Virgin of Garabandal. When this work, which he had spent a great deal of time composing, was rejected by the Catholic magazine *Vida Nueva*, Don Andrés, in a moment of compassion, told Father Ithacio that if he hadn't become a priest, he might have been a great poet. Rather than receive the compliment as it had been intended, Father Ithacio was devastated. It was true. He had spent his life among philistines when he might have achieved the kind of recognition bestowed on Góngora and Quevedo.

That afternoon he went to his study and began to drink. Not a glass or two, but a bottle of brandy. The following day he wore his vestments to the market. That night he wore them to O Galo. The next day he wore them to work in his garden. Even though the violet and gold silks of his chasuble were soiled and began to fray, he wore nothing else, as if he meant to demean his calling by demeaning its garments. One morning before Mass, he drank half a bottle of wine and urinated behind a headstone as several women were entering the churchyard. His nose was etched with bright red veins, his teeth had been misplaced or lost, and his eyes, that had once been so relentless, were now empty windows of inattention. On el Martes de Carnaval, he was so drunk he believed the grotesque corbels below the roof of the church had come alive and spent the better part of the afternoon battering them with stones until part of one broke away and landed on the statue of an angel.

This time the bishop listened. Early in the morning on the Feast of Saint Felicity, a large black sedan parked in the grass beside the churchyard. Three men got out and entered the rectory. An hour later, just as a heavy rain began to fall, they returned to the car with Father Ithacio and a portmanteau containing his personal property. One could only imagine what he was thinking as the car drove down the hillside and he saw the church that had been his home for the last thirty years disappear behind him. In an attempt to do the right thing by Rosa and her son, the diocesan authorities allowed them to remain in the rectory in return for maintaining the premises. And, like Facundo, she would continue to receive a small monthly stipend. An intelligent woman, Rosa knew the priest had taken advantage of her because of her eyes and must have wondered what life would have been like—whether she would have married and had a family—if she had been born without this stigma.

For the next month, the church of Nosa Señora do Mar went without a pastor. The day of Father Ithacio's departure, Don Andrés wrote to the bishop requesting a replacement, but never received a reply. Finally the mayor decided to take matters into his own hands, and with one of the Gallardo brothers, walked up the path behind Campo da Graza through broom as high as a man's head to a remote area on the north side of Aracelo where they found the reclusive Bachiario in a shepherd's cabin beside a spring. After a lengthy discussion during which Don Andrés expressed the needs of the people for spiritual leadership, the apostate priest agreed to serve until another could be found.

And so the man who had collaborated with General Molinero's forces during the war was replaced by the man the soldiers had come to arrest. By this point, however, the intrigues of that era and the danger to Bachiario had passed into history with the smoke and fire of war. As a young priest in Santiago, he had exhibited an unusual devotion to his calling and was soon sent to Madrid where he was recognized as a man of unusual powers. At some point he was introduced to General Molinero and accompanied him to Morocco. No one knows what advice or service he gave the general. Some said he could predict his future. Some said he interpreted his dreams. And some said he pacified the ghosts of those the general had killed. Perhaps all of this was true.

Because he had been so close to the general and was viewed with suspicion by those in his inner circle, a plan was made to remove him on the eve of the declaration of war. But Bachiario had foreseen this betrayal and, on the night before he was to be detained, escaped into the Rif Mountains. He returned to Spain on a Portuguese fishing boat and made his way back to the remote region of his birth a few weeks later. He slept in a watermill on the Deva and picked fruit from the orchards on the edge of town in order to survive. The people who saw this gaunt figure in the darkness left bread and lard where he could find it, and in return he devoted himself to their spiritual well-being.

When Father Ithacio realized Bachiario was living in Porto Lúa, he informed the authorities, and when Colonel Florentino was sent to seek out and subdue enemies of the state, he carried orders to capture or kill the fugitive priest. But as soon as the first shots were fired, Bachiario, like Uncle Teo and several other men, disappeared up the slopes of the mountain and eventually moved to Casa Xoana. Accessible only over steeply angled boulders, it is a tunnel carved by the forces of nature through a peak on the mountain like the eye of a needle. Because the soldiers did not follow the men, they had no way of knowing where they had gone. Nevertheless, they sat in the churchyard with binoculars watching for any movement in the open fields or among the boulders or trees. When they saw something, they fired. Many wild horses, goats, and sheep were lost in this way, and more would have been destroyed if Gustavo, the landlord of O Galo, had not given the soldiers bottles of wine to throw off their aim.

Most of the men who sheltered in Casa Xoana returned to Porto Lúa when they were confident the soldiers would not return, but Bachiario, who felt a close kinship with the creatures of the forest and spirits of the air, remained on the mountain. Over the years stories of his engagement with occult powers and participation in strange rituals were common. One shepherd claimed to have seen him surrounded by dozens of wild animals on the night of a full moon. More imaginative accounts of his powers alleged he was in touch with the old gods or that he walked in the night with the Santa Compaña, a ghostly procession of the dead who come for the souls of the dying. One night when a column of light appeared on the mountain, people said he had harnessed the fire of stars to create a path for souls to climb to heaven.

The period between Father Ithacio's departure and the arrival of Bachiario provided an opportunity to make some repairs to Nosa Señora do Mar. Over the years, several beams had begun to rot, and a number of tiles had fallen from the roof, which allowed rain to enter and more rot to occur. Father worked with Facundo and a few other men to replace the beams and tiles, and Aunt Fioxilda and I helped Rosa clean the altars and wash the windows and pews. In the gaudy Churrigueresque retablo of the main altar was a reliquary containing an ear of the donkey that had carried the Virgin Mary to Nazareth. On a side altar in an alcove to the right was a statue of Nosa Señora do Mar, and in an alcove on the left, a painted sculpture of Santiago on horseback with a sword raised over a vanquished invader. Along the walls were several granite sarcophagi whose lids were carved with the crude figures of recumbent priests or noblemen of the past. Their beatific smiles did little to ease the fear I felt when thinking about the dusty bones that lay on the other side of the stone. A few solitary lids were propped against an outside wall beneath the corbels sculpted to resemble hideous apes, demons, and *sheela na gigs* that seemed to follow people passing in the churchyard with their hollow eyes. The two I found most unsettling were a lascivious devil with a long, curling phallus and a stunted dragon with gaping jaws.

Because the repairs weren't finished on time, Bachiario said his first Mass in the town hall at a makeshift altar before a mural from the Second Republic depicting an amply endowed Liberty naked from the waist up. Dressed in a woolen friar's robe with a rope belt, he possessed a hearty, natural elegance, but was worn by his exposure to the elements. His flaxen hair reached to his shoulders, and he wore a white, uncropped beard perfumed by mountain air. Although he had not said Mass for twenty-five years, he still knew the Latin by heart, but delivered his sermon extemporaneously in Galician.

"Good men and women of Porto Lúa," he began, "I am here today because the Church has neglected its people. The sole task of His shepherds is to spread the word of God, and that task has gone unheeded. Looking to their own needs, they pervert and corrupt His teachings. Imagine a man were to steal a candlestick from the House of God. Would God allow his wickedness to prosper? And what if he were to steal the words of God and use them for his own ends? What say you? Would he not be damned a thousandfold in proportion to the gravity of his crime? The Church in our time is abounding with charlatans who would steal the truth of God and make it their own. Listen not to them. Suffer not the rebuke of the Lord. The wicked-doers will dwell in bondage, and the righteous in the light, the light that is the manifestation of the truth, truth visible, immeasurable, as vast as the emptiness through which it flows. 'I am the light of the world,' saith the Lord. We are all children of the light, and our dwelling place is not of this world. To know ourselves, where we have come from and where we are going, is to live in the light that has no beginning and no end. The world of gold and silver, of the pleasures of the flesh, of the hypocrites, is not yours, but belongs to another who seeks to bind you to his illusions.

"Do not be strangers to your souls. Listen to the voice God has given you. Scorn false prophets, the politicians and tyrants, the makers of war and dogs of luxury. Happy is the man, happy the woman, who can leave the path of the ungodly and return to the path of faith. Give up wicked manners and wicked ways. Give up the idols of darkness, the things of this world, and seek you the Lord your God. For the Kingdom of God is not a kingdom of this world, but a kingdom of faith. It is not subject to the ravages of rust or moths. It is subject only to human weakness, to ignorance, to vanity. A thousand tempests will not shake His Kingdom, but a single doubt in the mind of a man, of a woman, will rent its walls asunder. Will you be the cause of the destruction of heaven and of your own immortal souls? God has given us free will to choose what is right. What will we choose? Do not, I say, allow the devils of hell to enter your lives. Do not allow them to envenom your hearts with doubt and remorse, to blight your eyes and ears with distortions and greed. Given leave by God to do their mischief, they will work their way into the souls of righteous men and women like worms burrowing their voracious destruction through the foundations of a good house. Those who have done much wrong may make amends in the eventide of life if they seek forgiveness with contrite hearts, but why wait until it comes to that and risk the fires of hell? They are eternal and so are your souls. Make haste to the Lord your God."

When he concluded, Bachiario came forward from the altar and stood before the congregation. He brought his palms together before his mouth, bowed his head for a moment in prayer, and uttered the word, "Faith." Then, as he rubbed his fingers together, a small white flower appeared between them. He touched it to his nose, inhaled its scent, and, looking upward, clapped his hands. The flower dissolved into ash and disappeared, like drifting smoke, into the air.

The example of Bachiario reinforced my determination to become a saint. I wanted to spend my life breathing the musty air of sanctity sweetened by the fragrance of extinguished candles, and succumb to the enchantment of brass candelabra standing on white linen, and gold-plated chalices, and the purples and greens and yellows and reds of stained glass, and the echoing solemnity of every spoken word. While others were working in their fields or casting their nets over frigid waters for a few mackerel, I would produce flowers from my fingertips and communicate with the hidden agencies of spiritual power known by my grandmother and aunt. Ultimately, I would achieve salvation—even though I had no idea what that was—and forever be an inspiration to others to seek the path of righteousness. Aunt Fioxilda believed I had received a calling from God. Her plan was to send me to a seminary in Santiago, but my parents would not entertain such a notion, so, with their blessing, she decided I should begin my life of piety as an acolyte assisting Bachiario in the celebration of the Mass.

By the following Sunday, the repairs to the church had been completed, and the crucifix and altar cloths returned from the town hall. Facundo had attached a new rope to the bells in the *campanario* and was ringing them as people walked up Via Sagrada for the ten o'clock service. The altars were covered with white lilies and their scent greeted all who entered the building on that warm, sunny day in early April. My responsibilities were to light the candles before Mass, pour water over Bachiario's fingers during the offertory, ring the handbell during the elevation, and hold the paten during communion. I carried out these tasks according to my instructions, and when Mass was over, I put out the candles and took the cruets back to the sacristy.

As the last members of the congregation filed out through the portal, I checked the pews to make sure no one had left anything behind, and then wandered alone through the transepts and apse. Fascinated by the statue of Santiago on his horse, I clasped the gate of the alcove where he seemed to burst through the wall toward the iron bars covered with dust and the smoky grease of candles that had burned for generations and imagined proving my faith on the verdant fields of a great battle. When Bachiario locked the portal and walked down the hill, I stayed behind in the churchyard thinking about what I might do for God or how I might edify him while courting wrens flitted about the gravestones and ephemerids rode the light breeze, coupling in the air and dying by the day. Later that afternoon I asked Aunt Fioxilda what I needed to do to become a saint, and she informed me of the spiritual benefits of mortification, so I began going without breakfast, walking through dense gorse, and kneeling on the gravel outside church. When mother discovered what I was doing, she knocked me on the head and once again blamed my behavior on the night I had spent in El Conde's garden under the full moon.

Because he was increasingly involved in church matters, Bachiario asked if I would be willing to take care of a small herd of goats he kept on the mountain. I was more than happy to oblige, and though mother was concerned I might be exposed to some risk on my own, she reluctantly agreed. Three times a week, I led a dozen goats up a sloping meadow from his cabin to Val das Ruínas where they fed on the tender grass that grows in the freshness of the clouds. A few hours before sunset, I took the animals back down to their enclosure, locked them in, and walked home, sometimes passing Bachiario on my return. Though there were wild dogs and even a few wolves on the mountain in those days, I never saw any, and the only real threat to the herd was from human predators.

Early one evening, just as I was leading the goats into their enclosure, I saw Bachiario coming up the windswept fields on the back of his mule. His mastiff, wearing a leather collar spiked with nails, followed behind him. It was unusual for him to arrive before I had secured the animals for the night. When he reached the cabin, he told me to take one out of the pen. I chose a small brown and white creature that I favored for its shyness. He led the goat to the steps of the cabin and told me to hand him a large, round stone lying beside the door. He must have brought it up from the beach because it was pocked with small holes that still held grains of sand. I gave him the stone, and he told me to hug the goat to give it a human scent. Then he told me to grasp the tips of its horns firmly and turn its snout toward him.

The goat tried to shake its head, but offered no great resistance, and I was able to hold it steady. Bachiario lifted the stone over his head for a moment and then brought it down on the skull of the animal just where the horns emerged. I felt the jolt in my bones like an electric shock as the animal instinctively jerked back, pulling free from my grip, and dug in. Then it stopped moving and for an instant stared at me dumbly with its dazed yellow eyes. Bachiario lifted the stone again and, as he did, the goat backed up a step or two and charged, meeting the stone as he brought it down again, doubling the force. There was a strange, demonic cry as the creature collapsed beneath me kicking desperately at the soil in its death throes and flinging a loop of saliva through the air that landed on my foot. An eyeball attached to a thread of flesh rolled to one side as the rest of the body quivered violently. Legs kicked the air. The other eye, though seeing nothing, remained fixed on me. Without waiting, Bachiario lifted the stone a third time and crushed the head of the animal like a broken shell matted with hair and blood, then he dug his fingers into the pink and purple pieces of brain and threw them to his dog.

"Quick and easy," he said. "Good shots, all of them."

"Are you going to skin it?" I asked.

"No. We're taking it to town."

"To sell?"

"No."

He wrapped a rope around the torso of the goat behind its front legs and motioned for me to hand him the cord halter of the mule. He pulled the reluctant animal closer to the goat and wound the rope over the hame top to secure it.

"What are we going to do with it?"

"We are going to deliver people from the bonds of evil," he said. "This beast will attract the malignant spirits that prey on flesh and draw them out of the darkness where they wait to invade the loins and bellies and hearts of people. When we have passed through the streets and collected as many of them as we can, we will take them up the mountain, far from human souls, where they will do no more harm."

We dragged the carcass down through the fields of bell

heather along a path of gray mica dust as its hindquarters bounced limply over the stones. The dog trotted along behind us stopping every few minutes to lick the thread of blood that trailed the body and urinate on the side of the path.

By the time we reached Porto Lúa, the sun was going down, and lights were coming on in the houses. In Campo da Graza, we were joined by a pack of dogs drawn irresistibly to the scent of death. Bachiario clipped them with his walking stick as his mastiff bared its teeth and snapped, but to no effect. They continued to follow us, hackles up, barking and nipping at the goat. When people saw us dragging the carcass, they opened their doors and windows to purify their homes. My participation in the cleansing ritual was cut short when we came across mother in Rúa do Olvido. As soon as she realized what we were doing, she reproached Bachiario for exposing me to such danger and took me home where she made me strip off my clothes. Aunt Fioxilda went over my body with a crucifix while mother looked on shaking her head and then made me sit on the balcony in a cool breeze until she was convinced my body was no longer hosting any residual evil. From my vantage point overlooking the town, I caught a glimpse of Bachiario as he crossed the plaza and heard the dogs that followed him. After I had gone to bed, they passed close to our house and took the Roman road back up the mountain until the baying of the dogs disappeared into the night.

The next morning I learned that I was forbidden to return to the mountain with the goats, and whether I would serve Mass again was still being debated. Of greater concern to me, however, was the possibility of missing out on an education. Resolute in his desire to repay the people of Porto Lúa for their charity and protection, Bachiario soon announced his intention to reopen the school. The incident of the goat had so upset mother that her first thought was to keep me home, but after some reflection, she realized that doing so would be to deprive me of a crucial advantage in life because of something someone else had done. Father, who showed little interest in the goat, had his own reservations about the value of education. He had very little himself and believed that his life of labor was the best example for me.

"An education will offer him more opportunities," mother said. "At a minimum he has to be able to read and write, add and subtract."

"Fioxilda has already taught him how to read and write, and he can learn his numbers from her too. Anything more will put too many ideas in his head. You'll fill him full of disappointments and false horizons. He'll disdain hard work. And we need everyone around here to pitch in."

Aunt Fioxilda, who had no vote in family matters, did have some sway, and her strong advocacy in favor of education lent more weight to mother's position. As a young woman, she had studied Latin and religion as well as history, literature, and French at a convent school in Santiago, and she fervently believed in the value of her own education and the profound effect it had had on her life. Father, who was not convinced that Aunt Fioxilda had turned out all that well, privately maintained that the example of her life was evidence supporting his argument.

In the end father relented, but only if I agreed to spend my summers working with him on his boat. And so, on a cool, windy afternoon in May, I was registered in the Colegio de Primera y Segunda Enseñanza de Porto Lúa along with thirty-six other children of various ages. The building, constructed in the 1880s, was a solid, honey granite structure of two-stories with a vaguely Palladian façade. There was a palm tree in the front garden typical of returning immigrants, or *indianos*, as they were called, and a hedge of roses behind a rusted iron fence. In the middle of the walk leading up to the entrance was a statue of the founder of the school with his right hand raised before him like that of a bridesmaid declining a dance. The green bronze plaque on the pedestal read, "Don Pedro Ruiz Bóveda y Varela Valcárcel, Ingeniero y Filántropo, Benefactor de la Humanidad." He had made his fortune selling *Nobel's Blasting Powder* to the government of Bolivia to build its railroad through the Andes and fight its war with Chile.

Under the Republic the *colegio* had been a state school, but prior to its closing, it had been operated by the Church, which supplied four nuns, two to teach the lower level, essentially reading and writing skills, and two to teach the upper level, compromised of courses in catechism, history, science, math, Latin, and French. When it reopened, the staff consisted of Bachiario and two nuns hired by Don Andrés and housed in the community. Facundo worked part-time as a janitor and, despite his age, often joined us in class where he was a dedicated scholar. The youngest student was six and the oldest was seventeen. Among my classmates were Miguel and María, who was to become my rival for distinction, Andrés el Tercero, the mayor's son, four brothers named Mateo, Marcos, Lucas, and Alfredo, as well as Father Ithacio's son, Mateo Mateo. One story said his mother had given him the same surname and Christian name to obscure the paternity of Father Ithacio, but another said she had stuttered nervously at his baptism and his name was recorded twice.

Reading and writing were taught in one room by Sister María Benigna Consolata, an indefatigable woman of remarkable patience whom I remember, not unkindly, for the large front teeth that pushed past her lips and gave her the perpetual smile of someone happily confused. English and simple arithmetic were taught by Sister Mary Rose, an Irish nun from Glencolumbkille, who spoke broken Castilian and no Galician. On Tuesdays and Thursdays, Bachiario stopped by to provide instruction in Latin, religion, science, metaphysics, and history, which were, to his way of thinking, inseparable. When we answered one of his questions incorrectly, we were required to wear a necklace of stones that could only be removed when we learned the correct response. "If you wish to rise above a material state, you must earn the light of knowledge," he would say. The stones represented the material world that weighed heavily upon the soul. Sister Mary Rose, who was more gentle and caring, quietly objected to his unorthodox methods, but respected his authority. To her I owe my knowledge of English. She would often sit with me after classes had ended and help me pronounce the strange words. It was not her native tongue, for she had been raised in the Gaeltacht speaking Irish, but as a young woman, she had fallen in love with a man from America, and for her, the practice of this language was like the caresses of the one man she would ever love.

The classrooms had high ceilings and an abundance of natural light from a row of tall windows. Pale blue paint, like a martyr's vision of heaven, covered the plaster walls and flaked off in small showers as we brushed past. The only light in the hallway came from the landing on the stairs, and when we entered the building or left the classrooms, we walked through a darkness of mold. The bathrooms, dripping caverns of leaking pipes and condensation, were a source of terror to us, and our business lasted no longer than the amount of time we could hold our breath. Each classroom had a blackboard and a half dozen long tables with six chairs to each table. At the front of the room was the instructor's large wooden desk and a wood stove vented by a long flue. The rooms were otherwise empty. The floors were cold, rough cement, and despite the stoves and the southern sun pouring through the windows, we wore our coats indoors during the winter. On warm days late in the spring and early in the fall, we were kept cool by the high ceilings and the sea breeze that ventilated the building. Our supplies were meager. The municipality paid for a box of lined exercise books, chalk, and secondhand instruction manuals for the teachers, and we brought our own pencils and pieces of bread that we rolled in our fingers and used as erasers.

Although summer was approaching, Bachiario decided it was better to begin with an abbreviated semester than to wait until fall because some of the students might lose interest by then, so the first day of class was a Tuesday late in May when the spring rains had stopped and the air was fragrant with the flowers of the season. The morning fog had cleared, and from the schoolyard we could see fishing boats skirting the headland and the chapel on Illa da Luz. As we waited for someone with a key to arrive, we could hear a flurry of wings moving back and forth in the hallway, and when Sister Benigna finally appeared and unlocked the door, we discovered a flock of black-birds had come in through the windows and taken up residence in the building. By the dozens, they flew in and out of the classrooms and up and down the stairs alighting on the window sills and perching on the railings. We grouped at the far end of the hall and tried to chase them out the door, but they flew back over our heads or up the stairs—everywhere but out the door. When Sister Mary Rose arrived, she immediately sent one of the older boys to fetch Bachiario, but he was already coming up the walk. When he entered the hallway, he moved his arms gently, and the birds dropped to the floor as if tired. We picked them up one by one and took them outside where they recovered from their trance and flew up into the trees. Because the desks and floor were stained with droppings, it took Facundo the rest of the morning and most of the afternoon to clean the building, and so our first day of school came to an end before it began.

Though Sister Benigna and Sister Mary Rose followed regular plans of study, there was little structure in Bachiario's approach. Because of the events on that first day, we spent the rest of the week studying birds. We learned that parrots, like men, become impertinent and belligerent when drunk, and that wrens enter the mouths of crocodiles to clean their teeth. Swallows are used by God to send messages to his priests. And the brilliant colors of birds are caused by sunlight passing through filters of exudation in their feathers. This led to a lecture on the way God uses birds and flowers and fruit, the grass and sea and sky, to diffuse His presence into color, and for this reason we feel a greater love for colorful things. In Bachiario's classes, our education followed the variable course of nature, as unscripted as a child's summer day. When the chestnut trees began to flower, we learned how sap rises and why pollination occurs. When a white butterfly appeared on the wall of the corridor, we learned the secrets of metamorphosis and imagined ourselves transforming from a chrysalis to an imago. As we pass though time, he told us, we are like the instars of butterflies living not in one body or one way of perceiving reality, but passing through many and that each of us now was in a chrysalis of dreams and that one day, if we dedicated ourselves to learning, we would emerge through a forest of symbols and know the lasting truths of the stars.

One day he brought four granite stones to class. One was purple, one pink, one reddish-orange, and one gray. He asked us why there were different colors for the same stone. Everyone was afraid to answer because of the necklace, so he finally told us that, according to Thomas Aquinas, variety is a higher good than multiplicity and that is why God created not just different colors, but also different kinds of things. That is why instead of creating only angels, He created angels, people, animals, plants, and stones. That is why He created not just land or sea, but land and sea. And why He created mountains and islands, forests and deserts, and all the stars in the sky. To the question why God created Illa da Luz so far from land, Bachiario answered that the island and the mountain were created together. They were both lifted by the thrust of massive sheets of rock lying below the surface of the earth. And in that layer of rock is a fenster where the caverns of hell exist like the spongy hollows of bone. The ancients called it Tartarus. Once there was a vast sea, a different sea than the one we have, called the Rheic Ocean, but it disappeared into this abysmal realm below the earth where its waters race back and forth through great caverns and tunnels of eternal darkness.

When we asked him how he was able to make a flower appear out of thin air, he told us he did nothing of the sort, that he was merely an instrument of God's will. "No man can perform a miracle. Everything has a cause, and God is the cause of causes. I am the means of God's will," he said. "The flower that appeared and turned to dust was like every other flower that lives and dies. If what I did was a miracle, then all of nature is a miracle. All flowers appear from nothing. All life appears from nothing. And all living things return to dust. I simply hastened the time in which the miracle occurred. Right now those rocks are thrusting beneath us, but so slowly that you don't notice. If they were to move more quickly, you would feel a jolt like an earthquake and think it a miracle. Time is an essential part of the truth. God creates not only objects, but also the time through which those objects pass. This allows more of His creation to come into being and to depart from being. So the knowledge we seek is not just of things, but of how those things exist in time. To know an oak, we must know its seed. We must know the rotting log in the forest. On the hillside above us, there is a field of flowers that stretches as far as the eye can see. Nodding in the wind beneath the blue sky, they are too numerous to count. Time allows each flower to be. And when they are gone, more will come. In the same way, time allows each of us to be. Since God has no beginning and no end, we cannot know Him as we know an oak, a flower, or each other. To know Him, we must know as much of His creation as we can in the time we have, and we must never doubt the possibilities of what may come."

Although he could speak like this for hours, there were days when he had little to say. Sometimes he walked back and forth in front of his desk quoting the tractates of Priscillian or asking us riddles from the *Aenigmata* of Symphosius, and sometimes he took us on excursions along the lower slopes of the mountain to teach us its mysteries. On one of these occasions, he took us to the field where Aunt Fioxilda and I had seen the flat boulder covered with cupmarks. On this day, several of the cupmarks were filled with seeds, which Bachiario attributed to the current belief that birds receiving such beneficence will carry the petitions of people to heaven. When he asked if anyone knew the original purpose of the cupmarks, I said they were meant to call souls down from heaven. He confirmed this interpretation and went on to explain that ancient people made the connection between stars and souls because they believed the soul is that part of us which belongs to the realm of perfection, and the stars in their predictable, enduring movement are of that realm. What exists above is unchanging; what exists below passes through time. Souls are reluctant to leave their home for the chaos and change in this world, but the permanence of a stone, carved to resemble a woman's body encourages them to come down through the stars to enter the realm of life.

Before birth, he continued, the soul exists in an ocean of light, like the one described by grandmother, where there are no dates and no places, no names, no races, no individuality. No seasons, no days and nights. It then emerges from the light into the manifestations of the temporal the way a single truth may devolve into many falsehoods. When the soul leaves the light, its natural inclination is to seek good over evil, but as it descends through the constellations into darkness, its separation from the light is deepened by the illusions of earthly pleasures.

When we asked him what the ocean of light is like, he said it is as bright as the light of the sun. "Imagine," he said, "that everywhere you look, in any direction, whether at the sea, the sky, or the land, you are looking into the sun. But there is no sun. There is only the light. In such light, no one can see the flame of a candle, and yet in the darkness, the candle burns brightly. Compared to the ocean of light, we live in darkness, but everything we see contains some portion of the light. If you know how to see, you can find the light of creation in every object. In each of us, in every living thing, the light is there in the impetus that moves our hearts and souls, and it is there in the desire for the good. It is there in the desires of nature that lead to increase and renewal. It is the desire of the Virgin of Light that draws the Prince of Water to her and causes rain. This was a story Priscillian told to help country people understand the ways of God. Science would say that light, like desire, draws moisture into the air and causes it to precipitate. Both explanations reveal the same thing: that God created a world of desire, and we must learn how to distinguish between desire for the good and desire for illusions of the good. We must learn how to live in harmony with nature. Many of the stories of the ancients contain these truths if we know how to read them. Ovid told of the transformations wrought by desire in his tales. As Apollo chases Daphne through the forest, she turns into a tree. His desire for her is false, and when at last he reaches her, she ceases to be the woman he sought. The truth of this tale is that when we try to possess something with the wrong kind of desire, we possess only the desire and never the object of that desire."

Bachiario provided a thorough education on everything we did not need to know. We learned that to flatter princes, men collected mucus from a small vein in a snail's throat to make purple dyes. The Kolchians buried their dead in sacks they hung from trees. The Mytilenians would not allow the children of those they had conquered to learn to write or play music. In Boeotia there were two springs. Water from one caused people to remember; water from the other caused people to forget. Those who forgot never knew which spring to drink from. The Peripatetics observed that during the day the soul is in the thrall of the body and therefore cannot know the truth plainly, but at night it becomes prophetic and knows the truths yet to come.

When I returned from school one afternoon, father asked, "What did you learn today?"

"That Archidamos, the king of the Lakedaimonians, reproached a man from Chios for dyeing his hair, saying that he had not only a false head, but also a false soul, and that the Celts dropped the 'p's' from their words."

"Is that all?"

"There was once a ship that sank because of the quantity of flying squid that landed on its deck."

Bachiario came to class one day carrying a branch from an alder tree and a bottle of water. He held the branch up and reproached Fray Rosendo Salvado for sending the eucalyptus seeds that destroyed the indigenous forests of Galicia. It was a perversion of the natural order, he said. The bottle of water was related to grandmother's story of the king who journeyed to the land of the dead. In his version of the tale, Bachiario named the king Iapetus and identified the river where one forgets the land of one's birth as the Limia, known to the Romans as Lethe. He told us the bottle contained water he had collected from the river, and then lifted it to his lips and drank its contents. In what might be construed as a history lesson, he proceeded to recount the story of the Roman general Decimus Junius Brutus Callaicus who would not leave Galicia until he had seen the sun set in the ocean, but to reach the end of the world, he had to cross the Limia. When his troops were afraid to advance, he waded into the stream and drank a handful of the water. To prove his memory was still intact, he called out the names of his soldiers. When he finally reached the end of the world and saw the sun disappear beneath the waves of the sea, he fell to his knees in the sand and wept over the insignificance of empires and the futility of human endeavors.

After pausing briefly to allow us to consider what he had said, Bachiario set the branch and bottle on his desk and walked to the window. "Even before the arrival of Romans," he remarked, "our shores were a source of wonder. Our ancestors told of strange trees and nuts that washed up on the beaches as well as pieces of wood with indecipherable letters found along the coast suggesting the presence of a culture flourishing somewhere over the horizon. The sea is a great river carrying other worlds on its waves, dreams of lost civilizations, memories untouched by time. One of these ancestors was a fisherman who saw emerging from the horizon a boat carved from the trunk of a tree bearing men who had faces the color of wet sand and long hair as black as night. They adorned themselves with mollusk shells and fished with sharpened sticks and gut cordage. The fisherman gave them fresh water and watched as they turned toward the setting sun and made their way back across the ocean's expanse.

"Many stories from antiquity survive that describe the world beyond the horizon: a place called the Blessed Isles, Ogygia, Avalon, and Terra do Bacalhau. For example, the unknown author of *de Mirabilibus Auscultationibus* mentions a fertile island in the distant ocean where a variety of trees and unusual fruits flourish along great rivers. In his life of Sertorius, Plutarch wrote of two islands with a temperate climate, gentle breezes, rich soil, and trees full of ripe fruit, and during the Middle Ages, a Galician monk named Trezenzonio climbed to the top of the Tower of Hercules in the city of Brigantium with a sacred mirror in which he saw on the horizon the high peak of the Great Isle of the Solstice. Trusting in God, he sailed to the island where he was greeted by a mild climate and an abundance of wildlife. In a meadow of blooming asphodels, he discovered a basilica adorned with precious stones, and in the garden of the church he ate fruit from the tree of eternal life. Living outside time and lulled by the pleasures of paradise, Trezenzonio ignored the command of an angel to return to his community and a life of prayer. As a punishment, the angel caused the fruit to rot on the tree and forced Trezenzonio to leave the island without proof of its existence."

While these stories served to stimulate our imaginations, they were not what children typically studied in their religion, history, or science classes. The names were foreign to me and the moral lessons we were meant to learn often eluded me. As Bachiario once said, "Knowledge is like a river that passes through you. Some of the water soaks in. Some wets the surface. And some continues in its course without a trace." Most of what he taught us left no lasting impression, but enough soaked in that I still remember it, and perhaps it has had more influence on my life than I have realized. As for the rest of my education, the foundation in reading and writing I had received from Aunt Fioxilda made it easier to remember what I learned in those subjects, and I was also doing well in English and arithmetic. In fact, Sister Mary Rose was so pleased with the progress María and I were making that she soon took us aside for advanced instruction.

Beyond the hedgerows and garden walls, beyond the narrow streets and alleys, scenting the air that we breathed, brightening the sky above, lay the blue Atlantic extending as far as we could see, emptying our thoughts with its immeasurable distance, stirring idle dreams with intimations of other places, other times, like memories of a life before our lives, but that proximity left us vulnerable to its moods and madness. Crossing thousands of miles of ocean water, storms of relentless ferocity made landfall mere feet from our doors.

On a wall in the fishermen's cooperative was a map marking the locations of forty-three fatal shipwrecks between Illas Sisargas and the lighthouse at Louro dating back to the nineteenth century. But these were only the most prominent naval and commercial disasters. Family fishing boats were also lost, so many, in fact, that the number of men in Porto Lúa was noticeably smaller than the number of women. Sometimes the widows or mothers or sisters of those who drowned but were never found would claim unidentified corpses and bury them with the family name in order to receive compensation from the state, and when men emigrated and failed to write or return, their families secretly hoped a boat would sink so they could file a false report and receive a pension. To console themselves, widows would sit on rocks along the coast where their husbands had fished and sing songs to them about their children or the days of their courtship and throw bouquets of flowers into the water in the belief that the ghosts of their men would find the flowers and remember their love.

One of the most celebrated wrecks on the map occurred on a night in November shortly after I was born. A ship hauling guano from the island of Ichaboe foundered on the rocks off the headland in a late hurricane that had curled across the upper Atlantic from North America. The mephitic cargo, bound for the gardens of Europe, washed into the sea and dissolved into a viscous brown froth to be pitched over the seawall onto the streets and plastered in pungent crusts on houses and gardens as far as a mile inland. During weeks at sea in an open hold under equatorial sun and rain, the guano had fermented into an apocalyptic stew attracting flocks of birds that deposited the seeds of tropical flowers and fruits in the percolating sludge. The following spring, flowers from the forests of Africa sprouted in the gardens and wild verges, the roofs and walls, of Porto Lúa, blooming in rare and beautiful colors.

Another memorable storm occurred several years later when a rusty hulk ran aground on the group of rocks called Illotes das Gaivotas. No crew members were ever found, but the next day, the bodies of dozens of capuchin monkeys washed up in the harbor and surrounding beaches. When father came home with the news, grandfather and I walked down to see them for ourselves. The plane trees along the quay were still bending back and forth in the wind when we reached the port and saw men pulling the creatures, limp as rag dolls, from tangles of kelp and throwing them into piles on the ramp. Believing the bodies to be those of enchanted monks, one old woman began to shout there was witchcraft in the air. Those that had maintained a semblance of freshness were flayed, salt cured, and hung in the *bacalao* stalls of the market, but no one would consider buying food that had once had a human face. Called "the ghost freighter" because it lacked a crew, the ship seemed to appear from nowhere. Theories of its origin flourished because it had no flag and no documents to determine its registry, but a scrap of newspaper and graffiti in the toilets suggested it had drifted across the Atlantic from Central America.

When you make your living at sea, you learn to watch the sky. Cobblestone or pebbled clouds and a south wind presage rain. Streamers approaching from the western horizon indicate a storm. At dawn on the day of the worst storm in the history of Porto Lúa, neither was present. Brilliant sunlight filled the bay between the green promontories of the headland and the northern flank of Aracelo, but as I passed grandfather on my way to school, he sniffed the air and said, "Take an umbrella. I can smell Moroccan sand." Late in the morning, the first few bars of cloud appeared in the northwest like the vanguard of an approaching army. Behind them, close to the horizon, followed the massing legions, impatient for action. By noon, a dense haze had formed over the harbor. Then the wind shifted, and the air quickly cooled. When Facundo arrived with a report that the storm was intensifying, classes were canceled. From the schoolyard we could see rows of white-capped waves riding across the bay and crosscurrents of silvers and blues so strong they tore the surface of the sea with tracks of white foam.

I began to understand the seriousness of what was happening when I saw the measures my family was taking. Mother had shuttered the stall in the market and was in the fields behind the house herding the animals down to the barn. Grandfather was nailing plywood boards over the windows on the front of the house. Father was still in the port where the men were helping each other secure their boats. As I went down the hill to join him, the sky continued to darken. Shutters along the street clapped against their casements, and the drystone walls became wind harps, as if the granite itself were

170

moaning. By the time I arrived, the men were on their way to O Galo. From the expressions on their faces, you could tell what each was thinking. They were worried about their boats, their homes, and their livelihoods.

When the wind blew one of his tables across the plaza, Gustavo took the furniture inside and cranked up the awning. Then he ushered everyone out the door, pulled down the shutter, and locked the gate. Fortified with Ribeiro and *aguardiente*, the men exchanged gestures of resignation and went off in various directions to await the consequences of the storm. We walked back up the hill with María and Miguel's father, but stopped on the way so he could buy a pair of lanterns. On a table in the shop were tin and brass lamps salvaged from ships that had gone aground somewhere on the Costa da Morte. It was not unusual to see such objects. In fact, every house contained something taken from a wreck, like the Pickman china on our sideboard and the brass spittoon that collected cigarettes and ashes in the corner. Even the railing on our balcony had been taken from a British cruiser that came ashore in 1890.

Because the sea wreaked such havoc on the lives and property of the people of the coast, there was a long-standing belief that it owed some compensation in return. When it took a son or father, the survivors waited for it to indemnify the loss with a shipwreck that might provide cutlery, furniture, woodwork, brass plumbing, personal items like watches and jewelry, or any other item of worth—even if such bounty came at the cost of human life. In times when the poor were desperately so, and couldn't wait for a capricious sea to provide, they took their own measures to ensure its beneficence and the survival of their families. Those times are gone, but during my childhood, there was still a community that sustained itself by luring ships into ports that didn't exist. They had come from the east and settled in an isolated valley on the headland sometime during the fifteenth or sixteenth century. For generations, they had kept to themselves—speaking a dialect of their own and marrying within their tribe. Their contact with the outside world, apart from occasional bartering, came from the service they provided to the people of the coast: ferrying the souls of their dead to the afterlife. In the evening of the first full moon after the death of a loved one, members of the family would make the journey to Foxo Escuro with generous offerings of ham or cheese or eggs. After learning the name of the deceased, one of the ferrymen would wait for the Santa Compaña to knock on his door in the hours before dawn. He would call out the name of the soul, and if it was confirmed by a voice, he would guide the procession of the dead along a stone path that leads to a cove near the tip of the headland. There he would launch his *dorna* into the sea burdened with its unearthly freight. Passing from this world to the next, he would sail across Mar das Almas into the luminous path of the moon until he felt the buoyancy of his boat return.

This custom ended, however, when families began to ferry the souls of their dead to Illa da Luz on the Día de Todas as Almas, and the people of Foxo had to rely more on subsistence farming, fishing, and scavenging for marine life in tidal pools in order to survive. But the soil near the village is thin, and when shellfish were scarce, when blight took their grain, and mackerel weren't running, they had little to eat and were forced to grind acorns into flour to make their bread. They boiled nettles and harvested watercress from the stream in the village. They collected chestnuts in the forest. But this could not sustain them. So they became the salvagers of the Costa da Morte moving up and down the shore seizing whatever they could find, and when shipwrecks were few and far between, they did what was necessary in order to survive.

Evening came early on the day of the storm. Clouds covered the lower elevations of Aracelo and a driving rain began to fall. The men of Foxo filled their lanterns with oil, wrapped themselves in waxed canvas, and gathered oxen from the few who owned them, fitting them with special harnesses. A lantern was secured to each horn of each beast and then another hung on each side of its back. Through the rain and wind, they led their animals into the twilight "to earn a living from the misfortunes of others." Twenty beasts and a dozen men crossed the headland along a cart path through the gorse and pines to a cliff above a treacherous reef near the end of the cape. Through intervals of rain and scudding fog, the lights of Porto Lúa were visible to the east. The men spaced the oxen out evenly, tethered them to stunted trees, and left them to the elements as they retreated to a stone shed nearby. With a store of dry wood, they built a bonfire that warmed them as they waited.

The *Eucrante* sailed past Illas Sisargas in the morning sun and Cabo Vilán early in the afternoon. Heading south along the coast, it began to encounter heavy seas and strong winds off Touriñán. At first the captain thought he could outrun the storm, but by the time the sun was setting, he realized he had no choice but to find a harbor for the night. As the ship lurched and plunged over the gray-green swells, skimming sprays of surf broke across its bow. Against the darkening sky, shredded clouds blew past, ghostly over the battering waves. Porto Lúa provided the nearest shelter, but as the winds increased and visibility diminished, the lights of the town disappeared, and the captain became disoriented. Instead of steering toward the harbor, he guided the ship toward the lanterns on the headland. Swells now rose above the height of the bridge, while from their peaks, powerful gusts ripped airborne streams like waterfalls flowing parallel to a dim horizon. With every list into the wind, lace trains of water spilled across the deck until the ship heeled, and they withdrew in rolling crescents, foaming scallops. As the bow plunged and rose and plunged again, as if nodding its assent to the raging violence of the sea, the overhang of a massive wave slammed the deck with the tumult and force of a mountain torrent. One of the crewmen was knocked from his feet and slid to the edge of the deck where he caught the railing and held on as the ship heaved from side to side. Someone threw him a rope tied to a stanchion that he looped around his waist, but in the end it made no difference.

As soon as the captain realized he was taking his ship and the lives of his men toward a fatal illusion, he attempted to reverse course, but the wind and sea were at his back and the ship, instead of hitting the rocks with its bow and lifting up on a pivot, edged along the reef tearing a gash in its hull for half its length. We could hear the groan above the roar of the wind and waves and feel the vibrations through the air as the night resounded like a vast chamber of terror. Amid the thunder and concussive impact of the waves, the souls on board listened to the granite and steel sound the notes of their deaths. The lights went out, and a flood of black water poured through the gash like spate over a mill dam. Knee-deep, waist-deep in the water, those below deck searched for flashlights and lanterns. Those above held fast to winches and bollards and pipes, anything attached to the ship, drenched to the skin in the cold, pelting spray. Lightning flashed around them as if they were inside the clouds, but in the white flashes they could see nothing of the deck now covered by a deepening surge. Abandoned to the liquid night, the men felt an indescribable sense of helplessness as they battled an inescapable darkness. Any moment could bring the wave that would end it all, each seeming more violent than the last, crashing and thundering against the creaking hull, beckoning the men to end their wait and have done with it, to plunge into a gelid slip of death and open their lungs to a final breath of numbing water.

There was no task now that was not futile. The mindless insanity of the sea was the only rule. No power could shield its fury. No hope could survive its raving destruction. No human effort would matter. Thoughts of survival, of seeing the sun again, of holding a wife, of being at peace in one's dreams seemed like childish fantasies. The men, each in his own way, accepted that his life now meant nothing. That all he knew or would ever know, that all that he had done or would ever do meant nothing in the vast forces that controlled his destiny. Some men went to their bunks to wait for the water to cover them. Some made it to a lifeboat and dropped into the sea only to disappear in an instant. Some were washed overboard at their stations. The captain was last seen on the bridge, an indistinct presence in the darkness, true to his post, until a wave broke through the window and took him, like the others, into the night that outlasts every life.

In the darkness of downed lines, the men of Porto Lúa found their way to the harbor and risked their lives to save the drowning sailors. They launched two rescue boats into the storm, but the waves pushed them back against the seawall as a rain of sand and fish fell on the quay. Water stood in the plaza as far as the stairs to the alameda and the narrow streets of the old part of town had become canals. The bells of Nosa Señora do Mar rang to call for more help, but as they continued to ring, it became clear they were tolling for the dead. Few were able to sleep that night as the storm whistled through the roofs of the town and rattled its doors and windows. What unsettled Aunt Fioxilda, however, was not the violence of the wind, but the rabble of all those strange souls who had left their drowning bodies in the bay.

By morning, the storm had passed. The sun was out, the air was dry, and there was a light breeze along the coast. The sea was calm with hardly a ripple on its surface, and the only sounds were the gentle rush of waves in the port and the songs of a few stunned birds that had not been blown to Castile. As mother and I stood on the balcony assessing the damage to the houses below, a crab dropped from a strand of kelp hanging from the roof. It was only one of the thousands of creatures out of their element. In the yard were two small, silvery shad and a lavender jellyfish. All of our trees had survived, but the fig had lost a large branch, and there were numerous palm fronds scattered about the yard.

After we took the boards off the windows, grandfather and I walked down to the port to survey the damage. The streets were littered with the bricks of toppled chimneys, pantiles, broken glass, leaves, tree branches, and clumps of moss and ferns scoured from stone walls. One of the tallest eucalyptus trees in the alameda lay on its side and had taken a string of decorative lights with it. Rugs and curtains drying in the sun festooned the streets in the old part of town. Nothing more than a ragged edge of cloth was left of the flag on the town hall. Drowned seagulls were being eaten by small green crabs, which in turn were plucked off the stones by living seagulls. At several low points in the seawall, water poured back into the bay where men were bailing out the boats that had survived the storm. Father was there working on our boat, which had lost its rudder, but was otherwise intact. The beach where we played soccer had been reconfigured, and the boat in the narrow inlet of the Deva was gone. On both sides of the river, just below the Roman bridge, rose palisades of debris. Farther up the river, a buoy was standing upright on a granite boulder. A half mile to the southwest and thirty yards off the coast lay the half-submerged hull of the *Eucrante* surrounded by seabirds and a flotilla of small boats.

Oxcarts crossed the bridge in a steady procession carrying the dead animals, fish, birds, and tree limbs that were lost in the storm to a barren site on the headland where they were burned in a great bonfire that lasted for days. As we looked south down the coastal road, we could see men clearing fallen trees with axes and whipsaws. Rows of pines had been ripped from the earth and their roots had come up in balls of soil and stones leaving depressions in the turf people would come to call fairy graves. A small stream flowing from the mountains south of Aracelo had washed out a section of the road, and a landslide had leveled a fishing shed full of contraband cigarettes. On the path along the edge of the bay, the odor of death was palpable. The surf had tossed schools of hake and grouper high on the rocks, and smaller fry had been impaled on gorse hundreds of yards from the water. Oarweed hung from the boughs of trees like clumps of sea snakes, and a small skiff was moored between two boulders where kittiwakes and gannets made their nests.

The northern shore of the headland rises from the sea in cliffs that reach a height of a hundred feet. Crescent beaches and isolated coves wrought by wind and wave shelter between towering buttresses of granite steep on a vertiginous scale and patched with a soft baize of moss and algae, dark green in the shadows, yellow-green in sunlight. Growing on the less severe slopes of the cliffs where the soil holds firmly are rock samphire, sea thrift, and sorrel. Gulls drift back and forth lazily on the updrafts, and at the foot of the cliffs, small islands of stone are surrounded by white water and rings of foam. For much of the year, fog sits on these cliffs, and the fields above, though thin, are well-watered. Fermenting slowly through the ground, the seeping moisture turns tawny as it drips from stones and trickles out under carpets of moss and heather, then gathers in small streams that shower down through fern glades in long glistening threads carving deep ravines in the rock and eventually falling into the sea. Grandfather and I climbed down one of these ravines on a worn path twisting and turning through pedestals of rock, slipping on wet stones, until we made it to one of the coves near the wreck.

There were a half dozen fishing boats on a narrow beach that separates the sea from a green tidal pool deeper in the cove. Men shouted at each other in the salty air as they searched for objects that had come ashore and battled the gulls that brazenly dropped from the sky to plunder what they could. The bodies of several sailors had come to rest beside the pool. They were alabaster white, with faint blue shadows beneath the surface of their skin. Like statues of gods hurled from the cliff, they lay half-buried in the sand. But unlike alabaster, the skin of these bodies was soft to touch and easily torn by lifting hands. The blood was mostly gone or hidden in scarlet arteries beneath the bleached dough of an arm or leg. Bruises like blue and violet flowers spoke of the trauma they had undergone. Some still wore rags of trousers or torn shirts. One was naked but for a burgundy waistcoat. Another bore a tattoo on his back like a postmark on a white envelope. White toes sticking through the sole of a black boot. Pockets full of sand. Blond hair matted with tangled algae. Mouths open to the sky holding water like blue-rimmed cups.

Of the twenty-two crewmen listed on the manifest, all but four were British. Seventeen bodies were found. The rest were presumed dead. On the beach where we stood, we counted eight. A recovery team marked the locations with red flags tied to long poles in case the tide rose to cover them. When the men moved on to search for more bodies, two stayed behind to guard against crabs and gulls, and protect personal items from scavengers. In addition to the bodies, we saw a blue hat, several shoes, a biscuit tin filled with letters, a work glove, a metal basin, a shaving mirror, a pocket watch, jackets, shirts, trousers, and a scarf. One of the men handed me the biscuit tin and told me to take the letters home to dry.

"Perhaps someone will come for them," he said.

The acorn-eaters of Foxo were already on the ship lowering furniture and rations down to their boats. But the next night they were forced to abandon their work when a salvage ship with a large crane arrived from Ferrol. By the time the sun was up, it was unloading the cargo containers onto another ship. No one ever knew for certain what was in them, what the men had lost their lives for. One rumor said they were full of sewing machines bound for the Orient. Another that they were full of engine parts going to Africa. In the meantime, the coastal road had been cleared and a large refrigeration truck ordinarily used to transport fish had arrived to preserve the bodies that were being brought up from the shore.

School opened on the second day after the storm, and I took the letters I had dried to Sister Mary Rose, thinking we might return them to the person who had sent them. The pink envelopes were lined with thin paper printed with yellow roses and still scented with perfume. Though most of the letters had been destroyed by condensation, a few were still legible. They had been written to a man named Jack, and the first was addressed to a shipping office in Calcutta: "How are you my dear? I have wanted to see you so badly it hurts. All day I have looked forward to this evening when I could come home and write to you. Knowing your fingers will touch these pages, and your eyes will read these words helps me to feel we're together. I look at the moon and know that wherever you are, you're looking at it too. Today at work I calculated that if I can save four shillings a week, we can take a holiday in France when you return. We'll find a quiet little room in Paris and make the most of our time together. I long to hold you and to kiss—" At this point, Sister Mary Rose decided the letters were too intimate for us to read and put them back in the tin. When we learned that personal effects were being catalogued and stored at the fishermen's cooperative, I left them there.

In the plaza, members of the Guardia Civil were conferring with a man from the British Embassy who had come to retrieve the bodies of the sailors and collect their property. After a brief conversation, they escorted him to Rúa das Sombras where the man inspected the tables of merchants and pointed out the items of British origin that had likely been stolen from the ship. At his direction, the officers confiscated three bottles of Scotch whisky, an umbrella with an ivory handle, a tea set, a pistol, a maritime atlas, and two short-wave radios. When they returned to the plaza, they were joined by an Anglican bishop and his retinue from Madrid. After another conversation, they crossed the bridge to the refrigeration truck where the bishop sprinkled holy water on the ground and recited passages from *The Book of Common Prayer*. That evening, led by Don Prudencio, Don Andrés, and the Gallardo brothers playing a mournful dirge, the bishop, accompanied by acolytes carrying a makeshift altar and tabernacle, made the trek along the top of the cliff to a field near the reef to conduct a memorial service. As the sun descended over Illa da Luz and the wind picked up over the water, he hurried through his sermon emphasizing that no one can understand the mysteries of Providence and asked whether a wren blames God when its nest is blown from a tree. After the service, Don Andrés laid the first stone of what he promised would be a monument to commemorate those who had died.

Every evening of the following week, I walked along the path above the cliffs to the site where the monument waited to be completed. Sitting on a wide, flat boulder overlooking the sea, I watched the salvage crew working until the sun went down and the jeweled lights of the crane flickered on under an amethyst sky. I tried to imagine the fury of the storm and the hopelessness of those who had died. I thought of the fishermen who venture out on rough seas to feed their families and of my father. Had this place which had just sent so many souls to the next world been altered in some way? Were their ghosts here on the cliffs? Were they resting on the low haze that floated over the water? Were they responsible for the disappearance of fruit and vegetables from kitchen gardens reported by people on the headland? And then one evening when a soft, pink coral glow from the clouds lit the sea and cliffs, I noticed a white column of smoke rising from one of the ravines and heard the melancholy sound of a brass instrument. The men and women tending their animals in the fields heard it too.

No one knew the source of the sound until the following morning when a half-starved man wearing nothing but a pair of ragged trousers snatched a carving knife from one of the vendors in Rúa das Sombras and ran off through the narrow streets as startled shoppers watched. The next day he returned for cutlery, plates, and a pot that had been looted from the ship. When an ax and bucket went missing from a house on the headland, people connected the thefts and concluded one of the English sailors had survived and was living in the ravine where I had seen the column of smoke.

Thrown from the ship by the power of the storm, he had found himself in a moving labyrinth of waves, a sea of chance, until, against all odds, chance delivered him, lifted him from the depths and restored him to solid ground, to a beach rather than the rocks, and he was able to climb, half-conscious, above the waves before collapsing. When he finally woke, the storm had passed. Cold and bruised, his clothes hanging like seaweed from his limbs, he crawled to a damp cave in a narrow fissure of the cliff where even at midday the light is dusky. He drank water falling from the rocks and ate what he could find in the surf. When his strength returned, he climbed the cliff to forage at night among the farms and steal what he needed to survive. With the ax he made a spear. With the bucket he carried fire. He lived on octopi and the small fish that were trapped in tidal pools among the rocks. And one night, while walking through the fields behind an abandoned house, he discovered a grove of wild grapes and lemon trees. On the seventh day, while looking for shellfish on the beach below his cave, he saw a glint of sunlight reflecting off a piece of metal and discovered his trumpet nearly buried by sand in a crevice among the rocks.

He pulled it free and washed it in a braid of falling water. Though dented, it still played.

When the sea was calm and the breeze was out of the southwest, we could hear the lament of his trumpet in the streets of Porto Lúa. He perched high on the cliff in a natural hollow that added resonance to the sound as the sea broke on the rocks below and the waves pummeled the hapless stern of the ship on summer evenings when fine mists brought a pleasant chill to the end of warm days. He knew several melodies by heart, and we soon learned them as well. We called them the *cancións do inglés*, but years later, I discovered that these songs from my childhood were well-known works from the classical repertoire.

According to the people who lived on the headland, his music had a transformative effect on nature, charming not only the birds and creatures of the fields, but the trees and plants and shadows and clouds. The sea grew calm when he played, and the moon was brighter. Even the waters of streams slowed as if entranced. People said he taught the air to sing and could do the same for the sun and moon and stars. When their cows began to produce more milk, the farmers on the headland offered him baskets of cheese and eggs and potatoes if he would play in their gardens and fields. One couple who could not conceive asked him to play outside their window at night. In return, they would name their child after him. And they did.

To the people of Porto Lúa, he was *o náufrago*. To the people of the headland, he was *o estranxeiro*. In fact, his name was Henry Winstanley, second mate of the *Eucrante*, from Hornchurch, England. But that person disappeared on the night of the storm as he struggled for his life between the ship and sand. He lost, in a sense, his dream of himself, and was reborn on those rocks as someone else—living for the first time on his own and by his wits. The inward change was soon reflected in his appearance. Exposed to the wind and cold on the granite cliffs, and nearly starved by a meager diet, his body became that of an animal struggling to survive, thin and muscular. His ribcage protruded and his blue eyes deepened in their sockets. In time, his skin darkened in the coastal sun, and his blond hair grew longer and lighter. With sticks and vines, he made snares to catch rock pigeons, which he sold at the entrance of the market, and with the money, bought the barbed point of a harpoon which he fixed to the end of his spear. With this he hunted the shallow pools where, as agile as a creature native to the element, he leapt from rock to rock in the white spray of the surf. When the man from the embassy returned to take him back to England, Harry, as he was called, could not be found. Hiring fishermen to take him along the coast of the headland, the official searched the cliff without success. Then he climbed down to the cave from above and left a letter sealed in a plastic sleeve on embassy paper instructing Harry to contact him through the good offices of Don Andrés. Despite his efforts, the official never heard from him, and yet at night, the melancholy songs continued. It was clear Harry had no desire to be found, and people concluded he had lost his mind in the nightmare of the storm.

As fall approached and the nights grew cooler, he moved from the damp ravine to a more hospitable gap among the rocks in a narrow valley closer to Porto Lúa where he built a shelter halfway up from the water that allowed him to approach the sea more easily and reach the town without a long climb. He cleared the brush and reeds from a level area beside a stream that tumbled down from fields of bracken and gathered flat stones from the streambed to mark a foundation. Once he had the floor in place, he cut a sapling for a balance pole and hung a bucket on either end of it to haul sand and pebbles up the path from the beach. Then he took lime from a hut along the coastal road where it was stored for highway maintenance to make cement. Panes of glass he found in an old house with no roof.

The people of Foxo showed no remorse for their actions on the night of the storm. The ship had merely had bad luck. Fate had caused the deaths of the sailors. Where a man stood on the deck, where the waves hit, where the swells rose and fell determined who lived and who died. Nevertheless, they let Harry's pilfering go without consequence as if they thought letting him steal would balance their accounts with heaven, or perhaps they had a superstitious respect for the mad and believed they were closer to God.

What became known as *o museo do estranxeiro* began when Harry laid the first stone of his house. As he was building up the walls from the foundation, he grew tired of the smooth, flat stones he had found along the stream and the symmetry and form of their regular placement. It was, he later explained, as if he were writing a story with a single word repeated over and over again. So he looked for various anomalies in the stones, various forms and shapes, and put them together as if in a dream, free of the sovereignty of convention, free of the imposition of a plan, but not without some logic of their own. Meant to accommodate a man whose memory of himself was like a dream of one who had never existed, the house seemed to change, from moment to moment, in both its appearance and character.

There were already two museums in Porto Lúa. One was in a locked closet on the second floor of El Conde's palace and contained the French plan of attack on Corcubión, funeral wreaths from the tomb of Alfonso XIII, precious stones from the sword of Matamoros, a bone from the foot of Santa Trega, the skin of a *vákner*, and several portolan charts. Its contents had been acquired by the ancestors of Don Prudencio and visited so infrequently that even El Conde himself couldn't remember what was in the collection. If it hadn't been for the vellum tags written in cuttlefish ink, most of the objects would have been impossible to identify. The other museum was the house where Alonso Pinzón had slept after returning from America. Stories passed down from generation to generation claimed the new world flowers in the gardens of Porto Lúa were brought back by the *Pinta* and that there were colonies of butterflies in the valley of the Deva that had descended from those on the ship of the famous captain. When Don Andrés decided the house should testify to Porto Lúa's claim of being the first place in Europe to receive news of America, he chastised its current inhabitants for keeping chickens in the room where Pinzón had slept and for the condition of the mattress that was covered with inky splotches of blood and the dry husks of bugs. According to oral history, the claim was true. However, it was also true that when the explorer arrived in the port laden with wonders, he was soon driven away by the natives' excessive interest in his cargo and sailed south to Baiona, giving that city the claim of discovery. Nevertheless, Don Andrés paid to have a sign painted over the door of the house reading *Museo do Explorador Martín Alonso Pinzón Descubridor do Novo Mundo.*

Late in the summer, school let out for six weeks so children could participate in the annual harvest activities with their families. I climbed the trees in the orchard to shake down fruit for Aunt Fioxilda and went around behind father to gather the hay he cut with the scythe, but I spent most of my vacation in the market helping mother. Harry continued to sit outside the front gate selling his pigeons and crabs, calculating with his fingers and haggling with gestures. But one week he failed to appear. When mother noticed his absence, she put several sardines in a bucket and told me to take them to him. From the bridge, it was a ten-minute walk along the cliff path to the stony valley where he had built his house, and I covered the distance with a mixture of curiosity and trepidation. I had seen the house from the top of the cliff, but this was the first time I had approached it and the man who had built it. Aunt Fioxilda questioned whether he was even alive and not just the spirit of the man. When I arrived, he was turning a barrel into a stove and a pipe into a chimney. The English I had learned from Sister Mary Rose allowed me to communicate with a limited vocabulary and rudimentary grammar.

"Hello. My mother give you fish."

"*Gracias*," he replied, taking the bucket.

I taught him a few words of Galician that he could use in the market such as *pombas* and *cangrexos*, and he showed me the first sculptures of his museum. As I was leaving, he asked if I could come back to teach him more Galician and said he would teach me English in return.

Once my parents agreed to the idea, I began to spend two or three afternoons a week helping Harry learn the language and doing odd jobs as he expanded his museum with new projects. The first few weeks I was there, he was making thin columns or pinnacles and capricious sculptures by cementing stone upon stone. Then he built a bridge across the stream and a stairway up the opposite bank to a lookout with a bench, also constructed of round stones cemented together. On either side of the stairway, he made a wall leaving holes between the stones for birds to nest in. My job was to mix the mortar and hold the stones in place until it set. Wherever there were blank spaces of cement, he inserted pieces of broken mirrors and seashells as decorations. Unlike the museum, the interior of the house was unadorned. There was a stone table, a stone chair, the stove, and a metal basin that received water via a channel connected to the stream. Beside a window overlooking the sea, he hung a hammock woven from strands of sisal rope.

At the end of the summer break, I returned to school to start a new term. The warm days of autumn were nearly over, and the trees were already losing their leaves. Harry continued to add odd sculptures to his garden, and sometimes after school I stopped by with Miguel and María or other classmates to see them. For our pleasure and amusement as much as for his own, he created mythical animals and strange objects out of discarded farm equipment, driftwood, glass buoys, netting, and shells that he found on the beach. First he shaped a deer from heavy wire and gave it driftwood antlers, then a dinosaur with the bony frill of a shovel blade and horns of long thin pine cones. Every week there was a new sculpture and sometimes two. Birds with feathers of seashells, cement owls with basalt eyes, a rudder turned sundial, an angel with a porcelain face and wings of broken mirrors, a mermaid with spindle shell hair, a large cement starfish encrusted with chipped bricks, and a crescent moon cut from a ship's brass serving tray. On Sundays after Mass, people brought their children to see the museum, and when the weather permitted, they carried picnic baskets and bottles of wine. When someone posted a sign on the side of the coastal highway with an arrow pointing to the *Museo do Estranxeiro*, Harry put a frame around it and titled the work "sign."

Mirrors hanging from threads appeared on trees and bushes reflecting the sunlight as they turned in the wind. Faces of satyrs and fauns gazed from benches and fountains. Tin cans, cut and bent and painted blue and yellow to resemble songbirds, sat on fence posts and stone walls whistling in the autumn breeze. People claimed he could sculpt the wind and paint the sky.

When he wasn't making art, Harry worked with the farmers to gather their harvests and traveled over the rough lanes of the headland on their oxcarts to cut bracken for winter feed. On one occasion, he helped a neighbor retrieve the wheelhouse of a scuttled fishing boat and set it up as a shed for his chickens. The farmers grew so fond of him they left him stacks of firewood, cans of milk, and boxes of eggs. In return, he painted the sides of their houses and barns with green hills and blue skies and white clouds. When he made sculptures in their gardens, they considered it good luck and gave him a small plot of land on which to grow his own potatoes and kale.

His next idea was to turn the town of Porto Lúa into a museum. He proposed the construction of Gothic follies in the plaza, a Roman temple in the alameda, and Norman towers along the quay, but Don Andrés intervened to explain that people in the town lived by fishing, farming, and commerce and had no interest in towers and follies. Nevertheless, Harry posted descriptive markers throughout the town where the scene struck him as a work of art. For example, as one enters Rúa dos Olores beside Madame Zafirah's house, there is a view of a *galería* behind a palm tree that he labeled "Dreams of Southern Light," and in the passageway where one first sees the plaza of the olive tree, he posted a sign that read "Spanish Morning."

Although the museum of Porto Lúa failed to materialize, it did inspire Harry's greatest achievement: what came to be called the ephemeral exhibition. It began as a museum of the sea, but rather than contain objects from the sea, it was the sea itself. Near the site of the unfinished memorial to those who died on the *Eucrante*, he mounted several window frames of long, thin stones cemented together on stone pedestals. As soon as he finished this project, he proceeded to place similar frames strategically along the coast and in the fields wherever there was an uncommonly beautiful view of Illa da Luz, or Mount Aracelo, or the cliffs of the headland, or the clouds over the sea, or the rustic charm of houses, or the long beaches to the south, and just behind each window, he built a stone bench large enough for two. People working in their fields or who came out from town on their evening walks wondered what strange spirits possessed this foreigner that caused him to place windows around the headland, but when they were curious enough to sit on the benches and look through the windows, they discovered scenes of the sky and mountain, of the coastline and town, as beautiful as any painting, but real before their eyes. Each window he gave a name. Archive of air. Gallery of grace. Pool of sky. The latter required people to lie on their backs and look upward through a horizontal window five feet above the ground in order to watch the clouds move slowly across the heavens. The final window he built was on the highest point of the headland and framed the entire massif of Aracelo. It was unusually wide and instead of one bench, it required six spread out in an arc across a flat boulder. This was the Portico of the Moon.

Sitting on the bench he built on the lookout above his house, Harry continued to play his trumpet every night. Just as his music taught us to hear the sounds habit had caused us to forget, so his museum taught us to see the fields and cliffs and clouds with a clarity and freshness we had never known. Because the views of the sea and mountain were as common to us as gray city streets are to urban dwellers, it took the perspective of someone else to lift the veil. As a survivor of a deadly storm, as one who had been given a second chance at life, Harry saw it with the fresh perception of one who has been resurrected to its beauty. If this was madness, it was the madness of art.

Winnowed straw blows across a threshing floor. Fields of kale endure the chill as cattle stamp in steaming muck, crowding under the scanty shelter of a single pine. A smattering of rain smarts the fingers and ears of a few dark souls grimly tasked to labor in sodden fields. Smoke and mist hang over the patch-work of small plots where the boots of men and hooves of beasts pock the earth with muddy pools winking at the winter sky. Just as the atmosphere begins to brighten, heavy rain hemorrhaging from low clouds passes over the pewter burnish of the sea. All day and all night, all week without end, it drips and patters on roofs and porches, running in sheets, shifting in the wind, first driven, then suspended, then driven again. Sluicing the channels of empty streets. Greening the stone-work of houses and walls. The windows fog and drip. The sills are icy cold. The floor is colder still. Only the fire in the corner hearth allows us to survive beneath layers of clothes. Heedless of the rain, men grapple with the freezing steel of harnesses and blades in their bondage to the earth. Holding their hats against the wind, others work on the launch, a storm-battered slab of cement preserved a hundred years in a coastline mil-lions in the making. The hands of these men are pink and chafed, swollen flesh around arthritic bones, but as steady as the rain when mending a net or securing their knots. They have no thoughts of luxury and few of leisure.

For a day or two, a fitful sun warms the gardens and dries the stones. Its solstice light lies among the shadows of the forest like strips of buttered earth. But the respite is brief. High clouds edge eastward beneath a stubborn sun. As the sky closes, the mountain cliffs turn blue, the water slate, and the beaches gray. From far across the sea, icy shafts of light slice through black clouds like blades of transparent steel. Days of rain return. Boat by boat men venture out where there is no mercy, no godliness, onto a sea tossing its fury in arcs of white foam. The liquid tomb devours its victims in an instant, and each man knows of another gone below.

High on the mountain, fierce winds blow through barren forests buffeting the rocky peaks that rise above the clouds like granite islets above the sea. Through months of chill mornings and dull evenings, of incessant rains that stream down walls and murmur in the gutters, far from the reds and yellows of autumn, the heart hungers for color. When at last a warm wind strays north from Saharan skies. The mist burns off. Fields brighten. Twilight lingers. Clouds move slowly across the horizon in the late blush of a departed sun. As the moon rises over the mountain, its soft light invades the bedrooms of Porto Lúa to enchant the nights of sleepless children. Curlews cry out in the marshes, and in the blue-green hour before dawn, hearth smoke climbs to the stars. Shadows move from house to barn to field. A hasp lock rattles, a latch scrapes, a hinge groans. In the morning light over Campo da Graza, a lone hawk appears. Cuckoos call from mountain thickets. In the days that follow, the land is turned and seeds are sown. From rough-hewn carts staved with alder branches, chaff and green manure are pitched over the black soil to preserve the furrows' warmth on cold spring nights.

The lost blues of childhood return in the open skies and lengthening days, and in the still morning air, the sea horizon revives a feeling of timelessness like a premonition of the past.

Along the fringes of the forest, new buds of beeches and oaks push the copper leaves of autumn from their purchase. And from the buds, nascent leaves emerge in yellow bouquets before ripening to green, as the petals of wild apple and cherry blossoms fall through the forest in a fragrant snow. In worn pastures and barren tracts, mud hardens, and the earth turns from black to umber brown, from paste to powder. Fresh fields shine in the silken luster of morning dew, and delicate stems of green appear in the slush of dead leaves that cover the ground along the paths and in the corners of walled enclosures. Scattered across open meadows on the banks of the Deva and the lower slopes of the mountain, daffodils capture the sunlight in the cryptic beauty of their yellow flowers. If, as the ancients say, the first day of the newly created world was a day of spring, it would have been a day like these when the intoxicating air, scented with watery freshness, stirs a longing for distant mornings, the calm purity of cloudless skies, and the blue iridescence of the sea blossoming in white waves rolling across the shores of memory. The air rings with the echoes of kitchens, a mason's hammer, children shouting. Outlined with the pollen of maritime pines, pools left by passing showers dry like the silted estuaries of a yellow sea. Odors rise from sun-warmed hedges and mossy stones, beds of ivy and wild onions, like souls of the dead returning to life. A broad figure in black stoops behind the broken wall of a kitchen garden where broiling sardines send up a savory cloud of white smoke. Sparrows revel in licentious tumult as they flit and chatter around the eaves, in thickets and hedges, and in their flights between barns and houses, orchards and vineyards. At the end of the day, seabirds sail an idle course over the rocky cliffs of the southern coast, and high above the bay, a crescent moon embraces the falling Pleiades.

Beneath the pale indigo of midsummer noon, shadows shorten, birds grow quiet. From a cloudless sky, the sun hammers its foil of light over the granite of the quay and jetty, the bluffs along the cape, the tide-washed shores. In the intensity of the light, the stones of the seawall surrounding the blue water resemble a coast of ice. The pace of life slows. The air is languorous, the people listless, moving slowly, as if in a dream, through the depths of an incandescent sea. Flecked with mica, the stones in the streets and walls glitter like blocks of sand, and in the corners of narrow lanes, where geraniums and hydrangeas flourish, sunlight and shadows clash in blinding contrasts as men and women disappear into the darkness of open doors. Behind closed shutters, dishes clatter, voices contend, and flies exhausted by the heat seek the cool surfaces of walls and floors. The smoke of frying fish and olive oil fills deserted passageways as the warmth enlivens every odor, heightens every sound. The pavement smells of burning stone. Woodwork cracks. Paint flakes. Dogs lying in the plaza lack the energy to lift their tongues from the dust, and from the plane trees along the quay, sparrows and magpies drop down to pick at the market's sun-cured refuse of pork tripe and fish heads lying beside barrels of trash. The grass and wildflowers that grew in the gaps of cobbled streets and stone walls during the months of rain bow limply in the slightest stirring of air. In the back lanes that tunnel beneath eaves and porches beyond the reach of the sun, walls are peppered with black mold from the winter damp. And on the slopes of the mountain, sun-warped air blurs the yellow fields of blooming rapeseed while corn languishes in smaller plots, pine trees sweat an oozing sap, and haystacks, like tufted huts of straw, dry to the sound of trilling insects.

As the sun slips below the horizon, a luminous tide retreats into the offing. Over the bay, swallows on stiletto wings careen through the auric light. Like stars emerging from the darkening sky, the faces of couples, families with children, the elderly, appear in the darkening *rúas* for their nightly walks. A trumpet plays across the water. A woman wearing a black mantilla sells anise shortcakes on a corner. Children break away from their parents to race down the streets into alleys and lanes, circling, laughing, hiding. For them, lost in their games, the glow in the western sky seems unending, taking on a greenish tint as white gulls pass silently, dimly seen, like ghosts seeking their rest beyond the horizon. The orange filaments of bare bulbs flicker on in street lamps along the quay, and within moments, the string of lights stretching across the entrance of the alameda begins to brighten. Above the gravel paths of its gardens, an ivory moon moves through the branches of palms and camellias. The trickle of a fountain is the only sound among the shadows of green bowers where the white blossoms of sweet magnolias offer their scent to the night.

Autumn arrives in a sudden gust of wind chilled over northern ice that sweeps a few dry leaves along the gutters. A bank of clouds follows, rolling southward like a moving frieze of celestial marble. Slowing over the argent surface of the bay, it breaks into white archipelagos that linger over seashore plots of corn and kale before vanishing into mountain forests where leaves are turning yellow among the highest branches of the trees. The town becomes an apparition of moods changing from moment to moment, sculpted by capricious shadows and intensities of light.

Fog rises from the sea before the sun is up and lasts until noon. Fishing boats pitch at their anchors as dogs scavenge among the rocks of the jetty sniffing at clumps of seaweed. Moving in from the coast, a cool rain blurs the forest fringed with mist. The dampness carries the odors of fish, of earth and stone, of sewage and cigarette smoke, of eucalyptus that clings to hair and clothes. Anticipating daybreak all morning, a wren questions the weak light with its song. When the fog lifts, the sky is deep blue, blue above the pink sand at sea's edge where, grain by grain, the Deva brings the mountain down to dance in the cadent tide.

The days grow shorter and the shadows longer. Gardens and fields languish in a sunny lethargy of slow time. Yellow, orange, and brown, the boughs of chestnut trees bend back and forth in a fresh breeze, like bladder wrack tossed in tidal pools. When the light fades over a sea horizon of vitreous clarity, and the aureate sky matches the apple gold of orchards, the harvest weary take their rest with a heaviness approaching death. Night birds sing the stables to sleep, and a full moon embraces the rising Pleiades. At dawn a blond light filtered by the smoke of burning fields shines on lavender hills to the south. Blown husks that escape the fires scratch and clatter across dry stubble. Men and women dig for potatoes and gather ripened grapes to press, and in open fields, the last cut of hay is bundled onto oxcarts. When the harvest is complete, and the wheat is on the millstone, a cold drizzle begins to fall lashing through a rising mist stinging hands and faces. Cranes fly south. Pigs are lured to slaughter by children bearing apples. Winnowed straw blows across a threshing floor. Fields of kale endure the chill as cattle stamp in steaming muck, crowding under the scanty shelter of a single pine.

The elderly appeared first. Less inclined to walk very far, they took their evening stroll around the plaza. Circling in groups of two or three, the men debated the issues of the day with their hands as much as with their words, while the women followed in groups of their own, equally emphatic in their conversations but with lower voices as if surprised by secret revelations. After three or four slow passes, the men sat on benches under a plane tree on the north side of the plaza, and the women sat on benches under a chestnut tree on the south side. When the bells at Nosa Señora do Mar struck nine, the men stood up, separated with a few final words, joined their wives, and departed in different directions toward their homes.

Along the way, they stopped to speak with friends and neighbors who were just emerging for the night. Young couples leaning into each other walked down the streets drifting from side to side. Adolescent girls, self-possessed and scornful, passed in small, exclusive groups of three or four. Dark beauties for the most part, though some bore the blood of northern invaders, they were known as the *raíñas das rúas*. Thin with a calf-like gait, they were serious beyond their years and deeply jealous of the attention other groups might receive from the boys they pretended to ignore. Less concerned with their appearance, the boys followed behind them. Boisterous as a flock of crows, they spat and stumbled their way along, broadcasting their mock disputes and scuffles like serenades to disdainful ears. Indifferent to the youth around them, widows of all ages walked together, arms linked. Stout, modestly dressed in black, they had always been, and would always be, immortal fixtures of the streets and market.

In keeping with their rank, Don Andrés and María Dolores appeared in conspicuous but relative luxury. He in a brown gabardine suit and short butternut tie. She in her imported pelage. Unfailingly, the mayor addressed those who approached by name, asked about their families, and responded to any tale they might tell with more appreciation than the story deserved. If the person was a man, Doña María took his wife to one side and engaged her in idle conversation. If a woman, she stood impatiently beside her husband looking elsewhere. Her head barely emerged above her shoulders of fur as if she were drowning in a sea of pelts, and the bosom she had once presented boldly to attract, she now used, thrust forward, to intimidate or warn the faint of heart who stood in their way as the pair proceeded down the *rúas*. There too, moving with the crowd, were the inseparable Sister Benigna and Sister Mary Rose in their black tunics and white cornettes. Often heard before seen, Fulgencio, Horacio, and O Gordo stopped every thirty or forty yards to discuss a matter of politics or philosophy before agreeing to disagree and move on swearing reflexively without offense. The barber and the clockmaker both wore fedoras and overcoats thrown stylishly over their shoulders, while O Gordo struggled with his chair over the uneven paving stones shouting in his imperious manner for people to give way before him. Among the many others who walked in the nightly ritual were the jaundiced Constable Sampaio with his wife and children, Dr. Romalde humming a tango to himself, the Gallardo brothers and their families, the Carreiras, the Piñeiros, the Monteros, the Caamaños, pork sellers and fishmongers, lacemakers, masons, carpenters, members of the fishermen's syndicate, many of our neighbors, often my own family, and somewhere among the shadows, worse for drink, Facundo.

The highlight of the night was the appearance of the Two Marías. At precisely nine-fifteen, they set forth from their house in Rúa dos Santos to be greeted by the children who gathered in anticipation of the grand event. There were initially three sisters, called *As Marías*, who came to Porto Lúa barefoot over the mountain to live with a maiden aunt after their father, a prominent leftist, had been arrested and executed by the forces of General Molinero in Santiago. Their aunt died shortly after their arrival leaving them the house and a small shop where they worked as seamstresses, but this wasn't enough to support them, and they were forced to rely on the charity of others to survive. The youngest of the three died in her twenties during an outbreak of influenza, but the remaining two continued to speak of themselves as three, and no one ever dared to contradict them or to pass too closely in the street, even when it was crowded, for this was the space reserved for the third María. Because they considered themselves to be distinguished members of a more urbane society, they never found suitable consorts or even close friends among the people of Porto Lúa. Like hand-colored sepia photographs from the last century, they walked arm-in-arm down the *rúas* wearing brightly colored make-up fashioned from rice powder, beet extract, and charcoal, which, rather than hiding their age, only succeeded in exaggerating it. Every day the elder sister wore a different scarf and on Sundays a flower in her hair. When people stopped to talk to her, she spoke of their deceased father coming for a visit. The younger and taller of the two was more reserved, but tended to criticize other women for wearing too much make-up. Though their hair had thinned and their skin had loosened during the decades since their youth, in their own eyes, they were still irresistible to men, to young men in particular. But, like a soft chisel, the lamplight in the narrow *rúas* sculpted vesper shadows on their faces, accentuating the delusions of their aging vanity.

The sisters turned the corner into the plaza and passed O Galo at nine-twenty. As they walked by the bar, they smiled and gestured at the fishermen and laborers who stood in the doorway or sat at the tables on the terrace. And the men, accustomed to the ritual, played along.

"Who are these beauties?"

"Have they ever looked better?"

"If only I were young again."

The Marías nodded to acknowledge the comments and continued on their way carrying themselves with a dignity and pride that suggested they not only deserved the compliments, but were gracious in deflecting the praise as if it were too much.

One night when the men sitting outside O Galo shouted their compliments to the passing Marías, a young man who had had too much to drink stood up and told them to stop.

"Are you crazy? They're not beautiful. Look at them."

"Sit down, Chucho."

"Why play this game night after night?"

The Marías stopped.

"Why lie to a couple of old fools? Why tell any woman she's beautiful when she's not?"

"Sit down. You're drunk."

"What's wrong with you people?"

Then he turned to the Marías who were standing a few feet away and pointed his finger at them.

"You don't believe them, do you? They're playing a game with you. You're just a couple of old women past your prime who dress yourselves up like clowns every night. Your families ought to be ashamed of you."

Several men stood up behind him and were ready to restrain him, but the younger María, the one who rarely spoke, looked at him with eyes of stone and said, "We are as you see us, and from this day forward, you will see us as young and beautiful. Not only that, but you will see all older women as young and beautiful, and you will see all young women as old and broken, palsied, and infirm as they would look after a lifetime with you. Their hair will be white and falling out. Their skin will be dry and shriveled. Their eyes will be red and failing. They will have birthmarks and moles and liver spots on their faces and arms and legs. Those are the only women who will ever take an interest in you for the rest of your life."

She waited a moment for his response, but he looked around at the other people on the terrace and in the street and said nothing. As the Two Marías continued through the plaza toward the quay, nodding at the men who called out to them, Chucho was left dumbfounded. He paid for his drinks and walked against the flow of people passing in Rúa Nova. He stared at each woman he passed. Young and old went by, but he couldn't tell if the spell of the younger María had worked—whether the young were old and the old were young or not. He went up to a woman walking by herself and asked her how old she was.

"Old enough not to tell you my age," she laughed.

He decided the only way he could determine whether his eyes were deceiving him was to find a woman he knew, so he went to the house of a friend who had a young sister. When he knocked on the door, he was met by an old woman with wrinkled skin and asked if her daughter was home.

"My *daughter*, Chucho? Do you mean my *mother*?"

Although more than two years had passed since I'd accompanied Bachiario and his goat through the streets of Porto Lúa,

Aunt Fioxilda still refused to let him in on Día de Todas as Almas when he went from house to house purifying the thresholds with holy water. Living with our family and taking on some of the responsibilities of the household had tempered her religious fervor, but she still made her herbal salve from time to time and still inhabited a place, as she had once put it, "beyond the ordinary ways of seeing." She had stopped making dolls of martyrs as the demand from the Church had fallen, but she continued to practice the art of the *curandeira* healing crossed eyes, the evil eye, impotence, madness caused by love (not by God), thin blood, snakebites, seizures of all kinds, memories of death in previous lives, warts, and frigidity. She was equally adept at curing herself and had the uncanny ability to know the precise moment of an infection or breach in her constitution. Once after Mass, she said she had caught the cold of a child sitting behind her. And she was right. The one constant in her diet was the cod liver oil she took before breakfast, but over time she also developed a mania for chard and saltwort.

Challenged by the appearance of any anomaly in her idea of order, she welcomed the opportunity to marshal her resources against the intrusion. At this point in her life, she faced three great adversaries: a mysterious disk she believed to be buried beneath the floor of our house that disrupted her communications with the world of spirits, a flock of starlings that had taken up residence in our orchard, which she was convinced was the result of a neighbor's sorcery, and the ubiquitous presence of electric light as it began to play an increasingly important role in our lives. "If it's such a good thing, why does it have to hide in wires?" she asked. She was so deeply suspicious of what she called "the invisible blood of fire" that she refused to have the light bulb on in the kitchen when she was preparing food for fear it would somehow poison us. Although not opposed to candles made from beeswax, she often repeated the belief that "it is presumptuous to mock the power of the sun with human inventions." Not surprisingly, she had a similar attitude toward telephones and once asked, "Why would I want to speak to someone's voice when I can go down the street and see her?" and was afraid if she stood too close to the lines, someone would be able to hear her thoughts.

That fall the power grid in Porto Lúa was modernized, and, as a result, Gustavo bought a large refrigerator and the first black and white television most of us had ever seen. Once the antenna had been installed and he had built a platform above the bar, he invited the town to inspect what he called the first wonder of the modern world. Despite the fact that she typically avoided electricity on Sundays, Aunt Fioxilda agreed to accompany us to O Galo, I suspect more to safeguard our presence than to approve of the invention. If she had understood how televisions receive their sound and images from signals passing through the atmosphere, I doubt she would have been so willing.

The bar was a long, narrow room whose only windows were small shuttered openings in the granite at the front of the building. The interior was lit by several fluorescent tubes and whatever sunlight might pass through the door and shutters. There were nine tables and for every table six or eight chairs. The walls were decorated with curling black and white photographs of football teams, color lithographs of the bay, and shelves with bottles of exotic spirits. At the far end of the room was a kitchen, a storeroom, and a porcelain latrine behind a plywood door. Although there was a small vent in the back wall covered by a grate to keep the rats out, in the summer, the warm odors of olive oil, garlic, and urine passed through the room as if through a horizontal chimney.

We arrived early enough to sit in the front of the room near the television. Mother made me wear the bow tie she had bought in anticipation of my First Communion and told me not to ask any questions because some things are meant to be beyond our knowledge. Although the kitchen was closed, Gustavo was busy serving chilled bottles of beer. Doctor Romalde was there with his mouth open and his head tilted back as he peered through his glasses at the dark screen of the television. Miguel and María came in with their parents as well as several other friends from school. Don Andrés was at the bar speaking with Gustavo while María Dolores saved a place for him at the table beside us. People stood in the doorway silhouetted by the afternoon sun while others continued to push their way in, stepping past dogs and children.

Just as things were about to get underway, O Gordo entered playing a harmonica to clear a path through the crowd toward the table where Fulgencio and Don Horacio were sitting. Gustavo, who was afraid the commotion might detract from the momentous nature of the event, turned to O Gordo and shouted, "No music!"

"Music?" someone in the crowd shouted back. "That's not music!"

Emboldened by a wave of laughter, O Gordo continued to play, but Gustavo wouldn't yield. When he announced there would be no television until the music stopped, O Gordo held the harmonica over his head to signal defeat and put it in his pocket. Don Andrés gave a brief speech about his work with Fenosa to improve the power supply to Porto Lúa and then predicted that one day everyone would be able to own a television, a notion that was met with mocking skepticism and more laughter. After the mayor took his seat, Gustavo, who was not comfortable speaking publicly, thanked everyone for coming and reminded them it was not necessary to applaud what appeared on the screen.

Contrary to our expectations, Aunt Fioxilda was mesmerized by what she saw. Providing a chorus to the pageantry of the various programs, she echoed the announcers, loudly identifying everything on the screen: Real Madrid. Sailboats. A bullfight. I was half expecting her to discover the devil in a program about churches, but she never did, probably thinking this illuminated box too trivial a thing to house such a power. By the time the news came on, many people had gone home, but, at Aunt Fioxilda's insistence, we stayed until the broadcast concluded. Sometime during the news, she leaned over to mother and commented on the announcer's clothes which led mother to question whether he was wearing a full suit or merely a jacket. Deciding to put the matter to rest, Fioxilda got up from her seat, stood on the chair Gustavo had left below the television, and looked down the front of the screen. Then she turned to the room and with great satisfaction proclaimed that he was in fact wearing matching trousers.

On a rainy morning in early January an army staff car crossed the Roman bridge and parked outside the town hall. Four men, three in black suits and one in a military uniform, got out of the car and went inside for a meeting with Don Andrés. Nothing good was likely to come from such a visit, and several people gathered on the pavement to wait for them to leave. One man said he was afraid they were there to investigate what had happened during the war. Another speculated the navy wanted to build a base at Porto Lúa. A third believed there might be terrorists hiding on the mountain. When the car turned around in the plaza and drove away, Don Andrés came outside with the news. General Molinero wanted the house of Alonso Pinzón to be transported to his garden and had ordered the army to dismantle it stone by stone and carry it away on large flatbed trucks. Initially there was a sense of relief that the matter was no more serious than that. No one gave much thought to the house anyway. Despite the money allocated for a sign on the coastal road, there had never been more than a few tourists who had visited the house and the occasional professor.

"It's an eyesore."

"At least the city won't have to pay someone to tear it down."

"Who's to say Alonso Pinzón actually slept there?"

Don Andrés was of a different mind. "That house has been in the Pereira family for centuries," he said. "It doesn't belong to General Molinero. Alonso Pinzón landed here. In Porto Lúa. This is where he slept. Not in General Molinero's outhouse."

"When are the trucks coming?"

"Tomorrow morning."

That night the men gathered in O Galo to weigh various proposals, but none were feasible. They ranged from blocking the street with boulders to declaring a quarantine for small pox to barricading themselves inside the house. Some argued it was better to let the general take the house than risk incurring his wrath and sanctions against the town. Others believed it was a matter of principle. They had defied the general during the war and they would defy him again.

When they left the bar that night, the men were resigned to the fact that the house would be dismantled the following day and no longer be a part of the history of Porto Lúa.

Xesús Teixeiro's wife Amalia was waiting for him outside the bar to lead him home. On the way, they stopped in front of the house. She noticed something the men had failed to see, namely, that in the old part of town, many of the houses looked the same. They were two stories with small wooden doors between two shuttered windows. Upstairs was a porch resting on three stone corbels roughly aligned to the three windows of that floor. When she had put her husband to bed, she went back outside with a ladder, a can of black paint, a brush, and a lantern. The streets were quiet, and before dawn she had painted the words *Museo do Explorador Martín Alonso Pinzón*

Descubridor do Novo Mundo over the doors of twenty-three houses.

Shortly after the sun came up, two military vehicles carrying a captain and eight armed soldiers arrived followed by four flatbed trucks and a covered cargo truck transporting laborers and equipment. Surrounded by a small crowd of concerned onlookers, Don Andrés met them outside the town hall. The soldiers leveled their rifles and pushed the crowd back as the captain got out of his car and approached the mayor.

"We're here to remove the house of Alonso Pinzón."

"I understand."

As the entourage of captain, mayor, soldiers, drivers, surveyors, masons, laborers, and onlookers proceeded down Rúa do Porto, one of the soldiers called out to his captain that they were passing the house. The captain stopped, saw the sign, and asked Don Andrés where he was taking them.

"Is this some kind of trick?" he asked.

For a moment, Don Andrés was confused, but then noticed that nearly every house on the street had a sign over its door and gathered his wits.

"I wasn't sure which house you wanted."

"What do you mean?"

"According to legend, the famous Martín Alonso Pinzón was a man of immense appetite and slept in many beds in Porto Lúa."

The captain looked up and down the street and saw the signs as well.

"Since you won't be able to get all the houses onto four trucks, I want to show you each of them so you can choose the one you want to take back to General Molinero."

Sensing what had happened, the captain ordered his soldiers to inspect every house with a sign over the door for some evidence that it was in fact the historic house, but there was nothing to distinguish the authentic house of Alonso Pinzón from the other twenty-three.

"General Molinero will not find this amusing," the captain said as he climbed into his car.

"Let him know that if he ever returns to Porto Lúa, he will find a welcome to rival that given to the illustrious explorer and discoverer of America."

Despite our fear of retaliation, that was the last time we saw any soldiers in Porto Lúa until a contingent arrived a year later to install signs naming the streets after the general's friends.

The second time I sat in the upholstered barber's chair was the Saturday before my First Communion. Mother was particularly concerned that I should look nice for the photograph that was to be taken beforehand when all the new communicants were to gather on the steps of Nosa Señora do Mar to record the occasion. Because the ceremony had been in abeyance during the final years of Father Ithacio's tenure, thirty-nine of us, an unusually large number, were under the instruction of Bachiario to receive the Holy Eucharist. As a consequence, many of us made appointments to have our hair washed and cut. When I arrived, two of my classmates, Miguel and Ánxel, were already waiting their turn, and more would soon come in.

In addition to the schoolchildren, Don Horatio and Manolo Trillo sat along the wall facing the chair. Fulgencio was in unusually fine form because he had recently achieved his dream of purchasing a small plot of land in Extremadura sight unseen where he planned to retire under cloudless skies. Although his customers varied widely in age and interests, the manner and content of his speech varied little.

"To be happy in life, you need goals. If you learn nothing

more from your visit to my shop today, learn that happiness in life comes from having goals and reaching those goals. Not everyone can be a Napoleon or a Caesar. It's true—I am a barber. Some might be generous enough to call me a dentist because I have pulled my share of teeth or a surgeon because I have been known to set a fracture or two. Do not disparage the humble station. 'No man is more than another if he does not do more than another.'"

"Quixote."

"Correct, Don Horacio. The Knight of the Sad Countenance. Is cutting hair my goal in life? If it were, it would not be a bad one. But I have always had my sights set higher than most. It's just the way I am. To that end, as you may know, I have recently acquired a small estate in a distant province where the air is clear, and the sky is always blue. That has been my dream. That is what I have worked for. Why I have spent my life cutting hair. All you need to succeed is the determination to achieve your goals. When you have that, you can't go wrong. I have endured many things in life that would have destroyed a lesser man, but I was determined not to fail. Cutting hair is more than a means to an end. It is an art. They call Michelangelo a genius for sculpting stone, but I sculpt the living, the farmer and fisherman, who come to my shop. I give them their appearance. You know, without others we have no identity. When they see us as we wish to be seen, we have the identity we wish to have. It is important to be honest with yourself. That is everything. If you are honest with yourself, you can do no wrong. Have I made mistakes? Yes. They say that makes me human. I believe the phrase of the philosophers is 'To err is human.' Well, I admit to being human. I sit at my table in the morning, and I ask myself, what would I do tomorrow if I found the treasure of Montezuma today? Work. Therein lies fulfillment. Do not be afraid to work, young men. Anticipation paralyzes the soul. Work like bees. Do you think they anticipate whether it will be too hot or too cold? Do they worry the flowers will not have enough pollen? A calling is what every person needs. To live for a calling. It's the hesitation that leads to unhappiness. Life carries us along. Don't just move with the current—stay ahead of it. That's the best advice I can give. I've been cutting hair for thirty years summer and winter. I don't worry about every hair. How could I? Nor can you worry about every mistake. Life is made up of many moments. There are moments of greatness and moments of humility. Every head has black hairs and brown hairs and white hairs and even some red hairs. Like blades of grass. A poet said that. Some grow faster than others. Overcome your weaknesses. Believe in yourselves. Each one of you has something to offer. I can take more off the side if you like. What did your mother say? I remember my First Communion. Every other boy wore black trousers, but I wore gray. These many years later, I am still the boy in the front row with gray trousers. Perhaps that made me who I am today. You never know. Sometimes it's the small things that count. The priest who presided was from Paraguay and had a bicycle he never rode. He wheeled it everywhere. Perhaps it was considered sinful to ride a bicycle in those days. Nowadays even women ride them. Well, there you go. The world changes. It's not so bad. Do you have something to add, Manolo?"

"Only that Cervantes was a Celt."

"A Galician, certainly. The name Saavedra tells you that. I say this on no less an authority than Padre Sarmiento."

"The noblest of our kind."

"From San Román."

"Ancares."

"The Palace of Vilarello."

"A proud example for our youth to follow."

"Colón de Poio, Balboa, Alfonso the Great, Diego Gelmírez, Camões, Valle-Inclán, Fidel Castro, Castelao, Fernando Rey. All

Galicians."

"Rosalía de Castro."

"Yes, of course, Rosalía."

"General Molinero."

"But not a Celt, Don Horacio. Not a Celt. His ancestors were from the south. He's a Moor if ever I saw one."

"Cervantes is our greatest luminary."

"No doubt."

"'Hoping to tie the tongues of slanderers is like putting doors in open fields.'"

"Like the foreigner's museum."

"How so?"

"Windows in open fields."

"He too is a Celt."

"Or a Saxon. Let's not confuse a Celt with a Saxon. I won't deny he is a Celt, but I can't confirm it either. Only his blood can do that."

Despite his reputation as the most vocal proponent of Porto Lúa's Celtic heritage, Manolo was a short, darkly complected man with heavy-lidded bistre eyes and lank shocks of black hair that fell on either side of a central part. He called himself a writer of histories, but had never written anything anyone had ever read. He walked with his shoulders hunched forward and his arms hanging outstretched seeming to stroke the air like a swimmer and had a tendency to step in front of his companions like a cat. As Fulgencio once observed, he was so badly put together it was as if God had not been bothered.

"Being a Celt is a matter of blood," he said, "but it is more than blood. It is the embodiment of the ancient nobility of the European soul. The history of our people has been buried by the tellers of competing tales, dulled by the dust and ash of their fallen empires, but there is evidence enough of our greatness to redeem a vanquished glory. It is especially important for you young people to learn your history so you may carry this heritage of moral and spiritual eminence forward into the future."

"What evidence is that, Manolo?"

"Just look at Plato. After their terms as rulers, the guardians of his state went to live out their lives on the Blessed Isles. These were the people with gold in their blood, those known as inherently superior, and when they retired from public life, they went to the westernmost shore of the world. The Costa da Morte is that shore. Our ancestors, the people who settled this region long before the birth of Christ, were those selected to rule in ancient times by virtue of their exceptional nature."

"I have no quarrel with his islands and guards, but where does he mention the Celts?"

"Let me finish. Let me finish. I was about to say these people, according to other writers of the past, were Celts. It was Strabo—or Tacitus—Strabo who said that a Celtic tribe called the Artabri inhabited the region around Cape Nerium. Now this cape has been identified by scholars as the headland adjacent to the bay of Porto Lúa. The very cape you can see from the window of this shop. In the twenty-first chapter of the fourth book of his *Natural History*, Pliny called the great promontory of the western sea Artabrum. If the cape before us is Cape Nerium, then it is reasonable to assume the mountain behind us, Aracelo, or Altar of Heaven, is Artabrum, the mountain of the Artabri. Home of the Celtici. It was the poet Ennius or maybe Persius who identified a moon bay as a place of inspiration for Homer thousands of years ago, a place that became synonymous with dreams. To corroborate the accounts of Strabo, I will remind you that in the last century, shepherds found gold torcs and rings at Onde se Adora consistent with Celtic artifacts found elsewhere on the continent indicating they were living on the mountain before there was a written history. If this is not enough evidence for you, I will also point out that certain runic inscriptions testify to the presence of Celts in this region, and there are obvious similarities between the distinctive folklore and music we have here and the Celtic heritage found in other parts of Europe. Are you familiar with the village Valdebois? The name does not refer to the valley of the oxen. *Val* is a corruption of *bao*, the Celtic word for 'ford,' and so our ancestors knew it as Oxford. I put it to you that the originators of civilization were the Celtic tribes of our coast who survived the great flood on Aracelo and subsequently migrated eastward across the continent to become the Etruscan and therefore the Roman people who conquered the earth. Because of their isolation, those who stayed behind have maintained the purest gold in their blood, and we are the descendants of those people."

"And there you have it, children. The history of the Celtic people of Porto Lúa."

"You should be a teacher, Señor Trillo."

"I am proud to say I am no more than a fisherman and no less than a fisherman, a man who believes in the importance of knowing his origins."

"Tell them the story of the Lord of the Sea, Manolo."

Accepting the request with no more acknowledgment than a smile, he cleared his throat and began: "I should tell the children in advance this is a sad story, but one containing an invaluable lesson. Many years ago, right here in this port, lived a poor fisherman who because of his bad luck was barely able to make ends meet. He was unsuccessful in finding the best spots for fishing and consistently returned home with only a few small herring or smelt in his crates. On the rare occasion when he did find a good spot and was able to fill his net, it broke. One morning in rough seas, his boat struck the rocks off the southern tip of Illa da Luz and sank, forcing him to swim to shore where he survived for three days on mussels and watercress until he was rescued. After that, the only boat he could afford was unseaworthy and sprang a new leak every time he patched a hole. Then his wife became seriously ill and could no longer care for their home."

"What happened to him then?"

"Just when things were at their worst, and all hope was lost, his fortune changed. One evening as he was sailing back to port he heard a voice in the mist asking him if he would like to catch more fish.

"'Yes,' he said.

"'Then you must do as I say. Wake before the other fishermen and leave before the tide turns. Let your boat go where it will. When it stops, drop your nets and they will be full. In return I ask that you acknowledge the Lord of the Sea at the end of the jetty every day when you arrive.'

"The fisherman did as the voice commanded and the next day returned to port with a net full of fish. When he had unloaded his catch, he proclaimed from the jetty, 'I acknowledge the Lord of the Sea.' The other fishermen thought he was losing his mind, but the size of his catch did not go unnoticed. Every day he did the same thing, and every day he returned with full nets. Soon he was able to buy a new boat and then another which he leased to other fishermen. He bought shares in a wolfram mine near Figueiroa, hired a private tutor from Salamanca for his children, and paved the street where he lived. After El Conde's father, he was believed to be the richest man in Porto Lúa. Because she was able to receive the best medical care, his wife recovered fully and decided they would pursue the dream they had always had, to own the best bar and restaurant on the Costa da Morte, so they sold the boats and built a bar on the hillside above the coastal road with a stream running through the terrace and a beautiful view of the headland. The bar had every kind of spirit and beer and wine they could buy and a large billiard room and modern toilets. But no one came. They were too far outside Porto Lúa for people to walk and too far off the road for casual travelers to notice. They held on for more than a year hoping that people would discover them, but with no income, they found themselves with increasing debts, so they were forced to sell off their stock and fixtures and buy a boat. Just as he had done when successful, he woke before the other fishermen, left before the tide turned, let his boat go where it would and dropped his net, but it was empty. When he reached the pier, he shouted, 'I acknowledge the Lord of the Sea,' but the next day and the day after that his luck was no better. In fact it was as bad as it had been before he heard the voice. They boarded up the bar, sold the building, and moved back to their old house in town. His wife's illness returned, and he was still only catching a few small herring or smelt in his net. And there you have it."

"What's the lesson, Señor Trillo?"

"The lesson?"

"You said there was an invaluable lesson."

"Ah, yes. The lesson of this story is that you should never take anything for granted."

Much to the amusement of the fishermen working on their boats, Miguel, Ánxel, and I went out on the jetty with our new haircuts and shouted, "I acknowledge the Lord of the Sea," to the waves breaking over the rocks. The next day I received my First Communion, and when the photograph was taken on the steps of Nosa Señora do Mar, I was the only child wearing a bow tie.

With no idea of the precise time, Harry stood outside the gate of El Conde's house for half an hour in the rain. At two o'clock, Doña Esperanza's housekeeper appeared with an umbrella and opened the gate without saying a word. They walked down the long gravel path between box hedges toward the house. The wisteria that covered the granite walls around the house was not yet in bloom, but the air was fresh and spring was near. The housekeeper, who was accustomed to treating guests with disdain, wasn't certain how to treat a foreigner. She gave him a towel to wipe his bare feet and, despite the wet shirt and trousers he wore for the visit, allowed him to sit in a large leather chair in the foyer. He had come at the request of Doña Esperanza to schedule monthly recitals, but he also wanted to speak to her about his idea for a museum to the souls lost at sea. The housekeeper went to inform Doña Esperanza, who appeared at length and invited him into a private study where they drank coffee and discussed their favorite classical composers in English. To test his wits, she asked him what he would save first if her house were to catch fire.

"I would save nothing," he replied.

"Not even the art?"

"Nothing."

"Why?"

"Because nothing is worth saving."

"Is that why the people in town think you are mad?" she asked.

"That is why I am sane," he replied.

"How can you create art if you believe nothing is worth saving?"

"You will have to see my art before you ask me that."

She explained that she would like Harry to come to her house and play his trumpet in the drawing room on the first and third Sundays of every month at six o'clock in the evening.

"I don't have a clock."

"Well then, you will come just before sunset. I will pay you twenty pesetas for each visit."

"I don't need money."

"How can we pay you?"

"I would like a book that I found on your property."

"A book."

"Yes."

"What is the book?"

"It's an English Bible."

"A Bible?"

"An English Bible. From a shipwreck."

"And where is this Bible?"

"In a barn on your property near Foxo Escuro."

"Bring it to me and we'll see."

The next Sunday was the first of the month, and he arrived as the sun was going down with his trumpet and a plastic bag containing the loose pages of a Bible and its leather cover. Don Prudencio joined his daughter in the drawing room, and after Harry had played a concerto from memory, El Conde complimented him on his playing and asked if some arrangement had been made to compensate him.

"This book, sir," Harry replied as he placed the contents of the bag on a table.

"What is it?"

"A Bible, sir. I found it in a barn."

El Conde looked at the foxed and yellowed pages. "Is that all?"

"And some flat rocks for my museum. The round ones by the sea won't do."

"By all means, take whatever you need. You can use one of our oxcarts."

Doña Esperanza thanked her guest for coming and showed him out.

Curious to learn more about him, she used the excuse of wanting to see the progress of his latest museum to visit Harry on the following Sunday afternoon. She cut through the fields on cart paths she had known since childhood until she came to the rocky coast on the south side of the bay and then followed the cliff walk to the head of the valley that led down through brambles and gorse to his house. Tall, slender sculptures,

spindles and pinnacles of smooth sea stones cemented together, rose five or six feet beside the path to mark the way.
Along the side of the stream she noticed the embankments of
stone he had constructed like honeycombs with holes where
sparrows and songbirds nested. She found him washing his
dishes in the stream that ran alongside the path.

"I want to see your museum to the souls lost at sea."

He led her back up the valley and along the top of the cliff
farther out on the headland to a treeless point overlooking the
bay. There he had built a circle of stones that leaned inward to
a height of roughly eight feet. The stones on the rim of the circle were carefully balanced to teeter on its edge.

"There is nothing in your museum."

"There is nothing in my music."

"But I can hear your music in the moment."

"Then you must learn to see in the moment."

"I see nothing more than stones piled precariously in a way
that they could fall at any moment and kill someone standing
below them."

"Which moment?"

"What?"

"This is a museum to those who died at sea. How did they
die?"

"They drowned in storms."

"Some died and some survived. Were their different fates
a matter of chance or necessity?"

"I don't understand."

"If two people stand here beside each other and one of
these stones should fall, it will kill one, but not the other. I have
set them in such a way that a strong wind will knock them
from their place. Two have already fallen. Do you understand
now? In this museum dedicated to those who died at sea, I
have presented the question of whether a stone falls due to
chance or by some necessity. It's not something for people to

see, but to experience."

"Someone could be seriously injured."

"Most museums contain objects created by human beings that represent objects in nature. My museum doesn't contain any representations—only experience itself. I am alive because a single wave carried me to shore where I slipped past rocks that could have easily killed me. Men who stood next to me on the deck perished because they fell into the water a moment before me or a moment after me or were next to me in the water and caught by a different current. And yet I think of my survival as less extraordinary than my being born in the first place."

"You speak of chance. Do you not believe in Providence? You look for causes in nature, but I ask you, what caused nature? Would you parse the wind into a million causes for each blade of grass that bends, or would you ascribe its movement to the Cause of all causes?"

"We question when one man dies at sea and another doesn't or why one child is struck down by a fatal disease while others survive to old age, but in truth we would rather not know. All we can do is make the most of the time we have to alleviate the suffering of others and to appreciate the wonder of our presence in this world. That is why I made this museum."

"I too lost someone at sea."

"One stone and not another."

The following week when Harry played, Doña Esperanza was more subdued. Though polite, she was inattentive and spoke little. Two weeks later, she left the room before he finished. The next recital, she did not come down at all, and Don Prudencio sat by himself more out of his obligation as a host than out of any devotion to the music. The second Sunday after that, Harry did not return. Mistakenly thinking the music and not the man had affected his daughter, El Conde decided to ask

Harry to come back and play something more spirited. Although night had already begun to fall, he sent the housekeeper to fetch him with this request. But in the darkness, she stepped on a loose stone and stumbled off the path badly injuring herself. When she was discovered later that night, Paco Carreira rushed her to the hospital in Santiago in his taxi where she remained for several weeks with a broken hip.

It was Holy Week and because Don Prudencio was hosting friends from Madrid who had come to see him march in the procession, he needed someone to fill in for his housekeeper. After making several inquiries in town, he arranged to have Rosa, the housekeeper at the rectory, help out for the week and perhaps beyond. One afternoon while she was at work, members of the Order of Santa Lupa had taken the cross used in the procession from the storage room behind the rectory and left it in the yard leaning against the house. When her son, Mateo Mateo, saw the cross, he was moved by an impulse of religious fervor to emulate the passion of Christ. Creating a scene based on the crucified figure in Nosa Señora do Mar, he cut a half dozen blackberry switches and wove them into a crown, stripped down to a towel wrapped around his waist, and attempted to drag the cross, a pair of thick planks fastened by stove bolts, around the yard. But he only made it as far as the side of the church where he propped it against the wall and moved on to the final act of his passion, a re-creation of the crucifixion. To hold himself in place, he tied cord fetters at the ends of the crossbeam for his wrists and what was essentially a noose to secure his neck to the vertical beam. After he had inserted his hands in the fetters and his neck in the noose, his foot slipped on a wet stone, and he dropped, tightening the rope around his neck. Facundo, who was on a ladder inside the church cleaning the windows, heard him cry out and went to investigate. By the time he found Mateo Mateo, the penitent was turning blue and barely conscious.

Although he survived the accident, Mateo Mateo suffered irreparable brain damage that left him unable to walk or control much of his voluntary nervous system. When she realized the extent of the damage, his mother collapsed in the arms of Dr. Romalde. In addition to her poverty and the stigma of bearing the child of a priest, Rosa now had to care for that child as if he were an infant again. Over the next few days Facundo scavenged several wheels and boards and the handlebars of a bicycle and built a wheelbarrow that Rosa could use to take Mateo Mateo for walks. When she arranged to return to work for El Conde three days a week, she rolled Mateo Mateo down to the school and left him in a corner of the classroom beside Bachiario's dog. No one knew if he could understand what was being said, but sometimes he would begin to cry, and Bachiario would instruct one of us to take him for a walk around the schoolyard.

When Cotolay was not sitting in the front row of Capela de Santa Lupa, he could often be found in the rose arbor at the entrance of the alameda between Señor Morcín and a fenced shanty sheltering a pair of scurfy peacocks. For ten céntimos he would hand you a piece of paper where he had written what he claimed to be the truth. But the paper was blank. Two days out of every month, when the moon was full, he left his post to observe a self-imposed exile on the mountain as the result of an agreement he had with the town following an incident many years earlier. Like everyone else who had grown up in Porto Lúa, he had heard the story of the moon passing over the peaks of Aracelo to convey the souls of the dead to the next world and was terrified by the possibility that some night he too might be carried away. Over time, this fear had increased, and one night he broke the windows of several houses throwing rocks at the moon to keep it away. When the owners of the houses took him to Constable Sampaio, he agreed to leave Porto Lúa and spend two days on the mountain every month if the town would provide him with a gun to defend himself against the white stone in the sky. After consulting with other members of the community, Don Andrés gave Cotolay a rifle and a box of blank cartridges and presented him with the official title "Guardian of the Town" if he would keep a monthly vigil to protect it. For a few years distant reports could be heard on the nights when the moon was full, but they gradually decreased and then stopped altogether. When asked if he had run out of ammunition, Cotolay replied that he had not, but rather had come to terms with the moon: he would no longer attack it if it agreed to come no closer. Still, he said, he would maintain his vigilance.

His journeys up Rúa das Angustias to the Roman road were so predictable that when people saw him climbing the slope with his blanket and gun they would exclaim, "Has another month passed already, Cotolay?" One day when Aunt Fioxilda and I saw him in the street, I asked her what was wrong with him.

"He's mad," she said.

"Why is he mad?"

"Because he asks too many questions."

In fact he experienced many periods of lucidity, but a good day would be followed by a bad week. And intemperate weather, clouds and fog in particular, would often prolong that week to two or more. And then, invariably, came the crisis of the moon and his sojourn on the mountain. Even on a good day, he still considered himself to be the mayor of the City of God, and would proudly declare, "I have more power than any king of state because I am king of my mind, a kingdom that has no boundaries." He exercised his official prerogative by proclaiming that every evening clocks should be set at nine to coincide with the flight of seagulls. In addition to this, he refused to use words like *catarro* because he was afraid the sharpness of their letters would lacerate his tongue. Though he still spent hours sitting in Capela de Santa Lupa staring at the cross, he had stopped mortifying his flesh with mud, dung heaps, and horsehair garments.

Despite the relative calm his advancing years had bestowed, there was still disquiet in his soul. He was afraid the selfish motives and deceptive practices he saw wherever he looked in human affairs would create a distance between the human and divine wills that would lead God to abandon us to His adversary, and, as a result of this abandonment, the sea would rise to cover the summit of Aracelo or the moon would crash into the earth and bury the world under a mountain of white ash. One Sunday morning as he sat in the front row of Nosa Señora do Mar, his agitation became so great that he rose in the middle of Bachiario's homily, and, pointing his finger at the priest, asked, "Who is this man? He is a man with seed and no children. God will judge him." Then he turned to Don Andrés, who was sitting in the front row on the other side of the main aisle and asked, "Who is this man? He is a man who has abandoned his God for the illusions of prosperity, for fashion and false ambition. God will judge him." He went on to inveigh against the self-deception of humanity and claim the only way for us to save our souls is to return everything to nature we have taken from it. Return furniture and paper to the forest. Stones to the earth. Clothes to sheep. He went on like this as he left the church and continued without stopping to eat or sleep for the next forty-eight hours. He walked up and down the streets at night waking people from their dreams until finally, when she could take no more of it, Madame Zafirah went out in her dressing gown and, taking him by the hand, escorted him into her house. The full moon came and went and there was no sign of Cotolay. When at last he emerged, his hair and beard had been trimmed, and he was wearing a fresh cotton shirt. He had nothing to say about God or judgment or iniquity, and for the first time in many years, he appeared to be at peace, but it would not last beyond the spring.

In dry weather father paid me a peseta for every twenty stones I cleared from a field behind our house. But it was an endless task. For every stone I removed, another two emerged. We covered these with a bed of manure and kelp only to watch as heavy rains carried the richest soil down the hillside to the Deva and into the sea. I augmented the pesetas father paid me by writing letters for people who had never had the advantage of an education. My ability to read and write in both Galician and Castilian had improved significantly over the two years I had been in school, and I had a better understanding of English thanks to the time I had spent studying with Sister Mary Rose and speaking with Harry. So neighbors sometimes asked me to compose letters for purposes of employment or to make enquiries of government offices to claim benefits, and those with family members working abroad often sought my help when addressing envelopes.

A source of more regular employment presented itself one afternoon when father's toothache led him to visit Fulgencio. Don Horacio was there and asked if I would be interested in helping out around his shop.

Because of his arthritis he needed someone dependable who could wind his clocks and set them to coincide with his master timepiece. I agreed and was immediately taken on as a kind of factotum, not just winding and setting the clocks, but sweeping, oiling, wrenching, hammering, or assisting in a variety of other ways. The shop was a larger building than might be assumed from its frontage on the street and contained four rooms including closets that were filled with every size, style, and form of clock imaginable. There were baroque timepieces with gilded angels and acanthus volutes, a strange cyclopean dial in the middle of a teak cabinet shaped like the letter *phi*, a dial encased in a bronze sun suspended on wires from two bronze trees, a soapstone monkey wrapping the dial in its tail, and a porcelain seashell crowned by a golden Aphrodite holding the dial in her hands.

Rarely selling more than two dozen clocks a year, even Don Horacio admitted that Porto Lúa was an unlikely place for a shop such as his. There were only so many people in the town and most either had no use for a clock or already owned one. They were given as wedding presents, or as official gifts to visiting dignitaries, like the delegation from Camariñas that came to inspect the port, or adapted for maritime use when a new boat was launched. But money wasn't an issue for Don Horacio. He was rumored to be a member of the minor nobility in León and had come to the end of the world because he believed that time flows more intimately in a place so near the sun and moon and stars. As if the frenzy of urban activity or lazy rivers on dull plains could affect its natural course. Like the lover of food travels to Paris, or the lover of music travels to Vienna, the lover of time travels to Porto Lúa. Here, he said, he can watch the sun drop into the sea and stars appear over the evening horizon the way a gardener watches flowers bloom in his garden. Before opening the shop, he spent a year studying both the physics and folklore of time in the hope of someday making a clock that could not only measure its passing, but also distil its essence and regulate its temperament.

Whether it had a clock or not, every household in Porto Lúa operated according to its own time. As a consequence, many students arrived at school five or ten minutes after the first class started. The same was true of church. No one thought much about punctuality, let alone synchronizing clocks. And I was no different. But on my first day at work, I began to consider time more closely. As I wandered through the back rooms of the shop discovering boxes of maritime charts, metronomes, pendulums, and astrolabes, the hours became minutes, the minutes seconds, and, before I knew it, it was time to leave. The next day my assignment was to wind and synchronize all the clocks in Don Horacio's vast collection. As I inspected the hands of dozens of dials, listening to every tick of the works, every knock of every pendulum, the minutes became hours and I thought the afternoon would never end.

"Time is an invisible river," Don Horacio said, "flowing down from the sun and stars and through these little machines we build to measure its passage. And just as the flow of a river appears to be hastened or retarded by causes beyond our control, so appears the flow of time. I once tried to determine if it was affected by the alignments of the planets and moon or by the tides or the wind blowing fiercely over the sea, but my investigations were inconclusive. By what standard could I measure it? How could I accurately gauge if my clocks were slowing down or speeding up if time itself was slowing down or speeding up? The Greeks believed that Krónos, the god of time, slept somewhere off our coast, but how would we know? Perhaps time sleeps frequently, and we are unaware of it. Perhaps in the space between my two sentences, time stopped for as long as it took the universe to form. How would we know this?"

On an oak pedestal in one of the rooms at the back of the shop was a large clock of inlaid mother-of-pearl. It was trimmed with gold, and its dial was silver with gold numerals. On the left was a crescent moon and on the right a sun with needle rays. Don Horacio opened the wooden door to the works box with a silver key, but there was nothing inside.

"Where is the pendulum?" I asked.

"There isn't one."

"But how does it keep time?"

225

"Not by gears and levers, but as the wood ages, and the silver's gleam turns black. As the trees on the hillside turn green, and the clouds pass in the sky above. As the tides shift, and the planets move. Although time is invisible, you can see it in the shadow of the church and the rise and fall of rivers and in the flowers that bloom on old stone walls and in the growth of children like yourself. Time creates the longing in a piece of music, places Sirius in the summer sky, Arcturus in the winter. And moves the blood of men to sow and reap. We measure it by its passage through the things of the world and across the sky. And, like these boxes of wood and brass that rot and tarnish, we are one of those things. Time is as much a part of us as our hair and eyes. It gave us life and, at your age, fills us with a future. It allows us to move and change every day and every night, from childhood through old age, in the muscles of our hearts, in the paths of our thoughts."

"Are you afraid of running out of time?"

"I don't worry. When it leaves me, it will provide a future for someone else. And when it leaves that person, it will give a young tree in the forest the opportunity to grow and spread its branches."

"If I were old, I would want to stop time."

"There is no need to stop time when your soul is eternal."

One afternoon just before we closed the shop, I went to the town hall to check the mail and found a registered letter for Don Horacio. It was an invitation from the Salón de Cultura in Muros to present a public lecture on the nature of time in a series of lectures entitled *¿Qué es?* that included talks on the heavens, life, sound, and light. He was both surprised and flattered by the invitation and sent a letter accepting the proposal the next day. But over the weeks that followed, he began to have second thoughts.

"Don't worry, my friend," Fulgencio said, attempting to reassure him. "Just talk to them the way you talk to us."

When Paco Carreira loaned him several books on the subject from the library in the trunk of his taxi, Don Horacio was able to clarify his views on time by reading those of Plato and Augustine and other great thinkers from the past. To test his grasp of these sources, he decided to present his ideas to Fulgencio, Manolo, and O Gordo. As the three sat against the wall of Fulgencio's shop, Don Horacio stood in front of a chair representing a podium and began reading from his notes.

"Plato said anything that is made cannot be eternal. So when God made the universe, He made time as a moving image of the eternal, but it is not the same thing as the eternal."

"What does that mean?"

"He's saying time is a measurement, and the eternal is what is measured."

"Not exactly."

"Continue."

"Time can measure the past and future, but the eternal can never be in the past nor the future. It can never become anything other than what it is nor cease to be what it is. It exists outside of becoming. Time is unlike eternity because it allows things to change. The temporal world is inferior to the permanent world, but resembles it otherwise."

"That's what Plato said?"

"I believe so."

"Did time exist before God separated the light from the dark?"

"No."

"What did God do before there was time?"

"He didn't do anything before there was time. That's the point. When there was endless time, there was no time. Because God is eternal, He exists in endless time."

"Isn't existing doing something?"

"Doesn't God exist now at the present time?"

"In the eternal present. For God, the present moment has

always been and will always be. In His mind, everything happens at the same time and forever."

"I'm confused."

"Wait. Go back. If God created time by separating the light from the dark, wasn't He acting in time?"

"Plato said the Eternal Being exists outside time."

"Where is outside time?"

"In the Eternal Being."

"If there were no stars or sun or moon, would there still be time?"

"Yes, but there would be no days or nights, months or years."

Manolo, who had not been able to follow the discussion and was afraid he might embarrass himself if he said something, took advantage of a pause in the conversation to offer a comment without revealing how little he understood.

"God has put eternity into man's mind, but in such a way that he cannot know all that God has done from the beginning to the end."

"That's good. You should write that down, Don Horacio. 'Put eternity into man's mind.'"

"It's in the Bible," said Manolo, pleased with the success of his contribution.

"What if time isn't real? What if it only exists in our imagination or memory?"

"How could the sun rise and set if time isn't real? How could the planets move through the night?"

"Plato said the temporal is not real. Time disappears like the things that occur in time."

"The sun and moon aren't real?"

"Nothing is real except the laws of nature."

"Because they don't change."

"Yes. Because they're eternal."

"The *logos*."

"What did St. Augustine say, Don Horacio?"

"He said the past is gone and the future has not yet arrived. Since the present is all there is, whatever we have of the past and future must exist in the present. The past is memory in the present, the present is perception in the present, and the future is expectation in the present."

"That's true. Memories are in the present."

"The present is the past before you know it."

"Gone before you finish saying the word."

"In that case, do we ever live in the present?"

"Is the present never present or is it always present?"

"Everything is a memory."

"Except what's happening in the present."

"But you only know what's happening in the present by what's happened in the past."

"Maybe there is no time."

"Just clocks."

"You can tell them about your collection of clocks, Don Horacio."

"Take some to sell."

"It's a lecture, not a market."

The day before the lecture Don Horacio could think of nothing else. Both the morning and afternoon were devoted to working and reworking his draft. Every few minutes he changed his mind about what he had written or how he had written it, anxiously crossing out and reinserting metaphors and illustrations as he considered and reconsidered every word. "It is easier to eat soup with a fork than to fit my ideas into words," he said. However, late in the afternoon, his thoughts on his subject coalesced with impeccable timing, and he called his friends together in order to determine which passages of his lecture might elicit the warmest reception from an audience. Once again, Fulgencio, Manolo, and O Gordo lined up against the wall as he stood before them fingering his heavily annotated pages.

"Tell me if you find any weaknesses in the argument or presentation."

"Of course."

"Or contradictions."

He looked down at the first page and adjusted his glasses, then twice cleared his throat, the second time more emphatically than the first.

"We come to this life as a refuge from eternity. When our time here is measured against the timelessness of all time, we might be said to live in an infinitely brief moment of time, but because that moment is infinitely divisible, it contains an eternity within itself. Consider that moment and you will know eternity, and to live in that moment is to live forever. What do I mean when I say a moment is infinitely divisible? In the famous paradox of Zeno the Eleatic, Achilles can never catch the tortoise because when he reaches the place where the tortoise was, the animal has moved forward to another point, and when he reaches that point, it has moved on to yet another. Just as these intervals may be divided into an infinite number, so can an instant of time—"

"Beg your pardon, Don Horacio, but you said to interrupt you if we have any questions."

"That's not exactly what I said, but never mind. What is your question, Manolo?"

"If Achilles couldn't outrun a tortoise, why do people consider him to be such a great warrior?"

"It's a paradox. It's precisely because he was a great warrior that he should be able to outrun a tortoise."

"But he can't because, as you say, the tortoise is always ahead of him."

"That's right. That's why it's a paradox."

"Even Benito can outrun a tortoise."

"I'm faster than Achilles."

"May I continue?"

"By all means, but you might want to leave out that part about Zeno. People won't believe it."

"I'll keep that in mind. As I was saying, an instant in time can contain an eternity. But we have not yet established what we mean by *time*. Take ten sequential moments. Each passes in the present. But there is no inherent characteristic in each to distinguish it from another. It is only distinguished from those that come before and after it by the changes that occur in space. So time, properly speaking, is not a thing, but the opportunity for things to change. In a single instant, a person ages. Time is the medium of things that pass, the insubstantial avenue upon which we travel from birth to death.

"Does time change or does it only appear to change? Is it governed by immutable laws or does it too evolve unpredictably? I have long been of two minds on this matter. On one hand, there is the experience of our individual perception that would suggest time is inconstant, but on the other, there is mathematics that successfully employs time as a constant. But is mathematics merely a human interpretation of reality, an interpretation predisposed toward constancy and not an adequate means of understanding something larger than our singular experience in one place at one time in a vast and expanding universe? After careful study, I have concluded that while our individual perception of time does change, we cannot know whether time itself changes, for we lack the perspective from which we may observe it. In other words, the appearance of change depends upon the constant perspective of the observer both for our personal experience of time and for our scientific understanding of it, and no observer is ever constant. Not only does time seem to speed up and slow down, but through the lens of time the proportions of things seem to change as well. Just as the school where you studied as a child seems smaller now that you're grown and have seen more of the world, so the years seem shorter when we have more of them at our back. For children a year old, a year is a lifetime. At two, a year is half a life and seems to last forever. When you are ten, it is only one tenth of your life and goes by more quickly. When you are fifty, it is only one fiftieth and rushes by so fast you hardly notice it. So the first few years of our lives seem to comprise most of our existence in this world. When you are young, life is like climbing a mountain. At first you think you will never reach the summit. And then one day, almost without realizing it, you do and then begin the descent that will take you to the grave. The farther down you go, the faster you go until the days, the months, the years pass without clear distinctions. Time causes the young man to anticipate and the old man to regret. What lies between the two? Dreams that disappear. Time is part of who we are, one might say, what we are, like the blood that runs through us, like an invisible river that flows—"

"Sorry to interrupt, Don Horacio. Just one more question. Where does time go when it passes?"

"Where does it go?"

"Like a river goes to the sea. Where does time go?"

"It doesn't go anywhere."

"You said it's like a river."

"Yes."

"Where does it come from then?"

"It doesn't come from anywhere."

"It must come from somewhere and go somewhere."

"Why?"

"Because everything comes from somewhere and goes somewhere. A river starts on a mountain and goes to the sea."

"I suppose you could say it comes from eternity and goes to eternity."

"If it goes back to where it came from, why doesn't it just stay there?"

"Then it would be more like a lake than a river."

"Maybe it's like light. Where does light go? Does it ever come to an end?"

"At night."

"But the sun is still shining somewhere and the light of the stars travels forever."

"What about a candle?"

"I don't know, Benito. I'm sorry I can't answer all your questions. You've been very helpful though, and I now have a better idea how to present my lecture thanks to all your comments."

"Don't worry, Don Horacio. It's a very good lecture. However, I would leave out the part about Zeno."

"And the river that doesn't go anywhere."

"Yes, and the river. But your audience won't be as shrewd as we are when it comes to the mysteries of time, so they may not notice these things."

The lecture was to be held at six o'clock in the evening in the town hall of Muros. Throughout the day, Don Horacio busied himself around the shop, reciting lines to himself as he paced back and forth. He took deep breaths to calm himself, or perhaps to practice his breathing, and wiped his glasses repeatedly with a handkerchief. We closed early and found Fulgencio and Manolo waiting for us beside Paco's taxi in the plaza. A few other people had gathered to give him advice and wish him good luck. I was allowed to accompany them and sat in the back seat between Manolo and Fulgencio while Don Horacio sat in the front seat beside Paco. The drive was fewer than twenty miles along the coast, but there were always unexpected delays due to animals in the road or a lack of repairs, so we left promptly at five o'clock. When we arrived at Curro da Praza in front of the town hall, the building's lights were off, and the front door was closed, but there was a small group of people smoking beside a poster announcing the lecture.

"Will they be opening the building soon?" asked Don Horacio.

"Opening?"

"I'm here to give tonight's lecture."

"It's too late. The guard just finished his rounds and locked up."

"But it's not yet six."

"It's seven here. We changed the clocks to summer time last week."

"There you go, Don Horacio."

"What?"

"Now you have your proof that time is not constant."

Fragrances of sea and rain filled the streets and squares of Porto Lúa after an evening shower. As the clouds moved north, beyond the bay, their cream and coral reflections appeared in gutters and standing pools and in the steel-blue mirror of the sea's calm surface. Stirring gently off the water, a fresh breeze dispersed veils of haze that rose from the sun-warmed fields as the summer light began to fade. Like the drunken oracle of a drunken god, Cotolay careened down the streets and alleys with a copper pipe banging on trash barrels, drainpipes, geranium pots, and cans imploring people in broken Latin to witness how the souls of things were departing from their natural forms. From the besieged houses his exhortations were met with imprecations, while on the street people went about their business ignoring him, afraid they might be stopped. They assumed he was confusing the light shimmering on the pools and wet surfaces of the streets and houses and gardens with the departure of a spiritual presence. Despite their indifference, or because of it, he became more insistent, claiming the souls of stones and trees and flowers were abandoning their God-given natures to the counterfeits of evil.

"Beware the orient stars shedding their fires," he cried as he hammered a lamppost. "Beware the exhalations of light. The stones themselves are possessed. *Occupati a malo. Ubique lapides. Ubique arbores. Ubique floribus.*"

On the corner of Rúa dos Soños and the plaza, he came upon Dr. Romalde.

"What is it Cotolay? Why this rampage through the streets?"

"*Lux venit e rerum.*"

"The light of things is leaving?"

"*Mare est translucidus.*"

"The sea? Of course it's transparent. It's water."

"No. No. *Venit lux de mari.*"

"I don't know what you're trying to say."

Dr. Romalde took him to O Galo for a glass of brandy thinking it might break the spell and quiet his nerves, but a crowd of bemused patrons egged him on in what little Latin they knew from attending Mass.

"*Per omnia saecula saeculorum.*"

"*Dominus Vobiscum.*"

"*Et cum spiritu tuo.*"

Cotolay declined the brandy, still urging people to listen to him, but the men continued to enjoy the game until they noticed Bachiario standing in the doorway.

"Do you understand what he's telling you?" asked the priest.

"No."

"He says light is coming out of the sea."

"*Venit lux de mari.*"

"He's crazy."

"Abate, mooncalf."

"There's no moon tonight. It's something else."

"*Venit lux de mari.*"

"Can you show me where you see the light?"

Bachiario helped Cotolay up from the table, and with Dr. Romalde and several other men, they walked through the plaza to the port where a small crowd had already gathered. As they approached the quay beneath the twilit sky, they could see a blue glow cast upon the trees and buildings beside the water and a moment later were astonished to discover the sea was, as Cotolay had maintained, illuminated from within by a spectral light. Clumps of kelp, prowling fish and their prey, driftwood, and flotsam passed as black silhouettes on the tide. But there was no obvious source of the light. It seemed to be emerging from the water itself. More people arrived, some quietly, but some gasping and others crying with fear.

With no knowledge of what was happening on the quay, Aunt Fioxilda, who was sitting in the kitchen, got up and went outside intent on something no one else in the house could see or hear. Preternaturally sensitive to any alteration in her spiritual environment—the way one might notice a stone interrupting the flow of a stream—she was able to detect what Cotolay had already observed.

A moment later, father stepped out on the balcony. Calling to mother, he described how the water was glowing and added, "I've seen phosphorous on the tide, but this is something else."

Fearing a hidden danger in the light, Don Andrés persuaded the crowd to move to the plaza where a vigorous discussion ensued on the possible causes of the sea's transformation. Various theories were put forward ranging from the mundane to the miraculous. Dr. Romalde said a boat with a spotlight had no doubt sunk even though the entire bay as far as anyone could see was lit. Don Horacio was convinced Atlantic currents flowing in the subtropical gyre had carried luminous fish or crustaceans or plankton or other microscopic organisms to the shore from mysterious seas beyond the horizon. Then a chorus of voices speculated that the light was a supernatural discharge of electricity, or that a ship caught in a storm had spilled its chemical cargo, or worse, that radiation had escaped from a secret government project somewhere on the coast of Europe and that we would all be consumed by fire rising out of the water. Despite the vigor with which these theories were advanced, most people persisted in believing the light was a sign from God expressing His displeasure with His people. When Aunt Fioxilda reached the plaza, she marched straight to the steps of the alameda where Don Andrés was presiding over the colloquy of competing voices. Known for her engagement with the world beyond our own, she spoke with an authority on such matters few could equal. The light, she said, is not of natural origin, nor is it a punishment from God; rather, it is a sign that we are in the company of a malevolent presence, and we would be wise to heed this presence and counter it with increased devotion to all things sacred. When Ramón Montero, a lone voice of dissent, questioned why they should believe her, he began to cough violently and belched a cloud of black smoke and wisps of ash. For no apparent reason, the lights strung across the alameda went out, and then, one by one, the streetlamps along the quay.

In the strange blue aura, birds began to sing and people began to pray. Afraid to sleep, some kept a vigil in the plaza, while others, not knowing what to do, went home to protect their windows and thresholds with holy water and laurel branches. When grandfather discovered a drop of blood on the pillow where grandmother had slept, Aunt Fioxilda created fresh chaos points with verbena stalks to block the currents of evil and resumed her unorthodox battles with the legions of hell. I tried to sleep, but couldn't. Sometime in the middle of the night when the house was finally quiet, I heard the floorboards creak and felt the presence of someone or something standing beside me. I pretended to sleep, hoping this presence would take no interest, but it remained there. I was afraid to open my eyes for fear it would notice. My skin tightened, and my breathing nearly stopped as I waited out this brooding threat in the darkness. At some point I fell asleep, and whatever it was fled at the specter of dawn, but in my morning dreams, I saw the sky washed in blood and the sun burning through the red glaze like a demonic eye.

Those who boarded their boats at daybreak remained at anchor with dead motors. Wells and fountains filled with ice. The falls on the Deva flowed upward. And the television in O Galo showed only ghostly images and a maelstrom of shadows. Six-thirty Mass at Nosa Señora do Mar was crowded with people praying to God to shield His followers from the black arts of His adversary. But even there they found no sanctuary. The prayer books were written backward, and in the middle of the service, the chalice and candlesticks rose in the air and fell clattering to the stone floor. After Mass, as the faithful walked down Via Sagrada on their way home, their shadows separated from their bodies and rose into the air where they disappeared like black smoke.

When it was time for the evening meal, the sun was still in the east. So people ate another breakfast. Corn and kale wilted in the fields. Sunflowers stopped following the sun. Birds exhausted their songs. Night still did not come. A third breakfast came and went, and then, at last, when the sun had had enough, it left us for the western horizon and realm of the dead. No one knew what day it was. Having passed through a morning in the evening or an evening in the morning, people lost their assurance in the material integrity of things and studied their surroundings for openings leading to other worlds. They believed any inadvertent step could cause them to fall through the shadows of culverts and cul-de-sacs or the corners and closets of their houses, and for this reason they kept their children and household animals close at hand. They watched the movements of insects and the flights of birds to note whether, and at what point, they vanished. And they studied the patterns of fallen leaves and cracks in parched fields for any clues that might reveal where the solidity of stone and soil had been breached by malefic mischief.

When the tide went out one morning, a group of women digging for clams on the beach beside the Deva discovered the words *illumina sedentes in tenebris* written in strings of seaweed. Evidence of the disruption of the natural order was everywhere. Cows walked into the bay. Fish were seen in trees. Crows sang like songbirds. Parents found red tattoos on the arms of their children with words in unknown languages, while the constellation Perseus appeared in black dots on the chest of Xesús Fernández. Mars and Venus, pulled from their spheres, loomed large in the sky like bright marbles, and the boundaries that separate the dreams of people dissolved, so we found ourselves in the dreams of strangers and strangers in our dreams.

The sea-glow faded over time, and the bay returned to darkness, but mysterious lights began to appear in people's homes as if they had migrated from the water to the shore in search of human fellowship. As a neighboring family in Rúa dos Loureiros sat down to dinner one night, the mother noticed a light on upstairs and sent her child to turn it off. When he reached the top of the stairs, she heard him scream frantically and rushed up after him to find him lying on the floor covered by lights that moved like living creatures over his body and across the walls. When she waved a crucifix over him, the lights flew out the window into the darkness like shooting stars, but the child began to bleed from lesions where they had tracked across his body. The next morning his parents took him to Bachiario, who observed that while the manifest evil had been driven away, an underlying presence remained. To remove the lingering malignity, he led the child around Nosa Señora do Mar three times and then recited the following passage from the Gospel of Matthew as he cut the air around him with a knife: *Vade Satana: Scriptum est enim: Dominum Deum tuum adorabis, et illi soli servies.* Then he cut a branch of sage from the edge of Campo da Graza and, after setting it on fire, carried it before him as he and the child circled the *cruceiro* in the churchyard three times. He set the burning branch on the ground before the *cruceiro* and had the child pass back and forth through the white smoke as he shouted, "Get out. Go back to the depths of hell and leave this child alone," and cut the air around him one last time. To conclude the ceremony, Bachiario poured holy water over the child and for good measure uttered more violent curses to act as verbal grotesques to protect him from any additional threats. Within a few minutes, the lesions healed and disappeared as if nothing had ever happened.

While there were individual victories such as this, the collective struggle against the *potentia malum* continued. And as it did, Porto Lúa languished, overwhelmed by its inexplicable fate. All manner of supplication failed. All manner of appeasement. Nothing we did could prevent more prodigies of nature from occurring. Flowers faded. Fruit spoiled. The bull lost interest in the cow, the boar in the sow. Drops of fire fell from the sky burning through the boughs of trees and starting fires in the fields where the smoke rising from fresh grass smelled like burning flesh.

During a night of black wind, Aunt Fioxilda dreamt that an emerald green iceberg floated into port. It towered over the fishing boats like a mountainous island riven with deep valleys and lustrous hillsides. As the day progressed and the sun rose higher in the sky, the ice began to melt, and small streams ran off its surface through deep crevices. By the middle of the afternoon, enough of the ice had melted to reveal a caravel locked inside the dark green cavern at the heart of the floating glacier, and at the end of the day, when the last rays of the sun were beating down on the porous ice, the ship broke free of its cold prison and with sails extended rose up in the wind over the town as far as a bank of high clouds where it foundered on an airy reef and shattered. As the cloud bank moved inland over Mount Aracelo, splintered planks of wood and tatters of sails fell through the sky and landed in the forests. Without explaining why, she took this as a sign that our trials would soon be over.

The following morning, a stranger wearing a beige linen suit appeared in the plaza. No one knew who he was or what business he had, and rumors of his unexplained presence quickly spread. Because of his aloof bearing, many believed he was a monsignor sent in disguise by the ecclesiastical authorities in Santiago to report on the recent events in Porto Lúa. In fact his arrival coincided precisely with the appearance of warnings painted on the boulders along the Roman road instructing people to give up practicing pagan rituals at sacred springs, groves, and promontories or risk excommunication. But others thought his presence was more sinister and suspected he had come to witness the forgeries of the devil at first hand. Two people who passed him on the street late at night swore that the pupils of his eyes were red. Despite these suspicions, he spent his evenings at O Galo drinking and playing cards with the usual patrons, a mixture of fishermen, merchants, and farmers. He told them he was on vacation, but never mentioned what he did. When they asked him what he thought of the rare events that had transpired of late, he replied that he had heard several of the stories but hadn't seen anything yet with his own eyes that would suggest a malevolent force was at work.

"People are always looking to blame someone else for their problems," he said, "rather than take responsibility for them or make an effort to avoid them."

"How could people avoid a river that flows backward or a boy burned by strange lights?"

"Even though this world is a miracle in itself, they need to believe there is something more extraordinary in their lives. They need to believe they matter to something, good or bad, beyond themselves. That they are the victims of some evil or beloved by some good. And so they see these things and tell their stories, and where one leads, others will follow."

"You don't believe there is evil in the world?"

"I don't believe there is evil in nature. No evil in the storms of the sea. No evil in the fox killing to feed her kits. It lies in the hunger not for food but for the illusions of power and status, and for the couch of luxury. These things don't exist in nature. They only exist in the minds of your neighbors. Even in children lie the seeds. What would the devil hope to gain from tormenting people in this way?"

"He's a liar and a thief."

"What would he want that he doesn't already have?"

"The souls of men. The sorrow of God."

"I doubt if he has much interest in souls, and what would be the use of a grudge against God?"

"It's a strange man who stands up for the devil."

"If there is a devil, perhaps it's the folly of humanity that amuses him. The vanity. The self-importance. The presumption that somehow the charade of human affairs matters."

"It's more than that. He takes delight in the suffering of people."

"I suspect only because they are so ridiculous. They love the idea of redemption through suffering. Salvation and perdition. Like children desperate to win a game. Begging for forgiveness as if it matters. I can't help it if I find human pride to be so comical. How it leads to self-deception and hypocrisy."

To convince him of the hardships they were suffering, they took him to the home of a woman who was being visited by Bachiario. She was bedridden in a room with closed shutters because the touch of sunlight on her skin caused her to feel intense pain. Bachiario performed another ceremony with the knife and holy water and burning sage and succeeded in removing a black shadow from the woman that departed through the window.

"What do you think?" Bachiario asked the man after putting the knife and holy water back in his bag.

"I think you're wasting your time on this one. It's not the devil's fault. She's just crazy."

"What about all the other things that have happened? I have seen candlesticks rise in the air with my own eyes. Is that not the work of the devil?"

"I think you're being a bit melodramatic about all this."

"When there is no natural explanation for these events, witnessed by dozens or even hundreds of people, is it not reasonable to ascribe supernatural causes to them?"

"People see what they want to see. Perhaps even I am part of their dream, a character in the stories they tell themselves."

Bachiario understood this to be a tacit admission that the man in the linen suit was in fact an agent of darkness and that he viewed his activity in Porto Lúa, even his conversation with Bachiario, as trifling sport. Aunt Fioxilda agreed with this conclusion as did several other people. Don Andrés was not so sure.

"If he's really the devil, why wouldn't he come out and take credit for all these strange occurrences?"

"Because he prides himself on the virtuosity of his evasion, the success of his imposture. It increases his pleasure in our suffering."

"What should we do?"

"Go about your business, and when the next strange phenomenon occurs, express no fear, no anxiety, no interest. Nothing."

"Nothing?"

"For as long as it takes. He will have no reason to stay here if we don't respond with awe or despair. He will have no reason to be amused. We will drive him away with boredom."

"Shouldn't we pray?"

"No. No prayers. That will give him cause to mock us."

The people of Porto Lúa did as Bachiario instructed them. When the Deva dried up and the bells in the tower of Nosa Señora do Mar began to ring on their own and food came out of hot ovens cold, no one took any notice, not even when milk curdled in the breasts of new mothers, nor when Xosé Carrillo saw the image of his dead father in a mirror. We accepted all this impassively. When people suspected the man in the linen suit was cheating at dominoes, Bachiario told them to ignore their suspicions.

"What you think you see isn't necessarily what is there."

When the stranger met Bachiario one night in the plaza, he commented that he hadn't heard any more stories of miraculous events.

"People have become so accustomed to these things they no longer mention them. It's as if their perspectives have altered so much that they now accept the uncommon as common. The extraordinary as ordinary. We have endured the worst of this diabolical ordeal and exhausted it."

For the first time the man in the linen suit showed signs of discomposure, and while he agreed that the ability of people to accept their trials with equanimity was a good thing, he was noticeably agitated. As the conversation continued, he began to sweat and shake as though unaccustomed to his own body.

"It must be something I ate," he said. "You will have to excuse me."

When Bachiario bade him good night, it was the last time anyone in Porto Lúa saw him. The next day the fruit trees in the town blossomed despite the lateness of the season, bees hummed in the eglantine, and the water in the wells and public fountains possessed the sweet taste of jasmine. The prodigies ended as abruptly as they had begun. The sea and sky and fields ceased to be the stages of an infernal theater. In a celebratory Mass, Bachiario praised the forbearance and spiritual discipline of the congregation.

But that was not to be our last experience of the *potentia malum*. A week later, two women keeping a vigil in the shadows of Rúa da Morte heard a voice calling out but could not locate its source or determine what it was saying. Neither recognized it belonging to a deceased family member, and one woman said the stones themselves seemed to speak. The next morning, in Capela de Santa Lupa, a man by the name of Trofonio appeared behind the grate covering the entrance to the sea-caves. Cotolay was the first to see him and at the prompting of the exhausted fisherman went to find Don Andrés. By the time the mayor arrived, there were already several people in the church, and two men were busy sawing the rusty iron bars. When they finally broke through, the men pulled the fisherman out and laid him on a bench where he was given a mixture of wine and water and a breakfast of bread and anchovies. Famished and fatigued, like a castaway who has crossed the sea or a mountain climber who has reached the sky, Trofonio was slow to respond to the question of how he had come to find himself on the other side of the bars. So they led him to the fresh air in the shade of the great linden tree in the alameda where María Piñeiro dressed his wounds and covered the lump on his forehead with a cold compress.

"Friends, I thank you for your kindness and concern. You want me to tell you what has happened to me and where I have been, but you will not believe me. For few have seen what I have seen and returned to tell the tale. I have experienced the world below. I have passed through the realm of death."

It had long been known that the opening in Capela de Santa Lupa led to a network of caves the sea had cut into the granite of the coast, but at that time no living person had explored them in any depth. Because of the odors emanating from the opening, a mixture of sulfur and decay, church authorities had, sometime in the past, cemented a grate into the stone to keep the realms of darkness and daylight separate. So even though Trofonio's passage through the underworld seemed unlikely, there was some basis for his claim in the stories we had heard as children. Despite a murmur of disbelief among those who had begun to gather, people were willing to entertain the possibility that he had at least found a way to enter the caves.

"If you were able to get in, why did you need our help to get out?"

"I didn't enter here."

"Why didn't you go back the way you came?"

"Because I entered through Boca do Inferno."

"That's not possible."

"If you don't believe me, that's fine. Let me go home and sleep. You can crawl down through the rocks behind the grate and see for yourselves."

"Don't be upset, Trofonio. It's just hard to imagine such a thing."

"That may be, but it's what happened. If it will ease your suspicions, I'll submit my story to the judgment of Wilfreda and let her decide whether I'm telling the truth."

Whenever a major dispute arose and arbitration was needed, whether it was a legal or personal matter, Wilfreda was called upon to settle the issue. Because Colonel Florentino had forced people to serve on juries during the Civil War to try their friends and neighbors for acts against the state, the town had decided there would be no more juries and turned to Wilfreda—unkindly called *Sapa Virxe* by those who considered themselves the victims of her judgments—as the only means of establishing the truth or falsehood of a claim.

She was a giantess who could find a grain of truth in a desert of lies, but not command her own limbs. Her unusually large head rested on deep folds of flesh that spread downward over her body, one heaped over another in ever-expanding

247

waves. Due to her enormous heft and sway, she had broken several bones in her legs and feet, and when summoned for her powers of discernment, ten men had to carry her down the hill from her house in her bed. There were those who claimed the rolling white marble of her blind eye enabled her to see what others could not and those who believed her powers came from a swarm of bees that had lighted on her face during childhood. By whatever means, her ability to unravel the truth was uncanny.

When people were brought before her to tell their story, she listened closely, not so much to their words as to the timbre and tension of their voices while her lips tightened around her mouth like a cinched purse. Giving little away through her inscrutable demeanor, she would patiently consider their speech for a few minutes and respond in one of three ways. Sometimes she would wave her hand as a signal for them to stop and then spit indicating the petition, or petitioner, was of insufficient merit. Other times she would concentrate so intently that she appeared to fall asleep with her eyes open, and then suddenly shout out either "true" or "false." And on a few rare occasions, when the sound of the voice offered less than she needed to make a decision, she would question the petitioner before reaching her conclusion. There were no appeals, and after rendering her verdict, she was carried back up the slope to her home by the same ten men who had carried her down. Because people believed she had been given her gift through divine agency, no one, not even those whose claims were wrongfully denied, ever had the audacity to question her ruling publicly.

As Trofonio sat under the linden tree still somewhat disoriented by the bright sunlight and the growing crowd of people who had heard of his rescue, he invited those around him to ask questions. The first came from Antonio Loro:

"What is the sky like in the underworld?"

"It's like the ceiling of any cavern," Trofonio replied, "a dark hemisphere of clay and stone. The light comes from openings, like Boca do Inferno, that let the sun enter in long shafts. Imagine the rays of light that penetrate dark clouds in a storm. The farther you move toward the interior, the more distant the sunlight becomes and the darker the atmosphere. There you must rely entirely on the pale glow cast by pools of molten stone and the fires of retribution."

"I've spent my life at sea and never saw an opening in the middle of it."

"You wouldn't see an opening in the water, but rather on small islands or groups of rocks where there are caves and ancient vents in the stone. You could pass right by and never know they are there."

As Trofonio concluded his response, Wilfreda appeared coming down the slope of Rúa das Angustias in her bed. The ten men carrying her struggled under the weight, but as they entered the alameda, others came forward to help them lower the bed gently into the mica dust under the linden tree.

"Is this the man?" she asked.

"It is."

Wilfreda stared at him for a moment with her good eye.

"And your story? What is it about?"

"My passage through the underworld."

"Do you affirm that what you are about to say is true?"

"I do."

"Begin."

"Like others, I'm sure, I had long wondered what, if anything, lay at the bottom of Boca do Inferno, and, prompted by the disturbances of recent weeks, I decided to satisfy my curiosity for once and for all. So, on the tenth of August, with a calm sea and a light breeze out of the east, I sailed to Illa da Luz carrying a windlass I had salvaged from a wreck some years ago and two hundred feet of three-quarter-inch Manila rope. When I reached the cave, I anchored the windlass in deep cracks in the rocks on both sides of the opening and wrapped the rope over the drum in such a way that I could lower myself slowly down the shaft in a leather harness I had made. I wasn't sure how far down I would have to go to reach the bottom, but from the height of the opening above the sea, I guessed one hundred feet of rope would be more than enough. It wasn't. When I came to the end of the rope, I was hanging above an unfathomed abyss, and my arms were too tired to pull myself back up, so I swung from side to side trying to reach a ledge in order to rest. This motion must have loosened the windlass or caused it to break because I suddenly felt the rope give way and the awful sensation of falling helplessly into the earth. Although it couldn't have taken more than a few seconds, the fall seemed to last forever. I thought it was all over for me.

"At the bottom of the shaft my fall was partially broken by a thin dome of flowstone that had been formed and hardened by water seeping through the bedrock and dripping down the walls for untold years. Crashing through the brittle layers of this dome as one might break through a skylight of chalky glass, I fell another thirty or forty feet into a body of water. After rising to the surface, surprised by my good fortune in surviving the fall, I looked around to take my bearings and realized I was in a vast lake or subterranean sea illuminated by the rays of light I mentioned earlier. The shaft I fell through is a natural chimney, perhaps once a watercourse, in the ceiling of the underworld. The walls of this cavern are composed of columns formed by frozen tides of molten rock and fluted by millennia of falling water pouring down from the surface of the earth in streams. High on these walls are cliffs and ledges lined with hanging gardens where subterranean flowers grow in the indirect light. To the east, beyond the water's edge, are ridges of sheer stone and barren valleys filled with the fogs and mists of a world of perpetual twilight and the rivers of the dead. Deep in these valleys burn pits of sulfurous fire that are reflected in the seams of crystal overhead providing a kind of starlight in this granite tomb.

"To reach the nearest shore, I swam toward the dark landscape of these ridges and valleys. The water is saline and clear, and the only creatures to inhabit it are translucent, ghost-like fish. When I emerged from the water, I found myself on a wide beach where the streams falling over the rock walls gather in tidal pools and cut small channels in the sand. As I stood isolated in this strange world trying to determine how to get back to where I had come from, I heard a voice fill the chamber like the low rumble of thunder.

"'Who are you and what business have you in the realm of the dead?'

"As I looked into the shadows among the boulders at the foot of the nearest wall, I could barely make out the silhouette of a figure in form and height the likeness of some colossus.

"'My name is Trofonio. I am a fisherman from Porto Lúa,' I said. 'I fell into Boca do Inferno and am looking for a way to return to my home. Who are you?'

"'I am Berobreus of the evening land.'

"'Can you help me find my way out of this place?'

"'You must pass over the plain of the underworld and then ascend a path through the caverns of darkness. After a long climb, you will reach the underside of the world you know. There you will follow a long passage until you find an opening to daylight.'

"'How will I know I'm on the right path?'

"'I will take you there myself.'

"'Where are we now?'

"'The islands you see in the distance are the Cassiterides. They were called the Blessed Isles before they descended to the underworld when this remnant of an ancient sea was submerged beneath the ocean. Those who visited these islands in the past returned with tales of their abundance and beauty and the fairness of their climate but could never find them again. What they saw, in fact, were their own dreams of paradise as the islands offer no material bounty. Each exists for a particular virtue, and the rewards they provide for just souls are the ideas of those things rather than the things themselves. In such a way that nothing ever grows old or disappears.'

"'But if there are only ideas of things, are the souls too only ideas of themselves and not who they were in life?'

"'They are themselves no less than they were while living in the world above. Even when alive, they were never anything more than ideas of themselves.'

"'Is this Hell?'

"'No. This is the underworld. Hell lies beyond the rocky slopes that disappear in the darkness. Be forewarned. Unlike the islands, it is a region of material torments, and your journey to return to the living will take you on an arduous course where you may risk physical injury or worse.'

"As he emerged from the shadows, he remained a shadow, more a presence than a person. The details of his features were lost in the overwhelming impression of his stature and the hooded cloak that obscured his face.

"We set out across a salt marsh on the edge of the sea and then followed a path over an open plain where the coastal grasses give way to a rocky, black soil. As we approached the lifeless ridges and valleys of gray stone, I began to feel the heat of their burning pits and saw clouds of dark smoke enter the light the way a muddy stream enters the clear waters of a river. At the end of the plain, we came to a stone bridge that narrows at the midpoint of its arch to a width of no more than a yard. It is a natural formation with no rails or siding of any kind and the stones protrude haphazardly and are even loose in some places. Below the bridge is an endless expanse of blue sky, as if the world had been inverted.

"'You must be careful when crossing this traverse,' my companion said. 'If you slip and fall, I cannot help you. Here every soul denied the Blessed Isles must decide whether it will accept the consequences of its actions in life and endure an eternity of torture in the fellowship of other souls or avoid its rightful punishment and step into the pool of eternal time, this ether of blue oblivion, and fall where there is no up or down, where there is no rest or retreat, only time forever timeless, forever approaching nothingness. If you wait here long enough, one will pass, and you will see it either proceed to the other side of the bridge and the caverns of Hell or hurl itself over the side and disappear from sight.'

"Reluctant to witness the horror of such a fall, I chose not to wait, but before we could move on, a soul floated toward us on the path like a wisp of down and crossed the bridge, then another and another, and then one lingered for a moment on the bridge before stepping over the side, its faint white form quickly vanishing into the blue abyss below.

"'Who are they?' I asked.

"'Their names no longer matter. Anticipating eternity, they come from the valleys of Cantabria, the mountains of Granada, the gulfs of Ibiza. The lovelorn youth, the consumptive nurse, the palsied nun, the drowned sailor, the lonely widower, the prisoner shot by a firing squad. All are sinners. All are welcome. Here the monk and murderer pass together.'

"Afraid I might lose my balance on the narrowest part of the bridge, I got down on my hands and knees and crawled across. As I moved forward over the rough stones trembling and almost paralyzed with fear, I looked down into the sky below me, a seamless blue with no sun, no clouds, extending, it seemed, through immeasurable space. My guide, having more experience in this realm, followed me across the span indifferent to the threat of falling. On the other side, the atmosphere began to darken, and the heat increased. Through a sulfurous haze, I could now see the mounds of smoking scoria more clearly. Along the rocky slopes of the valleys were broken walls and the ruins of ancient houses and towers with crenellated battlements testifying to the ageless wars of Pandemonium. The path led us to a gate of mud and stone where a starving dog snarled and snapped at us flinging threads of spit from its ravenous mouth. Berobreus threw it a fish head to divert its attention, and we passed into the walled city of the damned. Seagulls that had found their way down the vents of Hell lay dead on the ground, overcome by the fumes. When I realized what had happened to them, I tore off the tail of my shirt, folded it in half, and wrapped it over my mouth and nose.

"Flitting through the darkness, anticipating the fall of another unfortunate, was the ghost of a woman less woman than form. Her hair was white. Her skin was white. Her eyes were the blue of an unbaptized infant.

"'Who is that?' I asked.

"'She is the first torment the damned will face as she harries them this way and that with the urgency of a bloodless will no more substantial than her ghostly form. Her role is to assign each soul to its eternal place. If you speak to her, she will convince you that you belong here. If you ignore her, she will disappear.'

"We entered a labyrinth of indistinguishable trenches and passed through a landscape more desolate than the worst nightmare of Hell laid waste by the privations of divine indifference. There was no life and no color except for the reflected light of fire and no variation in the scree fields or stone sky to relieve the tedium of a place without time. The path continued up an incline into the mouth of a cave where strange black forms like the shadows of bats stirred overhead. We passed a series of corridors and chambers, then crossed a stream fed by the dripping sweat of minerals that over millennia had built up a forest of smoothly sculpted spires. The ceiling here was opalescent, like polished flesh, and the walls were ribbed like a skeletal fossil of Leviathan. Each rounded corridor led into a darkness of its own, and each reverberated with the drubbing sound of labored winds as if we were passing through the lungs of a vast stone beast.

"'What lies down these paths?' I asked.

"'The chambers allocated to the punishments of particular sins.'

"'Is it possible to see them?'

"'I can guide you, but I cannot protect you. You may see them if you wish, but at your own risk.'

"At random I chose to enter one of the many passageways that branched off from the main corridor. The light was weaker here as there were fewer flares burning in the niches and hollows, but as my eyes adjusted, I could see subtle variations of hue in the walls and floor, so welcome in a place otherwise bereft of color: the blood red of porphyry, blue crystals, red garnet, golden topaz, and other stones that were clear green like lime juice in a glass. The passage opened up to a large cavern—a landscape hundreds of feet across where agate trees were leafed with jade, and the blades of grass were golden foil, and the clear blue lake was solid sapphire. But the abundance of these treasures meant they had no value, and there was insufficient light to waken their beauty. Here a single ray of sunlight, so common in the world above, was more precious than all the jewels of the earth. Nevertheless, there were souls walking through the fields and among the trees gathering as many of the gems as they could carry—nothing but handfuls of gravel in the dim aspect of that place—as insignificant as the souls themselves when bereft of light.

"'What sinners are these?' I asked my guide.

"'These are the avaricious,' he replied. 'Their greed will never end, and despite their delusions of wealth, they will never possess anything more valuable than worthless pebbles.'

"We returned to the main corridor, but stopped several more times to enter other passageways carved, according to ancient writers, by the churning rivers of Tartarus and tufted and spurred with calcite deposits. Led by my guide, I saw murderers boiling in a crimson lake fed by arteries of hollow stone. I saw the vain slicing and gouging their hands with the splinters of broken mirrors. I saw gluttons cut off their arms and legs to set their tables with steaming banquets of their own flesh. I saw those who had wasted their lives in apathy and ignorance confined to pillars of rock like anchorites in a desert forever isolated and unengaged from everything around them.

"We descended another passage to a crypt lined with the sarcophagi of those souls who had never sought another to love. Underfoot were veins of quartz druse like chunks of frozen slush, and, in the faint light, the room, coated with a patina of gypsum rime and leaching feathers of calcium frost, could have been an ice cave in a winter landscape. Lying unable to move in tombs of cold stone, with nothing to distract them but their own thoughts, these souls may rest in peace for the first few months or even years of their internment, but over time, those who avoided the upheavals of love eventually succumb to the misery of perpetual solitude. The only interruptions in the monotony of their existence are the fleeting earthquakes that rumble through the depths of stone a few times every century. Confined to their idle darkness, they wait hour by hour for decades to feel their coffins rock for a moment before coming to rest—stilled until the earth moves again in the slow progress of geologic time.

"We ascended the rocky slope of the passageway to the main corridor through a closed atmosphere laden with earthen moisture that grew warmer as we went higher. Tired from the climb, I stopped for a moment to ask my guide how much farther I had to go before reaching the end of my journey. He replied that we had traveled no more than a mile since the gate of Hell and several more remained ahead of us. Then he took the opportunity to explain what I had seen so far.

"'These punishments you have witnessed were not imposed by a higher authority, but are rather the fates determined by the characters of the souls themselves. You have experienced but a few. There are many more you did not see. For example, the sad fate of those who betrayed love. It is too disturbing to describe. But Hell is more than a place of punishment. It is also a place of creation. Because the souls of the damned have no hope of happiness, the demons who inhabit this place find greater satisfaction in undermining that hope among the living. In ways they never suspect.'

"'How is this done?'

"'You will soon see for yourself. Before you can return to daylight, you must pass the great halls of Pandemonium, the workshops of human misery. There you will encounter the legions of malfeasance, the sources of disorder and perversion in the world.'

"When we reached the end of the corridor that passed through the punishments of the damned, we entered a high open space between two elevations of barren rock and crossed a natural bridge of shattered limestone that arched hundreds of feet above a deep gash in the earth. From the highest point of the bridge I could see distant canyons and stone pinnacles where perpetual fires burned in a perpetual dusk. Below us were the villages of those who had sown dissension and profited from war. The prospect was similar to the view from Aracelo at night, but here the sky was like a stone oven blackened by soot and the pestilent air full of the fumes of burning rock. On the far side of the bridge we faced an even steeper climb up a narrow roadbed that wound around the side of the second elevation. As we came around the corner of a natural buttress formed by a cascade of frozen magma, we heard antiphonal choirs echoing among the stone draperies and canopies hanging all around us. Then through marble columns that rose into the darkness above us, we entered the great cathedral of the dead. The nave alone was larger than Porto Lúa and filled with a multitude of souls, hypocrites who had worshipped with the appearance of devotion while maintaining lives of deceit or violence or greed. From the portico, I could see members of the nobility and military officers, souls, as my guide explained, who had cheated in business or ignored the poor or who had attended church to display their wealth before others. There were too many to note individually, but Berobreus pointed out Colonel Florentino who, along with other officers, was standing in a vat of tallow illuminating the proceedings as a human wick. Torquemada was also there wearing a *sambenito* among as many priests as there are starlings in a summer sky. A member of the demon clergy approached and invited me to join the proceedings. He was covered with tarry fur, and his teeth circled his scabrous tongue like a ring of stubble in a closely cropped field. Both legs ended in calloused stubs, and his slightly crossed eyes seemed to burn the objects of their gaze. He led me through a sea of congregants muttering and bellowing in the fetid smoke of the burning wicks to the altar where they were celebrating Mass in backward Latin. The windows of the church were mirrors as there was nothing outside to see, and the ceiling dripped with an oily condensation from the tallow fires. In the sanctuary before the altar was an ornate chair of golden snakes writhing in anticipation of General Molinero's indurate flesh, and all the while, a chorus of lamentations and execrations shook the walls and columns with deep vibrations that sounded like the earth grinding backward against its axis.

"When I refused their perverted communion, the crowd of demons grew restless at my presence and began to taunt and threaten me. My guide, whose towering stature commanded their respect, shielded me from the congregation until we were able to leave through the transept on the left side of the nave. As we moved away from the church, my eyes were slow to adjust to the darkness, and I was forced to hold on to the hem of his cloak, trusting him to know the way. There are few fears in life comparable to the fear of Hell's darkness, and I could make out nothing of the stony detritus that we navigated nor the subterranean architecture that surrounded us. All I could see before me, floating around me, were words. Faintly, as if in my own mind. Not yet written nor spoken, but, rather, on the verge of expression.

"'Where are we?' I asked.

"'We have reached the place where language begins, the origin of every utterance.'

"Through the darkness the words passed like tangled nets drifting on an invisible stream, flowing together in ways both foreign and familiar. Each bore a unique character, like different tones of light in different climates, conveying distinct impressions and connotations. Some were soft like a forest floor of wet leaves, and some were hard like the edge of a mountain ridge, and some were fair like open fields beneath a summer sky. As we continued walking toward the source of this invisible stream, I noticed a faint glow, and then gradually, as my eyes became more accustomed to the darkness, I saw the demons at work. At first only their eyes appeared, like the yellow gaze of beasts in the forest at night. Then their hands bending and twisting the empty symbols before releasing them, like gossamer of the mind, to float freely, still unattached to any language, undirected by any will, but destined to be sculpted by tongues and weighted with intention.

"Surprised to discover language to be a source of disorder and perversion in the world, I asked my guide why it is such a scourge.

"'Words are a source of human misery because they separate human beings from their nature and lead them to believe they are different from their fellow creatures as well as from each other. When the myth of their mastery over the rest of creation is taken from them by death, they suffer more than all the other animals with whom they share their lives. Words have given human beings not only their art, their magic, and the tools of their success, but also the means of their destruction, the lies and false promises that lead to loss and despair. It is the promise of comfort, hope, and assurance, together with their denial, that makes human life more intolerable than all the others, and that is why the demons work so hard to keep languages from growing dull and falling into disuse.'

"As we continued through this room, it struck me how our thoughts are made of words, and the words that make each of us unique are not our own. Even the words that expressed this thought in this way had undoubtedly been used by others to convey the same thought in the same way before me. The idea that all words are lies, lies about ourselves, continued to trouble me as we entered a room where temptations of luxury were being formulated and refined. The air here was clear and the light soft. The furnishings were more accommodating.

"'These demons enjoy some of the greatest success in Hell because they have the skill and ingenuity to create material necessities where none existed before. Opulence is no easy thing to invent because the body only has so many natural requirements, but the illusion of greater comfort, greater pleasure, is so seductive that people spend their lives seeking it and will destroy each other in their pursuit. However, this is but a trifling diversion compared to the next room where we come to the most insidious of all the diabolical inventions.'

"'What is that?'

"'In the final precinct of the demonic imagination, higher than all the others and closest to daylight, we have the truth.'

"'Why is it the most insidious?'

"'Because as soon as you have what is true, you have what

is right, and as soon as you have what is right, you have to defend what is right—the right religion, the right political system, the right philosophy—and all the other sides then become what is not right—the wrong religion, the wrong political system, the wrong philosophy. Facts, the empirical observations people make, are then distorted to support their truths, and as a result, hundreds of millions have suffered and died. More than two thousand years ago, when I first came here, this was the room of dreams. Then Morpheus, Phobetor, and Phantasos, employing legions of the damned, set out to devise the perfect torment that would appeal to the pride and intellect of human beings. Carefully studying the alchemy of the human soul, they took fears and needs and subjected them to the fires of vanity and desire to create the dream of truth. Its pursuit became irresistible to the ancients seeking something more than superstition to improve their lives and even to give them meaning. Building on their belief in certainty and permanence, they developed science and philosophy. They kept records and histories. And yet, like a mirage sailors adrift will spy when weakened by calenture, the truths they sought disappeared as soon as they were reached, replaced by others. So they continued to sail, continued to search. Century after century philosophers refuted philosophers and science refuted science. Religions came and went. Armies perished and were left forgotten in the earth.'

"From the conjectures that filled the room with an atmosphere of uncertainty, from apprehensions and perceptions vague and cloudy, the demons labored to precipitate their truths. They ordered new words from those who crafted language and twisted the connotations of old words to suit their needs. Despite the alluring beauty of their immediate clarity, these crystalline structures of logic, capable of deceiving the most critical thinkers, are in fact as fragile as the human desires and perspectives from which they are derived, lasting no more than a generation or century or, in rare cases, an epoch.

"In addition to the first room we entered, which was devoted to philosophical truths, there were others where religious, academic, and scientific truths were being created. The so-called eternal truths expressed in axioms and equations were the specialty of a select group whose work supplied the basis of mathematics and geometry.

"'Focusing on simplicity and symmetry,' Berobreus explained, 'these demons polish their numbers to a luster of rare appeal, creating the appearance of harmony and predictability out of chaos. Lying at the heart of this appeal is the belief among many that truth is divine. With this advantage, the demons are able to divert the hearts and minds of human beings away from an imaginative engagement with the world to the illusions of final answers and solutions. When they have succeeded in planting a truth firmly in the minds of people, they oppose it with another, thereby inciting a series of arguments and counter-arguments that waste, to their immense pleasure and amusement, endless hours, even lives, on the empty contemplation of their hollow creations.'

"'I understand they are able to turn fears and desires into truths, but how do these truths then find their way into the debates of the living?'

"'That's the most cunning part of their strategy. They are living among you in all walks of life: politicians, lawyers, members of the clergy, petty bureaucrats vying for power, the buyers and sellers of land and chattels, and especially the demagogues who profit from sowing discord and division. Where you find hatred and intolerance, assume these demons are hard at work. Many more pretend to live by teaching and scholarship in the schools and universities: the opinionated academics who thrive on disputation, the condescending philosophers who unravel their proofs in airless rooms, the pedagogues who spend a lifetime writing books calculating the age of Shem or translating the thoughts of butterflies. These demons have countless connections to advance their agendas and members from their ranks on both sides of many questions. Those who follow them need to believe there is something certain in life, and that a refusal to believe in the truth leads to a life that is false. Once they have the truth, they will defend it, but they no longer need to question, no longer need to exercise their imaginations, and that is their downfall. Only those who deny the existence of truths, who live creatively amidst uncertainty, can escape the demonic influence.'

"Just outside the last room dedicated to the fabrication of truths, we came to another gate that marked the end of my journey through Hell. I was glad to be closer to my return to daylight, but unsure of where I was in relation to the world above. I had no idea how long I had been walking without eating or sleeping. While I knew I wasn't dreaming, time seemed suspended as if in a dream.

"Berobreus took two torches from their iron mounts on either side of the gate and handed one to me.

"'The way forward lies in absolute darkness. If you drop this torch, you may never find your way back.'

"Once through the gate, we followed a path along a stream that within a fairly short distance issued from the mouth of a cave thirty feet up the side of a bluff. We were close enough to the roof of the underworld to hear the sound of wind rushing beneath it and the echo of the falling water. From that height, I looked back into the darkness and tried to map the places we had been in my mind. Berobreus pointed to the cathedral and in the distance the faint light of the openings in the stone ceiling like pre-dawn light appearing through clouds far out at sea.

"'Follow the stream,' he said, 'and it will lead you back to where you came from. The entrance of the cave is too narrow to accommodate me, so from now on you will be on your own. Hold your torch high in case you slip and fall in the water.

Without its light, you will never escape this place. You came here as a fisherman more foolish than wise risking your life in Boca do Inferno, but now you have seen things no one else has seen, and you have knowledge unlike any possessed by those who live. Tell your story to those who will listen.'

"I thanked him for his guidance and climbed up the ledges of the bluff showered by mist off the falling water. Berobreus waited below holding his torch up to provide additional light. I turned and thanked him again when I reached the mouth of the cave and asked how far I would have to walk before finding a way out.

"'It is no more than a mile, but it will seem much farther because you will have to climb over rock formations and crawl through narrow passageways.'

"I looked out over the realm of the dead one more time and then lowered my head and entered the cave. For the first twenty or thirty yards, I was unable to stand upright, but then, as if emerging through the jagged teeth of a giant sea creature, I passed through opposing rows of stalagmites and stalactites into a spacious room and was able to proceed more quickly. I walked along ledges stained with ferrous plumes and around a corner where columns of flowstone were shaped like pipe organs and pleated curtains. The only sounds were drops of water in the clear pools of the stream that seeped through the rock and ran down thick stalactites and hanging straws and coral-like flowers. I continued to advance through a series of great halls where I could walk unimpeded through the stream until the walls closed in and I came to rocky palisades and berms ten or fifteen feet high that I had to scale and tight passages like bowels of stone that forced me to crawl on my hands and knees brushing the torch against the ceiling. The thought of losing my light or getting stuck in one of these passages terrified me, but I had no choice. The journey did seem like more than a mile. At times I wondered if it would ever end. As the cave wound like a serpent through the subterranean world, every bend led to another and that one to another. Finally, in the stillness of a large chamber, I heard the roar of the surf pounding against coastal rocks. I took off my mask and could smell the ocean for the first time and imagine the warmth and beauty of the sunlit shore. I hurried forward as quickly as I could along narrow ledges above the stream and down embankments where I searched to secure footholds in the loose stone and clay. When I heard people speaking above me, I climbed up a large boulder to get as close as I could to the sound of their voices and shouted as loudly as I could. But even if they had heard me, I don't know how they would have found me. I continued following the stream trusting it to lead me to an opening, but in my haste, I lost my footing on a ledge and slipped into the water extinguishing the torch. I sat in the darkness completely blind afraid to move for fear of falling down a hole and breaking my neck. I shouted and whistled to no effect and despaired of ever leaving this place however close I may have been to an opening. On my hands and knees, advancing no more than a few dozen yards an hour, I forced myself to continue. I did not know at the time that it was night, though soon enough I was able to see a faint glow in the distance. Over time it grew brighter, and my course became clearer. I left the streambed and climbed up a mound of damp boulders that smelled of brine. To one side was a chamber full of seawater and above me a natural vent in the rock. As I climbed up this opening, I recognized the grate in Capela de Santa Lupa. When I reached it, I saw Cotolay sitting in the front pew and called out to him. You know the rest."

For a moment after Trofonio concluded his story, there was silence. Even the birds were quiet. The people who had crowded around to hear him speak now turned their attention to Wilfreda. Half-lying, half sitting in her bed, she had rested her chin on her sternum impassively throughout the narrative.

She continued in this position with no movement except the rolling of her white eye as she contemplated the extraordinary tale she had just heard. After several minutes of thought, she rendered her verdict.

"If what he says is true, and there are no truths, then why am I here to judge whether he's telling the truth? Why would a man invent a story saying there is no such thing as truth if he wants us to believe the truth of what he says? He did not invent anything. Take me home."

Rather than concluding the matter, her pronouncement set in motion a wave of impromptu debates that sprang up in O Galo, on the quay, in the market, and everywhere else people came together. Many of the older residents of Porto Lúa had heard such stories in their childhood and said the existence of the underworld was common knowledge. Manolo Trillo claimed his great-grandfather had undertaken a similar journey in the previous century. Fidelia Amado remembered people on the mountain who prayed to Berobreus. Not surprisingly, Aunt Fioxilda believed Trofonio had experienced a vision from God. Bachiario was more skeptical. He argued that the story was too fanciful to be true and was similar to well-known fictional accounts of the underworld.

"There are no pagan gods residing below us," he said. "Even Cotolay knows that. It's more likely Trofonio wandered into a sea cave at low tide, fell asleep, and dreamt of stories he had read somewhere or made the whole thing up. He even gave himself license to do so when he said there is no such thing as the truth."

Many people wondered how anyone, even an educated person, could have invented such an improbable story if he had not had direct experience of such a place. But others agreed with Bachiario and said the sophistication of Trofonio's story suggested he had read accounts of the underworld somewhere and adopted them for his own purposes. Even if he had read books on the subject, his defenders responded, he could not have concocted a vision so extraordinary without seeing it and feeling it himself. Trofonio admitted he had read stories of hell during the years he spent in a seminary in Tui but claimed he did not have the knowledge to explain the agency of demons, and that he was merely conveying what he had seen and what he had heard.

People bought him drinks hoping he would let down his guard and tell them what had really happened. But he remained consistent through all the questioning. Why would he risk death to satisfy his curiosity? How could he have fallen so far without injury? Did he speak with any souls from Porto Lúa? Did he walk all the way from Illa da Luz to Porto Lúa? What his neighbors thought, however, was of secondary importance. The version of the story that reached Santiago appeared credible enough for the archdiocese to send two Church scholars to question Trofonio and examine the physical evidence that might support his claims. Arriving just before noon on the following Saturday, they set up an office in the rectory and spent four hours deposing the fisherman. The older priest with a severe gaze and tufts of white hair around his ears asked the questions while the younger sat next to him with a large leather-bound book recording Trofonio's responses.

"Is it true you were educated at the Seminario Menor San Paio in Tui?"

"It is."

"And that you abandoned your calling to become a fisherman?"

"Yes."

"As someone educated by the Church, you must know that several of your claims contradict its doctrine, especially the allegation there are demons masquerading as members of the clergy. The charge of heresy could be made against you."

"All I can tell you is what I saw and heard. It's also a sin to lie."

At one point the priest asked Trofonio if he understood the laws of physics. Trofonio replied that he did, but still believed the story of Moses parting the waters of the Red Sea. The second part of the inquiry was the collection of physical evidence that would either corroborate or contradict Trofonio's story. After conducting a series of interviews to establish the probity of several young men, the priests sent them into the cave equipped with lanterns. Once the men found the stream, they followed the trail of a person who had crawled in the sandy clay as far back as the large chamber where Trofonio first heard the roar of the surf and found both the mask he had made from his shirt and the burnt out stub of the torch he had carried. The search of Illa da Luz carried out later in the week yielded mixed results. They found Trofonio's boat on the beach, but no evidence he had set up a windlass at Boca do Inferno.

When the priests reported back to Archbishop Quiroga y Palacios, he directed them to replace the iron grate that had been removed from the entrance of the grotto and mount a plaque on it threatening to excommunicate anyone who attempts to enter the cave. No instructions were given pertaining to Boca do Inferno. However, two families who grazed their animals on the island in the summer built a stone wall around the opening, and both the penitent and merely curious began to make pilgrimages to the site.

As men were securing the grate, an emaciated dog trembling with exhaustion climbed up the rocks to the mouth of the cave and cautiously approached them. They removed the grate and coaxed the animal out with pieces of bread and sausage. Though it kept its distance from the men, it remained in the chapel pacing back and forth as they returned to work. When they stopped for lunch a little later, one of the workers took a bouquet of dead flowers out of an old can, filled it with water from the fountain outside, and set it down near the nervous creature. Remembering what Trofonio had said about encoun-tering a dog at the gate of hell, the worker found the fisherman on the quay and took him back to the chapel where Trofonio identified the dog as the one he had seen during his journey through the underworld. He fashioned a collar out of an oar tether, tied it to a rope, and led the animal down the street to O Galo where he fed it a ration of sliced serrano. When Harry stopped by the bar to deliver a sack of mussels, the dog strained at its leash to approach him and began to bark excit-edly. Harry crouched down and cradled its head in his hands.

"Winston. Where have you been?"

"He came out of the cave in Santa Lupa."

"He was on the *Eucrante* with us."

"He's yours if you want him."

"I do."

On a clear autumn morning just before noon, a black, chauffeur-driven Seat 1500 crossed the plaza and passed the curious patrons of O Galo before climbing the slope of Via Sagrada. Near the row of plane trees halfway up the street, the driver downshifted, and the gears labored as a carbonous plume rose from the tailpipe to cast a dark shadow over the gray asphalt. At the top of the street, the car swung around and stopped beside the gate to the churchyard, kicking up a cloud of white dust that floated off on the sea breeze through the funerary statues of angels and saints. The driver, a novice priest in a black, short-sleeved shirt and ill-fitting trousers, got out and opened the rear door for his passenger, a corpulent man dressed in a black soutane looking every bit the part of Mephistopheles with a tapered beard and self-assured gaiety in his eyes. He planted an ebony cane on the ground, leveraged himself out of the car, and sniffed the air like a scavenger searching for a meal. Breathing heavily in the warm sunlight and encumbered by his enormous girth, which rolled from side to side as he made his way through the churchyard, he stopped, red-faced and panting, to sit on an indecipherable tombstone as his driver carried his trunks up a series of steps and set them on the ground beside the rectory door.

Rosa was hanging laundry in the garden on the other side of the house when she heard the car approach and called to

Facundo who was scything grass at the far end of the church-yard.

"There's someone here."

He found the driver knocking on the door of the rectory and asked him what he wanted.

"Father Infante has arrived."

"Who?"

"Father has arrived to take up his appointment in the parish."

"I wouldn't know about that."

"Are you the caretaker?"

"I am."

"Well then, open the door and help me take these trunks inside."

"But there's already someone living here."

"Not according to the Archbishop," said Father Infante as he came around the corner. "I am here to take Father Ithacio's place."

"I don't know about the Archbishop, but Bachiario is our priest. You'll have to speak to him."

"I don't need to speak to anyone. This parish is in the jurisdiction of the Archbishop of Santiago, and I am here at his behest."

As he looked through the window into the blue shadow of the front room, he saw the white face of Mateo Mateo lying in his bed.

"Who is that?"

"Rosa's son. She's the housekeeper."

"We'll have to make other arrangements for him. Now let's get these trunks inside and find something to eat."

After deliberating on Trofonio's descent into the under-world and the various reports of prodigies, the authorities in the diocesan offices decided the congregation of Porto Lúa was at some risk of returning to its pagan past and hastened to find a replacement for Father Ithacio. Because of its status as an outpost in a wilderness of heterodoxy, the parish warranted a stout defender of the faith, but, at the same time, it did not rank among the most important congregations of the archdiocese, and its pastors had for generations been priests who, because of past indiscretions, were hard to place elsewhere. A solution consistent with this history was found in the orthodox but immoderate Father Infante, a rotund epicure from Madrid with bright, apple cheeks, smooth, amphibian skin, carefully curled bangs, and a taste for richly embroidered vestments.

As Rosa prepared an early lunch for the new pastor of Porto Lúa, Facundo went to look for Bachiario. After searching the school and O Galo, he found him speaking to Don Andrés in the plaza. When they reached the rectory, the car was gone, the door was locked, and Mateo Mateo was sleeping in his wheelbarrow under a fig tree in the garden. Although Bachiario could see no one through the window, he could hear Father Infante speaking to Rosa and banged on the door demanding to be let in. When this had no effect, he went to the church and locked himself in thereby initiating a standoff that lasted for a week when no one could enter the rectory or the church except for Rosa. Through her they each summoned Constable Sampaio to evict the other from the building he occupied, but neither would budge. Having heard of Father Infante's weakness for food, Bachiario proposed starving him out, but Rosa would not agree to such an act of impiety against a member of the clergy. His next idea was to propose putting the matter to a vote on the following Sunday by members of the congregation. However, Father Infante refused to agree to a public referendum. Since he wasn't well known to the people of Porto Lúa, he was aware that he had little popular support and decided instead to invoke the authority of the church and even St. Peter to argue that God had meant for the church to be a hierarchy and not a democracy, and he was the shepherd chosen by God's representatives on earth.

During that week, Don Andrés crafted a provisional agreement that allowed each man to leave his redoubt without the other taking advantage of his absence to seize the premises. Whenever they went out, they locked the doors of their buildings and posted Facundo and Rosa respectively at the church and rectory to keep watch and report on any attempt to violate the terms of the agreement. Having achieved this much détente, Don Andrés went on to propose that Father Infante stay with him as his guest until the matter was resolved and Bachiario could organize his belongings and move, but the priest refused, agreeing, however, to let Rosa retrieve the personal items Bachiario had left behind. After more negotiations, it was established that Rosa and Mateo Mateo would stay in the sacristy where Facundo lived, and Facundo would move to one of the empty rooms in the school. Bachiario, however, remained in the church.

With no access to Nosa Señora do Mar, Father Infante said the first Mass of his pastoral appointment in Capela de Santa Lupa on the second Sunday after his arrival. Beneath a pale blue sky, he walked down Via Sagrada wearing a black biretta and ornate vestments specially tailored by Mercedarian nuns in Rome. With his narrow beard and oiled black hair contrasting with his smooth skin, he could have been a masked *cigarrón* on his way to celebrate Entroido. The congregation was roughly half what it would have been in Nosa Señora do Mar on a typical Sunday, but that was more than might have been expected. Those who attended reported that two chairs had to be put together to accommodate Father Infante's bulk and that he suffered from a speech impediment causing him to drop his "l's" and "d's," so that he pronounced *mea culpa* as *mea cupa* and *Dóminus vobíscum* with unintended portentousness as *óminous vobíscum*. In his sermon he stated that his mission was to shore up the faith of the people in the town and reform those who lived on the mountain.

"I am aware of the old ways practiced in this region and must strongly assert their depravity. Where ignorance and superstition reign must shine the light of God's Scripture."

When he spoke, he had the habit of pausing frequently and looking at the ground as if searching it for the right words. Then a sentence would emerge with the effect of having been produced by deep thought, no matter how commonplace the content.

Father Infante believed all actions are either in concert with God's will or opposed to it, and the Church has the prerogative of determining which are among the former and which the latter—and this authority could not be compromised without compromising the spiritual well-being of his parishioners. Indirectly alluding to Bachiario, he went on to say that any attempt to wrest this power away from the Archbishop's representative was contrary to the will of God. To enforce his authority, he did not hesitate to invoke the certain torment of eternal fire for those who failed to heed his warnings.

For Bachiario, who believed the attempt to understand, and conform to, God's will was the purpose of each soul, the tactical leverage Father Infante employed to enhance his grip on the community was nothing short of spiritual extortion. At the same time, he was seeing his own authority diminish—and he was growing tired of sleeping on a cot behind a curtain of blankets in the alcove of Santiago. When Facundo reported that several dozen people had attended Father Infante's Mass on Sunday, Bachiario decided to act. To reassert his authority, he would appeal not to the congregation nor to Don Andrés nor any other human agency, but rather directly to the will of God. In our religion class he had once spoken of the life of Savonarola and described the scene on the piazza in Florence on a Saturday afternoon in April 1498 when Fra Domenico Buonvicini da Pescia had stood between two rows of timber knowing the only thing that would prevent him from dying in the black smoke when those rows were lit would be the miraculous intervention of God. He had willingly, even enthusiastically, exposed himself to such a death to validate the teachings of his master. As another example of the strength of faith that would lead someone to risk everything for his beliefs, Bachiario hung a framed print on the wall above the blackboard depicting Francisco de Asís's trial by fire. So the challenge he devised to settle this dispute did not surprise us.

Before presenting his proposal to Father Infante, Bachiario retreated to his shepherd's cabin on the mountain to prepare himself spiritually for what lay ahead. When he returned to Porto Lúa several days later, his face was half-shadowed by a rough flannel cowl, and he looked half-starved. Rather than burn with enmity, his eyes were glazed with contentment. Acting as his emissary, Facundo appeared at the rectory to arrange a meeting with the priest just as Father Infante was sitting down to his veal tenderloin and a glass of his favorite Mencía.

"Your presence is requested, Your Reverence."

"By whom?"

"Bachiario."

"What does he want?"

"He would like to discuss a proposal with you."

"I am going to finish my dinner, and then I'm going to read and go to bed. If he is in Porto Lúa in the morning, I will have time to meet with him. But not before then. Do you understand?"

"Yes, Your Reverence."

"Where is he now?"

"In Nosa Señora do Mar. Holding a vigil."

"A vigil? For what?"

"Purification."

"Tell him I'll be there in the morning."

Father Infante said the six-thirty Mass at Santa Lupa and ate breakfast as a bright sun cleared Mount Aracelo and appeared in his kitchen window. He could not have guessed how much his life was about to change. When Rosa arrived to do the laundry, he persuaded her to accompany him to the church because he wanted someone else present at the meeting. As they walked around the corner of the building and down the short path to the church, she warned him of the magical powers of Bachiario, but the priest dismissed her comments as the product of an uneducated mind. Upon entering the church, however, and seeing Bachiario for the first time, he grew slightly apprehensive. Bathed in the light of stained glass, the hooded figure knelt motionless on the step of the sanctuary. When he heard footsteps on the stone floor behind him, he stood and turned to Father Infante and without greeting him began to speak.

"You have questioned my faith," he said.

"Not your faith, but the lack of orthodoxy in your worship. The people of this parish are Christians, and those who provide examples of worship contrary to Christian teaching are risking their souls."

"I am confident in the state of my soul. And I am willing to test my faith against yours."

"I am not interested in contests. God does not play games."

"We'll find out whose faith is stronger by walking through a corridor of fire. You and I."

"I'll not test God with such foolishness."

"You will or you will lose these people."

"And you will be excommunicated."

"Your bishops might as well shoot their arrows at the moon."

Dismissing the proposal as more evidence that Bachiario was unfit to lead the people, Father Infante went back to the rectory and worked on his Sunday sermon. For naught. The next morning in Capela de Santa Lupa not a single person apart from Father Infante was present. After the service, he asked Rosa why no one was there.

"Bachiario said Mass in Nosa Señora do Mar while you were still asleep. He has convinced people that he is the rightful pastor of Porto Lúa. They resent your criticism of the old ways and think you should take up his challenge to prove who is right. His words are like rain, Father. They refresh the hearts of those who hear them. Yours fall on them like snow."

Later in the day, he decided to consult with Don Andrés and found him sitting with Gustavo at a table outside O Galo. In his initial comments, he wavered between appealing to the mayor to find some sort of compromise and demanding the respect his position in the Church deserved. He told them the proposal was an offense to God and a contest of immolation a barbarity of demonic proportions.

"I don't disagree with you," Don Andrés responded, "but if you won't agree to prove your faith, the people will not believe you are a representative of God."

"This is madness. As I told Bachiario, God is not interested in such games."

"That may be true. You know more about God than I do, but I know the people of Porto Lúa, and if you are unwilling to show them the strength of your faith, they will not return to your Mass, and you will have failed in your duties. Have you heard of Saint Savonarola?"

"What about him?"

"Bachiario said he was executed because he failed to undertake a test of faith."

"Savonarola wasn't a saint. He was a heretic. I will not imitate the actions of a heretic. God's power is not meant to be used as a trick. It is sacrilegious to assume He will perform a miracle to satisfy petty quarrels among His faithful. Miracles are signs of God's munificence and not to be demanded or expected by vain believers."

"But Francisco de Asís was no heretic, and he walked through fire to prove to the Moors that he practiced the one true religion."

"Is that correct?"

"According to Bachiario."

"I will have to look into this. If it's true that San Francisco walked through fire, then I will have to consider the matter more carefully."

"Remember, Father, this business will never go that far. If you call his bluff, you may be done with him for once and for all."

That thought must have stayed with Father Infante as he weighed his options and prayed for guidance. To act was to embrace his vocation. To fail to act was to deny his vocation. To act was to maintain his congregation. To fail to act was to lose his congregation. And while to act would be to risk death, to fail to act would be to fail to live, if life is the fulfillment of one's purpose. To save his congregation was not merely his vocation; it was a spiritual imperative. He had a mandate, not just from the Church, but from God Himself, to eradicate the old ways. The question was whether this mandate was cause enough for God to intervene to save him from the fire. If it was, the story of his miraculous salvation would circulate, and he would be respected as a living saint. But there was also the possibility that God might allow him to die in the flames to punish him for his pride in presuming he might be saved.

Two assurances convinced him he could accept the challenge. The first was that Bachiario was not insane and would not walk through fire. Don Andrés was right. He should call his bluff. The second was that the Archbishop would never allow him to participate in such a contest. So on Monday morning he walked to the town hall and informed Don Andrés he would accept Bachiario's proposal. He listened to the terms of the agreement and nodded his approval without comment: he would not wear vestments that had been blessed, carry holy water or a crucifix, or take Communion within twenty-four hours of the event. The course would run for twenty yards between two rows of combustible timber rising to a height of four feet and doused with kerosene. Neither participant could proceed faster than a normal walk. And finally, the event would take place on the following Sunday at eight o'clock in the evening.

When he returned to the rectory, Father Infante wrote a letter to the Archbishop explaining what he was being required to do in order to win over the wayward souls of the region and added that if His Excellency disapproved of such public exhibitions, he would defer to his judgment, but his superior would do well to send his disapproval by return post as the event was scheduled to take place in less than a week. Two days later he received a letter from a Monsignor Combarro saying this contest was the result of Father Infante's failure to take his pastoral duties seriously and visit the villages of the mountain. There was no mention of whether the Archbishop disapproved of the event. In the meantime, cartloads of timber cut from the mountain were quickly building up the corridor of fire in the plaza. People were even betting that due to their differences in body type, Bachiario would make it through the gauntlet of fire and Father Infante, with his laborious gait, would not. They said that even if his faith was not an impediment, his girth was. And they agreed with Bachiario when he said that if Father made it through the fire, he would respect God's will and instruct people to return to church.

Perplexed by the lack of a direct response to his offer to forgo the trial of fire, Father Infante wrote back to the Archbishop, addressing the envelope with the words "personal" and "urgent." There were four days to go before the event, and the last response had taken two. His agitation increased over the next two days and was only alleviated when Facundo ran up the walk with a letter in his hand. It was from the same monsignor, and it once again alluded to the need for a "more devoted ministry," but this time the monsignor chastised him emphatically for allowing the situation to get out of hand and urged him not to waste any more time on "vulgar spectacles" but rather to attend to his pastoral duties among the people of the mountain. Father wrote back immediately saying he could devote more time to saving the souls in the villages if the Archbishop would deny him permission to engage in the ordeal that faced him. In concluding, he pointed out there was no mail on Sundays, so an immediate response to his letter was essential.

By Saturday the preparations were nearly complete. In the plaza, running from north to south, were two parallel rows of timber approximately six feet apart. At the end of each row was a large barrel of water to be used in the event the life of either party could be saved. All around the plaza vendors had set up their stalls. There was every imaginable bread and confection, steaming pots of octopi, hand-crafted birdcages, baskets of horn buttons, porcupine brushes, hand-stitched boots with wooden soles, fried dough pastries, plastic handbags, straw hats, and tin jewelry. A man in a djellaba selling brass platters and teapots could have been the twin of Father Ithacio. Beside him stood the guardians of the alameda, Señor Morcín with his box camera and Xosé de Arcos with his wooden cart of fresh fruit. In the meantime crowds of people had begun to arrive from as far away as Malpica anticipating the immolation of at least one of the priests. Their children mixed with the locals, playing hide and seek and crawling under the tables of vendors. At low tide some went down to the beach to swim. Father Infante stayed in the rectory composing himself with wine and praying the letter forbidding him to walk through the fire might arrive in time, but as the afternoon turned into evening, there was still no word from Santiago. In his careless

thoughts he must have wondered if the Archbishop was deliberately ignoring him, and as he went deeper into the bottle of
wine, he may have even asked himself if he was being allowed
to die as a martyr for his faith.

On Sunday morning, when Aunt Fioxilda woke to the silence of larks, she assumed the spirit world was anticipating
the arrival of a new soul. Bachiario said Mass in Nosa Señora
do Mar, but Father Infante remained in the rectory until late
afternoon. Over the objections of mother, who called the affair
an affront to God, father and I went to the plaza to witness the
scene. He said it would be good for me to see the extremes to
which religious zealotry can take people. I don't believe he expected either man to die; rather, he was curious to discover
how they would back out of the trial at the last minute. Despite
the two wooden coffins leaning up against the wall of the alameda, Bachiario walked through the swelling crowd speaking
to people and appearing to enjoy the festive atmosphere. Carpenters were putting the finishing touches on a platform
where the ceremony would begin as two Africans wearing knit
caps and overcoats walked among the patrons of O Galo selling
wind-up dogs, rugs, and the antidotes to poisonous mush-
rooms. One of them claimed he could see the thoughts of people and for a small fee would reveal what they were. More vendors who followed the circuit of religious festivals from Portugal to Asturias arrived to fill the empty spaces around the plaza
with their booths and tables selling silk reproductions of the
veronica of Christ and rosaries carved from the *oliveiras* of
Gethsemane. Following in the wake of the caravan of vendors
came itinerant beggars who stationed themselves beside the
tables serving food, while in the middle of the plaza, a Romani
horseman wearing a feather headdress led children around the
Tower of Names on an Indian pony for fifty céntimos.

The men of Porto Lúa gathered in O Galo to listen to an
accordion player evoke bittersweet memories of the past with

a repertoire of pre-war tangos. Drinking *la fée verte* to ease the pain of his gout, Fausto Sarria told an incredulous audience he had seen Father Infante bathing in the sea at midnight. Not to be outdone, Xosé Carrillo claimed to have seen Bachiario walking with the Santa Compaña. At his feet, lapping at a bowl of wine, was his pig Hierónimo. Like many people in Porto Lúa, he bought a piglet late in winter, raised it in the spring and summer, and slaughtered it in the fall. He lived alone and kept it in the house as his companion, feeding it everything he did not eat. As fall approached, he would begin taking it to O Galo in the evenings, and, when he ordered a cup of wine, he asked for a bowl for the pig as well. Standing beside him, its belly resting on the floor, the creature slurped up the wine with relish. After several weeks of such indulgence, Xosé would take it to a neighbor's yard, hoist it on a granite post, and cut its throat. Then he would make sausages and smoke the ham to last through the next year. The wine, he said, gave the meat a special flavor.

When a Portuguese sailor by the name of Jerónimo Espinho, who had been drinking *aguardiente* all afternoon, took offense at the animal's presence, Xosé explained that Hierónimo was well behaved and only shit outside. Taking this as an insult where none was intended, the sailor struck Xosé across the jaw, which caused the pig to bite the sailor on the ankle and break loose from its tether wrapped around the railing of the bar. As Hierónimo knocked over benches and patrons, men attempted to corral the pig, but the animal crashed through the tables and chairs placed in its way and into the panicked crowd in the plaza. People retreated to stairs and doorways as the beast turned one way and then another, bewildered by its freedom. Dragging its belly over the stones, it trotted toward the pony, then veered off and crept under a table stacked with aniseed pastries. Coming out on the other side, it headed toward a circle of men behind the market who had set up a cockfighting pit sending several birds flying into the air. When one of them came down on the back of the pig, digging its metal spur into the animal's haunch, Hierónimo bolted back across the plaza, upsetting the table where the women of the lacemakers' guild were selling scarves and shawls, and stormed down the corridor of timber scattering the brush at the far end before running up Rúa das Angustias with Xosé close behind. Cut off by the Romani's trailer, the pig entered the alameda and, when finally cornered, forced its way through the stone balustrade and into thin air, plunging, as if from the sky, to meet its death on the stones of the plaza.

For a moment the crowd was silent. Then Aunt Fioxilda, who realized this was the death foretold by the larks, shouted, "Neither man will die today."

Falling in glittering arcs, a series of fireworks suddenly lit the darkening sky. Before the last was out, a deafening series of explosions boomed overhead echoing like thunder in the granite valleys of the mountain. Beneath a colorful snow of shredded paper and the smoke of black powder, Fanfarrias began to march down Rúa dos Santos playing a bolero while the Gallardo brothers entered the plaza from the opposite side playing a *muiñeira* followed by Leandro Feijoo cranking a hurdy-gurdy. The music blended like saltwater and freshwater into a general din as Don Andrés, Bachiario, and the newly arrived Father Infante mounted the platform. People pressed against a rope barricade surrounding the rows of timber. More were hanging out their windows and standing on the stairs leading up to the alameda. There were even children in the trees.

After taking a moment to confer with the priests, Don Andrés raised his hands to quiet the crowd. Once he had their attention, he turned to the participants and read the following statement:

"You are concealing no ostensorium, no ciborium, no

reliquary on your person. You are wearing no object blessed by a member of the clergy higher than a bishop. You are carrying no holy water nor cruciform object. You are clothed in no article upon which divine protection has been conferred. Do you avow the truth of these statements before God?"

"I do."

"I do."

Someone in the crowd shouted, "Now that they're married, light the fire."

Still hoping for an eleventh-hour reprieve, Father Infante maneuvered to delay the proceedings a little longer. Leaning in to Don Andrés, he said he had reason to believe Bachiario was hiding a secret amulet or magic potion on his person. Bachiario willingly complied with a brief search and then asked that Father Infante undergo a similar inspection. When both men's concerns had been satisfied and no spiritual advantages had been found, Don Andrés addressed the participants in a loud voice, saying, "You may now proceed to state your case before God and the people. Who would like to go first?"

Without waiting for a response from his opponent, Father Infante began.

"It is fitting that I have the joy of addressing you this blessed day commemorating the life of one of the greatest saints of the Church, Francisco de Asís, who was willing to walk through fire to prove his faith to the Sultan of Egypt. I think too of the saints in heaven who died by fire: Santa Inés of Rome, San Fructuoso, San Eulogio, San Augurio, San Policarpo, and consider myself a humble follower of such brave examples. It was San Policarpo who said to his tormenter that the fire of this world burns but briefly while the fire of God burns forever. Better a thousand times a thousand to burn in the fire of billets and coals than to renounce one's faith and burn beyond the Day of Judgment. So I am here, in the names of Francisco, Inés, Fructuoso, Eulogio, Augurio, Policarpo, and all the saints who gave their lives for the one true God, to lead those who remain in a bondage of error, who live every day of their lives on the brink of everlasting damnation, to lead them, I say, to the salvation and comfort of God's teaching. I claim the authority of the Church and Archbishop Quiroga y Palacios, who sent me to this remote and caliginous region full of cloud and Cimmerian gloom, into the darkness of superstition and heresy, where the orthodoxy of God's word is still in doubt, to bring its people into the fellowship of our Lord and Savior and banish the contagion of their ancient fears and false beliefs. Because perfection admits no flaw, these sins of ignorance, sins that resemble thorns of death in the body of God's love, end the life, the hope, the eternal glory of the soul. On this day, therefore, I reaffirm my faith in God our Father and humbly beg His mercy in showing us His will through the preservation of my life in this test of faith."

In his response, Bachiario set his eyes on the faces in the crowd, though he directed his words to his adversary.

"You subscribe to a limited, monolithic understanding of God because you have no understanding of your own. You have invested nothing of yourself in your beliefs. You were taught them by others. But the experience of God requires the direct experience of His creation, the opening of one's imagination to the multifarious nature of His truth. How else do we appreciate and come to love our Father? Without the imagination, there is no religion. Without the imagination, there is no faith, no love, no charity. Only the barren facts of a mechanical worship. Catholicism is more than a religion, and a religion is more than a narrow system of beliefs. Its catechism is the natural world, not rules. Each soul must have the freedom to worship in its own way. Like the creatures of the fields and sky."

"We are not creatures of the field and sky," responded Father Infante, "but beings created in the image and likeness of

God. And the unguided imagination is more prone to evil than to good. I have been told you drag goats through the streets of this town and encourage pagan practices by the members of its congregation. You have performed false miracles on the altar, claiming God's power as your own. You have made a pact with the devil to wield his iniquitous power over the innocent and simple-minded."

"What makes you think your power conferred by books and titles is superior to that conferred directly by God?"

"I don't claim anything for myself. The powers at my command are not my own. I save the souls of the faithful as a pastor and have been given the tools of salvation by the authority of God's one true Church."

"There are as many forms of worship, as many truths, as there are souls in this world."

"The only enlightenment is the enlightenment of scripture. The Truth. The Good. The Word of God. There are not many truths. There is but the single Truth of God."

"Your truth."

"The Truth of God."

"Of the Church."

"The Church is the ministry of God in this world."

"The individual soul is the seat of God in this world. He made us all different so we could understand him differently according to our different natures, not according to the nature of any one priest or even of a conclave of musty ecclesiastics cloistered in their narrow interpretations of life."

"Two thousand years of Christ's Church shows you are wrong."

"Two thousand years of Christ's Church according to the false prophets and Pharisees. Two thousand years of more and more rules and prohibitions meant to tighten their grip on the oppressed and stifle any creative encounter with their Maker. Two thousand years of divine authority usurped by the self-appointed keepers of God's kingdom."

"Christ himself gave Peter the keys of heaven."

"And his successors built palaces and collected art at the expense of the impoverished souls who gave their last lire and francs and pesetas to pay for this opulence. Why do you wear expensive robes from abroad?"

"Because I represent God."

"Christ represented His Father, not the tailors of Rome. He welcomed the people and didn't withdraw to a well-appointed home and well-stocked larder."

"We can't be exactly like Christ because the times are different."

"In what way are you like Christ?"

"I am celibate. I have given up union with a woman."

"Not by choice."

"Yes, by choice."

"But you haven't given up food."

"Food is necessary for sustenance. And like Aristotle's Milo, God made me to need more."

From the back of the crowd, someone shouted, "Gluttony is one of the deadly sins."

"There is a place for you in hell," Father Infante responded.

"Not if your fat ass gets there first."

"Enough," shouted Don Andrés as he raised his arms to quiet the crowd. "This is a solemn occasion before God. Two men of the cloth are putting their faiths to the ultimate test."

As the mayor spoke, Father Arias, who had just arrived from Santiago, pushed his way through the crowd to hand Father Infante a letter. Embossed on the envelope were the words *Pazo de Xelmírez*, the home of the Archbishop. Father Infante opened it with trembling hands and read aloud, "His Excellency esteems your pastoral service to the Church these many years and bestows his blessings on you and your congregation. May God's love be with you."

"Tell me, Father, did you speak with the Archbishop on this matter?"

"Briefly."

"What were his words?"

"In what respect?"

"On the sanctity of the cause."

"He didn't mention it."

"Does he approve?"

"He communicated to me his opinion that you are a soldier of Christ."

"I see."

"And that God has a plan for you."

"And willfully chosen death as an act of faith—might it be considered a suicide and therefore a mortal sin or does the intention purify the act and make it rather martyrdom?"

"If you contravene God's will, it would be a suicide. If you conform to it, it would be martyrdom."

"But what is God's will?"

"Only prayer can answer that."

Father Infante then turned to Don Andrés.

"How will the outcomes of the trial be interpreted and by whom?"

"Any outcome must be considered the dispensation of divine Providence," said Bachiario. "It is His prerogative to take us in any manner He chooses, and His judgment is not to be parsed. The fact is all that matters."

By this point it was well after eight o'clock. Darkness had crept down the *rúas* and alleys of the town, and only a bluish-white glow remained on the clouds in the sky above the open plaza. When the lights of the alameda came on, their orange filaments carved faces out of the shadows, distorting them with bright color and harsh contrasts. Cotolay later claimed he could see flames surrounding the priest as if his soul was already on fire. Through the speeches and discussions, Father

Infante had succeeded in drawing the proceedings out longer than anyone had expected. People had been waiting to see the trial all day, and, sensing their unrest, Don Andrés finally called for the timbers to be prepared. Each member of the crew carried two buckets of kerosene and was responsible for roughly twenty feet of one row. As they poured the contents of the buckets over the wood, Doctor Romalde, Sister Mary Rose, and Sister Benigna took their places at the end of the corridor with blankets that had been soaked with water.

Visibly affected by the kerosene fumes, Don Andrés gave each man a moment to pray and then covered his nose and mouth with his handkerchief. When the priests signaled they were ready, the mayor's only words were, "Let these walls of fire reveal the fate God has prepared for you." People held their children over their heads and approached the timbers so closely that Constable Sampaio had to push them back from the places where kerosene had pooled on the stone. Don Andrés lit a ceremonial torch made of tightly wrapped birch bark, but, fearing divine reprisals for his participation, handed it to Cotolay because, as an *inocente*, he could light the timbers without fault. As the torch flared against the darkness, Cotolay paused for a moment to watch an enormous crane fly overhead and land in a chestnut tree like a messenger from heaven. When he lowered the torch to touch the kindling in the row on his right, nothing happened. He inserted the flame below an arch of branches, but, again, nothing happened. Father Infante moaned and dropped to the platform. Cotolay tried the row on his left, but with no more success. Don Andrés took the torch from him and walked down the corridor touching it here and there on the piles still damp with kerosene. But still nothing happened. Cotolay looked around wildly and then ran the gauntlet with his arms raised, shouting, "*Un milagre! Un milagre!*"

The accordion player returned to his tangos serenading the

crowds as they set off for their homes. Those from villages on the coast or dwellers on the mountain bedded down in doorways and on benches in the alameda. Father Infante, who had been revived by Sister Benigna, sat on the stones between the rows of timber that had failed to light—in the very place where he had envisioned his death. As charcoal burners from the mountain hauled the wood away on oxcarts, he spoke to himself, lost in the mystery of his inscrutable fate.

"I am here because I was abandoned by the Archbishop, but God in His mercy has intervened to preserve my life. Only He knows how I have struggled to defend the faith and proclaim the teachings of the Church. If I have failed at that task, it is because my superiors have failed me. Because of them I have been reduced to this barbarous theater for the amusement of others. They sent me to this desolate place where they knew I could not succeed, where no one has ever succeeded, where, after two thousand years, Christ's teaching has had little effect on the pagan customs of these people. When they hear the story of my humiliation in the Archbishop's palace, they will drink their expensive wine and have a good laugh."

María Dolores took him a stool from her shop. Dr. Romalde checked his pulse and gave him a piece of chocolate to boost his blood sugar. Before locking O Galo, Gustavo took him a coat and a bowl of *caldo*, but he declined both the coat and the soup. And there he sat beneath the stars and falling dew. Early the next morning María Dolores left him a bottle of carbonated water and an earthen pot for his needs, which he attended to discreetly beneath his robe. Later in the afternoon, a child placed her doll in his lap as Madame Zafirah watched through her curtains. Day turned to night, night to day, and day to night, and still he sat, eating nothing, saying nothing. Then it began to rain. And went on raining. For two days and nights. He accepted an umbrella from Rosa, but remained where he sat. The dyes bled from his robe. Crescents of silt formed around the heels of his boots. A stray dog sheltered beneath his stool. Then the rain stopped. People passed on their way to work. Sparrows foraged at his feet. Red and yellow leaves fell from the autumn trees and rested on his head and shoulders. Then, on the tenth night of his vigil, in the hours before dawn, a bright light descended over the plaza and remained for several minutes. Cotolay saw it. So did several fishermen. No one knew what it was. Except Father Infante. By the time the sun was up, he had returned to the rectory.

Bachiario was already gone. On the morning after the trial by fire, he had retrieved his mule from Campo da Graza and his mastiff from Facundo who was taking care of it. Rosa opened the door to the rectory, and he filled two canvas bags with his possessions. I helped him secure the bags on his mule and walked with him up the path that led to his cabin. On the way, I asked him why he was leaving.

"I was never content within the confines of a church," he said. "Some people feel the presence of the divine in the shadows of a sanctuary or in the colored light of glass, but I need more than that. My church is the open sky. The columns of pines. The fonts of natural springs. For me God is not to be found in a box of stone. That is where we place our corpses, not where we find eternal life."

"What will you do now?"

"I'll do what I did before. I'll take care of my herd."

Halfway up the path, I stopped and said goodbye. He shook my hand and told me to visit him, and then continued his climb toward the meadows in the clouds where he found the spiritual fulfillment that eluded him among the streets and houses of Porto Lúa.

Though still weak from his ordeal and twenty pounds lighter, Father Infante said his first Mass at Nosa Señora do Mar the following Sunday. In his sermon he admitted he had taken the wrong approach to the spiritual needs of the people and vowed to address those needs with humility and compassion. Refusing the monthly stipend that came with his position, he would grow his own food in the rectory garden and gather his own firewood for the stove. This, however, would not prevent him from accepting tithes from the congregation as well as food and tools for his garden. He concluded by announcing he would be gone for a brief period in order to preach to the people on the mountain, not because this was his responsibility to the Church, but because it was his responsibility to those who lived there.

In preparation for his journey, Rosa made him a new pair of trousers and a new shirt to fit his diminished frame while Facundo found two mules to rent for a modest sum. The night before he was scheduled to leave, Father Infante convinced Facundo, whose family was from the eastern side of the mountain, to accompany him. As they sat in the kitchen of the rectory, the priest asked about the villages and churches he could expect to find and learned in greater detail of the poverty and waywardness of the people.

"Are there lodgings?"

"No. Nothing of the sort unless you are comfortable in the loft of a barn."

"There must be churches."

"There's a small church near Lonxe do Sol, a chapel at the shrine of Santa Locaia, and a grotto carved into the rock at Onde se Adora."

"They'll do."

"They're not what you might expect."

"Never mind that."

The next morning Father Infante collected an altar cloth and cutlery stored at the rectory as well as old candlesticks and a crucifix from the sacristy of Nosa Señora do Mar, and while looking for a box of unconsecrated hosts and a bottle of communion wine, he discovered a slightly tarnished silver chalice and an old ciborium decorated with images of the Last Supper.

The articles to be used in the Mass he placed in one large basket, and the altar cloth, together with a leather valise containing his vestments and a change of clothes, in another. When Facundo arrived, he fastened the baskets together with a leather strap, hoisted them onto one of the mules, and secured them with another strap under its belly. Then he led the second mule to a stone mounting block next to the rectory where Father Infante climbed onto the animal's back, but as he did, it lowered its hind quarters, and he slid to the ground to be struck in the face by the creature's tail. After the priest's second attempt to mount the animal failed, Facundo decided it would be better to take the mules back and borrow an oxcart. When he returned a short time later, we loaded the baskets onto the bed of the cart and wedged a large cushion from the rectory between them so Father Infante would have a comfortable place to sit.

Because Sister Benigna and Sister Mary Rose had gone to Santiago to find a teacher to replace Bachiario, school was suspended for the week, and when Father Infante told my parents he needed an acolyte to help with Mass, I was allowed to accompany him. We set out through the back gate of the churchyard and crossed Campo da Graza to the winding lane that passes behind Casa das Flores to meet the Roman road. As the cart creaked slowly up the mountain over one stone at a time, Father Infante rocked back and forth on the cushion between the baskets extemporizing on the health benefits of fresh air and the quality of sunlight on the coast. Facundo held the slack steering rope attached to the halter of the ox, and I walked beside him. His right leg was slightly shorter than his left, and to compensate for the difference, he wore a makeshift extension on the bottom of his boot which caused him to have an awkward gait as we climbed over the uneven granite of the road. He had blue eyes and light brown hair and was so thin the end of his belt, which was pulled tight to the last notch, hung loose by at least a foot and his pants still appeared to be falling down. The several teeth he was missing and the creases in his face from drink and black tobacco, caused him to appear older than his age.

After the heavy rains of the previous week, the ruts in the road had become trickling streams of silver reflecting the noon light. Metallic green dragonflies hovered over stagnant pools in the smooth hollows of stones while along the side of the road blue short-tailed butterflies fluttered over yellow-tipped fennel and purple loosestrife. Coming up from the sea on a light breeze, the scent of brine mingled with those of pine and eucalyptus and wet earth. Though the day was warm, leaves were falling from the trees, and there was a general lethargy in the air. We passed the stretch of road where Baltasar had collapsed and after more than two hours came to the path that leads to the tree of evil. Where the road curves and offers a panoramic view of the Deva gorge and bay of Porto Lúa, Harry had stacked flat stones as a resting place for travelers and set up several of his stone windows to frame the views.

When we stopped for our midday meal beside a boulder overlooking the valley, Father Infante, who by now was wearing a handkerchief on his head, advised us that one should never eat in direct sunlight, so we continued a few hundred yards up the road until we came to the thin shade of a pine grove where we spread a blanket over the ground among the cones and needles before sitting down to eat some of the tuna *empanada* we had brought with us. Within a few minutes we were joined by a group of five pilgrims who had walked all the way from Bierzo. They were surprised to discover a priest riding in an oxcart and concluded that Porto Lúa must be a very backward place. We assured them it was not and they would find all the amenities they would need if they inquired at O Galo when they arrived.

"Where did you spend last night?" Father Infante asked.

"In a bothy up the road," one of the women replied. "But I wouldn't recommend it as the place is haunted."

"Just as we were going to sleep," said another, "a ghostly woman appeared out of the forest and disappeared just as quickly as she came."

"Mother Ambages," said Facundo.

"Who?"

"Mother Ambages. Patron of the winding paths. Everybody knows her. You only see her when you least expect to—standing quietly in the woods or sitting near your fire waiting for you to sleep. When the wind whispers in the pines, when the crow flies, when the field mouse makes its nest, Mother Ambages is there. She feeds the birds when there is snow on the mountain. She plants new trees when there is fire."

"Have you ever seen her in Porto Lúa?" asked Father Infante.

"Not for a long time."

When Facundo took a moment to roll a cigarette, we knew to wait for the rest of the story.

"Many years ago people would see her in the streets and alleys at night or in the alameda or in the fields and orchards on the hillside behind Porto Lúa. She wore old rags tied around her feet, a scarf of discarded cloth on her head, and an oilcloth cape on her shoulders to keep them dry in the rain. People said she lived in an abandoned watermill on the mountain and would come to town to look after the wild creatures that had strayed from the forest. Some remember seeing her on rainy days taking shelter under the balcony of a house or walking through the market or sitting beside a grave in the cemetery, but I never did. I don't believe she has the needs that others have.

"At this time there was a woman in Porto Lúa by the name of Suzzain Sutania who had the power to cast spells, and she used it to intimidate people and even extort money when she needed it. She had been widowed at an early age and in her youth had taken several lovers. Because they had all perished at sea or in accidents, she was thought to have made covenants with the darkness to dispose of them. With age came bitterness, and increasingly she dwelt in the pit of her anger. The hair on her head grew like black wires and her face was covered with wens and warts like the skin of a dry gourd. Her mouth was drawn in a tight death smirk, which gave her the appearance of a shrunken head. And her breath was so foul it caused the leaves on trees to curl and fall. Rumors circulated that she practiced sorcery in a stone circle on the headland and at night raised her skirts and walked through fields to poison the harvest. Simple-minded people claimed she could steal the souls of children, hear every word uttered about her, and cast shadows she had collected into daylit streets to make them as dark as night. In the pocket of her waistband, she carried bones and garlic and hair and bay leaves to guard against the curses of others, an occupational hazard in a battle secretly waged.

"Although she lacked the power to make a river run backward or turn a person into an animal, she could cast the evil eye, and when a child was listless and had no appetite, the people who paid her to remove the spell often suspected she was its source. For a fee she would tell a man the secrets of women or diagnose a person's infirmity by tasting a drop of blood. Once when a young woman paid her to add a gray hair to her fiancé's head every time he uttered the name of another woman, the man paid her to take the spell off and cast it on the woman every time she became jealous. The woman soon looked twice her age and was abandoned by her fiancé. Such spells we could have lived with, but she went too far with the drought. When the fields were parched one summer, she claimed to have predicted it, which caused people to believe she caused it. Whether she did or not didn't matter. What did matter was that she eventually tried to use the drought to extort some payment. The scars from her years of battle with her adversaries in the dark arts had hardened her heart and made her resist any appeal that did not include money. From that pit within herself she excavated enough anger to take pleasure in the hardships and suffering of others.

"When Father Ithacio attempted to intervene, she cast a spell on him so that every time he spoke Latin, the words came out as lewd propositions, which made it impossible to celebrate Mass. For protection against her spells, people slept with laurel under their beds and spread it through their fields. After weeks of drought, the public fountains went dry, and those who had no wells were forced to walk to the Deva with buckets several times a day in order to drink and bathe, but then she turned its water brackish, and they had to climb the mountain in search of springs. No one wanted to confront her directly after what she did to Father Ithacio, but one night someone nailed a dead rat to the lintel over her door. The rat was gone by morning, and word spread that she had used it in one of her spells. The tide of public opinion turned to a demand for action. Led by the father of Don Andrés, the town elders decided to pay her to revoke her spells, but she said they had come too late and the money wasn't enough, so they sent a delegation up the mountain to search for Mother Ambages. Appealing to her on behalf of the wildlife threatened by the drought, they convinced her to intercede in their dispute and counter the malevolence of their adversary with charms of her own.

"The first thing Mother Ambages did after arriving was to freshen the water of the Deva. And though she couldn't make the clouds rain, she did make numerous springs appear and overflow at the foot of the mountain to water the fields. Suzzain Sutania countered by covering the fields with bad seeds which were meant to sprout and choke off the crops with a jungle of weeds, but Mother Ambages roused an army of mice to eat the seeds. In response, Suzzain Sutania conjured up a herd of cats to devour the mice, but as soon as she did, Mother Ambages called down a flock of eagles from the mountain to drive the cats away. The back and forth of move and counter-move went on for weeks, until, thwarted, Suzzain Sutania retired to her house in the woods."

"What happened to her then?"

"No one knows. She was never seen again. The house is still there, but it is covered in vines and the windows are broken. For a year or two her neighbors claimed they saw lights in the windows at night, but I never saw them. Perhaps she is still there. Perhaps she left. Perhaps she died. Once the natural order had been restored, Mother Ambages returned to the mountain where people still see her from time to time walking through the meadows or climbing sure-footed over the winding paths through the oak and chestnut forests."

After lunch, the pilgrims received Father Infante's blessing and continued their journey down the mountain toward Porto Lúa and Mar das Almas while we continued on our course toward Lonxe do Sol. I had forgotten most of the landmarks I had seen on my first ascent several years earlier and wasn't sure how much farther we had to go to reach Lonxe, but I enjoyed the company of Facundo who passed the time telling stories from his endless repertoire accompanied by fanciful gestures and exaggerated expressions as Father Infante sat on his cushion humming to himself. I learned that he was born in the village of Suevos and that shortly after he was married, he and his bride left the village to live in Porto Lúa, but times were hard, and when they couldn't make ends meet, she went to work as a domestic in France and never returned. He tried his hand at fishing, but was prone to seasickness, then failed as a mason's apprentice, a carpenter, a baker, and a waiter. As an indigent dependent on the parish, he was given the job of sexton at a small salary if he promised to live a life of temperance.

"I tried," he said, laughing, "but some things aren't meant

to be."

The ascent took longer than it would have if we had been walking without the oxcart, and the day was coming to a close as we reached the bothy. It was an old barn at the edge of an abandoned village sheltered from the wind by a bluff whose granite ribs stood out like a gallery of statues in the façade of a church defaced by time. Through the branches of the trees that had already lost their leaves, we could see the remnants of a few stone houses and a few acres of meadow that had once provided arable land for the village but were now covered by deep grass and volunteer fruit trees. The barn had been maintained better than the houses. The walls were still standing, and it had a wooden door that still shut. Its roof, though mostly intact, rested precariously on a single central beam, essentially the trunk of a pine tree, that held up four rafters supporting a crosshatch of slats upon which the pantiles lay—except for the gaps where they had fallen through. A frying pan and scorched teapot sat in a dry corner, and next to the door was a shovel to dig a latrine. A basket containing a tin of salt and dried cod hung from a thin chain in the middle of the room. Below it were benches made of rough planks and worm-eaten stumps. Lying beside a circle of blackened stones serving as a hearth, were stacks of dry firewood, and crowded around it, pine bed frames webbed with windowpane netting rising several inches off the ground. As Facundo built a fire and Father Infante gathered fresh ferns and grass for the beds, I went off to collect water from a stream that ran beside the village. Although the sun had just set over the Atlantic, the light reflecting off the clouds was enough for me to make my way through the piles of fallen stones that still bore traces of soot and fill the pot in a mill race where the water flowed with a strong current. Saving the rest of the empanada for another day, we ate a dinner of boiled rice, cheese, chestnuts, and watercress that I found in the stream. After dinner we sat by the fire listening to more of

Facundo's stories and then threw blankets over the fern beds and went to sleep.

The next morning the mountain was covered by a cold fog. As Facundo yoked the ox, I wandered among the foundations of the houses and discovered, of all things, a rusted anchor with one fluke buried in the earth and the other rising to my height. In the ivy-covered rubble of one of the houses lay a long rectangular stone crudely inscribed with the date 1315. There too, I found a piece of iron that Father Infante called a Roman nail. We ate a breakfast of bread and honey as we walked up the road through a gray mist that dripped from the overhanging trees. Around noon we reached the path that leads to Lonxe do Sol and followed it as it curved along the rim of the valley through shafts of granite that stand like faceless sentinels outside the village. Anxious about his mission, Father Infante pressed Facundo for information about the inhabitants of the mountain and was not encouraged by what he heard.

"They are not welcoming by nature, but rather suspicious and untamed."

"They are Christians, are they not?"

"That's what they would call themselves."

Perched on its promontory of rock in a sea of clouds, Lonxe do Sol appeared through the mist like the ancient citadel of a gothic tale. But the reality was quite different. The street was narrower than I remembered, leaving just enough room between the houses for a cart to pass, and partially paved with branches of gorse embedded in a mud of well-trod manure. The houses were barely more than ordered piles of stone with sagging roofs of weathered tiles. Beside them were heaps of gorse fodder for the livestock. Animal waste and decaying refuse fermented in standing pools surrounded by clusters of lethargic flies. Though the valley below was lush with hanging trees and clumps of ferns and gorse clinging to the rocks, there was nothing green in the village except the walls of the houses that had been stained by the relentless rain and mist. The only living thing in the street was a pink and black pig eating the scraps from a kitchen, until, alerted by our scent or the wheels of the cart, a group of barking dogs, teeth bared and backs bristling, appeared from the yards or barns behind the houses. As a wolf-like mongrel flanked us on one side, a man wearing a straw raincoat emerged from a house and struck it with a walking stick. The animal skulked away with its fellows sniffing the ground as it went and urinating on the side of a house. The man kicked at the air behind it and cursed.

"What did he say?" asked Father Infante.

"Ah, Father, they speak a different kind of language up here."

"Is he in charge? Tell him I've come to say Mass in the church."

Facundo raised his hand to quiet Father Infante as he and the man exchanged a few words. Then we went to a house where people were still eating their midday meal and stood in a light shower for ten or fifteen minutes before a second man came out and agreed to take us to the church and unlock the door. Facundo turned the cart around, and we walked up the same path through the fields of potatoes and kale that father and I had taken on my first trip to the mountain. But now several of the larger plots had been planted with eucalyptus saplings. Along the way, Father Infante broke in on the conversation between Facundo and our companion several times to ensure the purpose of our visit was not being overlooked.

"Ask him to tell the people that I will say Mass tomorrow morning."

"I told him why we are here, but he said we should return later in the afternoon and speak to the people ourselves."

"Will they be able to understand me?"

"They can understand some Castilian, but will speak to you in their own tongue, a version of Galician with many old words."

On the outside, the church had not changed much since the last time I was there. The finial was gone, but there were a few new tiles in the roof indicating someone had cared enough to repair it. However, the interior had suffered appreciably from neglect. On entering, we noticed a tangle of vines hanging above the altar and green stonework luminous with algae like a damp, living dust. The plastered wall behind the altar that had once been painted with primitive but colorful images of the apostles was stained with a felt of black mold. The room on the other side of this wall, entered through a low passage with a barrel vault, served as a sacristy and storage space furnished with an oak cabinet standing on three legs. In the rotting drawers were Latin prayer cards and a copy of the *Missa defunctorum*.

I cut down the vines and swept out the leaves and droppings and cobwebs with a homemade broom as Facundo took the baskets off the cart and Father Infante unpacked his vestments. While gathering grass to use for our bedding, I searched for my family name among the tombstones and found it on several. The grave that had been fresh on my previous trip was now overgrown with weeds, although there was a single bouquet of dry flowers next to the stone. After spreading the pile of grass and ferns over a corner of the church, I helped Facundo and Father Infante turn the baptismal font around so two of its sides, where a pentagram and a vulva had been carved, faced away from the congregation.

Father Infante dressed in a black soutane with a fresh white collar and purple cincture to impress the people with his probity and underscore the importance of his mission. Leaving the ox to graze in the mist, we locked the door of the church and returned to Lonxe. It was no more than five hundred yards down the path, but it must have taken us twenty minutes to reach the village. Sheltered by a patient Facundo holding a large umbrella, Father Infante leaned upon his cane and stopped to rest several times. He was pleased by the number of people who had gathered in anticipation of our return and through Facundo advised them that he would be saying Mass in the church the following morning. Although we had not seen a woman or a child earlier in the day, they now outnumbered the men and more appeared in the doorways of the houses as we proceeded down the street. In fact the quantity of people suggested some had come from outside the village. The women were dressed in black, wearing black scarves and black rubber boots, while, despite the weather, the children were mostly underdressed in soiled and ragged clothes, some with no pants. Because he could not understand their conversations, Father Infante failed to realize many of those who had come out to see us were there more for the novelty or spectacle of this obese man with the curling bangs and carefully trimmed beard making his way through the mud rather than as a display of piety or even respect. We were greeted by no open smiles and no overt gestures of hospitality.

A group of men led us to the public house, which was a dark, cave-like building at the end of the street. Like many other structures in the village, its walls, constructed of granite stones stacked one atop another, lacked mortar, and the gaps were filled with broken pieces of schist, so air and moisture were free to enter. The bar was an old door resting on two aged barrels. Two oil lamps hung from a rafter overhead. The landlord, to whom the others deferred, introduced himself as Régulo. Facundo, in turn, introduced each of us. Xosé, the son of my grandfather's cousin, moved closer to the bar and studied me for a moment. Then he stated my father's name and asked me if I knew him. I told him I was his son. The fact that I was a blood relative of people in the village changed how they viewed us. Régulo set a mug before Father Infante and another before Facundo and filled each with the house wine. When

Father Infante declined his, Facundo was happy to drink for both of them. As we spoke to the men, we discovered many of the people in the village were named after stars. In addition to Régulo, an Arturo and a Sirio were present. Several people asked us if we knew their friends and relatives in Porto Lúa, and one man revealed that he had lived there for many years but left when it became too crowded. Father Infante asked them when they had last attended Mass or received Communion. Some people were too embarrassed to answer. Some said it had been many years. And some said decades. There had been few opportunities, one of the men said. When we were ready to leave, Régulo invited us to a festival at Santa Locaia two days hence and said he would tell people about the Mass in the morning, but could not promise they would attend.

"I don't understand why they would miss this opportunity," Father Infante said.

"We have a different way of doing things here."

"Different from what?"

"Different from the ways of others."

It was now dark outside. The mist had risen and the stars were shining. Because a pack of wolves had been seen in the area, Xosé volunteered to accompany us to the church, but first stopped by his house to pick up his rifle and a lantern. When Father Infante asked him what Régulo had meant when he said they have a different way of doing things, Xosé explained, "We are closer to the stars and moon here, and we look to them as others look to churches and prayer books."

"But the Bible is the word of God passed down through centuries."

"The beliefs of the people here have also been passed down through centuries. To us, they are just as real as the stories told by religions. In the cities, people mock our beliefs, but are theirs any better? Their ways of knowing were unknown once and will be again while our world will continue to be as it has always been."

"And how has it always been?"

"A stone has an existence different from what you can see or touch because by seeing and touching, you make it something it is not. The same is true of streams and trees and fields of grass. Here we live with nature and let it speak to us. To survive we must learn to listen. Our ancestors taught us we can't make nature be what we want it to be. If we do, it will disappear."

"Do you believe that God created nature?"

"Yes, and He speaks to us through nature, not through books, because many of the people who live on the mountain have never learned to read or write. Come with me."

Xosé took us off the path and up through a field where potatoes had recently been harvested to an elevation of exposed granite. We climbed the stones, helping Father Infante as we went, until we reached a large flat boulder resting on top of the others. We could see the lights of Porto Lúa in the distance below and a pale blue smudge in the western sky over the horizon.

"When I was a child, my father brought me here, and we gazed at the sea. He told me out there lies a place beyond this life where my soul will pass through a gate of stars on its journey to God. These stones where we are standing are called the talking rocks. They are as old as night and speak of their origins, of the moon and stars. If you listen carefully, you can hear them. But we shouldn't linger. Many things happen here at night, and you may be robbed of your wits."

When we reached the church, we lit the candles we had brought and placed them in a rusty chandelier that I lowered with a rope attached to a bracket on the wall. Xosé had already bid us good night when Father Infante asked him to stay a little longer and tell us more of his stories about the mountain. We offered him a portion of the *empanada* we had saved for dinner and sat outside on stone benches in the weak light of the candles that shone through the portal.

"Most of what I know I learned as a child when the old people used to tell of a time before the Christians. It was the time of a great queen who lived in Casa Sagrada and ruled when there were many more people living on the mountain. During that time, the moon was much closer to the earth, and our ancestors were able to touch it."

"I was told the same thing," said Facundo.

"What do you mean?" Father Infante asked. "How could they touch the moon?"

"They climbed the northern peak of the mountain, which they called Porto Lúa, and the moon came so close they were able to touch it as it moved past. Because it descended through the realm of the dead every night when it set, people would come from far away to leave the souls of their loved ones on the summit so it might carry them to the life beyond this life. The village of Onde se Adora was near the northern peak, and its buildings were whitewashed with a glowing white paint made from seashells so the pilgrims could find their way to the peak even on a winter night. Then the queen, who was to remain a virgin out of devotion to the moon, slept with a young nobleman who turned out to be a wolf in disguise. The moon was very angry and retreated farther and farther into the sky so that she could no longer be reached. As a result, Porto Lúa languished, and soon the queen was forced to move her people to the coast. They carried the stones from the houses of Onde se Adora down the mountain and built a new town, which they named after the peak they had abandoned. Here the disciples of the new religion converted the queen, who was now called Raíña Lupa, to Christianity. Because the moon had abandoned her people, when the queen died, she was buried in a field on the mountain rather than taken to the peak to be carried across the sky. People who lived during the time of my great-grandparents claimed there was still enough paint on the stones left at Onde se Adora to allow them to see at night without any other source of light."

"That's a folktale made up to entertain children," said Father Infante. "Everyone knows it could never be true."

"I don't know if it's true or not, but people believe it, and if it's true to them, that's all that matters."

"Galileo proved long ago, hundreds of years before your great-grandparents, that the moon is higher in the sky," said the priest.

"But the Church said Galileo was wrong," said Facundo.

"That is not important. Many scientists have also proven this."

"So the Church was wrong?"

"Of course not. Science has one way of explaining things, and the Church has another, but they both arrive at the same truths."

"Then why did the Church—"

"I was there," said Xosé.

"What?"

"When they opened the tomb of Raíña Lupa. I was there. It was during the war. I was a boy like this one. Men had spent the better part of the day trying to loosen the stone lid of the coffin. It must've weighed several tons. Finally somebody showed up with dynamite from the wolfram mine on the other side of the mountain. By the time he'd fastened a fuse to it and found the best place to put it, the sun was setting, and it was growing dark. When the dynamite went off, there was a blinding cloud of dust. But that's not all. There was also a bright white light, like a star, that rose out of the coffin and danced around us before floating up into the sky and disappearing. All that was left inside was dust and chips of stone from the blast. Not a single bone or piece of gold. You can still see it. It's under an overhang near Chan de Lourenzo. I'm only telling you this now because it's true and nobody seems to believe the old truths anymore."

"A bright light?"

"Some things you can't explain."

"Those are just stories."

"All beliefs are stories."

The next morning we were awakened by a woman bringing fresh flowers for the altar. She was accompanied by her granddaughter and asked Father Infante to bless the girl, who was lame and deaf. Shortly after their departure, another woman brought us barley cakes for breakfast and told us we were wasting our time among her neighbors, whom she referred to unapologetically as pagans. When she left, we began preparing for Mass. I cleared the grass bedding from the corner of the room and, after wiping the altar with a wet rag, covered it with the lace-edged cloth we had brought with us. As Father Infante dressed in his best vestments in the small sacristy, I placed the chalice and ciborium on the altar, lit the candles, and filled the cruets with water and wine.

The first people to arrive for the service were Xosé and his wife María Amparo, who presented us with a potato omelet. Next were three skeletal women dressed in black who claimed to remember the time when a priest would say Mass in the church on the second Sunday of every month. Then came the woman with her granddaughter followed by the woman who had baked the barley cakes and who was jealous of the attention Father Infante paid to anyone else. An itinerant knife-grinder who happened to be passing through the village appeared and brought a half dozen pilgrims he had met on the road with him. The last members to arrive were two young women whose principal purpose seemed to be showing off their best clothes.

When he made the decision to preach to the people of the mountain, Father Infante began preparing his sermon, and during the course of our trip, he read parts of it to us and asked for our impressions. His first approach was to associate the poverty of the people with the lack of orthodoxy in their faith, but as he thought back to his experience on the plaza in Porto Lúa, he came to the conclusion that it would be inappropriate to link faith to material well-being. Rather, he would tell them the story of his trial by fire to demonstrate the power of faith and the active presence of God in our lives.

Despite the small number of people in attendance and the ruinous state of the church, Father Infante persevered and brought the word of God to the people who had long been deprived of it. In his sermon he confessed that, like everyone else, he had moments of doubt, but he overcame them through prayer. In fact, he declared, when he was recently tested by the prospect of a torturous death, it was the strength of his faith that had enabled him to triumph over his fear. After providing some background to the story of the trial by fire, he reached its dramatic climax revealing that just when the timber was to be set alight, a large crane came to rest in a tree overhead as a sign from God, and the wood failed to ignite. He would not, he concluded, be with them today in Lonxe do Sol if his life had not been delivered by the Paraclete.

Because none of those present had a clear command of Castilian and because Father Infante suppressed the letter "l" when he spoke, they thought he said he had been delivered by a parakeet. Rather than being moved by his story of faith, people thought it odd that God would choose a small, talking bird to rescue the priest, and some, noticing he had first said it was a crane and then a parakeet, even doubted the veracity of the story. As he stood by the door shaking the hands of the devout as they left, no one mentioned this, and he assumed all had gone well. Afterward, however, he complained that only sixteen people had shown up, and only ten were from Lonxe do Sol.

"I'm saying Mass for the sparrows on the roof," he muttered, "but I will not give up. Let's pack and go to Santa Locaia. Perhaps we'll have more success there."

I folded the altar cloth and took down the candles as Father Infante stowed his vestments and sacramental vessels in the baskets. When they were ready, Facundo hoisted them onto the cart and yoked the ox while I ran down to Lonxe do Sol with the key. By noon we were back on the Roman road eating the omelet María Amparo had prepared. When we passed through the gap in the rocks at Porto Ventoso, Father Infante asked why there was a gate in such a remote place, and Facundo explained the Church had put it there to deter people from practicing pagan rituals on the mountain. Agro Vello was just as I remembered it, but the trees were now mostly bare, and despite the clear sky, the air among their shadows was cold. On the other side of the forest, we entered fields of stone and stunted trees where a few scruffy sheep were grazing on the heather and passed the statue of St. Peter holding the keys to Paradise. Because we wanted to reach Santa Locaia before nightfall, there wasn't enough time to take Father Infante to the grotto chapel, but we stopped beside the purplish-white stone called A Noiva do Ceo to show him the small caves on the southern peak containing the bones of the ancient inhabitants of the mountain. From this height, with its view of the sea and the vast, open sky reaching to the edge of space, it was not hard to share the belief of those buried there in the benevolence of the heavens that received their souls.

The path to Santa Locaia turns north along the edge of Onde se Adora where the foundations of circular stone houses are tightly concentrated within a perimeter of scattered rocks that once made up the outer wall of the village. They would not have been much different from the houses of Lonxe do Sol except they were round and had grass roofs instead of tile. These stones placed one upon another are all that remain of the lives of their inhabitants apart from any beliefs or stories or customs that have survived among the people who still live on the mountain. From Onde se Adora the path descends to the west below the northern peak through a varied geography of forests and unspoiled meadows of harebell and bracken. As afternoon shadows filled the woods, we continued down through a grove of pines and ferns that grew waist-high. In an opening among the trees that shone like an oasis of light was a walled plot where a man and woman were loading an oxcart with hay. Facundo called out to ask if we were on the right path to Santa Locaia.

"Santa Locaia?"

"Yes."

"Follow the peth you're on thorow the bents and then head ayont the besom close agen the popple copse. Cross the brig and you'll see it."

Even Facundo was puzzled by this speech, but said we should stay on the path until we come to a bridge where the chapel will be visible. He was right. We arrived with just enough light to gather bedding and build a fire. Constructed of woodland stone mortared with a loose, sandy cement, at ten by fifteen feet, the chapel was large enough for us to sleep in and store the baskets, but not for Mass. We ate the last of the *empanada* and warmed stones in the fire before moving them inside to heat the building as we slept. Not that they made much difference.

It was a cool, cloudless morning when we awoke with no sign of the festival that would soon begin. The light conveyed a different aspect of the clearing than the evening darkness that had enveloped us on our arrival and had lent a haunted atmosphere to the valley. But even the bright sky did not entirely dispel the odd feeling of being in an unworldly place as I walked up the slope of the grassy yard. Perhaps it had something to do with the way the light reflected off the different hues of the granite peaks or the isolation created by the depth of the valley. Behind the church is a narrow gorge of mostly barren rock that drops from the highest elevations of the mountain. Through it runs a stream that falls over a shelf of granite and carves a deep pool in a crevice of rock below. On the banks beside the clear blue water people had left bunches of wildflowers, candles, and coins. I crossed the stream and climbed up through the gorse and bracken on the other side where I came to a large boulder in the shape of a recumbent bull. I don't believe it had been cut to this shape, but a fissure running along its length had been hollowed out to create a small cave, and there were cupmarks on either side of the opening suggesting some ritualistic purpose. Farther down, toward what would be the lower back of the bull, were two sarcophagi carved into the stone. When I returned to the chapel, I found Father Infante inspecting a large boulder that had been incorporated into its southern wall. The upper part of the stone had been hewn to form a flat surface where he discovered faint letters cut into the granite. When he realized they spelled *IOVI*, he picked up a sharp rock and attempted to scratch them out, but the granite was hard and the letters that had endured for centuries withstood his efforts.

By the middle of the afternoon, there were several groups of people lying on blankets in the grass with bottles of wine and baskets of food, and more continued to arrive on foot and in oxcarts through the rest of the day. Since there was no village or house in the immediate vicinity, they had all traveled some distance from places like Casa Sagrada, Lonxe do Sol, San Cibrán, Suevos, Louredo, and even smaller clusters of houses hidden in the valleys of the mountain or isolated in the forests. We saw people we had met in Lonxe do Sol, and Facundo discovered several of his relatives who had already begun to roast a lamb. The festival officially began with the procession of the Virxe do Monte. Two men mounted on horseback came down the path followed by a man playing a bagpipe and a woman keeping the rhythm with a drum. Behind them was a group of men, women, and children, and, carried in their midst on a platform with poles like a palanquin, a wooden doll of the virgin with a strangely grotesque face grimacing and cross-eyed. The palanquin was placed in the middle of the field where the grass had been beaten down by children and a few pairs of adults who were dancing to the music of the bagpipe.

Late in the afternoon, I spread the altar cloth over a flat boulder near the chapel and prepared the cruets and chalice for Mass. When Father Infante came out of the chapel wearing his vestments, I rang a bell to signal the beginning of the service. People were sitting on the grass eating and chatting, and even though the music had temporarily stopped, a few people, who perhaps had had too much to drink, continued dancing. During the sermon Father Infante repeated his story of the trial by fire and pronounced "Paraclete" as he had done before, but this time no one seemed to notice. The congregation was more interested in the series of fireworks set off by someone in the crowd. The length of the Mass was shortened considerably when out of the dozens present only three people came forward to receive Communion. Visibly disheartened by the response to the Holy Sacrament, particularly on a day honoring the saint of the site, Father Infante expressed his impatience to Facundo.

"How am I to take God to the people if they won't take themselves to God?"

"Father, try to understand that many of these people have received no religious instruction and have never made their First Communion."

"Then why are they here to celebrate the feast of a saint?"

"This festival has nothing to do with Santa Locaia."

"But that's what they called it. The Festival of Santa Locaia."

"*At* Santa Locaia. That's what they call the place, not the person. The chapel is the chapel of Santa Locaia, but the celebration is for the Virxe do Monte."

"The Blessed Virgin?"

"Yes, for those who choose to identify the Blessed Virgin with the Virxe do Monte."

It was true. When Father Infante looked up the feast day of Santa Locaia in his missal, he discovered it was in December. As Facundo was trying to explain, this festival was older than the chapel and perhaps even celebrated before the arrival of Christianity.

"Why didn't you tell me this earlier?"

"I thought you wanted to Christianize the people."

Despite his reservations about the purpose of the festival, Father Infante agreed to sit with Facundo's cousins and share plates of roast lamb and the wine they called *do monte*. After several *cuncas*, he was more amenable and agreed to accompany his hosts up a stone path to higher ground above the trees and watch the sun descend into the ocean south of Illa da Luz. Below us women were lighting oil they had poured into cupmarks in the rocks that bordered the stream leading to the basin beneath the waterfall. Realizing what was happening, Facundo handed Father Infante the bottle he was carrying and told him to drink the rest of the wine. People were coming up from the field and following the oil lamps to the pool where they left offerings to the local deity. There were grapes, sheaves of barley, the ears of pigs, piles of grain, bouquets of daisies, and more coins. Father Infante said nothing but did not stay for the brief ceremony that followed. Facundo and I joined him in the chapel where we found that all our food except for the rice had been plundered and scattered by an animal.

In the middle of the night, I woke to see a kaleidoscope of lights moving across the ceiling of the chapel and went out to discover a procession of people carrying candles passing by the window. They crossed the field and proceeded to the basin where the oil lamps were still burning. When I arrived, Facundo was already there. Some of the people were singing softly and throwing autumn flowers into the water. Some stood quietly. The full moon was high overhead and seemed as bright as the sun reflecting off a pool of oil. It must have been close to midnight. A young woman stepped forward with a silver cup to harvest the "cream of light" on the surface of the water at the moment when they believed it to be most plentiful. This cup containing the "dew" or "rain" of the moon was passed from person to person, and when it reached me, I took a sip and passed it along. As soon as I did, the plants and trees that had been faintly visible in the darkness brightened, and the water, moving past in silver waves, seemed to be alive. As if recalling primal sympathies, I felt a kinship not only with the people around me, but also with the essential presence of every object, every aspect of being.

For centuries people on the mountain had come here to cure the occlusion of their sight with the dew of the autumn moon. Free of the sensual appeals of daylight—the colors that provoke our appetites—the pure white light enabled them to see through individual need and desire into the commonality of life. While Xosé was the only relative I knew on the mountain, I shared common ancestors with the people from Casa Sagrada and Lonxe do Sol. Though more distant than Xosé, they were also my cousins, and, given the isolation of the people who lived on the mountain, the blood we shared had changed little since the time of those who built the houses at Onde se Adora and were buried in the caves on the southern portal. Facundo and I had come on a mission with a priest attempting to bring an orthodox faith to a more ancient mind, but we were in fact returning to our home, our history, and what was familiar to our blood.

We woke enveloped in another autumn fog that freshened the air with the blended scents of wet grass and pine. Father Infante had decided there was no point in continuing his work, and, after eating a pot of boiled rice for breakfast, we swept out the chapel and loaded the baskets onto the cart. A group of people from Lonxe do Sol told us we could avoid the more arduous return up the mountain past Onde se Adora if we followed them down the path through the woods that would eventually lead us to the Roman road in Agro Vello. And so we set out through the wet forest with Father Infante wrapped in a waxed tarpaulin rocking on his cushion, Facundo holding the steering rope wet with ox spittle, and me shivering beside him as the people ahead of us disappeared into the fog. Our mood reflected the weather. I was tired from the previous night, and Father Infante was subdued, no doubt disillusioned by his experiences on the mountain. Facundo, who had had too much to drink at the festival, kept to himself. After several hours, we reached the granite cliffs on the western side of Agro Vello where, if not for the trees, the entire coast would have come into view. Here we caught up with the group from Lonxe, who had stopped beside a small forest of granite steles to leave flowers. Father Infante asked a man wearing a straw raincoat who had placed the stones there. "*Os mouros*," he replied, meaning not Moors, but pagans of an indefinite past. Some of the stones were squat pedestals for votive offerings while others were tall and thin. Some were carved with primitive figures and some inscribed with irregular letters. One read, *DEVS LARI BEROBREO ARAM POSVIT PRO SALVTE*, and another, *PROTECTOR ANIMARVM IN EXCELSO CIVITATEM*. According to Father Infante, the first asked the god Berobreo for health and the second addressed the protector of souls in the high city, but it wasn't clear if that meant heaven or Onde se Adora.

We passed through the gate at Porto Ventoso with the people from Lonxe. When we reached the church, they gave us a stick of *chorizo* and took the path home as we continued down the Roman road. Tired and hungry from the descent, we stopped at the bothy for the night where we warmed ourselves before a large fire and cooked a dinner of rice, watercress, and *chorizo*. Though the fire had not had time to heat the room, Father Infante wrapped himself in his blanket and went to sleep almost immediately. Once he began to snore, Facundo, who had been drinking one of the bottles of wine his cousin had given him, revealed what had really happened on the night of the trial by fire.

"It wasn't the Paraclete at all," he said.

"What was it?"

"You mustn't tell anyone."

"I won't."

"Not your parents. Not your friends."

"I promise."

"And it must never get back to him," he said nodding toward Father Infante.

"No."

"I did it for him. And for Bachiario. I couldn't bear to see anything happen to either one of them, and they are both too proud to back down."

"What did you do?"

Facundo checked to be sure Father Infante was sleeping soundly and then leaned back and took a drink from his bottle.

"The night before the trial, I was in O Galo drinking when I felt the call of nature. The toilet at the back of the bar was so crowded that I went out to the alley behind the buildings that face the plaza. To be honest, it wasn't the first time. Before I was finished, I noticed a terrible odor and thought it had come out of me and that I might have been poisoned or dying of some terrible disease, but then I realized it was the odor of kerosene. By chance I had pissed in one of the buckets set aside for the trial by fire. Now I might have been drunk, but I was clear-headed enough to know what to do. If these two men wouldn't back down from their foolish contest, they might be burned to death. However, if I diluted the kerosene, it wouldn't light. I couldn't piss in all the buckets, so I decided to take them down to the quay two at a time and pour out half the kerosene and fill them up again with water from the fountain in the plaza. I was afraid that if I emptied them out completely, someone might get suspicious, and figured that half would maintain the odor and appearance without being enough to ignite. Just to be sure, I poured a little out in the street and tried to light it with a match, but it failed to catch."

As soon as Facundo finished his story, Father Infante turned over on his side and said, "Very good, very clever, but you have overlooked one thing."

Embarrassed, and confused by drink, Facundo tried to apologize and explain at the same time.

"It's all right," said Father Infante reassuringly. "You did the right thing, but you have failed to understand your role in this matter. Do you really believe that in your drunken state you could have thought of such a plan? It was God acting through the agency of His servant who spared my life. It wasn't chance, but rather God, who caused you to relieve yourself in that bucket."

"Yes, Father. Of course."

"But since many will fail to believe you were directed by Divine Providence, let's keep this among ourselves."

Both Facundo and I agreed.

"Good. Now let's forget about all this and go to sleep as we'll need to get up early tomorrow if we're going to make it home in time for dinner."

Despite his public interpretation of the cause of his salvation, it is unlikely Father Infante still believed the Holy Spirit rather than a drunken sexton had delivered him from a fiery death, so it was impossible to know what affected him more—

the realization that Providence had not intervened on his behalf or the failure of his divinely sanctioned mission to banish heterodoxy from the religious practices of the people on the mountain. Whatever the case, upon our return to Porto Lúa the following afternoon, he quickly reverted to his former lifestyle. Waiting for him in the rectory when he arrived dispirited and exhausted, were several large boxes of new vestments. When he asked Rosa where they came from, she handed him an envelope marked *Pazo de Xelmírez*. His superiors in Santiago wished to acknowledge the tenth anniversary of his ordination. He washed away the lingering traces of his ordeals on the mountain in a hot bath, oiled and combed his hair in the pier glass, and tried on the amice, alb, cincture, maniple, stole, and chasuble that still smelled like the ecclesiastical shop in Madrid. After some days of reflection, he decided to retract his renunciation of the stipend that went with his office and return to the fold. To demonstrate his renewed devotion to the authority of the Church, he published an essay in *Vida Nueva* entitled "Theophilus on the Mountain of Heresy" where he described himself climbing the mountain alone on horseback to root out the remnants of pagan superstition and convince the people there to embrace the one true religion. The authorities in Santiago were so impressed by his success that he was soon the second person in Porto Lúa to own a television. According to Rosa, he watched without fail *La tortuga perezosa* and *Sonría, por favor* and laughed so loudly that people visiting the churchyard thought him impious. His weight went back up and his cheeks were flush again. Witnessing this life of ease and well-being led me to decide on a new vocation. Rather than become a saint, I would become a priest. But the onset of puberty would soon change that.

No one had been more affected by the recent upheavals in the spiritual order than Aunt Fioxilda, whose fragile grasp on reality was becoming more tenuous. Vexed by the wavering boundaries between her worlds that allowed the material to dissolve into the spiritual and the spiritual to precipitate into the material, the future to exist in the past and the past to exist in the future, she moved through the house and gardens with a judgment clouded by the phantoms of a waking dream. She predicted the events of her childhood and confessed transgressions not yet committed, addressed ancestors long absent, and mourned the loss of those present. She made a soup out of compost scraps, brewed coffee with olive oil, fed chickens with handfuls of sand, and took clean towels from the clothesline to wash the floor. While I was on the mountain, she stole the cutlery and tried to sell it back to mother. And one morning she ran outside calling to the neighbors when she found a stranger in the house, but it was only grandfather sitting at the table smoking a cigarette.

The morning after my return, she removed a burner plate from the stove and, thinking she saw a covey of demons among the embers, reached into the fire and ignited the sleeve of her sweater. If mother hadn't entered the kitchen at that moment and extinguished the flames with her coat, Aunt Fioxilda might have set not only herself, but also the house, on fire. She stood for a moment staring blankly at her hand as if trying to under-stand what had happened. Dusted with ash, the skin on her fingers began to drip like potato soup. When Dr. Romalde ar-rived, he cleaned the wounds with vinegar, soaked her fingers in egg whites, applied a paste of baking soda, and dressed her hand with strips of boiled cloth. He told us to apply an oint-ment of stewed peppers when we changed the dressing and make milk thistle tea to alleviate her pain, but he could do nothing for her mind.

When he concluded his treatment, he turned to my parents and said, "The time has come."

Father asked me to bring him a piece of paper and a pen, and we wrote a letter to the abbess of the Convento de Las Mercedarias Descalzas where Aunt Fioxilda had previously lived to inquire whether there were rooms available in their retirement community. As we waited for a reply, I was as-signed to stay by her side to prevent any further incidents, watching over her the way she had once watched over me. She was no longer allowed to cook or clean or come in contact with any dangerous object or fire. So we spent the days sitting in church or harvesting late fruit or reading the holy verses cirrus clouds had inscribed across the heavens. When mother came home from the market one afternoon, she changed the band-age and asked Aunt Fioxilda if the pain had diminished.

"Pain is the penalty for being," she said. "It's the only thing that keeps me here."

A few days later we received a response from the abbess. A room was available and would be held. Father arranged for Paco Carreira to drive us to Santiago, and we wrote to tell the abbess we would arrive in two days, which gave the letter time to reach her. Now all we had to do was find a way to convince Aunt Fioxilda to put aside her aversion to motor vehicles and accompany us to Santiago. Father proposed a ghost wedding to some mysterious saint, but yielded to mother's idea that we ask Dr. Romalde to write a letter purporting to be from the Archbishop inviting her to Santiago to receive his blessing and commendation for her steadfast resolve in the battle against evil. When father gave Aunt Fioxilda the letter at dinner that evening, her only question was why it had taken so long to recognize her struggle. This was a Monday. On Wednesday morning, I took her to Mass while mother and father packed her clothes and essential belongings in her crate and put it in the trunk of Paco's taxi next to his books. The drive along the coast and the *ría* through Muros and Noia and over the mountains to Santiago took more than three hours and we arrived in the city just after noon. We informed the abbess and her assistants of our stratagem, and they played along offering Aunt Fioxilda a cup of tea with a sedative as she waited for the Archbishop to arrive. As soon as she was asleep, we carried her to her room, placed her crate in the corner, and decorated the walls with her color prints. Then I placed the bar of Italian soap on the table next to her bed. When she woke from her nap, we told her we had come from Porto Lúa to visit her. When she asked questions about the house, we told her she had been in the convent all along and must have dreamt she had been in Porto Lúa. Then mother showed her the crate in the corner with her things and the prints on the walls and the soap on the table.

She picked up the soap and held it to her nose.

"I remember now. There is a small house beside a waterfall in a forest. Above the waterfall, the river passes through mountains covered with snow. The sky is violet, and the scent of wisteria mingles with the scent of lilac, and I am home."

The abbess nodded and smiled. "We'll leave your soap here, and you can go home whenever you like."

By chance, Sister Benigna and Sister Mary Rose had been staying in the same convent while looking for a replacement for Bachiario and returned to Porto Lúa with us, sitting in the front seat with Paco while mother and father sat in the back with me wedged between them. I looked out the window to watch the countryside pass and thought back to the day when Aunt Fioxilda had entered the house and of her battles against evil and the ointment she rubbed on her arms and the lessons she taught me on language and life. But I felt no loss at her absence. The person I knew had been gone for some time. However, when we reached Noia and were in sight of the sea, mother began to cry, and, having said little on the trip thus far, suddenly exclaimed, "She's better off where she is." She was right. The narrow confines of her room and the limitations on her activity would reduce the risk of injury but not restrict her freedom when she could so easily escape the thick stone walls through the openings in her imagination.

Sister Benigna and Sister Mary Rose informed us they had found a new teacher who would begin later in the month, althhough we would resume classes on the following Monday. In addition to this news, the next day Father Infante announced that henceforth all children would attend Mass every morning before school and go to confession once a week on Fridays. For those of us on the cusp of puberty, this was a source of some anxiety. We had already been initiated into what was officially the Sacrament of Reconciliation at the time of our First Communion, but Bachiario had not been a very attentive confessor, and Father Infante had been occupied with the trial by fire and the trip up the mountain, so the regular practice of this sacrament had been put on hold, and we were now confronted by the disconcerting challenge of having to remember several months' worth of sins and divulging our deepest secrets to the amply jowled waxen face with curling bangs seated behind the silk partition of the confessional. The shame we felt was heightened by the instruction we received on the day we went back to class, for that was the day, as Miguel put it, that we became beasts.

On Monday morning when everyone had assembled in the front hall of the school, we marched double-file, arm's length apart, up a back lane to church. When we returned to school after Mass, Sister Benigna and Sister Mary Rose excused the older students until noon and then separated the remaining boys and girls and took the girls into our classroom and shut the door. The boys waited a few minutes for Father Infante to appear and lead us down the hall to a cold, damp room across from the toilets where a few long tables were stored. Awkwardly referring to the day's subject as a special class on science, he began by describing the mechanism of locks and keys and then drew confusing pictures on the board depicting the male and female "organs of increase." We had no idea what he was talking about until he mentioned bulls and cows, rams and ewes, and how the male and female must "unite" for "the species to continue." Then he told us about the consequences of self-love. Not only was hell waiting for us, but, he told us, there was an institution for the blind in Santiago for all those boys "who misuse their bodies." Proper use, we learned, was only in the Sacrament of Marriage for the purpose of creating children.

"What about people who don't get married? Are they going to hell?"

Father Infante blushed. "Not if they don't abuse their bodies."

"Do bulls and cows go to hell?"

"Brute beasts do not go to hell because they know nothing of God."

"Do they go blind?"

"Their practices do not include Onanism."

Because we had no idea what this word meant, the questions stopped there. When we returned to our classroom for the rest of the day's lessons, the girls were more distant, seemingly in possession of an extraordinary secret—as if flowers had bloomed in their bodies.

In the woods above Porto Lúa is a boulder that rises through the trees to offer a view of the rooftops of the town and the kitchen gardens where grapevines grow beside drying laundry. It was the place where Miguel and María and I would go to be by ourselves, a place where we could talk or simply sit and enjoy the afternoon sun. On the day of the lecture, Miguel and I went up the path among the pines and climbed to the top of the stone in order to consider the revelations of the morning more carefully. María was not invited. Instead, we decided to consult with Ramón, who was recently married and soon to be a father. Both Miguel and I had some inkling of the essential facts of reproduction from having spent our lives among domestic animals, but there were still many crucial details to clarify and errors to dispel.

"How did you know what to do?" I asked.

"That part comes naturally," Ramón said. "You'll figure it out. It's everything else that you need to worry about."

"What do you mean?"

"It's not as simple as you and her. There's consequences."

"Tell him what happened to you," Miguel said.

"You know my wife Euxenia?"

"Yes," I said. I knew she was a strong, large-boned woman who wore an apron decorated with roses.

"She and I had been going out for three years, and her family wanted to speed things up. So one weekend they left her at home and went to Coruña to spend time with their relatives. She said she didn't like being alone in the house and invited me over. Because it was so cold, she made a fire in the stove and boiled some milk, and then we sat down and drank some hot chocolate. We were both nervous and didn't have much to say. She doesn't say much anyway.

"Afterward she took me by the hand, and we went upstairs. I could feel my heart racing and my mouth go dry. The house was so quiet you could hear light rain on the windows. And so cold you could see your breath. Anyway, we went down the hall and into her room. There were photographs on the wall she had cut from magazines and a crucifix. We kissed for a while standing up and then awkwardly undressed each other. Finally we lay down and began to kiss all over. I placed my hand between her legs and touched what felt like a patch of dry moss and smelled like the ocean. As I was touching her, I looked at her skin. It was white and pink. Like something pre-historic. Rough and wrinkled, not smooth like her face. It all came down to this, I thought. All the years of courtship. And here I was, looking at these black hairs and pale skin with its chafed spots and pimples and tiny veins. The secret of women. What had been out of reach for so many years now seemed too compliant, too dull, almost indifferent, as if her body belonged to someone else. I felt like a puppet, dangling from the strings of a nature I hardly knew, a nature she was part of. Where was I among the strings? I was a proud, vain creature without a clue, without a will of my own. Then, despite the chill in the room, she said she felt warm and got up to open the shutters and a window.

"I almost lost my nerve, but then she kind of helped me get on top of her and guided me to the mark if you know what I mean. As she worked on things down there, I was suspended for what seemed like an eternity high above the world without a safety net. When I saw myself in a mirror across the room stretched out in my white socks, I looked like a skinned rabbit leaping over a wall. And then, just as we got things going, I heard the floorboards creak on the staircase. But I couldn't stop. I felt the impulse of desire driving me, pulling me down with an automatic spasm. The bed knocked against the wall. Our bellies slapped and everything was warm, like a warm bath, and I felt nothing else. Just the warmth. And then, a moment later, I felt a waterfall of light come over me, and she cried out. And then the door opened. There stood her father, two uncles, and two brothers. The next thing I knew, I was getting married and going to be a father. That's what I mean about consequences."

According to Miguel, their father gave Ramón a half-acre plot near the river, which, conveniently, was adjacent to Euxenia's father's property, two oxen, a wheelbarrow, an old plow, ten bushels of seed corn and potatoes, and eight hundred pesetas. The couple moved in with her widowed aunt who lived in a small stone cottage on a path just beyond the end of Rúa das Angustias near the plot of land. I thought about the story he told us and couldn't imagine myself as such a puppet. It was as if he had relinquished himself to become an empty husk through which life passes and disappears down the generations until nothing identifiable is left. Nevertheless, I began to look at girls differently, yearning vaguely for something I could not articulate, something inviting about their presence. Other boys in my class were equally curious, but burdened by fear at the same time. Since we were at the age when myopia sets in, some of my friends began to fear they were going blind and lined up outside the confessional to recover their eyesight.

On the last Monday of November, we entered our classroom to find Sister Benigna and Sister Mary Rose speaking with an older man in front of the instructor's desk. A mad plume of white hair rose over his cranium like steam rising from a boiled egg. Tall with broad shoulders, he wore a gray herringbone coat that hung to the shafts of his boots and a black scarf around his neck. Towering above us like a dovecote wrapped in wool, he left an indelible impression at first sight with his aquiline nose, large, inconsolably sad eyes, thick round glasses, a gray and black beard that trailed away like vines on the edge of a bluff, and irregular rows of teeth, above and below, like merlons in the battlement of a castle.

Sister Benigna wrote PROFESOR ARTURO LESTÓN on the

board in capital letters and introduced him to the class. But from that moment on, we knew him simply as *Mestre*. When the sisters left the room, he stood beside the desk staring at us with a look of bewilderment, and we stared back with quizzical expressions of anticipation. Time seemed to stop. He glanced at Mateo Mateo in his wheelbarrow, then walked to the window like a caged animal. He stood with his back to us for several more minutes contemplating the fog on the bay, then turned and took a Latin edition of Virgil's *Georgics* from his leather bag. He brought the text so close to his eyes that he appeared to be smelling it and squinted so hard that he pulled his upper lip back in a grimace. After selecting a passage, he wrote the following lines on the board for the class to translate:

> *tum pater omnipotens fecundis imbribus Aether*
> *coniugis in gremium laetae descendit, et omnis*
> *magnus alit magno commixtus corpore fetus.*

He turned around and asked for volunteers. No hands went up. He stared at us. We stared at him.

"I was told you had read Virgil's *Georgics* with your former instructor. How far did you get?"

"We never got this far."

"Where did you end?"

"We never started it."

"We can't read Latin, sir."

"Well then, what did you read?"

"We talked about Priscillian."

"All right. What can you tell me about Priscillian?"

"We learned that God presents the Virgin of Light to the Prince of Water to cause rain."

"The passage on the board is a similar poetic rendering of the cause of rain: 'The all-powerful father falls in showers to the womb of his happy wife and mixes with her great body to nurture the lives within her.' It is a description of the renewal of life in spring."

"Was Priscillian wrong?"

"They were both wrong in a scientific sense, but they were trying to explain something in poetic terms before the discoveries of science."

"Why don't we read science instead?"

"We read poetry to understand different ways of looking at the world and appreciate the beauty of how those views are expressed. Someday in the future, students may wonder why they have to read what you call science and not explanations more consistent with the discoveries of their age."

"How can we know that it's beautiful if we can't understand it?"

"That's what you're here to learn."

When he concluded his remarks, a hand went up. It was Alfredo.

"Sir, I have a question."

"Your name is?"

"Alfredo, sir."

"Alfredo, why are you wearing a necklace of stones?"

"Because I never know the right answers."

"You may take it off. What is your question?"

"Why is there a pebble on your ring?"

Mestre held his hand up for the rest of the class to see.

"It is set with a grain of sand from a dune in the Sahara Desert of Morocco. It was given to me to remind me that we are each like that grain of sand selected from a dune."

Although our new teacher was more orthodox in his manners than his predecessor, it was clear he was more comfortable in the quiet carrels of an archive than in front of a class of young students. In their search for someone to replace Bachiario, Sister Benigna and Sister Mary Rose had persuaded the priests in the diocesan offices in Santiago to provide a modest salary for a head teacher if daily attendance at Mass and religious instruction were part of the curriculum. They agreed that the person did not have to be a member of the clergy, but this did not make it any easier to find a qualified candidate. One of the priests suggested they inquire at the Rectorado, the Facultade de Ciencias da Educación, the concello's offices of education, and the Instituto de Estudios Gallegos Padre Sarmiento. They met with no success until their final stop where the librarian introduced them to Professor Lestón, who was researching the history of Raíña Lupa and had spent time in the vicinity of Porto Lúa cataloging the petroglyphs at Carnota, Mallou, and Louro. After considering the offer for a day, he accepted it thinking that establishing himself in the region and getting to know the people would be helpful in the pursuit of these studies.

He had arrived in Muros the previous Friday on the Castromil bus with the farmers taking their goats and chickens to market and then found a taxi to Porto Lúa. He stayed at the *pensión* on the plaza and on Saturday morning went with Don Andrés to see a house for rent on the edge of Caos. It was built into the side of a bluff, like a swallow's nest, about a quarter of a mile above the last houses of Porto Lúa in a narrow glen of oak trees untouched by the encroachments of pine and eucalyptus woods. At the bottom of the glen, watered by a small stream, was a deep brake of ferns and ivy. Though weathered, the two-story house was in good condition. A new roof and fresh mortar in the stonework had kept out the rain and dampness. In addition to a large kitchen on the ground floor, there was a storage room with a winepress. Upstairs were two bedrooms and a bathroom with white tiles, considered a luxury at the time. The yard was overgrown with saplings and wild grass, and the stone path that led to the house was nearly hidden beneath dead leaves. Thirty yards downstream, just off the path behind a copse of laurels and thickets of hawthorn, was a small field where the new tenant could grow his own vegetables.

Mestre agreed to take the house but stayed in the *pensión* until his trunks and crates of books and furnishings arrived the following weekend. In the meantime he enlisted the services of several of his students to sweep out the cobwebs and leaves and paint the walls in several rooms, and when his furniture and books finally arrived, we helped to load the wooden crates and a console piano on two oxcarts that Facundo procured for the final leg of their journey up the hillside. Mestre put in a new stove, had an electric line strung, and hired a carpenter to build bookshelves along two of the walls in what he had already designated his library, one of the bedrooms on the upper floor with a view of the bay.

Every morning he walked down the glen where the trees and leaves were wet from the night air or morning fog and through the freshened streets of Porto Lúa in the shadows of the houses to the Colegio de Primera y Segunda Enseñanza de Porto Lúa. Despite the warmth of the wood stove, he kept his coat on while teaching and paced back and forth before the blackboard where he conjugated Latin verbs, copied out the apothegms of Diogenes, drew maps of Greek history, and lectured on ancient creation myths, the origins of Porto Lúa, the history of Raíña Lupa, and the poetry of Virgil. In my exercise book from that year I copied the following notes:

The Creation Story

Before the sun and moon and stars, before the land and sea, the wind and clouds, man and beast, in the eternity before time, in the immensity before space, there was only God. God is everywhere and is the object of all hope. God is the limit placed on all possibility. The potential made actual.

Boundless without form, nowhere and everywhere, all things were one in God. Hot and cold, wet and dry, earth and air, fire and water existed together without distinction. Until nature, by its nature, began to separate, and time was born. Heavy, attracting heavy, fell to make the earth. Light, attracting light, rose to make the sky.

And of the emergent space were four corners: north and south, east and west. And each corner contained a wind: Auster, Boreas, Zephyrus, and Eurus, contending for domain, and, by their contention, they created the clouds that fell in rain that carved the hardness of the earth into mountains and valleys with streams and rivers.

Before the separation, there had been no loss, no gain. With separation came time and the blessings of growth and striving, but also conflict, death, and decay. Before time, whatever was had to be as it was and nothing else. The perfection of God. With time came change, with change came the mysteries of chance and necessity, and in the fallen order of imperfection appeared man.

From what could be seen with his own eyes and heard with his own ears, man created his world. He created destiny to overcome his fear of chance and free will to overcome his fear of necessity. There are no theories in science or philosophy able to explain the mysteries of being.

The Origins of Porto Lúa
Mount Aracelo was formed deep within the earth three hundred million years ago. The mountain was raised by

the subduction of the Gowanda plate beneath the Laurasia plate associated with the breakup of Pangaea. A pink and violet batholith of granitic magma containing biotite, orthoclase feldspar, and quartz in an equigranular texture, it rises dramatically above the Atlantic Ocean and is a singular geological phenomenon of this coastline where it creates its own weather.

Of the first inhabitants of the area little is known beyond the lowness of their state. Their bones, unburied and unmarked, are mixed with those of their prey, and their simple tools testify to a lack of technical skill. Of their culture, only flints for cutting and animal skins for covering have survived. The fate of these people is uncertain. Their deaths went unrecorded so far were they from civilized thought.

When the glaciers retreated and the warmth returned, another race made its way overland to the shores of the region and left more lasting remnants of its presence in the ceramic vessels and decorated tools found in caves and along waterways.

Five thousand years ago Neolithic people brought agriculture to Galicia and built the megalithic tombs that remain along with the concentric circles and cupmarks they carved in stone. People believe they were giants, but they were not. They were engineers who could move twenty-ton boulders to cap a circle of standing stones. They were followed by the people of the Bronze Age, who came here to mine the tin and fashion the bronze implements that characterized their epoch.

At the end of this period, roughly a millennium before the birth of Christ, people began to build circular houses behind high walls in communities we now call castros. *The artifacts they left behind and many of their place names lead us to call them Celts, and because of their presence, the Romans called the region "Gallaecia." Six hundred years before Christ, these simple hill-forts began to expand into larger communities, and by the second century before Christ, they were building larger urban areas called* oppida *with streets and running water. In the year 137 BCE, the Roman general Decimus Junius Brutus Callaicus invaded Galicia, and over the next hundred years under the leadership of Caesar and Augustus, the Romans pacified the indigenous tribes.*

The origins of Porto Lúa have been lost. There are several theories. Stories have been handed down through the generations that there was once a settlement on the northern summit of Mount Aracelo and when this settlement was abandoned, its inhabitants moved down the mountain to the bay where the current Porto Lúa is located. Other stories say that Onde se Adora was the original settlement, founded in the Neolithic period and abandoned when the castro *culture died out under Roman rule. Much research remains to be done.*

Along the Costa da Morte there is physical and written evidence of many ancient cultures: mussel-gatherers, Phoenicians, Greeks, Celts, Romans, Suevi, Visigoths, Moors, and Normans. Earrings similar to those in Iron Age Ireland were found in a field near Lonxe do Sol. The Romans had a port in the area called Dugium from which they exported gold. The ruined castle at Pedrullo was built to defend against Normans. The names of many places are Celtic, Suevian, and even Greek. The names of many people are Etruscan, Arabic, and Gothic.

For sea-faring people of the past, Galicia was the inter-section between northern and southern Europe.

The origin of the name "Porto Lúa" as told by a charcoal burner who lives in the woods behind Mestre's house: the moon, who was old and tired from traveling across the sky for so many years, began to fall from her path through the heavens. One night Raíña Lupa invited her to rest on the summit of the mountain and in return the moon agreed to carry the souls of the dead on the re-mainder of her journey to the distant shores of night.

Raíña Lupa

Raíña Lupa was born among the stars. Crowned by the Pleiades, she governed from her citadel on the moun-tain's summit, blessing the rains and softening the winds of winter storms. She called on the sun to warm the land to grow the grains and vines, and on the moon to give beneficial sleep. For her the earth put forth sap to make fruit and buried seeds to preserve life. It was she who ensured the fertility of the fields, the beasts, and the inhabitants of the country, and she who guarded the secret of the soul's immortality. To her the people of the mountain built a lost temple.

During her reign, a ship bearing the body of the Apostle Santiago landed on the coast. Teodoro and Atanasio, who had accompanied the body from the Holy Land, asked Raíña Lupa for permission to bury the saint in a sacred grove. Before agreeing to their request, she sent them to the priest of the sun altars who resented the intrusion of a foreign religion and took the disciples prisoner. With the help of an angel, they escaped, but were pursued by their guards. Just as the disciples were about to be overtaken, a bridge bearing the priest's men collapsed and they were drowned.

When Raíña Lupa heard of their escape, she decided to test the magic of the two disciples and told them they could find oxen on Mount Ilicino to transport the body of the saint, but when they reached the mountain where the oxen grazed, they encountered a guardian serpent spewing fire. They conquered the beast and the magic of pagan idols with the sign of the Cross and renamed the mountain Pico Sacro. The oxen they found were wild, but when the animals charged, the disciples pacified them through the intervention of the Holy Spirit. Then they yoked the creatures to a wagon and appeared at the palace of the queen.

Realizing the power of a greater God, Raíña Lupa allowed the disciples of Santiago to bury his body on an eminence to the east called Liberum Donum. She built a church over the sepulcher and abandoned her citadel on the mountain to spend the rest of her life in a hermitage near the shrine.

When the old gods allowed the season's crops to languish in the parched earth under the searing heat of the crab, the people of the mountain followed their queen and fled to the new religion. They built churches and shrines where the old altars had been and blended old feast days with the new.

When Raíña Lupa died, her body was carried from Liberum Donum to a secluded peak high on Mount Aracelo where she was buried in a stone coffin beneath the moon.

Virgil's *Georgics*
Book I

Before selecting a field to plow, you must understand the changing moods of the wind and sky in that place. And which plants are best suited for its soil. Alternate crops in the fields, use manure and ashes, burn the fields to give the soil strength. Dig ditches to irrigate the furrows.

Jove himself made the life of a farmer hard so that by labor he might keep his mind sharp and avoid lethargy and thereby win the blessings of the gods. The almighty father gave the serpent poison, made the wolves thieves, brought storms to the sea, and hid fire from humankind so that we might raise ourselves higher through our cunning and skills.

The hardships of the farmer are many. There may be mildew on the grain. Thistles and burrs and creeping vines crowding out the crops. Birds feeding on the seeds. Branches of trees cutting off the sunlight. A lack of rain. When these threats to his crops cannot be controlled, the farmer will subsist on a diet of acorns. But he can arm himself for his struggle with the land with a plow, a wagon, a sledge, a sturdy hoe, wicker baskets, and winnowing fans. To make a plow beam, bend an elm sapling to suit the form. Use linden for the yoke and beech for the handle. Pack the threshing floor hard with clay and roll it smooth so it will not crack or allow the mouse or mole room to dig a home.

Nature has a tendency to slip back from human cultivation. By improving nature, we improve ourselves.

Follow the stars to know when to plant. Sow barley when Libra balances day and night, and flax and poppies too. Plant alfalfa, beans, and millet when Taurus rules, and wheat when the Pleiades set at dawn. As Boötes disappears from view, he will tell you when to plant your vetch and lentils. In winter, hammer the plowshare straight, mark the bins of grain, weave baskets from briar switches, roast grain on the fire and grind it on the stone. Clear the ditches that water the fields, plant hedges to guard them, set out snares for birds, burn off the bramble thickets, and dip the sheep in a healthy stream. Winter is a time of leisure without worry, as when a ship comes in. But use it well to gather and hunt.

Learn to predict the weather through nature. Watch the seabirds and shooting stars. Note the actions of the crane, the heifer, the swallow, the frog, and even the ant that brings her eggs up from the earth. If a new crescent moon is bright, rain will follow. If a new crescent moon is red, there will be wind. If on the fourth day of its return from darkness, the crescent moon is clear and bright, good weather will last for the month. If the sun at dawn is hidden by patchy clouds, there will be rain. If the sun at dawn is fractured into shafts by breaking clouds, hail will fall during the day. If the setting sun is flecked by fiery red, a storm is on its way.

The sun is so closely involved in human affairs that it shrouded itself when Caesar fell. On that occasion people heard and saw the harbingers of doom: ill-omened birds, volcanic eruptions, disembodied voices in the woods, phantoms roaming the night, cattle speaking like men, icons of ivory weeping in temples, statues of bronze dripping with sweat, floods devastating forests, blood boiling out of springs, wolves invading the cities, lightning and comets. So many wars, so much crime, that farming was forgotten and sickles were bent into swords.

Book II
Like children, trees will put off their untamed ways and be willing to learn if properly taught. Each does best in its natural setting. Willows by rivers, alders in wet-lands, ashes on mountain rocks, myrtles on the open shore, yews where the cold winds blow. Soils have hu-man attributes and may be stubborn or torpid. Olives will thrive where thin clay is mixed with pebbles, and grapes do well in moist, rich soil on a southern expo-sure. Black soil is best for grain. To test for salty soil, put it in a strainer and pour water through it. Taste the water. Rich soil never crumbles, but clings like pitch.

On level ground, plant your vines close by one another, but on a hillside, give them more space. In both cases keep them in regular rows. Don't plant a vineyard on a western slope. Plant either in early spring when the stork is flying or around the first frosts of autumn.

The beginning of the world must have been an extended spring protecting cautious life from intemperate winds, hot and cold, when grasses first trusted the warmth of the sun, and the fields first opened themselves to west-ern breezes, and grapevines first reached out in delicate buds. The first cattle drank in the light, and the first men of the earth lifted their heads in stony fields.

One season begins before another ends. The farmer breaks the soil as he clears old leaves. Year after year.

Prune and weed and burn. But there is also happiness where the earth gives freely of her bounty. Far from armed conflicts, far from endless lines of petitioners, far from the luxury of curtains threaded with gold, of wools colored with foreign dyes, far from the anxiety and guile of the city. In the countryside the old ways are preserved. Young people are accustomed to hard work and ask for little in return.

Blessed are those who search into the causes of things, who overcome superstition and their fear of inexorable death. But the farmer's life is happy too in the company of country gods. In rural life there is no blind ambition for honor, no tyrant dressed in purple, no brother betraying brother, no poor to be pitied, nor rich to be envied. The farmer picks the fruit of his own trees unbound by the shackles of iron laws or undone by the madness of the Forum.

In the countryside, life is a remnant of Saturn's rule.

By his plow, the farmer raises his family. Fruit ripens all around. The herds are crowded with new lambs and calves. Grain is heavy on the stalks. The granary is full to overflowing. The olive-press is overworked. Foraging pigs have grown fat on acorns. Clusters of grapes mature in the sun. The udders of cows are full to sagging. In his simple home there is love and affection. This is how the Sabines lived and how Rome became strong. Before impiety led men to slaughter their working animals for indulgent feasts. Before the hollow pomp of trumpets and the ringing of swords on anvils.

Book III
*The ideal breeding cow will be ugly and fierce with folds
of skin hanging low from her neck, long flanks, and big
hooves. She will be feisty in a yoke and butt when given
the chance. Breed her from ages four to ten. Beyond that
she will be fit for neither breeding nor plowing. But during those years when the herds enjoy their lusty prime,
set the bulls loose early to produce as many offspring
as they can.*

*The best days of life for ill-fated mortals go by too
quickly. Soon enough they succumb to disease, debility,
and the struggles of old age. Until, in the end, a grim
death delivers them from all of this.*

*The ideal horse for breeding steps high and plants his
hooves lightly. He is fearless in the face of roaring waters and does not flinch at startling sounds. He holds
his head high, and his chest is taut with muscle. He lis-
tens keenly for the sounds of war, his limbs tremble
with anticipation, and through flaring nostrils he
snorts his burning passion.*

*Nothing wastes the strength of animals like the entice-
ments of Venus. Distracted by the presence of cows,
bulls will gorge each other to bloody ruins. To keep
them healthy, send them off to distant pastures before
it comes to that. All living creatures, including humankind, are slaves to lust. The lion will leave her cubs, the
bear will ravage the forest, the boar will roam with mad
ferocity, and the tigress is never more dangerous. Consider Leander swimming through churning seas at
night while a storm crashed overhead indifferent to his
parents' desperate calls and the fate of his lover who
would die weeping over his corpse.*

Burn cedar in the stalls and pens to keep vipers away. To avoid scabies, dip sheep in fresh currents or when they're sheared, rub them down with the dregs of olive oil mixed with hellebore, sulfur, and bitumen pitch. To venom and disease add the threat of plague. Once in a foul atmosphere of autumn heat it struck, wasting beasts both wild and tame. Hidden in the water, hidden in the forage, it dried the throat and then the veins, down through the limbs until the bones melted into a stew of death. Animals on the altar died before the sacrifice. Calves fell in fragrant fields. Dogs went mad. Pigs choked as their gullets narrowed, and horses starved amid plenty, kicking the dust as they died.

Book IV

To raise bees, shelter the hives from the wind and animals that graze among wildflowers. Protect them from lizards and birds, and place them in the shade of a palm or olive tree. Be sure there is water nearby whether cool springs or a mossy pool or a flowing stream. In the water place willow branches or stones where the bees may linger. For flowers, cassia, thyme, and violets are preferable. The hives themselves can be cork or wicker woven with a narrow opening. If the bees don't work, remove their king (queen) by plucking off his wings.

There was an old Corycian who lived on a few acres of unclaimed land, unclaimed because it was unsuitable for plowing or grazing or growing grapes, but in the brush he planted a garden of cabbages, white lilies, verbena, and poppies and considered himself as content as a king. And though he never went to market, his table was always well supplied. He had apples in the fall and honey in the spring when his bees were early to breed.

At his ease among the linden and viburnum, he planted pears and blackthorns laden with berries, and plane trees to shade his friends who came to share a drink.

When his mother hid the infant Jove in a cave on Mount Dicte, bees nursed him with their honey. For this he gave them a virtuous nature. They alone raise their offspring in common, share the quarters of their cities, and live under the rule of a higher law. They spend all summer at their labor, toiling in their meadows and hive, to provide a common store in winter. Some by agreement gather nectar from the flowers of forests and fields, some build the walls of their waxen combs, some tutor their youth in the ways of the world, some fill the cells with honey, and some serve as sentinels watching the sky or helping to unload returning foragers or dispatching the lazy from among their number. From the morning star to the evening star they work, as the hive, scented with thyme, bustles with a fever of activity.

Without exertion or travail, the female produces her young apart from males, gathering them, like nectar, from sweet blossoms. All members of the hive will sacrifice their lives for the common good. While a single life is short, no more than seven summers, the line can last forever. These are the qualities that lead some to believe that bees partake of divine wisdom and have drunk the ether of heaven.

They say that god exists throughout creation, in the land and sea and sky, and from birth, the beasts of the land, and the birds of the air, and the race of men and women live through his presence. And when they die, their lives return to the source of life, the divine among the stars.

343

When father asked me what I was studying, as he had done when Bachiario was my teacher, I replied, "A Roman poet named Virgil."

"Poetry?"

"About farming."

"And what does your poet say about farming?"

"That the life of the farmer is hard so he can win the blessings of the gods through his labor."

"That's true. What else?"

"That you bend elm saplings to make plow beams."

"That's right."

"And if you beat a young bullock and close it up in a room and starve it, bees will appear spontaneously from its carcass."

"The more you learn, the less you seem to know," he said.

Notwithstanding the farming lore found in Virgil, the study of poetry and history had little value in Porto Lúa. We were nevertheless acquiring knowledge of the broader world and coming to understand the place traditional ways of thinking had in it. When a scholar from Santiago valued our way of life, the stories we had heard as children were elevated in our eyes to subjects of serious study, and we took pride in collaborating with our teacher to document and preserve these stories.

During our class on Raíña Lupa, Mestre asked if we had ever heard our grandparents speak of her. There were several responses that he wrote down in a notebook he carried with him, but Facundo's revelation that my father's cousin had been present when her tomb was opened caused him to ask several additional questions and ultimately led him to organize a weekend excursion to the site. Eight weeks after my previous visit, on a wet, but unusually warm Saturday in mid-December, Mestre, Facundo, Miguel, María, Ánxel, Inés, Andrés el Tercero, Marcos, Lucas, Sara, Pilar, and I set out from the schoolyard loaded with blankets, sticks of *chorizo, empanada,* omelets, and bread. Establishing a brisk pace in his gray over-coat and black *boina*, Mestre led us through the fog-dampened streets and up the back lane behind our orchard where we came upon my grandfather. Mestre stopped and asked him several questions about Raíña Lupa, writing everything down in his notebook. As the interview concluded, they shook hands, and grandfather, surprised at the interest in his stories, re-marked, "I'm so happy you had the pleasure of meeting me."

Rising over the hills south of the Deva, a bleary sun burned through veils of moisture, lifting the fog that lingered overhead in daubs of gray and white cloud. Along the road, birch trees, alders and ashes, were bare, while the oaks were still laden with their russet foliage. The ground below was mulched with layers of wet leaves blown against tufts of grass and beds of nettles and ferns. In the cold promise of the low sun, the sap-less woods of deep winter possess a tenacious beauty unsur-passed by the forests of summer that flourish with indiffer-ence, too full to care, lush and spilling with ripeness, green to the point of darkness.

When we reached the path to the tree of evil, I told Mestre of my experience there and described the pool and rags in the tree. He listened carefully and asked the other students if they also had stories to share about the mountain. In this way we passed the better part of the morning and soon reached the overlook where Harry had constructed the bench and windows on the valley. On this climb, we made much better time than I had on my previous visits, and though we stopped once more when Mestre interviewed a group of pilgrims, we reached the bothy by mid-afternoon. My classmates stayed behind to rest and build a fire while Facundo and I led Mestre along the prec-ipice and through the granite sentinels to Lonxe do Sol, which at this time of the year was already deep in shadow. We found Xosé at home, and he agreed to take us to the tomb of Raíña Lupa the following morning. He invited us to stay for dinner, but Mestre explained that we were part of a larger group and needed to return to them before darkness. As we walked back above the high cliffs of the Deva, the winter sun dropped through bands of cloud leaving a wake of gleaming brass across the sea, scuffed and plaited by wind and current. By the time we returned to the shelter, the western horizon had darkened to a hedge of violet clouds, and the only light came from the colorless sky above it. We were greeted by a warm fire, and, despite the season, the night was no colder than on my previous visit.

We left the next morning before daylight. A white gauze of woodsmoke lay among the branches of the trees silhouetted against a porcelain sky as the first light of dawn appeared in the east. By the time we passed the church near Lonxe, the sun had risen, but was still behind the mountain. Crows circled, quarreling, above a ridge of pines while rattling across the forest floor, field mice searched for seeds in coverts of wet leaves. Descending from higher on the mountain, chilled by the stone landscape, the air was freshened by the scent of heather. We met Xosé and his son at Porto Ventoso and then passed through the gate and followed the path along the cliff to the cluster of steles that had been used as altars. Mestre marked the orientation of the site with his compass and drew a map showing the location of each stone relative to the others and the cliff. After completing his survey, he photographed the stones and speculated that this path was older than the road passing through Agro Vello. Before the birth of Christ, he said, people came from great distances to leave their offerings to the god of the evening land hoping to be blessed in the next life.

"Is the god of the evening land Berobreus?" María asked.

"Berobreus. Berobreo. Brioreo. Briareo in Dante. Briareus in Virgil. In Hesiod's *Theogony* and the first book of the *Iliad*, he is called Vriáreos and was worshipped in ancient Greece. In Latin, *vero* means 'in truth,' and *verius* means 'truly.' *Vero nihil verius* means 'nothing is truer than the truth.' When the Gallaeci referred to this god as Berobreus, did they see the words *vero verius* or something like 'truer than true,' or 'the ultimate truth' in the name, implying that nothing is more certain than the god of our final destiny? It is a question worth asking. Aelianus wrote that Aristoteles of Chalcis claimed the Pillars of Hercules were first known as the Pillars of Briareus, so the sailors who passed from the Mediterranean Sea to the Atlantic would have entered the unknown realm of the dead."

On the path to Santa Locaia, Mestre described two references in Homer to this realm. In the first, King Meneláos discovers he is destined for Elysium, which lies at the end of the world, and there his afterlife will be one of ease. It is a place without snow or the bitter cold of winter or pouring rains. Rather, a gentle west wind blows across the ocean to freshen the souls of men. In the second, Hermes leads the souls of the vanquished over a mountain, through the portals of the sun, and past the shores of dreams to fields of asphodels at the end of the world. In turn, we told Mestre what we could recall of Trofonio's account of the underworld and his guide Berobreus. When we finished, he replied that the story was consistent with many in classical literature, but he had never heard of such a tale in modern times. Respectfully expressing his skepticism, he suggested the man may have read more than he let on. In Santa Locaia, Facundo and I showed him the altar to Jove in the side of the chapel and the pool in the stream where we had stood in the night. Mestre reached into the water and took out a piece of white granite to show us it was rounded on one side—evidence it had once been part of a column, or even of a temple. He walked the perimeter of the meadow beside the chapel and marked the location on an ordnance survey map.

When several of the boys went to relieve themselves in a hollow between two boulders near the path, Xosé stopped them and explained that such places may be inhabited by spirits of the dead or local daemons and defiling them could bring misfortune. They should choose a thicket for their needs rather than a boulder or a stream where they could offend the invisible beings of the mountain. When we arrived at Onde se Adora, he issued similar instructions, pointing out a field where no one walks because it is thought to be sacred to the gods. We should also avoid the presence of daisies, he said, because they attract the souls of deceased children.

On the site of the ancient settlement, stone foundations emerged from the bell heather and wild grasses in both rectangular and circular formations. We walked quietly among the ruins as Mestre, with his trained eye, searched for evidence of those who had lived there in the past. Within a few minutes, on what may have been a doorsill, he discovered nine small cupmarks forming a square and suggesting a child's game or perhaps a simple abacus. Calculating the age of the village by the size and placement of the stones that made up the walls of the houses and pens where animals were kept, he decided that Onde se Adora was a Bronze Age community, but the area had been occupied by people for longer than that.

As we followed Xosé along the path to the tomb of Raíña Lupa, we came to what he called "the shepherd's hut," a shelter made up of four flat boulders—three sides and a capstone. It was, Mestre informed us, the remnants of a tomb dating back to late Neolithic times. We sat in the ferns as he traced the carvings on the side of one of the stones with a piece of chalk and then asked us if we could see any patterns among the markings. María noticed the big and little dippers as well as Cassiopeia. Mestre then explained that the carvings were a map for the soul of the deceased to navigate through the stars to return to its original home. He then pointed out the carving of a stick animal, possibly a deer, that was meant to be food for the soul on its journey. I held up a ruler to the markings as

Mestre photographed the wall. Then he went outside to photograph the structure and position of the tomb. He told us it was at least a thousand years older than the altars.

When he had completed his notes on the site, we proceeded another two or three hundred yards to the base of the northern peak. Under an overhang, as described by Xosé, was a long hollow stone, like a dugout canoe, partly covered by a flat stone of similar proportions that had been broken on one end. The break had been smoothed by decades of weather and was spotted with lichens, but it appeared consistent with his story of the dynamite. Mestre was less interested in examining the hollow, which would have been pillaged long ago, than in searching for inscriptions or petroglyphs in the vicinity of the stones. Seeing what no one else had seen, he pointed out shallow grooves in a flat boulder nearby as well as cupmarks, but further exploration would have to wait for another day. It was already early afternoon and if we were to make it to the bothy before nightfall, we couldn't afford to spend any more time at the site.

Our last night on the mountain we shared the bothy with two pilgrims who were returning to Brandomil. They had taken the souls of their deceased husbands to Porto Lúa and then on to Mar das Almas where they would be closer to their final destination in the afterlife. Mestre asked them if the custom was still common in the countryside.

"Only among the older people," one of them said.

"Why do you go to the headland? Isn't the mountain closer to God?"

"God is everywhere."

"Then why make the journey to Porto Lúa?"

"Because that's what people do."

We woke again before dawn and were back on the Roman road at first light. The descent was uneventful, and we reached Porto Lúa by the middle of the afternoon. Sister Benigna and

Sister Mary Rose had taught Mestre's classes to the students who were present, and our studies resumed their normal schedule the following day. The weather turned cold and rainy over the holidays and continued to be inclement during the darkest weeks of winter. Mestre wrote up his notes from our trip and interviewed Trofonio to find out more about his experience and determine to what extent it was based on his reading of classical texts, but despite its similarities to descriptions of the underworld in the works of several authors, he could find no specific source for his account and concluded it was a creative pastiche of several.

One weekend late in winter when the weather relented, several of his students accompanied Mestre on a walk across the headland to study the ancient path he believed to be a continuation of the original route over the mountain. María, Miguel, and I picked up Marcos, Lucas, Sara, and Pilar on the way down Rúa do Olvido, and met Mestre and Andrés el Tercero in the plaza. His father, Don Andrés, was also there. Declaring himself an amateur historian who read fondly of the people and events of the past, he had decided to join our expedition.

"While it is an obligation of my office to learn as much as I can about the history of Porto Lúa," he said, "I also have a personal desire to improve my knowledge of the lives of those who came before us. When I was a young man, I thought the world was also young and because of this, I had no interest in the past. I held it to be an invention of my elders. A constraint on the creativity of youth. Now that I am older, the past seems much closer, and a decade or two before my birth almost seems a part of my own life. Even the century that separates me from the grandparents of my grandparents is nothing from the perspective of time immemorial. If we do not communicate the importance of the past to the young people of today, will our own lives mean nothing to posterity? In short, those who forget the past, cannot blame the future for forgetting them."

His speech-making was lost on his audience, but I suspect he was practicing to deliver a similar address in the event that Mestre made a significant historical discovery—one which, Don Andrés hoped, would bring more visitors to the area. As we crossed the Deva and turned down the cliff walk, he continued, at Mestre's prompting, to expound on a past so far gone that no living person could confirm or deny it.

"While I'm not a scholar like Mestre, I have done some reading in my time, and I can tell you that since the beginning of history, we have been known by people in other parts of the world as, to use the words of Homer, the 'sunset race.' In some cases, we have been identified with the Cimmerians, who lived in a perpetual gloom at the end of the world near the entrance to Hades, or the Lestrygonians, who ate their guests. This may be due to the black legend which held that the people of the coast tore out the organs of foreign seafarers to frighten away pirates. But, consistent with the name of the town, we think of ourselves as people of the moon, peaceful and reflective.

"I yield to Mestre on questions of philology, but will add that, speaking of Homer, there was a teacher in Noia who claimed the town Outes was the home of the cyclops. However, 'nobody' can say for certain. That's a pun, of course, because 'Nobody,' or 'Outis' in Greek, is what the hero of the tale calls himself when the cyclops asks his name. This same teacher told me he had seen a skeleton with only one eye socket in private hands, but it was not an inch above three feet tall. I suppose cyclopes have children too. Not to be outdone, we have our own mysterious corpse locked away in our museum. Remind me to show it to you on our return."

He continued to speak in this vein as we followed the path along the edge of the cliffs. Though the day was clear, the wind was blowing hard from the open sea. As we neared the ravine where Harry had built his garden of stone, I suggested we stop to speak with him because he knew the paths of the headland as well as anyone. We found him in a field not far from his sculptures building an astronomical calendar of standing stones. Wearing nothing more than a pair of shorts, he was raising a large stone into an upright position. Mestre introduced himself, and they spoke cordially in English for several minutes. Running his finger along the southern horizon, Harry advised us to cross the ridge that runs down the length of the peninsula and follow the path westward from Foxo Escuro to the sea. We helped him set the stone in the ground and held it in place while he packed a foundation of rocks around it to keep it from leaning. On the way through the fields to Foxo Escuro, we told Mestre the story of the ferrymen who used to greet the Santa Compaña and lead the souls of the dead to the sea where they would carry them across Mar das Almas into the light of the moon.

The village was as dark and grim as Lonxe do Sol. It was essentially two rows of granite houses set on either side of a narrow lane strewn with manure. As we passed, people stared from their windows, but no one attempted to engage us or offer a word of acknowledgement. The size and placement of the stones in the roadbed, as well as the depths of the ruts carved by ironshod wheels, confirmed the antiquity of the lane. Outside the village, it lay three to four feet below the level of the surrounding fields and was bordered by mossy embankments and tangles of gorse and blackberries and small trees. Since the gorse was dense and shoulder-high, we didn't venture off the path to look for petroglyphs, but on a few boulders along the way we found cupmarks, used as oil lamps to guide religious processions in the past. At the end of the peninsula, the path dropped down through a grove of pines and a corridor of granite boulders to a narrow cove sheltered from the Atlantic by a natural breakwater of dark, tide-stained rocks skirted by beds of kelp where waves broke and fell in churning pools. A few colorful *dornas* were beached on a sandy slope surrounded by marram grass and clumps of rock samphire, while on higher ground a small shed open to the elements contained piles of weathered nets and lobster traps. We climbed over the rocks above the cove looking for evidence of an ancient presence, whether a submerged seawall or inscriptions or post holes for an altar, but found only small crosses carved in the stone to Christianize this place that had been a source of awe in the pagan world.

As promised, on our return to Porto Lúa, Don Andrés took us to El Conde's palace where Don Prudencio greeted us and unlocked the small room designated the official museum of Porto Lúa. As we crowded inside, he opened a cedar chest and took out a tin box containing a hand and ear and some of the pelt of a man-beast believed to have been killed on Mount Aracelo centuries earlier. The hand was more ursine than canine, but the ear was more canine than ursine. The fur was grayish-brown. According to the mayor, it was not an animal known to modern science.

"The country people," he said, "call it a *vákner*, a man-like creature with long hair covering its entire body and possessing superhuman strength. To this day there are reports of a wild man living on the mountain. In fact, Bachiario has seen him several times. Others believe the remains are those of the wolf who loved the Raíña Lupa, and some say they belong to a devil who emerged from hell to taste the sweet air and feel the morning sun and expired in that instant."

The origin of our next excursion, one that brought Porto Lúa the attention Don Andrés had desired, was a visit Mestre made to Fulgencio's barber shop. As a new customer, he was taken into the back room and shown the painting purportedly by Picasso, but Mestre immediately recognized it had no more value than an empty canvas and turned his attention to the other odds and ends in the room. He pointed to a rusty sword standing in the corner and asked about its provenance.

"This is the sword of a renegade Frenchman who fled to the mountain before the siege of Corcubión in the last century," Fulgencio said. "My friend Manolo found it and traded it for a year's worth of haircuts."

"It's not a French sword," Mestre said.

"No?"

"It's Roman."

"Roman?"

"Where did he find it?"

"In a field."

"Can your friend take me to the place?"

"Stay here and I'll go get him."

When Manolo arrived, he confessed that he had not found the sword, but had traded a pair of Waterloo dentures for it.

"Who found it?"

"Cotolay."

"Who is Cotolay?"

"An *inocente.*"

"Will he remember where he found it?"

"We can ask him."

After searching unsuccessfully for Cotolay in Capela de Santa Lupa, Manolo tracked him down in the alameda where he was selling his blank scraps of paper. Confronted by a growing crowd in the barber shop that included Don Andrés and Horacio, Cotolay at first denied any knowledge of the sword, but when assured that he had done nothing wrong, he revealed that he had found it in the woods on the mountain. When pressed for a more precise location, he asked for a sip of *aguardiente* to help him remember, but Don Andrés denied him even a drop until he showed them the site. If they could verify the location by finding corroborating evidence, he would reward him with a bottle from his own stock.

"I found it near Lonxe do Sol," he said.

Armed with shovels, picks, trowels, stakes, and string, a

group composed of amateur historians, students, and the merely curious made the trek up the mountain on the following Saturday. On the path between the bothy and Lonxe do Sol, Cotolay revealed he had found more than a sword. There had also been a human skeleton. When we reached the shafts of granite that guard the approach to Lonxe, he failed to recognize the place and claimed the stones had changed their shapes. Suspecting a subterfuge, Don Andrés began to grow impatient and told Cotolay to stop wasting time and concentrate on their surroundings. And then, as if on cue, the *inocente* noticed an animal trail through the boulders that he was certain he had taken before. We followed him down a winding path through the pale, tightly packed monoliths, not unlike an alley through a warren of whitewashed houses, to an opening among the stones that resembled a small square. Wild boars had dug a slough in the mud that had softened the ground and exposed several ribs and a cranium that had once lain beneath the surface. Also visible were the rusted tip of a Roman pilum and the green bronze of a belt buckle.

When he saw the bones, Mestre decided they should leave the site untouched and contact the civil authorities as well as the Facultade de Xeografía e Historia in Santiago. When Don Andrés argued the discovery belonged to the people of Porto Lúa, Mestre informed him that removing any bones or artifacts was a criminal offense, and the mayor quickly backed down. Before we left, Facundo was enlisted to guard the site. Well-provisioned with food, matches, and a heavy blanket, he was supposed to maintain a constant vigil, but retreated to the bothy shortly after sunset when the boars returned. Thereafter he stayed on site during the daylight hours and returned to the bothy to sleep.

On the following Saturday, Mestre led a group including two members of the Guardia Civil, four professors from the university, a graduate student, a donkey loaded with equipment, Don Andrés, Dr. Romalde, Constable Sampaio, Fulgencio, Cotolay, and a half dozen students to the site. The Guardia Civil inspected the body, declared the death was not due to criminal mischief—at least not in recent centuries—and left. The professors from Santiago cleared the space of plants and stones, plotted the entire enclosure, and took photographs from every angle before setting up a tent in a field nearby and retiring for the night. The people from Porto Lúa spent the night in the bothy imagining what had happened to the Roman soldier as we sat before a large fire.

At first light the archaeologists were back digging at the site and soon discovered a second skeleton and a small cache of coins. After working through the morning, they packed up their equipment and the material legacy of Roman occupation, less the skeletons, and anchored a blue tarpaulin over the excavation with a ring of stones. The plan was to reach Porto Lúa before dark, but just as they were leaving, a reporter from *La Voz* showed up with a movie camera to document the discovery, so they took the tarpaulin off and pretended to dig in order to preserve the moment of discovery for posterity. They left the tent and graduate student behind and gave Facundo enough money to take him fresh food twice a week and meet any other needs that might arise in their absence. Before departing from Porto Lúa, they reached an agreement with Fulgencio that they would not report him under the laws protecting cultural patrimony if he would turn over the sword that had been "stolen" from the site. To compensate him for his loss, they also promised to send him a card from the Galician Society of Antiquarians that would allow him to visit any state museum for free.

The archaeologists returned a few weeks later during *Semana Santa*. They carefully tagged and removed the bones and continued to strip off layers of topsoil to a depth of roughly three feet, but the earth yielded no more human remains and no additional artifacts. During their week on the mountain, they expressed an interest in exploring other areas of historical importance, so on their last day, Mestre and Facundo took them up the Roman road through Agro Vello to Onde se Adora and the tomb of Raíña Lupa and then back down through Santa Locaia to Porto Ventoso. They took photographs and notes at every site but were most impressed by the Roman altars where they spent more than an hour. On the way back to camp, they began discussing how they would move the stones down the mountain. Mestre conveyed both his alarm and displeasure at this possibility.

"Why do they need to be moved?"

"To protect them."

"From what?"

"From vandals or people who would sell them."

"They've been here for nearly two thousand years."

"But now people will know they're here."

"People have always known they were here. They leave flowers on the stones."

"What I'm saying is that once we reveal this discovery to the press, the wrong sort of people may come."

"Then don't reveal it."

"I don't think you understand why we're here. These extraordinary monuments of the past belong to the people of this country, and our role is to study and preserve them."

"If you ask the people who live here what their country is, they will tell you it's the mountain."

"That may be, but the state has a less poetic view of things, and the Ministry of National Education would find it inexcusable if we left objects of such historical value unprotected."

"The value of these stones is determined by where they are as much as what they are. Their location is essential to appreciating their significance. Before the trees grew up, this is where people coming over the mountain stood to worship their gods."

"When they're displayed, there will be an explanation of their historical purpose and photographs showing that location."

"It would have been better if I had never brought you here."

"The altars would have been discovered eventually and perhaps not by people who care about their preservation."

The archaeologists arrived in Porto Lúa early the next evening and loaded their equipment and two boxes containing the bones they had recovered into a van parked behind the market. Before leaving, they spoke with a number of people to arrange the removal of the altars the following week. There were twenty-four stones altogether, and they would need to hire twelve oxcarts and twelve men to dig them up and load them onto the carts. When Don Andrés got word of the plan, he tried to persuade people not to assist in any way, but they argued they needed the money, and if they refused to help, someone else would readily take their place. Remembering how they had defeated General Molinero's attempt to remove the house of Alonso Pinzón, the mayor pressed those who had been involved in the previous effort to come up with a plan to frustrate what he referred to as state-sanctioned theft. But the week went by, and nothing happened.

Officers from the Guardia Civil were the first to arrive, then two flatbed trucks covered with bales of hay, then a tow truck with a winch, then the professors. The men from Porto Lúa who would provide the labor for the project lined their carts up on the Roman road in semidarkness, and shortly after seven o'clock the procession disappeared up the mountainside. They reached Porto Ventoso late in the afternoon and worked until darkness, carefully placing two altar stones on each cart, cushioning them with bundles of straw, and securing them with cables. When the people of Lonxe do Sol found out what was happening, many of them gathered on the periphery of the grove to watch. A few approached the workers, but the Guardia stepped in and kept them from coming too close. The officers remained overnight to ensure nothing untoward took place, and early the next morning the crew finished loading the stones. After a descent slowed by the weight and value of their cargo, they were back in Porto Lúa that evening. With Dr. Romalde and María Dolores, Don Andrés stood in the plaza as the caravan of oxcarts came down Rúa das Angustias. Although he had known nothing of the altars or Roman remains a few weeks earlier, he now compared the removal of local antiquities to the pillaging of Compostela by Almanzor, and, as the carts crossed the plaza, his agitation only increased: "What will they want next? A tribute of a hundred virgins?" In an effort to calm her husband, María Dolores whispered, "There are plenty of stones on the mountain. We'll have someone carve a few Latin words on them and plant them in the ground where these were taken out. No one will know the difference." But Don Andrés took the loss personally and would not be reconciled to it. As the winch lifted the stones from the carts and eased them onto the trucks, he asked the Guardia Civil how they could stand by and watch as a crime was being committed. And when the drivers started the motors of the trucks and began to pull away, he ran behind them as far as the bridge where he threw his hat after them, awkwardly, given his girth, and shouted, "You can take away our stones, but you can't take away our history."

As he walked back to the plaza, hat in hand, wiping the perspiration from his forehead in defeat, he added, "Two thousand years of history gone in two days."

Having remembered the promise of a bottle of *aguardiente* for leading Mestre and Don Andrés to the Roman site, Cotolay followed him home and asked for his reward. Don Andrés was good to his word, and as he handed the bottle to Cotolay, he remarked how the sequence of events starting with the discovery of the sword had led not to the benefit of Porto Lúa, but to its deficit.

"Not entirely, Don Andrés. I did some digging of my own," said Cotolay as he took a handful of Roman coins out of his pocket. "You can put these away until the professors have forgotten about us and then add them to the treasures in the museum."

The closing chapter of this story was written the following week when Paco Carreira brought several copies of La Voz back from Muros after taking Father Infante to the dentist. In the section entitled Cultura, there was a full-page article celebrating the discovery of twenty-four Roman altars on Mount Aracelo on the Costa da Morte with several photographs, a crude map of the mountain showing the location of the altars, and an artist's rendering of third-century Roman soldiers in armor and commoners wearing tunics and sandals.

Mestre avoided the plaza on the evening the altars were taken away. Having seen his research lead to unintended consequences, he turned his attention from exploring the mountain to the books and stacks of papers in his study. Late in the spring, when he had gotten to know his students better, he invited those of us who showed an interest in reading to share his library. He understood that few homes in Porto Lúa provided an environment conducive to study, and fewer still had the resources to satisfy a natural curiosity in subjects that extended beyond the schoolroom. So on weekends and sometimes in the evenings during the week, several of us walked up the path to his house where we sat in chairs and on the floor reading or thumbing through his books as he worked at his desk. The shelves were bowed under the weight of a collection containing a variety of subjects from the religions of ancient Greece to modern poetry, from botany to geology. There were morocco-bound folios with gilt lettering on the spine, new and secondhand hardbacks, and broken paperbacks with loose pages. The older books exuded a dry odor exclusive to aging paper that filled the room and, at times, it seemed, the entire house. As the evening sun moved across the spring sky, its last rays moved across the room illuminating the row of books on top of one of the shelves. In the fading light, the gilt titles shone with a vividness that appealed to me like a secret language opening the door to a magical world.

Most of the volumes in the library were in the fields of literature and philosophy, both classical and modern. For example, one bookcase was dedicated to works by Homer, Heraclitus, Aeschylus, Plato, Aristotle, Diogenes, Epicurus, Catullus, Lucretius, Cicero, Virgil, Ovid, and Epictetus, and another to works by Montaigne, Shakespeare, Cervantes, Lope de Vega, Calderón, Voltaire, Goethe, Leopardi, and Tolstoy. Among the modern authors were Valle-Inclán and Pessoa. An entire shelf was filled with works by, and commentaries about, Virgil. Mestre's affection for the poet was based on his humanity and the beauty of his descriptions of rural life. His favorite philosopher was Diogenes. He said that his words kept him grounded, and sometimes, when we were challenged by intractable logic or unpleasant truths, he played the cynic, mocking the absurdity of such deliberations by asking what a dog might think of our struggles to understand.

But books weren't his only interest. Almost as soon as he took possession of the house in the glen, he set about cultivating a garden in the meadow behind the laurel and hawthorn grove. As the days grew longer, he spent the hours after school clearing out the leaves and winter weeds, and turning over rows of soil to expose it to the sun and air. On a Saturday morning, Facundo brought a cartload of seaweed and dung up the path, and the two of them spread it over the field. Then he planted carrots, potatoes, kale, and turnips as well as several apple trees, leaving the border around the field to whatever wildflowers might appear. Once he had surrounded the garden with a low mesh fence to keep the rabbits out, Mestre built four hive boxes and set them in a row on higher ground at the northern edge of the field to receive the warmth of the southern sun. He completed his garden by adding a simple weather station in the corner of the field to measure and record the meteorological information that could help him protect and care for his plants more effectively.

After working in the garden, he returned to the house, took off his muddy clothes, washed, and dressed in a clean shirt and jacket out of respect for the authors of the past he was about to engage. To write, he used the quills of seabirds dipped in a bottle of blue ink, because, he explained, the words came out with a flowing grace as if his hand could sense, still present in the feather, the currents of the winds over the blue horizon of the sea, and he could visualize his ideas better when they came through an object of nature. On his desk were several coffee mugs, empty tins of tuna fish—where he kept paper clips and rubber bands—a magnifying glass, two books of Etruscan phonology, one of Latin, the dictionaries of a dozen languages living and dead, numerous journals wrapped in plastic envelopes, and stacked shoeboxes of notes written on file cards listing Celtic, Etruscan, and Gothic place names, as well as surnames, the locations of hill-forts and tombs, and other historical monuments like the Roman altars. Scattered on the margins of the desk were piles of maps where these places were marked with tiny notes printed in red and blue and green and purple ink. His books were annotated with equal precision. Above all this was a light bulb hanging on a long cord from the ceiling. For a lampshade, he bent a box into a cone and lined the inner side of it with pieces of foil.

The room was crowded but uncluttered. Beside the desk was a cabinet filled with journals and correspondence. Against the walls perpendicular to the desk were two large bookcases.

On the other side of the room, opposite the desk, were two smaller bookcases, a tulip lamp, an armchair, two bentwood chairs, and a Hsinghai console piano. On the wall above the piano was a gilded icon of the Madonna and Child, and sitting on top of it was a replica of the Veii statue of Aeneas. As with the original, the terra cotta figures were indistinct, but captured the moment when Aeneas carried his father out of burning Troy, embodying the Roman virtue of piety toward family and the gods and depicting the burden of carrying one's history as well as one's destiny through the misfortunes of life.

Work as we knew it meant plowing a field or gathering a net, so an occupation of reading and writing where one could sit for hours lost in thought or be compensated for recording those thoughts on scraps of paper was a revelation to us. When Mestre spoke of his work, he did so modestly, comparing it to the skills of our parents. For example, when he demonstrated the Galician village of A Peroxa was named after the Etruscan city of Perusia or Perugia, he was establishing one of many facts, like a carpenter, he explained, cutting and trimming his boards, so that he could build an accurate argument on the history of Galicia. While working, he played Puccini or jazz in the background on a portable Victrola, and, when the mood came over him, he would sit at the piano and play an impromptu fugue, or, "Perché a lo sdegno" from Monteverdi's *L'Orfeo*, singing the following lines with feeling:

Nel sole e nelle stelle
Vagheggerai le sue sembianze belle

In the corner of the room was a long wooden box stamped with the words "Emil Busch AG Rathenow." When we asked him what it contained, he opened it to show us a brass telescope with a tripod and two eyepieces nestled in round nooks. Miguel, who was immediately taken with the instrument, asked how he had come by it.

"It was a gift from a woman I knew many years ago," Mestre said.

"Was she the person who gave you the ring with the grain of sand?"

"She was."

"What happened to her?"

"Like many people, she was lost in the war. Life was very hard then, and it was a struggle to survive. Our lives were no exception. Sympathetic to the Republican cause, we fled to Catalonia to escape the violence of the Nationalist offensives elsewhere, but then Barcelona fell, and because of the reprisals that followed, we made our way to Ripoll and hiked up Vall de Núria with the intention of crossing the frontier into France. In the mountains above Sant Gil, within a mile of the border, I stopped to look back at her climbing not far behind me in the cover of darkness. Unseen among the shadows were soldiers patrolling the border paths, and as I waited for her to join me, I was shot in the left shoulder a few inches above my heart and lost consciousness. That was the last time I saw her."

"Did she escape?"

"She did, but I only found out later. The soldiers took me to a military hospital where I spent six weeks recovering from my wound. When I was released, I was forced to serve with the Nationalists and sent to the front where I carried a note in my pocket reading, 'I am no man's enemy.' This was early in the spring of 1939, and the war in Spain was soon over, but I was kept on active duty until the following winter. I set out for France as soon as I could and looked for her in Céret, where we had agreed to meet if separated, and other towns and cities from Perpignan to Tarascon. I went to cafés and bars frequented by exiles showing people her photograph. Finally, one day I met a woman who recognized her and told me she had been interned by the government of the Third Republic almost a year earlier at a place called Camp Gurs. In danger of being detained myself and unable to see her, let alone free her, I returned to Spain to wait for the end of the war in France. Two years after the Vichy Government came to power, they handed many of their prisoners over to the Germans, and she was taken to Mauthausen, in the east, from which she never returned."

His voice faltered, and he paused for a moment before continuing.

"In the autumn of 1942, before she was sent away, I received a letter from her. She had been able to smuggle it out of the camp through a Basque guard sympathetic to the Republican cause. 'If you are still alive,' she wrote, 'and I do not survive this war, look for me among the stars.' This was her only request, and I have honored it more times than I can count. Even now, when the sky is clear and the stars are bright, we spend the night together as we have done for more than twenty years."

From the silence that ensued, Mestre realized how deeply we had been affected by his story and abruptly changed the subject.

"When the weather is clear and the nights are free of distorting vapors, we'll take the telescope to the top of the bluff, and you can see the stars for yourselves."

But such nights are rare in Galicia in the spring and summer when warm weather too often fills the sky with clouds or a blanket of haze heavy with dew that seems to shake the stars. As we waited, we pored over the drawings of the planets and constellations in Mestre's books on astronomy imagining the worlds that were floating in the sky overhead.

One evening, I inadvertently came upon notes he had written to himself when he received confirmation of his friend's death. I was in his study reading a translation of Cicero's *De re publica* and opened it to a bookmark in the closing section. At the top of the page, he had simply written the date, "June 12, 1945." And then in the margin, in small script, he continued, "Our lives have passed too quickly. She was everything to me." I never mentioned that I had seen the page, and put the book back on the shelf where I'd found it, but when the cold, clear nights finally arrived, and he stood in the darkness, faintly illuminated by the stars, I wondered if he was searching for one in particular or whether he found her in the vast emptiness of night.

Weeks before the first flowers opened, a premonition of their fragrance filled the night. Then winter returned with slanting assaults of rain that beat ceaselessly against the stone houses and budding trees and broken earth of the freshly plowed fields, washing away any thoughts of summer and sun. The saturate land was black, and the air was white with fog coming in from the sea hanging like drapes of lucent silk. Through rain-streaked windows and gossamer trails of falling mist, the lanes and roofs of the town were smears of gray stone and ocher tiles. When the wind finally subsided, the world around us was preternaturally still. The yellow lace of nascent leaves burned like cold flames in the forest slowly stirring to life. Tawny willows and groves of oaks and alders on the hillside conveyed the scent of musty wood and old wicker while the odors of damp straw and manure issued from the earth. In the calm, watery stillness of those spring mornings, cool air, cut off from winter's flight, pooled in the shadows of low-lying streets and streambeds. Over the mountain, gray-blue clouds, gravid but unthreatening, hung heavily, moved slowly, through the warming sky. When the sun broke through over flowering fields in saffron islands of light, larks and blackbirds opened a chorus joined at times by cuckoos hidden in the woods. Later, the sky would clear, its sapphirine depths softly blanched by the brightness of sunlight, and, like a sweet drug, the taste of spring, together with the hollow roar of waves on distant rocks, confused past and present in a place outside time where what we remember and what we perceive are one and the same.

Spring was also a season that demanded more intense labor in the gardens and fields. I was old enough now to do more than help grandfather watch the animals graze or chase birds off the feed corn, and father told me that for every hour I spent with Mestre on an excursion or reading outside of school, I was to spend another working on our land. So in addition to scything millet for the ox, feeding cured mangels to the pig, and filling in the muddy ruts of the cart path with flat stones, I was now to cut firewood for the stove, plow our pastures, and pitch marl and manure into the furrows from the back of the oxcart as grandfather led the creature back and forth through the small plots.

Despite the removal of the Roman altars, or, more precisely, because of the publicity surrounding their removal, the hopes of Don Andrés were realized when historians, both professional and amateur, as well as curious sightseers, descended on Porto Lúa with the arrival of warm weather. They mostly appeared on weekends and parked in the plaza, then walked the narrow streets noting the architectural details of the houses, the designs of the boats in the harbor, and any other unusual features of the town that caught their attention. Wherever they went, they stopped to ask people questions about the history of Porto Lúa or whether they could purchase old farm equipment they saw in the yards and fields, equipment they deemed it their responsibility to preserve. On one occasion a group gathered to photograph a stone in the wall beside our gate faintly etched with a Visigothic name indicating its past use to mark a grave. Many of the visitors who ate their midday meal at O Galo remarked on how fortunate we were to live in such a place.

Spurred on by his discovery of the Roman remains, Cotolay searched among the boulders and wild tracts of the mountain for similar finds, digging for coins and swords at various
sites where his voices instructed him to dig. Excavations appeared like anthills in the distance, and in some cases the holes
reached a depth of several feet. When he heard there were people inquiring about altars and dolmens in O Galo, he showed
up at the bar on Saturday and Sunday mornings where the patrons were more than happy to direct the curious to the man
they called the preeminent authority on the history of Porto
Lúa and discoverer of Roman artifacts. For his part, Cotolay
embraced the role of expert and welcomed the opportunity to
show the visitors where he was digging or lead them tramping
across fields or through the woods to look for elusive foundations or petroglyphs deep in coverts of gorse or brambles. One
Saturday he took a group of professors from Salamanca up a
path to the ruins of a medieval watchtower at Balcón dos Deuses. Along the way, he named the peaks and rock formations
and told them how he had discovered the Roman sword. Encouraged by their interest, he embellished the story of the discovery and went on to invent another about a coffin filled with
gold coins that had been buried beneath the ruins of the watchtower. When they reached the site, the professors found a
scree field of rock fallen from the tower and plotted a grid
within the original foundation. After removing hundreds of
stones and digging for most of the afternoon, they found nothing more than the bones of a goat and broken pottery of modern provenance but nevertheless decided to spend the night in
Porto Lúa and return the following morning to continue working. As they were packing their gear for the descent, Cotolay
climbed down from his perch on a boulder and turned to see a
pale gibbous moon rising over the mountain. He stopped,
transfixed, as if staring at the blue within his mind, until one
of the men called to him.

"What is it? What do you see?"

"The moon."

"What about it?"

"Don't worry. We have an agreement."

"An agreement?"

"To keep its distance."

Only then did the professors realize the preeminent authority on the history of Porto Lúa and discoverer of Roman artifacts was in fact an *inocente* and they had wasted their day laboring in his idle fantasy.

The attention he received from visitors led Cotolay to consider himself a *mestre* of the fields, and he began to entertain the idea of opening his own school. When he asked the men in O Galo for advice on how to go about it, Fulgencio tried to convince him to name his school the Academy of Erroneous Thinking where students with the most mistakes receive the highest grades. Xosé Carrillo told him the Corpus Juris Civilis requires all founders of schools to petition the king in order to procure his permission before opening. A week later, Cotolay returned to the bar with a letter authorizing his school signed by Don Juan, Count of Barcelona.

"Do you think this will do?"

The men passed the letter around, and, much to their surprise, could find nothing to indicate it wasn't authentic.

"What subjects will you teach?" Gustavo asked.

"How to extract gold from seawater."

"How is that?"

"If I tell you, how will you learn?"

"Aren't you a teacher?"

"I am. Are you a student?"

"Yes."

"Then you must study."

"He's not as mad as he looks."

"What else will you teach, Cotolay?"

"How to make stones."

"Do you mean how to make bricks?"

"I mean how to make diamonds."

"I could use some diamonds to decorate my house. When does this school start?"

"As soon as I can find a way to teach without words."

"How will you teach without words?"

"How can you learn anything new if you use the same words you've always used? I don't have time to make new ones, so I'll do without them."

While Cotolay dedicated himself to the discovery of a pedagogy surpassing language, Mestre took advantage of his free time at the end of the semester to return to the Instituto de Estudios Gallegos Padre Sarmiento and Colexio de Fonseca in Santiago. For two weeks, from morning to evening, he read through Latin codices as well as scholarly articles pertaining to the history of Porto Lúa and copied by hand ancient maps showing the land of the Artabri, the promontory of Nerium, and Namancos. By the time he returned to Porto Lúa with a stack of notes he had taken from the works of Strabo, Ptolemy, Jerónimo Contador de Argote, and Mauro Castellá Ferrer, he was convinced he had located the site of the lost port of Dugium and that it was the same city as Porto dos Ártabros. This was an ancient settlement built before the Romans, but enlarged by them for the exportation of tin and gold. When the mines played out, it lost its importance and finally fell in the fifth century when the Suevian invasion occurred. No one knows how it disappeared. Storms may have buried the streets and houses in sand, or a violent earthquake may have shaken it from its foundations and sent it to the bottom of the sea.

A seventeenth-century map showed a settlement on the coast north of Capela de Santa Lupa, called Extramundi de Abaixo, which we knew only as a beach and open pastureland. And on another map, farther up the coast, was a place labeled

Portus Artabri inhabited now by seagulls and sheep. Mestre believed either of these sites could be the mythical city of Dugium, but tended to favor the first because the rocks on one side of its cove were as flat as a manmade quay and the shore and seabed were more gradually sloped, lessening the impact of the waves. Before exploring the site carefully, however, he spoke with the men and women who collected goose barnacles from the rocks and hunted for octopi in the shallow water. Jaime Otero told him he had once seen a piece of fluted column, but could not remember exactly where, and showed him a badly rusted blade he had found submerged among the rocks. His wife, María Gloria, added that as a child she had heard stories of phantom ships being seen in the area that disappeared like the fog at dawn.

On a calm morning in June when the tide was out, Mestre and two dozen students walked along the path above Capela de Santa Lupa and down to the beach at Extramundi de Abaixo where we took off our shoes and socks and lined up hand-in-hand perpendicular to the beach in a chain that stretched for thirty yards into the sea with the tallest boys in the deepest water and the girls closest to the shore. For two or three hundred yards we walked through the waves that rocked us gently, looking for any unnatural patterns or formations of stone or pieces of metal, but we found only plastic bottles and bits of polystyrene and a small anchor. Then, stripping off our shirts and diving under the surface, the boys searched the seabed, digging in the sand between ridges of granite, but again found nothing of historical significance. Mestre extended the search farther up the coast, into deeper water, which made it more difficult to walk. One by one, we lost our balance in the waves, and when the line fell apart, we broke out in laughter and began to splash each other. Realizing there was nothing to be gained by continuing, Mestre called off the search and allowed us to spend the rest of the morning enjoying ourselves in the water.

As we waded through the rising tide, dancing buoyantly on our toes and chattering as the cold swells hit our waists and then our chests, I noticed something strange happening to me. I felt as though the sun and sea were enchanters calling forth the hidden dreams of my body. The stories of a former world no longer mattered, for a new one was opening before my eyes. The girls, cuffing the surface of the water to flail each other with bursting showers and laughing as they cleared the hair from their eyes, seemed transformed from the classmates I had known into creatures of color and light who provoked in me a pleasurable agitation, as yet more vague longing than acute desire, as if I had suddenly become aware of being incomplete. One of the girls was known for being fretful. One for brooding. One was loud and teased the boys. One made up stories. One never spoke in class. One talked without listening. But as I watched the movement of their bodies and responded to their laughter, they possessed an appeal, a beauty beyond their individual features, that lay in their very nature.

We sat on the white sand above the water drying out in the sun. A sea breeze stirred the sedge and thistle behind us, and the noon light glanced off the waves that rolled in below us breaking over rocks and spilling down in small cascades or spreading over the beach in lace-fringed slips that melted into the sand. On slabs of stone that stretched like searching arms into the clear blue water, gulls screamed like cats in the night while sanderlings and pipers raced back and forth at the water's edge. As my daydreams floated off into the summer sky, I was content merely to be in the company of the girls and listen to their voices. The presence of the feminine—not that which I associated with my mother or my aunt, or the nuns at school, or the feminine explained by Father Infante in his lesson on reproduction, but the appeal of play, the look in the eye, the form and movement, the awkwardness of emotion, and the novelty of it all—provoked a series of seemingly unrelated reveries that took me back to forgotten sources of happiness. But all the pleasures of the past now seemed a prelude to the pleasure I took in my companions, in the softness of their features, their laughter, and the breathlessness of their excitement. I wanted to be with one of them, but none in particular, and had no idea how that might happen.

Home became a place of exile. When I returned that afternoon, the kitchen where I ate, the bedroom where I slept, the hallway where I walked were as featureless as a prison offering nothing but cold, dull tedium. Hours of chores lay ahead of me before I could indulge my imagination again, but when I finally lay down for the night, I was able to escape my prison through dreams of girls sitting or lying in the grass as their hair dried in the wind. Although I would have been unnerved by such boldness, I wanted nothing more than to hold one in my arms.

Among my friends I was forced to feign an interest in subjects where I had none, and, at the same time, suppress what was more important to me than all the trivial interactions of daily life. I was once again living in two worlds. On one hand, there was the profane, the mundane and dreary, where I was dragged down by chores and schoolwork. On the other, was a world of intangible promise where my imagination could create an ideal without reference to material or social realities. As I indulged in this dream, the part of me that interacted with others appeared to them, by turns, irritable, indifferent, and disdainful, when, in fact, I was filled with uncertainty and doubt. Guilty of imagined transgressions, of moral conflicts I could not reconcile, I saw myself through the eyes of others as a collection of faults. My appearance, my family, my words were all a source of embarrassment to me.

I went on like this for weeks, suspended between the fictions of my aimless longing and the reality of the pig and mangels. These fictions were invariably more noble than carnal, for they were, as much as anything, a way of transcending the cold, muddy, malodorous life that appeared to be my destiny. In other words, I had no interest in being the beast Miguel said we had become, and thought of the objects of my longing not as I thought of the animals that give birth in the fields, nor as the women who bear us, but more as sunlight breaking through the fog of my isolation and despair. I wanted nothing more than to feel the warmth of that light, but in the absence of the feminine, my longing foundered, and the mud and manure of my daily life did nothing to revive it.

Everything changed unexpectedly one Sunday in the middle of July. Despite the calendar, the day began like a gusty spring morning when the ground is damp and the sun struggles to gain strength. I was walking through the churchyard of Nosa Señora do Mar with my parents on the way to Mass when I saw her. She was accompanied by an older woman who walked so slowly that we passed them and entered the church first. They sat in the middle of the second pew to the left of the center aisle. My family sat in the pew behind them beside the aisle. Inattentive to the Mass, I observed her out of the corner of my eye, wondering why I had not seen her before, why she was not in school. On my return from Communion, I saw her look at me, but rather than a furtive, embarrassed glance, she returned my gaze without looking away. Had she seen me before? After the final *Dominus vobiscum*, I dropped my missal to slow our exit. As I brought it up from beneath the pew, I caught her eye again as she looked back from the stream of worshippers filing past and smiled. The older woman with her delayed their exit, so I told my parents to leave without me as I wanted to speak with Father Infante who was conversing with members of the congregation. I watched as the crowd cleared the portal and then followed the stragglers down the hill.

Fool that I was, after waiting in order to be able to catch

up to her, I passed her without saying anything and couldn't even bring myself to turn and acknowledge her as I walked by. I continued as far as the market, which I circled debating whether I should walk back up Via Sagrada and pass her again or return home. To keep from embarrassing myself any further, I decided on the latter course of action, but as I was going up Rúa do Olvido, they were coming out of a lane between two houses and crossing the street just ahead of me. I looked down and pretended not to see her, but overheard the older woman call her "Laura" as they entered the yard at number 8. I continued up Rúa do Olvido to Rúa dos Loureiros thinking I would have to wait another week before seeing her again. But then it occurred to me that I hadn't seen her before because she was only visiting, in which case I might have lost the only opportunity I would have to speak to her.

Over the next week, I walked past her house as many as a half dozen times a day. Sometimes I only made it as far as the plaza before returning. Other times I wandered through the old part of town or stopped by the market on any pretext to talk to mother. On each trip I held out hope that I might meet Laura unexpectedly as we rounded a corner at the same time or crossed paths in the street, but that never happened. As I passed her house, the blue and white tile cemented into the stonework over her door bearing the number 8 was like a charm hinting at the enchanted world within. The iron latch on the door she touched, the cement threshold she crossed, the scent of the purple flowers she could smell from her window, the window itself, I envied for their place in her life. Even the neighboring houses of gray, weather-stained blocks of granite took on a luster by their proximity to hers. When I walked up and down the street, I pretended to be hurrying on my way to some important task, but my only task was to have her notice me if by chance she might emerge as I passed or happen to look out the kitchen window and see me hasten by preoccupied with my weighty affairs.

On Sunday morning as I walked up Via Sagrada and crossed the churchyard with my parents, there was no sign of Laura or the old woman. When we entered the portal, I looked at the middle of the second pew, but they were not there. We sat in the third pew beside the aisle as we had done the previous week. I glanced around to see if they were behind us, but they weren't. Father Infante entered the sanctuary, and the congregation stood up. I went through the motions of standing, sitting, and kneeling, but without much awareness of where we were in the service. Feeling light-headed, I eventually leaned back against the bench and sat down and remained seated until people filed out of the pew for Communion when I stood and followed them. As I was going back to my seat, I looked up to see Laura walk past on her way to the altar rail. Her hands were touching in prayer and her head was bent down so that the tips of her index fingers touched her upper lip. When she returned, however, her head was up. She saw me and smiled. I hadn't seen her earlier because she was sitting at the far end of the pew on the other side of the aisle near the back of the church, perhaps because they had arrived late. At the end of Mass, father stopped at the top of Via Sagrada to talk to one of his friends. As Laura went by with the old woman, she smiled at me again, and, on the way down the hill, looked over her shoulder to see if I was following. But I couldn't get away. Father had his arm around my shoulder as he was telling his friend a story he wanted me to hear.

I was reassured knowing Laura was still in Porto Lúa, but without being able to speak to her, I had no more idea of whether I would see her again than I had had the previous week. Knocking on her door required a reason, and I couldn't think of a good one, so I continued my walks past her house. As I went by late one morning, I saw the old woman sitting on a stone bench beside the front door. Like many women her

377

age, she wore a wide-brimmed straw hat with a black ribbon around the crown and a light blue smock over a black dress. At her feet was a pile of dry straw. With quick fingers, she was braiding the stalks to form a row in a circle that would become a hat. She had grayish blond hair and brown eyes that peered out of the shadows with an intense, scrutinizing gaze as if she were staring into the sun. Several of her teeth were missing and her face had shrunk inward with deep lines around her mouth. As people passed the house, she addressed them with a ritual *bos días*. I returned her greeting and went so far as to venture a subtle wave.

The next day when I stopped by the market to visit mother, I found myself in the good graces of fortune. Walking away from our stall with a parcel of fresh hake was this same woman.

"Who was that?" I asked.

"Your grandmother's friend, Filomena. She used to have a stall in the market selling cheese. She comes here every morning at the same time to shop and chat with her friends."

"I saw her with a young woman at church."

"That's her granddaughter from Muros." Mother looked at me as if she were reading my mind. "She's spending the summer here."

For the rest of the week, I timed my walks to coincide with her grandmother's trips to the market, hoping Laura would be with her, but I did not see her again until Sunday. By now it was August and even if she was going to be in Porto Lúa for the rest of the summer, time was running out. And still I had no idea what to do. But that uncertainty disappeared when my parents and I entered Nosa Señora do Mar on Sunday morning. Laura and her grandmother were sitting on the left side of the church in the second pew next to the center aisle, immediately in front of the place where she knew my family typically sat. As my parents and I edged our way into the pew, I caught her eye, but this time she averted her gaze. I knew instinctively what this meant. And she knew that I knew. Her bright red hair was tied in wispy pigtails separated by an irregular part that reached from the bangs on her forehead to the back of her neck. Her narrow shoulders and slender frame as well as the slight curve of an incipient bosom kept me from attending devoutly to the Mass.

Nature gives us this brief period at the end of childhood, this time of innocence, without the incentive of sexual pleasure, to live selflessly in the freedom of discovery so that we may be sustained by the dream of an ideal throughout our lives. Of all the mysteries of our first encounters with the world, the horizon at the edge of the sea, the storms that strip the mountain forests, the streaking lights that cross the meridian night, of all these and more, the initiation into love is the greatest because it renews the freshness of all things, restores the creative power of the imagination, the springs of wonder, at the very time in our lives when they begin to fade.

At the end of Mass she left her missal in the pew where I couldn't help but see it. I picked it up and considered returning it while she was still in church, but as my parents and I moved slowly down the aisle, we were separated from Laura and her grandmother by several other members of the congregation and more stepped into the aisle ahead of us, separating us further, so I decided it would be better to wait and take it by her house. Holding the prayer book tightly in my hand, I watched her pass through the bars of light from the stained glass that illuminated her face with blues and greens and yellows, transforming her appearance every few steps as if grace could be bestowed by color. From the shadow of the vestibule, she emerged into the sun, pausing momentarily in its light before continuing down Via Sagrada.

When I arrived home, I opened the missal on the kitchen table. She had written her name in the upper right corner of the first page. I studied the script for some clue about her character, and then turned the pages that her hands had turned and read the words that her eyes had read and then lifted the book to my nose and detected the smoke of beeswax candles. After lunch, I summoned my courage and set out down Rúa do Olvido, but began to experience nervous tremors in my legs and took a detour back up through Campo da Graza and the churchyard and then down Via Sagrada while I tried to compose myself. When I entered Rúa do Olvido for a second time, I continued past Laura's house to the plaza where I reproached myself for faltering and then went back up the street until I reached number 8. When I knocked on the door, she answered it. Without knowing quite what to say, I handed her the missal, uttered something about finding it in the pew, and then, to escape the vertiginous effects of my shyness, I quickly turned away, and, overwhelmed with relief, marched out the gate like a confused general triumphant in his defeat. She must have thought I was mad.

"Wait."

"What?"

"Where are you going? Come back."

"I just—"

"You have to give me a chance to thank you. Wait."

When she returned, she was carrying a plate of sweet buns.

"My grandmother made these this morning. Take one. They're still warm."

I took one and held it in my hand. I was too discomposed to raise it to my mouth or think clearly, but managed to say, "I don't remember seeing you before."

"I'm only here for the summer. I'm staying with my grandmother."

"It's nice in the summer."

She had let her hair down after church and now pulled it back with both hands and fixed it tightly with a rubber band which made her forehead look larger. Freckles stretched from cheek to cheek across her nose.

"Thanks for the bun," I said.

"You're welcome."

"I have to go," I said. "I just came by to return your missal."

"Come by again."

"I will."

I didn't have to go, of course, but feeling my façade of confidence give way, I wanted to escape as quickly as possible. As I walked up Rúa do Olvido, I turned and looked down the street. She was still standing at the gate.

"I'll come by tomorrow afternoon."

"I'll be here."

I caught myself at times floating through the day not fully conscious of anything only to realize I'd been thinking of her, but as soon as I was aware of these thoughts, I worried that I had misread her intentions. Perhaps she was only looking for someone to spend time with. A friend or companion. There was an inverse relationship between the growing strength of my feelings for her and the diminishing assurance I felt in myself. The next morning as I stood in front of the mirror in the hallway critically assessing what I found there, I began to think I would be better off not going at all. Perhaps, after all of this, I had been mistaken about her. Perhaps I had idealized someone who didn't exist. Perhaps she was like the girls in my class. Easily vexed or too talkative. Too demanding or begrudging.

As I walked down Rúa do Olvido, the sun was high overhead, and because people were just waking from their afternoon naps, the street was nearly deserted. When Laura opened her door, the house was still dark, shuttered against the heat and light, and her face was luminous against the darkness. She wasn't as calm as she had been when we first spoke, and I noticed her breast rise and fall from excitement. Rise and fall because of me. I was breathing just as heavily. My arms fell slack, almost numb, and my legs once again shook with a slight trembling. To hide our nerves, we set off walking at a brisk pace with no idea of where we were going. She was following me, and I was following her. Neither of us said anything at first, listening for the absent words of the other, and I felt my heart sink in the shallows of that silence. When I found my voice, it was far away, as if the words belonged to someone else. When I heard her voice, the words were like the tolling of a bell, clear at first and then fading on the air as I delighted in the sound and lost the meaning. By the time I recovered from this wakeful sleep, we were in Nosa Señora do Mar. Fearing that I might ask her what she had already told me, I began a new topic, repeating what grandmother had said about Andrade and his handlebar moustache and French officer's coat, and then, pointing out the skull in the stained glass window, I told her the story of Fidelio and his deal with the devil.

It was early evening before I knew it, and we had moved on to the alameda where we sat on a bench beside a row of blue hydrangeas. The air in the lavender shadow of an old larch was cooler than in the streets, and because the tide was out, the sea wrack below the quay smelled like rotten eggs. As we watched the fishing boats return to port, I asked Laura about her family and told her about mine. When clouds began to gather over the western horizon, we tried to guess what animal or mythical creature the other saw in them. Her eyes were the green of seawater beneath the foam of cresting waves, with the right slightly off-center, floating inward, which made her even more attractive. Shortly after sunset, the elderly made their way to the plaza and began their nightly rounds, circling the perimeter, men with men, women with women. Soon the swallows were out, gliding through the golden air, climbing as if seeking the surface of the sky only to plummet back to the depths of lanes and alleyways. When the lights came on in the alameda, we passed through the rose garden where Laura bought one of Cotolay's slips of paper. When she discovered it was blank, she laughed and said it was a small price to pay to learn what the greatest philosophers did not know. We shared a slice of watermelon from the stand of Xosé de Arcos and headed down to the plaza where I pointed out my stone in the Tower of Names. In Rúa do Porto, Laura asked why all the houses on the street were marked as the museum of the explorer Martín Alonso Pinzón, and I told her the story of Amalia González who saved the house for the people of Porto Lúa. We concluded our first day together watching the Two Marías leave their house and set off down Rúa dos Santos.

Early the next morning, Laura and I crossed the Deva and walked out the path along the cliff on the southern edge of the bay. The sea winds kept anything taller than deep grass and stunted gorse from growing and discouraged the cultivation of the land, but in the valley partially protected from the elements, Harry's garden flourished. We went down the stone steps through the forest of strange sculptures and found him sitting on the stoop of his shed sharpening the blade of a shovel. He took us back to the top of the cliff and showed us the museum to the souls lost at sea, which now looked like a beehive hut with an open roof. The astronomical calendar of standing stones was still not complete, but he explained how it would work. We thanked him for his time and continued along the cliff stopping here and there to look through the stone window frames of the ephemeral museum. To avoid Foxo Escuro on our way to the port at the end of the headland, we cut through the open countryside on narrow animal trails. As we made our way over the boulders and through the bracken and gorse, I felt her arm brush against mine. I pretended not to notice and so did she, but we both casually leaned in toward each other to ensure it would happen again. My body felt like an instrument struck on the keys of a perfect chord. Since touch is the only sense reciprocated, it was a means of communicating where words were too direct or in-sufficient. The next time it happened, we made a game of it, gently pushing each other off the trail with our shoulders. When we reached the cart path to the port of Foxo Escuro, I felt her fingers intertwine with mine, and we walked the rest of the way hand in hand. I told her how in the past the men of the village had ferried the souls of the dead from this cove across Mar das Almas into the light of the passing moon. As we stood on the rocks looking out at the Atlantic, dark clouds formed over the sea, and a cool wind began to blow. The open water turned an ashen gray as if the souls of the dead had come back from their colorless world to conjure up the storm, which, as the intensity of the wind increased, seemed a warning to the living, complacent on solid ground. When the waves crested in the shallows, they turned a chalky green and then white, aer-ated among the outer rocks where they danced, frenzied and foaming, before hitting the boulders along the shore and ex-ploding skyward, their arcs falling slowly over the stones, and the spray, driven by the wind across our faces, reaching up the beach as far as the fishing boats secured above the tidal surge.

Graceful curtains of rain began to fall between the cape and Illa da Luz, and we hurried back through the fields we had crossed earlier only to be caught in a passing shower. We con-tinued walking, laughing at ourselves as the water ran through our hair. When the clouds broke up and the sun returned, and the thickets of broom and gorse and the fields of bell heather sparkled with fresh drops of rain, we were like the first people awakening on the first morning, discovering a world newly made where the grass was the first grass and the clouds were the first clouds and the wet branches of the wild laurel along the path were the first to bend in the west wind that was the first to cross the sea. We did not care that the world can only be created once because this was that moment for us. Though we may seek it again later in life, with each attempt the glory of that discovery fades.

Because I had been neglecting the chores father had listed for me over the past week, I had to be home by the time my parents returned for the afternoon meal. I left Laura at her house and told her I would come by again as soon as I had caught up with all the responsibilities I had been ignoring. Once I had done this, I was able to work out a schedule where I could spend several days a week with her. On the mornings when I was free, I would walk down Rúa do Olvido and stand before her house and call to her through the open window of her room, and we would soon be on our way.

Carrying a pair of wicker putchers tied together and slung over my shoulder, I arrived at Laura's door earlier than usual on a cloudy morning when the streets and houses were still damp from fog. We went up Rúa das Angustias and down a path that cut between two houses and the walls of their gardens. As we descended to the Deva beneath the branches of sprawling oaks that sheltered an undergrowth of nettles and briars, the air thickened with humidity and the odor of fresh water. Gnats swarmed in hovering clouds along the wooded bank while blue-winged dragonflies rested on dry culms of grass hanging over the shoreline. The overcast sky, together with the low water and slow current of late summer, created a sluggish atmosphere throughout the valley. We climbed down over a series of natural steps in the granite, took off our shoes and socks, and waded into a shallow pool above a falls where two large boulders channeled the water down a ravine that dropped five or six feet below us. As we set the putchers and secured them in the rocky bed, two salmon shimmied up the white cascade to clear the edge of the pool and dart past us.

The path on the opposite bank led us up through a granite bluff and a tangled cluster of willows and alders. Here and there, through gaps among the trees, we could see light entering small clearings where people had planted sheltered parcels of corn and kale. We walked on through a village of a half dozen houses called Silvosa and more small fields enclosed by dry-stone walls before entering a forest where the trees had grown up among the ruins of another village abandoned so long ago that only a few foundations remained. In niches of the trees someone had placed porcelain eyes that appeared to mark the trail. We followed them as they seemed to follow us until we came to what was known as the house of Suzzain Sutania. We approached cautiously, our steps softened by the dampness of the leaves underfoot. The ochre tiles had long ago weathered to pale oranges and smoky grays, and patches of moss were scattered across the roof like tropical islands in a twilit sea. Many of the glass panes in the windows were broken, and the sound of the wind that passed through was as soft as the voice of a mother singing to her child. Although the house appeared to be abandoned, and the woman would have been impossibly old by now, we were too frightened to investigate more closely and continued up a mountain path, turning back toward the valley of the Deva as we did. After leaving the forest, we climbed through exposed fields of small stones and spongy turf where the grass had been cropped by goats, and by noon we had reached the remains of a medieval tower, a crude fortification built of local stone now covered with ivy. It had been situated on a high point for defensive purposes in the time of the Normans and was perhaps once paired with the ruined tower at Balcón dos Deuses on the northern side of the river. Below us sunlight broke through the clouds to flash off the ocean waves like clear notes rolling through the vivace of a piano concerto. To the right lay Porto Lúa and on its left, along the coastline of the bay, the valley where Harry had built his hut. Inland, half-hidden among the trees, was the *pazo* of El Conde and beyond that Foxo Escuro and the cove at the end of the peninsula. To the south we could see two more headlands reaching into the Atlantic and faint white beaches between them. At this height, the gorge of the Deva was marked by a series of high falls and above them, like the background of a Renaissance painting, were the crags of the canyon walls that surrounded the granite plinth where Lonxe do Sol was covered by a layer of clouds.

It was too late in the day to go much higher, so we took the same course down the mountain that we had taken up until we came to the edge of the forest. Avoiding the house of Suzzain Sutania and the village of Silvosa, we chose a more direct route to Porto Lúa that ran along the upper edge of the valley where the dense vegetation was watered by the mist that rose from the falls below. I showed Laura a rabbit's burrow in the brambles off the path and, in a pile of rotting logs, a fox's den. As we walked down the narrow trail that curled through the brush under a canopy of leaves, we stopped to pick wild strawberries and blackberries. She asked me the names of the wildflowers along the way, and I pointed out blue bells and calamint and wood sage, and when she asked me which birds were calling in the forest, I identified the species by their songs. I told her I could mimic them well enough to elicit a response, and to prove this, we lay on a stone half-hidden in the brake, and I called in several wood pigeons and a pair of curious blackbirds. But as we dropped farther down the slope of the valley, all we could hear was the roar of the falls. We made our way to the Deva beside a stream that passed through a cool grotto of watercress and pockets of ferns clinging to niches in the rocks and were able to cross the river without getting wet by leaping over deep channels the currents had cut into a flat plain of granite. We continued our descent along the northern bank of the river where I showed Laura the cave that had been an ice house and the millrace which we had once dammed and stocked with fish, and, finally, late in the afternoon, we reached the putchers we had set out in the morning.

There was a salmon in one. I put the fish in a net bag and hung the traps over my shoulder. On the way home, we stopped in the alameda and asked Señor Morcín to take two photographs of us standing awkwardly shoulder to shoulder against a blurred backdrop of shadow and sunlight. Laura promised she would keep hers forever, and I did too. We stood by the gate in front of her house talking until it began to grow dark and her grandmother called from the kitchen window. I told Laura to give her the salmon, said goodnight, and walked up Rúa do Olvido under the emerging stars.

Her birthday was the last day of August. It was also the beginning of her last week in Porto Lúa. I took the money I had saved from working for Don Horacio and the pesetas I had earned from writing letters and clearing fields to María Dolores's store on the plaza. There was a customer ahead of me buying baby clothes, so I waited patiently by the display case that contained the jewelry until she completed her purchase. Without leaving the narrow passage behind the counter, María Dolores crossed from one side of the store to the other, hurrying along stepping over boxes and past a rolling ladder in her curious, urgent way of walking.

"Bos días, cabaleiro."

When I told her I was interested in buying a piece of jewelry for a young woman, she took a wooden box with cantilevered drawers from under the glass and placed it on top of the counter. Then she opened each drawer to show me a large selection of brooches and rings and necklaces that she draped over her wrist. I had no idea what would be appropriate or customary. María Dolores sensed this and asked me who the item was for and if there was a special occasion. After I explained it was for a friend for her birthday, she took out a jet and silver necklace with a moon pendent in a double halo setting. I knew immediately that's what I wanted, but when I saw the price tag, my legs weakened, and I felt a rush of blood to my head as if needles had been stuck in my scalp. I had counted my money carefully before leaving home and knew I didn't have enough. I pretended to look at several other items, but was only stalling while I tried to think of a way to pay for the necklace. My disappointment did not go unnoticed. Delicate enough not to ask how much money I had, María Dolores feigned consternation, reproved herself under her breath, and then revealed the price was wrong and that this necklace was supposed to be on sale. When she told me the revised price, I asked her to repeat it. The second time she added it would be a little less if unwrapped. Suddenly able to afford it, I was exultant and told her I would have it wrapped. I counted out my pesetas, each hard-earned, on the counter as María Dolores took several sheets of decorated paper from a drawer and asked me to select the pattern I preferred.

Buoyed by my success, I hurried across the plaza, walked up Rúa do Olvido, and knocked on the door of number 8. When Laura appeared, I wished her happy birthday and placed the box in her hand. As she removed the ribbon and paper, she blushed, and as she lifted the lid, caught her breath, looked left and right, lowered her head, started to speak, but couldn't, and then abruptly excused herself and went inside. I waited, not sure that she would return, wondering whether I had misread her feelings. Perhaps it was too much, too presumptuous. When she came back down the stairs, she had composed herself, but still avoided my eyes. She thanked me shyly and told me she had shown the necklace to her grandmother who was resting in bed and put it in a safe place in her room.

"What did she say?"

"That a man is more than a hill of beans."

The following morning we set off for the northern shore. On the way, we picked lemons from a branch hanging over the back wall of a house in Via Sagrada and peeled the rinds as we walked through the churchyard and crossed Campo da Graza biting into the sour yellow pulp along the green paths of bracken and blackberries. A few thin cattle were grazing in a pasture of sainfoin on the edge of the pine forest that extends from the northern side of Porto Lúa to a granite ridge a half mile up Aracelo. Rather than continue on the path beside the forest, we cut down to the sea on a shaded trail feathered by the branches of pine saplings, ferns, and broom higher than our heads, and came out in bright sunlight a few dozen yards above the cove of Mestre's Dugium.

When we reached the shore, we took off our shoes and socks and walked barefoot into the waves that spread across the beach. I showed her a lagoon and littoral marsh where sea birds nested and told her about the Roman city buried beneath us and how the wind and waves and the sand yielding between our toes had wrought the destruction of the homes and shops of its sailors and ship-builders who once stood in the place where we were standing on a summer day not unlike that day. They would have seen the waves washing over the same shore and Illa da Luz and Aracelo beneath the same morning sky and perhaps even the same beauty of yellow lilies and white sea asters bending over the murky pool, reflecting like sunbursts in the dark water.

To the north, a mile beyond the lagoon, are an abandoned lighthouse and Cathedral Rocks, and beyond that, a towering dune called Monte Branco. Scattered among the low shrubs and deep grass along the path are stone enclosures, isolated plots where people once grew potatoes or kale barely sheltered from the wind. From there the shoreline rises in mist-darkened walls of granite dropping sheer from the green turf to the waves as if cut from the land by a flat spade. Below them are a few islets in the sea surrounded by white froth, rocks beaten and pocked by storms. From the lighthouse, the path descends and curves to the northeast around the base of Aracelo and Monte Agudo where wild horses graze on steep pastures. In the distance beyond the mountains, are the towns Malpica and Coruña, and, beyond them, cities like Paris and London, but those were still places of the imagination. On that day, as we walked through fields of gorse and coastal grasses, the endless realm of sea and sky, of northern blue, that lay before us was all the world we cared to know.

A fishing boat passed on the way to port followed by a flock of gulls riding the breeze behind it. Laura and I climbed Monte Branco, losing half a step in the sand with every step we took, until we came to the summit. Much of the dune was thinly covered with marram grass and carline thistles, but there was a gash of exposed sand that, seen from a distance, resembled a waterfall and gave the feature the name Fervenza Areosa. A cool breeze masked the heat of the sun, but when we stopped, we could feel the soles of our feet burning, and we quickly stripped down to our underwear, spread our arms, and let ourselves fall headlong into the white stream of sand tumbling, rolling, sliding, until at last we reached the foot of the dune where the tide, trapped behind a row of boulders, had formed a quiet cove cut off from the force of the waves. Except for a few wisps of algae that floated slowly in the current as green clouds might float across a liquid sky, the pool was clear, and we dove in to rinse away the sand. Laura swam to the bottom and then rose up through the surface tossing off streams of water that shone like a bouquet of light. I noticed the form of her small breasts through the wet cotton of her undershirt, and she saw my gaze and the wonder in my eyes. She kissed me on the cheek and ran across a field of stone and down a sandy path through the marram that led to tidal flats where a series of high schist arches stood like the ruins of a great cathedral. Flush with the mysterious arrival of an instinct deep in our blood, we swam out beyond the rocks into waves roaring louder than our shouts, cresting reefs of white foam crashing over our heads.

When the surf had finally exhausted us, we walked back up the ribbed tidal sand and rested under one of the arches that leaned overhead like a flying buttress and watched as the tide came in. Laura sat in front of me, and I wrapped my arms around her midriff and rested my chin on her head. Her skin smelled like the ocean, and her hair like sun-warmed cedar. We talked for much of the afternoon until the tide crept up to where we were sitting. Then we climbed Monte Branco to retrieve our clothes and sat for a little longer looking out over the sea leaning against each other. The sun touched the side of her face with soft yellow light, and her eyelashes were as luminous as filaments of glass. When she stood up, she took a handful of sand and, opening her fist slightly, poured it over me in a thread as slender as the sand in an hourglass until the wind blew it to one side and it fell like a curtain of fine rain. Catching the evening light, the grains of red and yellow and blue that made up that hill of white shimmered like small gems cut by the lapidary of time as if I were being baptized into the promise of eternity by a thousand suns. I poured sand over Laura just as she had done to me, and then, holding our clothes, we ran and tumbled down to the pool below where we bathed one more time, initiates to the life we would share together.

Laura's last week in Porto Lúa went by quickly. Because the summer had been unusually dry, corn was being harvested early on the coast, and I spent most of that week going through our fields picking the ears whose silks were already dark and storing them in the *horreo* beside the barn. But in the evenings when I was free, Laura and I walked the streets of Porto Lúa blending in with the crowd like any other couple. The Feast of Nosa Señora do Mar was the coming Sunday, and during the week preparations were already being made. Booths were built in the plaza, flags were hung, streets were swept, and a white van with the word *cine* painted on the side parked near the quay where the light of the streetlamps was blocked by the trees. In the evenings its owner set up a generator on the pavement and a projector in the back of the van and tied a bedsheet between two trees about thirty feet away. One night Laura and I joined the small audience that brought their own stools, and, as the light faded over the western horizon and the sheet billowed slightly in the breeze, we watched a film starring Gary Cooper. Afterward we walked across the bridge and into the fields of the headland, where we identified a dozen constellations. As the moon rose over the mountain, she said she felt she could hold it in her hands, and I told her Lucretius believed it to be no larger than it seems.

On the Feast of Nosa Señora do Mar, Laura invited me in to see her room while her grandmother was out. Since she was only there for the summer, she had brought few things with her: a pair of colored bottles containing perfume, which she never wore, a small make-up kit, which she never used, a pair of glasses, hair clips, a brush, and a suitcase containing her clothes open on a table. She took the necklace I had given her out of the box and lifted her hair so I could fasten it behind her neck. Then she stood before the mirror. I stood behind her looking over her shoulder and told her how well it suited her. She smiled and turned her shoulders from side to side to see it from different angles.

We left the house before her grandmother returned and walked down Rúa do Olvido as a series of fireworks exploded in rapid succession to start the celebrations. The schedule of events was the same as in previous years. The enactment of the rescue at sea was followed by the procession from Nosa Señora do Mar to the estate of El Conde de Curra. Laura and I watched the procession pass from the alameda where the African I had met with Uncle Teo was selling toy animals and framed pictures of Jesus while his friend sat in the shade of one of the eucalyptus trees with a talking parrot. There were booths set up on the perimeter of the plaza and bands playing on the street and in the alameda, but I wasn't as interested in the festivities as I had been in the past. I was thinking about Laura's imminent departure and how long it would be before I would see her again.

We followed an accordion player at the back of the procession to the grounds of El Conde's house where Fanfarrias was already playing on the western terrace. Father Infante said Mass in the family chapel, and people spread their blankets on the lawn in the shade of the great oaks and chestnuts. Laura and I sat on the front steps leading up to the main entrance of the house and ate salted ham and bread from a basket she had brought. Later in the afternoon, I showed her the walled garden and told her the story of the night I was trapped inside. When the band stopped playing, we returned to the front lawn where the last guests to leave were gathering their blankets and bottles, and joined the train of stragglers warmed by wine and *aguardiente* walking down the maple avenue, sharing their songs beneath the stately trees.

Laura and I stood by the gate outside her house until her grandmother leaned out the window and called for her to come inside. I waited in the street until her shutters opened and she stood silhouetted against the lamplight and whispered for me to go home. She would see me in the morning, she said. One of the customs on the night of Nosa Señora do Mar was for young men to leave plants outside the doors of houses to comment on the people within. Flowers for a lover. Weeds for someone ill-tempered. Beneath a waning moon, I gathered roses from our yard, careful not to take too many from a single bush, and left the fragrant bundle on the doorstep of number 8.

Father woke me, as I had requested, before dawn. As I dressed and ate breakfast, I considered what I would say to Laura before she left, but her departure was not how I had envisioned it. When I reached the house, Paco Carreira's taxi was already there, and the roses were gone. The sun was still behind the mountain, and the air was cool. I sat on the wall beside the gate until the door opened and then helped Laura with her suitcase and a box. Paco put them in the trunk of the car with a crate of fresh vegetables for her parents. The normalcy of the situation was at odds with the magnitude of the impending loss I felt. Just as the end of a life can occur among mundane events and conversations, its pivotal moments can be composed of commonplace gestures and banalities. As she stood beside the car, I wanted to kiss her goodbye or hug her, but her grandmother stood beside her patting her hand as she spoke to her, and out of courtesy, I stood back a little from their parting. Laura gave me a quick hug and then got in the car and lowered the window. Paco went up the hill to turn around, and then the car passed us on the way down. Laura, who was sitting on the right-hand side, leaned over to roll down the window on the left and wave, but by the time she did, they had passed. She turned and looked out the back window to wave one more time. And just like that, she was gone. Even today, after so many years, I can see her face clearly through the glass so deeply did that moment lodge in my memory.

The following summer seemed as far away as the next life. I looked at a calendar, counted the months, and thought of all the schoolwork and cold rainy days and tedious, backbreaking chores in the garden and fields that would fill the long interval, and couldn't imagine how I would make it to June without seeing her. On a wall in the fishermen's cooperative was an ordnance survey map showing the countryside between Porto Lúa and Muros. I studied it carefully and considered what paths I might take over the mountains in order to see her, but it was too far and my parents would never have approved. I thought about taking a taxi too, but had spent all my money on the necklace and didn't know where I would stay once I was there.

Everywhere I went I felt her absence. In Rúa do Olvido. In

Campo da Graza. In the alameda. On the path along the northern coast. But mostly in church where I first saw her. The stones of Nosa Señora do Mar had not changed, nor the odors of the closed, cavernous space, nor the rusty lightning rod on the bell tower, nor the purple flowers growing in the cracks of the outside walls. They were still the way they had always been. Their appeal, the attachment I felt toward them, now lay in their association with Laura, lay in that moment when she had looked away, and I knew she had felt the same thing that I had felt. I no longer had any interest in serving Mass or being a saint or a priest—rather than converse with God through prayer, I spent my time in church imagining what I would say to her in the next letter I would write.

School would soon begin and, drifting back to my former ways, I returned to Mestre's library where I found a book entitled *Historia de la costa de muerte* in Castilian that offered brief histories of all the towns along the coast from Muros to Malpica with maps of the town centers in pink. I studied every word of the text about Muros and on the map every street and the outline of every building. Laura's house was in Rúa Real near the Curro da Praza where Don Horacio had meant to give his lecture, so I could envision it, or at least its neighborhood, with some degree of accuracy.

When I returned to the fold of friendship, Miguel warned me I would end up like Ramón. I told him Laura was not like that. He replied that we are all like that. When I look back on those days from the perspective of middle age, I sometimes ask myself if what I felt was merely the enchantment of youth, the novelty of emerging desire, but if I am honest with myself, true to the person I was then, I know that what I felt was real and that I have never felt that way again.

One afternoon at the end of our final class of the day, Mestre walked to the window and gazed at Illa da Luz. After a moment, he turned to us and said, "It will be clear tonight and the moon won't rise until late. Those of you who wish to see the planets should come by my house after sunset. Bring lanterns and dress warmly."

We had anticipated this night since the previous spring, watching the sky on the clearest days only to be disappointed when clouds or fog or a high scrim of summer haze moved in from the sea. Wearing sweaters and jackets against the autumn chill, we met in the schoolyard a little before seven as departing clouds moved north across the western horizon like a cavalcade of sailing ships. Their vaporous rigging was pierced by the last rays of the setting sun, and soon their purple shadows darkened the peaks of Illa da Luz that rose above the silver water like a crown of amethyst. As we walked through the fallen leaves on the path to Mestre's house, only our lanterns and the depth of the worn path kept us from straying into the woods where the remaining foliage of the trees was darkly hued in shades of copper and rust.

When we reached Mestre's house, Facundo was already there. The two of them picked up the crate that housed the telescope while I carried the tripod and Miguel brought along a case of extra lenses. There were twelve students in addition to myself—Miguel, María, Ánxel, Andrés el Tercero, Amparo, Sara, Inés, Pilar, Mateo, Marcos, Lucas, and Alfredo. We followed Mestre and Facundo to a flat boulder well above the lights of Porto Lúa where we set up the tripod and mounted the telescope. Low haze over the southern horizon separated the fading light into bands of bluish gray, winter pink, and a pale, airy blue. To the east, the first stars were beginning to appear over the mountain. Mestre studied the sky and then consulted a book of astronomical charts he had received in the mail showing the positions of the stars and planets for every week of the year in Madrid, which was close enough to our location to serve our purpose. Then he looked back at the sky and wheeled the barrel of the telescope into position with two handles that moved it along two axes. The contrasting currents of warm air rising from the stones that had absorbed sunlight throughout the day and cool air falling from the mountainside circled around us like fish brushing past in dark water.

Pointing out the brightest object in the southern sky, Mestre told us we would begin by looking at Jupiter. He said we should note the four small stars surrounding it on an invisible plane that passes through the center of the planet. Facundo then moved a flat, rectangular stone next to the tripod so the shorter students were able to step up to the eyepiece without having to stand on the tips of their toes. The girls went first, and between each viewing, Mestre re-aligned the telescope to keep up with the axial rotation of the earth as the object in focus moved steadily across the field of vision and was soon out of sight. As I waited my turn, I gazed at the planet shining in the southern sky and imagined I would see oceans and clouds, but when I looked through the eyepiece, something much different appeared. Jupiter was a world of soft yellow light shining like a sun in the night and joined in the darkness by four smaller lights as faint as distant stars. When each of us had had a chance to see the planet, Mestre explained that between the seventh and thirteenth of January in 1610, Galileo had seen the smaller stars move around the planet changing their positions and configurations and realized they were not stars at all, but rather moons, that Jupiter was like Earth, and because of his observations, human beings realized they were not the center of creation, but merely one small part of it.

Holding it next to a lantern, Mestre examined the sky chart again and then identified the constellations above the southwest horizon. When he decided which point of light was Saturn, he moved the telescope in that direction working the handles deftly as he searched the black ether until the planet appeared in the field of vision. One by one my classmates peered through the lens, remaining longer than they had before, silent and entranced by what they saw: floating in the darkness was a sphere glowing like phosphorous, its rings clearly visible, cream-colored with a slight tint of green, a beauty unlike anything I had ever seen. I lingered, like the others, trying to comprehend the magnitude and distance of the object before my eyes. I still can't express the feeling of seeing it for the first time. The closest I can come is to say it was religious, but the experience challenged the very notion of religion. It's as if one were looking at an exiled god. The benign and familiar presence of one who shares our sun, but as otherworldly as a realm of mythic fantasy. Though small through the lenses of the telescope, the planet conveyed the majesty of night and the mystery of creation beyond our hills and fields, beyond the morning sun and evening moon.

Facundo, the last to look, was the first to break the silence.

"Is that really up there?

"What do you mean?"

"It's not some trick of the device, something painted inside it?"

"Between you and the planet, there is nothing but glass. You're seeing what is in the sky and has always been in the sky every night of your life."

"How big is it?" María asked.

"Hundreds of times larger than the earth."

"How far away is it?"

"Ten times farther from the sun than the earth."

Facundo returned to the telescope and gazed at the soft glow of the planet with its rings tilted like the brim of a *cordobés* hat.

"What do you see?"

"It is like a beautiful woman beyond a man's reach."

Mestre rotated the handles to re-center the planet for Facundo as we sat quietly on the ground gazing at the *Vía Láctea*, which shone like a trail of luminous smoke over the sea.

"How did it get there?"

"That's hard to say. How did anything get anywhere? How did we get here? Science provides an explanation, but it is no more intelligible than the creation stories of ancient people or one you might devise yourself."

"What does science say?"

"That at one time, before time, there was nothing, and after a vast explosion there was something."

"How could something come from nothing?"

"It might be better to say we don't have any way of knowing what, if anything, was before the explosion or even whether there was time."

"You are a learned man, Mestre, but some of the things you say don't make sense to me."

"I'm afraid these are the best explanations we have. Who's to say there won't be another theory in a century or two that will turn this one on its head? Even now some scientists believe there have been many universes eternally expanding and collapsing or that there is another universe right here among the stars that's too dark to see."

"What kind of universe would be too dark to see?"

"The universe of possibility. So there is the universe of things that exist and the universe of things that don't exist but could have existed."

"My aunt says there are two worlds," I said. "One of the body and one of the spirit. For every black crow you see there is a white crow you don't see."

"We each explain things in our own way."

"What about God?" Facundo asked. "Didn't God create the stars?"

"God is as good an explanation as any."

"And it would be the same God on all the stars?"

"It would if that's what you believe."

"And do you think Jesus was born on all those stars, and they have churches there like they have here?"

"I don't know, Facundo. That's a lot of places to be born."

"Or what if Jesus had been born on one of those stars and not here? How would we know about him?"

"That's a question you should ask Father Infante."

"But if there is a universe of other possibilities, wouldn't there be another God of that universe, a God that might have existed, but didn't?"

"That is a good question, Facundo. I don't know the answer to that. I can tell you there is a philosopher who said that God is what has limited infinite possibility into being. So you could say that all that is is God and that the universe of possibility would have a God of what never existed or no God at all."

"I think things are easier to understand if you believe in God."

"That may be, but imagine you are lost on the mountain and everywhere you look is only barren rock. Then you come across an opening in the rock and discover a beautiful garden hidden in a deep hollow. Fantastic fruits are growing all around you and extraordinary flowers of colors that you have never seen are blooming everywhere, and the air is filled with the fragrance of paradise. And you marvel at the wonder of such a place. Then I tell you it was created by a magician out of nothing. Would you not wonder more at the magician and less at the garden? So it is with the world. If there were no magician, it would surely command more wonder in its own right."

From this night forward Facundo's peace of mind was beset by rifts of doubt the way an old table is beset by cracks, and this doubt turned uncharacteristically into peevishness in a man known for his accommodating nature—a man whose wisdom had averted the immolation of Porto Lúa's priests, whose kindness had built the wheelbarrow of Mateo Mateo, and whose goodwill had dug the eternal homes of the dead for a generation. Punchy with drink, he confronted people on the street with incongruous remarks and questions. On one occasion he cornered Constable Sampaio to ask whether a drunken man riding a mule may be charged with driving under the influence. He neglected his job as sexton to spend his days on the terrace of O Galo drinking or sitting on the quay staring wistfully at the sky over the sea. When warned by Doctor Romalde of the damage he was doing to his health, Facundo was quick to reply: "As we grow old and time runs out, we can resign ourselves to the inevitable or we can take control and hasten our end through drink. One way or the other, we come to the same conclusion."

Several weeks after seeing Jupiter and Saturn, a small group of students returned to Mestre's house to help him carry the telescope and tripod back up the wooded path just as a Hunter's Moon was appearing over the darkened peaks of the mountain. We mounted the telescope on the tripod, and Mestre attached a special filter to the lens because of the intensity of the light at such magnification. Unlike the planets, the moon was so large we were only able to see portions of it at any one time, and as it moved through the field of vision, the details of the craters within craters and rays of ejecta and sunlit escarpments stood out so clearly we felt as if we were flying over the white surface at a great height. While Mestre was naming the seas and craters and mountain ranges, Facundo appeared out of the darkness, his face blazing as if the demon of alcohol were escaping through his cheeks.

"Do you mind if I look?"

"Of course not."

We sat in the cold as Facundo took his turn, losing himself in thought as the craters and peaks passed slowly by. In the moonlight our faces and coats appeared ghostly white like figures in a photographic negative, and the trees of the surrounding forest were black against the blue silver of the sky. Somewhere in the distance Cotolay shouted imploringly at the moon.

"It doesn't look that far," Facundo said.

"If the earth were the size of an orange, the moon would be the size of a radish about six feet away."

"Was it ever closer, as the old people say?"

"It was, but millions of years ago."

"How far would the sun be when the moon is six feet from the earth?"

"Again, if the earth were the size of an orange, the sun would be the size of a small house about a half mile away, and, although its distance from the earth varies, Saturn would be a boulder more than a yard wide four or five miles from the sun. And if the sun were the size of an orange, the closest star would be another orange as far away as Germany."

"How many stars are there?"

"More than all the grains of sand on all the beaches of Galicia."

"You said that God created the universe."

"I said that's an explanation that works for people."

"But if He created it, He must have been before it, somewhere outside of it. So where is the universe?"

"Where is it?"

"Yes."

"It's everywhere."

"Except where God is."

"I suppose."

"So where is God?"

"I don't know, Facundo."

"I'm sorry, Mestre. I know I ask a lot of questions."

"That's all right."

"Maybe you could tell me what book I should read so I won't have to ask you so much."

"We'll look through my books when we return to the house."

Because of the cold and a wind that stirred out of the north, we left for the warmth of Mestre's house as soon as Facundo had seen everything he wanted to see. When we reached the house, Mestre put a couple of logs in the stove and made cups of hot chocolate to warm us up. Then we went upstairs to find a book for Facundo.

"Let's see what I have."

"I want to read what others have said about God and the universe and time and the other things we talked about."

Mestre thought for a moment and then took a thin, paper-bound volume from the shelf.

"You can keep it."

"What is it?"

"The autobiography of a Russian writer who struggled with questions like yours. Read the entire book. Don't stop until you've finished it."

One evening late in October, I was in Nosa Señora do Mar helping Father Infante prepare the church for O Día de Tódolos Santos. As I was rummaging through a box containing vases to hold the flowers that would decorate the altar, I heard something fall from the roof. When I went outside, I discovered a ladder leaning against the side of the church, and when I looked up, I saw Facundo sitting on the tiles in a fleece coat smoking a cigarette. A bottle was sticking out of his pocket.

"What are you doing?"

"Thinking."

"Aren't you afraid you might fall?"

"No."

Father Infante must have heard the noise as well, for he followed me outside, and when he heard me speaking to someone, he turned his attention to the roof and saw Facundo in the darkness with his arms wrapped around his knees looking down at us.

"What's going on?"

"Nothing."

"Why are you on the roof?"

"I'm having a smoke."

"Come down from there."

"No."

"You've already broken a tile and the slats could give way at any moment."

"Have you ever seen Saturn?"

"What's that got to do with anything?"

"You should see it."

"I know what it looks like."

"Have you ever seen it through a telescope?"

"Come down, Facundo."

"No."

"I'll move the ladder."

"And in a few weeks, you can scrape what's left of me off the tiles when the crows are done picking at my bones."

"You're making a fool of yourself."

"As if we're not fools enough as it is. Look at us. Look at

our lives. Year after year I dig the graves of the dead. I replace the candles on the altar. I cut the weeds in the churchyard. Year after year. Winter, spring, summer, fall. I clear the leaves from the vestibule. I wash the windows. I dust the pews. Year after year. But what am I really doing? I'm digging my own grave one day at a time."

"The Bible says we should take pleasure in our toil. It is a gift from God."

"So you say, but it's not your fingers that are worn to the bone."

"Some praise God through works and some through prayer."

"I wake up every day and do my work. But I don't know why."

"You do it because that's what you do."

"It doesn't matter."

"Of course it matters. You provide an earthly repository for the Christian dead as they await their resurrection. But just as importantly, you work because you are human, and to be human is to persevere in the life God has given you."

"What do the stars in the sky care about the dead on earth?"

"God cares. His shepherds on this earth care."

"You care enough to play on people's fears."

"Don't mock the Church."

"Everyone is afraid to die, so you offer them immortality, and in return they give you the fruit of their labor. You frighten them with hell and comfort them with heaven and claim to have the keys to paradise. You grow fat on their labor, and they end up dying with false hope and rotting in the ground like everything else."

"You're drunk."

"Everything I'm saying is true."

"The Guardia Civil will know how to get you down."

"They've forgotten we exist."

"Or Constable Sampaio."

"You can call whoever you like, but that won't change anything. Ask yourself where you'd be if there was no hope of immortality. Who would kneel on your granite floor for hours despite the pain of arthritis? Who would send you a chicken or a flounder even though their own pantry is empty? Without the lure of false hope, you'd be no better than the rest of us."

"I do much more than you think. I counsel the members of my congregation and comfort them in many ways."

"You don't really believe all the things you say, do you Father? But you pretend to because you think your stories will bring peace to those who are desperate enough to believe them. You're like an actor on a stage who entertains people until the lights go off and reality hits them as they walk out the door into the night. You can admit it to me. The truth, I mean. I won't give your secret away."

"Of course I believe the teachings of the Church. I have sacrificed too."

"Have you?"

"I studied and sacrificed for many years. I have risked my own health nursing the sick. I have taken a vow of celibacy."

"You took a vow of poverty too, but you eat like a lord."

"Don't second-guess me, Facundo."

"I don't have to second-guess you. I guessed right the first time. You live in a dream. You hide from the truth and tell people stories of a future life as if they were children. But there's nothing you can say to me that will make any difference. You need to get drunk, Father. Only then can you bear the truth."

"I would rather not."

"I think about these things every day, but I'm only talking about them because I'm drunk. That's why I'm being honest with you."

"Just because you're drunk doesn't mean the things you're saying are true."

"Who can decide what's true?"

"The word of God is true."

"I have a question."

"What is it?"

"When we rise in our resurrected bodies, what age will we be?"

"The age at which we die."

"But what if we die in a terrible accident?"

"Climb down off the roof and you won't have to worry about that."

"Or what if the person dies old and decrepit? Who would want to be like that for eternity?"

"I'm sure if God can give us a healthy body at birth, He can give us a healthy body at our resurrection."

"What about a man who is drunk when he dies? Will he be drunk in heaven?"

"I think the odds are less than likely that he will go to heaven."

"Drinking is not such a bad thing."

"The body is the seat of God in this world."

"I can think of better places to put a seat."

"If you are going to blaspheme, you can sit out here by yourself."

"What if he goes mad before he dies? Will he be mad for eternity?"

"His soul will last for eternity, and that part of him is made in God's image, so it wouldn't be mad."

"But a person is made in the image of God and can still die in a state of sin."

"Sin is a choice and reflects the will, whereas madness is an affliction."

"But mad is what he is and mad is what he'll be."

"The soul is not a person's passing thoughts. For example, you can desire what is sinful or think licentious thoughts and still be a good person."

"If it's not my thoughts, then what good does it do me to have a soul? Who am I if not my thoughts? It doesn't matter. I wouldn't want to be around for eternity anyway. A dog could live forever if it were fed every day, but a man conscious of eternity could not bear the endless succession of days."

"It's not a man but his soul."

"And what is that?"

"Just what I said."

"Yes, but am I my soul?"

"Of course."

"But if I am mad or drunk, wouldn't my soul also be mad or drunk?"

"No. Your soul is not that part of you that is mad or drunk."

"Then it's not me. Because I am drunk."

"It is the essence of you. Not the temporary aberrations."

"But senility is not temporary. My grandfather was senile for many years, and he died not knowing who he was. So he would not know who he was for eternity."

"That is not his essence. You have a core self that doesn't change."

"But if it doesn't change, how can it repent or improve itself?"

"Facundo, you ask too many questions. There is a soul, and it is eternal. And if you're not careful, yours is going to be damned."

"If it's not my mad self or my drunken self or my repenting self or a self I can know, then I don't want a soul. If I can't be myself in the next life, then what's the point of having a soul?"

"So it can be rewarded or punished."

"These beliefs are no more real than the dreams I had last night. Why do people need all this? Why not just accept things as they are? The sun goes up. The sun goes down. What difference does it make if we go around the sun or the sun goes around us as long as it warms us and causes the apple trees to blossom? All these religions and philosophies are just words. And where do words come from? People. People invent things because they have too much time on their hands and are afraid to acknowledge there's nothing more to this life than what's here and now. Why is that so hard to admit? What if a star crashed into the earth and destroyed everything, where would all these beliefs go? They would disappear with all the people who made them up. That's where. Ask a dog if it has a soul."

"Human beings are not dogs."

"Only because we have words and can invent these stories to make ourselves feel better about ourselves. I've seen a dead dog, and I've seen a dead man. The only difference is the dog didn't tell itself some story while it was alive to convince itself it would live forever. Tell a dog about heaven and hell and it will stare at you waiting to be fed. We should be as honest as dogs. From now on I am only going to believe what I can see and what I can hear and what I can smell and taste and touch. There will be no more of these philosophies or religions to confuse me. Just the sea and the sky. When I dig a grave and touch the earth, I'll know my future. No more angels singing in the clouds for me. It's easier to face the truth than to try to make sense of all these stories."

"If it is so easy, why do you need to drink to come to these conclusions? Did it ever occur to you that these thoughts you have come from a bottle and not from the clear light of the mind that God gave you?"

"The night sky is a mirror. If you want to see the truth about your future, look into its darkness."

At Father Infante's request, I brought a bench that was just inside the portal out and placed it beside him. He sat down and rolled a cigarette as I leaned, half sitting, half standing, against the pedestal of a commemorative cross. After composing himself with several draws on the cigarette, Father Infante put it out underfoot and took a deep breath.

"So are you going to come down?"

"No."

He turned to me.

"Go and get Mestre. Maybe he can talk some sense into him."

But as I started to leave, he stopped me and whispered, "Wait. We'll pretend to go together and then come back. All he wants is attention. He'll come down as soon as we're gone."

We walked down Via Sagrada until we were out of sight and then looked back over the corner of a garden wall to see that Facundo was still sitting in the same place. Exasperated, Father Infante sent me off to find Mestre and returned to the churchyard. As I walked through the streets and up the path to Mestre's house, I did my best to recall the conversation between Facundo and Father Infante, and when I made my way back to the churchyard with Mestre, I was able to convey most of that conversation to him to give him some idea of what to expect. By the time we came within sight of the church, Facundo had climbed higher on the roof and was now sitting near the bell tower.

"Elpenor," Mestre whispered to himself.

"This is all your fault," Father Infante said as soon as he saw us. "Putting all this nonsense into his head with your telescope and books on philosophy."

"What are you doing up there, Facundo?"

"Trying to get closer to the stars."

"Wouldn't it be better to go up the mountain instead of disturbing Father?"

"I didn't think of that."

"Has he been drinking?"

"Of course he's been drinking."

"I can hear you."

"How much have you had to drink?"

"No more than usual."

"Do you think it's a good idea to climb up on the roof of the church when you've been drinking?"

"Is there a better time?"

As Facundo moved to lean against the bell tower, a tile broke free, and he slipped several feet closer to the edge of the roof. At the same time, the bottle of *aguardiente* sprang from his pocket and rolled down the roof and over the edge, and, after glinting for an instant in the light of a streetlamp, shattered on a gravestone in the yard.

"You're going to have to pay for that."

"Don't worry. I have another."

"Get down from there. Now. Fewer than five months into my appointment, I find my sexton on the roof of my church drunk on *aguardiente* and in danger of falling to his death. What will the bishop think? You're responsible for this, you know."

"For showing him the majesty of God's creation?"

"And I thank you for that, Mestre, but there's nothing more you can do for me unless you can show me how the stars are adornments to the glory of man."

"What brought this on, Facundo?"

"That book you gave me."

"What about it?"

"It said there is no aim or direction in infinity."

"Did you read the entire book?"

"I read far enough."

"I told you to read the entire book."

"What's the point?"

"He goes on to say we are a part of the infinite."

"What difference does that make?"

"You can look at it two ways. One is that the universe is vast beyond our comprehension, and therefore our presence here is insignificant. The other is that the universe is vast beyond our comprehension, and therefore our presence here is significant. The Church tried to gag Galileo because they were afraid the grandeur of creation would lessen our stature and turn God into a local phenomenon. But they were foolish. You could argue that the discovery of those moons around Jupiter made our presence here more miraculous and extended God's creation far beyond our limited knowledge."

"I don't see how there can be any purpose when the future is infinite. What's the point of doing anything?"

"Of course there is purpose. You seem to think the only purpose worthy of the name must be part of some extrinsic grand design. Isn't there a purpose intrinsic to each of us? To every part of creation? Consider the flower in the middle of the grassy plain that opens its face to the sun. It has no consciousness to ask whether it has a purpose. It opens and it dies. Its purpose is to be in that moment, to offer the sun its color and then fade and return to the earth. Life comes from the sun and is a part of the sun. And for human beings, because we are conscious and able to construct our lives, our purpose is to live as well as we can. Ask yourself if you are fulfilling your purpose. And if you aren't, don't blame the lack of a grand design for your failure to live. What is your purpose when you visit a garden?"

"To enjoy the flowers and trees or the coolness of the shade."

"And when you visit, you know you'll have to leave, but that doesn't mean you can't enjoy the time you're there. By the same token, even though you will have to leave this world one day, you can still enjoy the time you're here, perhaps even enjoy it more because it is not going to last forever. The Greek gods were frivolous because they had no limit on their lives, but we who live in time and suffer loss can live more profoundly and appreciate the narrow window we have in this world. If the trees in the forest were red and yellow every day, their autumn colors would no longer be beautiful. Their beauty only exists because it is fleeting. The young are only fair because their fairness will pass. Because we are only here for a short time, there is beauty in our being, and we should feel the same joy in our presence we feel when that flower opens for its day in the sun."

"I understand that a flower doesn't care that its appearance is meaningless, but I'm not a flower."

"Sit down, Mestre. Would you like a cigarette?"

"No thank you, Father."

"Can you throw one up here?"

"You can come down and get it."

"For a long time," Mestre continued, "I thought the accomplishments of people were futile because they only matter to other mortal creatures like themselves. A great general leads an army that conquers a country, and within a few years that country is reconquered. His name is in a history book for generations, but with each generation fewer people will care until he becomes an obscure name in an obscure book in a dark corner of a library—until libraries vanish and those who care are dead. And in a few millennia, when the bricks and stones of his civilization lie forgotten in a heap, the land he conquered will return to its natural state free of human scratches and scrapings. Nothing we do will ultimately make any difference to anything. At some point the planet will freeze, and miles of ice will cover our hair and bones hidden in scattered caches across the planet's surface. All this is true. The Hindus say that our actions support the world, that we must continue to act despite the illusion of attainment. We must support our column of creation, or the world will collapse and people will suffer. The shepherd, the fisherman, the priest, the women who mend their nets on the quay or search the forest floor for herbs must find their own ways to contribute to the common good."

"Those are just words, Mestre. They are wise, but they are

still just words. If the fool and the great man suffer the same fate, why work to achieve anything? People go about their lives harvesting their fields, raising their children, burying their dead, pretending that all this matters. They go through their routines day after day ignoring that it is all for nothing."

"Sharing one's life with another is fulfilling in itself."

"What does a woman think when she watches her husband die? What does a father think when he sees his child explore the world and knows that we return to the earth with no more consequence than a flower? Does he lie to his child and pretend that being human confers some special standing in creation? As if language and desire and dreams and love could guard us against the fate of all things. A child may provide some distraction for a while, but eventually the father wakens in the night and knows this distraction, this happiness, is no more substantial than a cloud and that prolonging his line for one more generation means nothing in the end."

"Maybe you're the problem," Father Infante said. "Did that ever of occur to you? Maybe other people don't feel this way because they don't think like you."

"Because they don't think at all."

"Maybe they have thought, and maybe they realize there is more to life than you know."

"When do you see them thinking, Father? When they are lined up like sheep waiting to enter church on Sunday? Is that thinking? When they are selling their fish in the market for money? Is that thinking? They are too busy saying their prayers or counting their money to think."

"Doesn't the fact that your way of thinking leads to unhappiness tell you something? Doesn't it tell you that you are living in a way you were not meant to live?"

"You're right. We weren't meant to live honestly. Somewhere inside us we know our presence is entirely random, and life is better if we never acknowledge that."

"If nothing else, I don't know why you can't accept the pleasures of the moment whether it's enjoying a good meal or the company of friends."

"Look at the stone walls running up the side of the mountain. Think of the labor that built them hundreds of years ago. They were meant to enclose the livestock of our ancestors so they could survive, so they could raise their families. They're gone, the animals are gone, and soon all their descendants who never knew anything about them will be gone. And someday in the future, the stones of the walls will be scattered over the slopes of the mountain. You talk about the pleasures of love and the beauty of spring blossoms, but for most people life is a struggle to survive the violence that nature inflicts from the time we are born. The winter storms that drown the unsuspecting sailor, the diphtheria that steals the child, the viper hiding under the haystack, the spiders in our beds. With so many forces competing against us, you have to wonder why we were born in the first place. I dig the graves and cut the grass that covers the bodies of those who suffered in the darkness and cold, freezing in their beds, half-starved by poverty, with rotting teeth, arthritic hands, bent spines, and broken spirits. But at least they survived the maladies of childhood. Why come into the world for that?"

"Have you never been in love, Facundo?"

"Have I ever been a fly caught in the honey that will drown it?"

"Is there nothing in this life of any value to you? You strip everything away until you're scratching at bedrock. And then what? Where does that leave you? Content to think of yourself as clay? Water and clay? And that you will dissolve into mud as the trees are flowering and the birds are singing? Just a shadow of nothing. That's the truth you seek. But if you wake up tomorrow and accept what the world has to offer, it will fill your lungs with a sweet sea air and your heart with its beauty."

"What am I saying that isn't true?"

"It's only half the truth."

"This world you want me to accept offers nothing more than a struggle to survive, an endless cycle of birth and death, predator and prey. In the calm of evening when the clouds are lit by the last rays of the sun, an eagle crosses the sky with a newborn rabbit in its talons, and deep within the forest, a wolf snatches the offspring of a fox while the fox snatches the eggs of a partridge. Every day we wait for it to happen to us whether by man or beast, illness or age."

"And yet here you are, surviving, as you say, with a job and a warm bed and friends and apparently enough money for all the *aguardiente* you can drink."

"Even with a job and a bed and enough money to live, I'm still being carried along toward a precipice like a boat on a river. So are you. And so is Father. We may be accompanied by family and friends, or we may be alone, but we are always moving helplessly toward the edge. We have an oar, and we dip it in the water and pretend to steer ourselves from side to side as if in control of our fate—just as we see a doctor when we're ill—but we're still being carried along. All we can hope for to ease our fear is sleep because only then can we forget what awaits us. Briefly we dream of standing on the shore, but we always awaken to that stream of water beneath us taking us closer to our destruction every minute of every day. I've put dozens of the dead in the ground beneath you. I've smelled the rotting flesh and chipped hundreds of bones with my spade. I have seen the precipice."

We sat quietly for several minutes looking at the sky—Facundo perched beside the bell tower, Father Infante and Mestre on the bench, and me on a headstone. Finally Mestre broke the silence.

"The sky appears empty, but in reality it is full of time and possibility. Dante called it *lo gran mar de l'essere*. The great sea of being. But it is more than that. Somewhere in the cold embrace of eternity is also what is yet to be. And there too, in a way, is what will never be. What is the difference, out of all possibility, between what is yet to be and what will never be?"

"Or who."

"Or who. What is the difference between those who are yet to be and those who will never be? The ancients, who believed our souls descend from the stars, asked the same question, and we are still no closer to an answer. And to this question, we could add those who have already been. What is the difference, essentially, between those who have been and those who have not yet been and those who will never be?"

"The two of you are speaking as if there is no God."

"With God everything is easier. Those yet to be and those who have already been are both present in His mind. The question is why are some destined to be born and some are not? The philosophers would say it's either chance or necessity."

"It's God's will."

"Let Mestre continue."

"We could ask the same question of those already here. For example, why did Harry survive the storm when so many others died? In a sense, he was reborn and others were not."

"Does it matter when we will all eventually be like those who are gone or those who will never be?"

"It doesn't matter to those who have never been nor to those who are gone, but it does to Harry. It does to us. It does to all those who have passed through the labyrinth of becoming to be here now."

"It's all the same. Here or gone or never to be. It's just a matter of time."

"Perhaps you are right, Facundo. But I think there is a difference between those who will never be and those who have overcome the odds to be here now. To have a unique body, a unique mind, at a specific time and place never to be repeated."

"Everything is here by chance. Birds. Insects. The fish in the sea. The only difference is we are aware of it and therefore deny it."

"What do you mean by 'chance'?"

"If I flip a coin, there's a one in two chance it comes up heads."

"If I told you there was a one in five chance you would be fatally poisoned by eating an oyster, would you take that chance?"

"No."

"What about one in one hundred?"

"Still no."

"What about one in a million?"

"I'd eat it."

"What if you flipped that coin one hundred million times and it came up heads each time?"

"That's not possible, Mestre."

"And yet the chances of that are better than the chances of you being born."

"What do you mean?"

"When you were born, the odds were hundreds of millions to one that it would be you and not someone else like your brother or sister. People call Harry's survival a miracle. What were the odds? One in five? One in ten? One in a hundred? And yet we take our own births for granted."

"The past took care of itself. It's the future that holds no promise."

"You're concerned about a lack of purpose or progress when the future is infinite, but you came from a past billions of years in the making requiring causes more numerous than all the stars in the sky. What brought your parents together?"

"They lived in the same village."

"Why did they choose each other and not someone else?"

"I don't know."

"Each parent and grandparent and great-grandparent and so on as far back as you can go was conceived against the same impossible odds, and each found the other despite countless contingencies and survived the hardships of life to raise their families. And what first brought them here? What forbearers came north from the Maghreb? What men and women from the forests of Europe? How many conflicts and famines over the millennia did your ancestors survive for you to be here? In school we are told to curse the villains of history, and yet without their effect on its course, the twists and turns they wrought, the villages burned, the animals slaughtered, the fleeing masses, the migrations, we would never have come to be. If Napoleon had not been born, he would not have invaded Spain, and history would have been different. Or consider the Black Plague that destroyed a third of Europe and the millions of others who died in war or from starvation or disease. Those who survived produced us. If those rats that brought the plague hadn't left the ship in Constantinople, millions of people who died would have lived and millions of others would have been born. Other wars would have been fought. Other people would have migrated. Millions of pairings going back to the mother of humankind were necessary for us to be here, and the same is true of the creatures that came before us. The small mammals on the plains of Africa. Even before there was life, the phenomena of nature that created the conditions for its appearance had to be precisely what they were. The composition of gases in the atmosphere, the iron in the core of the earth, the elements in the rock, the moderation of temperatures. All of this was necessary to produce life and, more to the point, the lives of those of us who are here today rather than countless other forms of life. Even the formation of earth from stellar debris and its distance from the sun were necessary for us to be here."

I thought of the telegram on the wall in our house. If my

grandfather had died in the hurricane, if he had not gotten drunk and missed his ship, I would never have been born. My father would never have been born. My mother would have married someone else and had other children. If my great-grandfather hadn't moved down the mountain from Lonxe do Sol, I would never have been born. If ancient people hadn't migrated westward and survived for centuries on the mountain in their cold stone huts, I would never have been born. Forbearers too numerous to count. Living among animals and smoke and ashes, losing children to famine or disease. Making their way through time for me to be.

"I don't know about Constantinople and the plague or Napoleon or iron, Mestre."

"Let's put it this way: If an afternoon shower had not driven a shepherd in from the fields centuries ago, you wouldn't be here. If a woman in the time of the Moors had stopped to remove a pebble from her shoe, you wouldn't be here. If a drop of contaminated water had reached the lips of a man before the time of Christ, you wouldn't be here. Countless events like these in the lives of your ancestors that happened or didn't happen were necessary causes for you to be here. Take all the grains of sand on all the beaches in the world and add them up, and they would not come close to the odds against your birth. And yet here you are. And you wonder how there can be 'aim and direction' in infinite time. How do we understand our presence against such odds?"

"And there you have it, Facundo," Father Infante said. "Whether he meant to or not, Mestre just proved the existence of God's Providence. How could an infinite number of possibilities produce anything if not directed by the will of God? We were meant to be here. Who we are, as we are."

"I'm not claiming this proves anything, but the odds against each of us ever being should give you pause in your most skeptical moments."

"A toad. A mayfly."

"What?"

"A toad. A mayfly. An ant. They have life. The world is full of life. Every living thing in the sky and sea and earth overcame similar odds, and every day in the sky and sea and earth those living things are dying unnoticed. Nature doesn't care about individual lives as long as life itself continues. The toad, the mayfly, the ant mean nothing to the blind forces that brought them into being. How am I any different?"

"The difference is obvious," said Father. "Human beings were created in the image and likeness of God."

"That's just another way of saying we have an exaggerated sense of our own importance. The pairings that produced the bees gathering nectar in the fields of Castile were just as random as those that produced each of us, but no one remarks on the extraordinary coincidence of their lives."

"God created all His creatures, but human beings have a special place in His order and are therefore distinguished for having unique souls."

"And if those bees living their lives among the flowers of Castile had brains large enough to consider themselves unique, they would also find meaning in the pairings that brought them into being. Sometimes I think our intelligence is what makes us stupid."

Mestre reflected on this exchange for a moment and then added, "That life appeared in all its variety over vast stretches of time on a planet of rock and gas, as unlikely as it was, does not astonish me. Given all the planets in the sky, it's almost inevitable that it would happen somewhere. Even in many places. That the impulse to flourish was sustained by adopting more efficient ways of surviving changing environments until it should reach a higher level of intelligence and self-awareness I can understand. That there should be toads and mayflies and ants and even human beings, as extraordinary as that is, is consistent with all the rest. That my grandparents and parents should sustain this impulse and have children also makes sense to me. But that I am one of those lives with a unique sense of my own being and that I could only have that sense of being through the incalculable conjunctions that were necessary to bring me about is what I cannot understand. And so each existence is a displacement. Not of one, but of millions, tens of millions, hundreds of millions, who might have been born in our place. Siblings who would have looked like us, but they would have been as different from us as we are from our siblings with different personalities, experiences, thoughts, and memories."

There was another long pause in the conversation. The night was so quiet we could hear dogs barking in the distance beyond the Deva and a motorcycle somewhere on the coastal road. The air had grown colder and the stars seemed to shine more brightly.

"What do you think now, Facundo?" Father Infante asked.

"I'm thinking about all those people who weren't born when I was. And where they are."

"They weren't born. They aren't anywhere."

"I don't know how it was that I was born and all those other Facundos were not. They would have had lives like mine."

"Very likely."

"But I am here in the fresh air looking at the night sky, and they are not. Perhaps they would have made more of the opportunity than I have."

"Or less. You never know."

"If there were millions, as you say, who could have been born, I'm sure some of them would have been like me."

"No doubt, but I prefer to think of you as the only Facundo."

"Perhaps they were born in another universe where I wasn't."

"I don't know if I would go so far as to say the universe

could not have existed without you, but it is true that each of us was produced by the same impetus that scattered the stars at the moment of creation, and we are connected to that moment by a chain of causes."

"Do you think we will ever understand these things?"

"I don't know, Facundo. Perhaps one day there will be those who do. And compared to us, they will be like gods. We are still creatures of the lower depths limited by our language and the conventions of our thought. Fish, with their gills and scales, will never breathe the air of snow-capped mountains. Our minds were formed to survive in the forests and fields of this earth, and, despite our dreams and aspirations, our understanding is limited by our natural element. There may be moments of insight when we glimpse what lies beyond our language, beyond our capacity to know, but we will never adapt to that rarified air of the mountain. Each of us will leave this world without knowing why we appeared in the first place. There is so much more to understand than we are capable of."

"What do you believe, Mestre?"

"What do I believe?"

"About God and religion. It seems to me most people don't know what to think, so they prefer not to think at all and let the Church answer their questions. But religion creates more questions than it answers."

"We have tried to make our world more manageable, more predictable, and because we can control the great rivers that have flooded the plains and the epidemics that have ravaged humanity, we labor under the illusion that we have achieved ascendancy over nature. There is a mechanical explanation for everything. We trust experts who assure us that if we haven't discovered a cure for a disease or a solution to a problem, one will appear in the near future. And yet, the one essential fact, the only one that really matters, we cannot explain, and therefore we ignore it. As I say, we are still at the beginning of understanding. If anything, our knowledge has only led to more uncertainty. To answer your question, I would say I try not to believe anything because once you have a belief, you no longer need to think. I prefer to remain in a state of doubt and open to wonder. There are some who profess to have enough knowledge to be secure in their beliefs, but if we cease to wonder, we will never learn more. The mystery of our presence undermines our arrogance and leads us to create the myths and metaphors of science and religion which are incapable of satisfying our most profound needs."

"Father Infante is asleep."

"He's been nodding off for a while."

"It's late, Mestre."

"You have a choice, Facundo. You can either get drunk and climb up on the roof of the church every night to howl your protests to an indifferent sky, or you can live in this world and accept it as it is. Accept the mystery and the wonder of your presence."

I don't know how long Facundo stayed on the roof, but I suspect he came down shortly after I left. He had sobered up over the course of the evening, and the conversation had more or less come to an end. The next morning before school, I went back to the church to retrieve my hat, but no one was there. If it hadn't been for the missing tiles and broken bottle, I might have thought the events of the previous night had been a dream. I returned a second time later in the day to wash and arrange the vases for the holiday flowers. Facundo was going about his business as usual. I helped steady the ladder as he carried a bucket of tiles to the roof to repair the damage he had done. The air was mild and the stones were damp with condensation. As he leaned over the roof from the top of the ladder, he whistled an old love song to himself and lit the stub of a cigar he had been saving in his pocket.

Having endured ocean storms and morning frosts, the last trees on the mountain to lose their color were the poplars that burned bright yellow on a high ridge in the waning days of autumn as blue and violet clouds approached from the north. Then fog and drizzle filled the landscape. On the cold, wet afternoons when roofs were shining in the rain and indistinct clouds passed through a sky of indistinct gray, Don Andrés crossed the plaza beneath a black umbrella and reached O Galo just as the television was warming up. He sat at a table reserved for him and gazed upward at the flickering blue light to have, as he put it, a front row seat on history. Though events in Madrid had once seemed as far away as the affairs of an Asian emperor, television had brought the anticipated death of General Molinero into the smoky, wine-scented heart of Porto Lúa, and the mayor, sipping *caldo* from his spoon, followed the slow decline of the general's health as closely as he might have followed his own—the bouts of pneumonia, the failing kidneys, the drug-induced stupor—not out of sympathy for the old man or an identification with the burdens of power, but because he believed the incident at the church many years earlier had caused the general to hold a grudge against Porto Lúa, and a regime change, he reasoned, might lead to a new highway or a modern port and an influx of visitors who could rescue the town from the enchantments of oblivion.

One afternoon he arrived several minutes after the broadcast had started. The woman reading the news had paused to compose herself as tears ran down her cheeks. With a breaking voice, she went on to explain the detailed medical history of the general and praise his accomplishments. Without waiting until the end of this long list of honors and military victories and cures for diseases and visions of the Holy Family, Don Andrés ordered a sandwich to go and returned to his office. He immediately took on the role of Reformer-in-Chief, abrogating the unpopular laws of the Molinero regime. His first act was to excuse all young men from military conscription even though no one in Porto Lúa had been called to duty since the assassination of Colonel Florentino. His second was to make Galician, which everyone spoke anyway, the official language of Porto Lúa. And his third was to replace the street signs General Molinero's soldiers had erected years earlier with temporary signs bearing their real names. And so Calle del General Mola officially returned to being Rúa do Olvido, Calle del Cardinal Isidro Gomá to Rúa das Sombras, and Calle del Colonel Juan Yagüe to Rúa dos Loureiros. When Dr. Romalde and Fulgencio saw Don Andrés standing in the rain watching Xosé Gallegos hang the hastily painted signs, they asked him what he was doing.

"Laying claim to our birthright of self-determination."

Looking down from his ladder, Xosé added, "The general is dead."

"He's not," Fulgencio replied.

"He's in a coma," explained Dr. Romalde.

"Not dead?"

"No."

"Not yet."

The replacement of signs was temporarily halted, and the vigil continued. Father Infante said the general had been spared through the intervention of the Blessed Virgin, Dr. Romalde believed he was in a vegetative state and being kept alive by machines, and the word traveling with the vendors from Muros was that the general had indeed died, but his staff had ordered journalists to withhold the information until a successor could be named. As men gathered in O Galo to bet on which organ would be the official cause of death, the only programming on television was a summary of the positive developments in the general's condition every hour on the hour followed by a documentary on his life with photographs of his childhood pets and schoolrooms and mustachioed forefathers presented in a funereal monotone that was as lifeless as its subject.

The first news that General Molinero had finally expired came from Cotolay. On a clear, cold, winter afternoon, he was sleeping in his usual place before the altar in Capela de Santa Lupa when he awoke to the odors of burning flesh and brimstone and turned to see a haze of yellow smoke drifting from the grate that covered the opening to the world below. He hurried out of the church and through the streets to O Galo where he urged the mayor to follow him back to the chapel to see the smoke for himself, but by the time Don Andrés had finished his braised lamb shank, there was no need—news of the general's death was official. Wearing a black *mantilla de encaje*, the grieving presenter read the plans for a funeral cortege that would travel by train through the major cities and provinces before the general was laid to rest in a state ceremony in the Valle de los Heroes, a large mausoleum twelve stories high carved from a granite escarpment and trimmed with gold and silver that had been looted from churches in defiant provinces during the war. These plans were repeated for the rest of the day as the national anthem played in the background. During the two days before the funeral, the only images on television were flags rippling in the wind, jets flying over the sierra, and tracer bullets fired across a battlefield as soldiers climbed out of a foxhole and ran over a berm. The only pieces of music playing on the radio were Chopin's *Marche Funèbre* and Mozart's *Requiem*. When the cause of death was declared to be an hepatic metastasis of colon cancer, Manolo Gallardo and Fernando Acuña, who had both guessed the colon because of its unflattering associations, came forward to collect the pool, but the three men who had guessed the liver called on Dr. Romalde to decide the matter. Having no idea, he suggested they call on Wilfreda. In the end, however, it was agreed all five would share the prize.

It was only after he had seen the casket slide into its vault, witnessed by the heads of state of seventeen sovereign nations and nine cardinals, that Don Andrés went back to replacing the street signs. Against the wishes of Father Infante, he also posted a plaque on the door of Nosa Señora do Mar, which, without mentioning grandmother by name, commemorated the rebellion of the people against the authority of the dictatorship.

Priding himself on his political instincts, he predicted a rise of nationalist fervor fueled by the pent-up demands of workers, and to embrace the spirit of this movement, he began to praise the underground *Fronte Revolucionaria* and wear a black beret. Still angry about the stolen altars, he considered breaking away from the rest of Spain and wrote a letter to Fidel, addressing him as "my fellow Galician," to ask whether the Cuban leader would send troops to defend their common patrimony. One night when holding court at O Galo, he proposed pulling down the statue of Don Pedro Ruiz Bóveda y Varela Valcárcel and melting the bronze to augment the town coffers on the grounds that the benefactor of the school had been an unconscionable capitalist. His conversations were now punctuated with criticism of the hegemony of western powers, although he wasn't sure what the word meant. When he suggested carving a giant bust of Karl Marx on an outcrop of Aracelo, he inadvertently inspired Cotolay to propose a bridge across the Atlantic using granite quarried from the mountain. The mention of Karl Marx was the last straw for María Dolores who locked Don Andrés out of the house for three nights until he swore an oath affirming they were members of Porto Lúa's *burguesía*, and if it weren't for her success as a business-woman, he would have no brown suits to wear and no leg of lamb to eat.

To express his sorrow at the passing of General Molinero and acknowledge the role His Excellency had played in maintaining the authority of the Church, Father Infante celebrated a memorial Mass to coincide with the national day of mourning. It had rained since dawn and few were present, but of those who were, one woman kneeling at the altar noticed something unusual about a painting of the Virxe da Cova hanging above the stand of votive candles. Where a chip of paint had fallen from the right cheek of the heavily lacquered icon, she saw a tear. When she pointed this out to Father Infante, he blessed the woman and told her she had been chosen by the Holy Mother to reveal her grief over the death of General Molinero. Despite the dearth of congregants that morning, word of the miracle quickly spread to friends and neighbors, and the next morning, when Father Infante went to open the portal for Mass, he found a crowd of people standing in the warm sunlight waiting to see what had already been dubbed the Weeping Virgin. Among the old women dressed in black were sickly children, a girl with a lifeless left arm, men and women on crutches, a blind man from Curra, and even a few pilgrims who stopped by on their way to Mar das Almas in order to pray before the image.

As was his custom, Father Infante returned to the rectory after Mass for a brief nap before setting to work on his weekly sermon. Because the number of elderly and disabled supplicants had increased during the service, he asked Rosa, who was beating rugs in the yard, to watch over the painting—

perhaps to keep the curious from coming too close and realizing the tear was in fact exposed canvas. She left Mateo Mateo under the fig tree in the care of Facundo who was taking advantage of the clear, warm day to dig a fresh grave for an anticipated death, but as soon as she was gone, the unfortunate *inválido* began to moan. Facundo put down his shovel and sang a *pandeirada*, clapping his hands to the rhythm. When his efforts failed to produce the desired effect, he lifted the handles of the wheelbarrow to take Mateo Mateo to his mother, but, as he did, he saw the ground beneath it was covered with bright flowers despite the season, and a wren he had taken for dead a moment earlier was now sitting alertly in the grass. When he wheeled Mateo Mateo into the church, the wren followed them, and when he dropped the wheelbarrow beside Rosa, the bird alighted on the unresponsive shoulder of the young man.

Those among the assembled who had never seen Mateo Mateo were disturbed by his appearance, but the girl with the lifeless arm walked over to him and, with her right hand, placed the limb against his forearm and stroked it gently. A moment later, she was able to open fingers that had been clenched for years and touch her face. She looked at Facundo in astonishment.

"There were flowers growing beneath him," he said. He turned to Rosa. "When was the last time you were ill?"

"I can't remember."

As Rosa wiped the saliva from his chin with the hem of her smock, the pilgrims reached out and touched Mateo Mateo's arms and legs. One of the women suffering from gout took off her boot and raised her foot to hold against his. As soon as she did, the swelling subsided. Another, who was doubled over with pain in her back, was suddenly able to stand erect. While the blind man from Curra could only claim a greater awareness of forms, those suffering from arthritis, gout, abscessed teeth, psoriasis, dropsy, and sciatica all confirmed a cure or at least a marked improvement in their conditions.

When Father Infante stopped by after his nap, he was initially heartened by the number of pious souls who had come to pay their respect to the Weeping Virgin, but he soon realized the attention had shifted from the painting to the bluish white body in the wheelbarrow wrapped in worn and tattered blankets.

"What is happening here?"

"Mateo Mateo is curing the sick."

"No one can cure the sick but God."

"See for yourself, Father. The lame are walking."

"If that is so, it is because Our Lord, through the agency of his Holy Mother, has chosen this humble means to bestow His blessings on the faithful, those who are tested with hardship, so that they might have the opportunity to strengthen their faith."

Vexed by the attention shown to Mateo Mateo and the disorderly presence of those who had gathered around him, Father Infante imposed a more orderly approach, telling the crowd to sit in the front pews and take turns coming up to pray beside the *inválido*. Throughout the rest of that day, the enfeebled and infirm drifted in and out. When it grew dark, Father Infante consulted with Rosa, and then ushered those still in attendance from their seats and out the door. As she lifted the wheelbarrow to move Mateo Mateo to the sacristy where they slept, the wren flew up to the rafters where it remained for the night. Father picked up a wicker collection basket he had left on the communion rail containing a bounty of coins. He told Rosa it is impious to profit from the blessings of God, but she explained it was a struggle to care for an invalid, and she believed God was helping her relieve this hardship by providing for her. Father Infante thought about what she said and suggested that since the church was her home, they might use the proceeds to mitigate some of the expenses incurred in maintaining that home. She had no choice but to agree.

As stories of Mateo Mateo's power to heal spread among the towns and villages of the coast, he became an object of both curiosity and veneration, and the devout made their way to Porto Lúa from as far away as Malpica and Noia to see him. Early on Sunday mornings, Rosa wheeled her son into the church and set him before the altar where the center aisle meets the sanctuary. After smoothing out the wrinkles in the linen cloth on the altar and opening his Missal to the *Introit*, Father Infante primed the donation basket with a few coins and small bills and set it on the communion rail beside the wheelbarrow. Then he opened the portal to let the people in who had been waiting, in many cases, since before dawn. And the wren too, waiting on a gravestone or funerary statue, flew in over the heads of the congregation to perch on the shoulder of Mateo Mateo. In this way, the weeks passed. Christmas and the Feast of the Epiphany came and went with unusually generous donations. But then one morning the bird failed to appear, and, despite the caresses of his mother to calm him, Mateo Mateo began to rock back and forth and became increasingly agitated. During the homily he began to moan and then laugh uncontrollably so that the church echoed with his guttural delirium. At first Father Infante raised his voice and tried to speak over the sound, but then Mateo Mateo grew louder, as if contesting his voice, and the two engaged in a competition of wills until the priest, who by now was shouting, stopped in mid-sentence and told Rosa to remove her cretin bastard from his church. A silence of collective shock ensued. Without looking at the priest or the members of the congregation, Rosa took the handles of the wheelbarrow, turned, and walked down the aisle to the portal and out into the mist. She didn't stop until she came to Capela de Santa Lupa. Two dozen members of the congregation followed her, and her friend Soledad defiantly took the donation basket from the communion rail. Father Infante stood at the lectern, his chin raised with the arrogance of authority, and waited until all who had decided to leave were gone before he continued.

Later in the day Facundo collected Rosa's bedding and clothing and personal effects and delivered the bundle to her on the back of a borrowed mule. She made a home for herself and her son in a dry corner of the chapel and hung a sheet from a fishing cable to separate her space from the rest of the church. Once she had settled in, Facundo took a black crayon and wrote *Mateo Mateo Bendicido por Deus* on the flap of a cardboard box and hung the sign on a string between the handles of the wheelbarrow. When it was raining, she set her son just inside the entrance of the chapel, and on warm, sunny days, she set him beside the fountain in the small square outside where they were often accompanied by devoted attendants—older women dressed in black sweaters and scarves whose vestal fires had long been extinguished.

The wren did not follow them to Capela de Santa Lupa, nor did the power to heal, but Mateo Mateo's reputation did, and that was all they needed. People continued to come from great distances in the hope that his innocent saintliness would expedite their petitions to God. On Sundays and holy days of obligation, Rosa's basket would contain as many as one hundred pesetas, and on festival days that number could double or triple. She paid Fulgencio to trim and oil her son's hair and bought him a tailored suit of gray flannel and a proper wheelchair. She even paid a traveling artist to paint a depiction of his crucifixion, which she hung on the wall of her alcove. By the end of the year, people had begun to lose faith in her son's curative power, but by that time she had collected enough money to buy a house in Rúa das Sombras and was considered, along with Madame Zafirah and María Dolores, to be one of the richest women in Porto Lúa.

Having banished his housekeeper by banishing her son,

Father Infante was forced to do his own laundry and shopping and cooking and cleaning. As a way to convince Rosa to return to her job without admitting that he needed her, he asked Facundo to tell her he wasn't sure how long he could keep her position open before filling it with someone else, but she wasn't interested. An old woman who was nearly blind helped out for a week, but she burned his roast and scorched his favorite chasuble with an iron, so he was left with no choice but to continue to look after himself. He attempted to revive interest in the Weeping Virgin, but more flakes of paint fell from the image until its mottled appearance led some to call her the Poxed Madonna at which point the priest removed the painting and stored it in the attic of the rectory where it was soon forgotten.

On the Saturday before *Semana Santa*, almost a year since the altars had been removed, a half dozen cars arrived in the plaza bringing fifteen professors and students from Santiago. Among them were experts in linguistics, the hillfort culture, petroglyphs, Roman masonry, ethnology, and megalithic tombs as well as a sketch artist, an historian from the Ministry of National Education, and a ranger from the forestry service. They had come for the week with their tents, sleeping bags, canteens, portable stoves, compasses, binoculars, cameras, carefully wrapped parcels of food, toilet paper, ponchos, flashlights, maps, plastic bags, and collapsible shovels to search the mountain for more artifacts. Facundo, Ánxel, and I helped them unload their cars while Mestre stood to one side speaking with two of his friends who were in the group. One was a foreigner with blond hair and sunglasses and the other an older man with gentle eyes, a graying beard, and wire-rimmed glasses who informed him his study of the Bronze Age petroglyphs at Pedra Longa written several years earlier was finally being published.

As soon as they had unloaded their equipment, the group went to O Galo for a coffee break, but it was already eleven o'clock, and Mestre encouraged them to hasten their departure because of the length of the climb and the challenges of the path after dark. Mestre, Facundo, Ánxel, and I led the way, and we made good time initially, but several of the professors were not accustomed to such arduous exercise and had to stop to rest and smoke. After the experience of the altars that were removed by the Ministry of National Education, Mestre was concerned about the presence of so many people on the mountain and wary of the harm they could do even if their motives were above reproach, and he wasn't convinced they were. He felt obligated to assist his friends, but troubled by the likelihood that any object of value would be removed. As the stragglers fell behind, he took his friends aside to share his reservations and explain that, because he could not prevent the arrival of such groups, he had decided it would be better to accompany them and counsel respect for the beliefs of the people who lived on the mountain.

"The outside world will come," he said. "The mountain will change and so will the lives of its inhabitants. We can't stop that. But we can mitigate the worst effects of these intrusions with courtesy and understanding. And perhaps one day our efforts will help to establish a conservation area."

We arrived at the bothy after dark, guided by the flashlights arrayed around us like the lights of the Santa Compaña. Those of us from Porto Lúa slept in the old barn on the rope beds that we covered with dry grass as we had done in the past while the rest of the group pitched their tents among the ruins of the houses and built a fire on the stone pavement of a threshing floor.

The next morning, we examined the site among the

sentinel boulders near Lonxe do Sol where the bodies of the Roman soldiers had been found and then proceeded to the village. We were at the same altitude as the clouds that float across the Atlantic and come to rest among the cool granite bluffs like weary travelers after a long journey, and, as a consequence, as we approached Lonxe, we entered a misting fog that thickened the closer we came to the cliffs of the Deva. The people of the village were surprised by such a large group appearing on their narrow street out of the clouds unannounced. Alerted by barking dogs, Régulo greeted us from a doorway and invited us to the public house with the door over the barrels serving as a bar. There was barely room for our group let alone the curious people of Lonxe who crowded in around us. Some were left standing in the mist, and some were pushed into the darkness at the back of the musty room.

The linguist questioned several of the men about their vocabulary and took detailed notes on the speech he heard while the other professors engaged the rest of the crowd in broken conversations with the help of Facundo. Ánxel and I were of some help as well, but the language of the mountain often eluded us. Most of the questions pertained to sightings of stones with unusual letters or marks and strange pieces of metal. When Mestre asked a group of men standing by the door if they knew any stories about a casque of gold buried on the mountain, one of them left and returned a short time later with a 1953 almanac from Argentina that had probably found its way to Lonxe from Porto Lúa after being acquired from sailors years earlier. The man opened the book to a paragraph on the history of Spain and pointed to a passage that had been underlined. He gave the book to Mestre, who read, "Celtic migrations into the Iberian Peninsula occurred as early 900 B.C. Archeologists have discovered an array of artifacts from the period including gold earrings and torcs characteristic of that civilization."

437

When he finished, Mestre nodded gravely and said, "That is something I will keep in mind. Thank you for bringing this information to our attention."

After the man was gone and we were standing outside, I questioned how he could possibly believe such general historical facts could be of any value to our investigations.

"It's not the facts that matter to him," Mestre said, "but what can be divined from the magic of the words. There is an ancient Celtic belief in their power and mystery. Because I am a teacher, he thinks I am endowed with the ability to unlock the secret meaning behind the words, which will tell us where to look for the gold."

The professors were disappointed by the lack of substantive information they received in Lonxe that morning. I assumed the villagers were guarded because of the altars that had been removed, but they did lead us to a black stone that was sent from heaven "in the time of Christ" and, according to legend, used as the seat of the throne of Raíña Lupa and then as a pillow in her coffin. During the invasion of the Moors, the stone was removed for safekeeping to a hidden location on the mountain and discovered again in the last century and set beneath the altar in the small church near the Roman road. And there it lay. With Régulo and my cousin Xosé leading the group, we walked up the path to the Roman road and the church. It had not changed since Father Infante had said Mass there on his trip to renew the faith of the people of Lonxe. Régulo inserted the chisel end of a mattock between two stones in the pedestal of the altar and prised one of them out to reveal a black stone rectangular in shape and rounded on the corners, not unlike a cushion or pillow. The object itself was of little interest to the professors since it was not that unusual, but they were interested in the story behind it and to complete the picture, asked where it was found. To that question, the unhelpful answer was "in a field nearby."

The most important discovery of the expedition occurred by chance later in the afternoon when one of the students was walking along the side of the stream that bordered the churchyard and noticed the shape of a long, narrow stone lying in a brush of alder saplings and russet ferns. She scraped off a partial covering of moss and decaying leaves to reveal a granite slab broken in half. After washing away the leaf mold and roots of small weeds, we were able to make out the images and letters that had been carved on the surface of a headstone. At the top was a human figure, presumably the deceased, with a square body and circular head surrounded by the sun of his paradise and a field of five stars that resembled sand dollars. The features of his face were simple, almost cartoon-like: small chiseled points for the eyes, their brows arched high in expectation, a bulbous nose, and a tight, wry smile. Below him was a square divided into four parts by intersecting diagonal lines with each triangular quadrant containing a large celestial body and two smaller ones. The twelve spheres suggested the journey of the soul through the constellations of the zodiac or perhaps months separated into seasons by the solstices and equinoxes of a timeless cycle. These symbols constituted a prayer cut in stone to ensure this soul would be as permanent as the stars of heaven lasting through all the seasons of eternity. In a narrow panel below the square were the letters *D.M.S.*, which stood for *Dis Manibus Sacrum* or "consecrated to the manes," ancestors of the deceased who had become gods. One of the professors speculated they might be the stars surrounding the portrait of the soul on the stone.

In the lowest panel were the letters

PRIMIANO

VITALES AN

LXXV

which Mestre translated as "Primiano, son of Vitales, age seventy-five." I could imagine this Roman Primiano in his own apotheosis looking down on us from the stars. He had made it, I thought, passed through the fear of death to the heaven of his distant sun where he has watched cities and civilizations come and go for nearly two thousand years.

We searched the area for the rest of the afternoon and found the fragment of another headstone twenty yards away that at first sight was nothing more than a nob of granite hidden in deep grass. Except for a notch on one side, it looked like every other stone nudging up from the ground: stained by damp soil and spotted with green and gray lichens. Removing a little dirt around the stone revealed that the notch was the letter *I* and part of the inscription *IOM*, signifying *Iovi Optimo Maximo*. As we gently pulled the fragment from the soft earth, rocking it back and forth, we saw a panel of decorations emerge, a poetry of granite—a sun with six rays like the petals of a flower, and below it, between two stars, a crescent moon resting on its back like a ship of sidereal seas whose stern and bow were its upright tips.

The professors and their students measured and photographed the stones and then, as the light began to fade, we went back down the mountain to our camp to spend the night. When we returned to the site the next morning, the stones were gone, but there were cart-tracks deep in the wet fields that were easy to follow. We found the three pieces undamaged in a recess among a group of boulders halfway to Agro Vello. The professors wanted to confront the people of Lonxe, but Mestre persuaded them to let the matter go. The stones, he argued, would be safe where they were and would risk damage if they were moved again before a cart could be hired to take them down the mountain. The professors agreed, but moved their camp to the field where the stones were found in order to keep watch over the site they were excavating.

Mestre, Ánxel, and I returned to Porto Lúa the next day while Facundo stayed behind to act as a translator and liaison of sorts. The excavations in the area where the headstones were found continued through the rest of the week, but nothing more than a few iron nails and shards of pottery were found. On Holy Thursday, the oxcart arrived from Porto Lúa. The plan was to take the stones down the mountain on Friday and transport them to a museum in Vigo where they would be studied and displayed, but Thursday evening, when several of the professors returned to the boulders where they had last seen them, the stones were gone. Accompanied by Facundo, they went back down the Roman road to Lonxe where they confronted Régulo and demanded their return.

"What stones?" he asked, shrugging his shoulders.

"The stones that were taken from our site."

"I'll ask around and see what I can learn."

"Someone must know. It would take several men to lift them."

"I'm sure it's just a mistake. We have lots of stones on the mountain, and it's easy to confuse them. Why would someone go to so much trouble to carry off your stones?"

"Because they're valuable."

"How valuable can a few stones be that are lying in the woods?"

"Are you attempting to extort money for them?"

"Why would I do that if I don't know their worth?"

"Because you know they're worth something to us. You do realize these stones belong to the state, and you could be arrested for stealing them."

"How can we steal something that belongs to us? I'd say the people stealing things are those who come from the city and take whatever they find."

"We'll see if the Guardia agrees."

"When the Guardia arrives, there may not be any stones."

"What do you want?"

"A fair exchange."

"Meaning?"

"We have stones and you have tents and raincoats and shovels and flashlights."

"I see."

The professors returned to their camp to consult with the rest of the group. After some debate, they agreed to leave much of their equipment behind. Facundo returned to Lonxe to confirm the deal. The next morning, the stones were lying in the Roman road where the professors lifted them onto the oxcart and secured them for the trip down the mountain.

According to his own account, Facundo had been standing beneath a white willow near the excavation site on Friday evening waiting for the rain to pass when the light of heaven, "brighter than a hundred suns," exploded the trunk of the tree and disappeared into the ground as mica sand sizzled into lumps of vitreous slag. Glowing threads of St. Elmo's fire danced in the blue smoke overhead, and then a large bough slowly split away from the tree and fell grazing his arm. His clothes broke out in patches of flame, his hair smoldered, his eyes were blackened, and one of his eardrums had burst, but he remained conscious. Those still on the site rushed to put out the flames and cover him with a blanket.

It was too late in the day to take him to Porto Lúa, so they moved him to one of their tents and dressed his burns. Because of the seriousness of his condition, one of the students kept a vigil beside him through the night. Sometime in the early hours of morning when he woke from a restless sleep, he had recovered enough of his voice to whisper to the woman that he heard laughter like that of a man who has cheated death, but she heard nothing apart from the wind in the pines. The next morning several of the professors examined him and speculated that the sound he heard was due to a constriction of the airways in his lungs or throat, air passing through a ruptured eardrum, or a disturbance of the fluids in his ear or in the circuitry of his brain. Though the extension to his boot had been blown off by the lightning, Facundo slowly regained his balance, and, accompanied by two of the students, was able to return to Porto Lúa under his own power. He refused to be taken to the hospital in Santiago, but accepted the care of Dr. Romalde who replaced his bandages and gave him a physical examination.

"In addition to second-degree burns, you have lost an eardrum and a great deal of hair," he said. "Both will grow back. I've never diagnosed a case of chronic laughter and can't tell you what to expect in terms of its abatement or a cure. In other words, it's something you'll have to live with until it goes away. If it goes away."

Facundo's hair grew back and his eardrum healed, but the laughter continued, and because laughter, by its nature, is infectious, when he heard it within, he laughed without. This, in turn, caused others in his company to laugh as well. When he tried to suppress his laughter on occasions that demanded an air of decorum, the result was often a more violent eruption. For this reason, he had to stand at the back of church on Sundays and avoid the mourners when he dug a grave. At night it continued and kept him awake, and, when speaking to others, he found it difficult to be taken seriously on any subject, no matter how solemn, when a smile invariably broke through his attempts to contain it. On rainy spring days shrouded in fog when his friends were dispirited, they looked forward to seeing him, for in addition to being a source of good cheer, he became an omen of good fortune.

One might have expected the dogs of Porto Lúa to take

exception to a man who had the appearance of a vagabond and laughed like the possessed, but the opposite was true. Rather than attack Facundo, they became submissive in his presence, tails tucked, ears back, and heads lowered to the ground. Since this was not the case before he was struck by lightning, we could only conclude that an imperceptible alteration in his nature had occurred as a result of his bad luck, if it could be called that. Rosa believed his eyes had taken in so much light so quickly that they were releasing it slowly over the weeks that followed, and because dogs have more highly developed senses, they were able to see this light emanating from his eyes not only in the darkness but also in daylight. When Don Andrés observed him subdue a pack of dogs fighting over scraps of meat outside the market, he asked him to stop by the town hall where he offered to hire him as a dog-catcher with a salary of thirty pesetas a month. Of more appeal than the money was an old blue vest he was given and the catch pole which was a long hollow baton with a loop of rope emerging from one end. Because he had no need for a pole, he used it to catch octopi at low tide and later in the summer to pick fruit for people for a share of their harvest. When he was wearing his vest on official duty, people gave him the nickname Hermes, but he was never really a dog-catcher since there was no place to put dogs once they were caught. Instead, his job was to separate them or calm them or take them home to their owners when they were unruly or in heat.

Although it was beyond his jurisdiction, one evening he responded to a request to investigate a report that a goat had been killed by a pack of dogs near Foxo Escuro and invited me to go with him. As we were walking down the path between Harry's museum and Foxo, we were set upon by three Alsatians appearing out of nowhere. I raised a large stick to threaten them as they approached barking fiercely, but when Facundo crouched down and extended his hand, the dogs stopped in their tracks and crept toward us, bent low as if paying homage to a lord. Even though I had seen Facundo subdue the dogs in Porto Lúa, I was still surprised by his power to pacify what appeared to be wild dogs in such a remote place. Trotting behind the dogs were two mangy pups and at some distance a shirtless man with long hair and a beard. When he reached us, he introduced himself as Hipólito and apologized for the greeting the dogs had given us and expressed his admiration for the way Facundo had been able to calm them.

"How did you do that?"

"I don't know. I've had the power ever since I was struck by lightning."

"Can you do anything else?"

"I suffer from bouts of laughter, although much less than before."

"Come with me. I want you to meet my brothers and sisters."

By "brothers and sisters" he meant a community of traveling people. As we followed Hipólito up the path over high ground between two barren mounds of granite, the sun was setting behind a low bank of lavender clouds that had gathered beyond the grayish green waters of Mar das Almas. In the east the rising moon resembled a thin chip of ice melting in a pool of pale blue water. From that height we could also see the dusty clearing in a grove of pine trees where these people had camped and smell the sweet smoke of their fire on the cool breeze. Among the pines were two vans in various states of disrepair and three tents patched with squares of canvas. Blankets were airing on a line hanging between two of the trees. As we entered the camp, Hipólito introduced us to the tall leader of the group who called himself Lobo. He was wearing an Inca hat with bells tied to its tassels. Brightly colored wisps of yarn were woven into his long hair and beard which reached down to the embroidered vest he wore over a hempen shirt. What impressed me most about him, however, were his hypnotic eyes set in a gaunt face only partially softened by an open smile.

"What brings you to our camp, brothers?"

"I was sent because a goat was killed by some dogs near Foxo Escuro. You should know that if your dogs are in that area, they may be poisoned or shot. The people in Foxo will take any measure to protect their livestock."

"We will keep them near."

"He has a power over dogs," said Hipólito.

"In Porto Lúa, they call him Hermes," I said.

Lobo invited us to join them and introduced us to Erasmo, Paqui, Tiago, Maruxa, Nerea, Arantxa, and Rocío, who were seated in a circle of stones around a large fire. Two other women were sitting at the opening of a tent playing a flute and small drum. Behind the tent, dancing to the rhythm, was my classmate Pilar, who had been absent from school for several weeks. Her eyes were closed, and she was waving her arms as if she were drowning in slow motion or in a dream. Tiago was shirtless like Hipólito, and Erasmo was wearing a hempen shirt like Lobo. The women wore loose, homespun smocks or pinafores and long skirts hemmed with mud. Their hair was unwashed, and Nerea and Arantxa wore theirs in braids interlaced with strands of yarn. Each woman was adorned with bracelets and necklaces of various metals, and Arantxa wore a large turquoise pendant over her breast, to "keep the sky close to my heart," she said. Some of them were barefoot, and all of them conveyed an odor of animal sweat. The mannerisms and speech of the women were slow, and in their conversation they gave undue attention to insignificant aspects of nature like the movement of the grass in the wind and the texture of the bark on pine trees. My interest lay more in the shapes and movements of their bodies beneath the light fabric.

Without knowing quite what to say to these people, and

curious about how they made a living, Facundo asked Hipólito, "What do you do?"

"We are preparing the way for others who will follow."

"Are you shepherds?"

"In a manner of speaking."

"We make marionettes," said Maruxa, "and sell them in the markets where we camp."

"I don't know about other places, but I don't think there's much demand for marionettes in Porto Lúa."

"We also knit wool caps and tell fortunes."

Nerea went to one of the tents and brought out a box containing several marionettes made from hand-carved wood and papier-mâché that they had painted and strung together with fishing line. Arantxa sat beside me and began to write on a scrap of paper. When she finished, she gave it to me: "You have been chosen by destiny to receive knowledge of Eternal Wisdom from the Golden Light. Let every moment of every day be your teacher. Let the flowers of summer and the wind-blown clouds be your scripture. It is the mind that separates us from the rest of creation, but through discipline, the enlightened mind can dispel the illusion of our isolation."

The clouds in the west had broken up and were drifting off as dark silhouettes across the dusky prism of the western sky. Someone placed a branch on the fire, and the flames rose casting our shadows on the trees surrounding us. When Facundo saw them passing a cigarette around, he assumed they were hard-pressed for tobacco and offered them some of his own, but they told him to try theirs. He took several puffs before handing it to me. I passed it to Arantxa without smoking.

"Hermes was struck by lightning and as a result has fits of laughter," said Hipólito.

"It's true," said Facundo. "Sometimes I weigh a lake at night because of it."

"How much does a lake weigh?" asked Erasmo as the

group, including Facundo, broke out in laughter.

"The professors think the circularity of my brain has changed, and that's why I have power over dogs."

"It is a gift," said Lobo, "to know the minds of other creatures. The reward of selflessness."

The conversation was punctuated by silences, and, as the fire died down again, stars began to appear. After some time, Hipólito turned to Facundo and asked, "What do you see when you look at the sky?"

"Mestre says the night is full of what is yet to be."

"Who is Mestre?"

"The head of the school in Porto Lúa. He says everything that will ever be and everything that will never be are in the sky. He calls it the great sea of being."

"There is more of what isn't than what is," said Erasmo.

"But we don't know how much of what isn't is yet to be."

"Is what is yet to be more real than what will never be?"

"Each one of those stars is like a grain of sand adrift in an ocean of emptiness," said Arantxa.

"Nothing is real," said Hipólito. "I don't mean there isn't anything real. I mean what isn't is real, maybe more real than what is."

"It's all nothing."

"Configurations."

"The harmony of spheres."

"Is there still harmony without spheres?"

They rolled and lit another cigarette.

"We're no more real than anything else."

"Except for all the things that will never be."

"For the moment."

"When you think about what could have been and wasn't, everything that exists is a miracle."

"Our presence is even more miraculous."

"We're no better than anything else."

"Except we're conscious."

"We value according to our nature."

"How do you know a tree isn't conscious? Maybe it has a consciousness different from ours."

"Is it conscious of the stars?"

"Who's to say it isn't? Who's to say our version of reality is the only one?"

"Maybe we're like trees to a higher reality. We say the night is empty because we don't know what's there."

"Can a tree be conscious of its consciousness?"

"When you're conscious of your consciousness, are you the consciousness you're conscious of or the consciousness of being conscious?"

"You can be conscious of being conscious or not conscious of being conscious, but you can never be conscious of not being conscious."

"What we know is the universe knowing itself. And when each of us dies, the universe loses part of itself, forgets itself forever."

"What you think of as a loss isn't a loss but a gain in another part of the whole," said Arantxa. "Loss is only an illusion of something separating from the whole because we think of ourselves as our own rather than as part of that whole."

"But if the universe is nothing, and we are the universe knowing itself, then we are nothing knowing nothing."

"Are our thoughts even our own? Maybe everything is a thought, and we are the thoughts of something else."

"To ourselves, each of us is what the world is not. We're what keeps the rest of the world from being whole."

Recalling his conversation with Mestre, Facundo observed, "When we were born, millions of others were not. Wherever we go, whatever we do, we're taking the place of someone else, of something else."

"We think we belong to ourselves but we don't. We belong to everything."

"We're all the lives that came before us and all the lives that will come after and all the lives we have encountered in our lives. We are less ourselves than we are all the others. They are as much of us as the food we eat and the air we breathe, and what are we without food and air and the body we were given by the bodies that came before us?"

"We can never be ourselves. We're always someone we can't recognize. We adopt a face like the faces that we see without ever knowing who we are."

"We are each a mystery to ourselves."

"When I look into my thoughts, it's as if I'm looking through a window from outside, and in the dark interior, I see a sky as vast as the one overhead. But rather than stars, it's filled with memories and dreams and images conjured as much as captured from every moment of my life sleeping and waking. It's hard to keep from falling into that sky and disappearing among its lights."

The moon seemed close enough overhead to be listening to our conversation. Lobo, who had been sitting quietly throughout the conversation, finally joined in.

"Science tells us our consciousness is a result of the way the minerals and gases that constitute our nature have been configured since the moment of creation. Our thoughts do not belong to us any more than they belong to the minerals and gases that make us what we are. When this configuration falls apart and the minerals and gases are dispersed to return to soil and air, they will be taken up again in the configurations of grasses and trees."

"And we are lost forever."

"When you understand the unity of all things in creation and your place among them, the illusions of separation and loss will no longer trouble you."

"I don't know how you wouldn't be troubled by death."

"We come into the world with a body that by necessity is different from every other body, but that differentiation is an illusion since earthly materials undergo constant change. By creating an illusion of individuality, our bodies mask our true being, which shares in the being of all things. The movement of our breath is the movement of the wind among the trees. The movement of our blood is the movement of the tide in the salt marsh. And the light that illuminates our thoughts is the light that enters our houses at daybreak bringing the objects of our lives back to life. No, we do not create a unique consciousness of our own. Rather, just as we share the movement of our breath and the movement of our blood, we share the greater consciousness of all things from the time of our birth."

"Are you from the university?" asked Facundo.

"I was a student once, but I left because I couldn't let others think for me. Since then, I have traveled the world learning the Mysteries of the Chaldeans, the Visions of Poimandres, the Vedas of Brahma."

"What do they say?"

"That the essence of all knowledge is the understanding that while our bodies are finite, the infinite is our parent, our source, and we return to it in time. Through discipline we can transcend our finite nature and remember our origin. If you can empty your heart of desire, of attachment to the transient, you will see the true nature of things without the dream of a self."

"Is that the same thing as the soul?"

"Each of us is a mixture of darkness and light, and our lives are a preparation for our journey into the light at that moment when the darkness overtakes our bodies. The soul is the moon of our lives, lighting our way through the darkness of matter in this world. We have come to the end of the world to prepare for our emergence. To learn the lessons of the sun and moon as they teach us the paths of light."

"What kind of light is that?"

"When consciousness is conscious of nothing but consciousness, when, free of all objects, it becomes the clear light of nothingness, like light seen through light. Then the world passes away, and we are free, liberated into the realm of pure consciousness, into the light."

"I don't think I can think of nothing."

"We are all children of the light. All minds exist in the original mind, and through discipline each mind can open to all possibility."

"People are so blinded by their petty concerns they fail to see the truth," said Erasmo.

"What about God and churches?" asked Facundo.

"There is a unity of all things. There is a spirit of being in all beings. Since we are part of that spirit, we are part of all things and all things are a part of us. That is God. Not the stories about men and miracles fashioned out of a need for love and a fear of death."

"Does that mean there is no hell?"

"Hell is just one of the stories."

"There's a man in Porto Lúa who says hell is below where we're sitting."

"A priest?"

"A fisherman."

"What he does a fisherman know about hell?"

"He's been there."

"He's been to hell?"

"He walked through the underworld from Illa da Luz to Porto Lúa."

Lobo thought about this for a moment and asked, "Do you know this man?"

"Everyone knows him."

"Can we speak with him?"

"Of course. I'll take you to him now if you like."

As we walked back to Porto Lúa, guided by what little light was offered by the moon, Lobo and Hipólito smoked another one of their cigarettes. When Facundo asked where he could buy some of his own, Lobo told him they were only available in the cities, but gave him one to try for himself.

Trofonio lived in a dilapidated fisherman's cottage with wildflowers growing from the roof in the old part of town just off Rúa dos Mortos. When we knocked on his door, he opened it reluctantly, but, recognizing Facundo and me, invited the four of us inside. Beyond a strip of floor, perhaps eight feet wide, that ran parallel to the front wall and provided just enough space for a metal cot and a table with two chairs, was a deep pit. Trofonio had removed the inner walls that had separated the rooms and the wooden floor and the older stone floor beneath it and dug down at least six feet below the level of the street. When Facundo asked him why he had removed the floor and foundation of his house, he explained that so many people had doubted his story that he had begun to doubt it himself, so he had decided to "excavate his memory." His original purpose was to create another opening to the underworld to prove to people that he had been there, but when he ran into bedrock, he decided to recreate the geography of his journey instead. What lay below us was a landscape of plaster and cement mixed with charcoal where Trofonio had sculpted towers and walls and molded tunnels consistent with his memory. He climbed down a ladder and lit more than a dozen candles in the tunnels to create a glowing impression of the burning city of the damned. The Sea of the Cassiterides was a large sheet of glass bordered by sand and grass in the corner of the pit, and its islands were small mounds of plaster painted green. With a broom handle, he pointed to where he had fallen into the lagoon and traced the path he had taken through the city. Despite his desire to prove the existence of the underworld, he was so afraid he might be damned for an inadvertent sin that he left his house only to provide for himself and empty the dirt from his wheelbarrow into the ocean.

"No one can imagine what hell is like unless they have been there, and I have been there. It is the worst horror you can experience. Worse than the worse nightmare you have ever had because it is real, and there is no redemption for those who dwell there."

Rather than doubting Trofonio's vision of the underworld, Lobo was unsettled by it.

"I know this place," he said. "I have seen it in my dreams. It is a manifestation of the darkness that keeps us from the light. And the voices. I hear the voices of that anguish as if they are beneath the ground where we stand. I see fires buried in the air, the dying light of dying stars falling all around us."

"I don't see anything," said Hipólito.

"They're here."

"Who?"

"The souls of the dead. I see their faces in the window. I see their faces in your faces."

Facundo whispered to Hipólito, "You need to get him out of here."

"This man is one of them," Lobo said pointing to Trofonio. "He is inhabited by the dead."

Once we had persuaded him to step outside, Lobo collapsed in the street unable to speak, unable to move, staring transfixed into the darkness. Hipólito spoke to him for several minutes about his friends and the beauty of the night and the freshness of the air, and slowly he came to his senses and was able to stand. His natural voice returned, but his mind was not quite clear as he claimed he had experienced his own death and the tortures of hell and that he had seen Trofonio's soul among the damned. As we walked up Rúa dos Mortos, Facundo invited us to a cup of coffee in O Galo, and when he was assured both Hipólito and Lobo had recovered from the ordeal, we accompanied them across the bridge and along the path as far as the point where it leaves the cliffs and turns south toward Foxo Escuro. On the way back, Facundo took the cigarette from his pocket and tossed it into the Deva.

The next day began clear and fresh like the morning after a storm. I had to go to school, but Facundo went back to the campsite to check on Lobo as he felt responsible for what had happened at Trofonio's, but the tents and vans were gone. All that remained were old newspapers and cans and smoldering ashes in the stone circle where they had made their fires. As he was about to leave, he encountered Erasmo returning to the site with a bucket to collect embers and asked him where the others had gone.

"They left for Muxía."

"What about you?"

"I'm going to work for Doña Esperanza. I met her walking in the fields."

"If there's anything I can do for you, let me know."

"Thanks, brother."

That evening in O Galo, Don Andrés asked Facundo if he had found the dogs that killed the goat.

"I don't know."

"What do you mean you don't know?"

"I found a camp of traveling people who had a pack of dogs."

"Did you talk to them?"

"I did. For more than an hour."

"What did they say?"

"I don't remember."

"You spoke to them for more than an hour, and you don't remember what they said?"

"We smoked one of their cigarettes and talked about the universe, and then we went to see Trofonio."

"You smoked one of their cigarettes?"

"I offered them some of my tobacco, but they preferred their own."

"That wasn't a cigarette, Facundo."

"It wasn't?"

"It was a *porro*."

"A *porro*?"

"A Moroccan cigarette."

"I don't think so, Don Andrés. They rolled it themselves."

"Let's just leave it at that."

When people woke to find the words *Espanha é a Nossa Ruína* painted on the side of the market and *Independencia* painted on the portal of Nosa Señora do Mar, their first thought was that Porto Lúa had been invaded by terrorists. Don Andrés said it looked like the work of ETA or GRAPA or SWAPA or some other insurgent operation. Father Infante blamed Protestants, but apart from the German tourists who had been seen on the beaches near Muros, there were no Protestants in the area. A few old people thought it may have been the French. Marcella said it was the Moors.

Later that day, the parents of Pilar went to Constable Sampaio to claim that gypsies had stolen their child. He reported the case to Don Andrés, who in turn questioned Facundo for information on the people camping near Foxo.

"They're not gypsies. They're traveling people."

"That's not the point. Is Pilar with them?"

"She is, but now they're gone."

"They're gone?"

"Yes."

"Where did they go?"

"Muxía."

"When did they leave?"

"Yesterday morning."

"That rules them out."

"Except for Erasmo."

"I thought you said they were gone."

"Not one of them is left, except one."

"Can you take us to their camp?"

"I can, but he's not there anymore. He's working for Doña Esperanza."

"We need to warn El Conde."

María Dolores, who had overheard the conversation, pointed out that the graffiti did not say anything that her husband hadn't said a few months earlier in his letter to Fidel.

"But that was when we were throwing off the yoke of dictatorship," he said. "This is different."

"The only thing that's different is your politics."

Don Andrés and Constable Sampaio paid a visit to El Conde after lunch and told him they believed a terrorist could be working for him. El Conde said his daughter had gone out, but he would speak to her when she returned.

Before dawn the next morning, the terrorist had struck again. When he arrived at the town hall, Don Andrés discovered the word *Fóra* painted on the front door. A small crowd of concerned citizens had already gathered in the plaza demanding that he take some action.

"Call in the Guardia."

"Sampaio can't deal with these people."

"If you don't do something, we will."

Don Andrés stood on the top step of the entrance to the town hall and waved his arms up and down to quiet the crowd.

"We are experiencing a threat unlike any we have seen before. With the end of the dictatorship and the emergence of new freedoms, new challenges have beset the authorities, and we will take strong measures to ensure the people are safe

457

from the menace of anarchy and a tyranny of the few who seek to intimidate with their slogans and crimes. This morning I have decided to call the Guardia and request reinforcements in this challenge to our Christian, democratic way of life."

After the crowd had dispersed, he called the Guardia, explained the threat of terrorism the town was facing, and asked for help in identifying and dealing with the culprits. As he waited for them to arrive, he began to examine the crime scene on his own and noticed that while the paint was still fresh, someone who was barefoot had stepped in a small pool that had dripped from the door and left a trail of broken prints that went around the corner and down the street. By the time he reached Capela de Santa Lupa, they had almost disappeared. He asked Rosa if she had seen anyone coming or going that morning. Only Cotolay, she said. He found a can of marine primer and a stiff brush hidden under a blanket behind the altar and went in search of his suspect. After looking for him unsuccessfully in O Galo, the alameda, the school, and Nosa Señora do Mar, he returned to the town hall, but as he entered the building, he saw the Guardia crossing the bridge, and, realizing the embarrassment he would face by calling for their help when the terrorist was Cotolay, he barricaded himself inside the building and pretended to be held hostage.

He quickly discovered that he had acted impulsively and had failed to consider that a staged kidnapping must have a credible exit strategy and account for unforeseen circumstances. As Don Andrés paced back and forth in his office on the second floor, the Guardia took up their positions outside in the plaza.

"This is Captain Martínez," shouted the officer in charge from behind their car. "If you are able to speak, tell us your condition."

"I'm all right," shouted Don Andrés from behind the door to the balcony.

"What are the terrorists' demands?"

"They want you to withdraw and allow them free passage."

"We can't do that."

"They're threatening to kill me."

When the Guardia didn't respond, Don Andrés looked past the louvered door where he was standing and saw Gustavo carrying a basket of food and a bottle of wine across the plaza to the officers. Cotolay was standing behind them.

"They're threatening to kill me," he repeated. "You need to withdraw at once."

"Tell them we've decided to wait them out," shouted Captain Martínez.

The stand-off lasted through the lunch hour and into late afternoon. Every now and then Don Andrés looked out on the plaza to see the officers chatting with people passing by. A spring shower came and went.

"Tell your kidnappers we're not waiting anymore. We're going to storm the building if they don't let you go."

"Don't do that. Don't do that. They're serious. They said they'll kill me if you approach the building."

"Sometimes the only way to get rid of rats is to burn them out."

"What if you burn the cat along with them?"

"You get another cat."

The Guardia had come prepared for a siege, and, with a battering ram improvised from the discarded mast of a sailboat, the officers forced open the front door of the building and threw a concussion grenade inside blowing out several windows on the ground floor. After the smoke had cleared, they entered to find Don Andrés on the staircase dazed and covered with plaster dust.

"They must have escaped through a back window," he said.

What he hadn't known at the time is that shortly after their arrival, Cotolay had confessed to the Guardia that he was responsible for painting the graffiti. Realizing he was harmless, they told him not to paint any more buildings and let him go.

Every evening after the sun went down, grandfather sat on the stone bench in front of the house where grandmother used to sit as if he were waiting for her to return. He wore a straw hat whose brim had been gnawed along the edge by field mice and a black woolen jacket he had bought in the market before the war. The one luxury he had maintained throughout his life was a "factory" cigarette at the end of the day. After settling on the bench, he tipped one from a pack of *Ducados* and smoked it slowly, saying to anyone who would listen, "If a hurricane can't kill me, I'm not going to worry about a stick of tobacco." Lost in the past, he would ask mother and father if they remembered the woman in the market who had a parrot that spoke Persian or the night a boulder rolled down the mountain and killed two cows in Campo da Graza, but they never did, and now, with Aunt Fioxilda gone, there was no one left in the family who had witnessed his early life. Sometimes Francisco the boat builder would join him on the bench. Because they had grown up together, this short man with a broad smile, eyes that opened wide, and a half-wreath of white hair around the back of his head was one of the last witnesses of those "better days."

In their youth, as they told it, they had been caught stealing fruit from the orchard of El Conde's father. When the steward took them to the old man, he threatened to have them arrested and pasted their hair with the pine tar he used on his horses. On the way home from their humiliation, they hatched a plan to get even. There was a ledge above the coastal road before the turnoff to the manor house where a dead tree trunk housed a large beehive. On a Sunday morning after Mass, when El Conde's father was passing by in his carriage, they pushed the beehive off the ledge onto the pavement beside the horse, sending horse, driver, and passengers on a wild ride down the road.

On another occasion a neighbor paid them to drive his pigs over the mountain to the market in Mazaricos. The afternoon of the second day, they fell asleep after lunch and had to make up for lost time by traveling at night. On a narrow lane through the mountains near Vilar, the pigs strayed from the path and walked onto the roof of an isolated farmhouse just below. The roof gave way, and several pigs fell through, landing in the kitchen of the house. When they went to retrieve them, the owner of the house kept one to pay for the damage and even though they sold the rest at market, they ended up owing the neighbor more money than they had earned.

However, the memory that overshadowed the rest, the one that could never be outdone, was the famous duel between Odilo Valmond and Eusebio Gaudet, two descendants of the French infantry in Corcubión who, in an extraordinary coincidence, each shot off the other's ear—Odilo's left and Eusebio's right. After the duel, the woman they had fought over eloped with a sailor, and the two combatants became inseparable friends and were known thereafter as the bookends.

Grandfather claimed he could no longer remember his age. When asked, he would say he was so old the breath of a baby could bruise his skin. When he awoke in the mornings, he was surprised to find he was still alive. Like the sibyl, he seemed to grow smaller every year and desiccated like a leaf late in autumn. When the subject of his longevity was brought up, his expression became apologetic, even sheepish, as if to say, it's not my fault that I continue to take from this world after so many years. God knows, if it were up to me, I would have obliged you all and disappeared long ago. Then someone put it into his head that he had won the favor of a goddess and been granted the gift of immortality. At first he wondered how immortality could be a gift when it seemed like a scourge, but then he grew accustomed to the idea and tried to imagine which woman in his youth could be the goddess. One had a sense of smell so acute she could find truffles in the woods. Another accidentally poisoned her husband with a love potion. A third became deaf as a post and squinted even in the darkness as if to help her hearing. Because she was the only one still alive, he decided it must be Faustiña, who wore an oilcloth cape and satin scarf and fed the pigeons every morning on the quay.

That spring was his last. We should have seen it coming, but mother and father were busy with their work, and I was so wrapped up in my studies and correspondence with Laura that we had failed to notice the changes in his mood and health. At dinner one night he said he was wondering how death would find him. Whether he would go mad like Fioxilda or lie in bed for months or fall over in the yard while feeding the chickens. A few days later, while sitting at the table, he lost all feeling on the left side of his face. Halfway up the stairs, he sat down. Mother and I helped him to bed, and he never got up again.

Doctor Romalde said it was a stroke and told us to keep him as comfortable as we could. And wait. I was enlisted to keep watch, which meant to fan the flies from his face and listen to his stories. He recounted the night in Havana and the hurricane several times, and how grandmother had locked General Molinero out of the church, and how when he was young, he used to dangle over cliffs on long ropes to collect gooseneck barnacles at low tide. This went on for a week. Then one morning just after dawn, when the air was cool and the dew was still on the grass, an egret entered the front door and walked up the stairs. It stood outside his room as still as a statue. Mother was too superstitious to remove it, so we walked around it as we tended to his needs. Shortly after she left the house, I sat beside him and noticed him clutching the sheets and blanket tightly, as if trying to hold on to the world as he felt himself slipping away. Then he sat up suddenly, looked at me calmly, and said, "Bring me a bottle of *aguardiente* and a loaf of knobbed bread." I did as he asked. He took a long drink of the *aguardiente* and tore the knob off the bread, smelled the pith that hung like a cloud before his nose, and swallowed it. Then he asked me to hand him grandmother's hairbrush, which he also lifted to his nose and smelled. Then he asked for a mirror so he could see what it's like to die. He studied the glass carefully and put it down on the bed. "I've been waiting for this my whole life," he said. "This is nothing." He took another mouthful of *aguardiente* and said, "I return to the earth the body it gave me. I have no more use for it. Dust to dust. There will never be another like me. *Besos para todos.*" He lay back with a smile on his face and ended his quarrel with death. The egret walked down the stairs and out the front door. It stood for a moment in the yard, then lifted its wings and flew away.

On Saturday mornings I was still sweeping out the shop and winding the clocks for Don Horacio, and now that school was over for the summer, I was going down earlier than usual. As I entered the plaza on the first Saturday in June, there was a cold fog over the bay, and people in the market were busy unloading fresh produce from the carts and vans that were parked haphazardly around the building. I reached the shop just after eight and found Fulgencio standing at the counter reading a letter.

"He's gone."

"Where?"

"He doesn't say. I opened the shop this morning when he didn't arrive and found this," he said holding up the letter.

Cotolay appeared in the doorway to tell us he had seen the clockmaker the previous night carrying a small suitcase as he locked the shop.

"I followed him as he crossed the plaza and then the bridge but stopped there and watched him continue down the coastal road until I could no longer see him."

Troubled by the disappearance of his friend and neighbor, the barber considered various reasons for his sudden departure and concluded that Don Horacio's precipitous flight was a direct result of his investigations into the mysteries of time.

"What forbidden knowledge had he gained from those

shadows?" Fulgencio asked. "After spending his life capturing the passage of seconds and minutes in his boxes of brass and wood, like mill wheels capture the flow of a river, did he discover a place outside time, a refuge from its inexorable progress? Or did he become the prey of his quarry stealing away before he was stolen?"

In his final act of friendship, Fulgencio carried out the instructions Don Horacio had detailed in his letter. After waiting a week, he placed an ad in *La Voz de Galicia* announcing an auction of the contents of the shop, which brought horologists from as far away as Asturias to bid on the clocks and tools and furnishings. The proceeds of the auction and sale of the building were sent to an attorney in León. Because I had worked for him, Don Horacio had stated that I was allowed to take any of the antiquarian books on the shelf below his prized astrolabe, but there was only one I wanted, a dusty volume entitled *Contos curiosos da costa da morte* by Ariosto Panches.

Throughout the winter and spring, I had lived in anticipation of the summer, and while the death of grandfather and departure of Don Horacio had affected me, my thoughts remained more on the promise of the future than the losses of the past. This promise depended on my contact with the world beyond Porto Lúa, which in turn depended on the regular appearance of a cream-colored Citroën van parked in the plaza outside the town hall. A woman Father Infante referred to as a "libertine" because she wore trousers and was unmarried left the letters and parcels of Porto Lúa on a shelf just inside the front door of the building, sorted not according to individual addresses, but by streets. Apart from a tinted linen postcard from Uncle Teo showing the Houses of Parliament, all my mail over the past year had come from Muros. Every Monday evening I had left a letter for Laura in a box beside the shelf and had received one in response every Thursday morning. But our correspondence had now come to an end because in the letter she sent the third week of June, she informed me she would be returning for her annual visit on the following Sunday.

She wasn't sure what time she would arrive, so she told me not to waste the day waiting for her, but I did anyway. After breakfast I walked down Rúa do Olvido to the quay where I sat on a bench in the shade of a plane tree observing every car that crested the bridge over the Deva hoping it would be Paco Carreira's taxi. Mornings of still heat had returned with the white ferns of cirrus clouds. Returning too in the spacious warmth were the sounds of distant shouts across the bay, the hammers of construction, and the motors of fishing boats, as well as the familiar scents of coffee and garlic and frying oil and the slightly acidic scent of onions and freshly cut hay and sea wrack and warming soil and the very moisture in the air, sounds and scents no less vivid than the colors of a garden in sunlight. From where I was sitting, I could see fishermen repairing their boats overturned on the beach beside the Deva, scraping off the old paint and applying fresh layers like colorful paste with thick brushes. And there too, on the mudflats where we used to play football, was a woman digging for clams and, farther out on the rocks below the southern cliffs, a man searching for octopi.

When the taxi finally appeared a little after four, I rose from the bench and waved. Laura saw me and waved back. I followed the car across the plaza and up the narrow slope of Rúa do Olvido, and when it stopped in front of number 8, I took the suitcase from the back seat and carried it into the house. While Laura greeted her grandmother, I waited beside the gate, and then she came to me, and we kissed each other's cheeks and agreed to meet in the evening after she had had a chance to visit with her grandmother. When I returned a little after nine, the sun was low in the sky, and the air had cooled a little. She was wearing the necklace I had given her the previous summer and a floral dress I hadn't seen before. After a few minutes of nervous conversation, we were once again easy in each other's company as if the intervening year had lasted no more than a week. Our steps and thoughts and words fell into a common rhythm as we walked through the narrow streets catching up and remembering what we had forgotten to say in our letters. We waited for the Two Marías with the children in Rúa dos Santos, and when they emerged from their house, we followed them down to the plaza where we watched the second half of a movie with Spencer Tracy and Katharine Hepburn on the sheet that was tied between two trees. When it was over, we became the Tracy and Hepburn of Porto Lúa, strolling up and down the streets leaning into each other as we used to do.

We woke before dawn the next morning and accompanied my father to the port where we boarded his blue and white *dorna* and set out for Illa da Luz. Unlike the trip the family had taken on Día de Todas as Almas several years earlier, our voyage this time was across a still surface of barely perceptible swells. When the sun rose above Aracelo, the day warmed quickly, and the sea breeze behind us was a welcome relief from the growing heat as we moved steadily over the open water of the bay. Father left us on the beach and continued to the banks off the headland where the mackerel were running. Laura and I first explored the chapel where I showed her the stone crypt called the vestuary of souls and then Boca do Inferno where I told her the story of Trofonio. From there we walked north along the base of the granite ridge that rises into the steeples and towers seen from Porto Lúa until we reached the ruins of the round houses where we ate an early lunch. I told her about the settlements on Aracelo, and she asked if it was possible to see them. We would have to spend at least one night on the mountain, I replied, and maybe more, and she said she would ask her grandmother for permission. After lunch I found the cave near the rock resembling a bell tower, which was still guarded by a host of angry gulls, and pointed out Laxe dos Defuntos, the last bit of solid ground the souls would know before their journey to the next world. I had brought Don Horacio's volume *Contos curiosos da costa da morte* in the bag I carried over my shoulder and took it out and read the first story in the collection to Laura. It was essentially the same story grandmother had once told me and Bachiario had repeated, a story that was no doubt much older than any modern version of it.

"In the time of the Moorish conquests, there lived a monk who, because of his devotion to God, was granted a vision of Paradise. His name was Trezenzonio, and he was a man of uncommon virtue. Early in his life, he had fallen in love with a young woman, but on the day before they were to marry, the Santa Compaña took her away. He promised her he would search heaven and earth to find her, and at night he dreamt of following the moon across the sea to the distant shores of Paradise, but then he would awaken and once again feel the sorrow of her absence. After living alone for many years, he took holy vows and withdrew from the world to lead an exemplary life of fasting and prayer. One night, because of his righteousness, the Lord God sent an angel to grant his prayers and show him the way to Paradise.

"The angel told him to go to a city in the west and seek a holy mirror that reflects the presence of the sacred hidden among the objects of the earth. He did as he was instructed, and after many days alone in the city with no sign from God, he gave his last piece of bread to a beggar sitting beside a shrine to the Virgin Mary. In return for this act of charity, the beggar offered him the tray he used to collect his alms. Because of his vows and the purity of his heart, Trezenzonio refused the gift. At that moment, the beggar was surrounded by a brilliant light that revealed him to be an angel of the Lord and the tray to be the mirror Trezenzonio had sought. Unseen by those not chosen, he led Trezenzonio through the forests of

Brigantium to a great lighthouse on the northern shore where he instructed him to climb the stairs to its highest point, and when the sun rose, to hold the mirror up to the western sea. When the eastern sky turned pink, and the dark blue waters shone with the luster of a new day, Trezenzonio looked to the west and saw nothing but the distant horizon. Then he held the mirror up to the brightening sea, and in its reflection, saw *Insula Solistitialis* bathed in the first light of dawn."

I glanced at Laura who was peering out across the wide expanse of blue.

"What do you see?"

"It's as if I can see the outline of the island."

"Many people in Porto Lúa claim to have seen it."

I leaned back against a rock as idle gulls wheeled overhead and waves crashed against Laxe dos Defuntos sending up towers of spray. We watched the currents of the sea move in lines of froth and silver coils across the indigo darkness of the deepest waters for a few minutes before I looked down at the book and continued to read.

"Guided by the angel of the Lord, Trezenzonio made his way to the Coast of Death where he built a boat of oak timber and fixed a sail. Sufficiently provisioned for his journey, he secured the holy mirror and set out for the Island of Paradise. On the first day he passed Illa da Luz and entered the open sea. Alone he sailed through storms and sun for a week before coming to a small island ringed with jagged rocks and colonies of seabirds. There he met a hermit who gave him fresh water and sun-dried fish and showed him the cave above the storm surge where he lived and the few acres of soil he farmed made fertile by the abundance of the birds.

"'How did you come to this place?' Trezenzonio asked.

"'I was delivered to this land after drowning at sea, and I have lived here alone through many lives. These small fields and the creatures of the sea have sustained me. I am blessed by the purity of the earth and light on this island. Far from the company of men, I have come to know the movement of each swell in the sea and the scent of each departing tide and how the gull fixes its wings in the wind, and I have learned we are nothing to the stones and sea and sky.'

"'Do you know of an island beyond this one?'

"'I do. I have seen it. And there are times at night when I can see its light glowing in the sky. It is the home of the souls of the blessed who have found eternal peace. God has preserved it in the state of grace that existed at the moment of creation, in the eternal spring that came before the arrival of death and decay. Covered by white asphodels, it is free of the relentless storms that strike fear in the hearts of living men. Not a single cloud has ever crossed its sky. If you go there, you will find the souls of the dead.'

"'God willing.'

"When the winds were favorable, Trezenzonio thanked his host and set out again for *Insula Solistitialis*. Navigating by the light reflected in the mirror, he took his bearings every morning at dawn and kept those bearings by the course of the sun as he sailed past golden columns of light that fell through broken clouds as light falls through an ancient forest of oaks. At night when the surface of the sea was the blue of a moonless sky and the aurora shimmered pink and green, he saw white whales, like islands of ice, following his boat and fish that leapt above the rolling crests of his wake. Feeling a kinship with the stars and moon that travel across the sky, he sailed on. He sailed through ivory chasms of fog and towering corridors of ice that floated by in the blue water. When the wind failed, he was carried by the currents, lost among the clouds that bloom on the far horizon.

"After twenty days, Trezenzonio reached the barren rocks of Thule, an island marking the edge of the world, and there he read, carved into a broad sheet of granite, the words *ne plus ultra*. Despite the warning, he continued his trespass into the unknown. In the solitude of the immeasurable emptiness of the sea and sky, he realized the inconsequence of his will, and, nearing death from hunger and thirst, he placed his life in the hands of God. The next morning he saw a gray cliff on the horizon, but as he approached, discovered it was a wall of cloud. His boat drifted into the darkness of the cold damp air, and for three days he lost all sense of direction and was only aware of the coming of morning and evening.

"On the fourth day, his boat came to rest on a beach of precious stones shining beneath a cloudless sky. Though weakened by his ordeal, as soon as he set foot on shore, he recovered his strength and no longer craved food or water. The land was caressed by fair breezes that blew through colorful fields of asphodels and the finest fruit trees he had ever seen bearing apples and lemons and oranges that were ripe and unblemished. The forests were gardens, and the streams flowed like liquid glass filled with an assortment of fish. At length he came to a city whose streets and walls were fashioned not of granite but of sapphires and emeralds and rubies, and on a great eminence in the heart of this city was a basilica of crystal.

"Trezenzonio climbed the stairs leading to the basilica, and as he reached the great portal of the church, the woman he had loved and lost many years before was there to greet him. Through the grace of God, he had fulfilled his promise to find her. Together on that height they watched the moon move across the blue sky and pass low over the treetops and houses bringing the souls of the dead to Paradise. Then they walked to the high meadows surrounding the city where larks were singing beneath a mild sun, and the colors of the sky and grasses and wildflowers were more vivid than those of a dream.

"'This is the life we might have had together,' Trezenzonio said.

"'This is not life, but death,' the woman answered. 'There is nothing like Paradise in life where change comes to everything.'

"'But we are together now and happy. There is no need to change. No appetite to satisfy. No thirst to slake. Here no fruit ever falls. No cloud ever darkens the sky. And your beauty will last forever.'

"'It is true that I will never change, but my beauty will only last because of my death. Though young forever, I will never live again.'

"'Then I will give up my life to be with you.'

"'But you have given your life to God.'

"'My only vow is to you.'

"As soon as he uttered these words, an angel of the Lord appeared before them.

"'Because you have broken your vow to God, you must return to the life you had before. It was through God's will and not your own that you arrived on these shores. You were granted a vision of Paradise because of your righteousness, but you have confused this state of grace with the illusions of material happiness. Go forever from this place and never seek to return.'

"And so Trezenzonio was banished from *Insula Solistitialis*. Without being able to speak to the woman he loved or turn to see her again, he was led to the beach where his boat had been provisioned. Once he was on board, the wind shifted to open the wall of cloud and hasten his return. Within days he passed the rocks of Thule and after two weeks, the island of the hermit, and less than a week later he saw Illa da Luz and heard its gulls. After reaching the mainland, he returned to his life at the monastery, but though he labored in the fields and workshops as before, his heart never returned to the living things that suffer from death and decay, the fruit that spoils, the crops that fail, the animals slaughtered for their meat and hides, and the men who grow feeble with age. Everything he saw, everything he touched, was a falling off from its perfect form in Paradise.

"On midsummer's eve, when the sky above the horizon is free of clouds, if you look west across the sea from the Coast of Death, you may see the sun set behind *Insula Solistitialis* and be reminded of the story of Trezenzonio."

I closed the book and placed it in my bag.

"There is a fog coming in, and father will be waiting for us on the beach," I said.

"If I died, would you go as far to search for me?"

"I would," I said. "I would go wherever you were."

On the longest day of the year, I rose before dawn and dressed in darkness. A wood pigeon was cooing softly in the trees behind the house as the first hint of light appeared behind the mountain. I went downstairs as quietly as I could, stepping on the edges of the boards. When I reached Laura's house, she was waiting for me in the doorway. After her grandmother had spoken to my mother in the market, they had agreed to let us explore Aracelo on our own, reasoning that my knowledge of the mountain would keep us out of harm's way and, at the same time, assuming we were either too young or too naive to compromise our virtue. Loaded with food and matches and candles and blankets and corked bottles for water, we walked up Rúa do Olvido and cut through the back gardens of houses to reach the Roman road accompanied by the chatter of sparrows. As we climbed, Laura tired easily, so we stopped after an hour in an open field and rested on a group of boulders. Below us Porto Lúa appeared sealed in an amber lethargy as the morning sun shone through a summer haze. We stopped again when we took the path to the pool where white rags adorned the tree of evil, and I told her the story of the purgation that nearly gave me pneumonia. Pausing to rest every half hour or so, we continued our slow ascent until we reached the stones Harry had arranged as benches overlooking the gorge of the Deva where we ate a late lunch with a group of pilgrims who had chosen the same place to stop. We passed through the sentinel boulders and arrived on the edge of Lonxe do Sol early in the evening, but avoided the village because of the dogs and cut back up past the church to our family house only to discover it had lost part of its roof since I had last seen it. We cleared a space in a dry corner of the kitchen and covered it with one of the blankets and ate our dinner by candlelight. Then we pulled the other blanket over us and lay on our sides facing away from each other, but touching along the lengths of our bodies. I could feel her bones pressed against me like a bank of warm boulders.

We woke early the next day and followed the Roman road through the gate at Porto Ventoso and up through the natural park at Agro Vello where I gave Laura a small stone of pink granite I found in the grass. It was shaped like the mountain and meant to be a remembrance of our time there. At the statue of St. Peter, I pointed out his keys, and we turned to look at the first glimpse of the Atlantic pilgrims coming over the mountain would see, and I told her how the solstice shadow of A Noiva do Ceo was believed to mark the way to Paradise and showed her the crosses and cupmarks cut in the base of the stone by pilgrims. To escape the noon heat, we entered the grotto chapel, but when Laura saw the empty sepulchers in the stone floor sculpted in the shapes of bodies, she said they looked like shadows of death and frightened her, so we crossed the valley between the peaks of Aracelo and ate our lunch under an oak tree near the round houses of Onde se Adora. When a summer storm rose over the western side of the mountain, we retreated to the megalithic tomb decorated with a map of the stars and watched as clouds moved past dropping blue sheets of rain.

Strung with droplets of water, gossamer nets hung like illuminated bridges from the tips of alder buckthorn and butcher's broom, heather and the trembling fronds of royal ferns as we followed a path around the base of the northern summit that was still encircled by clouds. We searched for a way to climb higher, but the peak, which reached more than fifty feet into the sky above us, rose in perpendicular walls of granite like a heavenly fortress, and so we continued on our course down through woods haunted by a ghostly fog until we descended several hundred feet and the sun reappeared through gaps in the leafy canopy. Late in the afternoon we entered Casa Sagrada, a village of no more than half a dozen inhabited houses and a greater number left to ruin. My maternal origins. The people who had remained in the shadow of the mountain farmed small plots of land among waves of boulders that had either fallen from above or emerged from the ground, and their houses and barns were crudely built of the same material. They were still living among stones that were part of the earth unlike those that have been tamed by plumb lines and levels, chiseled into the artifice of constructed cities. We met an old woman standing on the path who stared at us in wonder and questioned her unsuccessfully about the location of the cave associated with the birth of Santa Lupa. It was a small, half-naked child who ultimately led us to the site, a bluff behind the rubble of a chapel. The dark opening in the wall of rock was also the source of a spring that trickled down through a muddy field of close-cropped grass littered with manure. Hanging from a ledge above the narrow entrance were vines and ferns that continuously dripped on the stones below. Inside was a dark chamber roughly six feet wide and ten feet deep where no more than a dozen people could stand at close quarters. Cut into the far wall was a ledge that served as a simple altar occupied by two vases holding wildflowers that were dry and brittle. This was the *casa sagrada* where the Raíña Lupa of pagan legends, the Santa Lupa of Christianity, was believed to have been born.

We decided not to spend the night in such an inhospitable place, and since there were only another four or five hours of daylight left, we had two choices. We could try to return to the family house near Lonxe or circle around the eastern side of the mountain and look for a shepherd's hut or old barn to sleep in. Because there was little chance of reaching Lonxe before nightfall, we chose the second option and set off immediately through fields where sheep and cattle were grazing, but once again the uphill climb was fatiguing for Laura and we stopped so often that we were in danger of finding no shelter before darkness. When the sun went behind the mountain, we walked in the light reflecting off the eastern hills and clouds, and, as luck would have it, while some daylight remained, we came upon a small stone hut where someone kept a bin of dry straw for sheep or cattle in the winter. I built a fire to take the chill off the air and smoke out any insects or vermin that might be present, and we shared a loaf of dry bread and half an *empanada* and then placed one of the blankets over the straw before climbing into the bin and wrapping the other around us. From where we lay, we could see the silhouette of the northern peak above us, and behind it, a crescent moon that appeared close enough to touch the summit.

Morning broke tentatively with the weak light of a cold, dense fog. I lit another fire, and we sat beside it and ate another one of the small loaves we had brought. Unaware of the hour, we waited a little while for the fog to lift, but as time passed with no improvement in the conditions, we were afraid we might end up spending another day there, and so, without the sun or the landmarks of the mountain to take our bearings, we noted the position of the hut relative to the course we had taken the previous day and stepped up over a series of rocks to a path through a field believing we were heading toward Onde se Adora. As the path rose, we felt confident we were on the right course, but, without our realizing it, we gradually turned in the wrong direction and were heading away from Onde se Adora toward a peak on the eastern side of the massif. After walking fifteen or twenty minutes into a white wall unable to see more than a few yards before or behind us, we came upon Evandro the poet. He was holding a long stave and herding a dozen sheep toward us. We stepped to one side, and he stopped, puzzled by our sudden appearance out of the fog.

"*Bos días*," I said.

"*Bos días*."

I asked him if he could tell us the way to Onde se Adora, and he took us back up the path and pointed to another that branched off to the left.

"You will soon come to a group of boulders. Pass through them and bear to the right even if the way isn't clear. If you leave the path, you may see an old house overlooking the valley below. There is no way forward from there, so you will have to retrace your steps. If you lose your way, do not go back to the house."

"Why?"

"Because it won't be there, and if you try to return, you will end up lost. No one who has ever seen the house has found it again. I saw it once many years ago and have tried to return to it many times without success. How it came to be no one knows, and no one knows where it goes when it disappears."

Laura and I followed his directions, and when we reached the boulders, we continued through a labyrinth of alders and laurels and the clinging shoots of blackberries. As we entered a grove of birch trees, the air suddenly brightened, and we realized the sun was just coming up, and we had wakened and traveled this far in predawn light. The white bark of the birches and the white mist surrounding us were soon luminous in the pink glow of the rising sun, and every blade of grass and every leaf laden with condensation was crystalized with prisms of reflected light. Then the fog began to disperse, and the undergrowth of nettles and ferns began to thin, and the path straightened between two rows of laburnum trees whose blossoms hung from their arching branches like yellow rain in the rays of the strengthening sun. Able to see farther into the lifting fog, we detected the outline of a lane that had long been unused. To our right were beds of daffodils and ivy that had climbed the trunks of ancient trees, and, barely visible among wild grapevines, was a granite bench where the names Antonio and María were carved. Like children abandoned in the forest, the apple and pear trees flourishing on either side of the lane were the fugitive offspring of a neglected orchard that had learned to fend for themselves.

We emerged from the woods into an open area where the grasses and wildflowers were glistening with a selvage of dew. On the far side of the clearing, incongruous in this landscape, was a great house overlooking a bluff that seemed to drop off into the sky. Surrounding it was a wall crumbling along its span into thickets of blackberries and wild clematis. On the corner posts where a gate had been were ornamental urns large enough to hold small trees but now filled with a mixture of weeds and vines. A series of three stone terraces with a central stairway led down from the house to a park where pink and white camellias surrounded a dry fountain with a stone faun in its center. There was still a faint blush of rose in the flaking stucco of the house, colored here and there by a light green algae born of the mountain's rain and mists. Ivy covered the eastern façade except for the granite portal and tall windows that were blue with the reflected light of the sky, resembling sad eyes looking out from a distant past. On each side of the portal was a recumbent stag sculpted from granite, and carved on the lintel over the entrance was the date 1780. Laura cupped her hands around her eyes and peered into a window, but stepped back immediately and, without saying a word, motioned to me to look. On the landing of the stairs was a woman with a purplish-white face wearing a long white gown. In the shadows, her features appeared graven, as hard as granite. Thinking we had trespassed on the privacy of the woman, we hurried back through the garden and disappeared into the woods, but once we were some distance from the house, we couldn't agree on whether we had seen a living person or a ghost or perhaps the sculpture of a woman or goddess.

Guided by the sun, we made our way back to the path where we had met Evandro and returned to the hut where he was sitting on a rock watching his sheep.

"We saw the house," I said.

"And a woman," Laura added.

"I have seen her. Others have seen her."

"Who is she?"

"I don't know. No one knows. It's as if we see her in a dream."

I asked him for the second time in as many hours if he could tell us the way to Onde se Adora. He took us behind the hut and showed us another path over a ridge of boulders.

"Climb through here and you'll come to a small pasture. You'll see the path I told you about earlier. The way from there will be clear."

The ascent was steep and arduous, but once we reached the pasture, the return to Onde se Adora was fairly straightforward. We kept to a trail used by a small herd of wild horses that wound through a forest of oaks beside a narrow stream until we entered a cleft in a granite outcrop where the stream fell from a sheer wall of rock too high to climb, so we retraced our steps and found a way around the falls that took us over a flat bed of violet and reddish granite from which we could see the circular foundations of Onde se Adora.

We reached the ruins early in the afternoon, and rather than return to Porto Lúa through Agro Vello and spend another night in the family house near Lonxe do Sol, we decided we had enough time to take the longer route through Santa Locaia. When we reached the chapel, the door was unlocked, and we were able to enter and leave our bags on the floor. I showed Laura the altar to Jove and the pool where people skim moonlight from the surface of the water, and then, exhausted from the long day, we were ready to have dinner and retire. We made a pile of long-stemmed grass and brown summer leaves in the middle of the floor and placed one of the blankets over it and then ate the fennel cake we'd been saving and went to sleep as soon as it was dark.

When we woke to our final morning on Aracelo, we ate the last of the bread and what remained of a lump of cheese for breakfast and then cleared the grass from the floor and secured the door behind us. As we descended through the forest of altars, I showed Laura the holes where they had been removed and related their history. Thinking there might be more hidden in the woods, like the headstones that had been discovered beneath a layer of soil and decaying leaves, we briefly searched the undergrowth, but soon gave up, and, wary of the time, continued our descent. Near the gate at Porto Ventoso, we met Bachiario and his dog who were on their way from Lonxe to his cabin in the high meadows. He asked if we had heard any strange sounds in the night. We hadn't. The *vákner*, he said, had been seen near Lonxe do Sol, and we should leave the area before nightfall. I told him we would be in Porto Lúa by then.

On the way down, we stopped at the lookout where Harry had built his benches. Laura sat quietly for a long time gazing into the blue shadows of the gorge cut by the Deva. The sun shone like a white star through clouds that passed slowly beneath it, and a pair of hawks far off over the valley drifted in circles on the updrafts. "The world is so beautiful," she said and began to cry. Like a child experiencing nature for the first time, she touched the warm stone with the tips of her fingers and examined the wildflowers at her feet, and, with her mouth slightly open, listened to the summery lilt of a woodlark passing above the trees. She remained in a reflective mood during the rest of the journey down the mountain. We arrived in Porto Lúa just after sunset. A strange pink ochre afterglow settled in among the trees and buildings as I walked her to her door. Because we were both exhausted and hungry, we said goodnight without lingering and parted.

I didn't see her for several days. We had spent four in each other's company, and it was as if we had agreed, without needing to express the thought, to spend some time alone. When I saw her again, she had little to say. Her manner was indifferent, her expression distant. I tried to make up for the lapses in our conversations by recalling the places we had been on the mountain and our trip to Illa da Luz and the people she had met in Porto Lúa, but I began to repeat myself as I exhausted these subjects, and when I ran out of things to say, she had nothing to add. Because I had never seen her like this, I wasn't sure if I was being prompted to say or do something that I hadn't said or done. Or perhaps it wasn't something I had forgotten to say, forgotten to do, but something I had said or done thoughtlessly. I tried to recall the conversations we had had but couldn't remember her reacting to anything at the time. Perhaps I had overlooked her needs in some way or had been imprudent or inconsiderate about the challenges she had faced when we were on the mountain or did not show enough interest in her feelings when she began to cry. When I asked her if anything was wrong, she said there was nothing, but she was no longer as interested in our walks or exploring new places together. It seemed she was trying to distance herself from me or to provoke me to distance myself from her.

A few days later, she gave me an edition of *El ingenioso hidalgo don Quijote de la Mancha* printed in the eighteen-nineties that had belonged to her grandfather. On the front flyleaf, she wrote the following inscription: "My dear Quijano, never cease in your quest." At first I didn't know what to make of it. I thanked her and told her the book meant a great deal to me. But later, when I thought about the inscription, I realized her reference to me as Quijano was not so much an endearing way of describing my imagination as it was a comment on my unrealistic idealism.

On our walk that evening, she led me to a quiet corner of the alameda where she lingered over a bed of roses, seeming to smell each one. Unobstructed by the plane trees on the quay, the sun shone brightly just above the horizon. Painful to direct gaze, its light reflected off the windows of the fishing boats in the harbor and of the houses crowded together beside the port. For a few minutes everything around us, the branches of trees and the white walls and tiled roofs of houses, was transformed into a scene of golden light. Laura spoke to an elderly couple who had come to admire the end of the day and then sat on a bench beside the balustrade, placed her hand beside her, and told me to sit as well. Thin clouds like finely shredded cotton had turned pink in the greenish blue twilight. In the distance Harry played his evening concert. She studied my eyes solemnly for a moment, collected herself, and looked away.

"I'm leaving tomorrow and won't be back," she said.

"Why?"

"I can't explain."

"I'm sorry if it's something I've said or done."

"It's not that. I have to go back to be with my family."

I spoke with a calmness that failed to reflect how I felt. Like someone suffering from shock after an accident. Because she couldn't tell me her reason for leaving, I imagined any number of possibilities and told myself the circumstances that had caused her to depart so abruptly might change again just as quickly. Perhaps there was simply some kind of misunderstanding or crisis at home that could be resolved. More than anything, I wanted to believe I would see her again. I wanted to believe she felt the same way I felt and wanted to see me as much as I wanted to see her.

We walked through the alameda and up Rúa do Olvido. Neither of us said anything. I was thinking about the morning when I had followed her home from church and how the street had been transformed by her presence. I wanted each moment of that short walk to last, but suddenly we were there. Despite the growing darkness, I could see tears in her eyes. We stopped at the gate outside her grandmother's house.

"I'll be leaving early in the morning."

"I'll come by."

"No."

"Are you sure?"

"Yes. I'm sorry."

We embraced one last time, and as we did, I remember thinking how absurd is our fear of insignificance when the touch of another person can mean more to us than all the stars in the sky.

I watched her enter the house, then took a few steps up the street and stopped and turned around. The light came on in her room. She closed the shutters without looking to see if I was there.

I didn't eat that night and barely slept. As I lay in bed staring at the ceiling, a feeling of dread spread like black ink to infect every corner of my mind. In the hours that passed without distinction, in the slow minutes that made up those slow hours, I feared the coldness of life without her. Everything I cared about, everything I looked forward to, had been invested in her. The time we had shared now meant nothing. I drifted in the darkness searching for some assurance, some purchase.

Then, in the soft currents that carry us imperceptibly into dreams, I found myself speaking to her in her room. A stranger entered and stood between us. He took her by the hand, and the two of them walked away. I followed them down an unlit hall to another room where several couples were sitting on cushions on the floor. Some were embracing each other. Others were conversing quietly. One woman asked me why I was there. I told her I was looking for someone. You can't be here if you're alone, she said. Laura and the stranger were sitting in a chair in a corner. He put his arm around her, and she leaned her head against his chest. When I opened the door to leave, I sensed a vague threat as an animal might sense a predator in the night. Then the sky and earth brightened and an angel with the painted face of a doll appeared and led me through a forest where white petals were falling from the black branches of trees. When I asked where we were, he replied that we had crossed *Insula Solistitialis* and pointed through the silhouettes of trees to the city of rubies and sapphires. He left me at the bottom of the stairs leading to the basilica of crystal. When I reached the top of the stairs, the basilica had become the great house on Aracelo. I opened the door and passed beneath the lintel carved with the date 1780. There, on the landing of the stairs, I saw Laura wearing a long, white gown. Her face was smooth and purple-white and hard like granite.

I opened my eyes and gazed into the darkness. A white streak had appeared on the wall. I saw a sword. Then a candle. Then moonlight shining through a crack in the shutters. I had seen it many times before and yet still saw it as something other than what it was, something I had wanted it to be. How I could trust myself to know what is real and what is not? Perhaps her parents were to blame. Perhaps they favored someone else. Or they were sending her away to school. Or perhaps she had met someone else over the past year and had only returned to say goodbye. I could not dispel the dream of the stranger with his arm around her and began to consider the things I did not like about her. The misspelled words in her letters. The casual indifference of her departure. The face that had been the fulfillment of my dreams had become plain and unattractive, and the eye that turned inward now seemed lazy and unfocused. Yet a moment later, I remembered the tears in her eyes and was relieved by the thought that she was still nearby—that that face and those shoulders and those eyes were only a short walk away.

While the first light of morning dispatched the phantoms of my sleep, it also brought the hour of her departure nearer. I debated whether I should go to see her one more time. She had told me not to. But I couldn't bear the thought of never seeing her again. So I decided I would accompany my mother to the market on some pretext and then return home. This would give me two opportunities to pass her grandmother's house. The day could not have been more ordinary. People were walking down the hillside going to work or walking back up from the port. The house revealed nothing. The first time I passed it, the door and shutters were closed. The second, nothing had changed except for a pair of magpies harassing a crow on the roof. Because it was still early, I assumed Laura had not yet left. I continued to the top of Rúa do Olvido glancing back as I did to ensure no car came up the hill behind me without my knowledge. Then I cut between two houses and walked up a muddy lane paved intermittently with broken pieces of cement to a fountain surrounded by a stone wall where people who lacked plumbing or a well washed their clothes and drew water. I sat on the wall and kept watch. People passed on the street below, but the taxi never appeared, and I concluded that Laura had left earlier than I had expected. The next day the shutters were still closed.

I waited three days to write to her. She waited a week to respond. I said that I missed her and wrote about our trip to

Illa da Luz and the days we had spent on the mountain. She made no mention of her precipitous departure. She wrote that they were having their house painted and she had moved to another room, and it had been so cold on Sunday that she had worn a sweater to church. Perhaps I had been mistaken about her. Perhaps this was all there was to her. And yet I continued to write and continued to wait for her reply. It was as if the person with whom I had shared my love of the mountain and the sea, experiences I would never have again, no longer existed, as if that person had died, and in her place was a stranger who knew nothing of the time we had spent together or the things we had shared, who was as indifferent to me as any random person I might encounter in the street.

When mother asked why I wasn't spending time with Laura, I told her she had returned to Muros because of an illness in her family. I created the appearance of normalcy in order to avoid the admission of loss. The world looked the same to me, so I attempted to look the same to the world and went about my business as if nothing had happened. Since the year I had spent with Laura wasn't real, I reasoned, I might as well continue to live a life that wasn't real. However, despite the outward appearance of normalcy, inwardly I detached myself from everything around me with the kind of apathy found among the aged who, lacking vigor and desire, yield their ground in the world. When father noticed how much time I had on my hands, he put me to work on his boat. Several days a week, I rose before dawn when the damp air tastes like the sea and sailed out to deep water several miles off the headland. It was not the summer I had imagined. Alone with father, trawling with the wind at four or five knots, surrounded by rolling swells, I had little to occupy my mind but thoughts of Laura. What she was doing at any given moment and whether she was looking at the same clouds I was seeing slowly covering the morning sun or bringing rain from the south.

Toward the end of July she let me know she would be going to Madrid and wouldn't return to Muros until later in the summer or early in the fall. I wrote back to say I hoped she enjoyed her trip, but my first thought was to wonder how she could go to Madrid for weeks yet couldn't return to Porto Lúa for a day. During those weeks I imagined her meeting new people and visiting the museums and parks and historical sites of the city. I pressed several mountain daisies in a book with the intention of including them in a letter to her, but remembering the small stone I had given her on Aracelo, I decided the daisies would be another foolish attempt to recall our time on the mountain together. She wrote to say that her aunt and cousins had come from Vigo to visit and that she had gone out in a rowboat at Retiro Park. She asked why I hadn't written more often even though I was answering every letter she wrote. She told me I was a good person and a good friend, and she would never forget me. I was afraid my letters had not reached her and continued to write and asked her to tell me what she was doing, but she didn't respond.

I reread her last letter several times and asked myself whether something I had said or done had upset her. Had I been too attentive or not attentive enough? Weeks went by without any word. I wrote several more letters that I never sent. In one I said I understood that things would never be the same again, but I felt she owed me an explanation for why her feelings had changed. In another I said there was no point in continuing our friendship because she wasn't the same person I had known. One minute I burned with anger and decided I would never see her again even if she returned to Porto Lúa, but my anger was shortly followed by an impulse to send her something. A piece of jewelry or a scarf. Something to remind her of me. I continued to write my thoughts on scraps of paper and in the margins of unsent letters, but the result of these attempts to clarify my feelings, to somehow elevate them to the status of general truths, led to embarrassing sententious-ness as I declared that "The greatest harm one can do to an-other is to take away one's ability to trust" and "The person who knows me best knows me not at all."

More weeks passed with no word from Laura. I had thought by now she would have returned to Muros or at least informed me of her plans. I opened her grandfather's copy of *Don Quixote* and read the inscription again. I took the letters she had written the previous year from my dresser and read through each one carefully. I studied her expression in the photograph taken by Señor Morcín and the lines in her last letter saying I was a good person and a good friend she would never forget.

The inscriptions written in books, the letters, the special names for things we share, the photographs, the gifts, lose their enchantment and burden us as testaments to our folly when the feelings for that person have passed. When undying love has been superseded by another, we push the tokens of that love to the back of a closet or throw them away as we are obliged to do and admit that what had once given our life its meaning and purpose now means nothing. And if such feelings can be so easily abandoned, those of the present and those of the future may suffer no better. We can have no more assur-ance in the promises we make, and that are made to us, than we have in the most ephemeral things in our lives, and we are therefore no different from any other creature of the earth and sea and air that lives and dies.

With such thoughts in mind, I placed the photograph in-side the book and packed it in a box with all the letters she had written and wrapped the lot in brown paper and wrote the ad-dress of her house in Muros on the outside. Then I walked down the hill past the house in Rúa do Olvido and left the box on the shelf in the town hall with the other packages to be mailed. But that night I had second thoughts, and, realizing that I was not banishing my pain but compounding it, I woke early the next morning, and when Don Andrés arrived to open the door, I was waiting to retrieve the package. Once I was back in my room, I unwrapped it and placed the book and letters in a drawer and fastened the photograph to the frame of my mirror.

I decided I would not let chance be the architect of my life, and that night, after my parents had gone to bed, I slipped quietly down the stairs and out the door. The houses were dark and the streets were empty as I walked through the plaza and across the Deva. The sea was calm, and a half moon hung above the coastal road like a beacon guiding me through the night until the road curved around the beach at Carnota. After walking for two hours through the sleeping villages of the coast, I left the highway and climbed the ridge above Mallou on a narrow cart track that wound through rocky fields of broom and gorse past the embankments of an ancient hillfort. Sometime in the early hours of morning, I reached the crest of the ridge and lay down to rest on a large boulder that shown like chalk in the pale, white light. A cairn of fieldstones stood at the center of the boulder, and sheltering on its southern edge in a cluster of silvered pines was a small herd of wild horses. Apart from their occasional movements, the only sound was the light wind passing through the trees. From that height, I could see the beach at Carnota and the thin white lines of breakers in the moonlight. To the west and beyond was the night sea. To the north, the brooding massif of Aracelo and the dark gorge of the Deva. To the east, the lights of the port at Muros. Above it all were a few bright stars and the moon casting shadows from a sky as luminous as blue crystal.

I left a stone on the cairn as an offering to the local gods and followed a stream down through a wooded glen, losing my way from time to time in the dense growth of pine and eucalyptus saplings and broom that rose several feet above my head. As the path descended the hillside and the pools of the stream widened, willows and oaks appeared along the bank. Soon I could smell the sweet air of dawn, and, as the sky began to brighten, I stopped to drink from the stream in a wooded ravine above Serres. As I neared the farms of the village, the track was bordered by walls and hedgerows that enclosed small plots of kale and potatoes and late summer hay. The smoke from hearth fires rose from chimneys as roosters crowed and people emerged from their houses to begin their daily chores. I reached Muros just after six and went directly to Rúa Real where I found Laura's house. The windows were closed and the curtains drawn. I had expected to find something distinctive, something familiar that would reflect the person who lived there, but it was like all the other houses on the street. I stood outside a corner shop for a few minutes waiting to see if anyone stirred and then made my way through the narrow passage of Rúa do Sufrimento to the port where I sat at a table in an arcade and ordered a cup of coffee.

I lay my head on the table, but the traffic passing within a few feet of where I sat kept me from sleeping. Soon I was surrounded by morning shoppers and workers from the port, and the waiter asked me several times if I wanted anything else, so I got up and went for a walk along the waterfront. When I reached Curro da Praza, I entered Rúa Real from its southern end and walked by Laura's house one more time. The windows were still closed, and I noticed the geraniums on the balcony were dead. I couldn't decide whether I should knock. I had come all that way and yet wasn't sure what kind of welcome I would receive. But if I wasn't going to knock, there was no point in being there. I went back to the bar and bought a sandwich and a bottle of water and walked south along the coast where a car stopped and took me as far as Lira. As we passed Monte Louro and turned north around the cape where the *ría* opens to the Atlantic, I gazed at the coves of white granite and the blue water and the far horizon, and lost myself momentarily in the measureless reach of the sea. From Lira I took a path down to the beach at Carnota and walked for a couple of miles along the edge of the waves, crossing Boca do Río at low tide and then climbing back up to the road past the fishing sheds of Caldebarcos. I reached Porto Lúa late in the morning without my parents knowing I had been gone.

Seeing the house in Muros closed with dead flowers on the balcony led me to conclude that Laura's family had moved, and for some reason she had decided not to tell me. I knew that things were never going to go back to the way they had been, but it was hard to move forward when everywhere I went I was reminded of her. The wet streets of Porto Lúa in a shadowy mist, the gardens of the alameda beneath an ivory moon, the second pew on the left in Nosa Señora do Mar. Places I had known my entire life were transformed because I had shared them with her. They were more vivid, more evocative, because she had seen them, and in my mind they could never exist again without the thought of her. But while her presence had added so much to these places, her absence took just as much, if not more, away.

After speaking with Laura and writing to her for more than a year, I continued to think of what I would say to her, and, as if conversing, I imagined her voice in response. So great is our need for a witness that when we lose the person we are closest to, we re-create that person within ourselves. But as days turn into weeks and weeks turn into months, we lose that voice and resurrect in its place the witness who has always been within us, the person we are to ourselves, abandoned early in life when family and friends drew us out of ourselves and forced us to create a social self formed by their needs and desires, a self belonging to surfaces, adaptable but inauthentic, changing as the world around us changes, so that we became someone else to ourselves. We may resist the stranger on the surface who displaces us and fight for our survival, but most of us succumb to the demands of others, and, overshadowed by our social roles, who we are to ourselves languishes and fades, until forgotten, and our only witnesses are those who cannot know us. We find happiness in the illusion that we are sharing intimately, profoundly, with others all that life offers, and when we are once again alone, and that happiness is lost, we continue to hold on to the illusion of sharing, of being witnessed, for as long as we can. In Laura I believed I had found a witness to my deepest feelings, my passions, the wellspring of my imagination, but once she was gone, that dream was over, and I had to return to myself, like a prodigal son, to find myself again. And that, perhaps, was the beginning of the self-consciousness, the interior awareness, that would lead me to witness my life with the words I told myself about myself.

When school started, I was back in the company of María, Amparo, Sara, Loli, Pilar, Inés, María Jesús, Alicia, and Belén. I felt the same wonder in their presence I had on the day we went in search of Dugium. The appeal was strong, but not enough to overcome my reluctance to begin again, and part of me was afraid to disturb the sanctity of my memories. I saw a clear choice before me. I could betray myself or be alone. I could abandon the one witness who would never abandon me to follow another illusion, or I could renounce such illusions altogether and their false hope and withdraw into myself.

In a world of changing fortunes, we need to believe in what will last, a person who will always be there to share our lives with us. What I had found in Laura seemed more real than anything I had ever known, and therefore impervious to change, immune to the forces that wear us down. But such a person is only one of the many illusions we create to satisfy our needs. And when I realized this, when I lost the willingness to leave myself to chase another dream, my life was emptied of dreams. The streets became stale and the faces of people appeared dull and stupid. I became impatient with any show of sincerity and saw it as a ploy of vanity or a form of hypocrisy. Wherever I went, I went with the emptiness of mistrust. Everything I saw, I saw with the emptiness of mistrust. Everything I thought, I thought with the emptiness of mistrust. All I had was myself and the determination not to succumb to an illusion again. And to do that, I had first to avoid succumbing to desire. Blindly in service to life's blind ambition, we are driven by impulse among shadows and dreams to sustain the force that brings us here, fills us, empties us, and tosses us aside. The freedom to be ourselves is just one more illusion. We are compelled in life as we were compelled at birth.

At the end of the first week of school, Miguel and I climbed the boulder in the pine forest overlooking the roofs of Porto Lúa to share one of the *Ducados* grandfather had left behind. We hadn't seen much of each other over the summer, and since this was to be my last year in school, we talked for a while about the future. We tried to imagine where we would be in two years, five, and ten. Military conscription had returned to the isolated towns of the coast, and we assumed that after graduating we would be shipped off to another region in Spain to fulfill our obligation. After that Miguel saw himself back in Porto Lúa working on a fishing boat. His dream was to be a professional football player, but his limbs were too short and his body was more stout than lithe. When he spoke, he had a nervous habit of catching his breath as if trying to take in more air than his lungs would hold, and, however mundane his point, he conveyed it with the earnestness of someone trying to convince an incredulous auditor of an indisputable truth. I had no idea what I would do. Although unorthodox, our education had benefitted from small classes and Mestre's generous devotion to us. As a result, I had read many of the books in his library and was proficient in Galician, Castilian, and English and knew quite a bit of Latin. This, I hoped, had prepared me to continue my education and ultimately would lead to a better life than I could find in Porto Lúa.

We stopped speaking when we heard someone approaching on the path below. A moment later Ramón appeared climbing the small boulders that served as stairs.

"Hiding from Euxenia?" Miguel asked.

"As far as you know, I'm cutting hay."

"See. You're better off without that girl or you'd have to come up here with Ramón to get away from her."

"What girl?"

"A girl from Muros he's been seeing."

Though only in his early twenties, Ramón already looked much older. His face was dirty brown, as if permanently darkened by the sun, and scarred from a childhood case of impetigo. His hands were equally dark, scabbed, and stained from working in the fields.

"Listen to Miguel."

"She's not like Euxenia."

"Not yet. Give her time. Once they've got you, it's over."

"She's not like that."

"You'll learn. There's not a one of them that won't tell you where to go and what to do, but if you disagree or have a different opinion, God help you. They'll start crying and tell you you don't love them."

"They can't all be like that."

"But until you know them better, you don't know which one is and which one isn't."

"Women need to keep busy. Me, I'd rather sit up here and have a smoke. But when a woman's idle, her thoughts turn sour, so she keeps herself doing something. Washing something that doesn't need washing. Cleaning something that doesn't need cleaning. Bleaching the steps. Beating a rug. Telling me to fix something that doesn't need fixing or get something that doesn't need to be got."

"Once you get married, you're just a mule in a harness."

"How do you know?"

"Because I listen to what he tells me."

"I've got to get back, but I'll tell the two of you this: you need to get out of here. Don't be like me. See the world before it's too late."

Whether I was lying in bed at night or sitting idly in class, Ramón's words and the example of his life were never far from my thoughts that autumn. Heraclitus said that a man's character is his destiny, but how do we know our characters before we reach our destinies? What good is Providence if it only becomes clear after we have found our paths through life? I didn't know myself well enough to know what I should do. Perhaps no one ever does. I recalled the wonder I had felt when imagining the light of the moon on the towers and domes of Uncle Teo's distant cities and my childhood desire to cross the mountain beneath the stars. But my choices were limited. Military service offered one way to see the world. At least for a while. I wasn't really cut out for life in the army, and when I tried to picture what it was like, all I could see was myself in an ill-fitting uniform awkwardly carrying a rifle. With the possibility that I might accidentally shoot myself or someone else. Education was another possibility. I thought that if I worked hard enough, I could earn a scholarship to study in Santiago. I couldn't imagine how I would fare being away from the sea and the mountain, but I couldn't imagine how I would fare if I stayed in Porto Lúa either. I might be like Ramón with his scabbed hands and a wife like Euxenia or like my father risking his life every day in the Atlantic before coming home to a damp house and a meal of hake and kale and potatoes or the occasional smoked pork. But if I left, I might meet someone like Laura and live in a city like Madrid or Seville or even Santiago where there are theaters and museums and people who read and discuss the same books that I read.

I finally convinced myself I was better off without Laura. We didn't really have that much in common, and the more I thought about her, the more I realized that what had once seemed novel and charming could become strange or tiresome over time. As we grow accustomed to a companion in our lives, we adapt to the person and align our interests. Because of this, we become less critical and more accepting. Not just of that person, but also of ourselves. When we are suddenly bereft of that presence, it's like a blast of cold air. Defenseless and deprived of habitual reassurances, we are more vulnerable to self-doubt and self-criticism. At first it's a shock, but after some time, we adapt to being alone as we once adapted to being with another. The coldness is replaced by the pleasures of independence, and the thought of being with someone seems stifling. Though I was still thinking of Laura, I was now far enough removed from her company to find other sources of happiness and, more importantly, other sources of self-assurance. I felt relieved of the compromises and concessions I would have to make in order to accommodate her. She would have limited my already limited possibilities as I tried to determine what I was going to do with my life.

As I walked to school early one morning, a fresh breeze blew across the rooftops from the north. The clouds over the mountain were breaking up, and the moon setting over the sea cast a wake of buttery light on the soft blue water. I had seen the same colors of water and sky and the same light of the waning moon one morning on my way to school several years earlier, and for a moment I returned to that morning and felt the same way I had felt then, and I realized that despite everything that had happened, I was no worse off than I had been on that day.

El Conde leafed through a stack of letters that lay before him on his mahogany desk. After glancing over one, he licked his thumb and turned to the next. Though of average height, his stature was somewhat diminished by the great wing chair where he sat to conduct his business. It was a high-backed antique, like a throne, upholstered in oxblood leather hammered onto the wooden frame with decorative tacks dulled by the corrosive effects of sea air. Behind him was a portrait of Doña Esperanza as a child with her hands folded in prayer. On either side of her were more primitive paintings of their bearded ancestors darkened by layers of varnish. A Great Dane sat on the floor beside the desk, his forepaws extended, his haunches high, his bearing regal, as if he were guarding an Egyptian tomb. Long curtains shielded the room from the intensity of the morning sun which nevertheless brightened the languorous atmosphere with thin slices of light that exploited a series of gaps in the heavy fabric.

I have already described the palace. Upon entering, one crosses the mosaic of mermaids and leaping dolphins and proceeds past the locked doors of the residential rooms to the broad oak staircase that leads to El Conde's office on the second floor. Though a large room, it seemed smaller than I had remembered it. The dark wainscoting and deep green wallpaper decorated with classical columns and flowers, as well as

the chandelier and hearth, were the same, but I had no recol-
lection of the wall opposite his desk which was a large bookcase containing hundreds of leather-bound volumes behind
windows of pebbled glass. Nor had I noticed or remembered
the array of semi-precious stones in the ceiling above the desk
arranged to represent the constellations of the zodiac. His father, he would explain to anyone who asked, had believed in
the power of celestial influences on his decision-making faculties. The other wonder I hadn't seen or remembered was a cast
iron bathtub stored beneath a long table beside the bookcase.
Attached to it was a card written in barely legible script that
recorded its provenance. It had originally belonged to the
eighteenth-century poet Robert Dijon but had passed into the
hands of Victor Emmanuel II who left it to King Amadeo I who
loaned it to the grandfather of El Conde on condition that it be
returned to the House of Savoy upon the dissolution of the Italian Republic.

I found myself sitting at an antique writing table near the
door because Mestre had recommended me when El Conde
had asked if he had a trustworthy student who was adept at
writing in both Castilian and Galician. His custom was to devote Saturday mornings to his correspondence, and my job
was to take dictation, translate documents, and run errands,
but there was little work to do, and I suspect the real reason I
was there was to provide companionship. It was a poorly kept
secret that Doña Esperanza had left Porto Lúa with Erasmo,
and the loss of his daughter, especially under such circumstances, had caused the disconsolate father to withdraw from
society and neglect many of his civic responsibilities. Initially
he treated me with formal courtesy, but after several weeks
grew more familiar and, remembering me as the child who
was moonstruck in his garden, joked that he would try to avoid
locking me in the office at the end of the day.

From the letters he received, I learned that his full name

was Prudencio Froila Vermúdez de Traba y Támara, Conde de Curra, but most people referred to him simply as Don Prudencio. On the Saturdays when he was in residence, he wore a red bow tie, a white shirt so heavily starched that it crackled when he moved, and a gray flannel suit. His white hair was neatly parted but rebellious unless pressed in place by a hat. White too were the jutting eyebrows that gave him the appearance of a great horned owl. On the left side of his head was an old wound that he covered with gauze dressing when, like a tree oozing sap, it suppurated a watery fluid. He was proud of his heritage and naturally at ease in his place at the pinnacle of local society, but was affable with everyone he met, offering his hand to young and old, high and low alike without a trace of condescension. In addition to overseeing his estate, his principal pastimes included collecting farm equipment from previous centuries and writing an occasional column on various aspects of regional husbandry in *El Correo Gallego*.

On this morning El Conde began his day by searching his files for a response to a letter he had written several years earlier to the Archbishop of Santiago regarding the relic of Santa Trega in his possession. He had decided to donate it to the archdiocese in return for a weekly Mass for his soul in perpetuity. His desire for the blessings of the Church became greater as he grew older, and he sought to use his wealth to secure his well-being in the afterlife. Because I had never seen the object in question, he unlocked the closet that served as the museum of Porto Lúa and opened a silver box. Resting on a lining of burgundy velvet was a small yellow bone.

"Do you know what a metatarsal is?" he asked.

"A bone in the foot," I said.

"This one dates back to the city of Maaloula in the first century and was brought to Christendom by my ancestors during the Crusades. It has been an object of veneration ever since. Through the mediation of the saint, it has performed many miracles. I have personally seen it cure blindness and gout in my own family. In 1804 it banished a plague of mice from Porto Lúa, and in 1492 it led to the defeat of Boabdil in the siege of Granada. My ancestor, a prince from Asturias, was there."

"It must be very valuable," I said.

"It's value cannot be measured in this world. No price can be put on the salvation of one's soul."

"No, sir."

"My grandfather showed me this bone for the first time when I was your age. When he came to Porto Lúa in the summers, people would throw flowers on the road, and his servants distributed bronze céntimos to the children. That's when a céntimo was worth something. But times have changed. Now there is no respect for the nobility. There is no gratitude, and no matter what is done to alleviate the privations of the poor, it is never enough. My grandfather was a good man, like my father, and taught me the sport of falconry. That's his portrait there on the left. His father is on the right."

The only letter El Conde received of any importance that day was from "The Society of the Immaculate Conception for the Benefit of the Widows and Orphans of Seafarers," the charity that owned the row of houses along the quay. The origins of the society went back to the eighteenth-century when members of the nobility in Santiago, in association with the monastery of San Martiño Pinario—which owned a great deal of property in the area before the ecclesiastical confiscations of the nineteenth century—constructed the houses beside the port for the families of those who, as the name implied, had perished at sea. A pine tree carved into the cornerstone at the end of the row testified to these origins. As part of his charitable mission, El Conde had worked with the society over the last decade to improve the houses by installing indoor plumbing and electricity and replacing several of the roofs, so when any decisions regarding the property were made, he was contacted as a matter of courtesy. The letter opened with a long preface cataloguing the economic concerns of the society. As a result of these concerns, its governance was being assumed by the archdiocese, and it was being forced to sell off its assets. This letter served as the official announcement to the residents of the property that the society could no longer support its charitable work in Porto Lúa. The members of its executive committee requested that Don Prudencio serve as their representative in the community and give the residents notice that the property would be sold before the first of the year. The terms of the arrangement were that the current residents had the right of first refusal, but they all had to agree to purchase their homes for a modest sum, or the lot would be sold to the highest bidder at auction, and that person would be free to tear them down or rent them back to the residents at whatever rate the market determined. Unfortunately, most of the residents lived hand to mouth and couldn't afford even the reduced price the society was asking.

Believing that God had given him the role of overseeing the affairs of the people of Porto Lúa and the moral character to do so according to the highest principles, Don Prudencio sought to exercise his powers in a just manner as an agent of God's will in this world. He often consulted the Bible for advice and read the works of Aristotle, Augustine, Aquinas, and Thomas à Kempis for the wisdom needed to serve the best interests of the people. He asked me what the books I had read would say about this situation and offered the observation that Plato believed the artisans should be governed by those who have gold in their blood and act according to reason. After considering the letter for a week, he wrote back to the society and informed them he was certain the residents could not buy the property outright, but he would loan each widow enough money to buy her home at a low rate of interest as an act of

Christian charity. Instead of paying rent, they would be paying roughly the same amount of money on the principal and interest over a limited period of time and eventually own their homes.

With this in mind, Don Prudencio invited the residents of all ten houses to dinner one evening. After the meal, he read the letter to them and explained his proposal. The rate he cited was lower than the lending rate of banks, and he emphasized the difference in percentages would cost him money, but it was worth it to him to ensure the residents, people who had already suffered enough in their lives, could stay in their homes. His proposal was well received, and the gratitude of the women was enough to remind him of the affection the people had once felt for his father and grandfather.

However, the resident of house No. 3 had other plans. Though not a widow herself, she had moved in with a man who had been the companion of a widow who had died. When the man disappeared, she continued living in the house and established squatters' rights that no one ever bothered to contest. Because of her haughty manner and habit of chewing tobacco, she was mockingly called Condesa de Rumia. She was the mother of three children and worked in a bar owned by a smuggler known as Jefe on the hillside above the coastal road. In addition to serving drinks, she was rumored to be Jefe's mistress.

Less than a full day after Don Prudencio announced he would loan the residents of the houses enough money to buy them, Jefe had produced his own offer at a lower rate of interest that Condesa de Rumia delivered to each of her neighbors with a half kilo of *queixo tetilla*. When Don Prudencio received word of this offer, he assumed it was nothing more than a stunt to provoke him because he had once reported Jefe's attempt to build an illegal warehouse on protected land along the coast to the authorities.

There were few people in Porto Lúa Jefe had not bullied or conned. Most were convinced he woke in the morning looking for ways to cheat his neighbors and could not rest at night if he had not taken advantage of someone during the day. His name was Gunrod Moreno de la Granja, but he had been known as Jefe since his return from South America. He dyed his hair a waxen orange to match his waxen skin and told people he was German, although his thick black eyebrows bespoke his local origins. His eyes were like black peas and too close to his nose, which was lumped at the end with an irregular knob. To intimidate, he wore a fierce scowl that belied the vacancy of his mind. Like a sack of flour, his belly hung so far below his belt that no one could tell if he was wearing one. He left the top three buttons of his shirt unbuttoned so women could admire his chest and was quick to pull his shirt over his head to show people the tattoo of General Molinero that covered his back. The great man's only mistake, he liked to say, was not getting rid of the anarchists, communists, atheists, and gypsies when he had had the chance.

Originally from Foxo Escuro, he fled to Brazil before I was born and returned largely unnoticed ten years later with a Portuguese wife and two children vowing revenge against his enemies real and imagined. He was driven into exile by an ill-conceived venture that went awry. Hidden in the woods on the eastern side of Aracelo is a spring once believed to ensure the fertility of women unable to conceive. But it was cursed by a witch when her rival for the affections of a man drank the water and bore his child. Since then women have drunk from the spring in order to avoid conception, and young men who want to sleep with their girlfriends will make the climb to fill a jar with the water. So seriously is the enchantment of the spring taken that shepherds in the area built a wall around the pool to keep their animals from drinking there. Jefe believed he could make a fortune selling the water in the villages of the interior, so he collected one hundred empty wine bottles, borrowed a corking machine, and printed one hundred labels which read, "Anti-concepsion Water. Ingrediants: Water from the Pozo de Santa Artemisa, Monte Aracelo. Shake Well. Drink 10 ml Twise a Day for Best Results. 750 ml." He loaded the bottles onto two mules and went to the spring where he filled and corked them. Then he led his mules down the mountain and sold the bottles of various shapes and colors in the markets of Mazaricos and Pino and Brandomil for two pesetas. After selling out the entire lot, he bought more bottles and sold them in Dumbría and Muxía for five pesetas a bottle. When the women in the first villages he had visited started to conceive, a group of men armed with shovels and scythes crossed the mountain to look for him. He was on a steamship to Brazil by the end of the week.

Unlike many emigrants who returned to the Costa da Morte, Jefe did not come back to plant a palm tree in his garden and wait to die embraced by the ghosts of his ancestors. His plan, rather, was to invest his savings in a business that would make him the richest and most powerful man on the coast. His father had been an itinerant pig gelder and salvager who had left his family on a half-acre of land in a damp ravine on the northern edge of Foxo where they were too poor to afford a pig of their own and lived off whatever fish they could catch, mussels they could harvest, and the blighted kale and feed corn they were able to grow in the dank shadows of the slope. Upon his return, Jefe discovered the stone house in ruins, his mother and brother gone, and several truckloads of building debris dumped over the slope. He cleared away the debris, burned off the gorse, cut down a row of pine trees, and built a modern house where the old one had stood. The next step in his ascendancy was the purchase of a second-hand Mercedes, which he used to establish his authority over his neighbors by parking it wherever he liked blocking doorways and the narrow alleys and lanes of the village. The only person to confront him about it woke one morning to find his favorite rooster hanging from a tree. He slept during the day and at night drove down the narrow cart path to Porto do Foxo Escuro where he kept a skiff with a motor and where people reported seeing the running lights of ghostly ships in the darkness. On the weekends he would disappear for a day or two. Everyone knew what he was doing. No one said anything.

In Brazil he had been the foreman of a construction team in the Amazon and bragged that he had amassed great wealth by stealing from the natives in the villages where he worked. One night in O Galo when he had been drinking, he confessed to O Gordo that he had shot several Indians who had tried to block a highway they were building through the forest and buried them beneath the asphalt, and he would do the same thing to anyone who dared to cross him in Porto Lúa. Whether that was true or not no one knew, but the story spread quickly and had the desired effect. One night when Cotolay was roaming the headland, he came to Porto do Foxo Escuro and saw the skiff in the water below him. Imagining Charon had come to take his soul to hell, he pushed a boulder off the cliff that crashed through the hull of the boat sending it to the bottom of the shallow cove. When Jefe discovered the loss, he walked into O Galo and pointed a ten-inch hunting knife at every man present, then cut a deep gash in his left forearm. As blood dripped to the floor, he took the cigarette he was smoking from his mouth and cauterized the wound without flinching. "*No me jodas*," he said and walked out the door.

As his business became more profitable, he began to expand his operations and become more brazen, even reckless. He bought a van to transport shipments of contraband from the port to various towns in the province and hired Chucho to drive it, and after someone stole several cases of cognac from the shed where he stored his goods, he built a cinderblock warehouse the size of a large barn with a cement floor and a metal door. Because the cove at Porto do Foxo Escuro was shallow and there were rocks and small islets, the ships that appeared in the night could come no closer than a quarter mile from the coast, so Jefe decided to open a second base of operations on the northern side of the headland near the *Museo do Estranxeiro*.

Building was restricted on the shore of the headland by the law of public domain, and when Jefe began moving equipment down the cart path to lay the foundation of a warehouse, El Conde contacted the Guardia Civil to stop him. Out of spite, Jefe complained to the Guardia that Harry's museum was also illegal, and when they returned to investigate, several men cutting fodder for their animals stood on the path with threshing flails to block them. The Guardia, who had heard about the museum and the mad *estranxeiro*, were not interested in a confrontation over something so insignificant and decided a hut and rock garden built of native stone were not a violation of the law and sat down with the men to smoke and discuss a recent sighting of the *vákner*.

Frustrated by what he perceived to be a double standard favoring a foreigner, Jefe declared that his daughter Malvina, a short swarthy woman with bulging eyes in a face pocked as though scarred by burning sand, had had a vision of the Blessed Virgin at the very place where he had cleared the land to build a warehouse. After asking the girl several perfunctory questions, Father Infante confirmed the vision, and construction began immediately on a shrine to the Virgin—a stone cabinet with a glass window housing a statue of Mary and a bouquet of plastic flowers. Father Infante returned the following week in his chasuble to consecrate the site and say Mass. Following the lead of Harry, which had proven successful with the authorities, Jefe called it a museum to the Virgin. Taking the flat stones from Harry's museum to the souls lost at sea, Jefe's men built a small caretaker's house next to the shrine. When no one protested, he built a three-story house and terrace surrounded by a high wall overlooking the sea. He destroyed the old *camino* to Mar das Almas in order to have a larger driveway to accommodate his cars, and in the front yard, he erected a thirty-foot pole to fly the Spanish flag. In addition to the house, he built a warehouse and garage, and around the terrace he placed a series of statutes of naked women with grotesque heads of his favorite actresses. Then he invited off-duty members of the Guardia to hunt rabbits in the open fields and treated them to his best cognac. No one ever visited the shrine, and the glass grew moldy in the winter rain. The men who worked for Jefe eventually painted the statue black and hammered nails into its head and re-dedicated the shrine to Santa Muerte. As offerings, they left empty bottles of wine, cigar stubs, bullet casings, and hypodermic needles.

Harangued by his wife, who didn't want a mad, half-naked foreigner living so close to their house, and still vexed by the unwillingness of the Guardia to dismantle the museum, Jefe tried to buy the title to the property, but because it was public land, there wasn't one. So he considered less seemly ways to remove this obstacle to his happiness. Because he could see some financial benefit from maintaining the museum, he decided the best course of action was not to destroy it but to convince Harry to give it up voluntarily. This plan would have the additional benefit of providing an opportunity for his son to take a more active role in his affairs. At fifteen, Tomás was being groomed to intimidate. He was taller than his father and roundly obese with the pink skin of a suckling pig. His slightly reddish hair was short-cropped, his nose was knuckled, his ears were curled, and his pendulous lower lip glistened with saliva.

Jefe gave him a pick handle and showed him how to swing it and pat the fat end in the palm of his hand.

"Don't swing up or across. Always swing down. Like you mean it. And don't hit anything you can't break. You'll look like a fool if you do."

"What should I say?"

"Tell him you're a salvager and what you find is yours."

"Then what?"

"Say something about his kneecaps or how it would be too bad if one of his sculptures fell down. Then hit one with the handle. Then tell him he might be better off living somewhere where it's not as cold and damp. He'll understand."

Tomás walked along the path at the top of the cliffs with a swagger practicing his swing by knocking the flowers off the gorse and thinking about what he would say to the foreigner. When he reached the museum, he walked down the valley nervously tapping the rock sculptures with his stick to announce his presence. When he reached the hut, no one was there, but, overcome by his nerves, he defecated on the threshold. As he walked back up the path, Harry was waiting for him.

"Looking for something?"

"We're scavengers."

"Scavengers?"

"Salvagers. And what we find is ours."

"Are you the salvagers who lured the *Eucrante* onto the rocks?"

"No."

"Are you the salvagers who murdered my friends?"

"I don't know."

"What are you looking for?"

"We take what we find and what we find is ours. Watch your kneecaps."

With one quick motion, Harry disarmed the boy and held his wrist behind the middle of his back. Then he marched him down the valley to check his hut for damage or theft. The excrement had already attracted a cloud of flies, and the odor filled the narrow walls of the gorge.

"What I find is yours," Harry said, and took the excrement in his hand and rubbed it into Tomás's face. "You tell your father I'm the ghost of the man you're looking for, and if I see you around here again, I'll take you down to the sands where the ghosts of my friends lie buried, and he can dig for you there."

Harry broke the pick handle over his thigh and stuck the two ends upright in the waist of Tomás's trousers and sent him back to his father. Barely able to see through the drying paste of excrement that encrusted his face, the boy returned crying along the path. He was afraid to open his lips because the paste might enter his mouth, and he stunk so badly one might have thought his skin was permeable to the contents of his bowels. His father swore at him for entering the house before washing and told him if he hadn't been covered in filth, he would have slapped him for dishonoring the family.

"If you ever do that again," he said, "I'll kill you with my own hands."

To launder the money he made from contraband, Jefe restored an abandoned building on the coastal road that I had always associated with the story of the Lord of the Sea. Many of the roof tiles were missing, and the windows were broken, and the walls were covered with mold, but his crew cleaned it and painted it and replaced the tiles and windows. Once the electricity was connected, they installed a refrigerator and a Gaggia coffee maker. On the hillside behind the building was a small chapel beside a spring and a keystone bridge dating back to ancient times. Before they had even opened for business, Jefe placed a loudspeaker in the tower of the chapel so he could listen to "O Emigrante" and "S. João Maroteiro" wherever he was day or night.

The man who worked behind the bar and supervised the rest of the staff was called Morsa, a name indebted to his appearance. His chin was a knobby excrescence in an ample neck framed by a bristling moustache that hung from his upper lip like the wings of a swallow. Portly, quiet, and near-sighted, he provided a sharp contrast to the temperamental owner. Whether by chance or design, many of those who worked for Jefe had a nickname associated with an animal. In addition to Morsa, Condesa de Rumia, and Chucho, there was a waiter from Viana do Castelo known as Ganso who was very slight with short hair, a prominent Adam's apple in a long neck, and small, but noticeable, feminine breasts. Jefe also brought several young women over from Brazil to wash the dishes and dance in the evenings. They lived in a dormitory on the second floor with several children. There weren't many customers, but those who did frequent the bar said they rarely saw the women leave the building. During the day, Chucho closed the *persianas* in the storeroom and slept in a hammock among the cases of spirits or played dominoes with Morsa. When the women were working, he sniffed them with his eyes or stared at them with the smirk of one who is worth little and pretends to much. Still under the curse of María, he imagined the women who appeared old to his eyes to be younger and more beautiful than they actually were. In the privileged position of a driver, he rarely did any work in the bar and mostly sat in the same chair at the same corner table under the banners of football teams or stood in the doorway spitting through a gap in his teeth.

When a government agent appeared from Coruña to inquire why the owner had not applied for a liquor license, Jefe told him it wasn't a bar and took him upstairs to show him children playing in the hallway as their mothers slept. He was audacious enough to claim it was a religious hostel, and when he gave him a handful of ten-peseta notes, the agent agreed. To lend the establishment an air of propriety, Jefe took stones from the bridge to create an artificial grotto around the spring and placed statues of various saints on the rock ledges and a stand of devotional candles under the overhang. One day, to the great surprise of everyone, a bus from Portugal appeared. The passengers walked around the grotto and chapel, had a picnic in the field behind the spring, and departed. As word spread of the healing power of the water, more buses from the villages of northern Portugal climbed the narrow track up the hillside to deliver pilgrims to the shrine. This went on for months until one of the buses broke down, and the pious travelers had to spend the night among the dancers and drunkards and quickly realized the iniquitous nature of the place.

The final addition to the site was equally incongruous. When Jefe returned from Brazil, he brought back a parrot that he kept in his office and trained to curse in three languages. One could imagine him looking into the eye of the bird and dreaming of the jungles of the distant continent and growing nostalgic for the colors and sounds of its inhabitants. The ghost ships that emerged from the Atlantic darkness fed his appetite with blue and gold macaws, quetzals, toucans, and more parrots. Not satisfied with the birds, he ordered sloths and tapirs and iguanas and llamas. As the menagerie grew, he built a warren of structures to house the animals between the chapel and the grotto, covered the entire area with a canopy of chicken wire, and promoted it as Galicia's New World Zoo.

On a Saturday in October, just as El Conde and I were preparing to leave his office, Jefe showed up in the doorway unannounced. Chucho stood behind him in the hall with his arms crossed in a threatening pose that was undermined by the smoke from his cigarette that caused his eyes to water. Don Prudencio was cordial but formal, inviting them to sit down. Neither responded to the offer.

"What can I do for you?"

Jefe's tongue rolled around in his mouth like a pink slug probing the trough between his cheeks and gums for the remnants of his last meal.

"I heard your daughter ran off with a gypsy. You can borrow mine if you need one."

"Are you here to discuss the houses?"

"What's there to discuss?"

"Is your offer serious?"

"Ask me when I own them."

"The people who live there will have to agree."

"They'll agree."

"Why do you say that?"

"Because I know them. When the weak and ignorant and lazy come together, it's not because they like each other or share a common interest. Hell, they don't even know what their interest is. They come together because they hate the same thing."

"And what is that?"

"The ways things are. Whatever it is that puts people like you at the top and people like me and the rest of them at the bottom. They hate people like you who think they're better than them."

"You're not giving them enough credit."

"You're the one who's not giving them enough credit."

"They know what's in their interest and what's not."

"Their interest as you see it?"

"Their interest as they see it."

"You don't know them."

"And what do you offer them?"

"The opportunity to rise up for the first time in their lives and challenge the order that made you rich and them poor. The opportunity to be a part of something greater than themselves. Their lives are so small and insignificant that they need to believe in a cause or a person who shows them what they could have been. I can do that. You can't. You are who you are by virtue of luck. You were born to it. Somewhere in your past, there was someone with the guts that I have, and you're still benefitting from his strength. That had nothing to do with you. But I am who I am by virtue of hard work and a ruthless approach to life. Nobody ever gave me anything, and I curse the luck I never had. I'm like your ancestor, and you're like the people he defeated. Your blood is no better than mine, and someday there will be people who enjoy wealth and power because I earned it for them. They'll look back on me as their noble ancestor."

"That's what you want?"

"I want it all. The houses. The money. The respect. I want to know that when I piss I don't miss anybody. And I'll want that until somebody puts me in the ground and covers my bones with mud. I'm going to own those flea-infested houses. And I'm going to tear them down and build something more profitable. And there's nothing you or anybody else can do to stop me. Maybe one of these days I'll own you too."

"You boast about your strength, and yet the only way to get what you want is by lying to people. You can't win and play by the rules. I wouldn't call that strength. I'd call it weakness."

"What do I care what you call it? It doesn't matter what I tell them as long as it works. The truth is something made up by people like you to protect your interests. These people care more about getting even than they care about the truth even if they have to go homeless. They'll believe anything I tell them because they want to believe it. Your truth, my truth—it's all the same. What happens is all that matters."

"As long as you get what you want, you can justify anything."

"You make me laugh. Your ancestors used the same ideals to their advantage, but now people are free of all those lies that kept them enslaved for centuries."

"You can't win if you tell them the truth. It's that simple. The only way for you to succeed is to break the rules that others follow."

"I tell them what they want to hear."

"What you want them to hear."

"The lie is the fable that the meek shall inherit the earth. They know it's not true, but they're not going to give up on their dream because that's all they have. That's what they've been taught. That's all they know. Look at their miserable lives. They have to bank on heaven because there isn't anything else. If they had what I have, they wouldn't be so meek. They wouldn't be waiting around for heaven. It's not my fault. I'm offering them another dream to believe in. It's like the lottery. They're never going to win it, but they still play."

"And what are you banking on?"

"Myself. To take what I can get. I wasn't born better than them. I made myself better than them. I gave up all their nonsense and superstition to enjoy the world while I'm here."

"You made yourself better, as you say, by bringing contraband into the country that kills people."

"People die in the world every day. Sometimes it's fate. Sometimes it's their choice. What's one life? What are a dozen lives or hundreds? Smoke your poison. Drink your poison. Eat your poison. That's your choice. The world doesn't care. If they didn't get it from me, they'd get it from someone else."

"Are you utterly devoid of a conscience?"

"I look outside and I see trees and clouds, but I don't see a conscience. It doesn't feed me. It doesn't clothe me. It doesn't make me feel better. It doesn't do anything for me."

"Then no one has any obligation to you either."

"I never expected any."

"Why shouldn't I betray you to the people and tell them what you have said?"

"They'll never believe you."

"I think you are wrong. I have more faith in these people."

"That faith is misplaced. One day I'll prove it to you. One day soon."

"We'll see."

"You think you're the best judge of people and have the right to determine their lives, but you don't even know them."

"In my position I have a responsibility to—"

"Lord over them?"

"Consult and advise."

"By virtue of birth."

"By temperament and education."

"My temperament is to act. My education is the world. If I don't take what I want, someone else will. So why not me? You don't have to take anything because what you need was given to you."

"What I need can't be given. It can only be earned."

"What have you ever earned?"

"I hope to earn the respect of people by looking after their interests."

"Looking after their interests? Looking after your own interests."

"They know I have no intention of hurting them."

"Let them be hurt. They hurt themselves by failing to rise above their miserable lives. By allowing themselves to be limited by the morality that comes from people like you so you can maintain your privilege, so you can have a large house on the plaza with a coat of arms and another in the countryside with a garden full of strange plants and statues. So you can sit by yourself at a great table with a lace tablecloth and silver serving trays under a chandelier with two or three servants standing around at your beck and call. When you look at me, you see a peasant upstart. When I look at you, I see a bloodless shadow of greatness who's never earned a penny of his worth. Nothing will be easier than to turn these people who you think respect you against you. All I have to do is remind them of the injustice of their lives, and all your glory and power over them will disappear like the morning mist over a plowed field."

"You underestimate them."

"I'm going to prove to you that I'm not your inferior. I wasn't born with your privilege, but there's nothing lacking in my mind or heart. We'll choose the same goal, and my methods will defeat yours."

"It's true that I was fortunate in my birth. 'Privileged' as you call it. But what matters is what we do with what we have. I have tried to do the right thing in my life to help those less fortunate."

"You want the poor to believe you have their interests at heart. I can convince them you don't."

"My goal is not to convince them that I have their interests at heart but to have their interests at heart."

"What difference does that make?"

"You said you want to prove you are not inferior. You can only do that by acting according to your word."

"According to your rules. Not mine. God made men like me to rise above these superstitious fools to show them how to live like a human being. What are they going to do with money? Give it to the Church? Hocus-pocus. Save my soul. They sweat like mules for the better part of their lives working in their fields, dying in their boots. For what? To pay for their Masses and indulgences. A few days off in purgatory for some ghost they don't remember. As if the dead could care. In the meantime, the priests get rich. Go to Santiago and see what kind of palaces the labor of peasants can build. They make yours look like a shed. Blessed are the meek. Blessed are the fools. Let them turn it over to someone who knows what to do with it."

"Your god is the creation of your vanity."

"Better mine than yours. Look out your window and see how the farmers and laborers sweat and starve in their stone hovels so people like you can have your books and nice furniture. My god is the god of nature. The impulse to thrive. People like you see the beauty of a garden because you've never been a gardener. But I see a competition for light and water and the minerals of the soil. A bush overshadows a flower. A tree over-shadows a bush. Even an old tree of dead wood will kill a sapling in its shadow. The tree doesn't grow for the benefit of other trees. It grows for itself."

"A man is not a tree."

"But a man is like a tree. Just as the termites in the Amazon can bring down the tallest tree, the ants of the forest floor can bring down a man and strip his bones in a matter of minutes. All they need is one ant to lead them through the forest."

"And you're that ant?"

"All I need is one person to keep you from getting those houses. And she works for me."

"All I need is one person to keep you from getting them, and there are nine other residents. Two of them have worked for me."

"It will be easier for me to get those nine than for you to get my one."

"We'll see about that."

"To make it easier for you, I'll tell you what I'm going to do, and you can tell them. I don't care."

"I'm not interested."

"I'm going to loan them the money at a lower rate than you're offering, but I'm going to make it a variable rate. If they ask what that is, which they won't, I'll tell them it means the rate will go down the longer they're paying me. They won't know what I'm talking about and will want to believe me because their greed will get the best of them. After they sign, the rate will go up. They won't be able to pay and will come crying to me. The contract, which they'll sign without reading, will also stipulate that if they default for any reason, the deeds will go to the lender. When the interest is high enough, they'll all default and their houses will be mine."

"You don't care that women and children will have no

place to live?"

"They'll find something. It can't be worse than where my family lived. If I feel generous, I may rent them back to the people who live there now. I can collect their money and let the roofs fall in and the sewage back up. Then they can move out of their own free will. Why waste money on upkeep and repairs when I'm going to tear the block down anyway? Once they're gone, I'll own the best location in Porto Lúa and may build a bar or a hotel or a casino. What should I build, Chucho? What would you like?"

"A casino would be good."

"You see how that works? The voice of the people. That's the new way of doing things. Twenty years from now no one will remember those houses were even there."

"If you're so confident in your new way of doing things, let's present our proposals publicly and let the residents decide."

"Whatever you like, Don Prudencio."

"After we finish, they can vote openly with a show of hands, so no one can doubt or dispute their choice."

"You say when and I'll be there."

"A week from tomorrow in the plaza after Mass."

Before leaving, Jefe reached down and picked up the notes I had taken. He glanced over them briefly and then tore them into small pieces and dropped the bits of paper on the table as Chucho laughed.

When he heard them go out the front door, Don Prudencio pulled back a curtain and watched them cross the plaza. After a moment, he released the curtain and said quietly, "We are being invaded by barbarians from within."

There was something foreboding in the air that week. The days were unnaturally still, and the autumn trees quickly shed their leaves, denying us the farewell of color that eases the onset of winter. During dinner one night, father reported that

Harry had been seen in Rúa das Sombras buying a suit and second-hand luggage. Then we heard he had been sighted at Banco Pastor in Muros. On Friday, Paco Carreira told Don Andrés that he had driven him to the airport at Lavacolla. He said he had trimmed his hair and washed and looked like any other passenger. His dog Winston took up with Cotolay following him through the streets and sleeping with him in Capela de Santa Lupa, and for the first time since the wreck of the *Eucrante* there were no twilight concerts. People were afraid Harry had given up his fight against Jefe and returned to England, but when I went by his hut, I noticed a lock on the door suggesting he planned to return.

Jefe wasted no time trying to persuade the residents of the row of houses to accept his proposal. He sent Tomás around at night to give them canned hams and one hundred peseta notes and followed up these visits with visits of his own. In his conversations with the women, his strategy was to accuse El Conde of the very tactics he was using and of possessing the very faults which he possessed, as if to inoculate himself against the criticism he anticipated. He told them Don Prudencio had said he was going to increase the interest on the loans after they had signed and wanted the property so he could tear it down to build a new palace with a view of the bay. When one of the more skeptical residents said she found it hard to trust a man who was a smuggler and procurer, he told her it was an historical fact that the nobility had smuggled more goods and people into the country than all the little smugglers put together. If I cheat you, he went on, it will harm my business and cost me money, but if El Conde cheats you, he has nothing to fear because he can live off his inheritance unlike the rest of us. Jefe also paid a visit to Father Infante and made a charitable donation to the church that allowed the priest to buy new vestments. In return for this contribution, Father reminded his congregation on the morning of the presentations that Christ taught forgiveness and asked who are we to question Our Lord and Savior. As Cotolay, an *inocente*, often tells us, it is a sin to usurp the role of God and judge another man's heart. It was clear to everyone present that he was referring to the smuggler and not the devout nobleman.

The day of the presentations arrived with fog and intermittent rain. The houses, which were dreary in warm sunlight, were ruinous in the gray mist and not worth the trouble of so much contention. But the contention was about more than the houses. It was about the changing social order and seat of power in Porto Lúa. The event became more than an appeal to the residents. It took on the mythical status of a battle between the old and new, and many people who had no interest in the fate of the houses showed up to hear the speakers for this reason. No one liked Jefe, but no one had ever challenged El Conde, and people were curious to see how he would respond.

A swastika painted on the timber door of the palace greeted Don Prudencio when he arrived after Mass. From a table at O Galo where he was sitting with Chucho smoking a cigar, Jefe called out, "I see you've been redecorating."

I waited outside the door and carried El Conde's umbrella and a leather attaché case containing his notes and calculations to the western side of the plaza where a platform had been constructed from wooden crates and a large sheet of plywood. The stage was empty except for two chairs brought over from O Galo with the houses in question serving as a backdrop. Chucho handed out bottles of beer, and an old woman from Corcubión was hawking rosaries and holy cards she carried in a basket in the crook of her arm. In addition to the residents, there were as many as a hundred people standing expectantly in the mist under tented ranks of black umbrellas.

El Conde felt confident that by providing a reasonable proposal and explaining it in a forthright, sincere manner he could triumph over the emotional appeals of his opponent. To indicate who should go first, Jefe deferred to him with a sardonic bow. Slightly stooped with age, Don Prudencio shuffled his feet for a moment as he collected his thoughts. His white hair was matted to his skull, which shone with moisture, and his glasses were beaded with condensation. As soon as he began to speak, Condesa de Rumia shouted that his family had been exploiting people for centuries. He ignored her.

"Thank you for coming out on such an inhospitable day. As I'm sure you are aware, we are faced with an unexpected financial issue involving some of the most vulnerable members of our community, and I take my role, my responsibility, in helping to resolve this issue very seriously. As seriously as I would if these properties belonged to me. My family has long been a part of this community, and we have held the interests of its people to be inseparable from our own. You know me. You have known my family. Most of you have been to my office. Many of you have been to my home. I know your children, and I knew your grandparents. I have never wavered in my devotion to the common good, and I never will. Guided by my sense of obligation to the people of Porto Lúa and by my devotion to God, I have invested my time and resources in the preservation and maintenance of the houses you see behind me. As the plaque on the wall tells us, The Society of the Immaculate Conception for the Benefit of the Widows and Orphans of Seafarers laid the first stone on this site in 1760 during the reign of Carlos III. For more than two hundred years, these houses have been a godsend to those who have suffered the unimaginable tragedy of losing a loved one at sea. Through the benevolence of God and His agents in this world, these modest structures have provided shelter and comfort for those families. As many of you now know, the Society has experienced a series of financial setbacks, and while it is neither the time nor place to discuss the causes of these setbacks, it is enough to say the charity has been absorbed into the body of the Church, and in the reorganization of its assets, it has found it necessary to liquidate many of its properties. Because of my history of involvement with the Society's holdings in Porto Lúa, I have been authorized by its governing body to supervise the sale of the houses. To that end, I have offered to loan the current residents funds sufficient for them to purchase their homes at a rate of interest lower than that offered by the banks with the stipulation that all residents must agree to the arrangement. The term of the loans will be ten years. I believe it is better for the people who live in the houses to own them than for the bank to own them or for the residents to live under the constant threat that they may be evicted by an unscrupulous person whose only interest is financial gain. That is my proposal. Are there are questions?"

Don Prudencio waited for a moment, and when there were no questions, he sat down to light applause. Jefe stood up, tucked in his shirttail and stepped forward, stooping as El Conde had done and shuffling his feet. He tilted his head back and scowled in a mocking pose of arrogance, looked from side to side, and burst out laughing, much to the delight of several people in the crowd.

"I am what you see. For better or worse. I am like you. I don't pretend to be something I'm not. I can't claim to speak like an educated person because I'm not. My education comes from the people around me. People like you. My father was a salvager from Foxo as poor as they come. I have worked from the time I could walk, but we barely survived. Like many of you, I am an emigrant. I brought my earnings home and invested in our people. No one is more religious than I am. I have built a shrine to the Blessed Mary on the headland and a grotto to the holy saints at my restaurant. Now it is time for a change. It is time for us to control our own lives and remove the relics of the past. El Conde pretends to be one of us, but he looks down on people like us. He will lie to you and tell you what he thinks you want to hear. Are you going to believe him?"

"No," Chucho and Tomás shouted back.

"He tells you he wants to help you, but he is only helping himself. He has a manor house on the headland and a palace in town. How does that help you? Who built those buildings? Your ancestors who were starving while El Conde's ancestors were living in luxury. Do you want to be exploited like they were?"

"No!"

"He gets richer and richer by making deals with his wealthy friends and charging the poor rent to scrape a living out of his rocky fields. Everybody knows this. Now he wants to own your houses like he wants to own everything else in this town. If he doesn't get them, will you grieve over his gold-plated suffering? No. Let him lose once in a while so he knows how the rest of us feel. Last week I went to speak with him, and do you know what he told me? He said he was going to tell you one thing and do something else. He said he was going to promise you low interest on your loans and then raise the amount to the point where you couldn't pay, and then he would tear down the houses and build a new palace overlooking the bay. Then he looked me straight in the eye and said there was nothing I could do about it. He even told me I could tell you what he said because you would never believe me. Do you believe me?"

"I believe you are the Anti-Christ and these godless hypocrites are the followers of the Anti-Christ," shouted Cotolay as he walked in front of the stage. Chucho took him by the collar and dragged him off to the side of the crowd where he shoved him to the wet paving stones.

"If you trust me, I will loan you the money to buy the deeds to your houses, and whatever rate Don Prudencio is offering, I will offer less. And I will never raise the rate before the term of the loan expires."

Able to endure the effrontery of Jefe's attacks no longer, Don Prudencio rose and stepped forward on the stage. Jefe turned and coughed in his face hoping to incite or distract him, but El Conde proceeded unperturbed to instruct the residents: "Read the contract he offers very carefully and be sure not to sign away your rights. If you default on the loan, he will own your houses and can do whatever he wants with them. He told me he was going to raise your rates and had no interest in maintaining the property."

"Friends, that is exactly what El Conde confidently told me he would do, not what I told him. He is using his own words against me."

"Mark my words. He will take your homes from you."

"We don't believe your scare tactics," Tomás said.

"Why didn't you come talk to us before tonight if you care so much about us?" one of the residents asked.

"I invited you to my home for dinner."

"He is only interested in himself," Condesa de Rumia shouted. "These are just scare tactics."

In closing, Jefe raised his arms to quiet the crowd and said, "You must look into your hearts to know how to vote, and if you do, you will make the right decision."

El Conde was shaken and momentarily lost for words. He looked out at the group of people before him, some of whom he had helped their entire lives, and finally said he would agree to carry out whatever decision they reached. Jefe had created just enough confusion that the residents couldn't determine who was telling the truth and who was not, so rather than weigh the credibility of the speakers by any rational criteria, they relied on their feelings and, without exception, they responded most strongly to the thought that they were the victims of a privileged class.

El Conde asked the residents to come to the front of the crowd and, after brief deliberation, vote for their preference by a show of hands. When they did, all ten households voted to accept Jefe's offer. Keeping his promise to carry out their wishes, Don Prudencio told them he would communicate their decision to the authorities in Santiago and expected the confirmation and paperwork for the sale to arrive in a week or two. As the crowd dispersed and the rain returned, he stood alone on the platform. When I went to help him down, this great man, who had seemed to inhabit a world beyond ours, was at a loss for words. I thought for a moment he had suffered a stroke, but by the time we reached the palace, he had recovered enough to write to the archdiocese to inform them that the current residents would be buying their houses and to request ten copies of the contract. In the days that followed, he observed that people no longer saluted him in the street, and believed that to assuage their conscience, they had convinced themselves he was their enemy. So tenuous are the bonds of affection, loyalty, and indebtedness that they can be swept away by the lightest winds of malice, greed, and guilt. Don Prudencio had no society of peers in Porto Lúa, and without Doña Esperanza, his rejection by the people left him more isolated than he had ever been. Feeling the burdens of age and perhaps reflecting on his mortality, he remarked in a moment of candor that we are like the clouds above assuming the shape of grandeur one moment only to dissolve into nothing the next. When the office is not respected, he asked, what is the man?

The residents of the houses met with Jefe shortly after the vote to discuss the terms of the loan. He assured them he would keep his promise to offer them a rate lower than what El Conde had offered and explained that when the archdiocese had received their purchase agreements and completed the documentation for the sale, he would give them his own contract to sign and write a check equal to the amount for each house which they would deposit in their accounts and use to pay for the houses. Once in possession of the deeds, they would begin their payments to him on a monthly basis. On Thursday of the following week, they stopped by El Conde's office and signed their purchase agreements. That night in his bar, Jefe boasted that it had been easy to convince the residents to believe him and told Xosé Carrillo that his plan all along was to raise the interest rate as soon as the contracts were signed.

When the women heard this, they confronted him and demanded an explanation. He promised them he was going to keep the interest as low as possible and maintained that a slight increase was necessary to cover the taxes and fees. Several of the women appealed to El Conde to find something in the law to require Jefe to keep his word, but he told them they had entered into a verbal contract with him freely, and if they tried to abrogate that agreement unilaterally, he might take them to court, which could be very expensive. Nevertheless, they asked Don Prudencio if he was still willing to loan them the money to buy the houses. He pointed out they would have to convince Condesa de Rumia to go along with the change of plans because without her consent, he could do nothing. As they were leaving, he warned them that if they waited too long to purchase their homes, they could forfeit the right of first refusal in which case the houses would be sold to the highest bidder, whoever that might be. When Condesa de Rumia told Jefe the other residents had spoken to El Conde about buying the property, he said he would increase the rate of interest by two percent because of their bad faith.

Ten days passed with no word from the archdiocese. On the next Saturday when I stopped by the town hall to collect the mail, I found a large brown envelope from Santiago, which I assumed contained the documents necessary to complete the sale of the houses. No doubt Don Prudencio thought the same thing when I placed it on his desk, but it was a response to his second query about the bone of Santa Trega. As he read the information on the protocol and spiritual benefits of making donations to the Church and muttered under his breath about the incompetence of the curates, Cotolay entered the office carrying a leather bag over his shoulder. He passed me without saying a word and stood before the desk waiting to be addressed. El Conde took off his glasses and looked up.

"What do you have there, my friend?"

"Papers."

"What kind of papers?"

"The kind you're looking for."

"May I see them?"

When Don Prudencio opened the bag, he found ten envelopes. Each contained the deed for one of the houses on the quay.

"Where did you get these?"

"I can't say."

"Who told you you can't say?"

"Harry."

"Harry gave them to you?"

"No."

"Who gave them to you?"

"No one gave them to me. I traded them for Winston."

"For Winston?"

"Harry's dog," I said.

"Harry told me if I traded them with you, I could get something better."

"Where did he get them?"

"I don't know."

"Cotolay, I am going to make a trade with you. I am going to give you this silver medal of the Sacred Heart in return for these papers. Is that fair?"

"Yes, sir."

"But you can only keep the medal if you never mention a word of this to anyone. No mention of the envelopes or Harry or this conversation with me. You have to promise. If you say anything to anyone, that will cancel the trade and you'll have to return the medal. Understood?"

"Understood."

"Good."

El Conde elected to spend the night in the residential quarters of the palace and asked me to return sometime before midnight to distribute the deeds because he felt I would be less conspicuous if anyone appeared unexpectedly coming or going from the properties. Around eleven-thirty, when the streets were quiet, I opened the front door, which was slightly ajar, and went upstairs where I found him waiting for me in the office. He was marking the envelopes with the numbers corresponding to the addresses on the deeds and double-checking each to be sure it would go to the right person. The lights were already off in the houses, but we waited another half hour to be sure I would not be seen. As Don Prudencio stood on his balcony watching me, I made the short walk along the edge of the plaza and, in the faint light of the streetlamps on the quay, slipped the ten envelopes under the ten doors according to their numbers.

The discovery of legal documents conveying the ownership of the houses to their residents provoked a range of responses from bewilderment to suspicion. There were even tears. The deed itself was a single sheet stamped with the seal of the archdiocese and signed by various ecclesiastical functionaries. Most importantly, it featured the name of the resident in large chancery script. Those who couldn't read were apprised of what had happened by those who could. After Mass, the new owners were joined by their friends in the plaza to celebrate their good fortune and speculate about the identity of their benefactor. When Don Prudencio passed through the crowd, several of the residents asked him if the deeds were genuine or a joke someone was playing on them. He feigned surprise at the news and, after inspecting one of the deeds, confirmed its authenticity and congratulated the women. Informed of the changing circumstances by Condesa de Rumia, Jefe showed up with Chucho demanding to know who had purchased the deeds and delivered them to the houses, but none of the residents had any idea who was responsible for releasing them from their obligations to him. Some believed the archbishop himself had intervened on their behalf while others believed it was a miracle and the signatures of the prelates were forged by angels.

Later in the afternoon, I accompanied El Conde to the valley where Harry lived and helped him down the path to the stone hut. Winston began to bark as we approached and Harry came out to greet us. He acknowledged he had given the deeds to Cotolay, but maintained he had only done what anyone would have done with the same means at his disposal. When his curiosity overcame his sense of decorum, Don Prudencio discretely inquired whether Harry had independent means in the country of his birth.

"No. I come from a family of sailors."

"May I ask how you were able to acquire the deeds?"

"You paid for them."

"I paid for them?"

"Do you remember the Bible I found on your property?"

"No."

"You gave it to me as payment for my recitals."

"What does an old Bible have to do with the deeds?"

"It was a Coverdale."

"I don't understand."

"The Bible I found in the shed was one of the first printed in English. I rebuilt the spine, stitched the pages together with silk thread, and covered it in leather. Even rebound, a Bible from 1535 in good condition is worth more than enough to buy those houses. The rest I deposited at Banco Pastor in Muros. It can be used to improve them."

"Why would an English Bible be in Foxo?"

"Sailors would have traded it for grain or fruit or it was salvaged from a wreck centuries ago."

"How did you get around the right of first refusal?"

"I gave the priests the names of the residents to put on the deeds which matched the names on the purchase agreements. They assumed I wouldn't have had that information if I hadn't been authorized to negotiate on behalf of the women. And they probably couldn't conceive of an Englishman appearing before them in a suit with the names of the residents of a small town on the coast and a bag full of money being anything other than what he claimed to be."

Harry's explanation completed the story of the houses of the Society of the Immaculate Conception for the Benefit of the Widows and Orphans of Seafarers, but the story of Jefe did not end there. And it did not end well. Because he never knew who had purchased the houses he had thought were his, he suspected the entire town of being in on an elaborate ruse at his expense. He saw so many targets for his anger that he couldn't decide what to damage or whom to abuse. So his vandalism was indiscriminate. He broke windows in the town hall and El Conde's palace, urinated on the terrace outside O Galo, knocked tiles off the roofs of houses on the quay, and beheaded the roses in the alameda with a machete. When he was drunk, he believed he embodied the spirit of a jaguar, and when Constable Sampaio confronted him in the plaza one night, he knocked him to the ground and bit his arm. More and more he was convinced that Don Andrés was behind his humiliating defeat, so one day when María Dolores was serving a customer, he entered her store and dropped his cigar on a stack of sweaters. Knowing he would not pay for the damage, she did not send him a bill, but rather sent one to his wife for an expensive dress. When the woman protested there had been some mistake, that she had never ordered such a dress, María

Dolores showed her the original copy of the invoice and in-sisted her husband had picked it up for her. Aware of Jefe's relationship with Condesa de Rumia, his wife sought to avoid the embarrassment of admitting to her husband's infidelity and pretended to remember the dress and agreed to pay for it. But she seethed with jealousy and began to flirt with Chucho and other men in front of her husband.

When Jefe told Xosé Carrillo he was going to raise the in-terest rates, one of the widows cursed him with a prediction he would kill his mother in his own bed. He laughed it off at the time, but something strangely similar happened almost two months later. Suspicious that his wife and Chucho were romantically involved, he came up with a plan to catch them *in flagrante delicto*. His testimony in court provided the details. For weeks he had told both he was going to drive to Madrid for a business appointment on a weekend in December. But on that Friday afternoon, rather than go to Madrid, he went to Carnota where he spent the afternoon drinking in a bar. Later that night he drove back up the coastal road, left his car in Porto Lúa, and walked to his house where he stood in the dark-ness beside the garage watching the windows. The kitchen light went on, and a man walked past. Then the light went off. A moment later the light in his bedroom went on. A man and a woman walked past the window several times, and then the woman closed the curtain. A few minutes later the light went off. He felt his heart beating in his chest as he picked up a large stick he used to kill moles and entered the back door. He waited at the bottom of the staircase and listened as the people spoke in the darkness. A man and a woman. Strangely, he found his heart failing him, but when he heard their bodies shift and the springs of the bed creak, he tightened his grip on the stick and quietly climbed the stairs. He entered the bed-room suddenly and struck the woman across the head as she cried out in terror. He swung again, and the man fell out of bed. As he raised the stick for a third blow, he heard his wife scream behind him. A moment later the light was on. Her mother lay bleeding in the bed, and her father rose from the floor holding his hand on his head as blood streamed between his fingers. The injuries to both were serious enough that they had to be transported to the hospital in Santiago. Jefe's wife told the court she had asked her parents to visit from Portugal to keep her company while he was gone and had slept in her daughter's room so her parents could have the master bedroom. Because it was a case of mistaken identity, Jefe was only sentenced to six months in prison.

When he was released the following summer, both his wife and Chucho were gone. So was the cash in the safe. Condesa de Rumia had also disappeared. Morsa had kept the bar open for as long as he could, but without money to launder, it was deeply in debt. The animals in Galicia's New World Zoo were mostly dead, and the birds had flown away, though some were occasionally seen in the forests for years. Tomás was arrested in Coruña after hitting a street sweeper with the Mercedes early one morning. Malvina had stayed in the house on the headland with a boyfriend from Foxo but left when Jefe shot his reflection in a mirror. He had convinced himself that drug lords from South America were coming after him for their money and believed he could prevent his assassination by destroying his image.

Brooding over his losses, he became the sole consumer of the drugs and alcohol in his warehouse. To entertain himself, he dressed the statues on the terrace in his wife's clothes and used them for target practice or shot the seagulls that fed on the ditch of trash below the terrace. In his daughter's absence, he invited the dancers from the bar to live in the house. While indulging his whims and laughing at his jokes, they ransacked the closets and drawers, stealing handbags and jewelry and shoes and pills and anything else they could find. But fearing the air was poisoned by the exhalations of Jefe's decaying lungs or the toxins in his skin, they abandoned him—all except Aldonça, who remained as the only witness to his descent into madness. One night he convinced himself the Brevetto .22 he kept under his pillow had gone off and opened his skull to the empty silence of eternal loss. As he stared at the ceiling from the darkness of his soul, there was no doubt in his mind, delusional as it was, that he had died and become his ghost.

Having consumed all that he could consume and taken all that he could take, he had no more use for his earthly existence. What was material became immaterial, and what was unreal became his life in death, and in this life he had no rivals but one, the ghost of the drowned man. Still disturbed by his presence, but knowing nothing of the Bible or the deeds, Jefe went to the top of Harry's valley and challenged him to give up this world and join him in a race to the next. Harry was curious enough to play along. On the night of the next full moon, they met at Porto do Foxo Escuro where two dornas awaited them. As tidal currents ripped past the headland and the moon poured its light over the surface of the sea, they set out across Mar das Almas. When Harry, who knew the currents as well as any fisherman, could feel his boat drifting out of control toward the open water, he steered it back to shore. Jefe taunted him and continued to row as the will of the sea carried him outward on the silver path of the moon. Harry made landfall several hundred yards south of the port. Jefe's boat was never found. Of the fishermen who were there that night, several claimed Harry had conjured up the drowned sailors of the *Eucrante* to carry Jefe to the realm of the dead. One said he saw demons take him beneath the waves to hell. The next day his body was found in a rocky cove near Caldebarcos.

They hauled a cart of fish in front of the wagon carrying the body to cover the smell and placed it in a plywood box as a heavy rain began to fall. In the yard of Nosa Señora do Mar,

Facundo had dug a hole in the black earth lined with melting lumps of glistening mud. At the bottom of the hole, water pooled in shallow pockets reflecting the dull clouds overhead. As the coffin was lowered, Malvina, Morsa, Ganso, Aldonça, and Azucena, a mistress no one had ever seen before, stood at the edge of the grave. The latter was a large woman with the arms of a man and the neck of a minotaur. As she leaned forward to drop a rosary into the hole, the ground gave way beneath her, and she fell on the lid of the coffin, splitting it open to reveal the dead man's face, bloated and turning greenish-black, looking one last time at the sad sky. When Morsa reached in to pull her out, he slipped and fell as well. So did Ganso. Then Aldonça leapt in followed by Malvina. Standing on the broken coffin with only their heads above level ground, they put their arms around each other and sang "O Emigrante" until Father Infante chastised them for their impiety and told Facundo to fetch a ladder.

According to his daughter, Jefe had plans to commemorate his life with a mausoleum on his property, but the house was sold to pay his debts, and his grave was marked with a single uncut stone. The plot was near the wall where the fig tree grew and the grass was deep and wild. Though he scrupulously uprooted any volunteer bush or tree that took hold in the yard, Facundo allowed a camellia sapling to grow above the splintered wood and decaying corpse. Flourishing beyond expectation, within a few years it was twice the height of a man with sturdy branches and pink flowers. At night when the wind blew through its leaves, people claimed to hear it speaking in soft whispers of the secrets and crimes buried beneath it.

On a weekend near the end of our final semester in school, María and I went to Santiago to take the qualifying exam for admission to the university there. The results arrived several weeks later, and I did as expected. My strengths were languages, literature, and history. I did not do as well in science and math. Overall my scores were good enough to qualify, but unlike María, whose scores were higher, I did not receive a scholarship. Nevertheless, I held out hope that the financial impediments to my education could be overcome now that I had been accepted. If not, I was destined for military service and ultimately an inglorious return to my father's fishing boat.

In order to prepare for the exam, I had given up my job as Don Prudencio's assistant, but the Saturday after I received my results, I saw him in the plaza where he congratulated me on my success and invited me to stop by his office the following week. I took his invitation as a favorable sign and entertained the hope that he might help me secure the means to further my education. When I arrived for my visit, he was playing with his dog and in noticeably good spirits. After offering me fresh coffee, he gathered himself and settled into his chair to indicate he was now assuming his official role. He rested his elbows on his desk, leaned in, and, interlocking his fingers, flexed them several times.

"Dogs are better company than people," he said.

"Yes, sir."

"People disappoint you. It's not like it used to be. When my grandfather arrived to open the house for the summer, people threw flowers beneath his carriage. Now nothing you do is ever enough for them. Have you ever been disappointed by people?"

"Yes, sir."

"Well, I'm not going to disappoint you."

"No, sir."

"I have a bullet in my shoulder that is still painful, and I wear a gauze bandage on my head because there is a piece of metal lodged in my cranium. Did you know that?"

"I've seen the gauze, sir."

"Enrique, the brother of the Marías, died in my arms. Shot by the Falangists. He was a good friend when I was your age."

"I'm sorry to hear that."

"You think because I belong to the aristocracy that I was a Falangist?"

"No, sir."

"What are your plans?"

"I was hoping to be able to study in Santiago."

"Very good. Very good. I've been considering your situation and am going to make you an offer."

"I'm flattered, sir, that you would think of me."

"You needn't be so formal."

"No, sir."

"It has been my family's privilege to serve the people of Porto Lúa for generations. Our interest is the interest of the people here. The town is changing. You have seen that change in your lifetime. Some people think change is good. Some think it is bad. You are discerning enough to know the good from the bad. You must continue your education."

"Yes, sir."

"I have a friend who is a priest at Colegio La Salle in

Santiago. They are willing to offer you dinner every day in exchange for two hours of tutoring. It's a very good school. In addition to the meals, you would receive the spiritual benefit of serving the Church."

"Thank you for thinking of me, sir. The meals would be helpful, but my family isn't able to afford the matriculation fee and accommodations."

"I'm sorry to hear that. Very sorry. Higher education should be available to all who are qualified. That is the mark of a civilized nation."

"Yes, sir."

"What will you do?"

"Without a deferment, the only thing I can do. I'll be reporting for military service in August."

"That's unfortunate. That's the problem with this country. Talent like yours too often goes to waste."

"Yes, sir."

"Well, we tried, didn't we?"

"Yes, sir, and I thank you again for putting in a good word on my behalf."

"It's the least I could do."

So that was it. My future was set. With no other options, I had no reason to delay my military service. To mitigate the regret I felt over losing the opportunity for an education, I tried to convince myself I should look forward to seeing other parts of the country, but this openness to new experience faded as soon as I reported for duty. Because I had passed a university entrance exam, I was sent to Campamento de Monte La Reina near Toro in Zamora to live in a tent that from a distance looked like a Celtic round house with a peaked roof of camouflage instead of thatch. A Mongolian yurt would have seemed luxurious by comparison. No place on earth could have been more different from the Galician coast, and for the better part of a summer I was sorry I had ever been born. The temperature in the tents rose to 110 in the summer, and the ground was a dry yellow powder. When the wind blew across the plains of Castile, as it often did, everything and everyone was covered by a layer of dust. Dust in the mouth. Dust in the nose. Dust in the eyes. Dust in the hair. Dust in the breakfast. Dust in the dinner. Dust in the bed. Dust on the towel after a shower. Dust that was supposed to fortify us for a war against the threat of Morocco or the Polisario rebels in Spanish Sahara or whoever the enemy was meant to be. That was the theory. It was hard to imagine a less productive way to spend one's time.

Despite not being well suited to military life because of its irrational but unassailable way of doing things, after completing three months of basic training, I became a sergeant and was sent to Ourense where, because of my official status as a student, I was only required to spend a year before returning to civilian life. I was assigned to an office where I translated manuals for various pieces of equipment ranging from fork lifts to industrial washing machines, but spent most of my time in idleness. I experienced far more tedium than patriotism, and the thought of defending Andalucía from an invasion of Moors or Catalonia from Gauls was as foreign to me as defending Bactria from the Scythians. If we had actually gone to war, I would have been as ill-prepared as an Asturian milkmaid.

After my year of duty to God and country, of sitting at a metal desk in a storage room, I found myself back in Porto Lúa. Heartened by my return and the prospect of having his son as a partner and successor, father bought a larger boat with an outboard motor. No longer a book learner or a dreamer of Roman altars, I was now like him, a man inured to the elements, a diviner of capricious seas and skies, who earned his living with his hands. In the summer we woke at four and were on the water by five, weather permitting. Dropping the net, dragging the net, hauling in the net. Dropping the net, dragging the net, hauling in the net. Through burning sun and fog and mist and rain. Wearing a yellow oilcloth apron, I navigated awkwardly too close to the rocks, too far from the channel, hearing the admonitions of my father even in his silence. The sea, the sky, the birthplace of my imagination, became a prison. The sea, the sky, gray on gray, the incessant rocking, the gulls overhead like a mobile hanging from a ceiling of clouds, and the bitter winds bearing down, pouring across a continent of water. I went to bed smelling of fish. I woke smelling of fish. I picked the scales from my clothes and hair. My hands were red from the icy water and lacerated from the nets. I was no longer convinced of the greatness in my soul. I was a fisherman, the son of a fisherman, in a remote town on the northwest coast of a country I barely knew. The only value of my education lay in my occasional conversations with Mestre.

The year of my return he was removed from his position, the first casualty of our discovery by a distant bureaucracy. Education was the second. State inspectors from Madrid had descended on Porto Lúa, combed through the closest thing anyone could find to a curriculum, and declared it lacking in the assignments they deemed essential in their quest for uniform sterility. In a two-hundred-page report on the school, they characterized its offerings as "unstructured and undisciplined without a scientific basis," suggesting those of us who had been educated there had not been educated at all. This report led to a complete overhaul not just of the school, but of the way of life in Porto Lúa. All children were now required to attend classes until they completed their basic education. Those who would otherwise have been educated by the legends and tales of their families, life in the fields or on the sea, would now be educated by textbooks on natural history and in time the state-sanctioned study of science. Mandatory attendance naturally led to a significant increase in enrollment, and for the first time the student body was divided into twelve separate grades. All of this necessitated a commitment of government funding which in turn led to even more government intervention. Twelve professional pedagogues with the requisite degrees and certificates were hired to teach the twelve levels. A principal and six staff members were also brought in to administer what had never needed to be administered before. They kept Sister María Benigna Consolata and Sister Mary Rose on in auxiliary roles as librarians and monitors of the hallways and lunch hour. As the number of students increased, so did the demand for space. To meet this demand, the empty rooms that had been dedicated to the growth of mold were refurbished, and four new classrooms were added to the building. The tables and benches stored in the library were set in rows, and the donations of Mestre that partially stocked the bookshelf were supplemented by modern textbooks. Despite the dearth of resources, the room offered students whose homes lacked suitable conditions a quiet place where they could study in relative comfort.

When I returned from Ourense, I brought back several books, mostly biographies, in order to keep my mind active and to be in the company of those I admired. Leopardi in his confinement at Recanati and Cervantes imprisoned in the Cárcel Real de Sevilla were especially appealing given my own incarceration within the four horizons that had once been open to my dreams. Reading also gave me something to contribute to the conversations I had with Mestre when I wasn't too tired from working to walk up the valley and sit in his study.

Although his knowledge of history and literature and philosophy would have qualified him to teach the teachers who replaced him, he took his dismissal in stride and expressed no bitterness toward the authorities who deprived him not just of his livelihood, but of his chief pleasure. Rather, he turned his attention to his studies. For several years he had collected personal anecdotes of encounters with Mother Ambages, and, comparing these accounts to similar stories in other languages and cultures, he connected her to Cybele as well as to Druantia, goddess of the forest, or the White Goddess. The name "Ambages" comes from the Latin for "winding," and, he argued, she represents the presence of fate in our lives, the inexplicable, unforeseen paths we take that make us who we are. Because she inhabited the forests of the mountain, she was as much associated with trees as with paths, and this led him to identify her with Druantia, whose name is derived from *dhru*, the Sanskrit root for something firm and solid found in words as diverse as *dhrutiḥ* meaning "fixed destiny" and *dhruva* meaning "tree," even more specifically, oak tree, so that we find the word *druída* in various forms in Galician, Castilian, Latin, English, and the Celtic languages to mean one who knows oak trees. Even the word "true" in English, he argued, was derived from the same source, used comparatively to refer to something as firm and solid as a tree—such as a knight who is true to his lord—before a metaphysical need arose for the Truth. When I protested that I had seen Mother Ambages on several occasions, he answered that a woman who is a stranger seen obscurely in the woods or at some distance can take on this name, but the belief pre-dates any individual by thousands of years. Time may grow old, he said, but Mother Ambages never changes.

Less clearly defined than his thesis on Mother Ambages, but more personal and imperative to an aging mind, was his study of classical descriptions of the light that permeates all things and provides the medium for knowledge. In explaining his line of thinking, he began with Plato's metaphor of the sun and tried to draw a connection between the light that facilitates knowledge and the light the people of the mountain see shining from within the trees and stones and water. From Plato he turned to Plotinus who argued there are three natures, each comparable to a form of light: the One is the Good, above Being and Knowing; the Intellectual Principle is an image of the One and determines Being; and the Soul is an image of the Intellectual Principle. To illustrate this, Plotinus went on to say the One is like light, the Intellectual Principle is like the sun which carries light as if it were its own, and our Souls reflect the Intellectual Principle as the moon reflects the light of the sun.

Not satisfied with the similes of metaphysics, which he considered too abstruse, Mestre sought an explanation for the light that enables us to see in our minds and in his reading of the *Etymologiae* of San Isidoro discovered a description of vision that appealed to his imagination. According to the saint, ancient philosophers were divided over the nature of vision. One theory held that it is a product of external light while another held that it is an *interno spiritu lucido* originating in the pathways of the brain. Recognizing this as a theory of visual emission rather than as a theory of images recalled in the mind, in other words, a theory of *oculi carnis* rather than of *oculi mentis*, Mestre pursued descriptions of the latter in classical sources as well as in the lives of the saints. Whenever I stopped by for a visit, he wanted to discuss what he had been reading which ranged from Cicero to Philo to Origen to Capgrave's *The Life of Saint Katherine*. Sometimes he gave me a volume to read in order to offer him a more informed critique of the ideas in the work. Reluctant to affirm or deny the material presence of the inner luminous spirit, he could not deny the reality of that spirit in memory and dreams and the imagery we see when we read poetry or descriptive prose, describing it as a light that shines in the mind as undeniably as a shaft of sunlight in a dark wood. Self-consciousness is this light reflecting upon itself, a mirror of its own being. Because science still could not fully explain the phenomenon, he developed a kind of mystical appreciation for it and asked me whether I thought it could be the soul, whether, like the moon reflecting the sun, it reflects the nature of pure being emanating, as Plotinus put it, from the infinite One. I don't believe Mestre ever intended to publish his conclusions on this subject; rather, I believe his purpose was to use the knowledge he had acquired during his lifetime to come to a better understanding of his own nature and reach an assurance that some part of that nature would continue as he approached the end of his life.

On the days when I visited Mestre, I returned home to an early supper and an early bed. If the weather was fair, a lavender sea in the rose light of dawn awaited me. If there were storms or strong winds, I would stay in my room and read in the gray light beside the window, or sometimes I would sit in the fluorescent gloom of O Galo with the other idle fishermen and play *birisca* as the rain beat down on the plaza and the plane trees shook in the cold winds.

One evening early in the spring when it was already dark, I arrived home in a light rain to find mother and father sitting at the kitchen table speaking to a man I had never seen before. His name was Álvaro Quintero, and he had stopped by on his way to Vilar de Paraíso. Dressed in a black woolen jacket, a collarless white shirt, and a black *boina*, he was not unlike other rural travelers. My first impression—that he was an emigrant returning home to live off his foreign pension—proved to be correct. His clothes were worn, but well-tailored, and his self-assurance suggested a worldliness uncommon among laborers on the coast. Two suitcases sat on the floor beside him. One bore the initials of Uncle Teo. He told us they had worked together at a restaurant in London and lived together in a workers' hostel, and he had sought out Casa das Flores to fulfill a promise he had made to him. In addition to delivering the suitcase, he was there to inform us that Uncle Teo had died of pneumonia a few months earlier and was buried in a Catholic cemetery in West London. Because he had been traveling all day, mother prepared a tortilla for him, and while he ate it, he gave us an account of Teo's final days and told us about the restaurant and the neighborhood where they had lived and concluded with several humorous anecdotes about the social errors and misunderstandings of Galician immigrants in England. When I cleared the plate and glasses away, father placed Teo's suitcase on the table and opened it as Álvaro explained that he and another friend had given his clothes to charity and had only kept his most valuable possessions. Among these were a framed black and white photograph of Aracelo that had hung above his bed, a photograph of him standing beside a table in Don Pepe's Restaurant with his fellow waiters, his glasses, a watch, a gold ring, and a small humidor made of Spanish cedar. Inside the humidor were a half dozen Cuban cigars and an envelope with a moon drawn on it addressed to me. Beneath the moon were the words, "Follow your horizon." The envelope contained his life savings.

The next morning, I wrote to the registrar's office at the university to ask whether the results of my entrance exam were still valid. When I learned they were, I informed my parents that I planned to enroll in the fall to continue my studies. Father was disappointed that I had chosen to abandon the life he had established for me. Mother, I believe, was secretly pleased, but worried the expense of an education would never be justified if I did not become a lawyer or a doctor. When I told her a teacher can earn a substantial salary with a lifetime contract, she seemed resigned to that possibility.

At the end of the summer, I matriculated in the Facultade de Filoloxía in Santiago. While most students lived in the new part of the city on one of the streets lined with dreary eight-story apartment blocks, I preferred the old part where the houses and palaces had stood for centuries and found a *pensión* in Rúa do Cardeal Payá three doors down from Praza de Mazarelos. The room was only twelve feet by eight feet, but was large enough to accommodate a small bed, a wardrobe (unstable on the uneven wooden floor), a writing table, and a sink. Most importantly, it had a window where I could watch the life of the street pass below me. The excitement of being on my own in the city was short-lived. Much like my experience in the military, as soon as I was away from home, I longed to return. I knew no one in Santiago except for María, and because she was already in her third year, she had an established group of roommates and friends, and I didn't see her very often. At least once a week I went to the *mirador* on the western side of the alameda to look at the mountains between Santiago and the coast and think how the clouds in the distance were in the sky over Porto Lúa. Rather than study what I felt I already knew, I explored the narrow passages and hidden plazas of the city and discovered the architectural chimeras and anomalies and jokes embedded in its ancient stone known to generations of students before me: the bespectacled saint, the shadow of the pilgrim, laughing Daniel, the amorous gargoyle, *el trasero de un ángel*, and the crosses and scallops carved on walls and lintels by medieval pilgrims. At night I walked the *rúas* until the early hours often in fog and misting rain guided by the streetlamps that shone on the wet flagstones and standing pools like moonlight shining on the sea. Insomniac gulls circled past the spotlights on the cathedral, and on the steps of the Quintana, beneath the arch of Pazo de Xelmírez, behind the columns of arcades in Rúa do Vilar, lonely musicians played their sad ballads to passersby, silhouettes beneath umbrellas, whose steps and voices echoed off the walls of convents and churches. When the sky was clear and the moon was out, I would lean over the railing of my window and watch it descend behind the roofs of the houses at the end of the street and the end of the world.

My first year I was not an assiduous student because I did not need to be. The education I had received in Porto Lúa was

more than enough to earn *sobresalientes* in my languages classes. In my oral exams, I used colloquialisms I'd learned from
Harry and Sister Mary Rose like "not my cup of tea," "donkey's
ears," and "gobsmacked" to impress my examiners and convince them that even if my grammar was not perfect, I was
familiar with the spoken language. As I began to make friends,
the nights became dreams of dissipation. We wandered the
granite canyons of narrow streets under the stars and moon
singing, stumbling, laughing, and fending off the bone-chilling
cold with *tazas* of Ribeiro. We went from bar to bar, from the
barrel-vaulted cavern of Modus to the nocturnal fantasy of Paraíso to the smoky Dado Dadá to the dimly lit *tabernas* of
whiskered laborers with saddlebag eyes. We were drunk not
just on wine, but on life and the false certainty of an illustrious
destiny. It was an Elysium of stale smoke, sour floors, and in-
flated ambitions.

One night when I was sitting with friends at a bar in El
Franco at two or three in the morning, I noticed an aproned
waiter at the back of the room turning the chairs upside down
on the tables, waiting patiently for us to leave. My friends put
off my urgings to call it a night until I told them I had to get up
early the next day and rose from my chair. As I did, I left all
the coins in my pocket on the table. Walking up the street
through Praza do Toural and Rúa das Orfas, I thought of Uncle
Teo waiting tables for all those years in order to pay for my
education: the thousands of plates he had carried, the long
hours, the foreignness of his surroundings, and the looks he
received as an immigrant performing menial tasks. I felt humbled and embarrassed as I imagined how he had sacrificed for
me, a nephew he barely knew a thousand miles away, saving
his pounds and pence in the cramped quarters of a Notting Hill
workers' hostel that he shared with West Indians, Greeks, and
other Galicians. That night wasn't the last time I went out for
drinks, but from then on, I cut back on my carousing to the

point that when I did go out, bartenders asked me where I'd been, and with a zeal commensurate with my former prodigality, I devoted myself with uncharacteristic singlemindedness to my studies.

When summer arrived, I went home and worked for father, saving what he paid me to make up for what I had spent in the bars and cafés of Santiago. Returning after months of absence, I noticed not only how Porto Lúa had changed, but how I had changed in regard to Porto Lúa. I saw it with a more objective eye, an eye I had lacked when growing up because I had no basis for comparison or evaluation. As we experience more in life, and the light of discovery fades, different needs narrow our vision, and we see only what lies around us, not what lies behind it, not the place within the place where Aunt Fioxilda used to go. Used to the swept and orderly streets of Santiago's prelates and shopkeepers, in Porto Lúa I noticed the flaking paint and drab alleys, lanes encrusted with drying moss and the shadows of winter's mold, the dung of oxen in the lanes, pools of green water, the disintegrating tiles and rotting joists of roofs propped up on rotting pillars, and the mud, everywhere, the mud.

The people had also changed, and those I knew best seemed to have changed the most. Perhaps because I had seen them so frequently in the past, I hadn't seen them at all, and now, after a long absence, I noticed not just the alterations of a year, but those of many. Though I had seen Mestre often until the previous summer, the picture of him I had retained was of the teacher who paced back and forth before our class like a caged leopard, but since his dismissal, he had not been the same man. When he greeted me at his door, his embrace lacked vigor. His voice was weak, and a tremor passed through his cheek. Eyes that had always searched avidly for information now sought the distraction of distance. We walked up the stairs to his study where he sat in his armchair beneath the tulip lamp. He was wearing the same dark woolen shirt he was wearing the last time I saw him, darned so often that it was almost a different shirt. A striped alpaca blanket rested over the back of the chair. The light coming through the window was white like the light of a heavy fog—enveloping, not accommodating—soft, but not warm. The life had gone out of his skin, which clung to his bones more by habit than nature. His eyes were rimmed with yellow gound, his bottom lip was purple and cracked with sores, and the white hair that sprang from his eyebrows curled upward an inch or more like frayed wires.

He could see himself in my eyes and acknowledged, as if mystified by the effects of time on his body, "I am old. I have entered that strange time in life that had always been the province of others."

To change the subject, I gave him a copy of *The Book of St. Cyprian* that I had brought at his request and asked him what he was working on. As he stood up, the blanket fell to the floor. I picked it up and helped him across the room where he took down several books, heavily marked with marginal notations, and told me I should read them. Then he unfolded the scuffed and soiled ordnance map that he had carried on our excursions. Pointing to the annotations in a dozen colors of ink, he began to speak but lost his train of thought.

"The words are sometimes hard to find," he said. "You take them for granted when they are there. But when they are gone, you are like a child searching for a light in the darkness. To be deprived of words is to be deprived of ourselves."

"You were going to show me something on the map," I said. "Your current research."

"I am convinced the ruins of the original Porto Lúa exist."

"You don't believe it was mythical?"

"Not at all."

"But we've been all over the mountain."

"Will you do me a favor?"

"Of course."

"When you return to Santiago, go to the Departamento de Xeografía and ask for an aerial photograph of Aracelo."

"Anything in particular?"

"I'd like to see what's on the summit of the highest peak."

"It looks like solid stone."

"We don't know that. Unless someone climbs to the top or we have detailed photographs from the air, there is no way to know what's there."

"That's what you're working on at the moment?"

"I'm studying classical allusions to *Lunai portum*."

"Do you have enough material for an article?"

"I continue to work. That's all I can do. I can't worry about all the rest. You or someone else will have to carry on. I'm on the downward slope forgetting more than I can remember, looking into the fog where my thoughts used to be and wondering if I've made the most of the time I've had. When I was a young man, I gathered knowledge from libraries and from scholars I respected not knowing if I would ever be able to make something of it. It was all blind faith. And now that I'm coming to the end of my work, having succeeded in the life I sought, I ask myself whether it is better to be young with that uncertainty and the burden of producing such a body of work or to be old with that work in hand, but little time left to enjoy it."

"If there is something there, I'll find it," I said.

Mestre raised his hand and brought it down with mock formality on my shoulder.

"I, Grunnius Corocotta, bequeath to you my useless appendage, my desire to find Porto Lúa. It is a poor bequest, but the best I can offer."

"How can I inherit what I already have?" I asked.

"It is there," he said. "I know it is. I should have made more of an effort to find it when I still had the strength. When I was young, I believed that life gives us all the time we need, even more than enough, but I don't believe that now. The last few decades have gone by with the brevity of years, and the years with the brevity of months. And what about you?"

"What about me?"

"Are you learning anything in your courses?"

"That's a good question," I said. "The ambivalence I feel toward my studies is matched only by the ambivalence I feel toward returning to Porto Lúa which is matched only by the ambivalence I feel toward life. There's nothing I especially want to do."

"He drove out the man; and at the east of the Garden of Eden, He placed the Cherubim and a flaming sword which turned every way, to guard the way to the Tree of Life."

"Exiled to nowhere."

"Banished to a world without enchantment, without re-demption. Every day we find ourselves farther from the gar-den and what we can never have again. In the city you forget the admonitions of the stars, the divinations of childhood, and the infinite beauty of the simplest flower. You live in a cage of practicality moving over the surface of things and forgetting the essential that lies like light in the heart of every object. One day when you are ready, the mountain will take hold of you again, and you will return. Not to Eden, but to yourself and all that Eden gave you."

I visited Mestre several more times that summer. Each time I took fresh hake or sardines from our daily catch and once a scarf that mother had knitted for grandfather before he died. We spoke of the sacred sites on the mountain like places on a map of heaven. Each possessed a reason for reverence. Each satisfied a need of the soul. At the end of the summer, I promised I would visit more often, but my studies kept me from fulfilling that promise.

The last week of the fall semester, María came by my *pensión* with news that Mestre had disappeared. A rumor spread that he had died, and people were afraid to walk up the valley in case they encountered his ghost. By the time we arrived in Porto Lúa, he had been found and was back home, but it wasn't until the next morning when I met Facundo on the street that I discovered what had happened.

"Because Mestre had not been feeling well," he explained, "I was going up to see him every week or two. I took him whatever he needed. Sometimes it was mail. Sometimes it was matches. Sometimes it was fresh milk. One afternoon he didn't answer my knock, so I went inside. His coat was hanging on the back of the door, but his boots were gone, and I couldn't find him in the house. I went down to the garden and called for him, but he wasn't there either. I thought he had decided to walk into town on his own, but when he hadn't returned by dark, I told Don Andrés. The next morning I went back with Xosé Gallegos and several young people from the school to search the area. The ground was damp, and there were fresh footprints leading up from the house toward the mountain. We followed the tracks over the stone walls of abandoned fields and through stands of eucalyptus and pine trees, but when we came to a flat boulder, the tracks disappeared, and we had to spread out until we found them again. Just before dusk we heard him call to us from a shallow cave in a wild area near Onde se Adora where he had taken shelter after injuring his foot. It was cold, and he was only wearing his shirt and trousers and boots. He was confused and suffering from exposure. He told us the only things he'd eaten since leaving home were a chocolate bar and bread that he had taken with him and sun-cured chestnuts and watercress that he'd found. I asked him what he was doing out there in the cold by himself and he said, 'research.'

"'What kind of research is more important than your

health?' I asked.

"'I'll be fine,' he said.

"'And what would you have done if we hadn't come for you?'

"He didn't have an answer for that one. We were about a half mile from the Roman road and spent the night in the bothy before bringing him down the next day. His great-nephew came from Coruña to take him to the hospital in Santiago. He was there for about a week, but now he's back."

Before going to see Mestre, I picked up grandfather's cane that mother had set aside for him and then went by and got María. As we walked through the wet leaves that covered the path up the valley, I related the story Facundo had told me. She expressed her concern that Mestre was no longer able to take care of himself, and this concern was reinforced when we saw the vegetable garden he had always cared so much about overgrown with weeds. When we reached the house, Dr. Romalde was coming out. He stopped, peered at us through the bottom of his glasses, and sniffed involuntarily as he tried to recognize us.

"You were his students?"

"Yes. We've come by to see how he's doing."

"Much improved. Much improved. But time is catching up with him, and he must take care of himself. No need to rush the end. We all come to it in good time. Some sooner than others. My job is to delay that end, not to contravene God's will. There is only so much you can do, you see. Only so much."

"Yes," María said.

"You brought him a cane. A cane is a good idea. A thoughtful idea."

"So he can get around in the garden."

"He should enjoy the time he has. If this rain would only stop."

With that, Dr. Romalde took his leave stepping cautiously

on the stones of the wet path half-blind and talking to himself.

Mestre was in better spirits and health than I had anticipated. I apologized for forgetting to bring the aerial photograph of the mountain and to assuage his disappointment presented him with the cane, which he was delighted to receive.
He examined the pommel, a tarnished knob of sterling *re-
poussé*, but could not determine if the grotesque figure it de-
picted was a jaguar or sun god.

"My grandfather bought it in Cuba," I said. "But it was
made in Mexico."

"The Aztecs were very good with silver."

When María told him she had concentrated on philosophy
in her studies, he expressed his satisfaction with her choice
and told her he had been reading Epictetus and the epistles of
Seneca and had memorized all the maxims Montaigne had
painted on the beams of his tower.

"I plan to constellate my own ceiling with these same pre-
cepts."

As Mestre showed María his amber bottles of medicine and
described the "thousand indignities" of the hospital in Santiago where he was subjected to the tortures of needles, cathe-
ters, tubes, monitors, bedpans, fluorescent lights, and lavender
walls, I went to the kitchen where the only food I found was a
stale piece of bread covered by a damp tea towel. I took it to
the door and held it up.

"Is this all you have to eat?"

"There are some vegetables and potatoes in the wicker bin
and a can of beans in the cupboard."

I washed the dishes in the sink and made a fire in the stove
to warm the beans and boil the vegetables. María and I sat with
Mestre as he ate his first warm meal in two days and then followed him upstairs to his study. The spines of his books had
faded in the sunlight of hundreds of evenings and were worn
from rubbing against the palm of his hand as he carried them

to the fields to read when the weather was fine.

"These books are old friends. I can remember when I first met each one and what they have had to tell me. How they have changed me."

"What have they told you?"

"So many things. That you may grow old in your body without growing old in your mind."

"How have you felt since you've been back?"

"I started feeling better as soon as I left the hospital."

"People were worried about you."

"They shouldn't be."

"It was only by chance that they found you. What would have happened if—"

He waved off my comment as one would a persistent gnat. "The same thing that will happen to all of us," he said. "At your age it's hard to understand what it's like to live when there are few things left to live for. Sitting in this house is not one of them. So I decided I would climb the mountain and continue my search for the lost city. If something were to happen to me on the way, then that is where I would want to be. In a mountain field where the air is cool and the grass is green. You can't live in fear of what you may lose because you lost everything you will ever have on the day you were born."

"But if you take care of yourself, you can continue your work for years to come," I said.

"I can't pursue my work if I'm afraid to go outside because I might hurt myself. Two things that can take away our lives are fear and a lack of interest in the future. If we have something we care about, if we are still curious about the world, I sometimes think we can live forever. And when we exhaust our search for knowledge, our sense of wonder, we stop living. That's the only thing to be afraid of."

"Can we help you with your research?"

"Tell us where to go and what to look for."

"No. No. You have your own lives. I need to do it for myself. That's the only way I can keep going. But I tire so easily now. I feel like I'm wearing an overcoat made of cement. Whether I'm sitting in the morning sun dreaming or watching the rain fall through the forest or playing *L'Orfeo* on the piano, I can never take it off. It weighs not just on my body but on my mind. And I stop and think how long it's been since there was a quickening in my pulse because for so many years my heart has been dry like an old leather purse full of stale blood. All I have left is the hope for one good day when I wake up without pain or worries and feel like myself again, when I can sit and look at the warm sky and feel the simple pleasure of being."

Neither María nor I said anything. After a moment, as if waking from a brief dream, Mestre changed his tone and concluded with an exhortation: "It is you who must live, you who have the time to achieve what has been left undone by those who came before you. Make the most of that time. Find what has not been found. Remember what has been forgotten. It is you who must tell the story of Porto Lúa. If you don't, it will be lost forever."

This is what it comes to, I thought. If I work hard and sacrifice my life in a quest for knowledge, and learn half as much as Mestre knows, I could find myself of little use to anyone, neglected and living alone—finding solace, if it could be called that, by reading authors who advised their adherents on the noblest approaches to death, that is, to dispense with the defenses that shield us from the truths of our nature. If the quest for knowledge leads to loneliness rather than happiness, then perhaps it is best to abandon that quest and live a more active life among family and friends.

During the rest of the break, I continued to visit several times a week. In addition to fresh fish, I took Mestre canned fruit and beans as well as light bulbs, a bottle of ink, and black paint, which I used to write more than two dozen of

Montaigne's maxims on the ceiling of his study—in no particular order or pattern so that they seemed to float in that plaster sky like fragments of wisdom raining down from heaven.
Standing on a stepladder with my head bent back and paint
running down my wrist, I felt like Michelangelo on his scaffold
while Mestre sat in his chair checking my Latin orthography
and attempts to write Greek. As I painted, we recounted our
trips on the mountain, and he spoke of his desire to return to
the summit as soon as his foot was fully healed. From these
conversations I came to understand that despite his lack of
faith in a Christian afterlife, his dream of finding the original
Porto Lúa was not unlike the dream the faithful have of finding
heaven. Its discovery had become the purpose of his life.

The following spring I received a grant that would help pay
for the rest of my education, but it required me to stay in the
city over the summer to work with an instructor on a research
project. It was mostly a matter of looking up citations in the
library and proofreading, which was preferable to waking up
before dawn and hauling in nets of fish all day. Life was an
uneventful routine of work, sleep, and study with a few meals
thrown in at odd hours. María graduated and early in the summer passed her teaching *oposiciones* and was fortunate
enough to be sent to her first choice, Porto Lúa, because no one
else wanted to be that far from a major city and several of the
recent hires had already applied to transfer elsewhere.

When I returned to my room one evening in July, the land-
lady had slipped a message from María under my door that
read simply, "Mestre is dead." The next morning I took a bus
to Muros and a taxi to Porto Lúa. It had been six months since
I'd seen him despite the promise I had made to visit more often. I had told myself he would be there when I returned, as if
he would always be there, but death is indifferent to our plans
and promises.

When he was found, there was a vase of fresh *trachelium*

caeruleum, the ubiquitous purple flower of Porto Lúa, on his desk that he had picked from the wall surrounding his house. It was easy to imagine his last moment in this world was spent smelling the sweet scent of those flowers. On the kitchen table was a note that read, "I wish to apologize to you who were unfortunate enough to have come across my mortal remains. I have no idea how long they were here. Do not fear that you have intruded upon my privacy. You bear no responsibility for catching me off-guard, just as I bear no responsibility for what you find here, for I am gone."

Mestre's great-nephew, Francisco, arrived shortly after I did and arranged to have the body sent to Elviña to be interred in the family plot while María and I sorted through his personal effects. Facundo brought an oxcart up the path, and we loaded it with clothes and furniture to sell in the market. The piano was hauled off by a company in Coruña that specialized in estate sales. Disposing of the books and research materials presented a greater challenge. He had set aside a box of books for María and a box for me, but that left several hundred volumes as well as two wardrobes in his study that were packed with maps, journals, envelopes of academic offprints, and shoeboxes filled with thousands of notecards covered with red and green and blue ink. María and I spent two days sorting through the wardrobes and organizing their contents by subject in storage boxes. When I returned to Santiago, I offered the lot to the university and several institutes of Galician studies, but no one was interested. I was told that Mestre had never achieved the kind of reputation in his lifetime to warrant the archiving of so much material, and his writing was more poetic and personal than academic. In the end, the librarian at El Instituto de Estudios Gallegos Padre Sarmiento, who had introduced Mestre to Sister Mary Rose and Sister Benigna, agreed to store his papers and notes in her attic in the event that someday a young scholar might find them useful.

Francisco told us to take as many books as we could carry in addition to the boxes that were set aside for us. María and I selected a few additional volumes, and the rest we donated to the school. In each book was a file card with the date and place of its purchase and a brief description of its contents. Francisco also told me to take the cane I had given Mestre six months earlier and what appeared to be the loose sheets of a journal he had found on the nightstand next to the bed. I folded the sheets in half, slipped them into Mestre's copy of *Georgics*, and forgot about them until I was back in the *pensión* in Santiago where I took several of the books out of the box to examine the notes he had made in their margins. When I opened *Georgics*, I realized that what Francisco had thought was a journal was actually a letter. It was not addressed to anyone, but after reading the first page, I concluded he had written it to his unborn child.

> The house is quiet. The wind has stopped. The sea is calm. Shadows are falling. The stream in the valley is the only sound I hear. Today as I lay in my bath surrounded by white tiles, I lost myself in the morning light. The sky outside was a summer blue, and the rectangle of sunlight on the tiles beside me brightened the entire room. It was not the light of a single moment, but of all such moments. All such memories. As if my dreams were somewhere in that light. What religion calls a state of grace. If I had only been given a moment to live, I would want that moment to be in that light. And if I were to write about my life, I would want the words to contain as much of myself as is found in that light. I am of the age when no praise, no reward, no achievement has any meaning to me. The greatest gift I can receive is the benevolence of sunlight in a blue sky. I only ask for more time to enjoy its blessings.

You don't know me, but if you had come to be, I would have been your father. A woman I loved would have been your mother. She would have been a good mother. Though time has reduced her to a few images, and those images have faded in the evening light of an aged mind, I can still see the longing for you in her eyes and tentative smile. She brought the world into being for me, but was taken away too soon. As little as I have of her, that is more than I have of you. I will never know the color of your eyes, the sound of your laughter.

I have thought of you often. How you were deprived of all that is good in life. The love of a mother. The blue and lilac clouds of spring. The evening song of a thrush. The warmth of sunlight on a morning of bright frost. To ease the loss of your laughter and smile, I also think of the things that would have hurt you. The petty cruelty of people. Their absurd vanity. The irony of knowing the futility of knowing. You would have come home from school and entered my study to ask me questions about your classes, and I would have told you what I know. We would have gone on long walks together, and I would have explained the phases of the moon and the poetry of Virgil and how the stars are people who became gods. You would have grown up surrounded by books and music and maps and dreams. By now you would be in your thirties. Perhaps married with children of your own. You would be with them and not here with me. But you are here. And here we grow old together. Not in the light but in the blood. Together with your children and your children's children. And when my body returns to the earth, we will remain together. You having never been and me never to return.

A philosopher once wrote that whatever can exist

must exist. Or, to put it another way, what exists had to exist, and what does not exist could not exist. But I question what is it that can exist before it exists. If what it is can exist, then it must in some way already exist without existence. In the mind of God, perhaps. Like the belief in this part of the world that souls exist among the stars before they are summoned to enter the wombs of women.

Since you do not exist, you could not exist, and yet I imagine your existence like that of one who has yet to exist. Perhaps because I believe you would be here if not for the glance of a soldier in the darkness. Or perhaps because I can't believe that in the vastness of creation such a moment could cancel out the possibilities of your being. What cause was lacking for you and not the others, those here, those here and gone, those not yet come? Why the need for each gnat that plagues the garden, each ant that digs its earth and not for you?

You are in good company. Like you, the greatest writers and philosophers, the greatest artists and inventors, messiahs unknown, were never born. The greatest works of literature, countless Hamlets and Quixotes, were never written. What glory the world might have seen, what art and literature it might have known, if not for capricious fate, the twists and turns of one life, the whims and humors of another. You are among those who would have created a world different than the one we know. Would you too have made a difference? When you reached us from the depths of night, would you have kept the perspective of the stars, or would you have forgotten those heights as you descended into the narrowness of covetous flesh?

You would have come to us as a stranger among strangers, new to the forms of this world, new to its light and shadows, its whispers and laughter. When you felt bewildered by the discovery of your being, I would have soothed you with the gentle rocking of your cradle. Over the years you would have grown accustomed to the world and made it your own. You would have assumed yourself as much a part of it as the sea and clouds, the sun and moon, until at some point your family and friends and the places of your past would have begun to disappear, returning only in dreams. You would have become a stranger to the world again, only this time you would be leaving it rather than entering it. Would you have accepted this life if you had known this and been given the choice?

I enter another spring alone. Another summer. Another fall. Another winter. Another year. The young fear the contagion of age, and the old have lost their interest in life. When I was young, the demands of others on my time and attention were great, but now, though I am the same person, there is no interest in who I am or what I know. What is a life unless it is shared? Nothing more than survival. A long and anxious wait, a journey through hardship to suffering and extinction. As a shadow in the light, I have often welcomed the darkness, but a line by the poet Rilke, weil Hiersein viel ist, "Because being here is so much," reminds me that hopelessness is a failure to recognize the wonder in every moment of being.

I am a bystander at the spectacle of my own destruction, shedding myself one flake at a time, one hair at a time, one moment at a time. I am down to one good eye, one bad ear, and fewer than half my teeth. Every day the shelves of cartilage and bone in my spine collapse a little more. When it rains, as it does nearly every day, I feel it trickling through bones that grind against each other when I move. More of my hair lies on my pillow than on my head. My skin is thin and white like the paper where I write these words. Paper that is mark-ed with ink the way my skin is marked with small blue veins. Paper that will be all that's left of my memory. One day, my body will be found on the floor here or there, or perhaps someone will be foolish enough to take me to the hospital where they will strap a mask over my face and cut me open to extend my life a little longer. But it's all the same. A year or two more, perhaps a total of eighty. It's all the same. We are what is not.

Like a Hindu sage, I should have been a forest-dweller. I should have stripped myself of all my possessions and entered the forests of the mountain. I should have fed its insects with my blood and fed myself with its berries and seeds. But I have little left to renounce. I eat next to nothing. I am little more than the exhalation of a life. My feeble blood makes its rounds where it can, too weak to reach my marble hands and feet.

Despite the infirmities of age, it is still requisite to bathe, to shave, and to dress suitably. For in this way, one maintains one's sense of self. However weary. However heavy. Vitality has left me, and every thought is loosened by a loss of memory. Feeble, contrary, lazy, my body, like an old servant, is kept around out of a sense of loyalty. Most of the time we get along, but only because we have to.

At night when I lie down, I hear the murmur of time flowing through my veins, softly as the caress of falling leaves, the cadence of passing wings. My heart often flutters and staggers as if to warn me not to trust it to the night. Dreams offer some respite and the only good legs I will ever have again. As if I have ever been anything other than a dream. Without it, I am just another object in the room. A chair, a clock, a table to be removed one day.

The books that line my walls were once a source of satisfaction, a means of fulfillment. Their titles welcomed me with the promise of light. But I see them now through a fog of confusion, and though I continue to read, sometimes the words on the page look back at me like the faces of strangers in a crowd. Just as we reach the point in life where knowledge and experience coalesce into wisdom, our faculties begin to decline. Our thoughts defy our wills. We let go of things that keep us rooted in the present. But perhaps what we see as a decline, this withdrawal from the world, from its pettiness and vanity, is itself the source of wisdom. The acceptance of formlessness over form. Of unknowing over knowing. Of helplessness over control. Of what we are over what we would like to be. I ask myself whether nature softens the brain as we age to protect us from the pain of so much loss.

The old are merely the young who have been here longer and who have the advantage of being able to look back on those moments in their lives when chance made them who they are, when they became what is out of all that is not. I know I am not what I could have been. I have lived only one of many futures and possess but a single past. I look back from the narrow end of life and see what I will never be.

Sometimes I ask myself whether I have made the most of this life. I have undertaken many endeavors but left many more untried. I am beyond the languages I never learned, the instruments I never played, the people I never took the time to know. I am beyond the many understandings I might have had, ideas gained and lost. I live now with little desire and less intention.

The past is an abyss of books I don't remember, songs I have forgotten, satisfactions succeeded by desires. Meals eaten, sunsets seen, friends departed. It is better that you are not here as I would be a burden to you now. You would have to come and check on this tired old man who offers nothing of promise and who would speak to you tediously of these things while your thoughts were elsewhere.

To have children, you must believe in something. You must live for something. To sacrifice everything for the love of another, you must persevere in a faithless world and make your love your faith. Without it, there is no hiding from the emptiness, no diversion from the darkness. But even those who assess their worth by sacrifice, who live for something greater than themselves, find nothing to redeem their sacrifice on the other side.

When I have been absent from society for even a brief period and once again find myself in the company of others, I am struck by their impostures of speech, their evasions of truth, their strategies of will, and their false fears of giving offense. I see them as if they inhabit graves of air or had never lived. If they were nothing before this life and will be nothing after it, can they be anything but that now? You should know this about people: they celebrate themselves beyond measure. They find themselves in the world against all odds through no merit of their own and live off its bounty, spending their time indulging their vanity, while destined to be forgotten or at best remembered briefly by those who will be forgotten in their turn.

We are a contradiction of two natures. On one hand, we want to change and grow, to improve ourselves and our surroundings. On the other, we want to be what we are, or what we think we are, forever. We are lulled by habit and hope into a dream of timelessness beyond any reckoning, but beneath this dream flows an undercurrent of fear, for we know bodies like ours grow old and die.

I have seen paintings and sculptures noted for their beauty, but the faces of youth are endowed with greater beauty by the fleeting nature of life. There is a race of people still living at the beginning of time who believe their souls are not immortal, but alive like brilliantly colored birds in search of beauty. They believe this search is the purpose of life. They seek no heaven outside time, but rather a paradise of flowers that bloom and die. I understand this more with every year that passes.

There are many people in the place where you would have been born who believe that a man was God and appeared in the world to offer them immortality. This belief answers the questions they cannot answer in any other way and enables them to understand the awe they feel in the fact of their being. I was educated in the doctrines of this religion and for many years went along with what I learned burdened by a fear of transgressing laws I could not comprehend and of offending an entity I could not know. Until I stopped. Now, when asked what I believe, I reply, I try not to believe anything, for once we have a belief, we are no longer open to the possibilities that lie beyond that belief. It is true that to live among mysteries is to lose the comfort of our certainties, and yet, even if we are orphans of an empty sky, there is pleasure in the wonder of our origins and nature.

The Bible is the book of this religion. Though I put it aside many years ago, I have returned to it recently because it contains the wisdom of those who searched as I have searched. This morning I read the following passage from the second chapter of Ecclesiastes:

"I undertook great projects: I built houses for myself and planted vineyards. I made gardens and parks and planted all kinds of fruit trees in them. I made reservoirs to water groves of flourishing trees. I bought male and female slaves and had other slaves who were born in my house. I also owned more herds and flocks than anyone in Jerusalem before me. I amassed silver and gold for myself, and the treasure of kings and provinces. . . . My heart took delight in all my labor, and this was the reward for all my toil. Yet when I surveyed all that my hands had done and what I had toiled to achieve, everything was meaningless, a chasing after the wind; nothing was gained under the sun. . . . So I hated life, because the work that is done under the sun was grievous to me. All of it is meaningless, a chasing after the wind. I hated all the things I had toiled for under the sun because I must leave them to the one who comes after me. And who knows whether that person will be wise or foolish? Yet they will have control over all the fruit of my toil into which I have poured my effort and skill under the sun. This too is meaningless. So my heart began to despair over all my toilsome labor under the sun. For a person may labor with wisdom, knowledge and skill, and then they must leave all they own to another who has not toiled for it. This too is meaningless and a great misfortune. What do people get for all the toil and anxious striving with which they labor under the sun? All their days their work is grief and pain; even at night their minds do not rest. This too is meaningless . . . . And I declared that the dead, who had already died, are happier than the living, who are still alive. But better than both is the one who has never been born, who has not seen the evil that is done under the sun. And I saw that all toil and all achievement spring from one person's envy of another. This too is meaningless, a chasing after the wind."

According to scripture, better than being, better than having been, is never having been. I wonder if you would agree. It is easy to disdain life and wish for death while alive, but much harder to disdain death and wish for life when dead. Or disdain both having never been. Every night when we sleep, we cease to exist, but are granted the boon of a return by the same agency that brought us here from our eternal sleep. Do we waken to regret our brief reprieve, the sunlight of another day? When I pass from this life into the darkness that awaits me, I will reach into that darkness to take your hand. Knowing you are there assures me I will not be alone in being nothing.

The author of Ecclesiastes goes on to instruct us to "enjoy life with the wife whom you love all the days of your vain life which has been given to you under the sun because that is your portion in life and in your toil at which you toil under the sun. Whatever your hand finds to do, do it with your might; for there is no work or thought or knowledge or wisdom in Sheol, to which you are going."

The years lie in my bones like rings in a tree. What I will achieve in life, I have achieved already. A chasing after the wind. Millennia of chance and necessity contending in every grain of sand, every opening flower, every drop of rain, have brought us here, and yet we live unmindful of the struggle. Heedless in our vanity. Even if misbegotten in a world of indifference, I am content to watch the clouds cross the sky, to breathe

567

the scent of grass wet with dew, to see the sun shining on the stony bank of a forest stream, to feel it on my face, and to think of how far that light has traveled un-impeded to touch, to warm, to brighten my skin. If I were offered one additional day in the sun in exchange for all the learning of my life, I would gladly choose that day. So sweet is its light. So useless is knowledge in the grave.

As I sleep, the sun rises over the gorges of the Yang-tze and the plains of the Ganges. Through a haze of dust and smoke, through the lingering breath of night, it shines on market towns, on fishermen in painted dhows, on plowmen turning the yellow earth beside a grove of palms. It will shine whether I am here or not warming the stones beside the sandaled feet of beggars blind or broken in the grip of saṃsāra. If they are like me, when waking in the darkness, they question whether they have died in the night, and if they have, whether they should continue to act out the dream of their lives. For hell is not a privation of God, as Augus-tine claims and Islam repeats, but rather a privation of purpose.

When I dream, I return to a time when I took life for granted. Your mother is there and my mother and fa-ther. And my childhood friends. In places foreign and fa-miliar. A path beneath the trees at the edge of a field. Our old house with its damp stone walls. Evening light in the windows. Crows calling. Skies so distant now. And then I waken and am alone. But if I close my eyes again, I am there, waiting for my mother to call, worried that I might be late for school. The fresh scent of rain and the reflections of houses in the road. Sometimes I dream you are walking that road beside me.

The house was on the edge of town. It was cold and

gray. In the morning, the blankets were wet with condensation. We kept a white pony in the field behind the house. Every Sunday, I fed him a carrot my mother had given me. When he saw me nearing the fence, he would approach from wherever he was in the field. In the winter he took shelter in a small shed, and in the summer flies rested on his eyelids like rows of pebbles. One night he was attacked and killed by a pack of dogs. My father and I dug a pit in the corner of the field and buried the carcass. He said that if we didn't destroy the dogs, they would come back and kill another animal. Then he loaded his rifle and with several neighbors went to look for them. I heard the shots in the distance and imagined what happened. I was eight years old at the time. Not long after that, I began to have nightmares. I dreamt that a tiger stalked our house looking for me. I hid in various rooms, the cellar and outbuildings, and used various contrivances to ensure my safety, but the locks would break or the furniture would shift or something would fall and alert the animal to my presence. I can still see its eyes as it discovered me. My mother told me that tigers live far away and wouldn't bother me unless I went to them. I realized years later the tiger that haunted my dreams was death, and life is the path I have taken to find it.

I have been ill for several days. Lying in bed without sleeping. Subject to waking nightmares. Indistinct terrors. My pulse races as if my heart is trying to outrun death. Each beat sends a subtle shake through my body. I am struck by the strangeness of this life the closer I come to its end. In the middle of my chest is a cavity of blood, black in the darkness, but in the light, red like the sea beneath a setting sun. Behind the face by which I am known, gossamer nerves connect my eyes, turning in orbits of bone, to the folds of a brain fed by snaking arteries. We live on surfaces happy in our ignorance, but as we lose the cover of hair and skin, the more the surfaces resemble what lies beneath. Soon there will be no difference. Enough of that. You can go too far in thinking that way.

Don Andrés appeared today to inquire about my health. My nephew contacted him to suggest I might be better off in a home for the elderly in Coruña. I told him I would rather die alone where I am, comfortable among my things, than live miserably in a strange room in a strange building. I am like an old dog that trembles when taken from its home, when confronted by a place that is not its own. I use the same dishes I have used for more than sixty years. I remember when my mother bought them. The tulip lamp beside my chair belonged to my grandparents. My books have been my companions from the time I learned to read. I prefer to wait alone. Why inflict this on anyone else? Alone we come from the eternal. Alone we go to the eternal. Alone in the laps of our mothers. Alone in the arms of our lovers. Alone in the long hours of night. After a life among others. Waiting to wait no more. Sometimes at night when I am half-dreaming, I am careful not to pull the blanket to my side of the bed, vaguely thinking I am pulling it away from your mother.

There is nothing as satisfying as eating the bounty of one's own garden. From the dark earth one works with one's hands and waters with one's sweat come the color and savor of life-giving life—the carrot, the tomato, the pepper—and from the trees, apples and oranges and lemons, freely given so that we may spread their seeds and their offspring may flourish, sustaining us with a sweetness mined from the minerals and seeping moisture in a small plot of ground. A sweetness that enters us to become our life. Blood and muscle and bone. And thought. An alchemy more remarkable than the transmutation of lead to gold.

This morning as I was working in the garden, I decided I want my body to be buried on the lee side of the bluff and left a note to that effect on my desk. The earth there is good. The soil is black, and the grass is deep and cool. A few timid saplings have come down from the forest. I like them. Someday they will provide good cover. I believe there are Romans buried in this valley. They will also be good company.

Because we come from this world, because we have been made from its soil and air and water and light, it is beautiful to us. It is good to us. The greatest wonders of all are possessed by every person every day without travel or labor: the sun and moon and stars. However short our time or insignificant our place, each of us is blessed to witness the origin of all things when we look to the night sky.

I have always had a good relationship with the earth. I have been sustained by her generous gifts all these years, but with the understanding that at some point I must return what I have been given, and my soul, if I have one, must fend for itself without her. She has waited very patiently to reclaim what is hers. When I pass a plowed field, she reminds me of her presence. When I see the lush foliage in my garden and the dense thickets and forests of the mountain, I see her beckon to me ever so gently. She knows the last times are near. The last season planting the garden. The last visit to the market. The last conversation with a friend. The last book read. The last meal eaten. The last words I will ever write. She will be there at the end. She understands us better than we understand ourselves. Once we accept this, there is nothing more to be gained or lost.

Alone in the darkness. Haven't spoken to a soul for more than a week. Man nor beast. Facundo should be here soon. Once or twice a month he brings me a loaf of bread and a fillet of bacallau or a pan of tuna empanada. When I ask him, he brings me chocolate. We bury my trash in the woods. I keep a small store of onions and potatoes in a bin beneath the counter and coffee in a can that is rusted along the edges. My water comes from the stream. I carry it in a metal bucket and boil it on the stove with kindling I collect from the woods. I have lived in this house for nine years. Although what I know will soon be lost, I continue to read. I read in order to be. Lego ergo sum. Apart from Facundo and Don Andrés, I have no visitors. Except the sun and rain. The cold, dark clouds. The wind that strips the trees.

The day arrives when we accept that death is imminent. It may be the day of our death or months before. But it is the day when we know. When the eagle raises its wings but can no longer fly. As a young man, I studied the works of Epictetus, Marcus Aurelius, and Seneca. I considered their words carefully and prepared my mind for that day. I imagined the moment. I thought rationally of its necessity and told myself that a single death is nothing. As the Roman emperor wrote, "Do not despise death, but be well content with it, since this too is one of those things which nature wills. For such as it is to be young and to grow old, and to increase and to reach maturity, and to have teeth and beard and grey hairs, and to beget, and to be pregnant and to bring forth, and all the other natural operations which the seasons of thy life bring, such also is dissolution. This, then, is consistent with the character of a reflecting man, to be neither careless nor impatient nor contemptuous with respect to death, but to wait for it as one of the operations of nature. As thou now waitest for the time when the child shall come out of thy wife's womb, so be ready for the time when thy soul shall fall out of this envelope."

But now that death is near, none of that means anything to me. The works and lives of philosophers are just books on a shelf that will remain when I am gone. Old friends that stand in mute testament to a mind that is no more. No one can know what it is like to reach the end until it arrives. Those who are in the middle of their lives, still far from the day when death is imminent, seem innocent to me now. Like children at play. They go about their lives with no fear of what is too far off to be conceivable. Let them enjoy their innocence as I did because at some point they won't be innocent anymore. I will live my last months like those who went before me, knowing finally what it is like to lose everything forever. To lose ourselves and all we know and all we have and all we've done. For nothing. For nature. The price we pay for being.

Our lives are like libations poured into the ground. We plant vines, weave them along the wires of a canopy, pluck pests from their young leaves, gather and press the grapes, and ferment the juice only to return it to the earth, to gods whose existence we cannot confirm.

When we leave the world, whether from mud houses with tin roofs, or mansions on green hills, or crowded tenements, or hospitals with waxed floors, the world suffers no loss. The night sky is unmoved. A life ends as another begins. But if the purpose of nature is to create life, then we fulfill that purpose when we love, and for this reason it could be said that we exist in order to love. Religion, art, learning, customs, and rituals mean nothing unless they help us to achieve that end. And yet every step of the way, our attempts are frustrated by vanity, fear, anger, envy. And chance. We may believe we can create the life we choose, overcoming whatever obstacles arise by the strength of our wills, but we are nevertheless carried along through the years the way the wind carries insects in a storm.

If this sounds like madness, it's because I can no longer accept the strategies of sanity that deny what I know is true.

In a month or two or three, these hands, these arms, these legs, will be free from the demands of my desires, free to lie unmoved in the earth. We wait our entire lives for the waiting to be over, and yet nothing frightens us more than what we wait for. But kindly nature softens the blow. Life is only what we remember of it, and every year we remember less. By the time we depart, we no longer know the world we knew, and in that way, we can leave without knowing what is left.

Words are memories. Of when they were learned and when they were used. We live within them as much as they live within us. Like dreams, they appear from nothing and fill our lives with meaning. Making us who we are. Each is fashioned by every mind through which it passes, bringing with it a history of human thought and emotion. Each is a means to escape ourselves, and each is a form of confinement, for we can only go as far as the words can take us. The way is narrow, a compromise between common ground and the uniqueness of what we know and feel. As an artifice of convention, language dilutes complexities and renders absurdities.

It allows us to form and reform our intentions and make the world in our own image. Even as I write this.

I am wearing out my heart with insomnia, shaking as if possessed by a mischievous spirit.

Lost the feeling in my left hand today. It was only a matter of time. Before this or something worse. Still able to eat. Still able to read. Still able to write. I'm like the shuffling elders I stared at as a child. Enfeebled in every joint. Hollow in every thought. I move like a marionette among tangled strings. One by one I give up the things I used to do. No more cutting wood. No more walking through the forest. No more trips to the market. When I can no longer feed or bathe myself, it will be time to leave all this. But I worry about my mind. Let me not outlive it by a single day, a single hour. Clinging too long to this world, we devalue death. And life.

These setbacks are like clouds that darken the evening sky. There is still enough light to see, but not enough to believe in the illusions of the day.

The sun burns in a day without nights. Burns alone in the emptiness of its light. Source of life. The ibis in the glade. The rose among the rocks. Ageless and alone. Burning time timelessly. Our world is nothing to the sun. A distant reflection of light. Faint and blue. But we are more than the sun. We burn life. Contain worlds. Know the secrets of creation. The sun knows nothing. We expire. Knowledge expires. The sun expires. But we alone defeat time with memory. Conscious among the stars.

If there is only God and what is not God, His creation out of nothing, then, in a sense, we are like a god because we too distinguish ourselves from everything we are not, which we have also created. To be is to step outside God's creation into our own.

If there were another God somewhere beyond the stars, in a time belonging to another eternity, would He leave as much to chance? What souls would inhabit his garden? Would they be mysteries to themselves? Would their deaths be transformations?

Boethius said that we apprehend our world according to our nature. If this is true, and an eternal god knows eternity in the present, then a mortal creature must know its end in the passing of every moment.

When I close my eyes, I see a faint blue light fading in and out like the moon through passing fog. It seems to be waiting for me. Perhaps this is how the sun appears in the shadows of the afterlife.

The words I write contain what is lost. Beyond any gain. More appear. Coming and going. White birds flying through a forest. Flashing through the darkness. Disappearing before I can capture them. Until I am no longer the words but the darkness that surrounds them.

Each word together with another. Form. Formless. Sense. Senseless. I am losing my hold. Thoughts on their own. Coming on their own. Without me. In a cold austerity. No warmth in the words. No comfort in the heart. Where I go without going. Into all that is lost. Where I have been without being. Among all that is lost. Dream in the light. But that time is over. Lost in the night. I would. But that time is over. The time when I would. Dream in the light. Lost in the night. When I would. Dream of time before. Dream the timelessness of time before. Light pouring through me. The light of dreams. Pouring through me. Like light through glass. The scent of lilacs. The solitary wren. In the light. Pouring through me. Lost in the light. What good will come. What good. Nothing to be [illegible] And you. Without welcome. Unborn. Without welcome. Lost in the darkness. No wonder of welcome. She with you. Mother and child. Together forever.

To endure is the only answer. To endure until the end. Through the long days. Through the sleepless nights. Until back among the vast unborn. Those that never. And those that were. As if never. Wakeful once. Long ago. In the sunlight and the wind. Young in the sunlight and the wind. Briefly wakeful. She and I. Out of all the others. Those that might have been. Together forever. Rose in the twilight. Lost forever. Ever together. Among the stars. She and I. Among all that might have been. And you. There. Ever unborn. Memory in blue.

Two years after the death of Mestre, my father died of a heart attack at the age of fifty-eight. I was living in Madrid at the time and took a short leave of absence from work to settle his affairs and help mother move to Santiago where she would be able to live more comfortably and have better access to medical care. To pay for the new apartment and her living expenses, we rented our house and fields to Ramón. Although I visited Santiago over the Christmas holidays and occasionally on the Feast of St. James, for twenty-seven years I did not return to Porto Lúa.

My life followed the course of many lives of my generation. I left the countryside to receive an education, and from there I went where I was offered a job. In my case it was Madrid, but it could have been any large city. I was successful in my profession and well compensated. I woke punctually, worked diligently, returned home reluctantly, and slept anxiously. I saved my money. I spent my money. Sometimes after work I went out with friends, and during my brief annual vacations, I traveled to France, England, Italy, and Germany. Once, for a change of pace, I went to Malta and North Africa. In addition to these countries, I became familiar with Brussels and Strasbourg through my work. And the years went by.

It was not the life I had envisioned, and I wasn't the person I had expected to be. My professional life was like a play where

I interacted with others according to well-rehearsed conventions with little thought to what occurred offstage. I had an apartment like other apartments. I shopped like other shoppers. I argued and complained, as everyone else argued and complained, about things that aren't important. And I was alone. In the city, one lives concealed behind anonymity. I knew nothing of the lives of my neighbors and in some cases very little about the lives of my friends. I knew my routines. Weekly errands. Restaurants. The kiosk on the corner. The views from my windows. At home and at work. Work. The word that describes how we spend our lives as someone other than ourselves. I was busy, always busy, in order to have an excuse for not living. When I walked home from work or went out in the evenings, I passed families sitting on the terraces of cafés or on benches in the small neighborhood plazas where children play and felt inauthentic in their presence. There was nothing beneath me, nothing supporting me, nothing to lift me out of myself. Only a movement forward in a direction I never chose, but accepted. The richness of my childhood was replaced by central heat and modern furnishings and inexhaustible ways to spend what I earned. Circumscribed by the demands of work and the conventions of my society, I lived like those around me. I walked the same streets beneath the same trees; I entered the same doorways; I walked up the same stairs; I ate in the same cafés from the same plates and drank from the same glasses. I carried the same newspaper under my arm, the same money in my pocket, and breathed the same air. I went unnoticed, unnoticing, among the arms and legs and hats and coats of the city, and was to them what they were to me.

From the perspective of this life, Porto Lúa was a dream of another time, a place inviolable, beyond the murmur of traffic and moving crowds, a place where the colors of the sea and sky are clear and bright, a place secure against the unending urban winter of cement and shadows. A place still on the edge of the unknown where my ancestors had believed in the life of the sun, and the constellations of night were empowered with our destinies. Perhaps Aunt Fioxilda was right. Half mad between two worlds, she had freed herself from the constraints on her imagination and the narrowness of modern life, filling her world rather than emptying it.

That dream was recovered briefly one autumn afternoon when, searching for the mood of the season, I walked down the gravel path of the Paseo de las Estatuas in Retiro Park. A bright sun was descending over the yellow and russet crowns of the chestnut trees. The air was crisp and still, and in the shadows dusk was beginning to fall. Within that moment was another, brought forth from memory, of an autumn sun shining down the narrow alley of an apple orchard in Porto Lúa gilding the leaves of the trees and transforming the air into a luminous veil of golden mist. The trunks and branches of the trees were half radiant in honeyed light and half black in shadow. Memories as immediate as perception followed: the scent of burning oak, of wet grass and wild onions; a chorus of warring crows in the pines; the touch of earthy cold on my face and hands; my breath white before me; and beneath the trees, damp beds of violet and scarlet and yellow leaves.

A few weeks later in the rain and darkness of mid-December, I passed a church where a concert was playing just as someone opened the door. Within a few notes I recognized the music as the twilight song Harry used to play. Curious, I stepped inside and was handed a program. I asked the woman which song it was, and she pointed to the adagio from Marcello's *Oboe Concerto in D Minor*. It sounded more lively, less melancholy, on the oboe than I remembered it on the trumpet, but it was unmistakably the same song. I stood at the back of the church until it ended and then went home where I searched the storage space in the attic of my building until I found the box containing Laura's photograph and letters and the copy of *Don Quixote* she had given me. Beside it were the boxes of Mestre's books and his letter.

As I sat cross-legged on the dusty floor of the attic reading those letters under a dim light, I began the conscious process of recovering what I had feared was lost. Among the cold, indifferent streets, the shadows, and dreary winter nights of the city, the blue sea and coastal light had remained within me. The golden orchard. The twilight elegy. I realized too that in the faces of strangers I saw the faces of my childhood. The old man who sat beneath the plane tree outside my building was another Gustavo. The clerk at the post office, another Chucho. And every day as I passed through the city, I saw Laura in the faces of women I had never seen before and would never see again.

It was a custom in our office to go out after work on the last Friday of the month. Usually there was a core group of four or five and a few others who would occasionally appear. We went to a quiet café in the Barrio de las Letras not far from the Cortes. On a warm night in March, our number increased to nearly twenty because we had come from the funeral of José Manuel, a former member of the group who had died unexpectedly at the beginning of the week. His wife had heard him gasping for air in the middle of the night, and he never regained consciousness. His heart had simply stopped. There was no obvious cause. No blocked arteries. He was younger than I was, and I had been thinking about him all week. Living alone meant that I could have a seizure or stroke and no one would know. I could lie in the darkness indefinitely.

José Antonio settled into the chair where he usually sat and lit one of the Cohiba Esplendidos that he saved for special occasions. Javier took a copy of *El País* from the bar and sat at the same table. The rest of us remained at the bar sipping coffee as the conversation turned from cognac to cardiograms to the question of wills. Several people admitted they did not have one. Juan Carlos, who had stopped drinking coffee because of an ulcer, and Paco, who had been diagnosed with lymphoma, both chastised their colleagues for their oversight especially in light of the recent death of José Manuel.

"Do not ask for whom the bell tolls," said Miguel Ángel.

"Hemingway."

"John Donne."

"Did José Manuel have one?"

"I never thought to ask."

"What about his widow? Is anyone in contact with her?"

"She'll have his pension."

"For what that's worth."

"She has family in Asturias. Someone said she'll be going back to live with them."

"Any children?"

"Six. Three boys and three girls. The oldest is fifteen."

There was a pause in the conversation as we took a moment to reflect on our own families and fates. Then José Antonio broke the silence by changing the subject.

"What's the news, Javi?"

"'Ergot Suspected When the Devil Visits Arcos.' There's a village in Galicia where people claimed to see the devil."

"That's news?"

"Careful. There's a Galician in our midst."

"And the devil is his old friend," I replied, going along with the joke.

"Do they really believe such stuff?"

"Not so much these days," I said. "You know how the newspapers are. They'll look for the most obscure story and present it as commonplace. I suppose there are still some villages where people are superstitious, but the cities are like everywhere else. Of course, that doesn't make a very interesting headline: Santiago de Compostela Now Like Everywhere Else."

"This was a remote community on the coast of Coruña. It says here, 'Local people claimed to see the presence of malevolent spirits in their fields, and some even reported conversing with the devil. In addition, several people in the town claimed to see lights in the ocean and said their Bibles were written backward. The area has a history of such reports. Scientists have long suspected the role of ergot in these mass hallucinations and have worked with the government to drain fields in order to avoid damage to grains by the fungus. A bakery that uses locally milled grain is being investigated as the source of the outbreak.'"

"Magic pastries."

"Who needs ergot? *Aguardiente* on a dark night in Galicia is enough to see the devil."

"It's a failure of education in this country."

"It's a disgrace. The English don't have this problem. Not even the French."

"'Not even the French' should be our national motto."

"And yet," José Antonio said, "educated people go to museums to see the altars of the Romans and pride themselves on reading Ovid and Virgil where women turn into trees and ships turn into nymphs."

"You can't compare the two things. That was centuries ago."

"People living in cities today are no different," I said. "They still have their myths and superstitions. Illusions of love. Of immortality. Of their own importance. Even in a modern city like Madrid, we're surrounded by churches wherever we go. We just came from a Mass where we prayed for the everlasting peace of a soul."

"Religion is not the same thing as superstition."

"Where do you think the devil comes from?"

"I don't see the point in people wasting their time on folk tales and ghosts that don't exist. This is why we have education. To be liberated from ignorance."

"There are still plenty of things we don't understand," I said. "People are trying to make sense of their world in their own ways."

"It's a waste of time. There are no more devils or mysterious islands or giants."

"And so we spend our time more productively sitting around bars arguing about sports and politics and films and whether Sartre is still relevant. People in the countryside live much more intensely in their world than we do in ours. They have much greater knowledge of wildlife and husbandry than we do. They're not ignorant."

José Antonio brought this conversation to a close by offering several humorous anecdotes on our late colleague to lighten the mood before we went our separate ways. That was the last time I heard anyone mention José Manuel until we went to a meeting several weeks later to discuss who would fill his position.

It was still early when we left the café. I took a circuitous course home in order to enjoy the night air and to walk the conversation out of my system. I didn't succeed. Not because of the estrangement I felt from my colleagues, but because of the estrangement I felt from myself. Though I had offered a defense of people in the countryside, I had also made light of the subject and refrained from saying what I really think. It isn't a matter of the validity of believing in apparitions of evil or exorcisms or the Santa Compaña, but of the validity of living in a world of one's own making. It is easy to mock the attempts of people to explain the inexplicable in chance and fate, but much harder to provide explanations of one's own. And while the beliefs of country people do not stand up to scientific scrutiny, in their engagement with nature, they are exercising their imaginations rather than accepting the theories and arguments of others. Indebted to the lore of their ancestors, but not bound by modern conceits, they are like artists who, within the context of a tradition, create according to their individual needs. How impoverished by comparison are those who rely instead on received knowledge to explain their fortunes, their fears, their loves, their very presence.

The attempt to reduce the world to its constituent parts and examine it more "objectively" without the distorting effects of human need or desire does not result in more accurate understanding, but merely in a different kind of understanding. According to this way of thinking, the great cathedrals are not creations of grace and light aspiring to the beauty of divine perfection, but piles of stone erected according to the principles of physics by a creature marginally more intelligent than the termites who erect their mounds in equatorial forests. Similarly, ascribing love to physiological processes that ensure the survival of the species fails to explain the experience we each feel and feel differently and why we select one person over another—sometimes in conflict with the interests of nature and ourselves. The ancients ascribed our irrational impulses to the gods, and now we attribute them to the equally unfathomable god of psychology. We can read a thousand books on the subject and come away with no better understanding of ourselves than the people have who believe their souls are torn between forces of good and evil. Those who object to such beliefs and disparage as ignorant people who see hidden agencies behind their fates have simply replaced one inscrutable cause with another: gods with physics, myths with data. All of these explanations are products of the human imagination, and all are destined to be superseded by others. How many of those who rely on science to explain their world can grasp the subtleties of its methods and conclusions? How many can explain the roles of chance and necessity? How many can explain how they came to be? They see their form of worship as superior to others, but it is still a form of worship foiled by our most fundamental questions.

The death of José Manuel and Paco's diagnosis of cancer continued to occupy my thoughts and darken my mood as ominous reminders of my own mortality. I compared my lifestyle to theirs on the basis of diet, drink, tobacco, and exercise, and decided that while I had probably been more conscientious than my colleagues in looking after myself, I was still not doing as much as I could. Most concerning about the death of José Manuel was that he had been in good health his entire life, and there had been no alcohol or drugs in his system. My health, which was generally good, was therefore no assurance that I was not also at risk—a thought that occurred most often at night when I lay in bed. I had trouble sleeping for more than four or five hours a night, and more than once woke from a deep sleep fearful that I had stopped breathing. The cause of this panic, I eventually discovered, was a recurring nightmare where I saw myself slipping on a wet street and being hit by a car that couldn't stop. Thinking of Paco, I also noticed a dull ache on the floor of my pelvis, and in the shower I checked for lumps in my armpits and groin. My doctor ran a series of tests for each complaint and concluded that I had no serious health concerns.

"What should I do?" I asked.

"Go out and enjoy your life."

Contributing to my gloomy state of mind was the concern I felt over the deteriorating health of my mother. We spoke on the phone at least once a week, and recently I had noticed her memory failing and her speech faltering. So apparent was the change that every time the phone rang unexpectedly I was afraid it might be a neighbor or doctor in Santiago delivering bad news. That call finally came at four o'clock one morning. It was a night nurse at the hospital in Santiago. Mother had fainted on the stairs of her building and was spending the night in the hospital under observation. There were no broken bones. Her pulse and blood pressure were both elevated, but not dangerously so. Dehydration was believed to be the cause. I drove to Santiago and was there by two o'clock that afternoon. She was discharged the next day, and I took her home.

She was in her seventies and still independent, having insisted on living on her own for twenty-seven years, but I could tell by her voice that she had been shaken by the experience. She had aged, as country people do, with gout, poor circulation, and respiratory problems. A lifetime of pork had hardened her arteries, and though she had never touched a cigarette, the ubiquitous presence of smoke had forever scarred her lungs.

"Before going to bed," she said, "I took the trash down, and on the way back up, I don't know what happened. I was lying on the stairs, and my back hurt. If Mari Carmen hadn't found me, I might have been there all night, and it could have been a lot worse."

We sat at the kitchen table and discussed her options. She acknowledged she was having trouble with her memory and worried she might leave the stove or a heater on. Cleaning and shopping, she admitted, had become more onerous because of her arthritis. However, her greatest concern, given recent events, was falling and injuring herself when no one was around. I asked her if she would consider moving to an assisted living facility, and she seemed relieved that I had brought it up. Friends of hers had given her the names of two—one in Conxo and one in Pontepedriña. The next day we went to see them, but both had waiting lists, so we went to a third in Fontiñas that she preferred because it was on higher ground than the two near the Sar, and she was afraid the dampness of the river and its morning fogs would worsen her arthritis. Fortunately, they had an opening—I didn't ask—but the room wouldn't be ready for a week as it needed a fresh coat of paint and new fixtures in the bathroom. We would cover the cost by selling the apartment where she lived on Avenida de Castelao, and I could meet any expenses beyond that. It shouldn't have surprised me when mother added that she would also sell the house and land in Porto Lúa. There was no reason to keep the property apart from its sentimental value. I just never imagined being without it.

"Ramón has made me a good offer."

"You never told me that."

"He's been waiting to buy it for years. He's a big shot now."

"In what way?"

"He's got a company that's built several apartment buildings in Porto Lúa. When he offered, I told him I wasn't ready to sell, but I am now."

"I thought I might restore it someday and use it as a vacation home."

"You're not going to do that. You haven't been there since your father died. Your life is in the city and mine is here. Porto Lúa isn't the same anymore."

"You're right."

"Ramón will give us a fair price. We don't need to negotiate."

"I'll call him tonight."

"There should still be some old furniture and boxes in the house that you might want."

"I'll see what's there, but I doubt there's anything I want to keep."

"If you don't want it, throw it out. Don't bring it back here."

I called my office and arranged to take some time off. During the week that followed, we packed mother's clothes and personal items and found a second-hand dealer at the market in Padrón who agreed to buy most of her furniture and appliances. Whatever she couldn't take and we couldn't sell, we gave to the neighbors. I contacted the utility companies and listed the apartment with a real estate agent, and then we waited for her room at the facility to open. There wasn't much to read in the apartment, but I did find a single-volume encyclopedia in a box to be given away that contained the following summary: "Porto Lúa is a municipality in the province of A Coruña in the autonomous region of Galicia in northwest Spain. The principal industries are fishing and tourism. Mount Aracelo, the highest elevation on the Galician coast, is located nearby."

On Friday morning after a consultation with mother's doctor, I set off for Porto Lúa. The patched and cratered road we used to take to Santiago that was barely wide enough for the Castromil buses to pass had been replaced by a sleek highway where cars seemed to glide effortlessly past the green valleys of suburban developments and the ruins of dreary *aldeas* and over the ridge of mountains separating Santiago from the sea. The journey that had taken hours in Paco Carreira's taxi went by so quickly that I missed several landmarks. Within twenty minutes of leaving Santiago, I was coming down the western side of the ridge where I could see the *ría* and Monte Louro in the distance. On the northern shore, above Freixo, a row of windmills with slowly turning stiletto blades extended across an eminence of bare granite, and beyond it, to the northwest, rising above the sea haze, was the outline of Aracelo. I crossed a bridge over the Tambre and quickly passed through Outes, Freixo, Esteiro, Tal, and Abelleira before reaching Muros. Slowed in traffic, I looked over at Curro da Praza where Don Horacio had arrived late for his lecture and thought too of Laura's house on Rúa Real, which was just behind the buildings on the square.

From Muros, the highway skirts the *ría* and the beach at San Francisco before passing beneath Monte Louro to reach the shore of the Atlantic. There, for the first time, I felt the openness of the blue sky and the freedom of the ocean horizon. In the clarity of the coastal light, I passed a forest of maritime pines on the left and on the right wild tracts of gorse and broom rising to austere elevations that bore the brunt of winter storms. As I rounded the curve in the road at Lira and saw the beach at Carnota and the pink granite of Aracelo, I recalled the night when I crossed the ridge above Mallou beneath the stars hoping to see Laura again.

The outskirts of Porto Lúa now reached more than a half mile south of the bridge over the Deva. On both sides of the road, where there had been walled, patchwork fields and a few stone houses gray with dust and mold, there were new homes with bright second-floor *galerías* looking out over the headland and, behind ornate fences, palm trees and gardens with roses and blue hydrangeas. As a decorative homage to the past, some people had taken grinding stones from the watermills on the river and disintegrating oxcarts and rusty plows and placed them in their yards. The lots were narrow, and the houses were so closely crowded together that I almost missed the avenue of maples leading to the great house of El Conde. The shoulders of the road where we had walked as children and where barefoot women had carried their *grelos* and fish to market were paved with new sidewalks, and on the ground floors of new apartment buildings were cafés and bakeries and small supermarkets. As I approached the bridge, the road widened to four lanes divided by a median. Along its length the municipality had planted a row of trees and painted the curbs red and white. And there, like a reincarnation of Cotolay, stood a bearded man wearing a long white gown waving cars forward as if the people driving them were paying any attention.

The commercial center of Porto Lúa had shifted to the south side of the bridge where a number of new stores, hotels, and restaurants catering to summer visitors had been built. To protect the historical status of the old part of town, traffic was now restricted to residents and delivery vehicles, and to accommodate the cars of tourists, a section of the harbor had been filled in to create a parking lot. At the far end of the lot was a dock for an excursion boat that took sightseers to Illa da Luz, but the company that ran the service referred to the island as Isla de los Torres because that's the name that appeared on the maps the government produced in 1945 when employees of the Instituto Geográfico y Catastral went around the country naming geographical features and towns without consulting the people who lived in those places. At the other end of the lot was a bus station with six bays and a lobby with a snack bar and restrooms. Pilgrims who brought the souls of their loved ones to Porto Lúa could now ride in comfort as far as the terminal. From there, a paved trail led them to Mar das Almas.

As soon as I stepped out of the car, I felt the freshness of the sea air blowing across the warm asphalt, the same air that had caressed me as a child. The sky was summer blue, but behind a forested shoulder of Aracelo, a bank of clouds loomed like an avalanche of snow rolling down from more distant, more inscrutable, heights. On the bridge children were throwing pieces of bread into the water as scavenging gulls swept past crying with the insistence of habitual beggars. I stopped at the top of the arch to study the outline of the mountain and attempt to locate where among its gothic peaks and green meadows were Agro Vello and Onde se Adora and Santa Locaia, and I wondered whether Lonxe do Sol had succumbed to the same changes I saw around me.

María Teresa, the younger sister of Andrés el Tercero, kept a *pensión* in the building where their mother's store had been. I'd called the night before to make a reservation, and when I checked in, there was a message from Ramón asking me to meet him in his office in the new part of town at ten o'clock the following morning. Free for the rest of the afternoon, I left my bag in my room and went out to become reacquainted with the streets of my childhood. Though revived by fresh paint and new roofs, the buildings on the plaza were much as I remembered them. Except for a new addition. The row of houses built by The Society of the Immaculate Conception for the Benefit of the Widows and Orphans of Seafarers had been replaced, as Jefe had envisioned, by an eight-story condominium overlooking the bay. The old market was still there but had been converted into a "living museum" where craftsmen and women in artisanal workshops produced lace, jewelry, ceramics, and linen scarves for tourists who watched them through the lenses of their cameras. The Tower of Names had been dismantled and the stones repurposed to pave part of an esplanade that ran along the top of the quay. Walking slowly in and out of the shadows of the trees, I found many names I recognized, but many others had been worn away, obliterating the memory of those whose lives they were meant to preserve, and that was perhaps the fate of mine, which I never found.

I followed the same course through the streets I had taken with grandmother forty-five years earlier when she had said goodbye to the place of her birth. The *Museo do Explorador Martín Alonso Pinzón Descubridor do Novo Mundo* had been restored well beyond what it had once been. The walls had been whitewashed, and the wooden floor had been sanded and varnished. The bed where the great explorer had slept and the table where he had written to Ferdinand and Isabella on his return from the New World had been immaculately restored—or replaced—to educate a public that may or may not have heard of him. Capela de Santa Lupa, which had been renamed Capela do Salvador, had also undergone renovations that had changed its appearance as well as its character. The walls of the interior where Cotolay used to sit had been whitewashed, and the dolls of saints had been replaced by glass vases filled with fresh flowers. More importantly, the entrance to the underworld had been covered with cement shaped and textured to look like a wall of granite. As I continued through the narrow streets, I tried to imagine what Porto Lúa had been like when people came down from the mountain centuries earlier to make their living from the sea—which houses were among the oldest and what secrets lay beneath the paving stones. In the square at the entrance of Rúa dos Mortos someone had painted Falangist slogans on the house of *los conversos*, and in Rúa das Sombras, the flea market that had brought the treasures of the seven seas to Porto Lúa had been replaced by stalls selling inexpensive leather purses, belts, scarves, and cotton saris. Both the house where grandmother had been born and the house where Trofonio had dug his replica of hell had been torn down. As in the past, I entered the plaza through the alley of odors, but the only odors that day were of coffee and musty stones. On the left, the house of Madame Zafirah was a dress shop with voguish manikins behind plate glass windows staring blankly into the distance.

By the middle of the afternoon the only people walking around were foreign tourists. The large wooden door of the Information Center on the ground floor of the town hall was closed until five o'clock, but a newsagent's shop next to it was open. I bought a copy of *La Voz*, a book of stories on Porto Lúa, and a map that showed the ancient path from Santiago to the tip of the headland. The proprietor was from Toledo and spoke with the accent of that region. I asked him if he knew where I could find Casa das Flores. He apologized and said he was new to the town, but directed me to what he called the best restaurant in Porto Lúa. Though retaining its name and location, O Galo had changed in every other aspect. Over the door was an electric sign written in a frenzied script suggesting an energy and excitement at odds with the lethargy of the afternoon. The interior was decorated with maroon granite, brass railings, and new woodwork that gave off an odor of fresh varnish. Gone were the tubes of fluorescent light, the walls brown with ancient smoke, the scent of wine urine from an unkempt toilet, and the rough-hewn chairs and benches. A large family was seated at a table in the front corner where we had watched television for the first time with Aunt Fioxilda, and a young couple stood where Hierónimo, the wine-sipping pig, had bitten the Portuguese sailor and fled through the plaza upsetting the table of the lacemakers' guild before falling to his demise.

I took a glass of Albariño and a selection of ham and cheese to the terrace and opened the map to see where the pilgrims' route over the mountain had been plotted. For the most part, it followed the Roman road, but omitted the names of Agro Vello and Onde se Adora, while adding others I had never heard of. The chapel in the cave was indicated with the red symbol of a church, but A Noiva do Ceo was not marked. There was an *albergue* near the site of the bothy where hikers could sleep and another on the eastern side of the mountain as well as alternative routes marked in dotted lines of different colors. A modern pilgrim with a backpack and walking stick sat down at the table beside me. By the fairness of her hair and the fresh bronze of her skin, I guessed she was German or Scandinavian. She was reading *The Way to the Sea of Souls* and peeling an orange. As the scent of the fruit reached me through the briny air and metallic tang of broiled sardines, I closed my eyes and felt at home for the first time. Grandmother was right when she had said Porto Lúa would never be the same. Although the houses in the old part of town had been preserved, the preservation had destroyed what it was meant to save. But this was still the place whose boundaries had defined me. From the underworld of Trofonio to the heights of Aracelo, from the shore of Dugium to the cape at Louro, from the rising moon of Uncle Teo to Aunt Fioxilda's realm of spirits. In describing Porto Lúa, even now, I describe myself, as I have also changed.

Entranced by the scene before her, a woman drifting out of the bar declared to her companion that they were in a land of poets and artists. I imagined her sitting at a table sharing her lunch with Raíña Lupa as the *vákner* crossed the plaza and

Roman soldiers arrived on the beach. Hustling the tables for coins were the fallen angels of a distant youth rebellion who had become burnt-out alcoholics in rock and roll t-shirts. Avoiding the locals, they moved among the foreigners followed by a German Shepherd that licked scraps of food off the pavement. As the siesta came to an end, people lingered over drinks and coffee on the terraces while others began to emerge from the dark interiors of houses and bars. I paid for my lunch and set out to see what else had changed.

Just outside what was officially designated the historic district, where Rúa das Angustias, Rúa dos Castiñeiros, and Rúa do Olvido enter the plaza and the slope of the hillside begins, stood a cluster of five-story apartment blocks uniform in size and shape with the same aluminum doors and sashes distinguished solely by the patterns of mold staining the whitewash of their cement shells. The ground floors were bricked up waiting for commercial tenants or occupied by bars with names like *Breogán* and *The Atlantic* and grocery stores with molded plastic signs and colorful ads in the windows selling everything from detergent to powdered chocolate. Overhead networks of cables crisscrossed the streets like the wires of grape arbors.

The house at 8 Rúa do Olvido was among those torn down to make way for the multi-story blocks. Though a few of the old houses and barns of schist and granite had been restored with new roofs and windows and doors, fresh mortar and sealant, most were either gone or in ruins. Of the latter, some were hidden from the gaze of tourists behind the apartments, and some were barely visible higher on the hillside where, washed by sea mists, their stones and tiles blended in with the background of fields and forests. The poverty of the past, which had had an organic connection to the land characterized by untamed gardens and cold, austere houses of stone and oxcarts of decaying wood and the natural waste and refuse that fertilized the soil, had been replaced by a poverty of comparative luxury, of building debris and abandoned equipment left in vacant lots: sheets of corrugated fiberglass, tractors and roof cisterns, rusted cement mixers and plastic ground cover, crates and containers of all sorts.

I continued up the street where I had walked every day of my childhood, where I had often imagined walking again, walking where I had walked the last time I saw her, feeling for a moment the fanciful hope of seeing her again, even though the house was no longer there. It was as if my childhood had been a piece of theater, and the set had been changed so another play could be performed with another cast. As I reached the top of Rúa do Olvido, I caught the fragrance of Porto Lúa's purple flowers growing somewhere on a stone wall or among the ruins of an old house. It was the first time I had smelled their scent in more than twenty-five years. So much had happened in that time, so much had come and gone, but the perfume of that theater had remained the same.

I decided to wait until the following day to return to Casa das Flores and instead entered the lane where I had sat beside the fountain thinking I might catch a glimpse of Laura before she left. It was still there, sheathed in newly cemented stone. Next to it were several picnic tables and a plastic rubbish cart marked Concello de Porto Lúa. I looked out over the lower slopes of Aracelo, blond with summer grain. Edenic light was breaking through the clouds and moving across the fields. I cupped my hands and drank the water from the fountain, pure from deep veins of granite, and then continued to Via Sagrada and up the hill to Nosa Señora do Mar. A high, unpainted cinder block wall separated the churchyard from Campo da Graza, which had been converted to a football pitch. Softening the harshness of the wall were tangles of morning glories and eglantine where a wren was singing to the dead lying in quiet slumber all around me.

Unlike the villages that stacked their departed in niches or *panales* of death, the people of Porto Lúa buried their dead in the ground. The grass in the yard was so deep and the bell heather and briars so thick that many of the stones were hidden from view, as if the bodies beneath them had been buried again, as if they could be forgotten more than once. I went first to the graves of my grandparents and father and the undisturbed plot beside him waiting for my mother. After a moment's reflection, I moved on to an untended corner of the yard clearing dead leaves and roots and earthy debris from the stones with the side of my shoe. Harry's marker was there inscribed with the words *Náufrago e Músico Estranxeiro* and nearby was a stone marked *Cotolay, Alcalde 1936* and three graves decorated with fresh flowers containing the mortal remains of María Carballo San Martín, María Carballo San Martín, and María Carballo San Martín. North winds had blown years of autumn leaves into deep piles along the base of the wall where they lay decomposing in damp shadows. The splendor of so many summers. So many leaves. So many faces. On the wall, written in faded black paint, were the words *Cando as bestas están nas súas tumbas o mundo está en paz.* What the message may have lacked in delicacy, it made up for in honesty.

The roof of Nosa Señora do Mar had been replaced in the recent past, but the tiles, patched with moss and lichens, had already begun to fade from a bright orange to a weathered ochre. Beneath the roof, however, nothing had changed. Once again, it was a scent that brought back so much, a combination of the odors of old wood, damp stone, and the smoke of beeswax candles. As I walked up the main aisle, my footsteps echoed like distant explosions. I entered the pew where my family used to sit and knelt down. The altar where Father Ithacio had defended himself against Aunt Fioxilda, where candlesticks had danced to the tune of the devil, where the painting of the Virxe da Cova had wept for General Molinero, was in every way consistent with my memories of it. I leaned back in the pew and felt the worn oak polished by generations of the faithful press against my spine. How often I had sought the relief of that bench when overcome by the fatigue of kneeling on summer mornings. Like a refugee exiled from the past, I sat for a little longer seeking sanctuary in the afternoon light that poured through the stained glass coloring the wood and stone with virginal blues and harvest yellows and watery roses—a premonition of timeless heaven instilled during infancy, which even today brings to mind a place where I have been but could not be.

My retreat from time proved temporary as the light moved across the floor of the church and touched the opposite wall. I wanted to see the school again, and because it wouldn't be open on Saturday, I hastened down Via Sagrada before it closed. Don Pedro Ruiz Bóveda y Varela Valcárcel, Ingeniero y Filántropo, Benefactor de la Humanidad had maintained his pose and lost nothing of his coyness. The walkway leading up to the door was bordered on both sides by a well-kept garden, and the original building had been sandblasted to reveal a freshness I had never known. On the south side of the building was a parking lot where an old house had been and on the north side a new annex, a modern block of cement already stained by the weather. María and I had stayed in touch for several years, but not for the last decade or so. However, I rightly assumed Ramón had told her I would be visiting, so she wasn't surprised when I knocked on the door of her office. I could still see the awkward girl I had grown up with in her aging face, as I'm sure she could see the boy in mine. We greeted each other warmly and spoke with relaxed familiarity as she showed me the renovations to the original building and the new annex that was built when the local population expanded. The rooms were equipped with the latest technology, and, like the hallways, seemed much smaller than I remembered them. I asked her who among our contemporaries was still around.

"Most are gone," she said. "Andrés is the mayor. Pilar is working at El Árbol."

"Where's Miguel?"

"In Barcelona. Working as a pharmaceutical representative."

"What about Facundo?"

"He's around. The last time I spoke with him, he was giving tours of Nosa Señora do Mar for a euro."

"I just came from there but didn't see him."

"Look for him in the plaza or the alameda."

"I'll go by later."

"I bought him a hearing aid, but he refuses to wear it."

"What about El Conde?"

"He died more than twenty years ago."

"What happened to the house?"

"It's gone. So is the garden. After he died, a wealthy developer from Málaga bought the land and divided it up into lots. Doña Esperanza and her husband Erasmo live in the gatehouse and have several children who went to school here. The oldest, the current conde, is a research physician in New York."

"His grandfather would be pleased."

"Harry's gone too. He died four years ago."

"I know. I saw his grave."

"Where are you staying?"

"At the *pensión* on the plaza."

"If Andrés knows you're here, he'll probably stop by. He has the manner of a politician now. Just like his father."

"That doesn't surprise me."

"He's made a handsome life for himself distributing public money to contractors and receiving kickbacks in return. It's an open secret. You saw the sidewalks in the new part of town? Almost as soon as they were down, they were torn up again so pipes could be laid, and then put in for a second or third time. Each time more money was spent, more money was skimmed."

"Is his father still alive?"

"He is, but he's living with a sister in Ferrol. He was declared incompetent when he hitched a pair of donkeys to his old Mercedes. It was either that or an animal cruelty charge."

I told her how pleased I was to see the school doing well and asked about the students. She said they had sent twelve to the universities in Santiago, Coruña, and Salamanca in the last graduating class.

"That's better than two."

"But there will never be another two like those two," she said laughing.

She accompanied me back past our old classrooms to the main entrance where we said goodbye. I told her we would have to stay in touch, as people do. She nodded her assent, as people do.

The streets in the historic district had filled with tourists and local residents going about their business. The sons of men who had worn black woolen jackets and black *boinas* were wearing track suits and canvas shoes or the football jerseys of teams that played hundreds of miles away. I wondered what I had in common with them. We were born and raised in the same place and spoke the same language. We knew the same buildings, the same weather, the same views of the sea and mountain. We shared the odors of eucalyptus and pine and low tides, but we saw the world so much differently.

Standing on the corner where Rúa dos Castiñeiros meets the plaza, an old man with a white beard was leaning over a trash bin. He was wearing a long black overcoat patched with what appeared to be sailcloth and baggy gray trousers that rode several inches above his ankles.

"Can you tell me where I can find the Tower of Names?" I

asked.

"They tore it down," he said, "to make room for the visitors."

"I'm looking for the stone of a man named Hermes."

"There is no stone with that name."

"Well, then, can you tell me where I can find a man named Facundo?"

He turned to look at me. His eyes were blue like the color of glacial ice and sparkled as he moved into the sunlight. Cataracts.

"Why do you care about him?"

"Don't you recognize me?"

"I thought you were someone else."

"I am someone else. It's me."

"He was a boy, but you're a man."

"I'm that boy."

"You've changed."

"I'm afraid we've all changed."

"People think I'm a beggar."

"People once thought the gods were beggars."

"I'm only a gravedigger who can no longer dig graves."

"María said you're giving tours of the church."

"That's right."

"Where are you living?"

"In Rosa's house in Rúa das Sombras."

"And Rosa?"

"She's gone."

"I'm sorry. And Mateo Mateo?"

"The government took him away and put him in a home."

"Do you have everything you need?"

"I have enough."

"Let me buy you dinner."

We went to one of the new bars in the historic district, but were asked to sit outside at the end of the terrace, so we walked up Rúa das Angustias to a neighborhood bar where workers in blue coveralls were exchanging stories over white *tazas* of Ribeiro.

In addition to cataracts, Facundo had a tic in a drooping right eyelid that caused people think he was winking at them. I suspect the deafness María had mentioned went back to the time he was struck by lightning. It was most noticeable when he laughed in response to a question he hadn't heard, which he often did, especially in the bar where there were competing voices. As he ate a meal of merluza and boiled potatoes, he expressed his concern over the number of cars in Porto Lúa and asked me what becomes of them when they wear out.

"They keep coming and coming. More and more every year. Where are they going to put them all? And all the containers and paper and boxes. Where will all the trash go?"

I said I thought his concerns were well-founded, but assured him there was no immediate crisis. He confessed he had kept some of the books he had borrowed from Mestre. I told him Mestre would have wanted him to have them. He had also, in his words, assumed the responsibility of taking care of the telescope, which had been left behind. At the end of dinner I offered to buy him a new pair of boots. He was reluctant to accept any "handouts," as he put it, but I explained that I had been in his debt all these years and wanted to repay him now that I had the chance. When he asked what he had done, I told him he had given me memories of childhood that would last the rest of my life.

In the new part of town was a recreational sports store with rows of running shoes and climbing boots on shelves in the window. Cutting an odd figure in his overcoat among the aisles of hiking and camping gear, Facundo examined the display of boots and tried on several pairs before settling on a brand known for its sturdiness and bright green stripes. He wore them out of the store walking awkwardly without his extension on the thick, lug soles carrying the box under his arm and expressing some concern about adding to the mountain of trash that was overwhelming the world. We parted in the plaza. He thanked me for the meal and boots and I thanked him for his wisdom and friendship.

Before retiring to the *pensión* for the night, I climbed the stairs to the alameda and sat on the same stone bench where I had sat with Laura. In the west the sky was an indistinct wall of bluish haze and cloud except for a narrow opening where pink light shone on distant towers of cumuli that glowed like citadels of heaven, as if revealed to mortals by mistake, a city of light bounded only by the limits of one's imagination, before fading like embers cooling. I recalled that night in my childhood when the moon shone through a wreath of bluish-white clouds that surrounded it like a baroque altarpiece as the rain fell in sheets before it. Above the murmur of the terraces and bars, the hum of traffic beyond the Deva, I could almost hear Harry playing his nocturne to the sea and sky, the prayer of a ghost in exile.

María was right. Andrés el Tercero, now known, as his father once was, as Don Andrés, was waiting for me in the sitting room of the *pensión* when I entered. He stood with a broad, but chastening, smile as if to ask, "now where have you been?" and extended his arms to embrace me. He was never a close friend, but after so many years, it was good to see him. I have to admit, with a degree of guilt, that I enjoyed the memories he evoked more than his company as his manner tended to swing back and forth between official and familiar, between inauthentic and something slightly less than authentic.

"We've heard all about your successes here and have been waiting for you to come back to visit," he said.

"Since my mother is in Santiago, I don't get back as much as I'd like."

"Many of our peers sold the homes and land they inherited

and moved to the city where they live in cramped and noisy quarters. I could understand that at one time, but, as you see, we have caught up with life in the city. I mean, in terms of creature comforts, but without the crime and exorbitant prices."

"You've done a good job, Andrés. The town appears prosperous and popular with tourists."

"What can I say? We do our best. It's a good life. A good place to raise children. The European Community has been throwing money at us to improve the roads and restore the old houses, so that helps. You saw the boat to Isla de los Torres, I assume? That was my idea. The foreigners bring a lot of money. Mostly Germans and Scandinavians pouring down from the cold blue north like the Swabians, Goths, and Normans of the past. They buy summer houses and wander around in their gardens half naked carrying geranium pots and handfuls of manure like lunatics. There are books for sale about the mountain and legends of the coast in every conceivable language. Even Chinese. Many of the young people you see have walked over the mountain from Santiago and some all the way from France on the *Camino*. Modern pilgrims with backpacks and walking sticks can be found tramping through back gardens in search of the Roman road. Schoolchildren climb the mountain with their teachers as we used to do with Mestre, but they can stay in one of the *albergues* where they have beds and running water. The Concello has put up signs with descriptions of the historical sites. Unfortunately, the increasing number of pilgrims means an increased number of cans and bottles and plastic bags in the groves of gods, and, as you can see, careless hikers and campers have started fires that have killed off many of the old-growth forests of oaks and pines. The traffic is another problem, but we're working on that. We put in the roundabout last year."

"Facundo is worried there are too many cars."

"He's become something of a nuisance. Several times I've caught him going down the street hitting the 'walk' buttons at all the pedestrian crossings. Traffic can back up for half a mile when he does that."

"I saw a prophet on the median directing traffic earlier today."

"That's Alberto. He's harmless. Reminds me of Cotolay."

"I thought the same thing."

"I'll leave you alone now. I've got to go home and get some sleep as we have contractors coming in tomorrow to see what we can do about restoring the old guild hall."

"Thanks for stopping by."

"I could have gone, you know. I could have left and been successful somewhere else. I thought about it and sometimes still wonder whether that would have been better, but I stayed behind because I could see the promise of the town and, at the risk of sounding immodest, I knew that I could make a difference. We had to bring Porto Lúa into the modern era. It hasn't been easy, but, God willing, we're getting it done."

I told him he deserved a lot of credit for all that he had done, and he thanked me.

María Teresa had given me the best room in the building. There were double doors that opened onto a balcony that overlooked the plaza. To the right were the blossoming camellias and palm trees of the alameda faintly illuminated by the late summer light. To the left was the port. I watched as the last excursion boat returned from Illa da Luz. At one time I knew the name of every barking dog in Porto Lúa, but now I was a stranger even to the people, although the stones in the streets and back lanes, the old houses that were still standing, the garden walls overgrown with honeysuckle were as familiar to me as they had ever been.

I woke just after three o'clock, and when I couldn't return to sleep, I got dressed and went for a walk along the quay. In the calm of the hour, I imagined nothing in the darkness had changed. I closed my eyes and filled my lungs with air infused with the odors of sea wrack and brine. Small waves rolled gently into the stone wharf from far across the night, from the realm of the dead where souls gather over the dark water like white blossoms. Overhead in the clearing sky, the moon was almost full, my only company apart from the traffic signals flashing in the empty streets across the river. I closed my eyes again, and I was back in my apartment in Madrid imagining myself in Porto Lúa.

We are each the creation of a particular place, of a particular people and the contingencies of a land and sky, of a local air. And yet when I returned to the place that had created me, it was gone. What made me who I am was buried beneath new pavement and apartment blocks. And within me. Where what grandmother had called my western soul lay hidden. Where the summer sky was sacred and sunlight still possessed a presence, a character, a kindness.

I went back to the *pensión* and slept until seven. After a light breakfast in the dining room, I checked out and left my bag in the car. I wasn't scheduled to meet Ramón for another two hours, so I walked along the northern coast to the sands of Dugium and on to Cathedral Rocks and Fervenza Areosa. Far from any building, any road, any people, the clouds, the sea, the sound of the surf, the plovers running on the mirroring sand were as they had always been. But the day, nevertheless, had a personality of its own, its own unique quality of light, something I rarely noticed in the city.

I sat on a granite point overlooking the windswept shore for nearly an hour and then returned to Porto Lúa on the path that came down behind Capela de Santa Lupa. As I walked through the historic district on my way to see Ramón, the morning sun was beginning to warm the stones of the narrow streets, and vendors were setting up their stalls in Rúa das

Sombras. In the plaza vans delivering fresh produce and *mariscos* and beer to nearby bars and restaurants created an obstructive labyrinth as they vied for space. After crossing the Deva, I turned into a new street that curved around the car park and reached as far as the cliffs that rise above the bay, opening the empty tracts to future construction. At the end of the street, the town had erected a metal sign that read *Museo* with an arrow pointing west toward Harry's valley. On the bramble path above the cliffs, I passed a group of sightseers, and among the remnants of the museum, I met another. The roof of the house had collapsed, and the interior was littered with soda cans, broken glass, plastic wrappers, tin foil, and condoms. The walls were charred from fires, and people had painted their names and graffiti on the stones. Fortunately, most of the sculptures were still intact, but some had come apart, blown by sea winds or toppled by vandals, and the walks and steps were overgrown with rock samphire.

The path from the museum to the estate of El Conde, which passed through fields of bracken and gorse and the stand of pines where Lobo's traveling community had camped, had been widened and plotted with small flags to be paved. New houses and apartments had already encroached on the gate-house where Doña Esperanza and Erasmo lived, and the wall that had enclosed the garden was essentially a ruin waiting to be demolished while the garden itself was overgrown with vines and volunteer shrubs and trees. The avenue of maples had become a park where children played and the elderly enjoyed the sun on a warm summer morning.

Ramón's office was located on the ground floor of an apartment building a block from the highway. Mounted on easels in the windows were architects' drawings and the floor plans of buildings that were under construction. After checking in at the front desk, I waited in a lounge surrounded by ficus trees and out-of-date magazines. Ramón appeared a few minutes later dressed in a loose gray suit without a tie, balding and slightly stooped from a bad back. He greeted me cordially, sized me up as any good businessman would, and invited me into his private office where several black and white photographs of Porto Lúa's past were hanging on the wall. An assistant brought in cups of coffee as we sat in deep leather chairs. I asked about Euxenia, and he related several anecdotes to illustrate her fondness for their grandchildren. As he was speaking, I couldn't help but recall the story of the entrapment that led to the birth of the father of those children. He asked about my mother, and I informed him of her pending move. Then we addressed the business at hand.

"What are your plans for the property?" I asked.

"I haven't decided yet. I'll either sell it as part of a larger tract including our land or build on it myself."

"And Casa das Flores?"

"Raze it," he said as a matter of fact. "No one wants to live in a cold, damp house. You know what I mean. You live in the city."

"Would there be any demand for it as a weekend cottage?"

"The restoration and modernization would cost more than it's worth. The land including the orchard and fields is the only valuable asset. It's true there's some nostalgia for the old houses—there are a few that have been fixed up for a weekend getaway—but people around here want heat in the winter and insulation and a roof that doesn't leak. They want modern appliances and a half dozen electrical outlets in every room."

"Of course."

"How old is the house?"

"Close to a hundred and fifty years."

"That's what I would have guessed by the stonework."

"If you keep the land, would you build houses or apartments?"

"I'd put up something like the apartments in Rúa do

Olvido. Two of those buildings are mine. There's a good view up there at the top of the street, and that makes the property more valuable."

"Until someone builds across the street."

"Let's get these papers signed so you can get on your way and I can get back to work."

"Busy on a Saturday?"

"Especially on a Saturday."

Ramón took a folder from a file cabinet and showed me where to sign on more than a dozen documents. I gave him the keys, but he told me to keep them and said there wasn't any reason to lock the house since there wouldn't be anything of value left, and they would soon be "clearing the site" as he put it.

"Will any of the trees be saved?"

"No. They'd just be in the way. María thought you might want to take some cuttings with you and left a few garden pots in the kitchen."

"Maybe I will."

"Take everything you want now because we'll start working next week."

"I'll walk through and see what's there."

"Here's a one-day permit for your car," he said, handing me an orange sheet of paper, "so you can drive up to the gate and load it with anything you want to keep."

"Is that it?"

"That's it."

We shook hands, and he led me through the office to the street.

"Give my best wishes to Euxenia," I said.

"And to your mother from me."

Rúa dos Loureiros had undergone significant improvements with grooved pavement, curbs, streetlights, and new sidewalks in anticipation of the construction that was coming.

Where the muddy path to Campo da Graza had been was a metal gate. Hanging over it was a sign in the shape of a crescent moon that read *Campo de Fútbol Porto Lúa*. Below it in smaller letters was another: *Liga Fútbol de la Costa*. There were already two apartment buildings on the street, but they were down the slope from our house and neither obstructed the view. The ground floor of one was still bricked up, while the other housed a supermarket, a beauty supply store, and a café. Casa das Flores was just another neglected property on the street. One of the palm trees was dead, and the yard was overgrown with grass and pockets of bracken and heather. There was even a patch of gorse where the fig tree had been. On the north side of the house, someone had covered the entire wall with cement to prevent leaks in the mortar. It was now stained green and brown with algae. The old power line to the house was gone, but the white ceramic plugs remained embedded in the mortar beneath the eaves.

I opened the gate and walked to the front door. The wooden casements of the windows, whose blue paint had once protected us against witches, had been replaced by neatly fitted aluminum frames. The windows were shuttered, but I could still sense the abandonment within. Although it was the same structure built of the same stones that had sheltered me during my childhood, it appeared to be more primitive than I had remembered it. Two of the blue and white tiles naming the house were missing, leaving those that remained to read, Casa d s Flo es. The hinges on the front door were rusted and had bent under its weight, so I had to lift it up to enter and noticed soft clumps of meal-like splinters on the threshold where the bottom edge had deteriorated from dampness and woodworms.

As I stood in the doorway, the world behind me seemed to vanish. Crossing the threshold into a vacant shell of decay, I entered a dream of lost time. A century and a half. Of life. Of family. The sweet smell of suet from decades of fire and the scent of old wood, like the aromatic trees of the tropics, brought back the nights when I had climbed the stairs with my mother, when I had lain in bed listening to Aunt Fioxilda, when I had watched the stars rising behind the mountain from my window. As I looked around at the stones mortared into place and the damp plaster and the wooden beams, I thought of the family house at Lonxe and how I had witnessed its decline over the years. It would now be nothing more than a rubble of stones covered with ivy. The demise of Casa das Flores would occur more quickly. The stones that had protected me from Atlantic gales and freezing nights, that had cooled my room on summer days, would soon be hauled off and dumped in the sea or used in a landfill.

Tied together by their laces, grandmother's boots hung from a nail just inside the door to the stable. The old cart-wheels were still there and the lanterns and saws and scythes under the same undisturbed dust of the past and the layer added by a quarter century. Catching a beam of sunlight passing through the gap between the door and its frame, a strand of gossamer loosened by my entrance danced sinuously like a crystalline snake swimming through the light, floating beneath the ceiling before disappearing into the shadows.

The kitchen where my family had cooked and shared our meals for generations was smaller than I had remembered it. There was barely room for a table and chairs beside the window, and now the space between the table and stove was crowded with plastic crates, buckets, and forgotten bags of fertilizer gnawed by mice whose droppings littered the floor and whose nests filled niches and corners with straw and newsprint. The utensils were gone and someone had salvaged the brass handles and knobs from the stove. Although its metal frame remained, the small doors in front and the metal plates that had covered the openings over the fire had also been removed for what little they were worth. There were still ashes in the hearth where mother had carefully covered the embers every night before going to bed and a stack of kindling in the storage space beneath the counter where I used to leave what I had gathered from the edge of Caos. I examined a box on the table containing several rusty tools and hinges, a doorknob, and a padlock. Then, as I turned around, I saw the calendar with the photograph of the fishing boats hanging on the wall. Its once bright colors had faded to a pale blue monochrome, and it was limp from the dampness and covered with a thin veneer of mildew, but despite its condition, I put it on the table to remind myself to take it with me when I left the house. It was easier to take a calendar than the view from the window of my bedroom or the quality of sunlight over the fields or the scent of orange blossoms in the orchard.

I stood beside the table in the glow of sunlight leaking in around the shutters looking at the room as it was and, at the same time, remembering it as it had been years earlier when I had sat here thinking about my future in vaguely imagined dreams, as yet unaware of my life beyond Porto Lúa, of the distant places where I would live, of exile from the home I would not know again until it was gone. The mortar between the stones, the contours and shapes of the stones, and the stains in the plaster belonged to a present decades in the past yet vivid before me. After twenty-seven years, I still knew it all as well as I knew the features of my own hand. Memories un-prompted by sight or smell or sound came at random the way thoughts come when I try to think of nothing. The golden re-flection of the last rays of a winter sun on the windows, the dim light of the bulb above my bed, the smell of coffee as I woke beneath warm blankets, summer mornings, the taste of well water, the buzz of wasps in the orchard's rotting windfall.

I climbed the stairs that I had climbed so many times be-fore, instinctively sensing the irregular height of each, stepping lightly as the wood, saturated by the sunless damp, was so soft I could feel the rot giving way beneath my feet. To avoid falling through, I straddled the stairs with my right foot against the right wall and my left against the left much as I had done during my adolescence when, coming home late at night, I had attempted to outwit the creaking pine. The mirror and wooden tables in the hallway were gone, and a pane of glass was broken in the window at the top of the stairs. I entered my grandparents' room first and opened a door to the balcony. This was the last time I would stand where I had stood so often looking over the bay to Illa da Luz and the far horizon of the sea. I took it all in for a moment, the freedom one rarely feels in the city, and let the house breathe one more time before leaving it to its fate. The two single beds and their straw mattresses were the only pieces of furniture in the room. One was the bed where grandmother had feigned her death and later died. The other shared my witness to the death of grandfather. Each was stained by nights of illness and incontinence, sweat and tears. Before leaving the room, I checked one of the hives in the wall. It was empty except for the bodies of a few dead bees that stirred when I opened the door, lifted by a draft as if they were made of paper.

The door to Aunt Fioxilda's room was stuck. I pressed my shoulder against it and shoved it open breaking off a sliver of the jamb as I did—violating the sanctuary of her struggles with evil, a sanctuary blessed and preserved by her companion angels. In the silence it was hard to believe what had once taken place in that room. The first thing I looked for were the crosses on the wall where she had tallied her victories. They were there in a neat row as clear as if they had been cut the day before. When I sat on the bed where I had learned to read, the mattress exhaled a musty air trapped for years. I leaned over and opened the bottom doors of the cabinet beside the bed and found a chamber pot, a snuff box containing the dried herbs she had called "comestibles of the soul," and a cache of letters. The folded sheets were yellow and brittle and wrapped in a white ribbon that frayed along the edges as I tugged gently at the bow. I unfolded the first and read, "*Querida Amor.*" Out of respect for her privacy, I stopped reading. I asked myself whether I should leave them to be buried in the rubble or burn them in the hearth so they might find her in her other world. A third option was to take them with me. I chose the third.

There was nothing in my parents' room, so I moved on to my own. The laurel cross was still hanging from a nail above the door. The dresser was in the corner, and the bed was against the wall where it had always been. Two boxes were on the floor beside it. In the first I found the photograph of my great-grandparents that had hung in the hall, the telegram grandfather had sent from Havana, the antique mirror, two vases, and the black scarf grandmother had placed over the clock. I don't know why such relics of family history had been left behind, but assumed their abandonment was due to indifference rather than haste or forgetfulness. The second box contained memorabilia of my childhood: ribbons I had won in school, several report cards, exercise books from my classes, a card with the responses to the Latin Mass, and the prayer book I had received at my First Communion. In a smaller box was a dried seahorse grandfather had given me, and in a tobacco tin, the horseman coin Uncle Teo had brought from his journeys and the Roman medallion from the house at Lonxe. I put both in my wallet. At the bottom of the box, lying among dusty fragments of its ashen leaves and washed-out crimson petals, was the rose I had retrieved from grandmother's grave. There too, on folded sheets of brown paper, were the hieroglyphs that contained the tales of grandmother. A dead spider and the dusty pupae of dead moths fell from the pages as I unfolded them.

With a mixture of curiosity and nostalgia, I attempted to

decipher the first words I had written, if they could be called words, and was able to piece together the stories of the frozen waterfall, of grandmother barring General Molinero from Nosa Señora do Mar, and of Fidelio's encounter with the devil. The contexts of the pictures helped to guide me when one of them eluded comprehension, or perhaps I should say "recognition," for the experience was not so much one of reading as it was of re-imagining—not just the events of the story, but the moments of that life.

In the same box I found the exercise book where I had translated the stories into Galician. Returning to my early attempts to write in the language of my birth affected me as much as the discovery of the hieroglyphs. Each word was like the threshold of the house, a doorway into dreams and memories, like summer lands, where lifelong bonds between sounds and forms, myself and others, came into being. Something akin to love, something deep in the heart, was still evoked by words like *madressilva* and *volvoreta* where those who are gone have remained, where I still hear the songs Aunt Fioxilda sang to me. Words that contain the flowers outside my window, the autumn fruits of the orchard, the blue of the blackbird's eggs. Words spoken in my mother's arms, in the colorful light of stained glass, in shimmering fields of freshening dawns, and in that modest room where I heard them again as when I heard them first, reviving the dreams of all that language could be, all that it could contain, before the sky of my imagination was closed by the clouds of habit.

Grandmother had told me I would be her witness in the world. Father had told me to remember everything because one day I would be the only person who did. The people who had told me their stories were gone, but they had remained in their words. Words that I remembered. Words that would be gone when I too was gone. I felt that I owed something to these people and the places and the ways of life that were disappearing with every year that passed. I decided to take the hieroglyphs and the exercise book back to Madrid and transcribe them in clear, orderly prose and continue to write down what I could remember. Just as a house provides a place to store the objects one collects in life, writing provides a place to store the thoughts, the observations, and the memories of a life. Perhaps, too, I could find something like the freedom of the sea and sky that I had known as a child in the freedom to live in my own creation, by my own colors and light, the freedom to ignore the demands of others, the compromises of social bonds, and material imperatives. Even the freedom to forget the weight of years on my back.

My thoughts were interrupted when I heard footsteps on the staircase and a woman's voice softly call my name. I walked down the hall expecting to see an old friend or neighbor coming up the stairs, but no one was there. I called out, but there was no response. I began to doubt what I had heard. And yet I had heard it. Clearly. My name. It was not my imagination. I stood quietly for several minutes wondering what had happened. Had I misinterpreted a sound from outside? No. I had heard my name called as if someone had been on the stairs. While I was standing there, I noticed the distinctive odor of the black tobacco that grandfather used to smoke. I searched each room on the second floor. I looked out the windows at both ends of the hall. Then I went downstairs and checked every corner of the kitchen and stable. No one was there. I walked around the house. No one was in the yard. As I went back upstairs, I could feel a coldness descend over my arms and the back of my neck as I realized the voice I had heard was my grandmother's. Standing in the doorway of her room, I called to her the way I had called to the voices of my ancestors many years before in the house at Lonxe do Sol.

"I'm back," I said. "I know you've waited a long time for me to return. I'm sorry. I've come to say goodbye. Mother sold the house to Ramón, and he's going to tear it down. I live in Madrid now, and she lives in Santiago, and we can no longer keep it. He will probably cut down the orchard too. And sometime soon, I suspect, he or someone else will build an apartment building here. You will be disturbed for a while, but then families will move in, and children will once again play where I'm standing. Not the children of the children of the children you knew, but strangers. These days Porto Lúa is full of strangers who make a stranger of me, and the people I once knew are no longer the same. Nor the houses. Nor the streets. I waited too long to come home. I went off to make more of myself, but lost myself, lost the connections that could lead me back to myself, and now I am as far from myself as I am from the people I once knew. I'm sorry it has taken me so long to thank you for everything you did for me. I wish I could still be the child I was with you. Do you remember when you made the shroud of memories to dress your soul, and we walked through the streets of Porto Lúa together? The town has changed in many ways since then, but I have kept your shroud. I will be your witness.

"I have to leave now. This is the last time I'll be able to visit you and the ghosts who linger in the shadows, who once welcomed me into the world. All of this, like you, has become a memory, and like every memory, even memories of ourselves, it will change without seeming to change, but it will last beyond the mounds of rubble and dust, beyond the rotting woodwork, beyond the stones destined for roads and jetties."

I closed the door to the balcony. Even though the house would soon be gone, I couldn't abandon it to the elements. The boxes containing the treasures of my childhood had been weakened by the dampness, so I went to the car and brought back a plastic bin and carefully placed the letters, the fragile rose, the photograph, the telegram, the scarf, the school prizes and report cards, the hieroglyphs and exercise book, and the calendar inside it and carried it back to the car. I also retrieved grandmother's boots and several pieces of the Pickman china we had used during my childhood. They were broken and chipped, and I had no practical use for them, but couldn't leave them. We hold on to broken dishes we are never going to use again or an old shirt we are never going to wear again or a box of books we are never going to read again because they become the only witnesses to what is irretrievable in our lives. I closed the front door for the last time and walked around to the back of the house. The gardens had gone wild and the barn hadn't been used in years. I was glad to see the chestnut tree where grandfather used to smoke was still there. So were the granite post where we bled our pigs and the shallow depression in the grass where we buried Romeo. Most of the flowers that had given the house its name had died, and the yard was over-grown with weeds and vines, beautiful in their own right but not the flowers I had known. Despite the warm wind stirring the trees in the orchard, the cold stones of the house and walls retained a lichenous air reminding me of the long months of winter rains and excremental mud. I pressed my cheek against the side of the house and took the air deep into my lungs. Before leaving, I plucked a handful of blackberries that had ripened early and savored the sweetness of our land with each that I ate. I got in the car without looking back and told myself it is better that the house is destroyed because to see it inhabited by another family would be like seeing a first love in the arms of a stranger.

On the Monday after my return from Porto Lúa, I helped mother move to her room at the assisted living center in Fontiñas. Everything went smoothly, and she was happy to find an old acquaintance down the hall on her floor. A member of the staff gave us a tour of the building and answered our questions about the dining room and laundry service. Stressing the importance of staying active, she highlighted the regular exercise classes and program of events and the van that took residents to Santa María de Belvís for Mass on Sundays. After we signed the contract in the business office, mother went back to her room to unpack, and I went out to buy new towels, a shower curtain, and a floor mat as well as personal items and toiletries. As soon as I returned, she sent me out again to buy cleaning supplies including a new mop and bucket. Even though the apartment was spotless, to her way of thinking, nothing is clean if she hasn't cleaned it herself.

In the afternoon, the second-hand dealer from Padrón came by for the rest of the furniture. I went through the rooms and closets one more time to make sure we hadn't left anything behind, locked the door, and took the keys down to the real estate agent in San Roque. Then I checked in to the Hotel Costa Vella where I had reserved a room for my final night in Santiago. I stretched out on the bed feeling a mixture of relief and anxiety. Relief in knowing that mother would not be alone if she had another accident or any issues with her health.

Anxiety because the move to an unfamiliar place marked a watershed in the final stage of her life. Tired from the move as well as from the weekend trip to Porto Lúa, I fell asleep for an hour and then got up and went for a walk through the Acibechería and Antealtares to Modus where I stopped for a drink.

My plan was to walk through the old part of the city for an hour or two and then decide on a place to have an evening meal before retiring to the hotel. When I left the bar, I turned into Rúa do Preguntoiro and continued down the slope past the stationer's shop and pharmacy at the top of Rúa da Caldeirería. It was the time of the evening when the streets are crowded with shoppers and strollers, and the Caldeirería, one of the main pedestrian thoroughfares in the city, is among the most congested, especially where it narrows to a width of little more than the outstretched arms of a man. With no clear separation, one current of humanity moves up the street while the other moves down, the flow interrupted by those who stop, like stones in a stream, to greet an acquaintance or by children running freely with no regard for the bodies flowing past them. Jostled and jostling, following the path carved by one person, then another, I made my way down the street.

In the narrow strip of sky overhead, swallows flitted back and forth, and in the shadows of the street before me, heads bobbed like swells on the open sea. Carried along by the tide, I passed gift shops and dress shops, a jewelry store and bakery, modern, brightly lit businesses behind wide windows set in dark façades of granite weather-stained like stones in nature. And then I saw her. In the light where the Caldeirería opens to Praza da Fonte Seca. A woman with striking red hair. She was well ahead of me, walking quickly, moving deftly, past the people in her path, so quickly I could not keep up. My heart was pounding, and I could barely catch my breath as I pushed through the crowd as courteously as the urgency of my feelings would allow. It was the same urgency I had felt that Sunday after Mass when, holding her missal in my hand, I had desperately tried to reach her through the crowd of people exiting Nosa Señora do Mar.

I called her name and heard it echo in the street. There was no response. I called again. Still no response. As the distance between us grew, I left the Caldeirería to take a more circuitous but less crowded route past the church of Santa Salomé and down Rúa Nova hoping to find her emerging at Cantón do Toural, but when I cut back to Rúa das Orfas, she did not appear. She must have entered a store or turned into Rúa do Cardeal Payá. Like an impetuous schoolboy, I hurried through the oncoming crowd looking into the windows and doorways of shops, but I couldn't find her anywhere. I went back down Rúa das Orfas and crossed Rúa da Senra to check the parking lot in Praza de Galicia and then circled through the same streets several more times. When I could think of nowhere else to look, I sat on the edge of the arcade in Rúa Nova reluctantly conceding defeat.

I was surprised by the intensity of my feelings. That she still meant so much to me. After thirty-five years. Years of struggle and success, of aging and illness, the deaths of loved ones. New cities, new homes, new faces. Beneath it all were the same feelings. The same recognition. As if something in my blood was incomplete without her. Something no one else could ever satisfy. I had become the person I was by knowing her. And by losing her. And now it seemed I could repair that loss by seeing her again and sharing a past that only we could share. If only for a day or an hour.

As the streets grew dark in the long twilight, the buildings became silhouettes against a golden sky. With a renewed sense of loss, I walked the *rúas* of the old city. As I did, the excitement of the evening faded into sober reflection. I had failed to consider how she might feel about seeing me again. Or the life she had now. Whether she was married. Whether she had children. She was a middle-aged woman, perhaps a grand-mother. Still, I couldn't help but wonder if she ever thought about those summers in Porto Lúa, the days we spent on the mountain, the night lying beside each other in the house at Lonxe do Sol. I returned to the hotel sometime after midnight but couldn't sleep. I kept imagining the life we might have led. Could we have sustained the freshness of youth or would we have grown more predictable with each year, living by habit, raising children by habit, growing old by habit, and dying by habit? Would we have succumbed to the demands of life that render people lifeless?

After lying in the darkness for several hours, I got dressed and went for another walk. If I could tire myself out, I might be able to get at least a little sleep before the long drive back to Madrid. Rather than retrace my steps through the city, I de-cided that climbing Mount Pedroso would be a more effective way of exhausting myself, and so I set out down the slope be-side the hotel in semi-darkness. A delivery van passed in front of Convento de San Francisco, but I saw no one else until I reached the road to Portomouro where a few vehicles were coming in from the countryside with fresh produce or fish from the coast. I crossed the bridge over the Sarela and con-tinued up the incline on the other side of the stream. After a few hundred yards, the neighborhood becomes more rural, and behind the gray and white houses that line the streets are fields and hedgerows where the thin soil and abundant rain yield small gardens of kale and corn. By the time I reached Rúa das Casas Novas, the streetlights were going off, and a dull pink light had spread over the fields from clouds lit by a sun still below the horizon. Above the park at the top of Santo Ig-nacio do Monte, the gradient steepens, but the forestry lanes that cross back and forth along the contours of the mountain make the ascent easier. As the sky brightened, the pine seed-lings and ferns and open tracts of gorse and heather glistened with dew wrung from the damp chill of night. By the time I reached the summit, the sun was rising over the haze that floated above the city. The wide valley of woods and farms on the western side of the ridge still lay in blue shadow in contrast to the early light shining on the mountains farther to the west. Beyond them, above a mantle of ocean clouds, the highest peaks of Aracelo glowed in the amber rays of the warming sun.

I was still not tired enough to sleep, so after a light breakfast at a café in Rúa do Vilar, I stopped by the Locutorio de Telefónica in El Franco where I looked for Laura's name in the Santiago directory. When I couldn't find it, I tried several other directories, but without success, and assumed her number was listed under her husband's name. Then I looked up her father, but there wasn't a listing for him either, and I had forgotten her mother's second surname. I went back to the hotel and checked out. Before leaving Santiago, I paid a visit to the assisted living facility to see how mother was doing after her first night and say goodbye. I planned to be back in Madrid by late afternoon and hoped to go to bed early to catch up on my sleep, but when I reached the main highway leading south, I changed my mind and turned west onto the Autoestrada do Atlántico and then took the road to Muros.

Another family was living in the house in Rúa Real. The woman I spoke with said they had lived there for ten years but knew none of the previous residents. I asked several shopkeepers around the corner in Rúa Ancha if they remembered Laura's family, but none of them did. When I asked the landlord in a bar down the street the same question, he told me to talk to an old man sitting alone in the corner. From him I learned the family had moved to Vigo thirty-five years earlier. He had been their neighbor and known her father well. I asked him if there were any relatives of the family still living in Muros, and he told me Laura's aunt, the sister of her mother, lived in Miraflores, a short walk up the hillside.

"You can't miss the house," he said. "It's three stories high and stands on a lot ten feet wide in a bend in the road. There's a terrace on the top floor over the front door. Tell her Pelagio sent you. I'm the only one in Muros."

The house was easy to find from his description, and Laura's aunt was home, but she was blind and partially deaf, so I could only communicate with her through a caretaker. I presented myself as a friend from Porto Lúa who had lost touch with the family over the years. Rather than question me, she said she had been expecting me because of a dream she had had the previous night. When I told her I was hoping to visit them sometime, she confirmed the family had moved to Tirán, a village across the *ría* from Vigo near Moaña, but the caretaker wasn't able to locate the address. All she knew was that it was near a cemetery by the sea. That was enough.

I arrived in Moaña in a little under an hour and a half and followed a narrow road along the coast where banks of flowers crested garden walls like waves pouring over granite jetties. The oranges and lemons of hillside orchards were ripening in the midday sun, and purple hydrangeas crowded the porches of white cottages, all within sight of the sea, all under a brilliant sky, all in the light of paradise. A half mile west of the port, I caught sight of the bell tower of a church on a bluff just above the reach of high tide. By chance, an elderly priest was coming up the lane that led down to it. I stopped and leaned out the window to ask if there was a cemetery nearby. "Beside the church," he said. Then I asked if he recognized Laura's family name. He said he did and offered to take me to the house, which was about three hundred yards up the hillside. The lane was too narrow for me to park, so I left the car on an intersecting street, and together we continued up the slope until we came to a modest, white-washed granite house on the left facing the *ría*. Father opened a small gate set between a pair of granite posts, and we entered a yard that was overgrown with fennel and bracken. The windows were un-shuttered, but it was too dark inside to see anything. He knocked on the door, then stepped back and looked at me as we waited.

"*Quen?*"

"*Padre.*"

"*Quen?*"

"*Padre González*," the priest shouted through the door. "*E un señor de Porto Lúa.*"

The woman opened the door slowly as if afraid to let the darkness escape. Her hair, though mostly gray, retained a stubborn tint of red, and she had Laura's green eyes.

"*Que?*"

"This gentleman would like to speak with you."

Shielding her eyes with her hand, she inspected me impassively.

"*Que?*"

"I'm a friend of Laura's."

"Of Laura's?"

"From Porto Lúa."

At these words, her expression softened, and she invited me in. I thanked Father González who excused himself and returned to his work.

"You've come from Porto Lúa?"

"From Santiago. My mother is there now. She had a fall, and I came up from Madrid to help her move to a home for the elderly. On Saturday I was in Porto Lúa to sell our house."

"Laura's grandmother lived in Porto Lúa."

"Yes."

"Did you know her?"

"My grandmother knew her."

"Your grandmother."

"In the market."

"Of course."

"Is Laura here in Tirán?"

"Laura?"

"Yes."

"She's with her father."

"Will they be back soon?"

"*Ela está morto, meu fillo.*"

She pulled a chair out from the dining table.

"Sit down."

"I didn't know," I said. "I'm sorry."

"It was many years ago."

"The last time she wrote, she was in Madrid."

"She went there when the doctors in Santiago couldn't help her."

"I didn't know she was ill."

"She had a tumor. They said she was getting better, so we allowed her to visit her grandmother. We thought it would be good for her. Then she got worse and was sick again. She was very ill, but insisted on going back the next summer for a visit. She wanted to go so badly. She was so happy there. That's all she wanted. All she ever asked for. To go back to Porto Lúa. Shortly after she arrived, her condition worsened. She left us that October."

The old woman looked across the room as if there was an answer somewhere waiting to be discovered.

"So you're the boy from Porto Lúa."

"Yes."

"Well."

Her expression revealed a mixture of weariness and resignation that only country people seem to feel. We sat in silence for a moment, two strangers united by our bond to one who was gone. At length, she rose and went to the kitchen to make a pot of coffee.

Though it was a different house, the objects that surrounded me were those that had surrounded Laura in her childhood and still contained something of her presence. An embroidered tablecloth. A vase with fresh flowers in the center of the table. A bowl of fruit and ceramics from Sargadelos on the sideboard. And on the wall above them the reproduction of a painting of an old house with cypress trees. When Laura's mother returned, she set a cup and saucer on the table beside me and sat on the opposite side of the corner, close enough to pour my coffee.

"With milk?"

"Yes. Thank you."

"Those summers were the happiest days of her life. She was a good child. A mother couldn't ask for a better child. She wasn't for this world."

Almost as soon as she had poured the coffee, she excused herself and went to another room, returning with a small wooden chest. I recognized the two colored bottles containing perfume, the necklace I had given Laura, and the photograph taken by Señor Morcín. She opened the jewelry box the necklace had come in and took out a pink granite stone, the same stone I had placed in a warm hand thirty-five years earlier.

"Do you know why she would have kept this?"

"It's something I gave her."

She conveyed her puzzlement with a silence meant to elicit some explanation.

"To remind her of Mount Aracelo," I said. "I found it in a forest on the mountain."

"She carried it with her wherever she went, and we never knew why."

She picked up the necklace.

"And you gave her this."

"Yes."

"And this photograph," she asked, "is of you and Laura?"

"Yes."

"You should take it," she said.

"I have another."

"Then take the necklace."

"I couldn't do that."

"Then the stone. Take the stone. You should have something of hers."

"I have her letters and her copy of *Don Quixote*."

"Take the stone too. She would want you to have it."

I considered telling her about Illa da Luz and the story of Trezenzonio and of our days on the mountain and the house no one ever sees twice and how we had laughed rolling down the white sands of Fervenza Areosa. But I didn't. I had already disturbed her peace with my presence and the memories I had brought back. I asked her where Laura had been laid to rest.

"Down the road in the cemetery by the sea."

I thanked her and left her standing on the front steps. As I shut the gate, I looked back to wave, but she had already returned to her thoughts and was gazing into the light reflecting off the *ría*. When I reached the lane where I had met Father Gonzalez, I followed it down to the small Romanesque church I had seen earlier and walked around to the back of the building where I entered the narrow yard through a metal gate in a granite wall. The niches are stacked four or five high in tightly packed rows, and many are in a state of moldering disrepair, undone by the moisture and salt that creep into the stone and mortar. They are distinguishing from one another by the colors and qualities of their cover stones and the glass panels that protect them. The yard is so small that I was able to find the vault containing Laura's family in a matter of minutes. Engraved on the granite square covering her niche are her name, the dates of her birth and death, the letters "D.E.P.," and a religious inscription. A conventional testament that tells the rare passerby nothing of her life. Surrounding her niche are those of her father and other relatives, presumably her grandparents, uncles, and aunts. A blank stone marks the niche reserved for her mother. By their dates, the deaths of those who lie around her, the seafarers and farmers, seemed natural, but I felt the injustice of Laura's death and the near anonymity of her tomb and the inability of the simple words cut in stone to recall her presence in the world.

I sat on the ground beside her. It was the first time we had been together since her last night in Porto Lúa. We who had walked along the shore of Dugium imagining Roman ships as breakers crashed over the sand. Her red hair illuminated by the sun. In darkness now. Seen only in the light of memory. Soon only mine. The laughter in her eyes. Her narrow shoulders. Now things of the earth. Everything she heard, everything she saw, everything she touched, she knew she was hearing, seeing, touching, for the last time. The joy she took in the song of the lark. Those of us still in the sunlight are merely survivors. Inexplicably. Perhaps unfairly. For a time. And yet what good is life if we can't share it with those we love?

When I heard the latch on the gate, I stood up and touched her stone to say goodbye. Father González had entered the yard carrying a basket of oranges he had picked from a tree growing beside the wall.

"Take as many as you like," he said.

"Just a few. Thanks."

"The best oranges grow in consecrated ground."

"I believe you."

"I never knew her."

"I've never known anyone else like her."

"A tragedy in one so young."

"Yes."

"You'll have to come back to see her again."

"I will."

Before the journey home, I stopped at a café in Moaña for lunch. To enjoy the breeze coming off the sea, I sat outside under an awning that was too short to offer much protection from the sun that shone like a silent explosion in the cloudless sky, searing the plane trees along the promenade and blinding with incandescence the hills across the bay where the water's edge was jeweled with sparkling light. An old man lay sleeping in the shadow of a passageway next to the bar. He was emaciated, covered with sores, and probably drunk. But despite the abuses to his body, he was alive. While Laura was not. If the purpose of nature is to produce life, why would it take one so young and full of life, why, after millions of years perfecting its methods, would it fail with her?

I had blamed Laura for leaving, never imagining what she must have felt knowing she would never return and couldn't tell me why. She had promised to keep the photograph taken by Señor Morcín, and she had kept her promise. But she had done more than that. For the first time I realized I had not been alone in my life. By giving me those final days, she had given me everything she had. Without knowing whether I would ever know.

I had promises to keep as well. To Laura, to my grandmother, to Mestre. And to myself. From Moaña, the shortest route to Madrid is south through the suburbs of Vigo to O Porriño and then east to Ourense. I went north. In an hour and a half, I was back in Muros, rounding the coast at Monte Louro and arriving in Porto Lúa late in the afternoon. I parked in the new lot by the bus station and went to the recreational sports store where I bought a backpack, a pair of boots, and one hundred feet of climbing rope. I stowed the gear in the trunk of my car and returned to María Teresa's *pensión* where I was able to get the same room I'd had on Friday night. I walked around the old part of town until it grew dark, then ate an evening meal at O Galo and went to bed.

The next morning I stopped by El Árbol supermarket in Rúa dos Castiñeiros and bought two large bottles of mineral water, a couple of golden apples to go with my oranges, two hundred grams of cheese, and a round loaf of bread with a knob on top. Grandfather's favorite. The cashier was a stout woman with a large bosom and stringy hair wearing a bright green apron. Although María had told me Pilar was working at the store, I failed to recognize her until she recognized me. Word of my previous visit had spread. She asked if I was on vacation. I told her I had come back to sell the house. Most of our classmates had moved away, she said, but some returned in the summer to visit their families. I said it was good to see her again and assured her I would stop by on my next visit. When I was back on the street, I tried to reconcile the image of the woman in the store with the girl who had danced around the campfire of Lobo's itinerant band and caused her family so much grief when she disappeared with the group.

I ordered a tortilla from O Galo and returned to the car where I took a tarp and blanket from the trunk and stowed them in the backpack along with the food and water I had just purchased. I wrapped Aunt Fioxilda's letters in a plastic bag to protect them and carefully placed them in an inner pouch. Then I secured grandmother's boots to a strap. When I had everything I needed, I slipped the pack over my shoulders, locked the car, and crossed back over the Deva. To ensure pilgrims on their way to Mar das Almas passed his wife's store rather than the other side of the plaza, Don Andres had painted arrows on the paving stones indicating where the Roman road had gone from Rúa das Angustias to the bridge, and in the years since, neither time nor man had removed them. At the bottom of the street were two information boards covered in plastic misted by the morning dampness that related the history of the road and many of the beliefs of the people who had lived on the mountain with color drawings of the altars and Roman soldiers wearing helmets and carrying spears.

The house of Wilfreda was now a barn with a bright zinc roof as incongruous among the abandoned houses and sheds of Rúa das Angustias as a silver plate in a field of mud. New cement laid over the original cart path had extended the street a hundred yards up the slope. Beyond that, where the lane entered the forest of Caos, it had been widened and paved with gravel for the benefit of tourists and pilgrims. In the shadows of oak and chestnut trees, heavy pads of moss sat on ancient walls, thickly piled like miniature green hills among plains of gray stone, while along the margins of the lane sprang an abundance of wildflowers, mostly foxglove, fennel, and honeysuckle. I stopped for a moment to pick the scented purple flowers that reminded me of Mestre and look back over the sea where the crest of a distant fog bank appeared like a snow-capped range of mountains.

In a millpond above the Deva, a stork stabbed the surface of the water and came up clamping a frog in its beak. Stepping shyly, it looked around as if bewildered by this means of living. Through the trees I could hear the bells of Nosa Señora do Mar ringing the noon Angelus and thought of Laura. *Que os amores xa fuxiron, As soidades viñeron.* This was my first trip up the mountain since I had climbed it with her. The vegetation along the road had changed so much that I missed the path to the tree of evil until I went back and located the streambed beside it. Where pines had once grown, eucalyptus trees had taken over, like enormous weeds, desiccating the earth and robbing the soil of its nutrients. Strips of bark and small scythes of green and brown leaves covered the ground where there had once been brambles and ferns. The tree beside the spring was gone, but there were two rags tied to a eucalyptus sapling near the place where it had been. On the way back to the road, I saw a blue and gold macaw and wondered if it was one of the original birds of Galicia's New World Zoo or its offspring thriving on Old World seeds and berries.

As the shadows of clouds moved eastward over the mountain, swaths of sunlight passed across the canopy of the forest.

In the cooler air of the higher elevations, a few early leaves were beginning to fall. Harbingers of autumn. I thought back to the seasons of my childhood. The barren trees and icy fogs of winter. The blossoms of wild cherries covering cold stones in the spring. The midsummer windrows of hay on the lower slopes. And on autumn days, the approach of darkening clouds and the orange and yellow leaves falling through the forest like the souls of the dead in Virgil and Dante.

On my first trip up the mountain, I saw its highest peaks as the turrets of ruined castles in a fabled city forgotten by time. *Fortis imaginatio generat casum.* We make the world in our imaginations, but over the years, my imagination, the disposition of a young heart, had faded, and my world was too often reduced to surfaces of fact. Those moments when the spirit is lifted by a memory or sudden insight were increasingly rare, and Mestre's comment likening his heart to a dry leather purse effectively captured how I felt.

Early in the afternoon I began to pass hikers and pilgrims who had spent the night on the mountain before the final stage of their journey to the sea. They were equipped with the latest raingear and packs and boots and hats and sunscreen and dark glasses. I doubt any mistook me for a local. I was like them, a tourist wearing expensive boots and sunglasses, equipped with a nylon backpack and water bottle looking for what lies beyond. When one of them asked if he was on the right path to Porto Lúa, I replied that he was, but I wanted to tell him he had already passed it, that Porto Lúa was on the mountain above, not on the coast below. I told others I met along the way about A Noiva do Ceo and the pool at Santa Locaia and the star map on the megalithic tomb, but their goal was the completion of their journey, and they had no intention of turning back. I wondered what they were looking for and whether they ever found it.

The bench Harry had built at the lookout was still there,

but not the stones he had set up to frame views of the valley. It took me longer to reach this point than in the past because, slowed by the years, I had stopped to rest more often. And the weight of the pack didn't make the climb any easier. I ate a slice of the tortilla and some of the bread and cheese I had brought, but didn't linger since, at the rate I was going, I wouldn't reach the *albergue* until sometime in the early evening, and I wasn't sure if there would be any beds left. Despite heavy legs and incipient blisters, I continued climbing with a sense of urgency. A woodlark singing in a clearing among the trees reminded me of the bird that had enchanted Laura at the same place. As I walked, I could see her on the path beside me and recalled the journeys with Mestre and Facundo and Father Infante in the oxcart as clearly as I could recall walking across the plaza earlier in the day, but, curiously, I couldn't picture the desk and furniture where I worked and had only a vague impression of the building where I lived.

Although I was prepared to spend the night outdoors, I was relieved when I reached the *albergue* in daylight and learned there was still a bed available. The two-story cement structure near the site of the bothy was relatively new, but already stained by winter rains. There were three dormitories, each furnished with four steel-framed bunk beds, eight lockers, fresh sheets, and a boot rack. In my room were four young Spaniards from Seville, a Dutch woman, and an older couple from Germany. The hostel was operated by a husband and wife from Lonxe do Sol who served breakfast and a light dinner in a lounge with a dozen small tables. A communal atmosphere prevailed among the hikers who had already met on the path, and I was welcomed into their conversations until the lights went out at ten o'clock. The next morning a heavy rain darkened the sky. After a breakfast of croissants and bananas, we lingered for at least an hour over coffee waiting for it to stop. At the first sign the clouds were lifting, the hikers, who were well prepared for all weathers, slipped on their raincoats and parkas and set out for Porto Lúa. I was not as well prepared and waited until the rain had turned to mist before embarking in the opposite direction along a forestry road toward Lonxe do Sol.

Crudely cut through a plantation of pine seedlings, the road left furrows of torn roots and broken boulders in its wake, and because the rain had turned the loose soil into channels of muddy water, I went back to the old path that winds through the sentinel boulders and burial ground of Roman soldiers. In the narrow clearings among the corridors of stone, the earth was smoking in a sadness of mist and rising vapors. Water pooled and tumbled down sinuous courses through a terrain of rocks and gorse, slicing into grassy brakes, trickling through spongy turf, then slowing in ditches and seasonal bourns before falling from ledges to rain again on the canyon below—washing all the while from stony plots the thin but fertile soil, centuries of kelp brought to the mountain by teams of oxen, washing it back to the sea in an endless cycle of Sisyphean futility.

A reservoir and power plant built in the gorge of the Deva had brought the modern era to Lonxe do Sol, but at some cost as the grandeur of its setting above the swirling mists was diminished by the dam and turbines and the skeletal towers that marched across the landscape like an army of giants. New houses built for the personnel operating the dam gave the village a fresh appearance, and several others were whitewashed or painted different colors like houses on the coast. To bring in the equipment needed to construct the dam, an asphalt road had been built that connected Lonxe to a highway on the eastern side of the mountain. Cars and foreign-made tractors replaced the oxcarts of the past, and, offering greater protection against the elements and vermin, metal doors and window frames replaced those made of wood. More important was the arrival of electricity. Like spokes in a bicycle wheel, power lines fanned out from concrete pylons to every house in the village, and nearly every house was topped with a television antenna.

Although the street was still littered with manure and scattered forage, the asphalt surface allowed me to explore the changes in the village without wading through mud and filthy water. I stopped at a new brick building which had taken the place of the old public house in order to rest and taste the local wine, but their entire selection was commercially produced. I set my pack on a chair beneath a widescreen television and watched a football match for a few minutes as I sipped a glass of Albariño. The only other patrons were sitting at the bar talking to the landlord. It was almost noon, and I had no reason to linger after finishing the wine. As I was going out the door, I heard the landlord, who failed to recognize me as a native, say to one of the patrons, "there goes another one looking for the gods." To their surprise, I stopped and replied in the local dialect, "and he found them in a bar."

At the edge of the village was a school bus shelter and the ubiquitous plastic trash bins of the local council. Where the asphalt road diverged from the old path to the church, I followed the latter. As soon as I left the village, the clouds opened, and the sun came out dispelling the darkness that had shrouded the morning with gloom. The contrast was so great that roosters began to crow in the distance as if the day had just begun. Trees along the path and the grasses in the fields glistened with as many suns as there were drops of water reflecting the light while the streams ran silver and the flowers of summer rose from their submission to the morning weather. Freshened by the rain, open tracts of purple heather and yellow broom brightened beneath white clouds hastening across the sky, and the leaves of oaks and sycamores and sweet chestnuts were so intensely green they appeared to give off a light of their own.

The oaks in the churchyard where my ancestors lay were so old they seemed to have changed little since my childhood. As I walked among the graves, I counted a dozen headstones bearing my family name and noted some of the dates going back to the early nineteenth century. The church door was locked, so I continued down an overgrown path to the clearing where our family home had been. The stone walls were still standing, but the roof and upstairs floor had collapsed into a rubble of tiles and wooden slats. I entered the ruins through the front door and stepped carefully over rotten beams to avoid the rusty nails hidden by tangles of ivy and nettles. Looking for some object I could recover and keep as a way of remembering the house and the people who had lived in it, I shifted the tiles and lighter boards with my feet and bent down to lift the heavier beams out of the way. Through decaying floorboards covered with moss and fungus, I noticed a roll of tattered burlap. The moldy cloth was wrapped around a heavy object, and as I lifted the bundle from the ground, it fell away in strips to reveal a bolt-action rifle. I blew the remaining bits of fiber from the stock and barrel and recognized it as an M93 Mauser.

The bolt and barrel were badly rusted, and the stock was porous with worm holes. I took it with me as I set out for Porto Ventoso, and when I was several hundred yards from the house, I broke off the stock and threw it into a bog of standing water and, after walking deep into the woods, buried the metal components beneath a pile of rocks—where I hoped they would remain undisturbed as long as the Roman sword had been buried among the boulders of Lonxe do Sol.

The gate at Porto Ventoso was gone, but its hinges remained mortared in the rock. On the wall of boulders to the right of the opening, someone had painted the words *Nosa Terra*, and on the ground beneath them was a cairn of cans and bottles and sheets of foil that cradled a fetid tea of pine needles, cigarette butts, and dead insects. Although the asphalt road leading out of Lonxe had been marked as the official *camino* and was the route taken by most hikers and modern pilgrims, the Roman road was still known by local people and historians, but because it saw less traffic, it was more susceptible to vandalism. When I passed through the gap in the boulders and the series of Bronze Age walls, I discovered that fire had destroyed the forest at Agro Vello. Where Romans had cut through dense woods to build their road to the end of the world were the white spindles of burnt pines. The lilies and anemones were gone, and the open ground was an austere landscape of charred boulders and ashen soil creased by black and gray braids of mud. The stone I had given Laura came from this forest, but it now seemed as out of place as a pink orchid in a wasteland of foundries and smelters.

I went back to Porto Ventoso and followed the path along the top of the cliff where we had come across the granite altars. The forest below had been harvested, and for the first time I was able to see what the people who had carved those altars had seen as they stood at the edge of the world and looked out on the realm of the dead. Even though the altars were gone, the presence of the gods remained and would remain as long as people continued to climb the mountain and gaze at the distant horizon of the sea. There was no evidence of fire or logging in the woods above the cliff, and the path was engulfed by dense growths of ferns and broom, ivy and laurels, and the low-hanging branches of ash and alder trees. Because there were no paved roads to Santa Locaia, the site had not changed since my last visit. The altar to Jove lodged in the side of the chapel was inconspicuous enough to have escaped the attention of vandals. The interior of the chapel was empty, but judging by the number of bottle caps and cans around a recent bonfire, the field outside was still being used for annual festivals. I drank from the pool of the Virxe do Monte and sat down on the stone embankment where I ate a dinner of bread and cheese in the shadow of a willow. When I heard movement in the brush behind me, I turned to see an old woman watching me through the dense undergrowth. I called out to greet her, but when I went to speak to her, she had disappeared.

I reached the base of the summit of Aracelo early in the evening. A forestry road had opened Onde se Adora to cars, and people had hiked the rest of the way up the mountain to camp beneath the towering granite peak. There were stone circles of campfires here and there and more discarded cans and bottles. An anarchist had made the effort to climb this high in order to paint the lower rockface with diatribes against conformity. Earlier in the summer a fire had escaped one of the circles and scorched much of the grass and brush along the edge of the monolith, but had fortunately not spread more than a few dozen yards in any direction. From where I stood, there appeared to be no natural features in the rock that would allow one to climb it. As impregnable as the pillars of medieval stylites, it offered no fissures or ledges large enough for a foothold. Even with gear, an experienced climber would find it a formidable challenge. And above forty or fifty feet of smooth stone, the peak was crowned with mitred rocks presenting an even more difficult challenge, for if one could ascend the side of the peak, there appeared to be no place to rest among the sharply sculpted boulders. But I had made a promise, and I had come this far, so the only thing to do was walk around the area looking for an opening or at least lower boulders where I might climb up high enough to survey what, if anything, lay above. I sensed intuitively that there must be something on top of the peak and a means of access. Always in my dreams of the mountain, there had been a level higher, inaccessible, a terrace beneath the open sky.

Looking for any breaches in the wall of rock or signs of an ancient presence in the vicinity like petroglyphs or cupmarks, I descended a stone ravine toward Onde se Adora following the path of animals and hikers. Water flowed from beneath the rocks on one side and trickled down over the boulders making the path a stream in places and staining the rocks with reddish-brown algae. At the same time, dense clusters of gorse crowded the path, making it difficult to pass. Below me lay the saddle of open heath where the circular foundations of the houses at Onde se Adora had been excavated. Perhaps a half mile beyond was the road to Lonxe do Sol where I could see a passing car. I continued a little farther down the trail, but finding no gaps in the wall of granite that would allow me to ascend, I turned around and climbed back to the campsite.

The shadows of trees and large boulders had begun to lengthen, and I was already considering places where I might spend the night as I walked north on the path toward Casa Sagrada. It was the same route I had taken with Laura, but now the brush was too dense to penetrate. I tried burrowing under the broom where it had overgrown itself and left a hollow beneath its branches. Pushing through the undergrowth, I could see no more than two or three feet in front of me and suddenly found myself on the edge of a cliff. Lost in the thicket, I took my bearings from the sunlight and worked my way back through the tangle of broom and pine saplings until I came to a spring at the base of the peak. There was a split in the stone above the pool, and I was able to raise myself up by gripping the sides of the fissure, but my pivot foot kept slipping sideways into the crack and was difficult to extract. Then I tried wedging small stones into the narrow opening to create makeshift steps, but the fissure ended beneath a ledge about twenty feet above the ground, and I couldn't find a way around it.

Reconciled to the fact that I would be sleeping there that night, I began to gather kindling from the surrounding area and stack it under the overhang of a boulder where others had built fires in the past. As I was walking back and forth laden with sticks and dry bark, I noticed the sunlight had shifted slightly to create shadows in a series of shallow cavities lined up vertically in the face of the granite wall. Though granite often forms such depressions naturally, upon inspection I realized these had been cut into the stone, and, given how smooth they were, it is fair to say many centuries earlier. Because of their spacing, it was clear they were meant to provide a footing for people climbing the rock face, and the effort they had required suggested what lay above was important enough to justify it.

I tied one end of the rope I had brought to a belt loop on my pants and the other to a ring on the side of the backpack, which I left on the ground as I placed my right foot in the first cavity and my left foot in the second. After every two steps, I took a moment to rest, pressing my face close to the warm surface of the rock, which was covered with abrasive projections of feldspar. I climbed at least forty feet like this, trusting there would be another hollow in the rock just above me, while my palms and particularly my fingertips were chafed pink and bleeding from gripping the rough surface. Because the cavities were not deep enough to insert more than my toes, the muscles in my calves were severely strained just maintaining my position, and with no more than ten feet to climb, my legs began to shake from exhaustion. I thought about going back down, but that was probably more taxing than continuing up. As I pressed my body against the wall of rock, I asked myself why I was so foolish as to be in this situation alone on the side of a mountain with night approaching, but after resting for a few minutes and calming myself, I was able to continue.

From the ground below, the gradual curvature of the rock had kept me from seeing a cleft in the wall filled with grass and a talus of small boulders. Grasping the root of a stunted cedar tree, I pulled myself up into the crevice and tied the rope to the tree. Then I crawled along a grassy ledge that widened enough for me to sit and rest from the climb. I was still ten feet below the summit, but could see a passage through the rocks at a fairly easy angle of ascent. Hanging above the aqueous horizon like an alien planet diverted from its course, the sun shone through the forests below illuminating the needles of pine boughs that gleamed like golden crystals of ice against the gathering shadows.

Above the ledge, a gap between the boulders had been filled with dozens of small stones allowing me to cross where it would have been impossible otherwise and continue up natural steps in the stone over a threshold between two of the mitred pillars of rock that were several times my height. In the passage, sheltered from Atlantic storms, flourished blackberries and wild roses, and in every crack in the stones, tufts of coarse grass held stubbornly to meager pockets of soil as if strengthened by the harshness of the environment. As I came out of the passage, I entered the dream of Mestre. Within the palisade of stones was a level surface of pink granite extending more than two hundred feet, isolated from the world below but open to the sky like the floor of heaven. Masses of ivy covered mounds of rubble, but the chiseled stones of ruined chambers and walls were clearly discernable. An inch or two below a cover of decaying leaves and layers of moss and soil were the smooth stones of an avenue that led to a raised platform on the eastern side of the elevation.

Birds flew in and out of the enclosure as if they were flying back and forth in time. As I walked down the avenue thinking of the hands that had placed those stones one upon another, I felt as though I too had entered a different time, had joined those people in the sky where they had worshipped. At the center of the site was a square pool chiseled into the granite where rainwater collected from a system of troughs cut in the stone. It was surrounded by decorative motifs and cupmarks that would have been filled with oil and used to illuminate religious ceremonies. As I inspected the heaps of stones and tiles, I wondered whether the entire site had been one large temple. There were broken shards of pottery, a bronze vase, a badly corroded knife, indecipherable inscriptions or graffiti, and, beneath a dense cover of vines, the head of a goddess. As I tore the ivy away from a wall, I uncovered a marble plaque that stood out against the darker granite. Tracing the inscription on it with my finger, I was able to make out two words:

LVNAI PORTVM

Because I was still tired from the climb and the sky was beginning to darken, I decided to spend the night on the summit and went back to the ledge to pull my pack up from the ground. The setting sun covered the silver blue water of the bay with a crimson frost of light until disappearing below the horizon. The downy underside of clouds blushed softly, then brightly with scarlet light before fading quickly. A crow flew silently over the forest below. Soon the sky above the horizon turned a smoky pink, like the color of certain shells, and above that, pale yellow passing into green, and, higher still, as if coated with a clear glaze, a delicate blue streaked with the black silhouettes of clouds. The headlights of cars along the coastal road moved like streams of fireflies flashing in the night, and the streets of the port spread out like a cobweb whose gossamer threads were hung with tiny points of light.

While there was still light in the western sky, I looked for a suitable place to pass the night. Because the wind was out of the east, I crossed to the other side of the peak where I found a sheltered spot on the lee side of a boulder. I unfolded the tarp, filled it with leaves and moss and tufts of grass, and tied the corners together to make a mattress. In the faint light above the eastern horizon I could see the outlines of Mount Pedroso and Pico Sacro and, beyond them, the mountains of Ourense where night clouds rose like reefs of gray coral. On a high point near Santiago shone a bright light like the dome of a marquee at a summer festival. As I watched, it grew larger and then the edge of pale orange became a semicircle. A drop of light rising through a liquid darkness. It was the moon. Fossil of night. Bone of stars broken before the sun was born. As it rose, bars of cloud passed slowly across its face like foam breaking from invisible waves moving through the night. Illuminating the layers of cloud in its wake, it seemed to rain a golden dust over the eastern mountains.

I untied grandmother's boots from the strap on my pack and removed Aunt Fioxilda's letters from the plastic bag where I had wrapped them. Then I took out the bouquet of purple flowers I had picked on the road above Porto Lúa. From my pocket I retrieved the stone from Agro Vello that Laura had kept with her during her final weeks, and from my wallet, the coin Uncle Teo had given me and the Roman medallion. Near the corner where I had made my bed was a small cave sheltered from the wind and rain, but open to the eastern sky. I took the boots and letters and flowers and stone and coin and medallion and placed them in the cave where the moon reached in and covered them with its light. Someday, if someone makes it to the top of the peak, and looks into this cave and finds rotting leather and tarnished metal and a small, pink stone, what I had left will be gone, separated from the objects like the ghosts of love from a lifeless body, taken by the light that travels across the sky.

The breeze died down with the disappearance of the sun, and the only sound was a nightingale singing in the darkness. The moon had wakened me to the night the way the sun wakens us to the day. Having recovered from the exhaustion I had felt upon reaching the summit, I climbed the stone platform at the end of the avenue. As the highest point of the mountain, it commanded views in all directions. White light shone across the landscape from the mountain peaks and valleys to the sea and distant island. Shone on the pink granite and the yellow broom and purple heather, like the ash of spent sunlight, falling through the branches of pines, covering the surfaces of streams, pooling in the eyes of wakeful creatures.

As I lay on my back looking into the sky, falling into its emptiness, I recalled Trofonio's account of the souls slipping into the blue abyss from the narrow traverse of the underworld and imagined what it would be like to fall forever, to be one of the nameless souls crowding together as they chose their fate between a torturous afterlife and oblivion. The price of a life poorly lived. And yet every night we lie beneath a similar abyss without end, without bearings, but for that circle of light, which gives some focus to the darkness, some definition to the night—and to our lives falling through time, providing stations for our journey, months to mark our passing. A timeless measure of time, a relic of creation, reflecting our lives like a mirror that never ages. Where I see my grandmother holding me up to its light, a sleepless child watching it from the window of his room, marbled clouds opening to its presence in a mountain storm. Shining on the domes and towers of Teo's cities, on the boxwood camels, the statues and urns of El Conde's garden, on the pool at Santa Locaia, on the silver pines above Mallou. Shining on the roses I left for Laura on the night of Nosa Señora do Mar. Shining on my walk to school without her. Gathering those moments of our lives into its light somewhere outside time.

If the moon could know us as we know it, how odd we would seem. How foolish our vanity, our illusions of worth that die in the darkness like candles burning out among the stars. No wonder Cotolay was mad. Firing his rifle into that impassive face, he saw our lives through the cold eye of its indifference. Far beyond our births and deaths. Far beyond our wills and desires. Far beyond our self-importance. *Sub specie aeternitatis*. The eternal made visible. A dispassionate witness drifting upward toward the meridian night shining as it had shone on the earliest creatures, strange beasts that slept and fed like we sleep and feed and left their bones encased in rock. Looking down from its heights on the dust of our endeavors. On our lives coming and going like shadows come and go in the course of a day. As we seek gods to answer our prayers. To confirm with our presence. Our shrines a feeble defense against the night. The castles and palaces of our cities, the piers and jetties of our ports, the paths of our highways and canals, faint abrasions on a stone. We ply our tools with purpose, dig our earth for daily bread, raise our towers above the clouds, fill our rivers and seas with waste. The sounds of our machines and weapons, the voices of our teachers and poets, orators and demagogues, dissipate in the emptiness of night. So too our cries of love and howls of birth. Our arguments and laughter. And the laughter of forgotten gods buried with the faith of their followers. The centuries pass like minutes until all is lost and forgotten—all those who loved and dreamt of children and planned futures and suffered the tedium of their jobs and feared the losses of old age and waited in pain for the morning light. And yet, as Mestre wrote, just being here is so much. Being part of the presence of things. In the light. Of the light.

I saw the sky as a canopy concealing what lies beyond, like the canopy of bone that houses our thoughts and keeps us in this world. And I saw the moon as an opening in that canopy, and its white oceans and mountains as a glimpse into a world beyond the darkness, into a paradise of long forgotten light. Holy light. Cradle of the dreaming soul. Comfort before the fall. The light we have sought since the shadows of birth closed around us. The light we seek at the end.

Passing through layers of mist that rose from the forest, the light fell like a river flowing over shelves of white stone. Drawn by the appeal of its purity, losing myself in its austerity, I felt myself lifted into the white cataract, cleansed of earthly concerns. No longer subject to the bonds of nature, no longer burdened by a return to matter, I passed through the canopy of darkness into a sea of light as clear as the light of creation, into memories of depth and absence formed in the origins of consciousness.

Moving into the light, I moved with the light, looking down through the darkness to the silver lanes and roofs of sleeping villages, to the white waves cresting in rocky coves, to the vast sea shimmering to the edge of night. In a silence as perfect as that of passing clouds, I moved beyond the horizon, beyond the ivory shores of dreams. Where the light shines like a ghost of the sun. Where time outlasts itself, and the earth is a distant memory, the source and sustenance of a distant dream. And when that dream is gone, the light will remain as if it had never been, shining as if it had never shone.

About Atmosphere Press

Atmosphere Press is an independent, full-service publisher for excellent books in all genres and for all audiences. Learn more about what we do at atmospherepress.com.

We encourage you to check out some of Atmosphere's latest releases, which are available at Amazon.com and via order from your local bookstore:

Icarus Never Flew 'Round Here, by Matt Edwards

COMFREY, WYOMING: Maiden Voyage, by Daphne Birkmeyer

The Chimera Wolf, by P.A. Power

Umbilical, by Jane Kay

The Two-Blood Lion, by Nick Westfield

Shogun of the Heavens: The Fall of Immortals, by I.D.G. Curry

Hot Air Rising, by Matthew Taylor

30 Summers, by A.S. Randall

Delilah Recovered, by Amelia Estelle Dellos

A Prophecy in Ash, by Julie Zantopoulos

The Killer Half, by JB Blake

Ocean Lessons, by Karen Lethlean

Unrealized Fantasies, by Marilyn Whitehorse

The Mayari Chronicles: Initium, by Karen McClain

Squeeze Plays, by Jeffrey Marshall

JADA: Just Another Dead Animal, by James Morris

Hart Street and Main: Metamorphosis, by Tabitha Sprunger

Karma One, by Colleen Hollis

Ndalla's World, by Beth Franz

Adonai, by Arman Isayan

The Journey, by Khozem Poonawala

Stolen Lives, by Dee Arianne Rockwood

ABOUT THE AUTHOR

David Green is the author of *Atchley* and
The Garden of Love.

He lives in Massachusetts.

www.portolua.com

CPSIA information can be obtained
at www.ICGtesting.com
Printed in the USA
LVHW051454070323
741114LV00005B/263